THE LEGEND OF

ZERO

ZERO RECALL

SARA KING

ISBN: 1942929005
ISBN-13: 9781942929000

Published by
Parasite Publications

DISCLAIMER

(a.k.a. If You Don't Realize This Is A Work Of Fiction, Please Go Find Something Else To Do)

So you're about to read about alien war, life on other planets, and intergalactic politics. In case you're still confused, yes, this book is a complete work of fiction. Nobody contained within these pages actually exists. If there are any similarities between the people or places of *The Legend of ZERO* and the people or places of Good Ol' Planet Earth, you've just gotta trust me. It's not real, people. Really. Yet.

BOOKS IN THE LEGEND OF ZERO SERIES:

Listed in Chronological Order
(because nothing else really makes sense):

Forging Zero
Zero Recall
Zero's Return
Zero's Legacy
Forgotten

DEDICATION

For Stuey.
My Muse, my inspiration, my hope.
For Sarah.
She edits ~~gud~~ *(Editor's Note: good...or more correctly, 'well'. Furg.).*
For Buchanan.
Motivator through the hard times.
And for Chancey.
Who, in the space of a single afternoon, said, "You're going to write a book, and it's going to go like this..."

AUTHOR'S NOTE

Zero Recall is different. If you read it right the first time, it should blow your mind. If you read it right the second time, it should blow your mind again. It should still be perfectly entertaining the third time through. It was an experiment in layers. Like a cake. (Or an onion.)

THE PARASITE PUBLICATIONS GLOSSARY
(BECAUSE SOMEBODY'S GOTTA TELL YOU THIS STUFF!)

Character author – That rare beast who lets his or her characters tell the story. (And often run completely wild.)

Character fiction – Stories that center around the characters; their thoughts, their emotions, their actions, and their goals.

Character sci-fi – Stories about the future that focus on the characters, rather than explaining every new theory and technology with the (silly) assumption that we, as present-day 21st centurians, know enough to analyze and predict the far future with any accuracy whatsoever. I.e. character sci-fi is fun and entertaining, not your next college Physics textbook.

Parasite – The Everyday Joe (or Jane) who enjoys crawling inside a character's head while reading a book; i.e. someone who enjoys character fiction.

Furg – Anyone who believes the best fiction makes your eyes glaze over…unless the glazing happens because you stayed up all night reading it and you can't keep your eyes open the next day. ;)

TABLE OF CONTENTS

1

FORGOTTEN

Approximately three and a half billion thoughts raced through Forgotten's mind at the moment the Congressional ships surrounded him, but foremost among them was that if things did not go exactly as planned, he was finally going to join the rest of his species in prison.

He was very close to sixty-three percent sure he didn't want to join the rest of his species in prison, though that percentage had been on the decline for the last thirty nanoseconds. The loneliness had grown difficult for him to bear. The extreme solitude was depressing. The lack of conversation—however inane—was painful. He didn't want to contemplate what would happen when his desire to maintain his freedom finally dipped beneath fifty percent.

Thus, watching the ships converge on him, Forgotten was actually looking forward to the company, vile as it would be.

The vessels sliding out of the void around him had been modified to appear old and partially decrepit, but the uniform perfection of their dilapidation gave their true natures away. Even poor merchants took pride in their ships. If they couldn't afford a new heat shield or decent com equipment, they found other ways to pamper their ships—a lovingly-painted mascot, the addition of teeth, a flourished name, an unknown logo.

Instead, the ships pulling up from the blackness around him were perfect in their poverty. They had no shiny features, no new paint, no teeth.

Once Forgotten identified them for what they were, it was simple enough to peer through the disguises and analyze the armada Congress had sent against him. And it was certainly an armada. Manned by Huouyt and Ueshi, if their reaction times upon noticing his ship were any indication. He was somewhat impressed he had ranked so high on their list of Dangerous Criminals, considering how painstakingly quiet he had been all these turns. He did everything he could not to attract attention. Not to create waves.

Yet, Forgotten was lonely. And, he'd decided, it was time.

Therefore, he held course as sixteen battleships, five carriers, thirty-five cruisers, and a command flagship slipped into place around him. They were static metal and polymers instead of the sleek black, spherical Geuji-conceived nanotechnology favored by the Space Force. His enemies were hoping to catch him unawares, though their choice to abandon Congressional technology for the rougher, less versatile static materials greatly increased his chances of eluding them, should he try to escape.

Instead, Forgotten left his systems at idle and waited for them to surround him. He could have evaded them with only an infinitesimal chance of getting caught by stray fire in the chase that would follow, but, as time went on and his body grew, he was bored. And the Huouyt, psychopathic creatures that they were, were interesting.

As the strange ships slid into place around him, Forgotten idly calculated his chances of being sent to Levren to be with his people increasing with each passing nanosecond. The chance that his pursuers would simply kill him, out here in the cold of the Void, surrounded by Congressional Space Force, was increasing as well. If they did, he found a certain poetry in the fact that it would be as it always was—the Geuji were used and forgotten, their deeds taken for granted, then lost to history. Stuffed inside some cold, dark cell in silence for eternity as the world passed around them.

Still, he let them come. While Forgotten was by no means brave, he had reached the point he would do anything to break the solitude.

"Silence, *this is the Jahul trading caravan* Green Fist. *What is your purpose on this trade route?*"

The dispatch came from the flagship, though Forgotten doubted the true power lay on board the frontrunner. It, like everything else about the armada's appearance, was a decoy.

He scanned the other ships as he listened, finally locating the likeliest command center at the left rear of the group, a fighter that would have been inconspicuous had it not been for the single additional lump on its belly. The shape and size of the lump suggested a coded, long-distance communications node, the brand of which was only used by the power-players of Koliinaat, which meant Representative Rri'jan was along for the ride. As expected.

Forgotten stretched himself, enjoying as much stimuli as he could, in case the encounter took an unforeseen turn and they wrenched him from his ship and imprisoned him with the rest of the Geuji. If he failed, it would be the last time he would see, hear, or feel anything… possibly for the rest of his existence.

Because, as Forgotten had learned long ago, one and a half million turns after Congress had betrayed and imprisoned the Geuji, their existence was a myth. A breath of wind that brushed scattered minds here and there throughout the eons, only to disappear again.

Forgotten. His people were forgotten.

Only one creature in the universe still cared about the Geuji, and Forgotten had spent enough time thinking about them for the rest of the galaxy combined.

A Huouyt's musical voice hailed him. "*This is the Jahul merchant caravan* Green Fist *out of Whuo. Identify yourself.*"

Forgotten cleared his mind of everything but the task at hand. He could go back to worrying about his people later, once he had dealt with the Huouyt. He didn't like the Huouyt. They, aside from the Geuji, were the smartest creatures in Congress.

They were also psychopathic killers who did not play well with others, and Forgotten's desire to live had not quite dipped below the fifty percent mark just yet.

"*This caravan is armed*, Silence," the Huouyt replied, when Forgotten took an extra moment to reply. "*Please identify yourself.*" The pitch and crispness of the Huouyt's voice indicated a seventy-eight turn old Northern Gha'Salaoian from Sh'ai. It took only a moment to recognize which one. Da'najo, one of the sixty-eight billion Huouyt in his memory. This particular Huouyt had thoroughly failed his tests as captain and had paid off one of the administrators to switch his results with the stellar marks of a poor, common-blooded classmate. Evading Da'najo would be easy. It was the lower-class Ueshi pilots that made up the rest of the armada that would be challenging, should the upcoming meeting go unexpectedly wrong.

Forgotten watched the Congressional fighters get into position around him and, for one of the few times in his life, found himself wondering what the hell he'd been thinking. Conversation was one thing, but the probabilities were rapidly ticking further into the unacceptable range with each moment he waited to flee.

He, Forgotten realized with a pang of alarm, was beginning to get reckless.

It's the loneliness, he thought, as every mental pathway he had was suddenly overloaded with that bewildering, earth-shattering revelation. *Geuji were never meant to be alone.*

Indeed, on their home planet, they had spanned entire continents, sharing and discoursing and comparing notes as they analyzed the skies together.

Disturbed, Forgotten selected a Huouyt voice from his ship's database and said in Sh'ai-accented, Northern Gha'Salaoian Huouyt, "Shall I give you the AR controls or do you intend to board?"

The Huouyt captain hesitated. In crisp Congie he said, "*This territory is known for its space pirates. Our escort believes you might be hostile. It would put everyone at ease if you would identify yourself before we pass.*"

From the mid-sized fighter in the back left of the formation, a Morinthian, Va'ga-trained Huouyt said, "*He did identify himself, fool.*"

A mix of satisfaction and fear appeared in Forgotten's mind. He'd been right—and if he failed, he was going to die. Rri'jan Ze'laa did not leave a job unfinished. It was why he had replaced Representative Na'leen in the Huouyt Regency seat.

"I've been given quite an escort," Forgotten said in Morinthian, Va'ga-accented Huouyt. "A Va'ga-trained assassin. A hundred and forty-two turns old. The head of the Ze'laa, a title taken from your elder brother after his...problem...saw him sterilized and slated for execution. You prefer to drink water bottled from northern Astori streams and you have a personal phobia of flesh-eating bacteria and Trith. What did I do for Aliphei to send you to visit?"

"*Your antics do not unnerve me, Geuji.*" Rri'jan's voice was cold, lacking the characteristic musical quality of Huouyt speech. It was a trait that all Va'gan graduates maintained—flat, lifeless speech, giving nothing away, ever. At least to everyone but a Geuji.

"I never suspected they would, my friend," Forgotten replied. "I was simply being polite. After all, you are a murderer by birth and training. The fifth most powerful family in Congress. How could I ever intimidate you?"

This got under Rri'jan's skin. "*The Ze'laa is the* most *powerful family in Congress, as we have clearly shown. We have the resources and manpower to capture even* you, *Forgotten.*"

Capture, Forgotten thought wryly. *Truly, they do not understand what they are dealing with.* Not even the *Huouyt,* his closest intellectual rivals in all of Congress, truly understood. Which, he supposed, made his survival in the upcoming game easier.

"You are fifth," Forgotten replied, on the common frequency. "Mekkval, Gervin, Keddrik, and Fabara could each have accomplished as much, and they would not have had to empty out their coffers to do it. This little escapade probably took an entire seventh of your familial worth, did it not? What is Aliphei paying you? I will triple it, plus cover the expenses you took to make your warships appear so believably unrealistic, and it won't even skim the surface of my funds." Then he hesitated. "But wait. That would make *me* the most powerful 'family' in Congress, no? Which would make you...sixth. And that's only if you don't split the Ooreiki and Jahul into their royal lineages. And at least four Dhasha princes exceed the Ze'laa's base wealth. Bagkhal is a good example. You wouldn't know it by looking at him, but he owns three planets. Personally."

Rri'jan's voice was as lifeless as ever, but Forgotten detected the anger buried underneath. *"Prepare for boarding, Geuji."*

Forgotten initiated the sequence without complaint, knowing the next seconds were crucial. Noncompliance would result in a cold, dead Geuji floating around in abandoned space. Too much reluctance would make Rri'jan overconfident and prone to do stupid, violent things. Complying immediately would simply scare the hell out of him.

As expected, the other ship hesitated as Forgotten instantly completed his ship's mating routine. There was a very long pause in which the opposite ship remained undocked, hovering in space, just out of reach.

"Anytime you're ready, Representative," Forgotten said. "I recently replenished my supply of Sutharian microbes. Play nice, and we should get along fine."

The pause grew to several tics, and Forgotten monitored the dispute that instantly began to rage inside the other ship. The Representative finally had to pull rank to get his underlings to submit to Forgotten's lock. Somewhere in the scathing arguments that followed, Rri'jan's captain finally found the courage to complete the mating sequence. Forgotten waited, watching the airlock from his ship's camera system.

Rri'jan was a gifted Va'gan assassin before he took the Regency seat. He had the capability of producing nine hundred and thirteen different drugs and deadly chemicals with his body, which he could then inject with a multitude of body shifts—spines, excretions, biological syringes, gaseous emanations—that the Huouyt were known for. And, because Forgotten had pushed him, Rri'jan was likely to forego his original intent in approaching him and simply attempt to kill Forgotten in the most painful way possible, to salvage his dubious honor.

Of course, if Rri'jan did anything at all that Forgotten did not approve of, he would flush both of their ships with a load of microbes that would eat away a Huouyt's *breja* and put its owner in the worst pain he'd ever felt before he died.

Tit for tat.

Tics passed. More argument within the Huouyt ship. Forgotten used the time to access Rri'jan's secured link to Koliinaat and confirm the current political atmosphere towards using an ekhta. It was as he had predicted. While the Jreet and the Dhasha maintained Tribunal seats, the Jahul had recently been given four new, lucrative metals-planets by the Planetary Claims Board, and they—an entire species of empaths—currently held the most sway in Congress. Further, the Jreet would vote to physically fight, considering technology of any sort to be a coward's weapon, and the Dhasha considered themselves invincible on principle. Forgotten sent a few subtle messages to strengthen these positions as he waited.

The air-lock between their ships remained shut. A closed-circuit message came to him directly from the other ship.

Eventually, Rri'jan got on the com system. *"I want you to know, Forgotten, that I am not here to kill you."*

"The word of a murderer is unto the word of a Huouyt to me, and since you are both, forgive me if I find it hard to believe you." Forgotten considered the current predicament of the Geuji imprisoned on Levren and decided that they would want, at the very least, to be able to communicate with each other. That, of course, would never happen with Yua'nev at the helm of the Peacemakers. Yet the Huouyt—psychopathic monsters that they were—traditionally maintained the Tenth through Twelfth Hjai of the Peacemakers, and their assassins would simply kill any non-Huouyt who had the audacity to try to claim a higher rank.

"I am here to hire you," Rri'jan said, the truth ringing in his voice at a ninety-ninth percent certainty.

"I'm sure you are aware that the Huouyt are infamous for their ability to lie," Forgotten said as he accessed Rri'jan's ship's database and pored through Planetary Ops records. There were several profiles that interested him. Daviin ga Vora would make a good Representative—if he had financial backing—and the Baga Traxxalihania had the familial ties to regain for his people thirty-two planets from the Huouyt and Ooreiki, should the Baga become aware of the discrepancy. Corruption and payoffs were increasing throughout the Peacemaker accounts, with over fifty percent of high-profile Sanctuary cases being fraudulently performed to increase the populace's fear of Peacemaker reprisals, further suggesting the current Peacemaster needed to be replaced, preferably by someone with a conscience.

Rri'jan seemed to understand that he would die as soon as he stepped on Forgotten's ship without an invitation, for the airlock remained shut.

"The Huouyt want what is ours."

Forgotten monitored Dhasha missives in the Old Territory as he listened. Several denned princes were attempting to foment war using new Dhasha planets along the distant outskirts of the Outer Line as staging points, and were conspiring with kin entrenched in the central Congressional planets. As if that was anything new. Mekkval couldn't send a team after them, however, because nothing sent down a deep den ever came back, and, in desperation, Mekkval was considering going after them himself, which would mean his inevitable death. Considering how Mekkval was one of the only *decent* beings in the Regency at that moment, Forgotten wanted to avoid that if possible. To Rri'jan, he said, "You want me to arrange Mekkval's death."

If Rri'jan was unnerved at how much Forgotten had deduced, he did not show it. *"We want Na'leen's seat on the Tribunal returned to us. If you can do it more easily without killing Mekkval, then—"*

"Mekkval must be killed for the Huouyt to gain the Tribunal seat," Forgotten said. "Unless you would rather oust Prazeil. But you won't. The Jreet are much more easily manipulated than the Dhasha, and Mekkval has a personal distaste for Huouyt, so he would be likely to thwart you on every vote he could."

"Then you agree to help us?" Rri'jan demanded.

"I agree to nothing until I hear your terms." Forgotten continued to monitor food shortages around the struggling new colony planets along the Outer Line. The military had overreached itself again, and the Ground Force was even then taking rations from starving settlers, turning several non-aggressive species' planets into dwindling ghost-towns that would be easily swept up and re-colonized by Huouyt before the Planetary Claims board got around to making up the proper deeds. Further, Aez's charismatic new clan leader Prazeil had whipped his followers into a blood-fever and all three Jreet bloodlines were on the verge of a full-sector civil war that would boil over into eighty-six other planets, including three peaceful Ueshi pleasure-planets, the Bajnan banking planet of Faelor, and Ooreiki's hallowed temple-planet of Poen.

But Rri'jan retorted, "*I will only present my terms in person, and I am not stepping aboard your ship until I am sure you will not make the experience unpleasant.*"

"Then we are at an impasse because I am not going to be pleasant until I am sure you are telling the truth. As it is, I am only ninety-two percent convinced." Forgotten studied the other feeds coming in from the Outer Line. An enterprising Dhasha prince had secured a planet very close to Earth and had given Human scientists a massive amount of classified Congressional documents, and Humans had taken the bait. Using his information, they had begun top-secret genetics experiments that would get Earth a severe Congressional rebuke—and finally give the Dhasha access to Earth for slaves. The Kophat-trained Human was the best candidate to help stave off that disaster, but in order to fulfill that destiny, his Va'gan tormentor was going to have to forgive and forget. Or at least move on.

"*Ninety-two percent is not enough for you?*"

Forgotten set his studies aside. "With my slow, painful death at stake? No."

"*Very well,*" Rri'jan said calmly. "*What can I do to convince you?*"

"Take the pattern of a Takki and have your Jreet blindfold you and secure your hands behind your back with stasis links."

Anger hovered in the flatness of Rri'jan's voice. "*I am a Representative of Congress.*"

"And I am a myth. I would rather not be dispelled."

"*You realize that by angering me, you are only increasing the chance that I'll kill you?*"

"Probabilities are a tricky matter," Forgotten replied. "You see, for every moment I anger you, not only does it increase your chances of future rash decisions, but it changes the probabilities of how you will react to future situations, thereby giving me an edge in any future conversations. Your anger also reflects on how likely it is you are telling the truth, which has jumped considerably after your last statement, all things considered."

"*What probability will it take to convince you I come to bargain?*"

"One hundred percent."

"*And to do that, I must take the pattern of a* Takki." Distaste was thick in his voice.

"Yes."

"*And if I said I do not carry Takki patterns with me?*"

"Then you would be lying, though your probability would only drop slightly, since Huouyt have the tendency to lie uncontrollably and you still might be telling the truth, as much as it pains you."

"*Very amusing, Geuji,*" Rri'jan said coldly, "*but I understand the symbolism. I will have my ships annihilate you before I assume the role of your slave.*"

Which meant Rri'jan was telling the truth. In certain situations, the Huouyt were as prideful as the Jreet. Had it been an assassination attempt, Rri'jan would have had no qualms with donning a demeaning pattern, since he would have simply made Forgotten's death all the more painful for it afterwards. Being *forced* to wear the pattern of a slave, however, was unacceptable to a Huouyt royal.

"You may board, Rri'jan," Forgotten told him, deactivating the ship's defense protocol. "I will suspend any unpleasantries until I have heard your proposal. You have my word."

Rri'jan hesitated. "*That was a test?*"

"Of course."

Rri'jan said nothing. The airlock opened and he stepped inside. Forgotten immediately decreased the artificial gravity of the ship to be something more comfortable to the Huouyt's ancestrally aquatic, boneless, three-legged frame. If Rri'jan noticed or cared, he said nothing. As Forgotten watched through the ship's cameras, the Huouyt strode purposefully down the hall and stopped at the entrance to Forgotten's chamber.

"Open the door, Geuji."

Forgotten found the idea of having Death literally a few digs away strongly alluring. He opened the door before he realized how alarming that was.

The Huouyt stepped inside, dressed in the gold and silver garb the Ze'laa family preferred—a testament to his success as a Va'gan. The writhing white cilia that covered every ninth of his skin were utterly calm and still, despite the fact that they both knew Forgotten held the Huouyt's life in his hands. His eyes were the bright, white-blue shade that most species found unnerving, even going so far to suggest the Huouyt could read minds and peer into souls with their eerie gaze.

Forgotten preferred to think that the eeriness behind a Huouyt's stare was simply due to their soulless nature. Of all the species he'd ever worked with, he found his experiences with the Huouyt the least enjoyable. It had actually been very satisfying to see Representative Na'leen's grand schemes foiled on Kophat by a handful of raw recruits just over fifty-three turns ago. To think he might be working to regain what Na'leen had rightfully lost left Forgotten discomfited.

"I warn you, Rri'jan," Forgotten said, as Na'leen's replacement to the Regency looked idly around his chamber. "I do not like Huouyt. Your offer must do much to persuade me, and I do not need wealth."

Unlike most species when confronted with a Geuji's feature-less mass, Rri'jan's gaze did not fumble for some point of reference. Instead, it simply found a spot and stayed there, his unnatural eyes never moving.

"Then perhaps I should warn *you*, Geuji," Rri'jan replied casually, "that if our bargain here does not please me, I will tow your ship back to Levren and hand you over to the Peacemakers."

Oh, this was getting even better. Perhaps Forgotten would let the fool live...with permanent drug-induced mental instability. "You will not kill me?" he asked, as surprised as he could manage.

Rri'jan's expression was cruel. "Why would I do that? You are one of the most critically endangered species in Congress."

"So your offer is a threat?" Forgotten asked, amused. "Help you or join the rest of the Geuji in prison?"

"Help me and I shall use the Tribunal to see the Geuji freed."

Though Forgotten had long ago considered this as a possibility, to have another species say it out loud threatened to steal all logic from his mind. Hope flared like traitorous sparks in his core. It required all his effort to ground himself, to remember the past.

"Aliphei would not allow it."

"Prazeil and I can override Aliphei. 'Tis the nature of the Tribunal."

"Why would Prazeil care about the Geuji?"

"The Jreet have a soft spot for misfortune."

It was true. Forgotten realized with alarm that the sparks of hope had grown into something more. Rri'jan offered something Forgotten had always wanted but had never been able to acquire. Something that even his wealth had never been able to buy.

Freedom.

Despite his distaste for the Huouyt, Forgotten said, "The Huouyt will be given a permanent place by the Tribunal."

Surprise agitated his visitor's cilia. "*Permanent?*"

"Yes," Forgotten said. "I see no need for the Huouyt to continue to struggle and bicker with other species for a seat whenever one becomes available. We should make your station as permanent as Aliphei's."

Satisfaction rippled briefly across Rri'jan's breja. "How long will it take?"

"A turn."

"You already have a plan?" Though Rri'jan tried to hide his surprise, the ship's monitors picked up the steady increase in Rri'jan's biological functions.

"Yes. For the Huouyt to gain a Tribunal seat, we must kill Mekkval."

"How?" Rri'jan asked, intensely interested, now, and trying unsuccessfully to hide it.

"The first step is to start a war," Forgotten said, already seeing it in his mind.

"What kind of war?"

"The kind Congress has never seen before."

2

ZERO RECALL

Have you seen this man?" Joe held up the age-progression photo of his brother to the dirty glass window.

The hollow-eyed man behind the booth scratched his greasy beard and said, "A man like that don't come cheap. You a cop?"

"I'm his brother."

The man looked him up and down and snorted. "Yeah. Right."

"*Look* at him, damn it," Joe said, pointing at the picture. "We're obviously related. Same chin. I'm just trying to find him. I haven't seen him since the Draft. He could be going by the name Sam or Slade, okay?"

The druggie's hollow, skull-like gaze sharpened on Joe, for the first time taking in the rash that had developed around the newly-activated hair follicles of Joe's face and scalp. Immediately, distrust tightened his features. "You're a Congie?"

Joe closed his eyes to keep from putting his fist through the glass and strangling the doping bastard. "Not anymore. I was forcibly retired a couple months ago. Please. I'm just trying to find my brother. I hear he's still alive. Some sort of rejuvenation technology or something."

The druggie's face darkened. "Thought you sounded funny. Get out of here 'fore I get my gun."

"Listen, you sootwad," Joe snapped. "I've gone through eight other furgs just like you, all of whom said the same thing, and all of whom ended up telling me exactly what I wanted to know. Think about it. I was a Prime Commander in the Congressional army. Been working in Planetary Ops for fifty turns. It was my job for a good number of those turns to make vaghi like you sing like canaries. You *really* wanna piss me off?"

The druggie eyed him sullenly. "You weren't in no Planetary Ops."

Joe slapped his right palm to the window, displaying the tattoo of a green, single-moon planet with a headcom, a PPU, and a species-generic plasma rifle leaning against the debris ring. The tattoo glowed slightly, a cell-by-cell gene modification that caused Joe's skin to bio-luminesce. It was a government nannite tat, and no ink in the world could duplicate it.

Even as the druggie's eyes were widening with shock, Joe once more pressed his brother's picture to the window.

"Oh, shit, man." The addict behind the window looked paler than ever. "You're asking the wrong person. He's a big-timer. I'm just a wanna-be, man. I ain't got no idea where the Ghost is."

Joe had to fight back the frustration he had felt ever since returning to Earth to find his mother twenty years dead, his brother vanished into the world of crime. As of yet, every single person Joe had interviewed had responded in the same maddening way. They recognized his picture, but didn't know anything else about him. It was like Sam really was a...ghost.

"So tell me what you know of him," Joe said, as calmly as he could. "Everything you can remember."

"Shit, man. Shit. I ain't never *seen* him before, man. Just heard of him. Shit, I shouldn't even be sayin' nothin'." The guy swallowed and looked around like he expected the very walls to be watching them. "Don't care if you *are* his brother, he wanted to talk to you, he would've found you already."

"I've only been here a week," Joe growled.

The druggie nodded emphatically. "Yeah, man. If the Ghost had wanted to talk to you, he *definitely* woulda talked to you by now."

Joe was fed up. The last seven days of civilian life had been hell. Not only did they question him, but sometimes they outright refused to talk to him—something that had blown Joe's mind the first time it happened. People were rude to him, especially when they realized he'd been a Congie. His PlanOps tattoo tempered that a little bit, but the hostility was still there. While he got along with every alien species even better than a Jahul, Humans, his own kind, hated him.

Once more, Joe wondered if he'd made a mistake in coming back to Earth instead of settling on an Ueshi pleasure-planet like Kaleu or Tholiba. On Kaleu, he would've been treated with the same welcome and respect as any other of the three thousand, two hundred and forty-four sentient species in Congress. Here, he was just one of those kids that got brainwashed by aliens. Here, he *was* the alien. He might as well have Ooreiki tentacles or a Huouyt's breja for the nervous looks and outright sneers he got. Earth simply didn't want him.

And yet, the Ground Force didn't want him, either. Not anymore. Not after Maggie's final bitch-slap in front of half of Congress.

Thank you for your latest reenlistment application, Commander Joe Dobbs, but the Congressional Army is over-capacity and is no longer in need of your services. We've scheduled your shuttle back to Earth for tomorrow morning...

Bitterly, Joe said, "Just tell me what you know about him, okay?"

"They call him Ghost," the druggie said. "Not because he's hard to find, huh-uh. Because he—"

"—bleached his hair white and wears contacts," Joe interrupted. "Yeah, I know. What *else*?"

The druggie's greasy brow wrinkled. "No, man. Who told you that?"

"Look," Joe snapped, "Do you know *anything* that might be helpful? As I see it right now, you're just wasting my time. Just like I told all the other ghost-burning sooters I've come across, I grew up with the little furg and he's got *blue* eyes and *brown* hair. Even if he went all the way and had his eye color permanently changed—which, if he's really as smart as everyone says he is, he didn't—his eyes don't fucking *glow*. How stupid *are* you people?"

The guy raised his hands in surrender. "Man, I just know what I been told."

"Really?" Joe barked. "Then who told *you*? Maybe I'll get some answers from him."

"I don't know, man," the guy said, rapidly shaking his head. "I know a lot of people. I was prolly stoned at the time. Karwiq bulbs, you know? The one good thing Congress brought with 'em. You get a good one and it's like you died and went to heaven."

Joe narrowed his eyes and leaned in close to the glass. "You wanna find out what that really feels like?" Joe growled. "I'll show you, you Takki leafling."

The druggie sobered, really looking at him now.

Joe tensed, realizing that this could be the break he'd been looking for.

"Gum," the druggie said finally.

Joe waited, then when that was all that was offered, he blinked at him. "Gum."

"Yeah, you know." The druggie made exaggerated chewing motions. "I hear he likes gum."

Joe stared at him for several moments, then his face tightened in a scowl. "I should break your stupid neck."

"Hey, man, you asked."

"I asked for something I can *use*," Joe growled.

"You never know. Maybe the Ghost owns a gum factory or something."

Joe stared at the druggie for several moments before turning and stalking from the building. In the parking-lot, he took out the picture of his brother and threw it aside. He slipped inside his civilian *haauk* and pressed his head to the climate-controlled steering panel.

The hasty plans he had made of reuniting with his family and returning to his roots had crumbled to dust over the past week he'd been on Earth. Fifty-five turns after Joe had been Drafted, everyone was dead except Sam, and Sam did not want to be found.

Joe had spent over fifty turns—over *sixty-one years*—hunting down people who didn't want to be found, and yet somehow he hadn't even got a whiff of the little druglord soot's whereabouts.

"Damn this place," Joe muttered. For seven days, he'd been wandering the planet, wasting his retirement money, getting no more than four hours of sleep at a time, trying to pin down a ghost.

Joe gave a tired scoff and wondered what his groundteam was doing on Falra. It had to be more interesting than trying to find a career criminal who probably didn't remember him or even care he existed.

Joe lifted his head and glanced at the list of contacts he still had to visit. Six names, none of which he recognized, all of which had been given to him by the same unsavory sorts that in the last seven days had tried to murder him, rob him, drug him, rape him, and in one case, harvest his organs.

Joe had known from the beginning he wouldn't get a hero's welcome upon his return to Earth. What he had experienced here, however, left him feeling numb.

They hated them.

They hated every one of them. As if the Congies were responsible for Earth's woes. As if the kids who had been Drafted sixty years ago were to blame for Congressional rule.

They didn't understand. None of the Earth-bound furgs would ever understand. Congress was the only thing protecting them from something far more dangerous—the Dhasha, the Jreet, the Jikaln, the Dreit, the Huouyt, and all the other warlike creatures Congress had found along the way.

Sighing, Joe wiped the rest of the destinations from his *haauk* memory. He set it on autopilot and told it to take him home.

"You're back early," the smiling young receptionist at the desk of the hotel said as he stepped inside, "You find your brother, Mr. Dobbs?"

"No," Joe said.

Her smile faded. "Oh. I'm sorry, sir."

"Don't be," Joe said with a sigh. "He sounds like a prick anyway." He passed the ornate receptionist booth and took the plushly carpeted stairs to his room—Human buildings still hadn't fully adapted to the introduction of the *haauk*, with the older ones still requiring ground-level entry. Joe had had the poor sense to choose one of the more archaic hotels, longing for the memories of his childhood. At least the locks were reasonably high-tech.

They were biometric, forcing him to scan both eyes and a thumb before the door would open for him.

Not that Joe had anything to steal on the other side. He would have disabled the security measures altogether, because they weren't necessary. All his belongings—what little he'd acquired after a spartan life in Planetary Ops—were still in transit, carried on a much slower freighter. He was due to pick them up in just over a turn—sixteen months, in Earth-time—and until then would have to get his apartment ready without them.

Sighing, Joe pulled his father's knife from his pocket, then stretched out on the bed and stared up at the ceiling, rubbing its familiar red surfaces. He felt lost. It had been almost three rotations since he'd held a gun or worn his biosuit. Three rotations since Maggie finally got what she'd been aiming for, ever since Kophat.

Now, without his job, without his gear, without his *life*, Joe felt as if he were missing something. It was a burning ache in his gut, almost like the homesickness he had felt as a kid fresh off Earth. Congress could have chopped off an arm and he wouldn't have felt the same pangs of longing he did now without his rifle and his biosuit.

He felt lost.

Joe rolled over on the bed and squeezed his eyes shut, still gripping the knife. He wasn't going back. Maggie had seen to that. After fifty-three turns of completely screwing him over at every opportunity, she had finally won. *Might as well get over it, Joe. You're stuck on this heap.* As he mulled over that, the lack of sleep finally caught up with him. Joe unwillingly began yet another disturbing dream about his inexplicably bitter former groundmate.

The phone rang.

Joe jerked awake, at first thinking it was an invasion siren going off. When he realized it was the blocky device on his nightstand, he frowned. Back at the front desk, the receptionist could have seen he was sleeping. He'd paid top dollar for all the amenities, and she had said herself that the staff would divert all calls when his heart and respiratory functions indicated he was sleeping.

Joe dropped the Swiss Army knife to the nightstand and picked up the phone, trying not to sound groggy, poring through the list of possible emergencies in the back of his head.

"Yeah?"

"Joe Dobbs?" It was a woman's voice, girly, almost teen.

Joe checked the clock. It was 3:03 AM. "Let me guess. The freighter crashed and my stuff's missing."

"This is Samantha," the girl said, then giggled. "But you can call me Sam."

Joe's brows furrowed. "Do I know you?"

"You want to," the girl said happily. "I can make all your dreams come true."

Joe rolled his eyes and hung up. He was taking off his shoes so he could go to bed properly when the phone rang again.

"Look," Joe snapped, "I didn't give out my number so I could get propositioned by every whore in the East Side."

The girl on the other end giggled. "You couldn't buy my services if you wanted to, Joe."

"Then I won't." He hung up again.

When the phone rang the third time, Joe was just starting to fall back to sleep. He considered turning the ringer off. Instead, he yawned, lifted the receiver, and said, "I tell you, lady, you're starting to get on my nerves."

"And you're starting to get on mine."

Joe blinked. It had been a man's voice. "Who the hell are you?"

"Who the hell do you think I am, Joe?"

"I don't know...that little girl's pimp?"

"Oh my God, you have the mental density of a block of ruvmestin, don't you?"

Joe blearily glanced at the clock again. "Look, buddy, it's almost three-twenty in the morning. I'd be a lot more likely to buy whatever you're selling if you weren't pissing me off."

"I take it being a Congie wasn't very stimulating."

"What the hell are you talking about?"

"The last sixty years of what would have been my life, before I saw the light."

"So you decided not to join the Army. Good for you."

"There were hundreds of them. All different colors. Sounded like bombs going off overhead. I remember them because they scared me just as much as they scared the ugly creeps I was with."

As Joe's sleep-starved mind tried to make sense of this, the caller added, "So did you ever end up in that cave killing dragons? 'Cause mine pretty much came true."

He's crazy.

Joe started to hang up again, then an ancient memory tickled the back of his mind. A fortune teller, telling Sam he'd grow up to be a drug-dealer, and that Joe would grow up to slay dragons. With that memory came the memory of the fireworks Joe had used to distract the Ooreiki that had been kidnapping his little brother for the Draft—and of Joe getting captured in his place. Joe brought the handset back to his face in a panic, his exhaustion-haze vanishing. "Sam?"

The line went dead.

Joe's heart pounded like a hammer as he set the handset back onto the receiver. He sat at the edge of the bed, staring at the phone, willing it to ring again. He stayed up the entire night. It didn't ring.

Not that night, not that week, not that rotation.

The next time Joe spoke with his brother was nine weeks after Joe had moved into his permanent apartment.

It was a rainy afternoon in September when Sam called.

"Yeah?" Joe said curtly, trying to get a foot into one of the new tennis shoes he had bought the day before. He was late for his morning run.

A girlish voice giggled. "Do you always answer your phone like that?"

Joe dropped the tennis shoe, his heartbeat quickening. "Sam?"

"How bad do you want to meet me, Joe?" Her voice had a flirtatious ring to it, like a cheap, mail-order hooker.

Joe hesitated. "That a trick question?"

"No. It's a warning. You might not like what you see. I'm probably not what you've been picturing in your head." Her voice lowered, sad and seductive at the same time.

"Burn that," Joe said. "I want to see you." He held back all the things he had wanted to say to his brother over the turns, respecting Sam's wish for privacy.

"Thursday. I'll be working at the Hungry Kitten in Nevada. Talk to Mindy. She'll set you up with something."

"Sure," Joe said. Then, sensing his brother was about to hang up, he said, "Lookin' forward to it."

There was a pause on the other end, then, "Me too."

The line went dead before Joe could say any more.

Joe had to fight the impulse to hop on the first flight to Nevada. Instead, he forced himself to put on his other shoe and step outside for a jog.

Two five-foot-tall Ooreiki Peacemakers were waiting for him on his front steps, dressed in Congie black. Their long, tentacle arms were twisted politely in front of them, their huge, sticky brown eyes mournful, their fleshy rows of air-exchanges in their necks flapping as inconspicuously as possible, the way they always did before giving bad news.

Upon seeing him, the brown-skinned Ooreiki flinched. They had obviously been waiting on his steps some time, and yet neither had dredged up the courage to knock.

"Commander Zero?" one of them managed. "*The* Commander Zero?"

Joe's heart began to pound, his mind returning to the conversation he had just had with his brother. "What?"

The Ooreiki who had spoken glanced to his partner, who continued to stare at the ground, mute. The first one turned back to Joe. His huge oblong eyes were filled with humble brown apology. "I'm sorry, Commander, but you've been re-activated."

It took Joe a moment for that to register. "On whose order?"

"Prime Overseer Phoenix, sir."

Joe ground his jaw and twisted his head away. Even retired, Maggie was going to screw with him. "Look, if this is a prank, I'm not falling for it. Phoenix would rather lube up her ass with a plasma grenade than put me back into Planetary Ops. She's the one who *retired* me. Just walk your happy asses back to headquarters and tell the Overseer I thought it was very funny and she can go burn herself."

"It's not a hoax, Commander." The sincerity in the Ooreiki's sticky eyes was plain. "You...didn't hear?"

Joe stiffened at the outright fear in the young Ooreiki's wrinkled brown face. "What happened?"

"The Dhasha declared war, sir."

Joe's chest seized. Every Congie knew it was going to happen, and every Congie prayed it wasn't within their lifetime. "Ash," he whispered. He thought of all of his friends and groundmates who were going to die. Billions. "How many of them?" he finally asked. If it was just one prince, like last time, perhaps it wouldn't decimate the Corps.

The Ooreiki that had been speaking glanced again at his partner. The second Ooreiki hadn't taken its sticky eyes off the ground.

It was the second one who finally spoke. In a whisper, he said, "All of them."

3

DAVIIN GA VORA

"Time to die, Voran scum."

The announcement jolted Daviin awake as it was broadcast to thousands of spectators, not all of which were Jreet. He uncoiled his great length to face his latest enemy.

At first glance, he was stunned. At second glance, he was resigned.

The Aezi had finally tired of him defeating their warriors. They were ending it now. With a kreenit.

Beda's bones, Daviin thought, furious—but unsurprised—at the Aezi's cowardice. Even compared to the Welu Jreet clans, the Aezi were honorless vaghi.

Through the narrow bars of his prison, Daviin watched the scaly, rainbow-colored monster mindlessly grunt and tear at the floor of the fighting pit. The very ground shuddered with enough force to throw Daviin off-balance as its muscles bunched and its great weight slammed against the earth again and again. In its animal rage, the kreenit threw huge chunks of solid rock aside, some of which assaulted Daviin's scales through the bars separating them. Though this was not the beast's intention, it left Daviin with an understanding of the raw power behind the massive, flesh-shredding talons and a healthy anxiety of what was to come.

Daviin glanced down at his own claws and tried to subdue his nervousness. He had fought and killed to stay alive, though thus far all his opponents had been other Jreet. Knowing that in moments they would pit him against a creature that could tear his body to pieces with a single bat of its paw, Daviin felt a shameful pang of fear.

He closed his eyes and repeated the mantra he'd maintained since the Aezi captured him. *The day will come when I will see every Aezi ruler enter the ninety hells for what they have done, and I will follow them through it so that I may watch them suffer for every Voran life they took. Then I will return, challenge Prazeil for his seat, and make him dance on my tek before the masses.*

He still wasn't sure *how* he would accomplish the last part, considering the fact that it took a billion credits to secure a challenge for the Jreet seat in the Regency and Vora would pledge him a hundred million, at best, but it was a pleasant thing to fantasize about as he awaited his doom.

The door to Daviin's cage lifted, leaving nothing to protect him from the kreenit on the other side. The beast jerked at the sound and lunged, its soulless green eyes locating him in an instant. Daviin's skin tingled as his instincts reacted and plunged him into the higher energy level required to disappear from the visual spectrum.

The fighting arena went black.

No light, not even the tiniest sliver of shadow, marred the void that was his vision.

Before him, Daviin heard the kreenit hesitate, obviously startled that its prey had disappeared. Daviin slid forward, feeling his way along the edge of the cage, praying that the beast was too confused by his sudden disappearance to register the tiny, echo-locating pings that Daviin was now emitting on a supersonic level to help him navigate. He was not sure if kreenit could hear them, but he knew Dhasha could, and they were from the same planet, sharing the same common ancestor.

He had to strike fast.

Daviin slid around the kreenit, until he was the one outside the cage. He had no hopes of escaping—the sides of the pit were glass-smooth and sloped inward almost ten rods. As a Voran heir, the Aezi would keep him here until he died. What he needed, however, the cage could provide.

A distraction.

As the massive kreenit—over ten rods long from snout to tail, one and a half times Daviin's own length of seven—began to back out of the cage, Daviin located a chunk of stone that the animal had dislodged and carefully lifted it from the ground. As the kreenit snorted and huffed, sniffing for him, Daviin threw the chunk so that it clattered loudly against the bars.

With a roar, the kreenit began ripping through the metal that had held Daviin for so long, its mono-molecular black talons shredding it as if it were made of mud. Listening to it, feeling the curls of metal assail his scales as they were thrown aside by the mindless beast, a new plan formed in Daviin's mind. He abandoned his ideas of killing the kreenit and instead began moving across the floor of the pit, made rugged by the kreenit's claws. He moved as fast as he dared, keeping his movements as silent as possible over the rubble the kreenit had spread across the floor. Here, in the open, he had no protection should the kreenit realize where he had gone, and both he and his enemies realized it. All around him, he could hear the echolocating pings of the Aezi spectators as they excitedly charted his course to doom.

Daviin stopped near the center of the pit and picked up another chunk of rock. He hefted it once, pinged to judge the distance to the door to the vast underground Aezi gladiatorial pens, then threw it.

The kreenit turned.

Even as the stone was clattering to the ground, the kreenit was atop it, systematically tearing holes in the floor, the wall, the door. The monster that had, millions of turns ago, driven the Dhasha underground, now drove the Jreet guarding the exit of the pit deeper into the narrow corridor. He heard shouts of terror from the Aezi cowards inside the gladiator halls, which only drove the kreenit onward, through the hole it had created, into the chaos beyond.

Daviin waited. Three seconds later, he heard the kreenit's scream as its handlers activated its collar. Daviin lowered the energy level of his scales and instantly the scene appeared in gory color. Ivory Aezi body parts covered the inside of the tunnel, which was all but blocked by the enormous body of the ancient, iridescent-scaled kreenit. Daviin plunged through the opening, sliding over the kreenit's rainbow-colored tail.

The lone surviving Aezi on the other side had her back to him, her three-rod body stretched out in the corridor, staring at the monster spread out on the floor in unconsciousness, a dozen Jreet warriors lying in tattered shreds beneath it. Daviin pushed his tek from its sheath and slammed it forward with every ounce of his strength, puncturing the ivory scales of the Aezi's back, delivering every ounce of poison he had. Before his victim even had a chance to fall, Daviin was yanking his tek free and fleeing through the hall, seeking escape. He raised the energy level of his scales again and took random paths down the cavernous intersections under the fighting pit, backtracking whenever he ran into gladiator cells or beast pens.

He hid for days, killing the Aezi searchers if they were alone, avoiding them if they were in groups. He got no sleep—he spent his time slipping from tunnel to tunnel, relying on his sense of touch, knowing the Aezi were waiting for him to try echolocation.

Sometime later, Daviin had allowed himself a brief few tics of visibility to feed on a gladiatorial pit-beast when the Jahul found him.

Their eyes met, and a mix of horror and fear swept across the Jahul's face. Daviin raised his energy level to leave the visible spectrum, but not before the Jahul filled the room with the stench of his excretions.

Daviin listened to the six-legged creature back from the room. He could hear the Jahul's internal pressure stretch his inner chambers, threatening to burst them over its sticky skin in a fragrant display of filth. In instants, the Jahul would be out of reach, the first witness that Daviin was indeed alive.

Yet Daviin's honor refused to allow him to kill the Jahul. He was obviously a trader of some sort, a delivery boy. He had nothing to do with this war between the Vorans and the Aezi. To kill him would be almost as dishonorable as killing a slave. Still...

Daviin lowered his energy level again, whipped forward, and dragged the Jahul back into the room with him. He wrapped a ruby coil of his tail around the Jahul's midsection and shut the door of the dead beast's stall behind them, leaving them alone in the beast section of the gladiator pits.

Trapped in his coils, the Jahul soiled himself again, making Daviin's scales crawl where he touched the filthy creature.

"Do you know who I am?" Daviin demanded, wrapping himself further around his prey.

"No," the Jahul whimpered. "I came to deliver a few crates of food for your exotics."

"They're not *my* exotics," Daviin snapped, disgusted the Jahul would mistake him for an Aezi. Couldn't he see his scales were *red*, not a disgusting, pitiful white?

"They said this was the storeroom," the Jahul whimpered. "I'm sorry, I didn't know—" A new wave of filth flushed out through the Jahul's pores, over his quivering green skin.

Daviin released the Jahul disgustedly, intending to rid himself of the sniveling creature before he spread his reek all over Daviin's body, possibly lock him in the beast's old cell. Then he stopped, his brain only then registering what the sticky, revolting creature had said. "You are a trader?"

"Exotic feeds, sir," the Jahul said. He nodded at the box of food he'd placed outside the dead beast's stall. "I've got more in my cargo bay."

Daviin eyed the wooden box, which smelled strongly of some sort of alien meat. And metal. Daviin briefly wondered why a box of food would be filled with metal, then he cocked his head at the Jahul. "You have a ship?"

The Jahul seemed to sense something was wrong, for his beady black eyes went wide. "No, sir. I mean, yes, sir, I own a ship, but part of my agreement with the Aezi is I won't help runaways…"

"Do you know what it is like to dance on a tek, Jahul?"

The alien's black eyes went wide in horror.

"Unless you want to learn," Daviin warned, "you will help me. Understand?"

"But the other Jreet..." The Jahul started to back away, towards the door, and Daviin lashed out again, easily dragging him back with a single arm.

"I will kill the other Jreet if they try to stop us," Daviin said, only ninths from the Jahul's huge, bulging, wet black eyes. The eyes, like everything about the Jahul, disgusted him. He could not imagine having to eat the rank, dripping creatures, as were once their fate as a prey species before the formation of Congress.

"But I risk my livelihood," the Jahul babbled, soiling itself yet again. Daviin had to fight the instinctive urge to release the disgusting thing and wipe his hand. Which was, of course, the mechanism's purpose—make them too disgusting to touch, and therefore to eat. "It's all I have."

"Your livelihood or your life, Jahul," Daviin snapped, lifting the Jahul half a rod off the ground, until they were eye-to-eye. "Decide now."

The Jahul's bald, leathery, yellow-green skin grew splotchy and dark. It trembled in his grasp, its six spindly legs twitching for purchase. "I'll help."

Daviin twisted his head and neck until he was peering at the Jahul from the side. "You say that lightly, you betray me in any way, and I swear by Beda's bones I shall kill you before I die. I am a Voran, and my word is my bond. You have my oath on that, understand?"

"I understand," the Jahul whimpered.

Daviin lowered him to the ground and released him, shamed at how he had bullied the lesser creature. He would certainly serve penance in an extra hell for his crimes. "You will not be impoverished for helping me," he added, feeling somewhat guilty. "I am the heir of a great family. I will see you find trade with my clan."

The Jahul's small black eyes went wide and flickered to the diamond of white scales that marked the center of Daviin's scarlet forehead. "You are Daviin ga Vora."

Daviin watched him, saying nothing.

"They think you fled the pit...they're looking for you in the city." The Jahul's voice caught. "You have a two million credit bounty on your head."

"So little?" Daviin snorted.

The Jahul swallowed, then seemingly made a decision. He glanced behind them, at the closed door. "Come. Disappear. I will lead you to my ship."

"I warn you, Jahul, if you are misleading me—"

"You'll kill me, yes," the Jahul said. "You said as much already. Please, hurry. I can get you off Aez before they realize you're gone."

Daviin watched the Jahul's demeanor change with a pang of irritation. The Jahul would not willingly risk his life to help another in need, but as soon as credits were mentioned, he wanted nothing more than to serve. There was a reason why the immoral little monsters were often strung up by their legs to die of exposure upon the Voran homeworld.

However, Daviin was in no position to be choosy about those who helped him. The Jahul would serve his purpose, and once he had, Daviin would pay him and send him on his way, with all the blessings of the ninety gods. Anyone who helped Daviin achieve his revenge would forever have his gratitude.

And, as the Jahul led him through the underground prison, Daviin's body tingled with anticipation. His revenge would be soon in coming. In less than a turn, he would return with an entire armada of Voran elite and crush this honorless planet to dust. Getting his coils on Prazeil would be tougher, but Daviin might be able to take out enough loans with his brethren to see the disgraceful Aezi worm skewered, segments of his ten-rod body staked to fortresses all over Vora.

The Jahul got him safely through the gladiatorial tunnels and helped him onto the ship without even seeing another Jreet. Once their ship had left atmosphere and Daviin was sure the Jahul did not mean to sell him back to the Aezi, he allowed himself some rest.

Something slammed into the ship almost as soon as Daviin closed his eyes.

Daviin instantly hunched into a defensive position. If there was one thing that unnerved him, it was the idea of war in space. Bombs and ships, especially, were unnatural. Cowards' weapons. That he had to use ships at all was distasteful to him. "Were we caught?" he demanded.

"No," the Jahul whispered. He was staring at the controls. "Aez. It's..."

Daviin heard something strike the ship and he flinched. "Aez is firing at us?" He hated technology—so many things could go wrong with it. Even then, he could see the next missile puncture the hull and squeeze them all out into space.

"No," the Jahul said. "It's gone."

Something else struck the ship, making the entire vessel shudder. Daviin fought down panic and said, "Then who is shooting at us? The Aezi won't follow once we leave their space."

The Jahul's hand was shaking, and for the first time, Daviin noticed the thin sheen of excrement on the alien's skin. He was terrified.

Daviin snapped an arm out and dragged the Jahul closer, until he writhed under Daviin's sharp stare. "Tell me what is going on," Daviin ordered. "Who is shooting at us?"

"No one. That's pieces of..." The Jahul's skin slickened again.

"Pieces of *what*?" Daviin roared, shaking the little creature as something jostled the ship yet again. "Answer me, or I will fly the ship myself!"

"Aez!" the Jahul said in a strangled garble of terror. "It's pieces of Aez!"

"Pieces of..." Daviin frowned, wondering if it was some form of Jahul colloquialism he did not understand. "Beda's bones! What are you talking about, furg?"

"Aez is gone," the Jahul said, staring open-mouthed at the ship's viewscreen, where a debris field was now spreading in all directions, chunks of rock slamming into their ship as they passed. "Somebody just blew it up."

4

JER'AIT ZE'LAA

"Oh, my friend, come in. Shall I summon servants to file your feet?"

"No, Caus," Jer'ait replied. "The journey was not that long. How is business?"

The old Jahul allowed his inner gas chamber to ooze bubbles over his skin and moved to the other side of the room, four hind feet pattering the packed earth like some sort of unsavory pest. It reminded Jer'ait of the fact that he shared a similar body, a fact that Jer'ait despised him for. Of all the patterns to take, the Jahul was the most revolting.

"Business has been poor, my friend. Very poor." He eyed Jer'ait. "Are you hungry?"

"Thirsty, perhaps," Jer'ait said. Anything to get the old bastard drunk.

"Come," Caus said, heading to the door. "It is not safe to speak here. If they haven't bugged my house yet, they will."

Jer'ait cursed inwardly. He'd been told to keep the Jahul within the house for monitoring at all times.

"You are anxious about something," Caus said, eying him.

Damn the Jahul and their freak abilities. Jer'ait had been schooled to keep his emotions from his face and body, but such was not good enough with a Jahul. They could peer inside his very soul, and if he did

31

not say what he meant, they could sense it. Empaths, it was said. And when they used their talents to, say, create a ring of murdering slaver thieves specializing in sales of Congressional citizens to Dhasha and assassinating Peacemaker spies, it made infiltration of their network all but impossible.

That's why Jer'ait had been called in.

"I feel sorry for you, old man," Jer'ait said.

Caus oozed some more in pleasure. "Don't. They can monitor me all they want. Congress will never stop me."

"Not legally, anyway," Jer'ait said. "You're too good."

This seemed to amuse the old Jahul. "Their assassins cannot touch me. I can sense a Huouyt six marches away."

Jer'ait cocked his head at him. "Truly? I've been told no species in Congress has the ability to sense a Huouyt in pattern."

"I can. Like night and day," Caus motioned a stubby, three-fingered hand toward the door. "Huouyt are…missing…something, my friend. Come with me to my *haauk* and I'll tell you of it."

Though the proposition of figuring out the Jahul's very *irritating* secret for ousting his species in pattern piqued Jer'ait's curiosity, he said, "You have nothing to drink here?"

"I told you," Caus said, waving dismissively. "I have something I must tell you and this house may be bugged."

Jer'ait calmly got up and followed Caus out the door and across the swampy, alien yard. Even wealth did nothing to clean a Jahul of their filthy habits. Jer'ait tried to ignore the way the globular alien plants squished between his toes as they walked. It was supposedly a treat, something only the richest could afford. To Jer'ait, it was simply disgusting.

Caus led Jer'ait onto a ruvmestin-plated *haauk* and Jer'ait silently noted the ten *haauk* of mixed-species bodyguards that surreptitiously took up positions around them. No Jreet. At least Caus' corruption hadn't reached the halls of Koliinaat yet. Or, if it had, the Representatives were not confident enough to lend the criminal their Jreet.

Such was their own misfortune. Had Caus been guarded by Jreet and not a mishmash of former PlanOps survivors, Congress would never have been able to insert an assassin into the crime lord's ranks.

"This looks good," Caus said. "You in the mood for Ueshi cuisine?"

Jer'ait twisted to look down at the restaurant. "Never was a fan of that poison."

"You'll like this place," Caus assured him. "They make delectable ooma."

Jer'ait grimaced. "Won't that kill you if they prepare it wrong?"

Caus wrinkled the thin, splotchy green skin around his eyes—the Jahul version of a smile. "They won't."

They waited as Caus' men cleared the restaurant of its startled patrons and then seated themselves in a hidden corner. The Ueshi landlord who approached their table showed no sign at all that he was disturbed by the sudden visit from the most dangerous crime boss on Bolan. They ordered, then he calmly walked out of their booth.

"That one is good at hiding his fear," Caus said with appreciation at the Ueshi's retreating blue-green head. "I could use a man like him."

"For what?"

"A spy."

"He looks like he does well enough for himself here," Jer'ait noted, glancing at the lavish furnishings of the place. The restaurant even had what appeared to be a ruvmestin-plated chandelier—at least a fifty thousand credit item, if not more. "Doesn't strike me as a man who would devote his life to crime."

"I never said I'd give him a choice," Caus said, looking as if he found the idea quaint.

Jer'ait grunted and sipped the glass of water that appeared through the table's trap door. It, like all Jahul items, was small to compensate for a Jahul's short fingers.

"So tell me of this trouble you're having," Jer'ait said.

Caus quickly flicked the switch that closed their booth off from the rest of the restaurant. Once they were alone, he said, "It's bad." The old Jahul watched him and Jer'ait made sure to keep his emotions strictly under check. It wasn't very hard. Training at Va'ga had left him able to do almost anything with his body or mind. Now, he portrayed worry and pity.

"How bad?"

"This latest thing with the border planets." Caus made a disgusted gesture at the restaurant. "The foodstuffs. Congress was unappreciative of my involvement, to say the least."

Jer'ait glanced up at the vent in the ceiling. Caus followed his gaze.

"This place is not bugged," Caus said. "I've never been here before. Read about it."

"Ah," Jer'ait said. He motioned for Caus to continue. "So you stole some food from the colonies. Weren't they having bad times with the military overdraft?"

Caus snorted. "If the supplies were important to them, they would have spent more on guards."

"So several million citizens starved to death due to the shortages."

Caus blinked his inky black eyes. "Whose side are you *on*, Dagi?" He sighed. "We both know they all would have lived if it weren't for the military conscripting too many of our citizens and therefore consuming more than their share."

Jer'ait bowed his head in concession. "And now Congress wants you dead."

Caus snorted. "They've tried. Ever since I orchestrated that freighter of Nansaba colonists to go to the Dhasha."

Jer'ait schooled his features to show surprise. "You sold colonists to the Dhasha? Aren't the Nansaba rare? It takes them hundreds of turns to spawn a child, yes?"

Caus waved a disgusted hand. "They're worth almost a lobe of ruvmestin apiece and the freighter was completely unarmed. Eight hundred thousand of them. When I see a karwiq bulb, I pluck it."

"And it has made you very rich."

Caus snorted. "Oh, you have *no* idea."

Yes I do, you disgusting bastard, Jer'ait thought, but he didn't say it.

Caus mistook his rush of anger and laughed. "Why, my friend," he cried, slapping a filthy hand against Jer'ait's shoulder. "I do believe you are jealous!"

"I just fear for your safety," Jer'ait replied. "Something like that is considered a war crime. As is the stolen food, come to think of it. Will Congress not come after you?"

Caus made a sound of complete disdain. "Let them. Congress has tried before. Sixteen times. I killed every one of the Huouyt scum myself."

Which was untrue. Usually Caus huddled in a corner while his cronies did the dirty work, but Jer'ait wasn't about to remind him of the fact. "So how *do* you spot these assassins, Caus?" Jer'ait asked, knowing he was putting himself in danger with every tic he prolonged the conversation, but curiosity ate at him. He hated things that did not make sense. "I've always wondered. Your abilities are legendary, in that respect. As far as I know, there are only a couple creatures in all of Congress that are rumored to do the same."

His target snorted. "Between you and me?"

"Of course," Jer'ait said

The Jahul leaned across the table and lowered his voice. "I think the Huouyt are without *soul*, my friend. Either that, or their damn eyes... Something about their damn eyes shields it. Cuts it away. Covers it like a casket, you understand?"

Jer'ait immediately grimaced. *That* was something he would be cutting from the recording before handing it over to the Twelfth Hjai.

But Caus misunderstood his discomfort and lifted a hand to continue. "Now hear me out, my friend, hear me out. I'm not suggesting they're not sentient. Gods, no. Huouyt are smart. Smarter than you, smarter than me, smarter than those extinct slime-mold Geuji."

"Somehow I doubt that," Jer'ait said wryly.

"But their *eyes*..." Caus shuddered. "The only ones I've never been able to read have been the deformed ones. If Va'ga allowed the deformed ones to train, then people like me would be few and far between." Then he chuckled. "But the fools never let those breed. Sterilize them immediately."

"Their loss," Jer'ait said, unable to suppress his bitterness. "What of the foodstuffs? Did you already make your profits from it?"

Caus snorted, too caught up in his foolish philosophy to catch Jer'ait's discomfort. "I sold the food," he said, waving a dismissive hand. "Deal done, money made. Now I sit back and count my credits."

Jer'ait schooled his face and mind into worry. "But what of the assassins?" he insisted. "You said you caught *sixteen* already? How did you kill them?"

"Slowly," Caus laughed. "We tortured the last one for twelve days, as an example. The boys wanted to have some fun."

Jer'ait's hand tightened shamefully of its own accord. Man'ja had disappeared three weeks ago. They had hoped his death was quick. Some, including Jer'ait, had gone so far as to hope that he had somehow been kept alive. "I see," Jer'ait said softly, fighting a flush of fury.

Caus' black eyes flickered toward him with surprise...and nervousness. Jer'ait knew the empath had felt his unprofessional rush of anger. "Are you feeling all right, Dagi?" Caus asked carefully.

Twelve days. They tortured him for twelve days. Jer'ait found it difficult to concentrate through his anger, and chose a different poison for the Jahul than he had been planning. One that took its time to kill. "Not well, no," Jer'ait informed him. "They were my brethren. The last was my protégé."

Caus' tiny black eyes widened and he moved to flip open the booth once more. Jer'ait's hand fell upon his and rested there. Caus froze utterly as Jer'ait shoved a spine through his palm and injected a poison under the crime-lord's skin. Caus' mouth immediately fell open and his skin shifted from a gray to a yellow-green to a black as he emptied every wastes bladder he had over his dying body. Slowly, the crime-lord slumped forward on the table, bulging black eyes wide as they stared up at Jer'ait.

"Did it never occur to you that eventually they would stop sending amateurs?" Jer'ait said softly. He pulled a small black recorder from under his clothing and turned it on. He set it on the table in front of the dying crime boss.

"Caus Rathsaba, you have been found guilty of numerous crimes against Congress, including treason, murder, theft, smuggling..."

Jer'ait took Caus' personal planner and tucked it under his vest. Then he climbed onto the table with all the grace an ungainly sextuped pattern would allow, planted his two back feet beside the crime-lord's head, and tugged open the vent. It was large enough for his purposes.

He pulled himself up and pulled the vent shut once his feet were clear. Behind him, on the table, the recorder droned on.

"*...hereby sentenced to death by poison.*"

Jer'ait had disappeared into the inner workings of the Ueshi food-service complex and was on his way back to Levren before the crime-lord's underlings produced enough courage to break into their boss's booth and discover the body.

He was called for another assignment only two days upon his return.

Most would have found the lack of leave after such a long, danger-ous mission to be insulting, but Jer'ait detested idleness. He lived to hunt.

He stepped into the Peacemaster's office and sat when the Twelfth Hjai directed him to a chair.

"I don't suppose I have to tell you that was well done, Jer'ait." Yua'nev regarded him from behind his large desk, his perfect, electric-blue eyes utterly emotionless.

Jer'ait had never liked his superior. They had gone through training together and Jer'ait was the better of the two to have come out of Va'ga alive, but Jer'ait carried a deformity and Yua'nev did not. Thus, Yua'nev had the twelve-pointed star of Twelfth Hjai and Jer'ait remained for-ever ensconced at Eleventh. The disparity, however, allowed Jer'ait to continue to do field assignments, which he appreciated. "Who do you want to die next?"

The Peacemaster gave him an appraising look, then handed a small black reader across the desk. "A Human."

"A what?" Jer'ait cocked his head, wondering if he had misheard.

"Read it." Yua'nev gestured at the reader. "One of the newest spe-cies. Bipeds, dexterous, high lingual capacities—"

"I know what a Human is," Jer'ait interrupted. "I want to know why you need one killed. They are hardly major players in Congress."

"Apparently, that might not be the case," Yua'nev said, with all the poise of the Twelfth Hjai. "We've recently received a tip regarding this particular Human that we find disturbing."

That caught his interest. "What kind of tip?"

"The Trith kind."

Jer'ait stiffened as a thousand different thoughts hurled through his head at once. The Trith were allied against Congress. They were the only species in the entire history of the universe that had not fallen to the power of Koliinaat and the Regency. They managed to do this because, as a species, they could see every moment of every future incident from now until the end of time. That a Trith was involved was… disturbing. "Go on."

"You are aware that Aez was just destroyed?" Yua'nev asked.

"I heard as much."

"Along with the message about the Human, we received a prediction that Aez was about to become its own asteroid belt."

Jer'ait peered down at the reader, fixing the Human's features in his mind. "A Trith sent us this prediction? Why? They hate Congress."

"We are aware of that," Yua'nev said. The Peacemaster was in natural pattern, despite the inconvenience that a Huouyt's three naturally-aquatic, boneless legs afforded him.

Jer'ait watched as Yua'nev ran a paddle-like hand across the surface of his desk, trailing breja that writhed in white threads across the polished stone. It was a gesture that belied his superior's anxiety, and Jer'ait watched it with disdain and amusement. Even with his perfect eyes, Yua'nev allowed his thoughts to show.

"However," the Peacemaster said, returning his attention to Jer'ait, "a Trith does not lie. And, if even a fraction of what it predicted in its message comes true, this Human must be killed."

"What was the prediction?"

"It told us, before we even knew the Dhasha Vahlin existed, that this Human would vanquish it."

Jer'ait leaned forward, interested. "There was more. Otherwise you would give it your blessing and see it on its way."

Yua'nev's perfect, mirror-like eyes held Jer'ait's as the Peacemaster inclined his head. "The message also predicted that this Human would destroy Congress."

"Really." Jer'ait felt a twisting inside his head as tingles of alarm constricted his *zora*. "Did it say how?"

"He will fulfill the Fourfold Prophecy."

Jer'ait slowly let out his breath and fought to keep his *breja* from rippling against his skin like a raw recruit. "You are sure this is not a prank?"

"Aez was *annihilated,* Jer'ait. It was the only warning we had."

"Is it possible that the one who destroyed Aez sent the message?" Jer'ait demanded. "Perhaps it *wants* this Human dead."

"It was a Trith," the Peacemaster said. "A Trith has not been recorded in a few hundred thousand turns, either digitally or otherwise. Our language experts tell us it doesn't match the ancient Trith we have on file."

"*Doesn't* match?" Jer'ait asked, curious.

"No. It contained minor evolutionary changes natural in the course of language development. We had experts chart it. Every altered word has a root and an evolutionary path. The message was given by a modern-day Trith. One that learned the Trith language as it is spoken now, not a few hundred thousand turns ago. Our linguists confirmed it."

Jer'ait continued to frown down at the Human's picture. "It could not have been faked?"

"No supercomputer in the universe could do this," Yua'nev said, "even if it had somehow acquired an ancient sample, which is highly classified information accessible only by the Peacemaster, a few select Corps Directors, and Representatives of Congress. It was a Trith."

"Very well," Jer'ait said, still somewhat confused. Any fool knew that if a Trith prophesized an event, any attempt to prevent it would only force it to happen. "What do you want me to do?"

"The Trith warned us of one disaster and it came true. We've got two more predictions to go on."

Slowly, it dawned on Jer'ait what his superior was asking. "You want me to make sure the Human lives long enough to kill the Vahlin, then kill him before he can fulfill the Fourfold Prophecy."

"Yes."

"And you think we can somehow *change* this?" Jer'ait eyed the Human displayed on his screen once more. Its blocky face and tiny, dirt-brown eyes didn't appear to house the great talent and intellect needed to shatter Congress. "Just how many times have the Trith been wrong?"

"When they have been gracious enough to prophesize for us?" Yua'nev snorted. "Never."

"And what makes you think they'll be wrong this time?" Jer'ait asked, still confused as to why Yua'nev was trying to fulfill one prophecy and not the other...when the intelligent thing would be to simply kill the Human outright.

"Because if you fail, then I will send another," Yua'nev replied. "And another. And another. I'll send the whole of the Peacemakers after him, if I must. The Human will never survive to see his destiny."

"And you're *sure* this is his destiny?" This nagged at him. Trith were not usually so...generous...in their observations.

"There's another Human," Yua'nev said. "One who trained with him in Basic. She has been making similar complaints against your target for fifty turns, ever since she had a Trith visit of her own."

Jer'ait's *breja* rippled. "So long? Why has no one dealt with it before this?"

"Your target happens to be one of the most decorated soldiers in Congress," Yua'nev said with a wry look. "Six *kasjas* to his name. *Despite* his former groundmate's constant intervention. By all accounts, it should probably be more like fourteen."

Suddenly, the thought that this Human would fulfill the Fourfold Prophecy became much easier to imagine. Jer'ait glanced again at the blocky, pinkish face, trying to picture it earning one kasja, let alone six. It was difficult. When Jer'ait looked at the creature, all he saw were brittle bones to break, tiny eyes, and a fragile brain-casing.

Finally Jer'ait said, "Six kasjas? That would never have stopped us before."

"He also had a Dhasha prince backing him," Yua'nev said. "One we wholly respected."

"You mean you were afraid of him."

Yua'nev's electric-blue eyes showed no reaction. "He is Representative Mekkval's brother. Prince Bagkhal. Your target is Commander Zero."

Jer'ait twisted his face. "This sounds like it might be annoying."

"Not overly. Follow the Human. Become his friend. Then, once he fulfills the first prophecy, kill him before he has a chance to fulfill the second. Leave no trails back to us."

"Become his friend," Jer'ait said, idly scanning the information on the datapad. "How?"

"You will be assigned to his PlanOps groundteam starting tomorrow."

A...groundteam. Charged with killing Dhasha. The unpleasantness increased by several notches in Jer'ait's mind. He scanned the photo. "Has it occurred to you that I might die on Neskfaat before I have a chance to kill him? This might be a self-fulfilling prophecy, Yua'nev. You send me into a war that has a horrendous survival rate and you may not know I'm dead until after the Human has switched sides. If you ask me, I should kill him as soon as I see him."

"No," the Peacemaster commanded.

Jer'ait glanced up. "It is the wise thing to do."

"No," Yua'nev repeated. "This Dhasha Vahlin is what we've been fearing. He's uniting the Dhasha. Calling them to the systems surrounding Neskfaat from all across Congress. He *will* carve a hole in our society, unless we can stop him."

"Just because this Human is prophesized to kill him doesn't mean that someone else can't do it in the Human's stead," Jer'ait reminded his commander.

"You will not kill him until the Vahlin takes his last breath," Yua'nev ordered. "Understood?"

Jer'ait returned his attention to the Human. "That pattern looks as irritating as the Jahul. How long will I be required to hold it?"

"You will not take a Human pattern."

"I...won't?" He peered back at Yua'nev, frowning.

"No. You're going as a Huouyt. As yourself."

Jer'ait flinched, his *breja* curling tightly against his body. "Is that wise?"

"This Human spent time on Eeloir," Yua'nev said. "He is reputed to be able to spot a Huouyt."

Jer'ait snorted. He'd heard *that* before. "I just killed a Jahul crime lord. If *anyone* could've spotted me, it would have been him."

"You go as yourself," Yua'nev said again. "Your natural pattern. No disguise. Jer'ait Ze'laa vehn Morinth, younger brother of Rri'jan vehn Morinth. Va'ga-trained. Number one in the kill rankings. A Peacemaker on loan from the Twelfth Hjai, due to Overseer Phoenix's request."

The reader began to tremble in Jer'ait's hand before he calmed himself. "You are the only one outside of Va'ga who has seen my true form. I should at least take the shape of another Huouyt—"

"No," Yua'nev interrupted. "You will be on Commander Zero's groundteam. You will need to change shape in front of him. You will go without a pattern."

Jer'ait had never allowed anyone else to see him for what he was. To do so now…

Slowly, he said, "Since leaving Va'ga, I have made certain to keep my deformity hidden, remaining in borrowed patterns, giving my shame no chance to assault another's eyes. It's the only reason the purists have overlooked the fact I left Morinth. If I flaunt my deformity in public, the other Huouyt will call for my death."

"Will this be a problem for you?" Yua'nev asked. His perfect eyes were like cold mirrors.

Shame and anger twined within him like lovers. "No," Jer'ait said, locking his misery away. "I can kill in any pattern."

5

THE HUNGRY KITTEN

Joe listened in silence as the Ooreiki Peacemaker described the various Headquarters installations he would have to visit to reactivate his enlistment term. He said nothing as they summarized his itinerary and his new command system. The Corps Directors were panicking over the Dhasha rebellion, ordering Planetary Ops to put together teams of their best soldiers—regardless of species—to make up the first wave of the Congressional attack. Phoenix wanted Joe in the midst of it. Of course. Because everyone going to Neskfaat was going to die.

Joe listened, but said nothing. The two Ooreiki Peacemakers expected him to leave with them that night. Two days before he was supposed to meet his brother.

The Ooreiki seemed to notice Joe's silence for the first time. The huge, slitted pupils of its sticky brown eyes dilated to massive black ovals, its leathery face anxious. "Commander? Is everything all right?"

"I'd like a couple extra days to take care of my affairs."

"Sorry, sir." There was real anguish in the young Ooreiki's dark brown face as it twisted its eight boneless fingers together. "Overseer Phoenix gave me orders to ensure you arrive on the staging planet of Jeelsiht as soon as possible. We've already talked to Relocations for collection and long-term storage of your belongings. They'll take care of the details. Right now, Phoenix wants you to get acquainted with your new groundteam. Your Battlemaster and your acting Second are waiting for you in the barracks here, and the rest are waiting on Jeelsiht. You'll only have a few weeks to get to know each other before they'll be sending in the first wave on Neskfaat, so Phoenix wants you to begin as soon as possible."

Joe didn't give a damn what Maggie wanted, but he nodded anyway. "Understood. Anything else?"

"No, sir." The Battlemaster handed him a thin black sheet detailing his orders.

"Very well," Joe said, reading them. "I'll see you again in a couple hours."

The Ooreiki Battlemaster's face wrinkled in a relieved alien smile. "Yes, sir." He had obviously expected—and feared—resistance. "Sorry to bring bad news, sir. We'll be waiting for you in the shuttle station."

Joe nodded and watched them leave. As soon as they were out of sight, his polite façade faded. He glanced down at the orders in his hand, then climbed the stairs to his apartment. He set the note from Command on the bed and began packing his meager possessions. When he was finished, he threw the duffel bag over his shoulder and tossed the thin black government sheet into the trash on the way out. He knew it was the final straw Maggie could use to get him permanently thrown in the brig, or executed, but he didn't care.

God hates a coward.

After fifty-three turns of wondering, Joe wasn't leaving Earth without seeing his brother.

Twelve hours later, Joe was in Nevada. He found the Hungry Kitten half an hour outside of Las Vegas. He set the *haauk* down in the sun-baked parking-lot and stepped into the dusky interior.

Music and the scent of cigarettes wafted back to him as a bulky man in sunglasses stopped him to check for weapons. He grunted at the tattoo on Joe's right palm, but otherwise said nothing. Joe paid the cover charge and walked through the heavy red curtain into the din of the dance room. Finding the contorting, skimpily-clad women strange without the hormone-induced musculature and bald, pale skin of a Congie, Joe found a quiet table and sat down.

"Any idea where I can find Mindy?" Joe asked the mostly-naked waitress who came to take his order.

The overly-tanned woman gave his pale skin a suspicious look. "Who's askin'?"

"Joe Dobbs."

"Never heard of you."

"I was told to come here."

"Sure you were. You look like a cop."

"I'm a Congie." Joe held up his right palm.

The woman snorted. "Fake."

"You know it isn't."

She gave him a patronizing smile behind too much makeup. "Look...guy...I've got other people needin' drinks. You gonna order or what?"

"Just tell Mindy I need to meet our friend sooner than expected."

"I don't know no Mindy. You gonna order or what?"

Joe hurled the table across the room as he got to his feet. Into the silence following the crash of the table and broken glass, he shouted, "Look, they're calling me back and I just want to see my brother before I gotta go die on some burning Dhasha planet. Why's it gotta be so goddamn difficult?!" He kicked over a chair, sending it careening across the room to shatter against the wall.

Even after rotations without the Congie nanos and drugs, Joe was still stronger than most.

The bouncers converged on him, and Joe, already in a foul mood from going AWOL, threw the first punch. He was doing all right, knocking out three and keeping the rest at a wary distance, until one of them drew a taser and fired it at him. Then the three that were still conscious began pounding his face into hamburger.

Joe passed out long before they tossed him on his head in the dusty parking lot and took to tearing apart his *haauk*.

When he woke up, Joe was sprawled in the dust behind the building, curled amongst the trash bags. He grunted and righted himself, then stumbled around to the front.

Six police *haauk* lined the parking-lot. Two more hovered near the road. Joe ducked back behind the building, his heart pounding.

"Hey!" a Human voice shouted. "You there!"

Joe clenched his right palm tightly to keep the tattoo from showing. Then he turned back to face the officer that had spotted him.

The uniformed man looked him up and down, then his face twisted. "This is a crime scene. Go sleep it off somewhere else."

Joe blinked, then realized the man thought he was drunk. He knew that could very well work to his advantage, but he was puzzled as to why they hadn't arrested him yet. "Crime scene?"

"Yeah. You didn't know? Biggest takedown in twenty years. Crime boss called Ghost. Was gonna meet his brother or something. We're still looking for him."

"The crime boss?"

"The brother."

Pain arced through Joe's chest. "You arrested him?"

"No, I just told you we got the crime boss." The guy gave him a disgusted once-over. "Man, you look like you got worked over by a Jreet. Go home and clean up. This place won't be open for a while. Maybe never. Looks like Ghost was using it as a front. Got a roomful of counterfeit bills in the back."

Joe felt his world crumbling.

"Say," the officer said, "You're all banged up, but you still look a lot like..." The man made a quick grab for his pocket. "Stay right there."

Joe watched as the officer fished out a reader from his pants. "Sonofabitch, you're the brother, ain't you? The renegade Congie."

Joe saw the officer's eyes widen as he realized the two of them were in the alley alone. The officer was fumbling for his gun when Joe slammed his fist into his solar plexus and followed it with a roundhouse to the temple. The officer went down with no more sound than the thud of his body hitting the ground.

Grunting, Joe dragged the man over to the pile of trash and left him buried amongst the fly-covered plastic bags to sleep it off.

Then he went looking for Sam.

• • •

"I hear you know quite a bit about Prime Commander Joe Dobbs." The green-eyed man sat easily upon Phoenix's couch, neither overbearing nor anxious in any way. He had a calm masculinity to him that seemed to dominate the room. That, and he had hair. Curly black waves. He clearly wasn't a grounder.

Phoenix hadn't seen anyone so sexually appealing in thirty turns. She had to suppress a little heart-flutter, uninvited. Odd.

Then she realized what he had said and her thoughts soured. "You want to talk about Zero," Phoenix said, immediately getting a bitter taste in her mouth.

"Yes," the man said. "Interesting name, isn't it?" The way he moved his hands, the slow grin—she could have sworn he was flirting with her. That brought Phoenix instantly back to her senses. She was wearing her rank of Prime Overseer. No man in his right mind would flirt with her, especially one that had somehow bypassed all the safeties and appeared in her office without warning.

A Peacemaker, then.

"How did you get through the security checks?" she asked coldly. "I see no rank."

The man smiled easily, his casual charm almost disarming. "I hear Zero got his name from a traitor. Odd, that he kept it even after the Ooreiki was tried and slain."

Phoenix's face twisted. "He's a traitor himself."

The man leaned forward, his green eyes intense. "Oh?"

Understanding dawning on her, a slow smile spread across Phoenix's face. "So why now?"

"Excuse me?"

"Why now?" Phoenix repeated, leaning back in her chair. "I've been trying to get the Peacemakers to investigate him for fifty turns. What made you finally decide it was important enough to come speak to me?"

The Peacemaker seemed taken aback. "You mean no one has interviewed you before this?"

"They have," Phoenix said, "but never more than a tri-point. You're a what, Sixth Hjai? Seventh?"

The man's only response was a smile. "Explain to me why you have lodged thirty-seven complaints against him in the last fifty turns."

"I don't see a rank, Mr...?"

"And you won't," the green-eyed man said, flashing a charming grin. "Suffice to say I'm not a tri-point."

Phoenix grinned, despite herself, finding his charisma refreshing. She looked him over, imagining him without the sleek blue civilian clothes. *He's got an even better body than Joe*, she realized with a little start. She thought about how much she liked sex, and how damn little of it she'd gotten since accepting Prime Overseer. Then she checked herself. She'd been at this too long. She was beginning to get soft. Becoming too complacent. Too...lonely.

Secrets, she had learned over the last fifty-three turns, were not good for the soul. Nor the digestive tract. Especially the kind she carried.

"You have access to my previous interviews," she said, fighting that carnal urge to open up to someone, anyone, after fifty-three turns in hiding.

"I want to hear it from you," the man said. "In your own words."

Phoenix took a deep breath and trailed her delightfully sensitive fingers across her glistening black Congie desk. The man watched her hand, seemingly bemused. Then, with a sigh, Phoenix said, "Back in basic. Kophat. I—we—were visited by a Trith."

The man nodded. "Uncommon, but not unheard of."

"This Trith showed me something...horrible." She closed her fingers into a fist. "I still can't explain it. I just felt...scared."

"You were still a child," the Peacemaker said. "It could have affected your judgment."

"No!" Phoenix snapped, hitting her desk with her fist, that old anger rising again. That betrayal. "No. This is something I will *never* forget." Ever. She remembered watching her friends die. People she'd sworn to protect. People she believed in, people she would have given her life to save in an instant. Because of Zero. Because he'd gone to the enemy.

"Try to explain it," the man said calmly. Then, when she still showed reluctance, he urged, "You can tell me. I want to get this fixed."

His friendly smile, his easy demeanor, the husky overtones... Despite her disgust for Zero, Phoenix smiled, deciding the man deserved something interesting for his troubles. "The Trith showed me Zero holding a planet in his hand. A purple one, like Kophat. He held it up, like he was showing it to me. Then he crushed it in his palm. I *felt* all those people die. I heard them screaming. Blood ran from his fist and covered the ground. When I looked down to watch the blood, I realized we were standing on skulls. Skulls and bones and Dhasha scales. Then, before I could look away, he plucked another one from the sky and brought it down in his fist. He held it out to me and smiled. Then he crushed that one, too. I will never forget those people as they died. It was as if I were in their minds, feeling it happen. I think he's going to destroy Congress."

The man's eyes flickered across her face. "You did not include this in your report."

Of course not. She had to hide a smile. "I knew the Ueshi tri-point would not believe me." Phoenix leaned across her desk. "Somehow, I think you will."

The man winked at her. Flirting again. Phoenix couldn't help but wonder what dinner with him would be like. It'd been a while since she'd been with a man. She fought the irritating emotions that surged forward at that, an unfortunate byproduct of unevolved body chemistry. A problem that, to her chagrin, a good portion of the more advanced species of the universe did not share. Unable to ignore the sexual appeal of this man, instinctively desiring his big, masculine hands on her body, not for the first time in the last fifty-three turns, Phoenix found herself wishing she were not Human.

Steeling herself, putting herself solidly back into her professional façade, she said, "So I ask you again. What changed?"

The green-eyed man stood and gave her a beaming grin. "Thank you for your time, ma'am."

She felt a pang of loss, despite herself. If nothing else, sex was excellent stress relief. And, with the Vahlin gathering his forces for war, very possibly about to succeed where Na'leen had failed, she needed all the relief she could get. "Before you go…"

The man stopped in the doorway and glanced back.

"Would you like to share dinner with me sometime?"

"I'm sorry," he said, "I've gotta go interview Commander Zero."

"What about afterwards?" she blurted, desperate to get that relief. *Damn*, she thought immediately. What was *wrong* with her? It was almost like her hormones were cutting off her brain.

The Peacemaker gave her a patronizing smile. "I'm not your type."

Phoenix did a startled double-take. Oh, he was *good*. Realizing exactly what she was dealing with, Phoenix quickly pushed away from her seat and stood, her hand automatically reaching for the weapon on her belt.

"Careful," the Huouyt said calmly. "If I'd wanted to kill you, you would be dead. I'm interested in Zero, nothing more."

Merciful dead, Phoenix thought. *That's another Va'gan.* Phoenix had wondered when Koliinaat would take interest enough to send a professional, and she cursed herself for letting her guard down so far in the meantime. She began calculating which assassin it could be as she watched him much-too-casually pick up a Human carving from an end-table beside her door, following the nervous tics, the body language.

She let her hand fall from her belt, knowing she needed to keep him in the room for a few more tics to make an accurate ID. With as much indignance as she could muster, she said, "You were using hormones, weren't you?"

Her visitor cocked his head, seemingly bemused she had caught it. "It is nothing new. Your species releases such scent chemicals all the time." The Peacemaker put down her statuette, which she would incinerate later. The charming smile had vanished as quickly as it had come, leaving an unnatural void in its wake. "As I said. Thank you for your time."

She scanned his face. "You're going to kill him?" She wasn't sure how she felt about that.

The Peacemaker turned slightly, to look at her. "Zero is a Congressional hero."

"You're going to kill him." There was something about this assassin's mannerisms that she knew, something she had seen before. But *where?*

The assassin smiled. "I'm going to be his groundmate."

Phoenix gasped, and this time she didn't have to fake it. "*You're* the one they sent me?" Then she sputtered, anger and outrage hitting her at his audacity. "You're under my command and you *drugged* me?" That, just tics ago, she had wanted nothing more than to take this furg home with her—and the fact that he knew it—was almost humiliating enough for her to draw her weapon and kill him anyway.

"I am a Peacemaker," the Huouyt said, his borrowed green eyes suddenly seeming alien and horrible even as his drugs continued to trigger her base Human instincts. "Even in this Human's groundteam, I will never be under his command." He gave her a wry smile. "Or yours."

The over-cocky furg. Phoenix felt a rush of satisfaction at her visitor's lack of observational skills, despite herself. Fighting inner disdain, Phoenix snorted. "Then you don't know Joe."

The Peacemaker eyed her. "Enlighten me."

Phoenix laughed. "Enlighten yourself, if you can find him. Joe's been missing for two weeks. We found his wrecked *haauk* in Nevada and there's an investigation as to whether or not a few bouncers killed him that night, but I personally think he went AWOL. There was a government takedown staged for Joe's younger brother the next day—a big crime boss who's been causing the planet a lot of problems.

He was going to meet Joe at the bar. They caught the brother, but Joe went missing."

"Zero's brother is a crime boss?" The Peacemaker asked, leaning his big body thoughtfully against the door. Phoenix couldn't help but notice the sexy muscles of his arms where he crossed them over his chest. *Merciful dead!* She had to shake herself and concentrate on stillness to resist the urge to cross the room and mash her body against his like a common whore.

"Biggest hacker in the Human race," she gritted. "Changed his own damn genome using Geuji nannites and information from classified Congressional genetics experiments."

The Peacemaker gave her a long, flat look. "Interesting."

"It's something in the blood," Phoenix said sweetly.

"As far as I am aware," the Peacemaker said slowly, "Commander Zero is a hero, not a criminal."

"Yet," Phoenix sneered.

He glanced at the wall, obviously in thought. It was the stiffness, the quiet, awkward respect for his pattern that finally gave him away. Phoenix smiled inwardly. It had been a long time since she'd seen Jer'ait Ze'laa. The Peacemakers' greatest assassin, Jer'ait had never missed a target. She wondered how he would fare against the creature destined to destroy Congress. The epitome of Va'gan training faced off against the prophecies of the Trith.

This should be interesting.

"His brother's people could have thought Commander Zero was involved in the sting," Jer'ait told her. "Perhaps they killed him."

"I don't think so. One of the officers disappeared for a day. They found him later, under a pile of trash. Couldn't remember how he got there, but had a huge bruise across the side of his face. Someone cracked him pretty good. PlanOps good. Bastard was lucky to be alive."

The Huouyt cocked his head at her and flashed her another sexy smile. "Perhaps you could give me the location of that bar."

Phoenix knew she was allowing the Huouyt's chemicals to manipulate her, but at that point, she really didn't give a damn what happened to Zero as long as he arrived on Jeelsiht on time. She *had* to stop the

Dhasha Vahlin. "Perhaps I can." She found it, scribbled the address on a slip of paper, and put it on the desk for him to take. She took a step backwards as he approached, keeping the assassin out of arm's reach.

The Huouyt watched her step back, then took the paper. This close, the hormones were like a pounding, insistent wave in her head. She stifled the insane urge to step forward, into the stranger's reach. She cursed herself inwardly for not noticing it sooner. *Soft*, Phoenix thought. *You're getting soft in your old age.* She decided she needed to start dating again, to get the stress out of her system before it killed her.

Still standing on the other side of the desk, the Huouyt slowly folded the paper in half, watching her with an amused smile. "My thanks."

Phoenix narrowed her eyes at the disdain in his face. "Just get out."

The Huouyt gave a sarcastic bow and left.

He, Phoenix thought, more than a little impressed, *has gotten better.* She glanced at her open door—where the assassin had appeared uninvited—then glanced at her personal web link. She'd wasted precious seconds on thinking about his eyes, his chest, his sexy hands…

Yes, it was definitely time to start slaking her body's thirst for hormones elsewhere, lest she allow her judgment to slip like that again. She thought of it happening around Zero and she felt sick.

Definitely time to start dating again, Phoenix thought, pulling over her personal console and sitting back at her desk. *Just as soon as this war's over.*

• • •

Joe found out very quickly that he was not going to free Sam. At least not alone. They had his brother under the strongest lockdown on the planet. Congressional forces were being used to supplement local police, leaving a wall of bodies three digs thick around Sam's prison.

News crews covered the capture full-time, leaving Joe staring at his brother's image in shackles every time he turned around.

The knowledge that Joe had gotten his brother captured burned in him. Every instinct told Joe he had to help Sam, but everything he knew about Congress and security told him he'd be wasting his time. Sam wasn't going anywhere. He was the first major Human criminal Earth had seen since its induction into Congress.

They wanted to make an example out of him.

Joe went to bar after bar to watch the news-feeds, ordering a drink or two every time to keep the bartender happy. Once the drinks came, he'd set the whiskey aside and draw up plans on how to free his brother on the little napkins that came with it. When he wadded them up in frustration, knowing that his plans were desperate and stupid, he would finish his drink and order another, all the while watching the newscast portray his eerie-looking brother as some sort of homicidal psychopath.

Fluffy white hair. Like a goddamn cotton ball. And his eyes... Where they used to be sky-blue, they now resembled the electric white-blue of a Huouyt.

What the hell did the scaleless wonder do to himself? Joe wondered, aghast.

As the days wore on, Joe abandoned the little napkins for the drinks they came with. He forgot all plans of rescuing his brother and began instead to routinely drink himself into a stupor each night.

Damn Maggie. Damn Sam. Damn Earth. Damn Congress.

He said each in his mind like a toast as he tossed back shot after shot. Oblivion began to come as naturally to him as breathing.

It was sometime at night—Joe wasn't sure how many days it was after he'd fled Maggie's recall—when his hackles suddenly went up.

Joe was well on his way to being drunk, but he still knew something was wrong. He set down his glass and glanced around the room. Nothing out of place.

He was about to go back to his whiskey when a man took a seat beside him at the bar and ordered a drink. He looked as half-dead as anyone else in the room, but Joe's senses were on high-alert. He might as well have been sitting beside a ticking bomb.

The man caught his stare and nodded, giving him a polite smile.

Joe leapt backwards, grabbed his stool, and swung it at the man's head with every ounce of muscle he had. The man's face showed a twitch of surprise before the metal slammed into the side of his skull, knocking him from his perch and sending both of their drinks flying.

Joe dropped the stool and ran.

He took the first alley he came to and peeled down the cobbled stones with every ounce of speed he could muster. Joe heard something big crash into the trash piles behind him and men shouting, but he didn't look back. He kept on running, taking three more odd turns and climbing onto a roof.

From there, he began the dubiously intelligent task of jumping from house to house, losing his pursuers in the fences and walls behind. On the ground beneath him, he heard another crash and what sounded like a fence being ripped apart, but he wasn't sure it wasn't his drunken imagination playing tricks on him.

Joe ducked into an unlocked rooftop storage area and huddled amidst the tools he found there. His fingers found a hammer and he waited.

Outside the storage shed, he heard the roof groan with a new added pressure. Joe held his breath, and soon he began to make out the sound of something being dragged across the rooftop where he had just been.

Dragged? Did he have more than one pursuer?

The sound stopped, and Joe waited, scarcely willing to breathe.

It began again, progressing to the other end of the roof. Then, like someone had thrown a sack of rice over the side, he heard a thump as something hit the ground. The huge pressure continued to groan and slide over the edge after it, every once in a while making a sound like pebbles against Dhasha scales. Whatever it was, it was *big*. Joe let out a slow breath and stayed where he was.

For a very, very long time.

6

JOE'S SECOND

"Who the hell are you and what the hell are you doing on my roof?"

Bright light shone into the shed, blinding him. Joe groaned, lifting his hand to shield his face.

A bald man carrying an aluminum watering pail was silhouetted in the sunlight, frowning in at him. Seeing Joe's palm, the man suddenly took a couple steps back, putting a good ten digs between them. "I know that mark. You're a Congie."

"Not anymore," Joe muttered, pulling himself from the pile of junk where he'd fallen asleep. He stepped to the edge of the sunlight and peered over the edge of the building. He noted the displaced bricks on the cement below, pushed over the edge by whatever had been following him, then looked dubiously up at the sky. "You know what time it is?"

"Twelve-thirty."

Joe grunted and reached into his pocket to pull out the remains of his cash. His savings were either flagged or frozen—probably both—and as he unwadded the bills, he found himself growing more depressed. Three hundred and eighty-seven credits. Not even four hundred credits to last him the rest of his life.

"You give me a ride to the next town and I'll give you three hundred, cash."

The man peered at him. "You kill somebody or something?"

Joe gave him a crooked smile, realizing his nose had begun bleeding again. "Nah. Just a barfight. Need to find another bar."

The bald roof-owner grimaced. "You should use that money to clean yourself up, not to buy some booze," the man said.

"Guess that means you'll drive for free?"

The man smiled, despite himself. "Maybe I will. My sister was a Congie."

Joe hesitated in wiping the sleep out of his eyes. "Was?"

"Died on Eeloir. Huouyt killed her."

Joe grunted. "That was a bad one."

The man's attention sharpened. "You were there?"

Groaning, Joe put his hand up to shield his eyes again. Confirming that the place wasn't swarming with Peacemakers, he lowered his hand and said, "Wish I wasn't, but yeah. I was there. Eight turns of Hell. Makes you really learn to watch your back."

The man gave him a look like Joe had just sworn his mother was still a virgin. "I heard the Human Ground Force didn't have any survivors."

"There were a couple. It was bad. You don't want to be on the opposite side of a Huouyt. 'Specially if the Huouyt knows what he's doing." Joe shook his head, then eyed the man. "What was your sister's name?"

"Tertiary Commander Tammy Schroder."

"Wheaties?" Joe asked, automatically.

The man's sharp look became painfully acute. "Some people called her that."

Joe chuckled. "Small world."

"Why?" the man demanded, suspicion tight in his face.

Joe shrugged. "She was in my PlanOps battalion, under a different Prime. She was Rat's Second. Really athletic, could outrun most of the guys in the battalion games. Sharper than a goddamn tack. Saved Rat's life a time or two, and mine more than I'd like to count. Was a deadeye shot. Put down more Huouyt than all her groundmates combined. They all called her Wheaties. Don't ask me why—she got the name in Basic."

For a long time, the man said nothing. Finally, "You some sort of con artist or something?"

Joe grimaced. "No sir."

"And you knew my sister." He still obviously didn't believe him.

"The Ground Corps is a big place," Joe said. "I knew a lot of people."

The man's eyes scanned his face, then, eventually, he grunted. "Eeloir wasn't nearly as bad as this Neskfaat thing. I can't believe those assholes at the news stations. We've got the biggest war Congress has ever seen brewing right on our doorstep and instead they're going on about this Ghost guy. Who gives a shit?"

"Yeah," Joe muttered.

In the end, the bald man led him out to his personal haauk, then fired it up and flew him an hour east, dropping him off in a housing district in the next town over. As Joe was getting out of the *haauk*, the man stopped him. "Your name Joe?"

Joe stiffened. "Who's asking?"

The man leaned forward against the straps holding him to his *haauk*. "I know for a fact only two Humans survived that Eeloir thing. One of 'em was a woman. Are you Commander Zero? The one they're looking for?"

Joe winced.

Seeing his expression, the man reached into his pocket and pulled out his wallet. Taking out all the bills he had, he passed them through the window to him. "It's about fifty bucks," the man said. He hesitated, his eyes searching his. Finally, he said, "Clean yourself up, Joe." Then he pulled the haauk into the air and departed.

Watching him go, Joe's hands fisted on the cash. *Self-righteous prick.*

He promptly went looking for booze.

Joe found it later that night, after he'd been walking for nearly six hours. He sat down, ordered a whiskey, and began his blissful return to oblivion.

• • •

Jer'ait watched the Human down his sixth vial of poison for the night from the comfort of a darkened booth. He wasn't going to make the same mistake twice.

The Human had recognized him. *How*, though, was still grating on him. Not once in his life had Jer'ait been recognized for what he was until he was ready. And sure as hell not that *fast*. Jer'ait was better than the best. He held the highest kill-rate in Va'gan history. He was always the first on the list when it came time to kill a Jahul—the most notoriously hard creatures in Congress to kill—and not once had Jer'ait ever been outed.

And yet, this Human had done it. Half intoxicated.

And then, as if swatting a Va'gan assassin in the face with a barstool was no more out-of-the-ordinary than slapping a lovely waitress on the ass, his commander-to-be had hunkered down in another bar *a single town* away and gone right back to drinking himself into a stupor.

Getting up after being knocked from his stool, listening to the Human's running footsteps as he departed...it was the single most humiliating moment of Jer'ait's life. He would pay for it later, Jer'ait promised himself.

Still, the oath did nothing to assuage the bruising to his pride. Jer'ait wanted blood. Watching the Human down glass after glass of poison, he imagined the painful ways he could kill him and still make it look like an accident.

Someone in the Peacemakers had to have tipped the Human off. It was the only explanation. There was no other. None.

The Human had certainly spent enough time in the ranks to have made a few friends in the service. He was a living legend. The more Jer'ait had read about him, the more he found to read. His men followed him into battle with a devotion that any Corps Director would envy. He'd earned six *kasjas* in his lifetime and was credited with eight personal Dhasha kills. Jer'ait could ask any of a million Human recruits who Commander Zero was and they could tell him the first six battles he was in, the awards he won, and the number of craps he took during each mission.

And yet the fool had gone right back to poisoning himself as soon as he had escaped Jer'ait. Such an error in judgment was mind-boggling. It had been no effort at all for Jer'ait to call every bar in the area and ask if they had seen his brother—a man with a luminescent PlanOps tattoo on his palm was hard to forget. Upon receiving his location, Jer'ait had found him and hid in the back of the place to watch.

Yet, in all the time he'd watched the Human, no one had approached him. No spies came to whisper in his ear. He carried no communications unit, received no clandestine messages taped to the bottoms of glasses. He looked truly and utterly alone. And miserable.

A tingle of fear crawled its way up the spine of Jer'ait's Human pattern. Could his target have recognized him without a tip-off?

No. Not possible, he immediately told himself.

Yet the thought ate at him, gnawing at Jer'ait's nerves. As the night wore on, he could not stand it any more. He had to know. He got out his reader and called Yua'nev.

"How many people know of this Human and my mission?"

"Where are you?"

"Watching the Human try to kill himself. Tell me."

"Can he hear this?"

"No. But if he could, he's too intoxicated to understand what we're saying."

"You said he's killing himself?"

Jer'ait lifted the reader and showed Yua'nev the Human at the bar.

"Ah. A filthy habit."

"Who else knows I'm supposed to kill him, Yua'nev?"

The Peacemaster's perfect, mirror-like eyes showed nothing of his thoughts. "A handful of Peacemakers. No one below Eleventh Hjai."

Jer'ait frowned. "Give me their names."

"Bek'kiu, Gov'aan, Gra'fei, Elv'uu, you, and I."

All of whom could keep a secret. Jer'ait scowled, the situation making even less sense. "Who did the Trith deliver the message to? Could it have been overheard?"

"No. It came to me directly, secure-feed." Yua'nev cocked his head. "Why? What's going on?"

Reluctantly, Jer'ait said, "It appears you were correct in telling me he could sense Huouyt."

Yua'nev was not amused. "Do the job, Jer'ait. This is more important than all your other targets combined. Do not allow your pride to cloud your sense."

Jer'ait cut the feed and glared at his target.

He would wait, he decided, for the Human to be too intoxicated to run.

The Human was halfway through his seventh drink when Jer'ait's hard grip on his neck made him stiffen. Jer'ait extruded several drops of a potent interrogation drug into his victim, then sat down beside him.

"Let's try this again," Jer'ait said.

The Human's dark brown eyes registered surprise but he made no move to speak, even though they both knew he could.

Jer'ait ordered a drink from the bartender and casually took a sip as he eyed the Human. "My name is Be'shaar," Jer'ait said. "As you probably already guessed, I am a Huouyt. I am also Va'ga-trained. Do you know what this means?"

"It means you know how to square dance," the Human slurred.

"Oh yes," Jer'ait said, "I'm very good at square dancing."

The Human peered at him. "How good?"

Jer'ait set his drink down and, leaning forward so he could stare into the Human's brown eyes, said, "The very best."

"You're working for my brother," the Human whispered.

Jer'ait frowned at the Human. "You must have interesting family ties, my friend. What makes you think your brother could afford me?"

"So you're not working for my brother?"

"I didn't say that."

"So who are you working for?"

Jer'ait began to get irritated. "I didn't say I wasn't under your brother's employ."

"Yes you did. So who are you working for?"

Jer'ait watched the Human for several long moments, then retrieved his drink from the bar and took a sip, observing him over the glass. "I can see why so many people find you troublesome."

The Human's mouth fell open. "*Maggie* sent you?"

Calmly, Jer'ait said, "Either you are doing me an injustice by suggesting a creature like you could have enemies powerful enough to pay me for your death, or you have a very unhealthy ego."

The Human watched Jer'ait watch him, becoming increasingly confused. "Maggie didn't send you."

"I never said that," Jer'ait said, rankling.

"Yes you did."

You're in charge here, fool, Jer'ait reminded himself. *Act like it.* Jer'ait thumbed the whiskey glass, gathering up his composure. When he was ready, he met the Human's eyes once more. "Tell me more about yourself, Joe."

"I'm eighty-one Earth years, being assassinated, and rapidly losing my buzz." Joe glanced at the bartender.

"He can't help you," Jer'ait said.

Joe gave Jer'ait an irritated look. "I need another drink."

That surprised him. Like being paralyzed meant absolutely nothing to the Human. *Then again,* Jer'ait thought, *if he survived Eeloir, he is probably accustomed to such things.* "You want to get back to poisoning yourself."

"Sounds like so much more fun when you put it that way."

Jer'ait set his drink on the bar and leaned forward. "I know you've had experiences with my kind before, on Eeloir. Therefore, you know exactly what kinds of horrible things I can do to you, should you piss me off. I'd think very carefully about your answers from now on, Human. Each one may be your last."

"Good, this interview is boring me anyway."

Jer'ait had to resist the impulse to inject something more potent—something more *painful*—into the irritating Human's system. Instead, he allowed no reaction to the Human's sarcasm and said, "You ran from Congress. What did you think we were going to do?"

"Give up," Joe said. "Sign a few warrants, seize my assets, forget you ever tried to recall me."

And normally, Jer'ait realized, that would have been the case. Trying a new tactic, he said, "Why did you run?"

The Human laughed. "'Cause God hates a coward."

Jer'ait blinked at the distinctly Jreet sentiment. It seemed strange, coming from a small, bulbous-headed weakling. "What?"

"Tell you what," the Human said, ignoring the question completely. "Tell me the drug you just used on me and I'll tell you how I blew your cover."

Jer'ait scanned Commander Zero's eyes and found, to his surprise, not an ounce of fear within them. He'd heard of such things before, especially in PlanOps, but to have it happen to *him* was unnerving. He might as well have been interrogating another Va'gan.

"You should not be worried about the substance I used," Jer'ait said. "I studied Human anatomy before taking this pattern. It could be any of a dozen different chemicals, all of which bring the same result. What you *should* be worried about is whether or not I'm going to let you live."

"You are."

"Oh?"

"You haven't killed me yet," Joe said. "And this is the wrong place to conduct an interrogation."

"So?"

Joe sighed. "So, if I had to guess, I'd say you're probably some poor bastard who was passing through on his way to his groundteam on Neskfaat when headquarters flagged you down to go out on a wild goose-chase for a retired old vet nobody cares about anymore because some Prime Overseer happens to carry a really long grudge."

"You are partly right," Jer'ait said. "Earth was a temporary stop-over and eventually, I *will* be going to Neskfaat to join with the rest of my groundteam."

"Figures. That's Congress for you, eh?" The Human sounded almost jovial. Utterly unafraid. The lack of fear grated on Jer'ait's nerves just as much as being recognized had. "Always putting its foot in the little guy's shit."

Collecting himself, Jer'ait said, "But right now, I am trying to figure out how to get my ground leader back to headquarters without anyone realizing that their fabled Commander Zero was actually drinking himself blind these last two weeks, instead of exchanging loyalty vows with his Second."

In his inebriated state, it took the Human a moment to realize what Jer'ait had said. When he did, he squinted at Jer'ait and began blinking hard.

"So you're not a Huouyt?" he said finally. "Ash, I thought you were a Huouyt."

Jer'ait rankled at the Human's simple statement—as if it were like recognizing a Jahul in a herd of melaa. "I was not aware Va'ga trained Humans," he gritted.

"But..." For the first time, the Human looked truly unnerved. "Multi-species units always fail. They end up killing each other. They were outlawed a million turns ago."

Jer'ait tipped his glass at Joe and smiled. "Desperate times. The Corps Director was not about to let Aez go unpunished. You *do* know what happened to Aez, don't you?"

"Not really. All they've been covering on the news is my brother's fat ass."

"The Dhasha Vahlin blew it up."

The Human laughed. "Good for him. Jreet are ashers."

"You don't believe me."

"Look..."

"Be'shaar."

"Be'shaar. No offense, but your kind are a bunch of lying spawn of Takki. You'll tell me anything to get me back to Headquarters so they can try me and you can get back on with your life."

"No offense taken, Commander," Jer'ait replied. "Normally, you are correct."

"Just cut the furgsoot," Joe snapped. "There's no way in the ninety Jreet hells a Va'gan assassin would get drafted for my groundteam. Maggie doesn't have the pull in PlanOps, as much as she'd like to think she does." The Human looked like he was getting irritated. Jer'ait wished it were fear, instead, but irritation was a start.

"I wasn't drafted, Human. I volunteered for your team."

Joe snorted. "Right. Just kill me, okay? I know that's what you came here to do. It's all over your face."

Jer'ait had to fight down a brief moment of panic, telling himself that there was no way the Human could read his intentions, none. "I'll be truthful with you, Human," Jer'ait said. "I'm not here to kill you. I am here to help you destroy the Dhasha Vahlin."

The Human stared at him.

Jer'ait decided to use the Human's confusion to catch him off-guard. "This was my first Human pattern," he lied. "It was a difficult pattern to get used to—it took me an entire week to learn all of the intricacies of Human interaction. I am pretty confident, however, that it was not my smile that tipped you off. Who is working for you at headquarters, Commander?"

"Huh?"

"Who told you I was coming? Last night. With the stool."

"Are you kidding?" Joe snorted. "I haven't spoken to anyone but Jim Beam since some prick broke my nose in Nevada."

"Who is—"

"Tell me what drug you used on me."

Jer'ait felt himself growing irritated. "Trade secret."

"Oh, huh. Guess you'll just be left wondering why I was able to pin you, then."

Jer'ait held the Human's flat stare for almost five tics. Then, grudgingly, he said, "It was *jasanbic-4*."

"Really? I thought you guys used *vembiridol*."

"*Vembiridol* is a novice's drug. After Eeloir, PlanOps have built up their grounders' resistances to it. A good dose barely lasts five tics anymore." Jer'ait looked the Human up and down, trying to figure out what it was about this creature that had allowed him to be one of only two Human survivors in that miserable war. Reluctantly, he said, "Considering your history, I didn't want to take the chance." When the Human offered nothing, Jer'ait leaned closer to his target. "Now tell me about this Jim Beam you've been speaking to."

"Ask the bartender. He'll know."

Frowning, expecting some sort of trick, Jer'ait said nothing. When it was obvious Joe would say nothing more, however, he motioned the bartender over. "Excuse me. What can you tell me about Jim Beam?"

The bartender broke into a toothy grin and took another bottle of poison down from the rack.

"No," Jer'ait said. "I don't want any more."

"Jim Beam," the bartender said, thumbing the bottle. "Not much there is to know you can't figure out for yourself."

"Where can I find him?"

The bartender's face changed into a glare. "Funny. Every guy who comes in here thinks he's a real comedian. As if I ain't heard it all before. Sheesh." The bartender put the bottle back and left to help another patron, giving Jer'ait an irritated look as he passed.

Jer'ait realized Joe was watching him very closely. "You can't read English."

Jer'ait stiffened. There were things he did not like about this Human. Things that reminded him of *him*.

"What kind of signal did I just give your friend behind the bar?" Jer'ait began to stand, glancing around them for an attack.

"Relax. The bottle reads Jim Beam. It's a type of whiskey. I've been drinking a lot of whiskey."

Jer'ait stared at him. "You're trying to tell me you have no spy with the Peacemakers?"

"That's right."

Meeting the Human's flat stare, Jer'ait did not know which was more disturbing—the fact that the Human was either lying and he couldn't see it, or that he was telling the truth.

Jer'ait reached out to give the Human another injection.

"How about you kill me and say I resisted?" the Human interrupted. "That'd be kinder than turning me in to PlanOps, though you pricks don't have a conscience, so I guess you wouldn't care either way."

Jer'ait frowned. "I'm not turning you in."

"Right. You think I believed that multi-species groundteam soot?"

"You will." Jer'ait put the Human to sleep and carried him from the bar. Outside, once he had deposited Joe in his *haauk*, he opened his reader and called Yua'nev.

"I really think we should kill him now."

"Why?" Yua'nev lowered the orange nutrient wafer back to the plate and waited.

Jer'ait glanced at the Human's sleeping form. He knew the Peacemaster would ask, but he had no answers. Just a feeling. It was a tugging in his zora, an urge to kill the Human right now, and deal with the repercussions later.

"Jer'ait," Yua'nev said, when he didn't respond, "you kill him and we'd be risking billions of lives."

"You are making a mistake if you don't," Jer'ait said. "Believe me in this. I would put my reputation on it."

For a long moment, Yua'nev remained silent, and only static crossed over the feed as his superior considered it. Eventually, Yua'nev said, "We have been given a rare opportunity to pick our future, Jer'ait. And the future that I prefer does not contain a Dhasha Vahlin carving out an empire within our boundaries. Understand?"

Jer'ait smoothed his features. "Perfectly." *Moron.*

"Good. I heard he ran off. You brought him back?"

"In the process now."

"Don't let them see you do it. I want as little suspicion as possible concerning his whereabouts the last two weeks."

"Phoenix filed a complaint that he was AWOL."

"Her complaints are nothing new," Yua'nev said. "I'll make sure her superiors ignore it."

"But it's her team. She's following us to Neskfaat and will be in charge of picking our assignments for us. It would be best if I killed her before she can make things difficult."

"I doubt he's going to kill the Vahlin because it's easy," Yua'nev said, sounding amused.

"Very well." Frustrated, Jer'ait ended the transmission and glanced at the Human crumpled in the seat of his *haauk*. "Merciful dead. What is it about you that makes people stupid?"

The Human, drooling against his seat, said nothing.

• • •

"If you're my Second," Joe growled, "where's our Battlemaster?"

"He's coming."

Be'shaar turned to the door and began entering a code into the wall, each number preceded by a distinct, toned beep. A personal access code. Then he stepped away and they were locked in. Waiting for backup.

Joe sank into the bunk in the corner of the room, ignoring the way the assassin was standing guard by the door. His head hurt too much to notice anything other than his immediate surroundings.

Somehow, under the dark of night—and while Joe was unconscious—the Huouyt had snuck him back into the military barracks, despite the fact he was missing an identifying tag. Now, rubbing his throbbing skull as the aftereffects of the antidote hit him like a sledgehammer, Joe could not help but feel rising irritation toward the heavyhandedness of this creature that claimed to be his Second.

That, and a tiny bit of apprehension. He hated Huouyt. Eeloir had given him a healthy appreciation of why the slippery, psychotic ashsouls all needed to die. To even *think* about working with one was making him ill.

"You didn't need to drug me," Joe said. "I could've walked here."

"You wouldn't have." The Huouyt stepped back and leaned against the now-locked door to watch him, crossing his arms over his chest in a perfect imitation of Human irritation.

Joe lifted his head to peer out from underneath his hand. "Are you really my Second?"

"I have that dubious pleasure, yes." The Huouyt continued to watch him over his crossed arms.

"Why?"

"You hit me with a stool."

Joe sighed. "You gonna stay in that pattern forever? If you're my Second, I'd like to know what you really look like."

"You mean you'd like for me to leave so you can escape again, and this time go into hiding with me and my talents in mind." The Huouyt gave him a flat look.

Joe waved his hand at the industrial metal door. "My tag is busted, my head hurts too bad to see straight, this place is on lockdown at this time of night, and you've got a personal access code set on that door—I wouldn't get far."

"Yes you would." The Huouyt continued to watch him, tapping his fingers on his borrowed bicep.

Joe grinned, despite himself. "I think I'm starting to like you."

The Huouyt gave him a long, utterly unamused look. "Let me make something clear to you, Commander. You are due to depart for Neskfaat tomorrow at noon. I intend to see you get on the ship as planned. No amount of cajoling, sweet-talking, or bribing will convince me to do otherwise."

Joe grimaced. "I was serious."

"And so am I."

"Scratch that," Joe growled. "I don't like you. You're a real pain in the ass."

"As are you," the Huouyt responded. "If you didn't have the drinking habits of a Cu'it slave, I don't think I ever would've found you."

Joe cocked his head at Be'shaar, who was still leaning against the door, barricading it. "Was that a compliment?"

The Huouyt twitched, but only momentarily. "Why did you run, Commander?"

"Why didn't you tell them I ran?"

"I enjoy lying to people."

Joe laughed. "Now that I believe. Was it the only reason?"

"Yes."

"You're lying."

"Perhaps. You'll never know."

Joe dropped his hand from his temple with a sigh. "Listen to me, Be'shaar. I know why you saved my ass. It was a challenge. You wanted to bring back the legendary Joe Dobbs so you could whip it out and throw it in my face whenever I got uppity as your Prime. That's fine. I deserve that much." He stood up and stumbled toward the Huouyt, his head on fire. "But if we're going to work together, you and I are going to have to come to an understanding. We're going to have to start trusting each other."

The Huouyt looked him up and down. Be'shaar's voice was laden with disdain when he said, "Huouyt trust no one."

"Good."

Joe rammed the blade of his knife into the Huouyt's lower leg and yanked up hard, severing the large artery that led from the thigh to the heart in several places. The Huouyt's eyes flashed open wide and he began to collapse, forced to focus his attention on mending his pattern before he bled to death.

Joe stepped over the body of the assassin and punched in the sound combination he had heard the Huouyt enter to lock them inside. The door slid open with a high-pitched beep, then slid shut again when Joe activated it on the outside. Then he changed the Huouyt's passcode to a code of his choice and hit LOCK. He heard Be'shaar struggle to reach the door just as the door made another high-pitched beeping sound and sealed the Huouyt inside.

Joe opened the intercom. "You all right?"

"No," Be'shaar said, panting. His voice sounded strained. "I'm bleeding bad."

Joe laughed. "I thought Huouyt were better liars than that."

"I'm not lying. The artery you cut was too large—there was too much internal pressure to stem the flow of—"

"Can it."

The Huouyt waited in silence.

"Look," Joe said, "I know you aren't here to be my Second. You're some poor bastard Phoenix sent to hunt me down so she could make an example out of me. That's fine. I don't hold it against a soldier for doing his job."

"Commander, listen to me," the Huouyt growled, dropping the act completely. "They're not trying to kill you, but they *will* hunt you down."

"No they won't," Joe laughed. "They don't give a rat's ass about some retired grounder Prime who went AWOL. Not when they've got bigger fish to fry. I disappear, they'll let me go without a fuss and we both know it."

"I'm your Second," the Huouyt snapped. "Look it up."

Joe laughed. "Nice try. I'd have to come back inside to do that."

"Here, I'll read it to you."

"Don't bother. You're a Peacemaker, not my groundmate. I'd recognize your kind of nasty anywhere. You were pretty convincing, though. I was actually picturing a multi-species groundteam before you put me out. I gotta give you credit—you're good. Better than most Huouyt I've seen, that's for sure. Hell, maybe you *did* have a little Va'ga training, who knows. Fact remains, you intend to take me to Levren. I've got more important things to do than sit around answering questions while one of your friends carves on me. Sorry."

"I can help you free your brother."

Joe laughed. "Would that be before or after I open this door and you drug me and stuff me on a shuttle bound for Levren?"

"I'm not sending you to Levren," the Huouyt said. "You have my word."

Joe snorted. "The word of a Huouyt is ash to me."

"Then you're truly one of the wisest people in the Army, Commander, but it makes it no less true. I'm to fight with you on Neskfaat."

Joe sighed, almost believing him. "Sorry. I'm retired, Huouyt. The only reason they called me up in the first place was because one of my old groundmates has a small mind and a big grudge."

"And which old groundmate might that be, Commander?"

Joe got a rush of icy, skin-crawling goosebumps at the glacial feminine voice in the hall. Fists tightening, he turned.

Maggie was walking towards him, the silver eight-pointed star and four inner circles of a Prime Overseer stark against her crisp black Congie uniform. Joe gave a startled twitch as their eyes met. Dancing over her pupils and irises, slow-moving orange flames flickered and twisted like twin glimpses into an inferno.

Specialized contacts, but unnerving nonetheless.

When she made no move to call security forces, Joe cleared his throat. "I like what you did with your eyes. Real sexy. Bet the Jreet eat that right up."

Her unnatural eyes scanned Joe's body lazily. "Why are you not in uniform, Commander?"

"Be'shaar and I were just chumming it up at the bar."

"And your Battlemaster?"

"Working out some things with Supply."

"Like what?"

"Like finding me a cool set of contacts like yours."

Maggie watched him from behind her glowing flames, her face expressionless. "Come with me."

"I'm a little busy."

"Now."

Joe had to withstand the urge to tell her to go hump a karwiq bulb, knowing that the easiest way to get back out of the barracks did not include being locked in the brig for the night. He followed her. They wound through the corridors of the barracks, and after a moment, Joe realized they were entering the Overseers' quarters.

"Shouldn't you have gotten me drunk before taking me home? It would be kinder."

Maggie gave him an irritated look and opened the door to her chambers. "There's something you need to know about Neskfaat."

Joe gave the security scanner on the door a wary glance. Untagged, it would go into lockdown the moment it registered him. "Tell me here. I don't plan on hanging around."

"Come inside."

"I'd rather not."

"I'm not giving you a choice."

Joe glanced at her Overseer's star, gauged just how much trouble she could get him into if he disobeyed, and reluctantly did as he was told.

Immediately, the sensors recognized that Joe no longer carried a working chip and alarms in the room began screeching. An artificial Ooreiki voice said, *"Unknown intruder. No identifying tag. Containment steps taken. Please advise."*

All around Joe, a blue-black field popped into being, giving him approximately six ninths in any direction before it began cutting off body parts. Joe held as still as possible as Maggie walked up and shut the door behind him, but made no move to free him from the field.

"So," Maggie said, coming to stand back in front of him. "How did you lose your tag, Joe?" At full height, she was only five digs, same height as the average Ooreiki. Even stretching, her nose was at about the same height as Joe's left nipple. She was stretching now. It didn't make much difference. Joe still towered over her.

"I didn't," Joe said. "I scrambled it."

She laughed. "Really? Why?"

"Because I spent the last two weeks AWOL, drinking myself into a stupor in every bar I came across."

Maggie flashed him an irritated look. "I'll have someone replace your tag for you."

"How about you let me out of this containment field before I cut off an elbow," Joe said pleasantly.

"I want to make sure I have your complete attention," Maggie said, through a forced smile.

"Actually, it's the proximity of the energy field to my ass that's got my complete attention."

"The Dhasha Vahlin is on Neskfaat, Joe."

Joe yanked his eyes away from the glowing blue-black containment field to stare at her. The Huouyt had been telling the truth?

Maggie saw the shock in his face and nodded. "The Vahlin exists. And Bagkhal took up arms with him. Against Congress."

Joe felt the breath slip out of his lungs. *"Bagkhal?"*

His mentor. His friend. The only decent Dhasha that Joe had ever known. The only one who had looked at Joe and seen anything other than food. Joe had served under him as a recruit on Kophat, then again as an Overseer on Eeloir. Joe would have given his life for him.

Maggie seemed to find his reaction amusing. "Bagkhal and a hundred and thirty-three other princes. Each one with dozens of side-dens, thousands of followers, and millions of Takki. They're carving out a section of space as we speak."

"Bagkhal *defected?*"

"Every Dhasha within that sector defected. They've got a ban on all Dhasha travel in the area, but some of them are still getting to Neskfaat anyway. Their numbers increase with every day we wait."

"Bagkhal wouldn't defect."

Maggie's reply was a smug smile. "Your pet Dhasha commandeered the ship that was taking him to his next assignment. Forced the pilot to set him down on Neskfaat. Then he killed everyone on board."

"He wouldn't defect."

"We found his ship last week when we began maintaining surface superiority on Neskfaat," Maggie said. She leaned back against her desk, watching him. "Search and rescue teams took vidchips of Bagkhal killing the crew off the ship's security systems. Scale patterns match Bagkhal's."

Joe let out a breath. "We're so burned."

"Excuse me?"

"Who's the Vahlin?" Joe said. "How did he get someone like Bagkhal to fight for him?"

"You know the legend."

"He's a reincarnate of the warlord that first subjugated the Takki," Joe said. "Destined to free the Dhasha from their 'servitude.' How about you let me out of this cage now?"

"Why?" Maggie laughed, plucking a cherry from the bowl on her desk and popping it into her mouth. Spitting out the seed into a bowl beside her, she smiled at him and said, "So you can run off and your Second can go bring you back again?"

Joe stiffened.

"Yes," she said, a malicious grin forming on her face, "I knew about that."

"Then why—"

"Because I'm smarter than you, Joe," she said, taking another cherry. "I knew you fried your tag." She put it between her lips and pulled the fruit free of the stem.

Joe groaned. "Why'd you leave the Huouyt locked in his room?"

Maggie spat out the seed and grinned. Shoving herself from her desk, she strode over to him almost seductively. "Because I wanted a few private moments with you." She smiled and made as if to stroke his chest, only she did it six ninths away from the blue-black barrier. "It's been so long since we've talked."

"Cut the furgsoot and send me to the brig. You keep me here much longer and I'm going to end my misery." He made a motion like he was about to step through the containment field.

Maggie's flickering orange eyes darkened. "Peacemakers are investigating you, you know."

"The Peacemakers are always investigating me." He gave her a tight grin. "Thanks."

"This time it's different."

Interesting. Joe thought of Be'shaar and how he doubted he was anything less than Eighth Hjai. "Oh? How so?"

Maggie smiled up at him, her teeth carrying the malice of a cat's. Instead of answering his question, she said, "I received an order earlier today concerning your last two weeks. Seems someone important's been deceived by your pretty *kasjas*." The orange flames dancing in front of her pupils flickered. "They told me to drop the AWOL charge."

"So I'm free to go?"

"Oh, absolutely."

She walked to the wall and de-activated the security system, leaving Joe free to move once more. She motioned at the door. "By all means, Joe. Go back to drinking yourself stupid. I won't press charges. I'd enjoy seeing you waste the rest of your pathetic life away."

"Great. Thanks, Mag. You're a doll." Joe turned and left.

• • •

"You still there?"

Jer'ait twisted around to stare at the intercom. The Human had switched on the camera on his side. He was looking in at Jer'ait, somehow stifling the smugness that Jer'ait knew he was feeling.

"What do you want, Human?" It was more curt than he intended, and he cursed himself for once again allowing the Human to get under his skin.

"Haven't called for help yet, huh?" The Human sounded intrigued. And amused. Damn him. "How long you planning on sitting in there alone in the dark?"

Jer'ait felt his pride prickle before he squashed it. "It's not dark."

The Human fiddled with the console outside and the room around Jer'ait went completely black.

Jer'ait felt a flicker of rage for the first time in turns. "You didn't come to bait me."

"No, but it's fun." The Human grinned at him. "You really here to be my Second?"

"I already told you yes," Jer'ait gritted.

"What's your real name, Be'shaar?"

Jer'ait felt like strangling something. He knew that the Human would have found out eventually, but he had wanted to reveal it at his own pace. *Damn* the Human.

Realizing the Human was still waiting, he reluctantly said, "Kha'vola."

The Human laughed, and it sent waves of fury coursing through Jer'ait's borrowed veins.

"Is that so," the Human said, once he had stopped laughing.

"You've heard of me?" Jer'ait demanded.

"How about I let you out when you feel like telling the truth."

"That *is* the truth," Jer'ait snapped.

"Well, don't be too upset, but I've been around too many Huouyt to think you tell the truth on the second go. Maybe the seventh or the eighth, out of boredom, but not the second."

Jer'ait smiled, despite himself. "We're to be groundmates. We'll have to learn to trust each other." *And then I will carve out your liver, you miserable cretin.*

The Human snorted. "Yeah, right." He glanced at his watch. "Look, I got an appointment with Jim Beam. Like, any tic now."

"Your brother is due to be executed in three weeks," Jer'ait said, leaning forward with interest. "I can help you rescue him," he promised. "You'll find no one better."

The Human laughed. "You're probably right. But, like I said, I don't trust you."

Jer'ait frowned. "I am not lying. I'd enjoy assisting you."

The Human continued to chuckle. "Look. I'm just a PlanOps thug and you're just a wannabe Va'ga reject who heard too many rumors about Jer'ait Ze'laa and thinks he's a trained assassin. We'd never stand a chance and I know it."

Jer'ait scowled at the Human, fighting his frustration. "Your brother is going to die if you don't let me help you."

"I'm not falling for it." The Human shifted his attention to the door as he punched something into the access pad on the other side. "And unless you swallow your pride and call some tech guys, the only way you're getting out of that room is by figuring out what Kophat means. I'll even leave you access to the net, to make it easier for you." The Human punched in a few more commands and the net option appeared before Jer'ait. Then the Human's face tightened. "Me, I'm going to go watch my brother's execution on primetime. I hear it's going to have a light-show."

"Kophat?" Jer'ait asked, trying to stall him. "That's where you were trained."

The Human laughed and walked away.

Perplexed, irritated that the Human had refused his offer to help, Jer'ait went to the net and began to search files of Kophat.

It was a basic training planet for thirty-two different species, plus had held high-tech Congressional weaponry as a depot before the last major Huouyt rebellion.

Jer'ait frowned when he realized that the dates of the Huouyt rebellion coincided with the date of Joe's basic training on Kophat. Joe had gotten his first *kasja* in helping a Dhasha prince retake the planet from Representative Na'leen.

Jer'ait sat back, frowning at that page. It made no sense. Why had Representative Na'leen allowed the Human recruits to penetrate his bunker? Why, when he could have simply sealed himself inside and launched an *ekhta* at Koliinaat without fear of any reprisals?

Huouyt were intelligent, more so than any other species in the universe aside from the legendary—and nearly extinct—Geuji. Na'leen had been smarter than most, ruling the Huouyt from the Regency on Koliinaat for almost three hundred turns. Jer'ait knew this, yet as he began making connections between the dead Representative Na'leen and Joe Dobbs, he began to feel a coldness creeping along his *breja*.

Na'leen invited Joe inside. It's the only way Joe's groundteam could have gotten past his Sentinels.

Confused, Jer'ait closed the common net and accessed the Peacemaker records.

Jer'ait scanned the files for hours, but out of all of them, only one other Huouyt, a meager four-point, had found it at all suspicious. But at the time, the Huouyt had been generally despised for their attempt to fulfill the Fourfold Prophecy, and when he had received the report, Prince Bagkhal had sent the four-point off to count Trosska in the ruvmestin mines. Before he left for the mines, the Huouyt Battlemaster had tried to get Joe court-martialed, but his Secondary Commander had simply denied the request. After all, Na'leen was dead. Killed himself after Joe trapped him. Twelve witnesses said that Joe had saved Congress. Only one little girl had said otherwise.

Maggie. Immediately, Jer'ait typed her name into the room's passcode prompt. The system immediately rejected it.

Frowning, Jer'ait leaned back. Maggie's account that Joe had betrayed them all did not make sense. Yet the more he looked at the reports, the more the official story didn't make sense, either.

There were at least a dozen eyewitnesses that said Joe had killed a Jreet by himself, with nothing but a knife.

Impossible.

Impossible, unless the Jreet hadn't tried to defend itself…

Jer'ait's eyes widened. Could Na'leen have had access to the same prophecy that the Trith had delivered to Yua'nev? Could he have expected Joe to help him fulfill the Fourfold Prophecy? And Joe had turned him down?

It would not make a difference to Yua'nev, even if it were true. Still, it provided an interesting insight into the Human's mentality.

But how does this help me? Jer'ait wondered. *Does it help me to understand what Kophat means?* Then, frustrated, he thought, *Means to who? Means to Joe? Or means to Congress? Or did he study linguistics and knows Kophat means 'Violet Sky' in Ooreiki Common?*

There were just too many options. As Jer'ait stared at the console, he imagined all the different passcodes having to do with Kophat that the Human could have used to lock the room. He began entering them as he thought of them, beginning with the names of his four dead groundmates, then his instructors, then Representative Na'leen and the names of his five closest advisors. When that didn't work, he began entering cities and areas Joe had visited while on Kophat. After getting nowhere with those, he tried the names of all the gear and items a Congie had to use while training on Kophat. He tried every keyword he could imagine.

He probably spelled it wrong, Jer'ait cursed finally. *Nothing but a stupid, uneducated Congie.*

He blinked.

Joe had chosen Congress over the rebels.

Joe had chosen to become a Congie.

Tentatively, Jer'ait typed in the new password.

With a quiet hiss, the doors of the room opened and the light from the hall pierced his prison.

"Where is he?" a deep voice demanded immediately, from the air almost half a rod above his head.

Jer'ait stepped into the hallway and looked up at his Battlemaster. "No need for alarm."

"You let him escape, didn't you?" A massive crimson fist smashed into the wall beside Jer'ait's head, shattering it to dust.

"I know where he is," Jer'ait said calmly.

"That's it. No more coddling this Human. You've tried twice and failed twice. Now we do things *my* way."

Jer'ait opened his mouth to argue, then, seeing there was no argument, sighed. "Very well."

7

JOE, MEET DAVIIN

Joe slipped out of the barracks needing a drink.

He'd logged into the news network after leaving the Huouyt in his room. What the Huouyt had said was true. The Vahlin had blown up one of the three Jreet planets. A third of the Jreet population, dead.

Not only that, but he had somehow gathered one hundred and thirty-four princes to his cause. Not loners, not young, but *princes*. Every one of them with his heirs and kin and mates and Takki in tow.

Joe had heard of wars that had lasted over a hundred turns just fighting *one* prince. The idea of fighting over a hundred was enough to make any man's gut queasy.

Congress would need every man they could get.

"Damn it," Joe muttered, finding a seat at the bar. He ordered whiskey, and gladly locked his hand around the glass when it came. He closed his eyes and drank, trying not to listen to the ongoing news accounts of his nefarious younger brother constantly blaring in the background.

He had no more taken his first swallow when a massive scarlet hand clamped down on his wrist, almost breaking bones.

"The Huouyt said I could find you here."

A force like a Congressional cannon ripped Joe away from the bar and threw him across the room. Patrons of the bar began screaming all around him. Joe's aggressor let him hit the ground hard in a sprawl and began dragging him before Joe even realized he had fallen from his chair.

"Son of a bitch!" Joe screamed, twisting. Whatever was holding him was *strong*. He kicked out, knocking tables aside, breaking chairs. "Let go of me, asher!"

"Of course." Whatever it was lifted Joe off the ground and hurled him into the wall twenty digs away. Joe caught a glimpse of red—a *lot* of red—before he was being torn out of the wreckage. "I am done chasing your soft, oily hide across the planet, Human." A red and gold blur filled Joe's vision, before disappearing again. The harsh voice continued, "The Huouyt might have the patience to pamper you, but I'm tired of your Takki crap. They won't let us go to Neskfaat until we collect our groundteam. You will get on that shuttle if I have to drag you there by your bulbous head."

Whatever it was threw him again, this time slamming him into a pool table. Joe felt the air go out of him and he gasped. Aside from flashes of red, he still hadn't gotten a look at his attacker. It was as if he was being attacked by thin air.

Groaning, Joe picked himself off the pool table and glanced around the room. Half the tables were shattered, the stools knocked over and tangled. There was a hole in the wall where Joe's head had gone through it.

Joe slowly twisted around, eying the bar. Except for the bartender, all the Humans who had been patronizing the place had fled. Not a good sign. It meant they'd seen something Joe hadn't.

Joe's eye caught on the Huouyt. Be'shaar was leaning casually in the doorframe, watching with an amused expression. Joe felt a brief flash of surprise that he had guessed his password before the force slammed into him again, rolling him across the floor like a wayward pencil.

Directly above him, the disembodied voice bellowed, "But, since dragging you by your weakling neck might kill you, I decided it would be easier just to pummel you until you can't move." One heavy hand grabbed Joe by the leg, but by this time, Joe was too dazed to think about defending himself.

"But, since you've got the annoying habit of disappearing even while puking drunk, I'm thinking I should probably break your legs, just to be safe."

Behind the counter, the bartender's eyes were wide and he was backing away from whatever held Joe. Thinking of his leg, Joe frantically jammed his elbow into his attacker.

His elbow hit solid steel.

A massive, serpentine flash of scarlet, then a sharp, diamond-shaped head was filling his vision. Small, bright golden eyes fixed on him with a dangerous intensity between deep, diamond-shape audial-ridges that took up most of the creature's head. A predator's fangs showed behind scaly red lips. A patch of white dappled its brow above its metallic eyes. *"Should* I start breaking legs, Human?" The grip on his leg tightened, and Joe had the sick feeling it would only take a slight twist to snap his femur in half.

"Burn me," Joe said when he realized what was holding him.

A Jreet. A burning *Jreet.* Even with two planets, they were rarer than Humans. They had no massive cities, no sprawling megaplexes. Even as one of the founding races of Congress, they were as close to primitives as a sentient race could come—he'd only ever seen them once before, during his time in bootcamp, the bodyguards of a Congressional Representative who decided to rebel. That he was seeing one here, on *Earth,* left him thinking the bartender had slipped him a little something extra in his drink.

"Only break one of his legs," the Huouyt said calmly from the door. "The last thing I want is to have to carry him around the shuttle while he heals."

"Stay out of this." The Jreet flung Joe across the room by the ankle. Joe collided with a tangled pile of chairs, but by that time, he was barely conscious. The Jreet picked him up again, this time by the front of his T-shirt, and lifted him four feet off the ground, until his head was crammed up against the ceiling—and he was looking directly into the Jreet's angry golden eyes.

Ninths from his face, the crocodilian mouth said in heavily-accented Congie, "I won't break your legs. But if you make me miss my flight, Prime, I will hunt you down and you'll wish I had." Then the Jreet dropped him to the floor, grabbed him by a foot, and Joe was being dragged again.

Joe saw the Huouyt sigh and follow them into the street before he passed out.

● ● ●

"See?" Daviin dumped his battered cargo inside the shuttle. "Some things are better done with force."

The Huouyt did not seem to share his satisfaction. He was giving the Human an appraising look. "He's going to be commanding our groundteam in a couple weeks, Jreet. I don't think pounding him unconscious did much to ingratiate him with you."

"Bah." Daviin disgustedly began forming coils, the coolness of the shuttle interior irritating him. "The fool needed it."

"I agree, but he might not see it that way."

Daviin laughed. "What do I care what a soft-skinned little weakling thinks?"

"He's your Prime." The Huouyt was in his natural form once more, his birth defect plain for all to see. Knowing what Daviin knew about Huouyt society, this Huouyt's purple eye was a badge of shame beside his normal, electric-blue one. He wondered again why the Huouyt did not take another Huouyt's pattern to spare himself the disgrace.

"He's not my Prime until we get to Neskfaat," Daviin said. "And even then, I won't give a *melaa's* snort what he thinks of me." Then, looking down at the battered pile of flesh and bone, he said, "My goal is the Vahlin. The only reason I'm here is that the Ground Force wouldn't clear me for a shuttle ride from Jeelsiht unless I was on a groundteam, and *this* is the fool they chose as my Prime. They can all be damned. These pathetic weaklings and their politics mean nothing to me."

The Huouyt's odd-colored eyes flickered to the broken Human. "Obviously. You should administer nanos, in case he's bleeding internally."

Daviin flinched. "They do that?"

"Not everyone can be a Jreet."

Daviin stared down at the Human. "How could they put *him* in charge? A *Takki* could best him."

"They give Humans biosuits, just like Ooreiki."

Daviin's face twisted with disdain. "Dose the weakling."

"I give the orders here, Jreet," the Huouyt said calmly. "I told you to do it."

Daviin straightened, until he towered over Be'shaar. "Oh? Do you see a rank upon my chest?"

"You're a Battlemaster," the Huouyt said, looking completely unperturbed.

Daviin laughed. "I'm a Sentinel-trained Jreet warrior and heir to Vora. Your ranks mean a Dhasha's fart to me."

He and the Huouyt locked gazes. Daviin waited. Tics marched by, neither of them moving. On the floor, the Human's lungs began to rattle.

Sighing, the Huouyt broke the deadlock and went to the shuttle's emergency supplies set into the wall. He found a nano kit and, as Daviin watched, he administered a dose to the unconscious Human.

He was putting it away just in time for a young Ooreiki to step through the door of the shuttle. The creature's eyes widened as he glanced between Daviin and the Huouyt. Tentatively, he said, "Is one of you our Prime Commander?"

"There's your Prime." Daviin waved a disgusted hand at the crumpled Human on the floor.

The Ooreiki froze, obviously thinking the war had already started. "What happened to him?" the Ooreiki whispered.

"He tripped."

The Ooreiki's eyes scanned the bruises and bloody scratches and he opened his mouth to say something stupid. The Huouyt interrupted him. "Are you Galek, then?"

The young Ooreiki straightened and gave a sloppy Congressional salute. Nothing like the sharp, swift motion that every Sentinel knew by heart. Daviin's disdain for the other creatures in the room grew by the tic.

"I am Be'shaar. The scaly red beast filling up the room is Daviin. And, as the Jreet said, that is Joe Dobbs, your new Prime."

"A Human?" The Ooreiki's liquid brown eyes were fixed on their ground leader with confusion. "What will we do with a Human?"

"Obey him," Be'shaar said.

Daviin snorted and gave the Human a derisive look. "I'll dance on my own tek before I obey that fool."

"You'll obey him, or I'll send you back to Vora so you can return to your petty bickerings with Welu."

Daviin lashed out, dragging the Huouyt off his three boneless legs, until his huge bi-colored eyes were only ninths from his own. Into the Huouyt's face, he said, "And as soon as Congress releases me from my oath, I'll gladly spit you, Huouyt. If there's one thing I hate more than a Welu, it's a Huouyt." He pushed his tek from its sheath, until the poisoned tip was visible only ninths from the writhing white cilia on Be'shaar's chest.

Be'shaar did not even spare a glance at the tek. The Huouyt's eyes were cold, utterly calm. "Release me."

Daviin continued to hold the Huouyt off the ground. He lowered his face until their eyes almost touched. "If anything gets between me and my revenge on Neskfaat, I will hold you personally responsible."

"Now, Jreet."

Daviin dropped the Huouyt. Twisting to face the Ooreiki, he said, "You say your name is Galek?"

The Ooreiki watched Be'shaar as the Huouyt slowly got back to his feet, then looked again at the crumpled Human. Returning his eyes to Daviin, he whispered, "This isn't going to work, is it?"

"There's a reason why Congress has never made a multi-species team before this," Be'shaar said tightly, never taking his eyes from Daviin. "Some don't play well with others."

"I can see that," Galek replied. His eyes dropped to the Human. "Are they giving us a full six?" He did not sound like he was looking forward to it.

"Yes," Daviin said, coiling into a corner as the shuttle launched. He locked eyes with the Huouyt. "You're young, aren't you?"

It took the Ooreiki a moment to realize he was talking to him. "I, uh. Yes." He shied away from Daviin's coils, getting as far from him and the Huouyt as possible. It didn't do much good. In such a confined space, Daviin had to wrap his body over itself several times in order to fit.

"What'd you do to get this assignment?" Daviin asked, gaze still locked with the Huouyt.

Out of the corner of Daviin's eyes, he saw the Ooreiki's sudah begin to flutter. "I guess, I uh…"

"Your Battlemaster asked you a question, boy," the Huouyt snapped. He, in turn, never took his eyes off of Daviin.

"Watch your own spears, Huouyt," Daviin snapped. "I'm a Sentinel, not a Battlemaster, and it's the boy's choice whether to answer. Jreet do not stoop to using our rank to force furgs to do our will."

"You mean those Jreet who are smaller than you obey or you kill them." The Huouyt had righted itself and was casually smoothing the cilia that Daviin had displaced with his grip. "How honorable."

"I might kill them anyway," Daviin said, still holding the Huouyt's stare. "If they continue to prattle." Disgusting. That he had been paired with a Huouyt was…disgusting.

"Jreet, if you are trying to suggest you are my superior in any way," the Huouyt said softly, "you are sadly mistaken."

Daviin cocked his head. "Your name is not Be'shaar. I recognize the name from my training. Your voice does not match." Then he laughed. "Too cowardly to give your true name, assassin?"

Jer'ait scowled at him. "You asked the boy a question. You wanted to know what a raw Ooreiki recruit has in comparison to a decorated Human hero, a top Va'gan assassin, and a Voran worm."

Daviin slid out of his first coil, intending to introduce his fist to the Huouyt's innards.

The young Ooreiki cleared his throat tentatively. In the silence that followed, with Daviin and Jer'ait dueling gazes in ka-par, he said, "I guess I got what they call tunnel instinct."

Ka-par instantly broken, Daviin and Jer'ait both whipped their heads around to stare at the Ooreiki, who immediately found the corrugated steel floor at his feet intensely fascinating.

"Interesting," Jer'ait said finally. He cast Daviin one last look, then left the room.

"Coward," Daviin snorted. He peered at the Ooreiki again. Tunnel instinct. That was as rare amongst Ooreiki as a black Jreet was amongst Vorans. Trying not to look as slack-jawed as he felt, Daviin grunted and returned to his coil.

"Sir?" the Ooreiki ventured.

"I am not a sir," Daviin snapped. "I volunteered. The rank they gave me was arbitrary."

"But aren't you…royalty?"

Scoffing, Daviin said, "On my planet, the only ones who call others 'sir' are slaves and cowards."

He might have slapped the Ooreiki, the way Galek flinched. "Sorry si—uh, what do you want me to call you?"

"Daviin."

"Not lord Daviin? Prince Daviin?"

"No. Daviin."

"So who is the Human?" the Ooreiki ventured. "I know why Overseer Phoenix picked Be'shaar and you…but who is he?"

Daviin made a dismissive grunt. "Some call him Zero."

"*That* Zero?" The pupils of the Ooreiki's huge, sticky eyes dilated until they were petrified ovals of black. "Prime Commander Zero? From Eeloir?"

"Or so I'm told," Daviin said, a little confused by the creature's reaction. He returned his attention to the pile of Human. "I was not very impressed, myself."

The Ooreiki's sudah were fluttering as if he were about to fly away. "Who else is on our team?" he whispered.

"I suppose we'll discover that on Neskfaat."

● ● ●

Joe woke with a headache that screamed for aspirin. He sat up and groaned, holding his temples.

Immediately, a massive red blur moved in front of him. "It wakes."

"Are you the bastard that attacked me?" Joe growled through a thick tongue and swollen lip.

His assailant snorted. "If you consider that an attack, you're sadly out of your league."

Joe frowned, trying to focus his eyes. There was something about the voice he didn't like. Something that sounded familiar.

A ruby-scaled, diamond-shaped head solidified in front of him, hard golden eyes peering down at him mercilessly. "Is that better?"

"Fuck me," Joe blurted.

"Are you sure you want that, Human?" The Jreet's small metallic eyes glittered, the pupils contracting to pinpoints. "Could be painful."

Peering up into the ridged, scaly red face, Joe had to laugh. It hurt. He held his side and groaned. "Help me up. I need to get to medical."

"You'll have to wait 'til we get to Jeelsiht."

Joe paused in rubbing his temple. "Get to…Wait. Where am I?" His eyes scanned the tiny space around them and his jaw dropped. "You asher."

The Jreet moved closer, his forehead almost touching Joe's, danger emanating from its golden eyes. "Excuse me?"

But Joe was furious, now. Beyond fear. "You ghost-burning farmed Takki *vaghi!* Maggie gave me a *choice!*"

"And you chose to accompany us."

Joe surged to his feet and the Jreet lifted his big, chest-sized head with him, staying level with his own gaze. They glared at each other, neither so much as blinking.

"Turn the ship around."

"In your dreams, Human."

Joe swiveled and yanked open the door to the cockpit, intending to go speak with the captain. A red fist suddenly slammed the door shut, almost wrenching Joe's arm from its socket. An instant later, a ruby wall barred his path. "You should've said something while we were on the shuttle," the Jreet said, crocodile-like teeth bared. "We're in deep space now. No way to turn around."

Joe was so angry he sputtered. "My brother is going to be *killed*. A Prime Overseer gave me a choice! I don't remember anyone *asking* me!"

"He asked," an Ooreiki said solemnly. "Three times. You didn't say much."

Joe whipped around to glare at the Ooreiki, who flinched away from him as if he expected a blow.

"Who are you?"

"Grounder Galek, sir," the Ooreiki whimpered. "Your groundmate."

Joe's eyes caught the rank and he scowled. "A boot? Biggest mission in Congressional history and they send along a *boot?* When did you graduate, kid?"

The Ooreiki squirmed under his gaze, his sudah working furiously in his neck. "Last turn."

Joe frowned. "And Maggie picked you?"

"Prime Overseer Phoenix, did, sir." The Ooreiki looked like he was about to explode with discomfort. His tentacle arms wrapped around each other in anxiety, the four boneless fingers of each hand writhing together in a knotted mass.

Joe watched the Ooreiki a moment, then grunted. "Then you must be worth your stuff."

The Ooreiki tore his gaze from the floor, looking startled.

Joe shrugged at the young Ooreiki's shock. "Maggie hates my guts, but she's the best judge of a soldier I've ever seen. It's how she made

Prime Overseer without a single *kasja*. If she put you here, I'm sure you're gonna kick Dhasha ass."

The Ooreiki's big, boneless mouth opened and closed in mute surprise.

Behind him, Joe was suddenly aware of the Jreet watching him. He turned back and prickled, not liking the appraising stare the Jreet was giving him. "You, on the other hand…She'd go for *any* Jreet, as long as it had scales."

The Jreet's eyes narrowed. "I am Sentinel-trained, Human."

Joe flinched. "You're lying."

The Jreet indignantly lifted itself from its bed of coils until he was glowering down at Joe from the ceiling. "A Jreet does not lie."

"No, but they'll kill little kids in the service of a Congressional rebel," Joe said bitterly, remembering the slaughter on Kophat.

The Jreet snorted. "Sentinels swear allegiance to a Representative for life. It is understood that oath comes before their oath of citizenship. Not even Aliphei begrudged those Jreet their allegiance to Na'leen."

The Jreet had researched enough about him to know his history? Joe found this the biggest surprise yet. "They can't draft Jreet," Joe said, looking him up and down. "So why are you here?"

"Revenge," the Jreet said. "This Dhasha Vahlin stole my vengeance from me."

"You volunteered." Joe was stunned. The Jreet didn't volunteer. They became Sentinels or they gathered their clan members and went on raiding parties to kill other Jreet, and Congress left them alone as long as they didn't bother anyone else.

"Yes. To kill the Vahlin."

"Why?"

"He killed my enemies."

"And that pissed you off."

"Immensely."

"So you're gonna what…tunnel crawl with us as a volunteer until we find him?" Joe demanded.

"Yes."

SARA KING

"Someone else might kill the Vahlin, you know."

"They won't."

Joe snorted. "I get the shot and I'm taking it, Jreet. Might actually make all this furgsoot worthwhile."

The Jreet straightened, his muscled body seething anger. The burgundy tip of the poisoned fang protruded slightly from the Jreet's chest. "The Vahlin is mine. You are free to kill the pathetic Takki that grovel at his feet, but the Vahlin will be *my* kill."

Joe narrowed his eyes at the Jreet's threat. He walked up to it and stabbed his finger into the creature's warm, cream-colored underbelly, his finger ninths from the poisoned tek. "I didn't want to be, but since you didn't give me a choice, I'm in charge, Jreet. You are under my command, and I'm not letting any insane Jreet vendettas get in the way of our job. If I think Be'shaar or Galek has a better chance of killing the Vahlin, then they will kill him and you will burning watch."

A low, rattling growl—the beginnings of the enginelike Jreet battlecry—emanated from the Jreet's chest. His poisoned fang slipped further from its sheath, until it was almost touching Joe's chest. Joe could see the muscles and tendons in the limb straining, putting almost six thousand lobes of pressure into a single strike. The slightest release would drive it completely through Joe's body.

And even a scratch from the poisonous tip would kill Joe where he stood.

"The Vahlin is mine," the Jreet repeated, rising until he had to curl his head against the ceiling. The appendage extruded further, two full joints from its sheath. The tip came to a rest near Joe's left eye.

"The Vahlin," Joe said, reaching up and shoving the poisoned tek out of his face, "Is whoever's I say he is. I've been leading groundteams down tunnels for over fifty turns. My Ops teams have claimed three *prince* kills—that ties any other ground leader out there, past *or* present. You're just a tool, Jreet. A tool that's useless to me if you don't do your job. You don't like it, leave." His eyes never left the Jreet's.

They held each other's stare for several moments, the Jreet's anger visibly increasing with every heartbeat. The Jreet made no motion to retract his tek.

Very quietly, Joe said, "I'll let the command know of your decision. Perhaps someone else will be stupid enough to take you on their team."

The Jreet snorted in complete disdain. "You wouldn't leave me behind."

"I'd do it in a heartbeat." Joe leaned closer, holding the Jreet's gaze. "In a goddamn heartbeat. You won't follow orders, I don't want you. Even if you are a Jreet."

"You're bluffing," the Jreet snapped. "We both damn well know I'm worth a thousand of whatever other weaklings you can con into serving on this farce."

That did it. Joe went to the wall pad, opened the PlanOps database, accessed his ground-team record, and changed the configuration. "There," he said, stepping back so the Jreet could see. "You're off the team. Officially. Now headquarters is looking for a new assignment for you. I'm sure they'll find some two-bit Takki slave for you to push around. Hell, you'll probably have every Prime on the planet get into a bidding war over your useless hide. In the meantime, *we'll* be down plucking the scales off the Vahlin. We might sell you a couple of his scales afterwards, if it will make you feel better."

The Jreet stared at the five names on the screen for long moments. Then, with an enraged cry, he ripped Joe off his feet and hurled him into the wall with all the force of a wrecking ball. Joe hit the corner, then crumpled instantly because too many bones had been shattered to hold him upright.

A Huouyt with an odd-colored eye rushed into the room at the sound of the Jreet's scream, then paused to give Joe's unnaturally twisted body a startled glance. Joe thankfully blacked out before his broken bones could get over their shock and make themselves known.

• • •

"What next?" Rri'jan asked, pacing the floor of Forgotten's chamber. "I'm not seeing a clear goal from all of this, Geuji."

Forgotten endured the imbecile's interruption calmly. "Now we have a war, we use it as a testing ground."

"A testing ground." The Huouyt was trying to maintain his façade of control, but he clearly didn't understand.

"Yes," Forgotten said. "Now that we've tied their hands, they'll have to send in ground troops. They'll try different combinations of Planetary Ops groundteams hoping they find a group that works well enough to take out the princes. With Aez destroyed, a handful of the strongest Jreet will go to Neskfaat seeking vengeance. Those will be the ones we need. Finding a team that can reach the Vahlin will only be half the battle—only a Jreet will be able to kill Mekkval in hand-to-hand combat."

"So we're using this war just to pick a Jreet to fight for us?" Rri'jan sounded disbelieving.

"There is more than one method to kill a Dhasha, Rri'jan. We're using this war to find the combination of species that is most successful at finding those methods. Ayhi, Jahul, Ooreiki, Huouyt, Baga, Ueshi…"

"Why don't you just decide what the best combination is and spare us the war?"

"I could. My personal choice would probably be a Human leader, a Huouyt assassin, a Jreet heir, an Ooreiki with the phenomenon called tunnel-instinct, a Baga scout, and a Grekkon burrower, though if I were to simply pick them out of hand, they would not have the experience working together that they will require when we send them against Mekkval."

Rri'jan's face wrinkled with distaste. "The best leader would be Human? You are sure?"

"No. That is why I will allow the war to make the selections for me. There are one hundred and thirty-four princes. Planetary Ops will assemble approximately two and a half million inter-species groundteams, all with different mixtures of killing talent. However, I believe the leader to successfully reach the Vahlin will be Human. There are several Jreet capable of taking out a large Dhasha, foremost among them are the Voran and Welu heirs. I have several Ooreiki candidates in mind, though any with the tunnel instinct will do. Same for the Grekkon. Burrowing is a straightforward process, and as long as his companions can protect him, any Grekkon will suffice. The Baga will be trickier."

Rri'jan gave Forgotten an irritated look. "What is a Baga? Are they even citizens?"

"They are. They've colonized seven planets, though they technically own sixty-five, most of which were colonized by Huouyt or Ooreiki due to the Baga's lack of understanding for numbers beyond six. They have only rudimentary mathematical skills, so advanced civilization is beyond them at this point."

"You would entrust our plans to a barbarian?"

"Baga are pranksters and risk-takers, but they are not stupid. Despite their appearance and lack of mathematical capacities, they are one of the six most intelligent species in Congress, and like to use that advantage over others. In fact, they will need someone to keep them in line or they are quick to offend species not so well versed in their mischief. Unfortunately, their particular talents make Baga more dangerous than over ninety-two percent of all other Congressional species, so I would not be surprised if they kill groundmates in over half of the inter-species experiments. In particular, I believe the Baga will target the Ooreiki for some of their crueler jokes, due to their terraforming history. I give Baga-Ooreiki pairings a projected failure rate of eighty-nine percent, over four-fifths of which will end in the Ooreiki's death."

"Ooreiki breed like vermin," Rri'jan said dismissively. "They can afford to lose a few."

"But *we* can't," Forgotten informed him. "The death of any member of the team will result in death for all of them."

"Really? Why is that?"

"Because I've engineered it that way. This is a testing ground. We don't want failure before we can use them."

"Then why put an Ooreiki and a Baga together, if you already know the result?"

"Because their separate skills will both be necessary to our team's final success. It will be up to the team's leader to keep the Baga under control."

"And the Huouyt?" Rri'jan demanded. "I can give you my best assassins."

"Do not concern yourself with the Huouyt."

Rri'jan's electric-blue eyes sharpened with displeasure. "I want this to succeed, Forgotten. If the Huouyt must take part in this experiment, I have the influence to do so."

"You have your personal assassins, but you do not have access to the one I want."

"Who?" Rri'jan snapped. "If he is Va'gan, I can hire him."

"You can't hire this one. No one can."

"Why not?"

"He works for the Peacemakers," Forgotten explained. "And, unlike the overwhelming majority of his kind, he cannot be bought. He works for Congress or not at all."

Rri'jan gave him a long look, the look of a creature that did not believe him. "Anyone can be bought, Forgotten."

"Don't concern yourself with the Huouyt. I've already stacked our odds, so to speak."

Rri'jan watched him, finding his words carefully. "You hand-picked your own team? Already? How could you possibly—" He trailed off, apparently realizing that he was showing his own ignorance, and that Forgotten was enjoying it.

"I chose two teams," Forgotten said. "Each with equal chances of survival."

"How?"

"I have contacts and money and the power of suggestion."

"And what will you need from me for your plan to work?"

"Not to question my decisions."

The former assassin peered at him, unblinking. "Are you thinking of one decision in particular?"

"I arranged it so that Jer'ait will be on one of the groundteams going to Neskfaat."

Rri'jan stiffened. "Jer'ait is a cur. I have better assassins."

"Better than the top Va'ga?" Forgotten asked. "Better than your own blood?"

"*Never* suggest that infectious pustule shares my blood!" Rri'jan trilled, his musical voice going high in rage. The Representative looked dangerously close to doing something stupid.

"We both know he does," Forgotten said. "I also know that the only reason he is not here devising a way to acquire his Tribunal seat instead of you is his birth defect. He surpasses you in every other way."

Rri'jan's voice was calm with fury, now. "For the sake of our plan, I will allow you to choose whatever filth you wish. But if you fail, Forgotten, I will destroy you. I swear it."

"I will not fail."

8

DAVIIN, MEET JOE

"Interesting, Jreet. It seems our Human had a spine, before you shattered it."

Jer'ait's eyes followed the Human's mangled body as the medics took it away, a smugness seeping from under his Va'ga-trained, expressionless features. The doctors had cursed and complained, but had accepted the Human out of the shuttle stasis with few questions, saying that the multi-species groundteams had been the biggest Takkiscrew they had seen since first giving the Dhasha Congressional technologies. Apparently, every room in the hospital was full, and not one injury had been from the enemy.

"Beda's bones. Let it rest already," Daviin growled.

"You know the Human won't take you back, don't you?" Jer'ait continued, without pause. "If there was any question before, it fled the moment you drove his sternum through his shoulder blade." Jer'ait watched him intently. Only the Huouyt's purple eye was out of place, like the mask that was a normal Huouyt had been torn away to reveal a trickle of his thoughts through this one odd-colored window.

Daviin was still furious with himself that he had allowed the Human to get under his skin, even more furious that the Human had actually followed through with his threat. To have the Huouyt rub it in, however, was too much. He turned on Jer'ait with a snarl.

"Let me deal with the Human," he growled at his annoying companion.

While the Huouyt's blue-white eye remained expressionless, the Huouyt's purple eye oozed amusement. "Considering whether your vengeance is worth more than your pride, my friend?"

"I am not your friend."

"On that I agree," Jer'ait said. "It was a figure of speech."

Daviin peered at Jer'ait, wondering if the Huouyt's mismatched eyes contained a key to the Huouyt nature heretofore undiscovered by the rest of Congress. The right one seemed completely aloof, eerie, unnerving, like all normal Huouyt. The malformed left one, however, had none of the unnaturalness of a Huouyt's normal gaze. Instead, it felt almost harmless, like an Ooreiki's, seeming to betray Jer'ait's thoughts like a leak within a canteen. A slow leak, but a leak nonetheless.

"Is that why those with defects are not allowed to sit in the Regency?"

Daviin had murmured it, almost to himself, but Jer'ait stiffened immediately. His violet left eye betrayed anger, frustration. His right betrayed nothing.

"That's it," Daviin whispered. "Your eyes. They're like a shield from your thoughts. Except your left is broken."

Jer'ait stepped closer, until he was only a foot from Daviin's coiled torso. "And what am I thinking right now, Jreet?"

Daviin ignored the threat. "Why are you here, Jer'ait? I recognize you from Sentinel training. They made us memorize your voice."

The assassin flinched, obviously taken aback. "How long have you known?"

"Since I saw you," Daviin replied, looking him over. "Who are you here to kill? Me?" He doubted as much, because Jer'ait was well-known as a Peacemaker's tool, refusing even the highest bids for his service, which, for a Huouyt, was enough to create a smudge of respect within Daviin. In a species of lying, backstabbing betrayers, Jer'ait was almost...

…honorable. Almost.

"I have better things to do than dabble in Jreet clan warfare."

"That's what I thought," Daviin said. "But the Twelfth Hjai wouldn't send you unless it was someone special."

Jer'ait gave him a long look before saying, "I am here to make sure the Vahlin dies."

Daviin felt his body stiffen reflexively, feeling his vengeance on the Vahlin sliding through his fingers. "You're next in line to the Twelfth Hjai. Don't the Peacemakers have underlings to do this?" An underling would fail. Jer'ait would not.

"Don't fret, Jreet," the Huouyt said. "I'm not the Human. I won't stand between you and your revenge if I can avoid it. All that matters to me is that he dies."

Daviin scanned the Huouyt's odd violet eye, watching his thoughts leak from him in a slow but steady stream. "The truth is there for anyone who would see it. A Huouyt's eyes…they act as a distraction. They bar natural communication, natural reading. It's why Huouyt with the defect are not allowed off your planets. Tell me I'm wrong."

It was impossible to miss the tightening of Jer'ait's paddle-like fists. "It is unwise to antagonize me, Jreet."

Daviin had a brief moment of nervousness, realizing what he was dealing with. It was creatures like Jer'ait that were sent to assassinate creatures like him.

Jer'ait's vertical slit of a mouth puckered. "Since you are to be my groundmate, Jreet, I'll spare you the mental anguish and I'll tell you another secret. My disability does not keep me from reading *your* eyes as well as any Huouyt."

Daviin flinched as Jer'ait strode away. This was a mistake. He should have gone straight back to Vora, gathered up a party of warriors, and come back here to do battle. Instead, he was going to have to rely upon five strangers, creatures infinitely weaker than himself.

Weaker…but possibly more useful.

Daviin understood his limitations. He glanced down at his long, ungainly bulk and squeezed his claws together. His kind relied upon ambush or distraction to kill. Once located, he could not move away fast enough to avoid a Dhasha's claws. He was not agile. He was not quick.

The Ooreiki and the Human were.

Further, due to the Dhasha's ability to hear his echolocation, Daviin could not penetrate a Dhasha den undetected. Jer'ait could.

Last, he had neither the capabilities of flight, nor a faculty for digging. They had discovered the nature of their last two teammates upon landing on Jeelsiht, and though Daviin had been curious as to why they needed a Baga underground, he was not going to question Phoenix's choices. With its burrowing skills, the Grekkon had been an obvious advantage. Galek had gone to meet them in the barracks while Daviin and Jer'ait had stayed to admit the Human to the Congie medical system.

Daviin decided to wait for Joe. Though he dreaded the moment, he needed to offer his ground leader an apology for losing control. Honor would allow him nothing less. He went looking for his commander's regen chamber.

After a long, frustrating search through the hospital corridors, many terrified Ueshi doctors giving directions that made no sense, and many dead ends, Daviin finally found the regeneration rooms deep in the hospital core. In full view of the Ooreiki guards in combat gear patrolling the hospital, Daviin passed repeated written warnings of Sensitive Area, Authorized Personnel, Staff Only, Escort Required, and other, more dire warnings to trespassers. The guards watched him, but none tried to approach him. If anything, they went in the other direction.

Annoyed at their cowardice, Daviin stopped outside the door that reeked of Human. There, he folded his body into a coil to the left of the door. The medics of the hospital eyed him askance as they passed, but none tried to tell him to leave.

Daviin felt irritated the way they left him unchallenged. It was a sensitive area, highly classified. What if he had been an assassin? What if he was here to spy or steal technology?

Beda's bones. No wonder the Vahlin managed to steal an ekhta, Daviin thought, brooding at doctors and staff from over his coils. *Congress is filled with fools.* A Ueshi doctor saw him from the far end of the hall, where it was just a blue-green blob to Daviin, and let out a high-pitched squeal and quickly departed the way it had come.

Fools and cowards, Daviin amended, his irritation building.

Several hours later, with still not a soul willing to come and demand his purpose in the restricted area, two heavy-limbed Ooreiki in gleaming, ebony Congressional biosuits stalked up to him, each toting a complex array of weaponry. Looking at their chests, he saw they were both four-point Battlemasters. Daviin perked up, looking forward to an incident after stewing for hours in his irritation.

Instead, the Ooreiki gave him nervous glances, and, without a word, went to the other side of Joe's door and waited. The Human's escort. Daviin could feel their eyes shift to him warily, but they said nothing as they waited for Prime Commander Zero to waken.

Irritation began to change into anger. *Do none of these Takki have the courage to say something to me?*

The tics continued to pass, with no one saying a word to him. Finally, Daviin could stand it no longer.

To the two Ooreiki, he casually said, "If this were a Jreet planet, every soldier in this hospital would be killed. Then we would research who trained them and their instructors would all be killed. Then we would find their families and *they* would all be killed."

The two Ooreiki's huge ovoid pupils dilated with obvious terror. One of them whispered, "Why?"

Daviin motioned at the uniforms of passersby. "I don't belong here. I wear no black. I carry no gun. Why has no one said anything to me?"

"You're a Jreet," the other one said.

"So?!" Daviin demanded.

"Jreet aren't traitors," the Ooreiki babbled. "Everyone knows this."

"Not until our ward turns traitor," Daviin reminded them.

"But..." The nearest Ooreiki stared up at Daviin, his hahkta and sudah trembling. "*Are* you a traitor?"

"Just shut up." The conversation had only made him want to drive his tek through their spineless bodies.

And they did. As they waited outside the door together in silence, Daviin seethed.

His disgust had reached a fever-pitch when the door to the regeneration room opened and the Human stepped out.

Joe's gaze was automatically drawn to Daviin, whose mountain of bright scarlet scales stood out in the black Congie hallways like a green Takki on a food farm. Then, as if he had simply been glancing Daviin's way, he turned back to the Ooreiki, ignoring him.

"So. Can one of you jerkwads tell me why one of you didn't escort this Janja pile back to the waiting area?"

Under the Human's stare, the Ooreiki's sudah began to quiver. Their big, sticky brown eyes flickered to Daviin, then to the Human, then back. "He didn't appear to be hurting anything, sir."

"Oh." Joe seemed to think on that a moment, then said, "So the fact that he can go into creepy inviso-mode and rip this entire hospital apart means nothing at all to you?"

The other Ooreiki said, "We thought he was with you, sir."

The Human turned back and met Daviin's gaze with flat disdain. "He's not." He continued to look utterly calm, but there was an edge to his voice. "Did you check his tag, men?"

The two Ooreiki babbled a negative.

"Why not?" The Human's deep brown eyes seemed to be holding back the weight of mountains as they glared up at Daviin.

"He's a *Jreet*, sir." The Ooreiki's sudah were now fluttering in their necks, betraying their nervousness.

The Human snorted, eyes still holding Daviin's gaze. "A Jreet turns traitor the moment his ward turns traitor. And when they do, they're the best enemy we'll ever get."

Daviin felt stabbed and vindicated at the same time.

Joe jabbed an arm at Daviin. "Check his tag."

"I don't carry a—" Daviin began.

Joe held up a hand, cutting him off. To the Ooreiki, he said, "Check it."

"C-Commander Zero," one of the Ooreiki managed, "We're here to escort you back to the waiting area, not to—"

"You're here to *protect this hospital*," Joe snarled, turning on them. "*Check* his *tag*."

The two Ooreiki seemed frozen in place for a moment under the Prime Commander's stare. Then, sliding sideways around him, they moved to Daviin, obviously more terrified of the soft-skinned Human than they were of Daviin's mountain of coils.

Daviin was impressed. He held still as the two petrified guards walked up and quickly ran the scanner over his torso, giving the sheath of his tek a wide berth.

"Nothing, sir."

"You didn't check all of him," Joe said. "Do it again."

The Ooreiki swallowed hard, looking at Daviin's seven rods of length. "But that would take—" he cut himself off and swallowed again, hahkta wriggling from the sides of his head. The battlemaster quickly glanced at the floor.

"I'm sorry," Joe said pleasantly, cocking his head. "Were you about to say it would take too long, Battlemaster?"

"Uh," the Ooreiki seemed to whimper, "no sir."

And liars. Congress was filled with liars. Daviin *hated* liars.

"Then you won't mind doing a thorough search," Joe said. "Now."

The two Ooreiki nervously did, running the instrument up and down Daviin's length for almost forty tics before giving the negative.

"I don't—" Daviin began.

"Shut up." To the Ooreiki, he said, "Check again."

"But, sir—"

"Check it!" the Human snapped.

The Ooreiki reluctantly did as they were told, this time trembling as they brought the instrument over Daviin's chest, hovering over the sheath of his tek as if they absurdly thought that touching the flesh there would make it spring out and hit him.

"No tag?" the Human asked once the Ooreiki was finished. "Hmm. Why can't you find a tag? Any ideas?" Before anyone could respond, he snapped, "Because he doesn't burning have one, that's why. And you know what that makes him?"

The Ooreiki shrank under his stare.

"*Unauthorized!*" Joe roared.

Daviin was impressed at the Human's vocal range. Every creature in the hall stopped to stare.

"You!" Joe snapped, turning back to Daviin. "Come with me." He started walking and Daviin uncoiled to follow him.

After three steps, Joe swiveled suddenly and made Daviin run into him, slamming the sheath of his tek against his chest.

Unfazed, Joe's eyes found the two Ooreiki who were still standing against the wall. "You two Takki slavesouls better the hell escort the both of us out of here properly or when I have my talk with your Prime, I'll remember names."

The Ooreiki jumped forth.

"And put a depressor on him. He could raise his energy and go invisible at any second. Who knows who he's working for? He'd have full run of the hospital and you wouldn't be able to do a damn thing about it. Is that what you want?"

"No, sir." One of the Ooreiki fumbled with the mass of gear strapped to his belt, then stepped in front of Daviin. "Uh, sir?" He held out a black device that looked like a small coin.

"Don't ask, *do it!*"

Daviin flinched away from them, his scales tightening against his skin instinctively. Never before had he worn such a device—it was dishonorable, despicable...*humiliating*. "This is not necessary, Commander."

"Really?" Joe asked, turning to face him. "Which terrorist network do you work for, Jreet?"

"That's ridiculous," Daviin snorted.

"Sure it is. Battlemaster, why aren't you depressing the Jreet?"

The sudah of the Ooreiki between them began fluttering like wings in his neck and looked like he wanted to flee down the hall, but he was fixed in place under the Human's merciless stare.

"I've taken my oaths to Congress," Daviin said. "I'm not affiliated with a Representative in any way. I'm a member of your groundteam. I don't need one of those."

"You're not a member of my groundteam."

The cool, even way the Human said it, it almost sounded as if he were serious.

An excellent bluffer, Daviin decided. "Very well, Human, let's get this stupidity over with."

The Ooreiki reached forth with a shaking tentacle, a small black device clasped in his four-fingered hand. He moved to place it on his back, but Daviin straightened, offering his stomach before the fool could place it somewhere he could not reach it. The Ooreiki did not complain, and meekly affixed it to Daviin's chest, where he could easily swat it away if he had to. Daviin flinched as the device took effect—the sudden, leaden feeling like a thousand lobes of stone had been pried under his scales. He had an instinctive pang of panic that the effect might be permanent before he fought it down.

He gave Joe an irritated look. The depressor was hardly necessary and they both knew it. However, he left it where it was, enduring the deprivation of his ability to leave the visible spectrum with as much grace as he could muster.

But Joe had crossed his arms, having observed Daviin's maneuvering. "Just what kind of Takki foodyard is your Overseer running here? You let the Jreet manipulate you into putting it on his stomach. He could fling that thing off him in a second. You stupid jenfurglings, put it on his back, between his shoulder blades, where his arms won't reach."

Daviin stiffened. "I'm not going to remove it."

"But you *can* remove it, can't you?" Joe growled. "Now get on the ground and let them place it properly. You're lucky they don't shoot you for being a sneaky Cu'it."

Daviin narrowed his eyes, but complied. The momentary relief as the Ooreiki took the depressor from his stomach was immediately ruined by its even more deeply unnerving presence in the unreachable area between his shoulders. Daviin spent the rest of the trip out of the hospital glaring at the Human's back, wondering what it would be like to make the fool dance on his tek.

Outside, once the Ooreiki had removed the depressor and left the two of them alone in the waiting area, Daviin growled, "Was that fun, Human?"

Joe rounded on him and jammed a finger back at the hospital. "Fun?! Those sootwads back there are in charge of some of Congress's most sensitive equipment—stuff they're gonna give the rest of us full brain-wipes for, just for being *near* it, and they let just anyone waltz around back there like they own the place."

"A seven-rod Jreet is hardly just anyone."

"It's the principle," Joe snapped. "They lack discipline. This planet is the staging area for Neskfaat, for the Mothers' sakes. Biggest goddamn war we've ever seen and one smart sonofabitch leading them, and our guys go and leave all of Congress's goodies out in the open for anybody who wants to walk in and take 'em. The whole lot of them should be shot. It's incompetent furgling dumbasses like that who get grounders sent to their deaths in the first place."

Daviin stared at the Human. "I couldn't have said it better myself."

Joe looked him up and down. "I know why you were waiting for me. My answer is no."

Daviin blinked. "What answer?"

"I'm not bringing you back." Joe turned to go.

Daviin's arm shot out, catching his shoulder. The Human paused and glanced at his shoulder before giving Daviin a dark look. Daviin quickly released it.

"You need me," Daviin said, trying to instill some logic into the situation. "I'm the only one who stands a chance against a Dhasha in hand-to-hand combat."

"We'll make do without you."

Daviin stared at the Human, stunned. It almost sounded like...he was serious. "You're turning me down? Truly?"

"I'm not taking on someone who's got no respect for authority." The Human turned to go again.

"I respect authority," Daviin snapped, his irritation returning. "If this is about my attack, I did it after you discharged me. It should have no bearing on this conversation."

"It doesn't," Joe said. "I'd made my decision long before you busted me up."

Daviin felt himself losing his grip on his fury once more. "If this isn't about your pride, Human, what *is* it about?"

"You're a volunteer." The Human seemed to recognize his anger, and was disdainful of it. "Volunteers don't follow orders unless they feel like it."

"I trained as a Sentinel." Daviin hated the way it sounded like begging.

"This is Planetary Ops," Joe said. "I don't give a rat's ass about the Sentinels."

Daviin's body coiled behind him in frustration. "If you had any idea how hard the training was—"

"I don't care how hard it was," the Human snapped. "What I care about is you following orders—*my* orders. Right now, if you got half a chance, you'd leave the rest of us stranded while you went after the Vahlin. That's fine, but you sure as hell aren't going to do it on my team. I've already put the order in. It's final. Cannot be undone."

Daviin felt a sinking in his gut, the same kind of sinking he felt as a Sentinel when he failed in his training. He stared at the Human, stunned the creature could make him feel that way. The Human stared back, his brown eyes unwavering.

*Beda's bones...*Daviin realized he'd made a mistake.

"So, where's the rest of my team?" the Human demanded.

"The barracks." The words slipped from Daviin's lips on a wave of misery.

The Human grunted. "What other useless jenfurglings did I get stuck with?"

"A Baga and a Grekkon."

"Bones." The Human cursed and glanced at the ceiling. He closed his eyes and took several long breaths. "Goddamn it, Mag."

"What?"

"She's playing with me," Joe said. "A Baga's the most annoying, uncontrollable, *smart* little creep you'll ever see. And dangerous as hell. Maggie's doing it to torment me."

"Who is this Maggie?" Daviin said. "Do you want her killed?"

Joe laughed. "I wish." Then he frowned. "And no, you will not buy your way back into the group by killing my enemies."

Damn.

Joe sighed again. "A Baga? You serious? Who's with it?"

"Galek," Daviin said. "I'm not sure about the Huouyt. He doesn't tend to stay with the group."

"You've gotta be kidding me!" Joe looked as if Daviin had just told him the Ooreiki was dining with a Dhasha. "You sent Galek in there? *Alone?* With a *Baga?*"

"I sent no one, Human," Daviin said, confused. "He went on his own. Wanted to welcome our newcomers. What difference does it make?"

Joe made a disgusted sound. Without waiting for him, the Human strode quickly from the hospital, his pace almost more than Daviin could meet. As if he didn't even notice Daviin following him, the Human took a shuttle to the barracks. Daviin shadowed him in silence, his mind working. The Human was not what he expected. His first impression of a drunken fool had been wrong. In another life, he could have been born a Jreet.

The Human turned on him suddenly. "Why are you still following me?"

"I want to be on your team."

"No. Begging will not change my mind." The Human kept walking.

Daviin followed, his fists clenching in frustration. "I made a mistake."

"Yep."

"I'm sorry."

"Is that what you'd say to the Sentinels, Jreet?"

Daviin felt shame descend upon him in a sickly shroud. "No."

"Then don't say it to me." The Human did not stop walking.

Daviin lowered his head and followed. He knew he should have salvaged his pride and searched for another group to descend after the Dhasha, but his gut told him this was the group he wanted.

They entered the barracks to the sounds of Ooreiki screaming.

Joe broke into a run, leaving Daviin behind.

When Daviin caught up, he had to bodily push a crowd of black-clad Congie gawkers out of the way to even reach the room.

Inside, Joe had a gun in his hand, the weapon charged and ready, his finger on the trigger. He was aiming at something over Daviin's head.

9

OF BAGANS AND BOOZE

"Give it back, you little janja pile." Joe aimed the gun at the football-sized alien's head.

"Why?" the Baga demanded in startlingly good Congie from its insect-like head. "The counter can grow a new one."

"That isn't the point, is it?" Joe demanded. "Put it down. Now."

The Baga buzzed its wings at him in a sign of disdain. "We both know you fire that weapon and you're in the brig for the next three turns. This is a non-discharge area, *Human*, and your threats are worthless."

"I haven't threatened you, sootwad," Joe growled. "You'll feel it when I do."

The elegant green, humming-bird creature let out a vibrating, contemptuous laugh and spat a gob of grayish slime at him from its tubelike ass. Joe dodged it, but just barely. Goosebumps sprang up on his arms as he watched the stuff solidify on the floor. Had it touched his skin, Joe would have had to cut it off with a laser, taking a ninth of skin and muscle with it.

"There's something you should know," Joe said, as calmly as he could, watching the alien glue fuse to the floor. *Become* the floor.

"Oh?" the Baga asked, holding up the still-wriggling Ooreiki tentacle and calmly snipping one of the four writhing fingers from the end with its razor beak. "And what's that, counter?"

Joe refused to allow his eyes to follow the finger to the ground as the Baga wanted, so he could glue him again. *Smart little bastard*, Joe thought, despite himself.

"You should know that I'm sixty-six turns old."

The Baga snipped another finger from the Ooreiki's arm, leaving two intact. "And why the crack should that matter to me, Human?"

"Because it means I'm too old to deal with little pricks like you." Joe popped the canister from his borrowed pistol and, as the Baga watched him in confusion, threw the gun.

It hit the Baga square-on, crushing the glittering green creature to the wall like a wayward spider. Its tiny clawlike feet released Galek's arm and the severed appendage fell to the ground, still wriggling. The Baga followed it down, landing in a glittering, stunned heap.

Joe walked up and stomped on the creature's tubular rear snout, effectively cutting off its spit supply. The Baga's beak, situated on the opposite end of its body, opened and it let out a high-pitched, almost supersonic scream. In the hall outside, the Jreet groaned and put his huge scarlet hands over the cavernous audial chambers taking up most of his skull. "Seventh hell, make it stop!" Daviin shouted. "Beda's *bones*! Kill it already…"

Ignoring the Jreet, Joe squatted in front of the Baga, peering into its faceted red eyes. "Listen very carefully. I'm a Prime. I've got fifty-five turns in service. One of my groundmates turns up missing, I get a slap on the wrist, no big deal. It happens. You, on the other hand, are a soot-wad Squad Leader who's never seen real battle. You disappear and they'd maybe make me fill out a couple forms, maybe not. You with me so far?"

When the Baga simply stared up at him with baleful, faceted red eyes, Joe ground the tubular snout with the toe of his boot. It screeched again and nodded.

"Good," Joe said. "So I hope you'll take me seriously when I tell you there's very few things in this life I hate more than a Baga. One of them's Huouyt, and the fact I'm gonna be working with *both* of you on this mission puts me in a very bad mood. One of you will probably push me over the edge before this is all over with, and frankly, since the Huouyt isn't stupid, I'm guessing it's going to be you."

The Baga watched him with unconcealed malice.

Joe leaned closer. "In case you've got some grand scheme to spit in my eyes once I let you up, I've got news for you. I spent two turns keeping the peace on Neen. I've seen it all, you little furg, and I'll make you regret it. But, since I know you charheads don't learn the first time, I'll give you two attempts. The first time, I'll break every bone in your body. The second time, I'll tear off your wings, cut off your spitter and feed them to you. Got me?"

The Baga watched him balefully behind ruby facets.

Joe let the Baga up.

The Baga pulled itself to its feet. It checked the damage Joe had done and, finding none, nodded solemnly. Then it spat.

Recognizing the pulsing motion in the creature's glands, Joe was ready for it. He twisted out of the way as the gray substance shot across the room to solidify on the wall. Then, with the heel of his boot, smashed the Baga into the ground. Even as the creature screamed and dragged its abdomen around to try and soak his boot, Joe brought his other foot down, crushing the lower half of its body.

He left the head intact. The Baga, like cockroaches, were almost impossible to kill. He proceeded to stomp and crush every moving part, every joint save the head. Then, once he was finished, he glanced up at the room.

The Jreet was staring at him, Galek's severed appendages hanging limply from his claws. A Huouyt was with him, one odd purple eye watching Joe with disdain.

"'Woe to the Takki the day the Dhasha stubs his toe,'" the Huouyt intoned. "You wake up during surgery, Commander?"

Joe scanned the Huouyt's face. "My thirty-two shattered bones had nothing to do with this. The little fool was going to spit on me."

"Of course." The Huouyt continued to watch him smugly.

Joe shoved his toe under the Baga's flattened corpse and flicked it toward Be'shaar with his boot. "Get this dumb prick to medical."

"It was just an arm," the Huouyt said, ignoring Joe's command. "He could grow it back."

"Believe me," Joe said, "you'll thank me later."

All around him, other barracks inhabitants were staring at him. Even Galek, whose truncated arm still dripped sticky brown Ooreiki blood onto the floor, looked at Joe like he'd lost his mind. "You didn't need to do that," the Ooreiki whispered.

They're all questioning me. Furious, Joe tossed the energy cartridges on the floor beside the broken Baga and headed for the door before he said something he regretted.

"Where are you going?" the Jreet asked, blocking his path with an arm that might as well have been made of half-dig rebar.

Joe merely followed the arm up to the Jreet's face and waited.

The Jreet lowered his arm and looked away.

"The doctors will have questions," Be'shaar said, nodding at the Baga.

"Tell them the truth," Joe said. "He pissed me off. Oh, and while you're there, get your chip synched up with our com system. If the Baga doesn't have one, have them put one in while they fix him up."

The Huouyt watched him with a strange expression oozing from his odd purple eye.

Joe turned back, frowning. "What?"

"Va'gan Huouyt do not get chipped."

"What?" Joe frowned at yet another mention that the Huouyt was supposedly Va'gan-trained. "You're getting chipped."

"Check the rulebook. We are exempt."

Joe frowned. "Exempt? Why?"

"Be content to know that we do not."

"Like hell," Joe snapped. "You'll get a chip if I tell you to get a chip. The last thing we're gonna do is go down a deep den and not be able to communicate with each other."

"Legally, you cannot order me to do that." The Huouyt seemed utterly at ease. "Congress has so few Va'gans sign up for service—they're willing to make a few sacrifices to keep us."

"So you'd get us all killed because you don't like surgery?" Joe demanded. He took a step towards the Huouyt. "Try this, smartass. You get chipped or you aren't going."

The Huouyt looked completely unaffected by his statement. "Further, you cannot discharge me based on my refusal. Look it up, if you do not believe me."

Looking into the Huouyt's flat, alien stare, Joe felt his mood deteriorating. *Damn* the Regency bureaucrats. A million turns of experience, and yet they couldn't leave Planetary Ops the hell alone. They had to go mucking it all up. As if a Huouyt would ever work well with *anything*, much less a goddamn Human. And a Jreet? Taking orders from anything but a *bigger* Jreet? It was ludicrous.

"Fine," Joe told the Huouyt. "You can stay. If you don't get a chip, I'll just find something *very* important for you to do in the barracks while the rest of us are down in the tunnels." He glanced at the other members of his team, the maimed Ooreiki and the flattened Baga, then put his hand to his head, the implications of commanding a multi-species groundteam still staggering him. "Damn I need a drink." He turned to go find one.

The Huouyt stepped in front of him, cutting off his escape. "Jim Beam has cancelled his future appointments, Commander." The Jreet joined him, putting his huge ruby body between Joe and the door. Seeing them work together to undermine him, Joe began to seethe inside.

"Get out of my way."

The Jreet didn't move. "I want back on the team."

Joe looked up into the Jreet's sincere golden eyes. "Not a chance."

The Jreet held steady, though his diamond-shaped head lowered in defeat.

"Move," Joe growled.

"Where are you going?" the Huouyt asked.

Joe's fury built as he looked from the Jreet to the Huouyt, acutely aware that he couldn't *make* them move. Every moment that he, the legendary Commander *Zero*, stood there, stymied by his own groundteam, he lost respect with both his groundteam and Planetary Ops in general. He glanced over Daviin's bulk at the observers in the hall, who were still watching the proceedings with interest. Obviously, they thought someone was about to die. A lot of that had been happening lately, if Joe's surgeons could be believed.

Only the Grekkon, whose horse-sized, insect-like body was crouched in a corner, didn't appear to care about any of the goings on. His four beady black eyes continued to stare at the wall. He hadn't even attempted to stop the Baga from chewing off the Ooreiki's arm. As far as Joe knew, he hadn't even *twitched*.

Keeping his voice as level as possible, Joe turned back to Be'shaar and said, "I'm doing some reconnaissance."

"You mean you go to poison yourself?" The Huouyt snorted. "Why bother paying? I could accomplish the same for free, plus it won't get you killed when the squads find you breaking the code."

"A few drinks isn't illegal," Joe snarled.

"No, but being inebriated in a time of war is." The Jreet had recovered, and now he sounded like a man chastising a child.

"I'm not going to break the goddamn code," Joe snapped.

"You want to mourn your brother, go ahead and tell me," Be'shaar said. "I'll make you feel miserable quite a bit faster than a few shots of alcohol."

Joe prickled at the way the Huouyt so casually threatened to drug him. Huouyt drugged creatures they didn't respect. He tore his eyes away from the Huouyt, realizing that it was the Jreet he needed to convince. With the Jreet's huge ruby body still blocking the door, he wasn't getting out of there without his cooperation.

"I'm on duty," Joe told the Voran. "I don't drink on duty."

The Jreet immediately relaxed and pulled away from the door. "My apologies, Commander." He sounded utterly contrite. Rounding on Be'shaar, the Jreet snapped, "You see, Huouyt? You question him needlessly. A true warrior would not drop his spear before a battle." That the Jreet was so trusting left Joe feeling ashamed.

The Huouyt continued to stare at him with his screwed-up eyes.

Suspicious bastard, Joe thought. He shoved past the both of them and went to find something to take his mind off his brother's upcoming execution. Over his shoulder, he shouted, "And find another groundteam, Jreet. It's the last time I'm going to tell you. You're wasting your time."

At his back, the Jreet said nothing.

Joe went into town fully intending to stay dry. He coasted the streets, spoke with the nervous grounders about the upcoming tunnel crawl, patted a few backs, offered a bit of wisdom or an anecdote here and there, even found another Prime and spent an hour with the Jahul discussing the mission on Neskfaat.

In the end, however, Joe sat on a stool by himself, the vidscreen in the bar in front of him tuned to Earth's news frequency.

"...*execution of the most wanted criminal in Earth's history. Spectators are already lining up outside the central plaza, hoping for a good view of what is sure to be—*"

Joe shut off the newscast and took another drink. They were executing Sam in two hours. Even if Joe hopped on the first shuttle he found, he would never get there in time.

My fault, he thought. *I got Sam caught.*

Joe slammed a fist into the bar, drawing looks from several broad-faced Hebbut down the row. He glared at them until they looked away.

Got Sam killed and what do I have to show for it? A groundteam that's gonna kill itself before it even smells a Dhasha. He snorted and took another drink, relishing the way the alcohol burned on the way down. *I can't do this.*

The Jreet had shattered his spine with one swipe of its arm. The Baga had tried to fuse his face together when he tried to stop him from maiming the Ooreiki. The Huouyt had outright refused to obey him. Even Galek, the youngest and most open to having a Human in command, had no qualms with questioning him in front of everyone. A *boot*, for Mothers' sakes.

Joe knew he didn't stand a chance. He was smaller, weaker, lighter, and, in the Huouyt's case, stupider.

Closing his eyes, Joe downed another whiskey, trying not to listen to the news feeds, trying not to think of Sam.

His team had automatically thought him cruel when he flattened the Baga. The Huouyt had asked him if he were taking out his frustrations like a spoiled child. The Ooreiki, who had just lost an arm, had given him a look like he'd lost his mind. Miserable, Joe knew he would continue to receive the same treatment as long as he did not have their respect.

But how did he gain an alien's respect? If they'd been Human, he would have started on a common ground. He would have shared common strengths and weaknesses. He would have established a rapport, exchanged stories of women and home, taught them little tricks with their weapons, and told jokes about aliens in their native language of Earth, so the aliens couldn't understand them.

Yet his new groundmates weren't Human. They came from different planets, had different breeding habits, spoke different languages, and used different weapons.

They *were* the aliens Joe and his grounders used to joke about.

When Sam stepped out onto the platform, the crowd in the bar cheered. Joe's fingers tightened on his glass. When a brutish Ooreiki shoved Sam to his knees and forced his head to the block, Joe lowered his eyes to the tabletop.

When the other Humans in the bar let out a ragged cheer, Joe cried.

• • •

Eight whiskeys later, Joe was still in tears, regaling the bartender with the story of how he'd saved his brother from the Draft, and had gotten taken to Kophat in Sam's place. The Ueshi bartender was nodding in all the right places, but Joe could tell he didn't believe a word of it. He became emphatic, motioning with his arms as he told of his training, his time as a Dhasha slave, the fight with Na'leen and his Jreet. In the middle of his tale, he knocked over his drink and wondered disgustedly if he'd have to pay for it.

"Look," the Ueshi bartender finally said, shoving another glass full of amber liquid at him, "You ain't weaseling any free drinks tonight. Maybe other guys've fallen for it, but I'm not stupid. You're a Human, but that's the end of the similarity. You're a drunk. Zero's a warrior. You can have this last one, but any more furgsoot and I'll have you kicked out."

Joe sobered as the Ueshi walked away. All around him, aliens were laughing. He stared at his drink, unable to tug his eyes away. Then, furious, he slapped it across the table, showering half the bar with glass and whiskey.

"That's it!" the Ueshi snapped. He motioned two Ooreiki to grab Joe, then they continued to hold him as the Ueshi dug in his pockets for his credit stub and dialed in a number six times what Joe owed and pressing Joe's finger to the confirmation screen. When Joe protested, one of the Ooreiki doubled him over with a blow to the gut.

"Well, what do you know," the Ueshi said, smugly tucking the credit stub back into Joe's pocket. "You really are Zero. Now get him out of here. Right out front, where the squads can find him."

The Ooreiki dumped Joe in the street outside the bar, badly scraping his knees and face on the concrete. After the others left, one of the Ooreiki pooled beside Joe and began easing his Planetary Ops jacket from his back.

"No," Joe mumbled, trying to fight.

"For your own good," the Ooreiki said. "This is Jeelsiht, not Kaleu. Corps Director's ordered squads out in every city to enforce the code. The squads saw you like this, they'd kill you as an example. Wouldn't matter how many kasjas you have, Commander. Now keep that tattoo out of sight and go get an antidote. They sell them at Jei'Jei's Liquids, right down the street. Come back when you're all sobered up and your jacket'll be in my locker. If I'm not here, just ask the Ueshi at the bar."

The Ooreiki finished removing the jacket and stood once more. He folded Joe's jacket under his arm and disappeared back inside the bar.

Joe lay there shivering in the filth, staring down at the bloody pavement.

Sam was dead. He had seen his headless corpse, hefted up by one foot, naked, hung by a crane so the entire Times Square could see it.

Sam was dead, and Joe had done it.

Slowly, he picked himself up and began wandering the streets.

I got my brother killed. The shame ate at him like worms roiling in his insides. *I led the Peacemakers right to him.*

After everything else that had happened to him—losing Sam, his groundteam's disdain, Maggie's constant betrayals—Joe felt as if his soul had been worn down.

He wandered down the street, intending to find Jei'Jei's Liquids and acquire an antidote before heading back to the barracks, but when he stopped outside the store, he saw a squad taking a break inside. Six Jikaln warriors, their naturally chameleon-like bodies blending with the racks of liquids as they padded along the rows on all fours, the neon green lights of the store gleaming off their teeth and claws.

Joe slid into an alley across the store and waited.

Tics went by, five or ten, Joe couldn't tell, and still the squad remained.

An elderly Jahul, stinking despite the heavy scent of soap, scuttled into the alley with him and prodded him with one of its six feet. "They do this before every mission. You better go, son. That squad ain't gonna leave. Even if it looks like they left, they still there. Tryin' ta catch guys like you." His marble-like black eyes shifted to the luminescent tattoo on Joe's right palm, upraised for all to see.

Joe grunted and closed his fist. "Thanks."

The Jahul hesitated in the alley. "You want a ride home? I got time to take you anywhere in Dayut. Congie barracks, methinks?"

Joe dreaded the look the Huouyt would give him when he arrived drunken and bloody. "No. I'll walk it off."

The Jahul eyed him. "Your purification system is equipped to handle such a high dose?"

"It'll handle it," Joe muttered. "Just get out of here."

"Son—" the Jahul began.

"Go!"

With a reluctant glance over its shoulder, the wet-skinned, six-legged Jahul climbed aboard his *haauk* and left.

Joe got to his feet and stumbled into the light. One of the Jikaln inside the shop looked his way, but made no motions to follow. Joe began to wander, wondering how he'd managed to be so stupid.

I just watched Sam die, he thought as he walked. *I just watched him die and it was my fault. I should have stopped them. I owed it to him to* stop *them.*

The longer he was on the streets, the worse he felt. It wasn't long before he couldn't take it anymore. Joe stopped in the first bar he found and ordered another whiskey. He drank it in silence, shame boring into his soul. *I should have stopped them.* Once he finished his drink, he ordered three more.

Joe felt yet another set of bouncers dropping him onto the cold stone street outside by the time he finally succumbed to oblivion.

10

A STUBBORN PIJI SHELL

"Then where is he, Jreet?" The Huouyt assassin made a lazy gesture at the open door. "Please, enlighten me."

"He's doing what he said he would," Daviin retorted. "Reconnaissance."

Jer'ait snorted. "You're a furg."

"He said he didn't drink on duty," Daviin said, growing irritated.

"He was lying."

Daviin prickled. "Why do you think so little of him?"

"Because he was *lying*, furg," the Huouyt snarled. "He left the barracks with every intention of drinking himself into a stupor. He has a chemical dependency. I recognize the symptoms."

Daviin prickled. "His file said nothing about a dependency."

"He developed it when he got his brother arrested. It's why he kept going back to those bars on Earth. It's the only reason we could *find* him."

"He got his brother arrested?" Daviin gave him a curious frown.

"He was a criminal, being tried for treason," Jer'ait said. "Execution was today."

Daviin flinched, realizing he would be sentenced to another level of hell for interfering in a matter of blood-debt. "They were going to kill his brother? Is that why he went AWOL?"

"I suppose during his sober moments he was probably trying to make a plan to save him, yes," Jer'ait admitted.

"Why didn't you say something?" Daviin demanded. "We could've helped him!"

Jer'ait laughed. "You know who I am."

"Yes. Exactly my point."

"You know who I work for."

"One's brothers must come before one's country," the Jreet intoned. "Without a tribe, you are nothing."

"Huouyt do not have tribes," Jer'ait retorted. "We have ourselves and we have our employer. I have a job to kill the Vahlin. It is Huouyt code that I must remain loyal to my employer until I've finished the job I accepted of him."

Daviin snorted. "That code is Dhasha flake."

"It is the only code we live by."

"The regen medicine from his operation would have removed the dependency from his system," Daviin said. "He went to gather intelligence."

"It's mental, Jreet," the Huouyt said. "Our fearless leader has succumbed to the pressures of his job. He's nothing but a lying, useless cur."

Daviin's body tightened into constriction position. Coldly, he said, "You're wrong." He had seen something better. Something that had made him wish to swear allegiance to his damned soft hide.

The Huouyt laughed at him. "We shall see, Jreet. Go looking for him, if you're so sure. I doubt you'll find him in a library. I, on the other hand, am going to attend the briefing. It will not be my *breja* they pull for missing it, and I think at least one member of our team should stay informed."

The Huouyt departed, leaving Daviin's claws digging into the scales of his palms.

In all reality, probably the easiest way to be re-instated in the Human's groundteam would have been to go to the briefing and complain to the Overseers. Daviin knew the tekless cowards would buckle to his demands in an instant. Yet, as desperate as he was to get back on the team, Daviin did not want to go behind the Human's back. He knew that as soon as he did, he would lose all hope of gaining his Prime's respect.

After a moment of indecision, Daviin turned and took the opposite hall, toward the city.

Without Jer'ait to ask questions for him, Daviin found it difficult to locate a single citizen willing to stand around long enough for him to get close enough to ask directions, and Daviin was too slow to run them down. Thus, finding the Human took a mix of instinct, smell, and luck. Humans were not common on Jeelsiht, so their scent was distinctive. As Daviin ignored the bars and wandered the most likely gathering places in vain, however, he had a growing, unhappy sense that Jer'ait had been right.

When Daviin finally found the Human, it was well into the evening.

Joe was face down in an alleyway, stripped naked, his valuables gone. The reek of alcohol and vomit was everywhere. Daviin stilled in the entrance to the alley, staring at the Human in disbelief.

Beda's bones...He lied.

Daviin was stunned. He had thought the Human honorable. He had thought him a warrior. He had *respected* him.

To think he had thought him worthy of a Jreet!

As Daviin watched, the Human stirred and vomited into the puddle growing at his side. The fresh scent of half-digested alcohol wafted back to where Daviin lay.

Daviin almost left him there, content to let the fool find his own way home and seek out another groundteam, but anger overrode his logic. He wove his way up to the Human and grabbed him harshly by the arm. As the Human groaned slightly, trying to bat him away, Daviin leaned back on himself and lifted Joe with him. He dangled the protesting Human out in front of him and brought his head down until their faces almost met.

"On Vora," Daviin growled, "we thread liars on sharpened stakes and let the vermin eat them alive. It takes days for them to die."

The Human opened his eyes long enough to see Daviin's face, then squeezed them shut again. "The answer's still no."

Daviin shook him until he felt the joints in the Human's shoulder dislocate. The Human screamed and tried to fight him, but Daviin was unaffected by his weak struggles. He watched him writhe pitilessly, ignoring his cries. Behind him, several passers-by peeked into the alley at the noise, then, upon seeing Daviin's coils filling up the space, quickly found somewhere else to be.

Once the Human's screams had died down to unintelligible drunken sobs, Daviin leaned down and said into his face, "Liars are scum. You lie, you make yourself as honorless as a Huouyt. A warrior is nothing without his honor."

"Fuck honor," he heard the Human whisper.

Daviin jerked back, stunned. "What did you say?"

"I said *fuck honor!*" Joe screamed, opening his wet brown eyes. "It never got me anywhere."

Daviin whipped back and threw him across the alley. Joe tumbled into the wall, then lay in an inebriated pile, groaning. Before he could right himself, Daviin was atop him. "Honor," he said quietly, "Is everything."

The Human shuddered. It took Daviin a moment to realize he was crying. Daviin pushed him over, furious, intending to give him something to cry about, when the Human said, "Yeah." His sobs grew to wretched wails, like a spitted Takki.

Daviin hesitated, realizing the Human cried out of a deeper pain than his physical bruises. He cried out of shame. Daviin grasped Joe's good arm and wrenched him back off the ground. "Lie to me again," he said into the Human's face, "And I will kill you."

Softly, the Human said, "I'll be dead by next week."

"Not by my hand," Daviin said.

"By mine."

Daviin peered at the Human as he said this, and realized he spoke the truth. He analyzed the Human a moment, then said, "No."

Joe laughed again. "No?"

"No," Daviin repeated. "You'll live."

"Sorry to tell you this, asher," the Human spat, "but you can't stop me. You're not even on my team."

Peering into the Human's stubborn brown eyes, Daviin saw the warrior's spark once more. Intoxicated, naked, dangling six digs off the ground by a limb, unable to move his other arm, the Human might as well have been on even ground, his spear at Daviin's throat.

"Someday," Daviin said, "You will tell me why you poison yourself." He dropped the Human, who crumpled on the pavement with a grunt of surprise. "Until then, you will walk."

From his awkward pile, the Human laughed. "Burn you, Jreet."

"You will walk," Daviin said, "or you will be dragged."

The Human stopped laughing.

Naked as he was, his soft body would be shredded on the sharp black gravel, and they both knew it.

"I hope you rot in hell," the Human finally muttered.

"Which one?"

The Human peered at him for a while, considering. "How many are there to choose from?"

"Ninety. If I found myself in your situation—which I wouldn't— I'd curse me to the Frozen Hell. Rii. It's one of the very last. There is very little that is more uncomfortable to a Jreet than cold."

The Human used his good arm to drag himself into a squatting position. "Soot my head hurts."

"It will hurt much more if you don't start moving."

The Human peered at him through one puffy brown eye, then reluctantly stood. He teetered a moment, then steadied. "You're not on the team."

"Walk, Human."

The Human muttered something under his breath, but he walked. Slowly, but steadily, he padded barefoot toward the edge of the alley, then balked, seemingly realizing his current state of undress.

"I can't go out there like this."

"You can. And will."

"Ghosts of the Mothers, what are you, some avenging angel come to cleanse me of my sins?"

"No, I am a Sentinel-trained Jreet who has little pity for inebriated fools."

The Human laughed. "You know, I might just start to like you, sooter."

"My name is Daviin."

"I'm Joe."

"Walk, Joe."

"Right." The Human took a deep breath, eying the bustling street. Bracing himself, he muttered, "God hates a coward."

And walked.

• • •

"Commander Zero, if you're not down here in *three tics*—"

Joe shut off the Overseer's snarl and leaned back into his cot, staring up at the ceiling of his barracks room. He heard the wall creak as the Jreet shifted outside his door. Joe lifted his head off his pillow and shouted, "I said *get lost!*"

The Jreet—who had the best hearing in Congress—ignored him. Instead, he said through the door, "You should go to the meeting, Joe."

They were going down the tunnels in two days. Two days, and the Jreet hadn't let him so much as step into a bar in a week.

My own personal nanny, Joe thought, miserable.

Outside his door, the Jreet shifted again, and this time the door slammed open. Joe sat up, outraged that Daviin had somehow managed to hack his password.

A furious Ooreiki stood in the doorway, its *sudah* whipping in its neck. It jammed a tentacle at him. "You!" Ooreiki Secondary Overseer Moskin snapped. "Do you want to be tried for disobedience, as well as drunkenness?"

Joe lay back down and returned his eyes to the ceiling. "It's all pretty much the same to me."

The Ooreiki's voice lowered to a dangerous whisper. "Zero, you are one of the most decorated soldiers under my command, but I swear to the ancestors' ghosts, if you do not show up for your trial, we are going to demote you."

"Wouldn't be the first time," Joe said to the ceiling. "And it would save me the hell of trying to keep my Takkiscrew of a groundteam from killing itself."

In a fury, the Ooreiki strode across the room and easily ripped him off his cot. Not even trying to keep him upright, the Ooreiki stormed out the door, dragging him by an arm.

A ruby hand bigger than Joe's chest suddenly blocked their path.

"Where are you going with my Prime?" The ominous sound of the Jreet's voice even made Joe flinch.

The speed of the Ooreiki Overseer's sudah suddenly took on a new intensity. "Where did you come from?"

"The asher's been squatting outside my door for the last week," Joe muttered. He yanked his hand free from the Ooreiki's grip.

Overseer Moskin's pupils expanded to enormous, terrified black ovals. "Then this is why you would not leave your room?"

"No," Joe said.

At the same time, Daviin said, "Yes."

When Joe frowned at the Jreet, Daviin lowered his head to face the Overseer and said, "If he leaves his room before he returns me to his groundteam, my honor demands that I kill him, as well as everyone around him."

The Ooreiki took two nervous steps backwards. Almost meekly, he said, "We need Joe to make an appearance for his toxicity trial, my lord."

"The trial is cancelled," Daviin said. "Leave."

"But..."

"*Now!*" the Jreet snarled.

The Ooreiki Overseer fell over itself trying to escape down the hall. Joe watched it go, then returned his attention to Daviin. He looked the big Jreet up and down, taking in the mountain of ruby

coils stacked outside his door before returning his eyes to the Jreet's diamond-shaped head. "So why are you still here?"

"I want on the team," Daviin said.

"I've already said no."

"I intend to make you change your mind."

Joe sighed, expecting as much. "I don't suppose you'll let me out for a drink?"

"A meeting, yes," the Jreet said. "To poison yourself, no."

Joe gave him a disgusted scowl. "I should check on the others. They haven't heard from their Prime in over a day."

Daviin bobbed his chest-sized head. "That you should. I'll come with you, in case the Ooreiki returns to harass you."

Joe squinted at the Jreet, wondering just what the chances were he could slip away from the Jreet and go get a drink. Probably infinitesimal. He sighed. "Just how badly do you want to be on my team, Daviin?"

The Jreet raised itself up proudly. "I would go nowhere else."

Joe eyed him a long moment. "Tell you what. The Huouyt is being difficult and I need a scout, and you've got inviso-mode, so you could work."

Daviin perked up instantly. "And?"

Reluctantly, Joe said, "And, you want back on the team so bad, I'll make you a deal. I have several important meetings with a long-time associate coming up. If you can manage to follow me between now and then, without losing track of me, but without me seeing you or noticing you're there, and can give me a full report of what my friend and I said at the end of the day, I'll let you back on the team."

The Jreet hesitated so long that Joe wasn't sure he had heard. Finally, he said, "And if I fail?"

"You'll leave. Permanently."

The Jreet's enormous coils tightened. "I won't fail."

"A full day," Joe reminded him. "I can't see you or notice your presence. If I do, you will leave and find some other fool to haunt. Agreed?"

"Agreed," the Jreet said. Its small golden eyes watching him, the Jreet suddenly vanished. Joe found himself unnerved at the way the Jreet's monstrous red body had simply disappeared and he was suddenly facing an empty hall.

Joe grinned. "Now to go find Jim Beam."

• • •

"You tricked me, Human."

The sound had seemingly come from the thin air beside him. Joe sighed and put down his glass. "And you were doing so well, too."

Daviin lowered his energy level, making every head in the bar suddenly turn at the mass of red that had appeared beside him…

…and filled up the rest of the bar, rolling over tables and booths and filling up inconspicuous aisles.

"I've been following you for the last six hours, and I know for a fact you no more intend to have me on the team than you do to have me document your secret discussions with your long-time associate. Jim Beam is a form of poison. I just heard the bartender discussing it with a Human in the corner."

Daviin had taken the time to form most of his body into a huge coil overlapping several pieces of furniture, leaving Joe feeling acutely aware at just how easy it would have been for the Jreet to kill him while he drank on, oblivious.

From the looks on the other patrons' faces, Daviin made them feel the same way. There was an air about Jreet that left everyone else feeling insignificant and weak. Most of the patrons quickly got up and found something else to do.

Prime Dhasha destruction, all two thousand lobes of him. Inwardly, Joe considered allowing Daviin to join them in the tunnels, then cursed himself for being a fool. The Jreet would not follow orders. He had just proven as much.

"You've been here awhile," Joe agreed. He hefted his whiskey and wiggled the glass. "But not long enough for me to finish my meeting with my long-time associate. You failed, Jreet. Go home."

The Jreet didn't move. "I figured out why you drink yourself to death."

Joe glanced at the infoscreen, which only moments earlier had contained sentimental memoryclips of his brother Sam that his mother had sent to Joe while he'd been across the galaxy, fighting Congress's wars for it. Immediately, he bristled. "Get out, Jreet. I was giving you an honest chance, but you screwed it up. I'm serious about keeping you off the team."

"I know." The Jreet lowered his head until he was at eye-level with Joe. "That's why I want you. There isn't another Prime on this planet who has the courage to turn me down and mean it, or the audacity to make me bumble around for six hours like a soft-skinned hatchling, utterly alert, thinking I'm looking for some mysterious Jim Beam."

"You mean the stupidity." Joe sighed. "Look, I've seen what a Jreet can do. I know you could wipe the floor with a Dhasha. You could kill more of them in an evening than I'll ever hope to kill in my whole life."

The Jreet waited, listening.

"But I can't take you back on," Joe said. "You're a risk to everyone else who goes down there with you." Then he laughed out of frustration. "Who am I kidding? I've got a Huouyt assassin who won't get chipped, a cocky little Baga nutcase, an Ooreiki who looks at me like I shit ruvmestin but questions me like I don't have two spare brain cells to rub together...About the only one who doesn't question me is the Grekkon, and as far as I know he doesn't have an opinion on anything...which worries me even more than the Huouyt."

"He doesn't question you. A quality of a good soldier."

"No," Joe said. "This isn't infantry. This is an elite squad. I need grounders with the ability to make their own decisions if they have to. You saw how he just stood there when the Baga was pulling his crap? Like he didn't even give a damn."

"He probably didn't," Daviin said.

"That's exactly what I'm talking about!" Joe cried. "If we were all Humans, somebody would have put that Baga in his place. Hell, they all woulda helped me re-arrange his face. But everyone just stood around and watched. Even the MPs in the hall didn't do a damn thing. Nobody did."

"Except you."

Joe sighed. "Yeah."

The Jreet turned to the bartender and ordered a round of something foreign. The Jahul bartender first brought out a regular-sized glass, then looking his newest customer up and down, got out a two-gallon canister and set it on the table beside Daviin.

Joe sniffed it and wrinkled his nose at the toxic burning-tire smell. "What is it?"

"Deadly." The Jreet lifted the canister and took two long swigs, then set it down half full. He smacked his scaly lips and stretched his huge, diamond-shaped hearing cavities in Joe what he recognized as a Jreet smile. "And delicious."

"Huh," Joe said. "I guess you have no reason to worry about the Tox Squads."

Daviin snorted. "It would take more than a few Jikaln to scare me."

Joe sighed. "That's one thing I didn't miss on Earth. You can drink 'til you pass out every day and no one will cart you off to the brig."

"It's the same on Vora." Daviin glanced out the door. "At home, they would have rioted if the clan leader outlawed enjoying oneself with friends."

Joe grunted. "Don't worry about it. Volunteers are exempt from the Director's stupid rules."

"I am not a volunteer."

Joe glanced up. "You told me you were."

"I pledged to serve." The Jreet's golden eyes were watching him carefully. "They accepted my Sentinel training in lieu of Basic. Took my oath this afternoon, after I realized you'd tricked me."

Joe felt his mouth falling open. "Why would you—ghosts! You became a *Congie*? Don't you know that's stupid?! They'll send you down every rat-hole they can find and charge you extra time for every trip to medical. They'll never give you up."

"I gave them a condition."

"Recruitment doesn't make conditions," Joe said, frowning.

Daviin smiled. "They do for me."

Seeing the two thousand lobes of twisted alien muscle, Joe decided the Jreet was probably right. "Huh. I'll bet." Joe sighed and tilted his glass. "Well, I hope you made it a good one."

"I did," Daviin said.

Seeing his smug look Joe stiffened. "If you conned them into putting you on my team—"

"The condition was that I be allowed to modify my Sentinel oath."

Joe frowned. "I don't get it."

"There is nothing to get." Daviin took another swig of his toxic sludge, downing it in one gulp. Then, without lead-up or segue, Daviin pulled a crystal dagger from the leather sheath in his chest and sliced open his scaly ruby hand. He then reached out and grasped Joe's arm before Joe could pull away. Holding Joe in place, he tore Joe's coat open and smeared the bluish blood beading on his palm across the bare skin of Joe's torso. In this, he scratched a symbol with a scarlet claw over Joe's heart, cutting bloody paths in the skin with a talon. Joe was so stunned he could only sit there and watch the Jreet carve on him.

"There," Daviin said, releasing him. "You didn't flinch. That's good."

"Wait," Joe said, pulling away. "Now just hold on. What'd you do?"

"Joe Dobbs, I am now your acting Sentinel."

Joe stared. His eyes traveled from his drinking companion's face down to where his blood was mingling with the Jreet's over his heart in stinging red-blue pathways. Then he laughed.

Tics went by and the Jreet's eyes never wavered. Joe realized he was serious.

"You're saying you swore an oath...to obey me?"

"This was why you were hesitant about having me on the team, am I correct? Because I was a volunteer? Unbeholden to you?"

"Now *hold on!*" Joe set his drink down and stood up. "You're a… my…*Sentinel?* As in a Representative of Congress Sentinel?!"

Daviin grinned at him and ordered another drink.

"Are you *nuts?!*"

"The Sentinels thought so, yes. Frankly, though, they could not stop me. A Sentinel chooses his ward."

Joe held the Jreet's eyes for a heartbeat, then threw back his head and laughed.

"What, Human?"

Joe pulled up his stool, relaxing. "You just made my job a hell of a lot easier, Jreet. I thought I was going to have to run you off. Now all I have to do is tell you 'git' and you have to git."

"I told you they allowed me to make my own oath."

Joe frowned. "And?"

"And I made certain provisions." The Jreet's crocodile-like jaws opened in a big Jreet smile. "That was one of them."

Joe's brows knotted. "I can't tell you to leave."

"No. You can't tell me to leave your side, except as strategy in a battle situation." Then the Jreet cocked his head. "Well, I suppose you *can* tell me to leave. I just don't have to obey you." He stretched his hearing-chambers and displayed his fangs in a big Jreet grin.

Joe closed his eyes, suddenly having a headache. "You son of a bitch."

"Now," Daviin said. "Is that proof enough of my intent to follow your lead in the tunnels?"

Joe opened one eye. "I'm checking this out as soon as I get back to the barracks."

"Why wait?" Daviin said. "It's all over the news." He touched the blank infoscreen with the back of his claw and selected universal news.

There it was, prominently displayed on the first page, a Jreet had sworn to Sentinel for a non-Representative for the first time in a thousand turns. Names and location had been withheld for privacy. The reasoning the Jreet had given was that it was "mutually beneficial" for both parties.

"The Mothers' ghosts," Joe said, staring. He wondered if the newscast could be faked.

Apparently reading his mind, the Jreet said, "It's not fake."

Joe took a deep breath, watching the words scroll across the screen. "Jreet, you're out of your mind."

"My name is Daviin."

"Daviin." Joe shook his head. "Ghosts, Daviin. I'm just a grounder." He felt awed, unnerved, and overwhelmed, all at once. "I'm nobody."

Daviin curled his head under his neck in a courteous gesture. "I will enjoy serving you a thousand times more than my brethren enjoy serving their fat, pampered wards on Koliinaat."

He swore to me. Voran royalty. As a Sentinel. The fact left Joe dumbstruck. Struggling not to look like an ignorant country bumpkin, Joe pulled his shirt closed over his bloody chest. Taking a steadying breath, he whispered, "All right, you bastard. You win. You're on the team."

Daviin's scaly face drew back in a grin. "I knew you would come to your senses."

Immediately, Joe said, "But nobody's gonna know. You get me? As far as the others are concerned, I swallowed my pride and let you back in. I don't want them to know about..." Joe gestured at Daviin's palm, which was still bleeding a blue puddle on the floor under the bar.

"Very well." Daviin bowed again, the gesture too close to subservience for Joe's liking.

Joe glanced around at the gawking aliens surrounding them in the bar. "And hit me."

Daviin froze, cocking his head. "Excuse me?"

"Hit me," Joe said hurriedly. "Do something a Sentinel wouldn't do. I don't want these sooters to get any ideas."

Daviin seemed to consider, then swiveled and slammed a meaty arm into Joe's torso. The blow threw him across the room to land in a heap amongst tables and chairs. Joe's head hit something hard and his world exploded into stars.

Out of the corner of his eye, he saw Daviin's sixty-foot length barreling down on him. All around them, aliens were getting out of their seats, not to help but to get out of the way.

"How *dare* you insult my oath of brotherhood, Human?!" Daviin roared above him, towering at least ten digs into the air. "You spit on my customs?! Spit on this!" He wrenched Joe out of the debris and flung him into a startled group of black-clad Ooreiki.

Thankfully, some of their soft, boneless bodies slowed his fall. Still, Joe was pretty sure he was bleeding internally by the time the Jreet grabbed him by the collar of his coat and began dragging him from the bar.

"You're lucky one of my provisions was to remove the part where I could no longer spill your blood," Daviin said once they were back outside and he was dragging Joe through the streets by his neck.

Joe didn't feel very lucky. "I think you broke some more ribs."

"Really?" Daviin dropped him suddenly, allowing Joe's head to connect painfully with the sharp gravel road. "I was trying to be gentle."

Joe would have laughed, but it hurt too much. "Remind me not to piss you off."

"I'll try." Daviin lowered his head so that it was filling Joe's vision. "You really are fragile creatures, aren't you? Did I go too far?"

"Nothing some nanos won't take care of," Joe muttered. He struggled to sit up, pushing Daviin back. Groaning, he got to his feet. "Mothers' ghosts, you pack a punch like a freight train."

"Can you walk?"

"Yeah." Joe began limping towards the barracks. Daviin slid along beside him, a disconcerting back-and-forth weaving motion that left him feeling like he was walking alone one moment and about to be run over the next.

"I'm surprised, Joe. Someone else in your situation would want everyone know of what I've done. Having a Sentinel...that's quite impressive. Why do you wish to hide it?"

Joe saw six shadowy Jikaln of a Tox Squad watching them from an alley as they walked. They saw Joe staggering and began to spread out to surround him, but checked their approach when they noticed he was talking to the Jreet. Like six translucent wolves realizing they'd just surrounded a grizzly bear, the lithe quadrupeds wandered off to find easier prey.

"Maybe I'm hoping you'll change your mind."

"A Sentinel can't change his mind. You know that."

Joe sighed. "Because I know what I am and I know what you are. Don't get me wrong—I'm proud of my species—but Humans are farmed Takki compared to a Jreet."

The Jreet's huge clawed hand engulfed Joe's shoulder, drawing him to a halt. "I didn't choose to Sentinel for you because you're a farmed Takki, Joe. You had the courage to stand up to me. Not many do."

Joe laughed. "You mean the stupidity."

Daviin's scaly face stretched in another fearsome Jreet smile. "Perhaps."

Joe peered up at the Jreet, then grunted and kept walking. "Lucky me."

"There is one thing I would ask of you for my services, Joe."

"What?"

"Allow me to kill the Huouyt."

Joe stumbled to a halt and peered up at Daviin. "What?"

"The one who helped me find you back on Earth. Let me kill him."

Joe squinted up at him. "Why?"

The Jreet paused a moment, as if considering. "I don't like his story. He is not here to kill the Vahlin."

"None of us are. The chances we'll get assigned to the Vahlin's den is like one in a million."

"One in a thousand. Much, much less if we are assigned more than one den."

"You mean if we survive more than one den." Joe laughed. "Daviin, I hate to say it, but aside from you, Be'shaar's probably our best bet of getting out of there alive."

"It's not the tunnels I'm worried about, Joe."

"Huh?"

Daviin cocked his head at Joe. "You don't know who he is, do you?"

"Who? Be'shaar?"

"As part of our training, Sentinels are taught to recognize the quirks and idiosyncrasies of the top assassins trained in Va'ga. The idea is for us to recognize them before they get a chance to strike."

"And?"

"I recognize him. His real name is Jer'ait. He was at the top of the Va'ga list when he graduated. Still is."

Joe flinched, suddenly feeling dirty all over. "Jer'ait? *The* Jer'ait?"

Daviin nodded solemnly.

Joe whistled. "Well, that makes him even more useful, doesn't it?"

"You don't understand," Daviin said. "He's at the *top* of the lists. Even now. He's killed more targets than any other assassin living. His specialty is befriending hard-to-reach targets and then murdering them. No remorse."

Joe frowned. "He was after my brother?"

Daviin's metallic gold eyes narrowed to pinpricks. "If he was, I don't see why he left Earth."

"So he's after the Vahlin."

"If he were after the Vahlin, he wouldn't tie himself down with the rest of us. He'd simply go and kill him."

Joe frowned. "So who's he after? You?"

"Joe, I think he's after you."

11

DAVIIN LEARNS TO LIE

Joe stared at Daviin. Instead of laughing, the Human just said, "Why?"

"There is a prophecy—"

Joe interrupted him with a foreign curse. "Will that follow me to my grave?! Who told you? Maggie?!"

Daviin hesitated, cocking his head at his ward, trying to judge how to proceed. Then, he said, "You know of it?"

"It's soot," Joe said viciously. "I told Na'leen to go to hell and we won Kophat back despite what the little gray slimeball tried to tell me. It's crap. You mention it again and I'll order you to go suck Dhasha dick, get me?"

Daviin flinched. "I was talking about the Vahlin. You mean you've had other things prophesized about you, Joe?"

Joe blinked. He looked like Daviin had knocked the wind out of him.

Hastily, Daviin said, "Every once in a while, maybe once in a thousand turns, a black Jreet will be born. These Jreet are different from the rest. They refuse to fight. And they—"

"What the hell are you talking about?" The Human looked confused.

"Only other Jreet know about the black one. But, since she spoke of you, I suppose you have the right to know. They see the future, Human. They read thoughts."

The Human's face grew angry. "You mean you breed Trith."

"What are Trith?"

Instead of answering, Joe said, "What did she say about me?" He sounded resigned. Angry.

Daviin analyzed Joe's reaction, then lowered his voice. "When they're born, the black ones are taken into seclusion. Worshipped. It is the black ones who ordain the next clan leaders, as well as the Representatives. It was a black one that warned us of the Ayhi thousands of turns before we expanded into space."

Joe gave him a suspicious look. "Warned you? From what I've seen of the Ayhi, they wouldn't hurt a Takki."

"Exactly. Don't you wonder why we assign four times as many warriors to defending their Representatives than we give Aliphei himself? It is because the black ones say they will one day need us, and if we are not there to save them, the Jreet will be annihilated to the last."

"Why?" The Human was obviously confused, not understanding what it had to do with him.

Daviin shrugged. "The seers don't tell us why. They simply tell us that we must do to prevent it."

"So this black one said something about me and you're gonna mindlessly hold it against me just like—"

"No," Daviin said quickly. "That's not the way of it. They never predict the future—only a fool does that. They offer us choices. Before I left the Sentinels, I asked the black one what path I should take to earn a place in my people's history. She said go to Aez, that my path there would lead me to one who could help me."

Joe snorted. "And you think that's me."

"And you do not?"

"Look at me, you son of a bitch. I'm a grounder. I've been Prime for most of my life, and I've got no hopes of climbing the ranks—ever. I've got an Overseer who hates my guts and does her damndest to get me executed. I don't have power, I don't have money, and you can break every bone in my body by flicking your pinkie. I can't get you anything you can't get by yourself."

Daviin felt himself liking this Human. He was growing more confident in his decision by the tic. "It's you. I know it."

"Then you're stupider than I thought."

"She said if I chose the path to Aez, I would come across a great and unstoppable foe, an opponent worthy of a Jreet heir—"

"That's not me," the Human snorted.

"Obviously," Daviin replied. "She said that I shall one day hold his fate in my hands, and my ward will help me give him the sentence he deserves. Depending on what I decide that day, I will kill the one who would shatter Congress...or I will discover what it means to be forgotten."

The Human's head jerked up sharply. "What?"

"So I ask you, Human, what is this other prophecy that makes you able to help me stop an unstoppable foe who would destroy Congress without our intervention?"

To Daviin's surprise, the Human lunged at him, grabbing him by the sensitive ear-crest and tearing him down until they were eye-to-eye.

"Let's get one thing straight," Joe said, his oily face ninths from Daviin's snout. "If I believed in prophecies, I wouldn't be breathing today. I despise them and everyone who believes in them, and the fastest way to piss me off is to say I'm destined to do something. I've had burning enough of that. I hear one more word about a prophecy out of you and you won't have to wait for some 'unstoppable foe'—I'll kill you myself."

"I can see why the seers like you," Daviin said, grinning. He nodded as much as the Human's grip would allow, pleased.

The Human released him and backed up, glaring. "You're lucky I didn't bring my gun."

"One thing I should warn you," Daviin said. "The Sentinels don't take it kindly when their wards kill one sworn to protect them. If you do kill me, at least have the sense to make it look like an accident. If you don't, and the Sentinels catch you—which they will—you're going to wish yourself dead long before they get around to letting you kill yourself."

"*Letting* me kill myself." The Human gave him a dubious look.

"Yes. More shame in it that way. And they'll do it all without spilling a drop of your blood."

"Classy."

"Very. It's impressive, when you see it in action."

"So I take it it's a common problem."

"Only amongst conniving politicians who would kill their own clanmates if it meant their own personal gain." Daviin grinned down at the Human. "I'm not too worried about you."

"You should be," the Human growled.

"I can break every bone in your body with my pinkie." He held it up, for the Human's clarification.

His commander looked at the crimson digit that was as thick as his bony Human arm and grunted. "Speaking of that, not to alarm you, considering you're my new Sentinel and all, but I'm rapidly losing the ability to stand up straight." As if to illustrate, he began to blink rapidly and weave on his feet. Catching himself on the wall of the alleyway and peered much too intently at the buildings across the road.

"Funny, Human," Daviin said.

"Yeah, I'd think so, too, if I wasn't all of a sudden feeling like someone was trying to shove a baseball bat through my ear." The Human kept blinking. "I'm thinking maybe using my head to splinter that chair wasn't such a great idea back there…"

Daviin glanced down the road, judging the distance to the barracks. "Can you walk?"

Joe peered up at him suspiciously. "Or what? Be *carried?*" He snorted. "Of course I can walk." The Human straightened, took a step, then his eyes rolled up into the back of his head and he slumped forward like a wad of wet rags. Daviin caught him before he slammed face-first into the packed gravel.

"Such delicate creatures," Daviin murmured. He threw the Human under one arm and made his way back to the barracks, ignoring the stares he received along the way.

Daviin let himself into Joe's room and dropped him on the bed. He had just administered the nanos when he heard a voice at the door.

"So our good Commander resisted your charms again?"

Daviin stiffened and twisted.

Jer'ait stood in the doorway, leaning casually against the frame. His features sharpened when Daviin turned to face him. "What happened to your palm, Jreet?"

Daviin immediately clasped his bloody fist shut. "I was in a fight."

"Oh?" the Huouyt asked, amused. "And where was the Dhasha?"

Daviin frowned. "What?"

Lazily, Jer'ait left the doorway and walked over to him. He took Daviin's palm and, when Daviin tried to flinch away, Daviin felt a tiny sting as the Huouyt injected a poison under his skin of his arm.

Fear warred with anger as he suddenly found himself helpless to resist as the Huouyt casually opened his palm and peered down at his cut with his unnatural, bi-colored eyes. *He drugged me*, Daviin thought, enraged. *I, a Sentinel, allowed a Va'gan to* drug *me!* The shame was overwhelming.

"Ah," Jer'ait said, as he examined his palm. "So my eyes did not deceive me. There are only two things that can cut through scales like this. A Dhasha's claws and a ceremonial *ovi* knife."

Jer'ait dropped Daviin's hand and looked up at him, smugness stretched across his downy alien features. "We both know what an *ovi* is used for. And we both know there isn't a single Dhasha on Jeelsiht. Did you really want to be on the team that badly, Jreet? Which politician did you swear to, to get the assignment?"

Daviin said nothing, seething. It was everything he could do just to squeeze his fingers back together and hide the wound. The Huouyt could kill him at will, and both of them knew it.

"You can speak, you know," Jer'ait said, obviously amused. "The poison does not inhibit linguistic capabilities."

Daviin merely watched him.

Jer'ait sighed. "Very well." He calmly touched Daviin once more, freeing him.

Daviin slammed his fist into the side of the Huouyt's head, knocking him to the floor. "I should make you dance on my tek, Huouyt."

Slowly, the assassin picked himself up. He had an open cut from one of Daviin's claws, but it mended as Daviin watched him. "You know, I have killed for much less."

"As have I," Daviin snapped.

Jer'ait cocked his kreenit-penis head at Daviin. "Fair enough," the Huouyt said. "Where'd you get the cut?"

Daviin begged forgiveness from the Ayhi, then lied. "There's another Jreet on Jeelsiht. Welu. He and I had an argument."

The Huouyt watched him, then slowly his eyes moved to Joe. "And the Human?"

"Tried to separate us."

The Huouyt cocked his head. "You escaped, so somehow you must have killed this Welu. Shall I check the report?"

"I didn't kill him, but go ahead."

Jer'ait went to the wall and scanned the files he found there. Slowly, he turned back, a look of confusion on his face. "Huh. I thought…"

"It was a furgish idea," Daviin snapped. "For you to suggest I would ever take a ward to get on this *Takki's* groundteam, it makes it harder and harder for me to find reasons not to kill you."

Jer'ait gave him an amused look and bowed. "Then I shall not push my luck." He cast one last look at the Human and departed. When he reached the door, however, he stopped and turned back. "Just out of curiosity, he didn't let you back on the team, did he?"

"No," Joe groaned from his bed. "Get the asher out of here."

Jer'ait gave the Human an amused glance. "I think I'll leave that task to someone more capable than myself, Commander. Good to see you did not crack like a *piji* shell to his whining."

Daviin stiffened, but the Huouyt turned and left. Daviin immediately went to the door and locked it behind him.

"So," Joe said, sitting up, "I thought Jreet did not lie, Daviin."

144

"I'm sure I will burn in several layers of hell for it," Daviin muttered. "But you gave me an order not to let others know. I hope it was worth it for you, Human."

"It was. Answer something for me, Daviin."

"What?"

"Why did Jer'ait drop it? Did you kill a Welu in between shattering my spine and swearing fealty to me?"

"We had an argument," Daviin admitted reluctantly. "Broke a few houses."

"And you won?"

"Of course I won!" Daviin snapped. "It was a *Welu!*"

"But you didn't kill him." The Human sounded...intrigued.

"He did not have Sentinel training," Daviin gritted. "It was not a contest."

"You let him live."

"If it can be called that," Daviin snorted. "The poor little furg will go home in disgrace. One of his older brothers will probably come for me later, to reap vengeance from my hide. Him, I'll have to kill."

Joe rubbed the sides of his head with his soft fingertips. "Damn Jreet vendettas. Why'd you start the fight in the first place if you knew it wasn't a contest?"

"I didn't. The little Welu furg attacked me on my way to find you."

Joe peered at him. "Is this going to be a common thing?"

"Depends. There are five other Jreet on Jeelsiht. All Welu. They will attack me on sight, and I them. Congress knows this, so they tried to put us in different staging areas. The Welu was on leave with his groundteam when he saw me."

"So why don't they just post your locations so you can avoid each other?"

Daviin stared at the Human, wondering if he was simple. "That would give us the obligation to seek each other out. They hide it from us intentionally."

"Ghosts." Joe gave an unhappy laugh and said, "How do you guys survive as a species?"

"It is hard," Daviin admitted. "Mortality rates are high, especially amongst youngsters. We gain one, maybe two thousand a turn. That was before Aez."

"One or two *thousand?*" the Human cried. "For your whole *species?*"

"A Jreet's life is hard," Daviin replied. "At least up until you get to be my age."

The Human peered up at him. "And just how old are you?"

"Almost a thousand, now."

His ward whistled. "I thought you were a little bigger than normal."

"Not at all. We have histories of normal Jreet reaching up to sixty-three rods. The black ones often get bigger."

The Human's eyes widened. "Ghosts of the Mothers. I'm not even a rod. I'm like two *thirds* of a rod, Daviin."

"You're a weakling."

He said it in all honesty, but the Human narrowed his eyes. "Sixty-three. That's what, nine of you?"

"Approximately," Daviin said, shrugging. "The breeders grow very large, once they swear off war and give up their teks. But nobody really counts them because they're forbidden to fight. Warrior-wise, I am about half the length of the biggest recorded Jreet with a tek. The Aezi representative, Prazeil—may he endure every level of the coldest hells—is very close to thirteen rods."

"Huge."

"To a Human."

"Huh." The Human sighed and stood. "We might as well come up with a convincing way for you to crack my stubborn *piji* shell."

• • •

"Are you sure, Geuji? The last time a Jreet decided to Sentinel to a non-Representative, it was the Age of the Jahul."

"The Jreet will do it," Forgotten replied. "It will be the only way he can change the Human's mind and therefore rejoin the team."

"We need a Jreet," Rri'jan argued, visibly losing his composure. "And you are betting everything he will swear himself to an inconsequential alien grounder."

"I would not call him inconsequential." Forgotten took a fraction of a nanosecond to monitor Syuri's life-signs, to make sure the poor Jahul wasn't suffocating.

"And if you're wrong?" Rri'jan snapped.

"I tire of that question, Huouyt," Forgotten said, deciding that the trapped Jahul was highly upset, but not dying. "Until some part of my plan fails, please try to refrain from asking it."

"Don't be flippant with me, Geuji. *I* decide whether you will ever see your people alive again."

"I'm aware of your inclinations to that effect."

"Yes, but do you really understand?" Rri'jan watched him. "No. I don't think you do." He reached for the com unit attached to his cloth-of-silver cape.

"Don't," Forgotten said. "I know what you're going to do, Rri'jan. You have no need to prove it to me."

"Oh, I think I do." Rri'jan activated the unit. "Cha'vai, kill one of the Geuji. The oldest."

Forgotten felt a flood of anger at Rri'jan's words. It had been so easy. So *easy* for the Huouyt to give the order to end the greatest mind in the known universe. Such petty ignorance sickened him to the core. Forcing himself to keep his voice in check, Forgotten said, "You didn't have to do that."

"You needed to fully understand who is in charge here, Geuji," Rri'jan said. "Now you do."

"Believe me, Rri'jan, I understand who is in charge."

Rri'jan scanned Forgotten again, then once more activated his com unit. "Kill another one. The youngest."

"Stop!" Forgotten snapped. "You have my attention."

"I'm not as stupid as you believe," Rri'jan said. "My species is known for its intelligence."

"Your species is known for its conscious cruelty."

Rri'jan tapped the com unit. "You should learn to think before you speak, Geuji. It would serve your people well in the future." Then he cocked his head, enlightenment suddenly crossing his face. "Unless you *are* thinking about what you're saying and are intentionally provoking me. Now why would you want to do that, Forgotten? I was under the impression we'd agreed upon a mutually beneficial business arrangement."

"We have an arrangement," Forgotten said. "It's you who's breaking the terms of that contract."

"The terms of the contract are that I free your people once gaining the Tribunal," Rri'jan replied coolly. "It says nothing about killing them to discipline you."

"You are treading dangerous ground, Rri'jan," Forgotten said, feeling himself despising the creature sharing air with him.

"Not really. I don't stand to lose anything if we fail." He tapped the com unit again. "Now tell me more about this plan of yours. Why do we sic my esteemed brother on this Human?"

"How else would I get the top assassin in the universe to join a common groundteam for the purpose of killing Dhasha?"

Rri'jan pointed the com unit at Forgotten. "Excellent point. But that leaves another question. Va'gans do not allow themselves to be put under anesthesia in any way. Just how do you plan on making Jer'ait get a grounder's chip?"

"I won't. The Human will."

Rri'jan snorted. "How?" He obviously thought it was impossible.

"With his winning personality."

Rri'jan tapped the com unit against his cilia-covered cheek, then said, "I'm going to give you the benefit of the doubt and assume you meant that literally."

"Thank you."

"So tell me," Rri'jan said. "Why do you put so much faith in this Human?"

"He's like me," Forgotten said.

Rri'jan laughed. "Oh? An immobile blob of mucous?"

Forgotten ignored the insult. "He's what's called a vortex. The Trith cannot see his future, so they attempt to make it for him. He's fought them every step of the way."

"And how does this remind you of you?"

"The last Trith that visited me, I killed and ejected into space."

That wiped the smirk off of Rri'jan's face. "You've killed a Trith?"

"Several of them. It took them a while to realize why their fellows were going missing."

Rri'jan looked...more subdued...than usual. "And this Human... he could also kill a Trith?"

"Yes. And he probably will, if he's ever visited again. I think they learned their lesson from me, though. They'll visit those around him, try to alter his path that way. A much safer alternative. Especially now, when they see our paths have crossed. That will cause them no end of anxiety, which pleases me very much."

Rri'jan's eyes glittered. "I assume it would. So tell me, Geuji. You've put together this perfect team, going to elaborate lengths to get just the right members, yet you continue to act as if the results of your little experiment are uncertain. What makes you think the Dhasha will give your brainchild any problems?"

"That's simple," Forgotten said, "The Dhasha will be expecting them."

12

TO CHIP OR NOT TO CHIP

"**Y**ou forced Daviin from our groundteam." Jer'ait watched the Human closely, wondering if he was a fool or something worse. "It was amusing for a while, but you're actually serious, aren't you?"

"He didn't want to follow orders," their Prime told him dismissively.

Jer'ait gave his target a long look. "Did you make this decision before or after he broke every bone in your body, Commander?"

A glimmer of irritation showed in the Human's face. "The Jreet is out. No discussion."

Jer'ait glanced at the other three members of their team. The Baga sat in a corner, watching the Human with unwavering curiosity. To Jer'ait's surprise, he had not only survived Joe's assault, but he seemed to find their Prime's attack to be nothing out of the ordinary. Further, Jer'ait had heard the Baga actually use the word 'sir' to the Human, earlier that day. Behind him, the Ooreiki was staring at the floor, trying desperately not to be noticed and therefore not to be called on to take sides. The Grekkon seemed oblivious to or unconcerned with the conversation, or both.

"You expect the five of us to kill a Dhasha prince, wading through possibly hundreds of his underlings to get to him, without a Jreet?" Jer'ait finally demanded.

The Human's small brown eyes found him and he gave him a grin. "Think of it as putting your skills to the test, Huouyt."

"I think of it as suicide," Jer'ait retorted. "They will not allow us to use explosives. That leaves hand-to-hand combat. Only a Jreet can kill a Dhasha in hand-to-hand combat."

"Then I suppose we'd all better pack up and go home, because there's only six Jreet on this whole planet."

Jer'ait stared at him. "Only six?"

"That's right," the Human said. "I checked. Six Jreet against a hundred and thirty-four Dhasha princes, plus a carrier-load of followers and young. If we're gonna win this thing, we're gonna have to come up with some brand-new ideas or we're all gonna die."

"You gave up one of the six Jreet on the entire *planet* because he bruised your pride." Jer'ait knew right then that the message was a Trith's cruel joke. As soon as this moron took them down the tunnels, they would all die.

"He wouldn't follow orders," the Human repeated.

"He's Sentinel-trained," Jer'ait snapped. "He *shouldn't* follow the orders of a soft-skulled Takki imbecile. Had Phoenix been in her right mind, *Daviin* would have led this group, not some weak, inebriated clown."

"I'll give you the same choice I gave the Jreet," the Human said, his tone going as cold as a Va'gan's. "Follow orders or I'll transfer you."

Jer'ait laughed. "You would go down the tunnels with four."

"Damn right, I would. In a heartbeat."

From where he sat, Galek looked up nervously, but he said nothing.

Jer'ait wondered if the Human had destroyed brain-cells with his sipping of toxins. "The Jreet and I are your two best chances of killing something down there," he said. "If I leave, you will have nothing."

"If you leave, I'll have more than I started with," Commander Zero said.

Jer'ait examined their leader and saw what the Jreet hadn't—the Human was deadly serious. Jer'ait could almost admire him, the way he could meet the gaze of a Va'ga assassin without flinching.

"Very well," he said softly. "What do you want me to do?"

"Flea, get over here." 'Flea' was an earth name that the Human had attached to the Baga the moment it returned from medical. The Baga had liked the sound of it, especially after Jer'ait had explained that a flea was a nuisance insect from Earth. Jer'ait wondered if the Baga was quite sane.

The Baga dropped onto Joe's shoulder, his entire body about the size of Joe's head. If the Human had any nervousness due to the proximity of the Baga's spitter, he did not show it.

"Flea, you'll be working with Be'shaar. You two are on recon. Be'shaar, go to the morgue and start picking through the bodies. Grab whatever patterns you think you'll need."

Immediately, Jer'ait felt every one of his *breja* stiffen. "Huouyt of my sect do not use patterns off of dead we did not kill ourselves."

The Human grunted. "That's right. Forgot some of you are superstitious about that."

"I will find another source," Jer'ait replied, trying not to sound as irritated as he felt.

"Good. Flea, you're too damn colorful. I want you as black as a Draak turd by the end of the day. You and the Huouyt will need to be in constant contact with each other, so you each get a chip—I'm told you already got yours, so that just leaves Be'shaar."

Jer'ait stiffened. "I told you Va'gans do not undergo operations of any kind."

"You do now," the Human said brusquely. "Galek, you and I will be the middlemen. It'll be our job to protect Scarab from whatever they throw at us. He's our lifeline—the only thing getting us out of there should something go wrong. He won't be doing any fighting."

'Scarab' was another nickname, one the Human had given after trying to pronounce the Grekkon's name three times and failing. Though he usually detested monikers, Jer'ait had to admit that it was easier, and the Grekkon didn't seem to mind.

As a matter of fact, the Grekkon didn't seem to mind anything. Though it was fully equipped with an artificial voicebox and a chip, it hadn't said more than its name since it had been introduced.

Jer'ait's *breja* rippled across his body in waves as he listened to the Human outline their plan. It didn't sound like a bad plan…except for the fact he expected Jer'ait to submit to an Ooreiki's scalpel. Finally, he could stay silent no more.

"Huouyt of my profession do not allow themselves to go under another's knife. Not for any reason. I will do without."

The Human's face darkened. "Flea, Galek, Scarab, go get some dinner."

The Ooreiki and the Grekkon were happy to oblige. The Baga was more reluctant, giving Jer'ait a curious look before the Prime's scowl sent him hurrying out after the other two.

Joe went to the door and shut it. When he turned, he crossed his arms and said, "Why?"

Jer'ait watched the Human a moment, considering whether to reply. "The gasses and medicines they use. In training, Va'gans are overexposed to every substance that could be used against us in the field to give us a greater resistance. Therefore, Va'ga-trained Huouyt do not allow another to introduce foreign chemicals into their bodies."

"So it's a pride thing."

Jer'ait almost left right there, but he forced himself to endure the conversation, if only for the sake of his mission. "No. That same resistance makes it extremely hard to put us into any sort of chemical-induced state without giving us a lethal overdose. It's a very effective safeguard against enemy interrogation. Ooreiki doctors may be able to accurately estimate the capacities of their other victims, but I guarantee you they cannot estimate mine."

"A medical patient is hardly a victim."

"Anyone allowing an intoxicating substance to enter their bodies is a victim."

The Human's face wrinkled. "That's an interesting way to look at it."

"It is the basis of our training," Jer'ait said.

"You're no good to us without a chip, Be'shaar."

Jer'ait felt his irritation rising. "Even in groups, Huouyt work alone. My PlanOps teams would usually go out by ourselves and meet afterwards in a certain place to discuss what we had learned. If it would make you feel better, we could take a look at the maps of the tunnels and choose six meeting times and places. I will be there—you can count on it."

The Human gave him a flat look. "You're not going down there without a way to communicate with us."

"PlanOps signs are universal amongst all its member species," Jer'ait said calmly. "I could leave them behind for you to find."

"When you were with other Huouyt, on your old PlanOps groundteam, what would you do when one of you got injured?"

Jer'ait said nothing. He watched the Human closely, wondering why he continued to push the matter when most would have long since stood down and agreed to his compromise.

"Because I know for a fact you did not allow each other to bleed to death."

"Why do you push it, Human?"

"Why?" The Human snorted. "You just said it yourself. PlanOps uses universal signs. Yesterday I chatted with an Ooreiki Prime who told me those signs haven't changed in six millennia. As soon as I found that out, I almost ashing crapped myself. All we'd need would be one Takki down there who'd been trained to read signs and we'd all be toast."

Jer'ait studied the Human. Sober, he almost seemed intelligent. "There is very little chance anyone has ever trained Takki in PlanOps protocol."

"You want to bet your life on that, Huouyt?" the Human demanded. "They told me this Dhasha Vahlin is over a thousand turns old. That's an awful long time to pick up PlanOps symbols, even if he *wasn't* in the military, which I'm pretty burning sure he was."

"Why's that?"

The Human gave him a long look, then stalked over to the table and switched on the satellite map. "Mark. Neskfaat. Random. Fifteen ground units." The map that appeared showed several areas cleared of vegetation surrounding the black pits of a collapsed den entrance.

"See anything?" the Human asked, watching his face.

Jer'ait didn't. He peered closer, however, not about to allow a Human to best him at something as basic to his trade as observational skills.

His eyes caught on the darkened patch in the forest and he frowned. "Mark. Remove foliage."

The screen shifted, leaving only the black pits on three-dimensional brown terrain.

Every hill, every high point of land, had a pit. *Open* pits. The area around the pits on the hills, however, were not cleared in the typical Dhasha manner. They were completely hidden by trees. Jer'ait could even see the rainbow smudges of several Dhasha sitting in the entrances to the tunnels, waiting. The entrances themselves wove an octagonal pattern across the surface of the planet, the sight of which made Jer'ait's *breja* tremble in waves across his skin.

"That is unnatural," Jer'ait whispered.

"That is *smart*. The whole planet's like that. If the Vahlin isn't intimately aware of battle tactics—*our* battle tactics, I'm a purple-pelted Takki."

"Our grounders are going to get slaughtered." Jer'ait glanced up, studying the Human. "Did you see this or were you briefed?"

The Human gave him a flat look. "It may be hard to imagine, but I do have the mental capacity to notice a pattern. Every visible deep den entrance on Neskfaat is on low ground. Every hidden entrance is on high ground. On every other Dhasha planet I've ever seen, the entrances are wherever the hell the Dhasha happened to sit down."

The Human was telling the truth. That *he* had caught this...Jer'ait began to wonder if indeed the prophecy was true. "Did you tell headquarters of this?"

"Do I look stupid to you? Space Corps is out there now, bombing the hell out of them."

Jer'ait glanced back at the maps. For a long time, he said nothing, merely scanned the honeycomb pattern of Dhasha tunnels industrious

Takki had dug within half a turn. "We would never have these problems if we could simply find a way to destroy the Takki."

"No," the Human said. "They'd find someone else. Ooreiki. Ueshi. Huouyt. Humans. About the only ones who wouldn't bow to them would be the Jreet."

Jer'ait glanced back at the Human, instinctively ready to object, but gave a tired nod instead and recited, "Under a Dhasha's claws, even a boulder crumbles. We can't all be Jreet."

"Thank God." The Human let out his breath slowly.

Reluctantly, Jer'ait said, "We have a companion stand watch."

The Human twitched, frowning.

Softly, Jer'ait continued, "Throughout the procedure, he observes and makes sure the doctors only use the chemicals that we have prescribed for ourselves before we go under. Should the doctor make a mistake, should he use the wrong chemicals or dosage, the companion is sworn to slay all who participated, right down to the lowliest assistant."

"How often does that happen?"

Jer'ait glanced up, scanning his face. "Often. Huouyt have a weakness to chemicals. Our constitutions are never constant, as with other species. One day, a dose might not be enough to achieve the desired effect, whereas on another day, half that dose would kill us. Even our self-prescriptions are mostly guesswork."

The Human grunted. "I always wondered why they never let us drug enemy Huouyt. Thought it was a stupid bureaucratic thing."

"It's so that you don't kill them." Jer'ait left out the fact that, as an Eleventh Hjai with his particular…idiosyncrasy…there were plenty of parties out there who would try to take advantage of his helplessness.

The Human watched him for some time. Finally, he said, "I think I can help you."

Jer'ait snorted. "I did not tell you the story so you could make false offers, Human. I'd expect you to kill everyone involved and I can tell if you're lying to me."

"I'm not offering to kill anyone. To hell with that. I'm offering to set you up so you can drug yourself. Then I'll stay and make sure no one adds to the mix. Hell, I'll order some damned robots, let you program them yourself, if that would make you feel better."

Jer'ait frowned at Joe. "You can do that?"

He tapped the eight-pointed star on his chest. "Sometimes rank's got a few perks. I get the feeling if I took a dump in the middle of the mess-hall, they'd laminate it."

Jer'ait peered at the Human for a moment before saying, "Why have you never moved past Prime?"

"Ask Phoenix." The Human's voice held uncontained bitterness.

I did, Jer'ait thought. *And what she said made no sense.* Curiously, Jer'ait said, "What does she have against you?"

"I don't know."

Jer'ait was taken aback by the sincerity in the Human's voice. "You mean you have no idea?"

The Human gave him a sharp look. "Do you?"

"There are rumors…" Jer'ait said quickly, cursing himself for once again allowing the Human to get the upper hand.

To his relief, Joe didn't follow up on his statement. He sighed, instead.

"Mag never bothered to tell me…just every promotion board I was ever nominated to stand before." Joe shook his head. "She was too young when we lost our groundmates on Kophat. It's the only reason I can come up with that makes any sense."

Jer'ait looked back at the map. "Arrange the operation. I'll get the chip."

The Human actually gave him a surprised look. "I honestly wasn't expecting you to say that." He gave a huge, relieved sigh. The pressure of holding together his groundteam, Jer'ait decided, was beginning to show in the Human's features. *He actually wants us all to live,* Jer'ait thought, more than a little stunned. What kind of alien cared about… aliens? "I'll go get that started now." Commander Zero turned to go.

"But Joe," Jer'ait warned.

"Yeah?"

Jer'ait hesitated, considering again how much trust he was putting in this alien he was tasked to kill. An alien that was, in all ways, weaker than any Huouyt in existence. "Keep them—" he swallowed, his voice cracking with unexpected fear of what he intended to do. Jer'ait looked away and gathered his composure, fighting shame. Once he had collected himself, he tried to appear bored and said, "Just you and me in the room, understand?"

He felt the Human's eyes sharpen in a way Jer'ait did not like. "It's not about the drugs, is it?"

Jer'ait felt his breja ripple once before he reined them in. "Just us," he said again. "Or your team will be down to four." Let him take that however he would. Then, before the Human could ask anything else—or deduce any more about his state of struggle with the rest of Huouyt society, he left to gather the proper drugs.

• • •

Joe was watching the robotic arm inject the Huouyt with a third small dose of the chemical of his choice when a Ueshi in gray doctor's garb overrode Joe's lock and entered the room. Instantly, every tiny hair on Joe's neck and arms stood on end.

"We're almost finished," Joe said, deliberately putting space between him and the Ueshi. "Shouldn't be more than another ten tics, doc."

"You shouldn't be in here," the Ueshi snapped. "I don't know who you think you are. This is *not* accepted procedure. This operation is not registered. The medicines were not approved. You *stole* that chip, Commander. I tried to stall them, but you need to go down to security right now and explain what's going on."

Joe eyes only briefly passed over the Overseer circles before settling on the envelope he carried with him. "What's that?"

"Medical records," the Ueshi said, tightening his arm over the envelope ever-so-slightly. "Be'shaar is highly sensitive to several different drugs. Fatally so."

"We know," Joe said. "That's why he's dosing himself."

The Ueshi seemed to relax a bit. "Go deal with the administrators. I knew Be'shaar from Eeloir. I'll watch over him. He'd feel better to have me here when he wakes up than some alien he barely knows." The Ueshi reached for Joe's arm, gesturing towards the door, but Joe quickly pulled it out of reach and stepped back.

His eyes fell back to the envelope under the Ueshi's arm. "Seems a little lumpy for a medical record. What else is in there?"

The Ueshi turned to Joe, for the first time taking his eyes off of where Jer'ait lay helpless on the table behind him. "You will leave now, Human. This matter does not concern you." The anxiety was gone, replaced with cold threat.

Joe took another step backwards, towards where Jer'ait lay helpless, and braced himself. "Yeah, it does."

The Ueshi's blue eyes were startlingly empty as they fixed on Joe. "Be'shaar was my patient on Eeloir. I know his metabolism best. I'm here to watch over him."

"Go ahead and watch," Joe said. "I'm not moving from this table."

A flash of amusement crossed the Ueshi's blue face and it stepped toward Joe.

Joe brought his plasma pistol up and held it between them. "Get out. And quit the act. We both know you're not Ueshi."

Amusement vanished, replaced once more with an unreadable mask. "You would raise a gun to a superior officer?"

"I didn't know Va'gans joined the army. Aside from Be'shaar, of course. But he's a Peacemaker, so he doesn't count."

"You think I'm an *assassin*?" The Ueshi's little blue-green face showed perfect surprise.

"Show me what's in the envelope. Then we'll decide."

The Ueshi's head-crest fluttered in annoyance. "I can have you thrown in the brig for impudence."

"Then do it."

The Ueshi and Joe locked gazes for several tics, watching each other in silence.

"Jer'ait's almost awake," Joe said. "I'm sure he'll just *love* to see his old buddy from Eeloir."

The Ueshi cast one more look at Jer'ait, then leveled his dead gaze back on Joe. "You've been marked."

"Funny, I never felt a thing."

"You will," the Va'gan promised.

Then, in silence, the Huouyt turned and exited the room. Joe holstered his weapon reluctantly. He knew deep in his heart he should have shot the bastard.

"Joe?" Behind him, Jer'ait's voice was groggy and disoriented.

Joe turned to him, catching him when the Huouyt tumbled off the bed. "How do you feel?"

"Fine." Jer'ait tried to stand, obviously not wanting Joe to see his weakness. He toppled forward again and Joe threw his arm over his shoulder to hold him up. "Need a few more tics?"

The Huouyt glanced at the door, then glanced at Joe, then nodded miserably. He almost seemed like a small child that had badly cut himself. He acted scared.

"You want me to wait outside, I can," Joe said. "If you need some time alone."

Jer'ait nodded silently, unable to meet Joe's eyes.

Joe almost turned to go. Almost. Instead, he dropped into a squat, so that he and the Huouyt were eye-to-eye. "There's no shame in it."

The Huouyt's head came up, his violet eye full of electricity. "There *is*." Jer'ait's speech was slurred and he turned away in humiliation.

"No," Joe said. He reached out and touched Jer'ait's arm. "You're my groundmate. You can trust me."

Jer'ait's gaze fell to where Joe touched his downy, cilia-covered skin. Then he looked up at Joe. "Human, I could kill you in an instant, just as you are now. You'd be dead before you felt the prick. Knowing this, knowing the power I have over you, I cannot trust you. Simply because you cannot trust me."

Joe did not remove his hand. "Listen to me. We're gonna see each other in a lot of awkward situations. We're gonna see each other battered and bloody, naked and crying. It's what we do. I don't like it, since I always thought Huouyt were evil bastards, but I've got to trust you. You're gonna have my back in the tunnels." He laughed. "Besides, Jer'ait. If you'd wanted to kill me, you'd have done it already."

"Perhaps," Jer'ait said softly. Then he stiffened, cocking his head at Joe.

"Yeah," Joe said. "I know who you are."

"The Jreet told you."

"Who else?" Joe demanded. "He was trying to bribe me into taking him back on the team."

"I suppose it was too much to expect for his Sentinel skills not to—" Jer'ait cocked his head at Joe's shirt. "What happened to your chest, Commander?"

Joe glanced down, then cursed inwardly. He'd left the collar open to cope with the heat inside the hospital room. "A few scratches from Daviin."

The openness the Huouyt had showed him quickly slammed shut behind a look of steel. Joe knew in that moment that Jer'ait had pieced together what Daviin had done.

Sighing, he opened his shirt, displaying the scabby symbol Daviin had carved into his flesh. "The furg wanted to play with my blood."

"He bound to you." Jer'ait's steely gaze melted again, replaced with simple shock. "As your Sentinel."

"I didn't know what he was doing until it was too late," Joe offered.

"Is he here now?" Jer'ait gave the room a wary look.

"No, he's outside in the hall somewhere, pacing like a nervous hen," Joe replied. "He doesn't like me being in here with you alone."

Jer'ait's look hardened again. "As well he shouldn't." The Huouyt began to stand.

Joe held him in place. "Is there something you want to tell me about mysterious Huouyt doctors visiting you while you're out, Jer'ait?"

The Huouyt jerked around to stare at him, horror oozing from its defective eye. "You let him attend me?"

"Hell, no," Joe said. "I convinced him to leave. Nicely. With a gun."

"How?" Jer'ait snapped. "Did he touch you?"

"No. I'm not stupid."

Jer'ait's gaze sharpened. "Did he carry anything with him?"

"Yup. An envelope."

Jer'ait's breja rippled. "And you're *sure* he never touched me?"

"There was a pissed off Congie with a plasma pistol standing between you and your enemies the whole time." Joe squeezed his groundmate's shoulder. "Don't worry. I've got your back."

The Huouyt lowered his head, saying nothing.

"So who was he?" Joe demanded. "Something going on I need to know about?"

"No," Jer'ait said abruptly. He stood.

Joe tried to help, but Jer'ait shook him off. The openness was gone, replaced with the same cold, hard indifference Joe had always seen. "Thanks for your assistance, Commander. I will see you at the next briefing."

"You jackass," Joe snapped. "I just saved your life, you know that?"

"No you didn't," Jer'ait said. Then, seeing Joe's face, he amended, "He wouldn't have killed me."

"Well, he wasn't there to chat war stories," Joe snapped.

"Goodbye, Commander." Jer'ait turned to leave.

"How about dinner?" Joe called after him. "You've missed every single team chow. The others would like to get to know you."

"No they wouldn't." Jer'ait walked to the door and left.

Daviin stuck his head in immediately. Locating Joe, he immediately seemed to calm. "The Huouyt did not look happy. The surgery failed?"

"No," Joe said. "I asked him to join us at chow. Anyway, you might as well show up for dinner tonight. No more point in pretending you won't be going down the tunnels with us. He knows what you did."

"You told him?!" Daviin roared.

"He saw the mark you carved into my chest, thank you very much."

"You mean you didn't cover it up? Vara's tek, Human, I *lied* for you. That's at least four levels of hell for every syllable."

"Good," Joe said. "So you won't have any problems doing it again."

Daviin stiffened. "No, that's not what that means."

"We had a visitor," Joe said. "I think it was a Huouyt. The nasty kind."

"Damn you, Joe!" Daviin roared. "I *knew* I shouldn't have allowed you to ban me to the outer hall."

"The Huouyt was here for Jer'ait, not for me."

"But you stood in his way," Daviin growled. "He would've killed you, too."

"Probably." Joe puzzled over Jer'ait a moment more, then sighed. "Be at dinner tonight. I want you to regale them with the tale of how you finally made me crack like a *piji* shell."

Daviin wrinkled his scaly snout in distaste. "A lie."

Joe winked. "How'd you guess?"

13

SYURI

Syuri stormed onto the ship, all six legs working in barely contained fury. His internal pressure had been at critical levels for the last two weeks, ever since the Jreet had tortured him until he gave up his real name and identification numbers. Even now, the authorities could be looking for him. The knowledge had left him unable to sleep, a constant, nervous wreck all the way to his employer's ship. The constant strain was going to give him a rupture.

As soon as he stepped into the dank room, the Geuji said, "You look unhealthy, Syuri."

"That was stupid, Forgotten. That Jreet almost killed me. He thought *I* had delivered that bomb."

"You did."

Syuri's internal pressure skyrocketed. He felt a slickening of his skin as his chambers voided themselves, then a sharp, blinding pain in his lower back.

"Careful," Forgotten said. "You're going to rupture your liquids exchange."

"You had me..." Syuri was so stunned he could not think. "That was *not* a part of our bargain." He had destroyed a *planet*?!

"If I had told you about it, you wouldn't have been able to sound so convincing when the Jreet interrogated you."

"He took my *identification.* He knows who I am!"

"He'll do nothing with it. You assured him of your innocence."

Remembering the horrible hours wrapped in the Jreet's muscular body, the poisoned appendage almost touching him as the Jreet asked his questions, constricted within the Jreet's coils until Syuri's internal chambers threatened to burst…Syuri shuddered and fought down nausea. "I've never felt so helpless in my life."

"Stands to reason. You've never *been* so helpless in your life."

"Getting squeezed until I voided myself was not part of the bargain!"

"I told you it was dangerous," Forgotten retorted. "You told me, and I quote, 'Danger?! Gimme your worst, corpse-rot. I *live* for danger.' You are, after all, a mercenary."

"I'm a pirate," Syuri muttered.

"Technically, you aren't. You don't ambush and murder innocent caravans for their goods. You steal, smuggle, and rent your services out to the highest bidder."

"Last time I make *that* mistake," Syuri snapped. "You're going to get me killed."

"You will not die in my service, Syuri," Forgotten replied solemnly. "A loyal agent is worth more to me than a dead one."

"Nice try," Syuri snapped. "I'm done doing business with you, Geuji."

"Then why are you here?"

Syuri opened his mouth, then closed it again. It was true. Forgotten had transferred the money into his account the moment Aez had exploded. He had no reason to be here, other than to vent, and both of them knew Syuri wouldn't waste valuable ship fuel to vent. Muttering, he said, "Last time I was here, you mentioned another job. Eight mil if I succeed."

"Yes," the fungus replied. "I want you to visit the Space Academy."

Syuri's jaw fell open.

"No, Syuri," Forgotten said, sounding amused, "I don't want you to blow up Levren. This is a personal matter."

Syuri's attention sharpened. He was good at reading people—it was the talent that had kept him out of Peacemaker hands for over twenty turns of high-profile thievery. He never worked for someone unless he felt sure he could read them like an open book. Forgotten was the only exception, Syuri only gaining brief glimpses of the Geuji's intentions before they were shut off again, but Forgotten's money had been generous enough that Syuri had been able to overlook that inconvenience.

"How personal?" he asked carefully.

Syuri's sivvet were hit with a startling rush of something that felt like...unhappiness...before it was shut away again. "I am currently involved in a scheme with creatures of very dubious integrity," Forgotten replied. "I want you to ensure their side of the bargain is still intact."

"What do they have in the Space Academy?" Syuri demanded. "That place is a fortress."

"What interests me is kept in climate-controlled vaults in the basement," Forgotten replied. "I want you to get in and verify they are what they are purported to be. I can give you the access codes to all the security points along the way, then the bypass codes to the vaults themselves. It will be a simple operation."

It didn't go unnoticed to Syuri that the Geuji hadn't answered his question. "What's in the vaults?"

Another startling wash of misery. And...loneliness? "Something very important to me." The rush of truth was overwhelming, like cool water upon his sivvet. Syuri liked that in Forgotten—he was always truthful. In that sense, he even reminded him of the infernal, self-righteous bastard that had spent three hours threatening to turn him into a pincushion—and meaning every word of it.

This made Syuri hesitate. Forgotten had only paid Syuri two mil for Aez. If a *planet* was worth two mil to Forgotten, Syuri could not help but wonder what was worth eight.

Tentatively, he said, "So you want me to steal what's in the vaults?"

"You can't." More misery hit his sivvet in a tide before the Geuji locked it away.

Feeling the sheer strength behind that raw emotion, Syuri actually found himself feeling a little bad for the fungus. Whatever it was, it hurt him. A lot. "There's nothing I can't steal," Syuri offered gently. "Whatever they took from you, I can get it back."

"You can't steal them," Forgotten repeated.

Syuri considered this. If he could put it in a ship, he could steal it. He supposed it was possible Forgotten was trying to convince him it was impossible so Syuri wouldn't take them for himself.

"I do not lie, Jahul."

"But you omit facts when it suits you," Syuri retorted. Then, at Forgotten's lack of an answer, he added, "Like, oh, say, exploding the planet of a clan of invisible, poisonous, strangulation-prone super-warriors that are irrationally blood-thirsty even for Jreet?" That *still* rankled him. Good thing there were no survivors, or he would be *dead*. Simply dead.

Forgotten said nothing.

Syuri knew he should leave right there, let the fool blow up his own planets, but something about the job fascinated him. It was Forgotten's reaction more than anything else. What could be more important than a planet? It...tantalized him.

"So you're telling me all I have to do is get into the Space Academy and check out the vaults in the basement and then come back? Do you want documentation? Photographs?"

"Visual confirmation is all I need." Forgotten almost felt...tired. Old.

"And nothing will explode," Syuri said pointedly. "No one will *die*. I don't like it when things die, Geuji."

"Nothing will die." When Syuri's gaze sharpened, the Geuji added, "Or explode."

"I don't get it. Why is it worth eight mil for me just to look? They find the Stone of Youth or something? There's some sort of plans you want me to read? You might find this surprising, but a Jahul's brain isn't as sharp as yours. I can't just look and take a picture in my head."

"Just make the visual confirmation and you will have your money." Again, Syuri's sivvet caught the briefest glimpse of...sadness.

Syuri hesitated, frowning up at the black mass hung across the walls around him. "What the hell is wrong with you, Forgotten?"

Syuri got blasted with a brief flash of shock. The Geuji hesitated. Then, "You can feel my emotions? Even when I try to hide them from you?"

"You know of some *other* way I became the greatest pirate in this sector?" Syuri demanded.

"You're a mercenary," Forgotten replied. "Pirates kill people." Then, belatedly, "*Knowingly* kill people."

Syuri waved a hand dismissively. "Technicalities. Besides. Everyone knows the Aezi are self-righteous zealots. Now answer my question."

"I have...a problem...that has bothered me for a while," Forgotten admitted.

"And?" Syuri insisted.

"...and I'm working to rectify it," Forgotten replied. "But I need your help."

Syuri tapped his hard, callused fingers against his chin. "Is this some way to get rid of me, now I've suited your purposes?"

"If I'd wanted to get rid of you," Forgotten said softly, "I'd have killed you as soon as you stepped aboard my ship, ejected your corpse into an uncharted area of space, and abandoned your ship in an area frequented by pirates."

Syuri felt his internal chambers tighten and a new slick spread over his skin. "Is that what you're going to do if I refuse?"

"No." Around the room, Forgotten's body seemed to ripple with a glossy black wave and Syuri felt another tang of misery before it went still.

"No, what?" Syuri prodded. "You're gonna kill me somewhere else?"

"No, I'll leave you free to live your life however you choose," the great mold replied. "I do not kill my agents."

Even though the Geuji emanated truth, Syuri snorted. "You won't let me go my own way, not after telling me about the bomb. I could tell the authorities."

"They'll have worse things to accuse me of before I'm through."

Syuri peered at the Geuji, realizing with a cold prickle that he was serious. "Worse than blowing up a *planet*?"

"Yes." The Geuji sounded tired. That scared Syuri more than anything. What could exhaust a *Geuji?*

"Why are you doing it?" Syuri asked softly. "You don't need the money—you bought me a new ship to take to Aez like it was nothing to you."

"You'll see soon enough." Again, that wash of...exhaustion. Strong enough to make Syuri himself want to take a nap.

Syuri debated it. He knew that a normal employer would kill him as soon as he declined, regardless of what he said. Forgotten, however, was different. It seemed as if he truly did not care what the authorities knew about his activities.

Maybe he didn't. Maybe he was too smart for them to catch him.

"Where are the rest of your kind?" Syuri finally asked. "You'd think with a brain like yours, I'd hear about you ruling planets and managing companies. You'd be better at regulating the economy than the Bajna, if you wanted to waste your time at it. Your arts would humble the Ooreiki. Your sciences would shame the Ueshi. I mean, if you weren't focused on avoiding the Space Corps, you could bring our civilization into the next golden age all by yourself. You said you're only three hundred and eleven turns old. So where're the rest of you?"

Syuri could feel a sadness emanate from the Geuji, though Forgotten said nothing.

"They're dead, aren't they?" Syuri said softly. He felt genuine sympathy for the great creature.

Instead of answering, Forgotten said, "Syuri, answer me something truthfully."

"I'll try."

"Does everyone think like you?"

Syuri laughed. "I break the law for a living, Geuji."

"I'm serious."

Syuri sobered.

"Would anyone else, stepping onto my ship and seeing me for what I am, see anything other than a way of getting what they want? Would they see anything other than something to fear? Something that would try to control them? Take over?"

Now Syuri understood. Tentatively, he said, "If you're thinking about straightening out, I don't think Congress'll ever forgive you. I mean, you've been a major pain in Congressional ass for like, what, two hundred fifty turns?"

"Three hundred and four, if you believe their propaganda," Forgotten said. "They didn't know I existed until then."

Syuri grimaced. "My point is Congress doesn't screw around. They'd execute me if they found me, but you...I think they'd keep you alive."

"I know."

Syuri cocked his head at Forgotten's answer. "Then I've got a question for you, Geuji."

"What?"

"Would you go straight if you could?"

It took Forgotten several moments to respond.

Finally, he said, "Yes."

14

NESKFAAT

"We're uncoordinated, just as likely to blow holes in each other as in the enemy." Joe took a deep breath and kept pacing, his father's knife a smooth comfort as he rubbed it in his hand. His gut was not liking the situation at all. Something was wrong...*very* wrong, yet he couldn't put his finger on it. "Unfortunately, I guess something about having a top-classed Va'gan and a Jreet the size of a Congressional tank—and no team casualties so far—gave them the idea we had our shit together." He made a disgusted snort. "They're treating us the same as a groundteam that's been working together for six turns. Our first assignment is a prince's den."

Daviin broke into an immediate, fearsome Jreet grin, but Jer'ait simply waited, silently holding Joe's gaze. He had still not bothered to hide his defective eye, which, Joe knew, meant something important. He was still trying to figure out what it was.

"Once we get down there, we're gonna be doubly blind," Joe continued, setting the mystery of the Huouyt's eye aside for more consideration later. "The rock surrounding us on Neskfaat has just the right striations of minerals in it to make imaging difficult. They can only see down the first twenty, thirty rods. From there, we'll have to rely on our PPU's to get us around." He glanced at the Ooreiki. "That, and Galek."

Though the Ooreiki outweighed Joe by about a hundred and twenty lobes, the youngster glanced at his feet in embarrassment, his dark skin sticky and splotched with orange.

Jer'ait, however, was watching the knife. Damn. Joe hated Huouyt.

As casually as he could, Joe stuffed the worn-smooth knife back into his pocket. Then he sighed. "It's hard to believe, but I think Maggie actually wanted me to survive this."

"Of course she did," Jer'ait said, his creepy gaze lifting back to Joe's face. There was no mistake—his Second had seen his weakness. And the knowledge had left him smug. *Damn.*

"Then you don't know Maggie," Joe said, willing the Huouyt a thousand deaths by a thousand Jreet. "She's hated me since basic."

"Whether she hates you or not is not the issue," Jer'ait replied. "Whichever PlanOps Overseer puts together the team to take out the Vahlin will be rewarded with a multi-species Corps Directorship. Of course she wants you to survive."

Joe's jaw went slack. "No."

"Why else would she put a Jreet royal, a Va'ga assassin, a Grekkon, and an Ooreiki with tunnel instinct on your team?"

"Don't forget me," Flea said, from Joe's shoulder.

Looking directly at the Baga, the Huouyt said, "A Jreet royal, a Va'gan assassin, a Grekkon, and an Ooreiki with tunnel instinct."

On his shoulder, the Baga bristled, but Joe quieted him by touching his carapace, its once-iridescent beetle-green shine now painted pitch black. To the Huouyt, he said, "You have a very poor sense of humor, Huouyt."

"I'm not laughing," Jer'ait said. "In fact, I find it slightly irritating that while Phoenix gets a Corps Directorship, we will only get *kasjas*, maybe a pat on the back and a few rotations' leave. Doesn't seem fair, does it?"

"Daviin, is he telling the truth?" Joe whispered.

The Jreet shrugged. "I thought you knew."

Joe hurled the info-unit against the wall. "Son of a *bitch!*"

"I don't understand..." the Ooreiki said, blinking at the equipment that had clattered to the floor. Like all Congressional gear, it was sturdy enough to take whatever beatings all three thousand, two hundred and forty-four species of heavy-handed Congie grounders could dish out.

Joe broke into a string of invectives and shoved the Baga off of his shoulder. He began pacing the room, throwing and kicking anything he could reach. Maps, equipment, supplies…he was so enraged he saw only Maggie's face. Once again, she was going to get the last laugh. No matter how well he did, she would always outrank him. Always.

Joe didn't realize the Huouyt had come up behind him until he felt the sharp prick and the Huouyt's firm grasp on his neck. His body stiffened.

Jer'ait twisted Joe around to face him. The room was empty except for the two of them, the door locked. The Huouyt looked him up and down with a flat look, and Joe couldn't tell if he were amused or bored. "If your goal was to show your groundmates you have the temper and mental capacities of a Dhasha turnling, Commander, I think you succeeded."

Joe closed his eyes, ignoring the Huouyt's multi-colored stare. "There's something you should know, Huouyt."

Jer'ait cocked his head. "What?"

"It was a pain in the ass, but I immunized myself to *jasanbic-4*."

As Jer'ait's odd violet eye flashed with surprise, Joe slammed his fist into the sensitive slit in the Huouyt's face. As Jer'ait made a startled cry and crumpled, Joe pressed his boot over the sheath that housed the Huouyt's *zora* and gave it a few warning lobes of pressure.

The Huouyt reached toward his leg. "Put your arms down," Joe said, leaning on his leg a bit more. "I'm feeling a little off-balance."

The Huouyt dropped his arms and stared up at him, malice burning in his violet eye.

"That's twice you've poisoned me since we met," Joe replied. "I might be an uneducated grounder, but I know Huouyt like to poison creatures they don't respect." Joe leaned down so he could peer into Jer'ait's eyes. "Are you saying you don't respect me, Jer'ait?"

"It was to calm you down," Jer'ait muttered. "You were throwing a tantrum like a Dhasha turnling."

"I'm Prime," Joe replied. "I'm allowed to do that. But, since you're a low-life assassin and you've never had to be a boot who's had to work up through the ranks, you wouldn't know that. Therefore, this time I'll only give you a warning. Next time it happens, I'll educate you on what a Human does to reciprocate disrespect."

The Huouyt's face twisted. "Very well."

Joe lifted his boot from the Huouyt's face and stood back while he sat up. "Further, I think we have a problem."

Jer'ait gave him a dark look as he got back to his feet. "You realized you just threatened a Va'gan assassin with your heel?"

Joe grinned and ignored the statement. "You haven't told the rest of the team your real name."

Jer'ait paused in brushing himself off. "That's a problem?"

"I'm not calling you Be'shaar in the tunnels, and I'm sure as hell not explaining who 'Jer'ait' is. You're lucky I've played along this long. Go fix it."

With a malevolent glare, the Va'gan started toward the door.

"Daviin," Joe said once the Huouyt had left, "You can come out now."

• • •

Daviin waited through the meeting in the corner, listening to every word. He had moved to step in the moment the Huouyt paralyzed his ward, but had been pleasantly surprised when Joe had socked the conniving bastard in the face.

I like him, Daviin thought, proud of his ward. *He's stupid as a* melaa, *but he's got a tek.*

"Daviin, you can come out now."

Daviin lowered his energy level.

"And what did you think about the way I handled the Huouyt?" Joe asked, clearly proud of himself.

Daviin hesitated.

"Tell me."

An order. Damn the Human! "I thought it was wise of you to immunize yourself, and impossibly stupid for you to tell him about it. You could've used it later."

Joe's face clouded. "So I should've just let him keep poisoning me whenever he felt like it? No, I needed to make my point."

"But you gave up the advantage you earned by immunizing yourself."

Joe snorted. "He's not going to try to kill me, Daviin."

"I think he is."

"Well, he's not," Joe retorted. "Besides, I can take care of myself. You saw how he couldn't move after I pinned him."

Daviin winced, wondering how much to tell the Human. "The only reason he didn't move was because he knew I was hovering over him ready to shove my tek through his face if he didn't obey you."

The Human deflated. He opened his mouth, then closed it again. Frowning, he said, "Were you?"

"You can count on it."

"Damn it, Jreet! That was *my* fight!"

"Don't be ridiculous, Human," Daviin laughed. "You're not a match for him."

"We're never gonna know unless you keep your pointy snout out of it!"

"Oh, I know," Daviin said, sobering. "He could have slapped a needle through the leg of your pants and you would've been down for the count."

"Not before I creamed his brain."

Daviin blinked at Joe. "His brain is located in his chest. You were simply straddling his *zora*. An inconvenience, if that."

His commander's mood had become increasingly foul. "I'm not gonna get his respect if you keep babysitting me, Jreet."

"You're not gonna get his respect anyway. He's a Huouyt. Let me kill him, Human."

Joe frowned. "No."

"Please. He's obviously—"

"*No.*"

Daviin wanted to argue, but the wall com unit began to beep.

"No," the Human repeated as he went to the intercom. Then, once he read the inscription across the bottom of the call, he sighed and said, "Yeah?"

"Is that how you address a superior?" a Human voice demanded.

"Must have slipped my mind, Mag. What do you want?"

"I heard you kicked the Jreet off your team."

Joe sighed and dropped back onto the bed. "What about it?"

"The Jreet goes down the tunnels with you, Zero," the Human—female, if Daviin wasn't mistaken—on the other end stated. "That's an order."

"Sorry," Joe replied, shrugging his bony shoulders, "Seems he took off. Wish I knew where he was. You know how I'd *love* to see you get that Corps Directorship you've always wanted. You've definitely earned it."

"Cut the crap, Joe. Scanner says he's in your chamber right now."

"Really? Funny, I don't see him."

"His energy level isn't elevated."

Joe glanced at Daviin. "Oh yeah. There he is." He shook his head. "Man. How could I miss that?"

"You'll let him back on the team or I'll have your ass on a plate," the female bit out.

"Well, since you've tried to have my ass on a plate for the last fifty turns, Mag, this must be very exciting for you." Joe cut the feed. "That's just what I need. Maggie to get a Corps Directorship."

"The gods are not always just," Daviin agreed.

Joe glanced up at him. "No shit." He sighed and went to his pile of gear and began to strip. "So. Your chip is working?"

Daviin flinched at the question, but managed to avoid lying. "I hadn't tested it."

"Well do so." The Human took off his shirt and threw it aside, revealing a criss-crossed array of raised white lines. Daviin forgot himself and stared.

The Human continued, oblivious. "We've got three hours 'till takeoff and I want everyone synched up so tight their balls—" Joe paused at the look Daviin was giving him. "What?"

"Those scars," Daviin said when he found his breath. "Only a Takki—"

Joe sat down on the lower half of his biosuit and activated it. Immediately, the two halves of the suit slid into place, hiding his butchered skin from sight with a smooth wave of glossy, rock-hard black that swallowed him from toe to head before sliding apart at the mouth and eyes to allow him to breathe.

When Joe did not respond, merely continued preparing, Daviin could not help himself. "You didn't get those in battle, did you?"

"No," Joe said.

"An interrogation?"

Joe laughed. "You think I'd be here, were that the case?"

"Dhasha, then?"

"No," Joe said. He eyed Daviin for a long moment. "It doesn't matter."

But it did, to Daviin. His innards were screaming at him that no warrior could endure those kinds of scars. They were too perfect. Too…calculated. "What was it?"

The Human sighed and threw his pack over a suit-encased shoulder. "Takki."

Daviin hesitated, his mind in turmoil. "You were captured by a Dhasha's Takki?"

"I *became* a Takki," Joe muttered. "For a while, anyway."

Daviin reeled away from his ward, horrified. "You allowed yourself to be *enslaved?*"

"I wasn't really given a choice," Joe growled, bristling.

"There's *always* a choice! There's—" Daviin checked himself, though he couldn't stop staring at his ward. He felt unclean, like he'd suddenly been doused in sewage. "You *served* a Dhasha?" He found it hard to think. The act was so completely dishonorable it left him struggling with disgust.

Joe's flat stare told Daviin he was on dangerous ground. "I did."

"You should have killed yourself," Daviin roared, appalled. "Any true warrior wouldn't—"

"We can't all be Jreet," the Human snapped at him, looking irritated.

"But no warrior would allow—"

"That's right," Joe retorted, "I stopped being a warrior the moment they stripped off my biosuit and left me naked and bleeding amidst creatures that would happily eat me alive. My choice was to serve or die."

The stark horror of the Human's statement made Daviin's coils twist in shock. Softly, a horrified whisper, he said, "And you chose to serve."

The Human looked him directly in the eyes, utterly cold. "Are you regretting your oath already, Daviin?"

My ward was a slave. The cold reality of that hit like a spear through Daviin's chest. He had bound himself to a slave. There was no greater disgrace. The humiliation was enough to drag the beginnings of a war-cry from his chest.

Hearing the rumbling, the Human softly said, "What is it, Jreet? Your Voran pride can't stand the fact that you, pride and glory of the Voran princes, just bound yourself to someone who used to pick a Dhasha's scales to survive?"

Daviin looked away, ashamed that the Human saw his thoughts so clearly. "I…" His pride was screaming at him to kill himself, to kill Joe, to end the dishonor before Vora discovered his shame. Even a whisper of it would ruin his family name. The Welus would lunge at the chance to disgrace the Voran line by spreading the tale of his shame. What had he *done?*

Daviin forced himself to unclench his fists and return his tek to its sheath. "I'm sure you had no alternative."

Joe gave a bitter laugh. "Sure I did. But I wanted to live." Then, after giving him a long look, the Human made for the door. Though it was his duty to follow him, Daviin let him go, horror and self-loathing closing on his soul.

His ward—his Commander—had been a *slave.*

• • •

Daviin was the first to the shuttle. Instead of following Joe to make last-tic arrangements with Supply, Daviin had gone directly to the transport. Daviin knew he should have stayed with him. His duty as his Sentinel required it.

But he was unwilling to look at the Human, as half of him was still screaming for Joe to dance on his tek for misleading him. He had made his oath to a *slave*. That made him a slave's *servant*. Most Jreet would have killed themselves as soon as they had found out. That Daviin hadn't, yet, was an act of cowardice in the highest degree.

An uncomfortable sticky feeling traveled down Daviin's flesh as he considered that. He was a coward as well as Sentinel to a slave. The Welus would thrive upon it, using it as a war-cry in every battle for the next thousand turns.

A Voran prince. Sentinel to a slave.

Daviin fisted his hands and tried to put it out of his mind. No one knew, yet. The Human had told no one. Perhaps he could still get the Human to transfer his loyalties to some Representative in Koliinaat. Even the most honorless politician would be better than a slave.

…Wouldn't it?

His mind reeling, Daviin raised his scales' energy level and wove his way through the maze of the shuttle staging area. He found the one his team was to take and slipped inside. Daviin slid into an inconspicuous corner and coiled himself as tightly as he could go. He felt his internal organs grind against each other, but endured the discomfort. All he could think about was the Human's scars.

Sentinel to a slave.

He'd been brooding for over an hour before the door opened again. The Ooreiki stepped inside first, oblivious to Daviin's presence. He could tell it was the Ooreiki just by the plodding sounds it made as it moved, but it was to Daviin's benefit that none of the creatures on his groundteam could hear his echolocating pings.

Galek sat down and began making last-tic adjustments to his equipment.

The Baga came next, alighting on the seat across from the Ooreiki. The Grekkon followed, settling in a corner across from Daviin, facing him directly. Daviin had a brief fear that the Grekkon could smell him, but the creature's blank stare never shifted. In time, Daviin relaxed.

The Huouyt and the Human did not follow them.

"Anyone care for dice?" the Baga asked. "Brought a set with me." He shook the miniature dicing cup, rattling the ten-sided pieces inside. Daviin's interest piqued and his heart rate increased despite himself—he loved a good game of dice. Then he remembered his predicament and his mood deteriorated again. He needed to kill something.

The Ooreiki lifted his head. Tentatively, he said, "I'll play."

"Good," the Baga said. "What do you want to bet?"

"I don't want to bet anything," Galek said.

"You have to bet something, Ooreiki," the Baga snapped. "That's the fun of it."

"Let's just do a practice-run first," Galek said, sounding cowed. "I'm kind of rusty."

The Baga gave a huge, condescending sigh, and they began their contest, the sounds of their game growing more intense with each rattle of the dice. The Ooreiki was lucky. He won much more often than not. Still, Daviin only half-listened to their game. He grew more and more agitated as the Huouyt and the Human failed to appear.

"You're good at this," the Baga finally said. "I thought I was good, but you're whipping me like a lazy Takki."

A lazy Takki. Daviin coiled tighter, humiliation grinding at his soul. *Sentinel to a slave. How could I do this?*

"I'm cheating," the Ooreiki admitted.

"Cheating?" There was a curious note to the Baga's voice. "How? I had these dice rigged myself. I'm the only one who knows the probabilities at which they should fall."

"I can tell what fell in your cup before you see it." If the Ooreiki was irritated with the Baga for trying to cheat him, his voice didn't show it.

"Oh?" The Baga sounded interested.

"Spatial awareness," Galek said. Daviin heard him pick up the cup. "Each side of the dice has a different feel when it's in your cup because of the amount of the surface has been carved out with a symbol. I'm just reading it like I'd read a Dhasha's den."

For a long moment, the Baga said nothing. Then, finally, "I'll have to find some painted dice. Could you read those?"

"No," the Ooreiki said.

"Good." Then, after another moment of silence, the Baga said in sudden excitement, "You think you could do this in a professional setting? Say, a Jahul gambling den?"

"I was blacklisted from all professional casinos as soon as Congress diagnosed me," Galek said woefully. "They won't even let me step inside the door."

"Damn," Flea said. "You could've made a lot of money at that."

"Still could. Soldier's halls can't ban me. Wouldn't feel right about it, though. I always pick cards so I have a fair chance of losing."

"Cards, huh? Only guys I know who like cards are Jreet. Now *there's* somebody I'm looking forward to relieving his accounts of a few credits. I heard Jreet royals got more cash than Aliphei himself, and are dumber than dirt to boot."

"I don't know," Galek said, sounding nervous. Daviin pinged, and frowned when he realized the Ooreiki was turned in his direction. "There's a reason they're rich."

"Sure there is," Flea went on. "They kill off all their brothers and sisters so they only get one inheritance. Jreet are built for strangling and stabbing things, not for using their heads. I could take twenty thousand credits from him in less than a night, easy."

"I heard they kill cheaters on Vora." Galek definitely sounded nervous. Daviin heard him begin twisting his wriggling brown fingers together again.

"Who said anything about cheating?" the Baga said, his tone growing dangerous. "I'm not stupid. Do you think I'm stupid, Ooreiki?"

"No," Galek said quickly. "I'm just saying maybe it'd be dangerous to play with a Jreet."

Flea scoffed. "He'd just hand over the money and never say a word to anybody. As long as you beat them fairly, you can take the scales right off their back and they'll play you again next time you ask. Their honor won't let them turn down a game. Makes for some pretty easy marks. I love playing with Jreet. Stupid oafs."

Daviin tightened his hands into fists and considered following the Human's example. The Baga could use another attitude adjustment.

The Ooreiki continued fidgeting nervously with his tentacles, the sound registering in Daviin's mind like leather ropes twisting together. After a moment, the Ooreiki said, "Think we should go see what's keeping them?"

It took Daviin a moment to realize the Ooreiki was talking to him.

Galek gently tried again. "What do you think? They're gonna miss the shuttle."

"Who are you talking to?" the Baga asked.

Daviin lowered his energy level, allowing the world of light and color to once more flood into being around him. The Ooreiki was looking right at him, and as soon as their eyes met, the Ooreiki lowered his gaze. "You're in charge, after Joe and Jer'ait."

"How the hell did you...?" the Baga said. Then he hesitated, focusing his faceted, gemlike eyes on Daviin. "How long's he been sitting there?"

"Long enough to challenge you to a game of cards after we finish this hunt," Daviin said. "I can always use another twenty thousand credits."

The Baga's faceted red eyes glittered and Daviin was sure the insane little creature was smiling. "You're on, Jreet."

"They're sure taking a long time," Galek said, just in time for the doors to open and the Human and the Huouyt to step aboard.

Jer'ait entered the ship with barely a glance at Daviin, then moved to take a seat. The Human, however, stopped in the entrance to the shuttle, forcing the doors to stay open. He locked gazes with Daviin. "Get out."

Daviin did not move. "What?"

The Human narrowed its eyes. "You told me you got chipped. Get out."

Daviin stiffened. "I never said that."

The Human's brown eyes were icy. "*Did* you get chipped, Daviin?"

Faced with a direct question, Daviin constricted. "Jreet don't get chipped."

"Neither do Va'gan Huouyt," Jer'ait said, his eyes focused impassively on Daviin.

"All that trouble to get Jer'ait under the knife and you never so much as made a peep about it," Joe said. He looked enraged. "I knew it was a bad idea to let you back on the team. Get out. You're not coming with us until you can learn to obey orders."

"Jreet don't get chipped." Daviin said, desperate. That's—" *Humiliating. Unmanning. Worse than being Sentinel to a slave.* Lifting his head, Daviin said, "I'll obey any order you give me but that one. I give you my word."

The Human's face cleared instantly. "Very well. Then stay right here." He stepped inside and sat down, levering his black Congie rifle onto his lap, relaxing completely.

Daviin had a sinking feeling he knew what the Human meant. He ducked his head in silence, knowing he'd lost the fight. He sat out the rest of the flight, listening carefully, but adding nothing as the group discussed the elements of their plan. They were landing in an uninhabited area and were going to make a ground incursion into enemy territory. They'd picked a collapsed tunnel near a stream, so the Huouyt had free access to water in case he needed to negate his patterns. The Grekkon would get them past the blockade. From there, the Huouyt and the Baga would infiltrate the tunnels and determine exactly what they were dealing with while the Human and the Ooreiki guarded the digger.

Daviin, he noticed, with a constriction of shame, was not given a part in the plan.

When the shuttle came to a stop, Daviin lifted his head slightly as the Human stood up, but Joe stepped off the ship without even glancing in Daviin's direction. The rest of the group followed, leaving Daviin coiled in his corner. Daviin watched the door shut, fighting the urge to follow them anyway. They were all going to die without him. He knew it like he knew the five of them would be the ones to get him to the Vahlin.

But he had given his word.

The Human had played an underhanded game, but if Daviin got off the shuttle, he would lose every ounce of respect he sought to gain.

His duties as a Sentinel warred with his duties as a grounder, which warred with his status as a Voran warrior. If he let the Human go without him, Daviin would not be able to protect him. The Human's death would solve many problems, but it was the coward's way out. Yet, if he followed, Joe would never trust him again.

And through it all, he had the nagging reminder he was bound to a slave. He was agonizing over the respect of a *slave*.

The very idea baffled and angered him. Had he grown so soft he actually *cared* what this slave thought of him?

The simple answer was yes.

Whatever the Human was before, he was a warrior now. Daviin wanted to earn the Human's respect, and he couldn't do that by disobeying yet another order. Though it pained him, Daviin lowered his head back to his coil and closed his eyes.

The Ayhi protect them.

The shuttle's engines rumbled to life and the ship jerked. Daviin ached inside, knowing he was leaving his five companions to die. He felt the shuttle roar back into the sky. Felt the jiggle as it lifted through atmosphere…

The door suddenly opened and Galek stood there, sudah fluttering with anxiety in his neck. "He says you can come out now," the Ooreiki said.

The sound of the engines roaring through the door left Daviin momentarily confused, knowing they should be in deep atmo by now. It wasn't until he saw the foliage in the background that he realized that the shuttle hadn't lifted off at all. The engines were blasting in neutral, aimed nowhere. It had been a ruse.

Daviin's mouth fell open.

"Can you turn those off!" Galek shouted at the tiny Ueshi pilots inside the cockpit. The engines died, leaving the world in a muted silence. Tentatively, the Ooreiki said, "Are you coming, Daviin?"

Hope flared with suspicion in Daviin's mind. Was following the Ooreiki's word considered taking orders from the Human? "I want to hear it from Joe," Daviin said, wary of a trick.

From behind the Ooreiki, the Human shouted, "Get your ass out here, Jreet! You have Dhasha to kill."

Daviin slid out of his coil, trying to hide his embarrassment. Galek scrunched his face in a shy, wrinkled Ooreiki smile, then jogged away from the shuttle. Daviin followed him, and when his eyes met the Human's, he realized he'd passed some sort of test.

And he was proud of it.

Ayhi save me, Daviin thought, stunned as he stared at the Human's soft, squishy face, *but this bastard has the soul of a Jreet.*

"Let's get this show on the road," Joe went on. "Daviin, I want you in inviso-mode the whole time. Since you're not chipped, Flea's wings will guide you. No echolocation. Dhasha can hear it."

The Human wanted him to enter the tunnels blind and deaf, but Daviin merely nodded and complied. The Baga hovered somewhere near his eye-level and Daviin followed the sound of his flight. He found, to his surprise, that the high-frequency vibrations of the Baga's wings that he had found so annoying in the barracks gave him a decent picture of his surroundings, if he could keep up.

"Galek, you've got the eyes in this operation. Take point. They've got Takki combing these woods all the time. Flea, stay behind Scarab. I want the Jreet at his back. Jer'ait, go do your thing."

The Huouyt dropped down to all fours—from the outline the Baga's wings showed him, Daviin assumed he'd taken the pattern of some sort of native creature—and disappeared into the foliage. The band began moving, and Daviin heard Joe drop back to walk beside him. They walked in silence for a moment, then the Human said, "Were you really gonna stay on that shuttle?"

"Yes."

The Human moved away, saying nothing else.

They found the first Takki body a few tics later. The Baga paused a moment, hovering over it curiously, so Daviin heard a clear picture of the Takki's throat ripped open. They had never heard a sound.

"Here we go," Joe whispered. "Daviin, you burning furg, you're getting a chip as soon as we get back."

"I know."

"Stay close." Then, like a wraith, the Human followed the Huouyt into the brush.

Up ahead, something screamed.

• • •

"Abandoned, my ass," Joe said, eying the twelve Takki corpses lining the ground. Two still oozed blue slime from plasma wounds—the Huouyt and the Jreet had gotten the rest. "Scarab, get us underground before the Dhasha come looking for them." Fighting Dhasha in tunnels, where the huge scaled creatures had no room to maneuver, was one thing—fighting them on the surface was suicide.

The Grekkon backed up to the site they had chosen to bypass the blocked entrance, then hesitated. As Joe watched, the skin of the creature's bulbous head—or butt, considering it had a set of eyes at each end of its body—began to excrete a pitch black substance that seemed to eat the light itself. Everyone near the Grekkon took a nervous step away from it.

The Grekkon lowered its rear into the ground.

Not *onto* the ground, not *atop* the ground, but *into* the ground. The back end sank into the dirt as fast as the front legs could push it, leaving a perfect, circular tube of earth wide enough for a man to walk through if he bent over. The Grekkon disappeared at an angle parallel to the main shaft, at an easy slope for them to follow. He was gone from sight in less than three seconds.

Everyone stared down at the hole with a mixture of unease and respect.

Through the headcom chip, the Baga voiced what they were all thinking. "*So what happens if he accidentally brushes up against one of us with that stuff?*"

"*You make up a will yet?*" Joe asked, falling back into the familiar routine of silent, chip-to-chip communication.

"*I'm serious,*" Flea insisted.

"*So am I.*"

The Baga stared at the hole in silence. Finally, it said, "*I bet Congress would just love to get that in ammo form.*"

"*They tried. Can't figure the stuff out. Kinda like the Dhasha's scales and the Jreet's invisibility.*"

"*And my abbas.*"

"*And your glue, yeah. Help me get these out of sight,*" Joe said. He grabbed a dead Takki by the wrists and began dragging it into the tunnel. Moving their dense, static bodies—probably two, two hundred fifty lobes each—was a struggle even with the aid of his biosuit. Joe tried not to wince as Galek and Daviin both grabbed a Takki in each fist and began casually throwing them into the tunnel as if they weighed no more than pillows. Jer'ait and Flea had already followed the Grekkon into the tunnel.

Joe had the Jreet slide deeper into the shaft while he and Galek disguised the entrance with a hologram of the spot as it had been before the Grekkon had disturbed it. Then Daviin and Galek stood back as Joe triggered a minor collapse, sealing the tunnel behind them to trap the smell of dead Takki inside, where it wouldn't attract attention from the surface.

"*Let's go,*" Joe said mentally over his head-com, breaking into a bent-over trot. "*Air is short.*"

Though the Jreet did not pick up the thought, Joe heard him slither along behind them, moving a pebble here, a clod of dirt there as he followed them. Here, bent over as they were, the Jreet actually had an advantage. Where Joe and Galek could outrun him in an instant on the surface, here the Jreet could keep up, if not pass them entirely.

Once again, Joe wondered if changing his mind about the Jreet had been a bad idea. Without communications, the Jreet wasn't going to do them any good as a scout. He'd have to stay with Joe at all times.

Probably exactly what he wanted, Joe realized, disgusted he hadn't seen it earlier.

Jer'ait's call broke him from his thoughts. "*The Grekkon broke through a downward shaft. The Baga and I investigate.*"

Joe hurried his step.

They found Scarab backed into a side shaft it had created, poised like a trapdoor spider in its lair, its two spearlike arms pointed outward. Looking at it, Joe realized that the Grekkon probably didn't need much protection. It could impale a Takki, and a Dhasha wouldn't be able to dig fast enough to catch it.

As Joe and Galek took up positions on either side of the Grekkon's hole, the Jreet slid out into the rough, Takki-dug tunnel and waited.

A young Ooreiki voice broke the silence in Joe's headcom. *"First and Second Battalions, this is Groundteam Two, Squad 43 of Third Battalion. We've reached the entrance to the main shaft. No enemies encountered. Haven't heard a peep from anyone in our Battalion. Is everything all right out there?"*

Joe frowned. There were six battalions assigned to the deep den. Five and a half thousand people should have had *something* to say before this.

"Can anyone hear me?" the request came again.

No one responded.

Though PlanOps teams were not governed by the same ranking rules as normal groundteams, Joe determined this was a good time to take control. To Second Battalion only, he said, *"This is Prime Commander Zero. Someone open your burning mouth and say something."*

Silence.

Joe's skin began to feel clammy. He switched channels to all six battalions and repeated his call.

"Praise the ghosts, we're glad to hear you, Commander," the young Ooreiki said. *"We can't get ahold of anybody. Think we mighta got some faulty com equipment."*

"It's working fine," Joe replied. *"Keep your eyes open. We hit seven Takki before we reached our shaft site."*

"So where is everybody?" the unknown squad leader insisted.

No one answered.

Joe did a quick mental calculation. One hundred and fifty groundteams per Battalion. Six battalions assigned to this deep den. That meant there should've been nine hundred groundteams out there responding to him.

"*Listen,*" Joe said, "*I want you to get into the tunnels as soon as you can.*"

"*We've got to blast a way in. They've sealed everything, even the slave tunnels.*"

"*And you didn't see anybody coming in?*"

"*Affirmative, the place is abandoned.*"

Joe felt a coldness seeping under his biosuit. On the local channel, he said, "*Unless somebody back at headquarters is screwing with us, everyone else in this attack is dead. We're not gonna get any help on the prince.*"

"*But I just heard a team on the com,*" Galek said.

"*They're dead,*" Jer'ait said. "*Dhasha are closing in on them as we speak.*"

"*How do you know?*"

Instead of replying, Jer'ait said, "*Downward shaft clear. Connects to a larger tunnel about six hundred rods past the Grekkon's puncture.*"

"*Flea, how's the way up?*"

"*We're good. No other connecting shafts for a long way.*"

"*How much of a way?*" the Huouyt asked, sounding irritated.

Flea hesitated. "*Maybe sixty ferlii lengths? A good long way.*"

"*Sixty* lengths?" the Huouyt cried. "*You've only been down there twenty seconds!*"

"*I said it was a good way,*" the Baga snapped.

"*Give us a* number, *pest,*" Jer'ait snarled. "*There's no way you went sixty lengths.*"

"*No?*" Flea retorted. "*Then come down here and find out yourself, you wet-eyed worm-tree,*" Flea retorted.

"*Perhaps I will,*" Jer'ait said smoothly, "*And end your useless existence in the process.*"

Joe interrupted, "*Baga have no sense of numbers, Jer'ait. Anything beyond six or seven and they're lost.*"

There was a very long pause. "*You jest,*" Jer'ait finally said.

Immediately, the Baga said, "*Is that something you do with yourself in the shade of the* miga *tree?*"

"*What is the pest talking about?*" Jer'ait demanded.

Joe had no idea. "*It's an insult of some sort.*"

"*Well, obviously,*" Jer'ait growled. "*What good is the little monster if his primitive brain cannot comprehend numbers?*"

Joe winced, hoping that the Baga didn't take it upon himself to stick Jer'ait next time he saw him. *"Can it, Jer'ait. Everyone else, let's go."*

Joe led the others from the Grekkon's tunnel and took out another hologram to mask the entrance. He took an image of the wall beside it and then set that same image over the opening to the tunnel. He eyed his handiwork a moment before nodding. To see it, one had to know where to look. He leaned down to mark the floor in front of the entrance, but the Ooreiki caught his arm. Joe looked up, irritated.

"I can find it," Galek said.

Joe shook his head. *"It'll be different in six hours, when we're running for our lives."*

"No. I can find it." Galek's sticky young eyes pleaded for trust.

Joe glanced back at the unmarked floor, then at the entrance itself. He'd disguised it well. Without a marking, he would never find it again.

He sighed and straightened, leaving the floor unmarked. *"Our lives are in your hands, Galek. Stay alive. Flea, get back down here."*

The Baga complied, and in seconds they heard the high-pitched hum of the Baga's wings. He was moving fast, at least forty lengths an hour. He passed by them without stopping and soon was gone down the tunnel following the Huouyt.

Joe nodded toward the others and began moving deeper into the tunnel.

Behind him, the Ooreiki was all but oozing pride.

Ghosts, what I wouldn't give to be young again, he thought. *God I hope Galek doesn't die down here.*

15

THE FIRST PRINCE

"I was told there would be five thousand three hundred and ninety-four. Six battalions minus one team that destroyed itself in a fight as they were boarding their shuttle. Why are six Congies unaccounted for?"

Tevval's lieutenants looked away, trying to do anything but catch his attention. Their iridescent, rainbow scales glittered in the light of the lamps that Takki had installed in niches along the walls, their blocky bodies perfect but for a few missing scales from minor dominance scuffles. Not *one* of them had the balls to ka-par.

Cowards, Tevval thought.

It had been six turns since one of them had even physically challenged him. *That* fool still carried his shame in his mangled jaw, the multiple rows of triangular black teeth twisting in on themselves where Tevval had sliced apart his face.

Tevval growled and began to pace. "Why have we only seen five thousand three hundred and eighty-eight Congies? That is precisely the right number to constitute an extra groundteam crawling through our tunnels as we speak."

"Perhaps they held another team back, my lord," one of his oldest heirs said, his hard, egg-shaped green eyes glittering hatred in the lamps. Aside from the one with the broken jaw, he was the largest. His left horn was a deformed black mass where Tevval had disciplined him as a child. Tevval decided it would probably be this one to try his luck next. The heir continued on, oblivious of his appraisal. "Maybe it destroyed itself like the first one. The experimental species combinations are extremely volatile. It could have been a last-tic change."

"Our information has never been wrong before," Tevval said. "They're here. An entire groundteam. Why haven't we found it yet?"

The room fell into a nervous silence. As he paced, a glimmering purple Takki skittered from a slave tunnel and rushed forward, blue eyes betraying its panic at being in a room filled with Dhasha. It stopped beside Tevval, head down, and waited.

"Speak!" Tevval roared, resisting the urge to tear the beast apart for wasting his time.

"Twelve slaves are missing from the surface, master," the Takki said. Its voice quaked with terror.

Bones. "Which entrance?"

"Entrance Six, master."

"Scour the main shaft and all the side shafts."

"We already did, master. We've found no markings. The tunnels are still sealed."

"Then they haven't punctured yet."

The Takki quivered, head down. "Eight more are missing, master. Searchers we sent to scour the tunnels."

Tevval's scales tightened against his chest. "They're inside?"

"The entrances are still sealed," one of his lieutenants rumbled. "I've got a Takki stationed at each with com equipment. They tell me they've heard no attempts to open any of the shafts since we killed the last team."

"All are still in position?" Tevval demanded.

"Yes, sire."

"Could one of them be a Huouyt? I was told we would have thirty-nine teams with Huouyt on them. How many Huouyt have we recovered?"

"Forty, sire."

"Forty? One had two?"

His heir looked embarrassed. "No, sire. Two teams had two Huouyt on them."

Tevval swiveled to frown at his lieutenants. "So only thirty-eight teams had Huouyt?"

"The slaves easily could have made a mistake in the count."

Tevval snorted. "There's a Huouyt loose in the tunnels. Are you certain one of your Takki monitoring the entrances is not actually a Huouyt masking his companions' approach?"

"Our slaves are using closed-circuit chips, same technology as the Congies, sire. It can't be an intruder."

Tevval began to pace again. "Tell me which species you recovered thus far."

A Takki dutifully held out the list for his lieutenant. The lieutenant cleared his throat. "Sire, there were seventy-two species represented in this attack. The main components were Ooreiki, Ueshi, Jahul, and Jikaln."

Tevval snorted. "They send Takki to fight warriors."

"The list also consists of a few Grislek, Dreit, Hebbut, and Grekkon."

Tevval grunted. "At least you found both Grekkon."

Instantly, his lieutenant looked stricken. "We only found one Grekkon, sire."

Tevval twitched. "You missed one? They should have been your *first* priority. A Grekkon can penetrate our tunnels." He began to pace again. He was not liking this. The final team had a Grekkon and a Huouyt. A bad combination.

"Perhaps we should contact the Vahlin, sire."

"The Vahlin will contact us," Tevval snapped.

"But it's been over a week since we've heard anything from him. Perhaps he was wrong and another of the teams stayed behind."

"The team is here, you leafy furg," Tevval said, his voice low. "Do not make me repeat myself again."

None of his lieutenants would meet his eyes to ka-par. Not one. *Cowards. Declawed, bony cowards.* It put him in the mood to kill one of them.

"The Vahlin has never been wrong," Tevval continued, irritated. "A week ago, I was told they would attack today, midway through the third hour. They did. In that same conversation, I was told to watch for thirty-nine teams with Huouyt and two Grekkon. We already have one dead Grekkon and forty Huouyt."

"The Vahlin said nothing about Jreet?"

Tevval swiveled to face his heir with growing irritation. "I think the Vahlin would have found that fact important enough to mention, don't you?"

His lieutenants seemed to relax. Tevval gave a disgusted snort. They were all descaled by the thought of an oversized worm. "Get out of here, vaghi. Go patrol the shafts."

His heir bowed his head slightly. He stood at Tevval's shoulder, but he still did not have the courage to challenge him. "Sire, wouldn't it be wise to leave a few of us here to guard you?"

Tevval roared and slammed the smaller Dhasha across the room, tearing away scales in a rainbow shower. As his heir slowly picked himself from the floor, Tevval said, "I can protect myself."

His heir retreated in silence, leaving Tevval alone. Even the Takki had departed while he'd been distracted with disciplining his heir. A shame. Tevval had been looking forward to a meal.

• • •

"He's got eighty-two adult young," Jer'ait said. "I'd say the oldest six will have to be killed, including the prince. We can let Congress bury the rest."

"You learned all that in thirty seconds?" Joe asked the Huouyt. "I'm impressed."

"I'm a professional."

"Describe the prince," Joe told his Second.

"He's a large one," Jer'ait said. "Less than a rod at shoulder. Probably five hundred turns."

Smaller than Bagkhal. Joe took a deep breath, relieved beyond measure. *"Flea, what about you?"*

"They're looking for us," the Baga said. *"I'm spending most of my time clinging to the ceiling now."*

Joe cursed. *"What gave us away?"*

Jer'ait was utterly calm when he said, *"Nothing. The Vahlin has an agent inside PlanOps. The prince not only knows how many teams would be attacking, but he also knows which species to look out for, and how many of each. Further, the Dhasha prince has had this information for over a week."*

Joe's heart began to pound. *"We haven't even been on Jeelsiht for a week."*

"So it would appear."

What in the ninety hells was going on?

Joe relayed the Huouyt's report out loud for Daviin's benefit.

The Jreet nodded, but offered nothing. He'd been almost demure since the confrontation in the shuttle. The perfect soldier. Except, of course, for the fact he didn't have a chip.

That still rankled on Joe.

"It is possible that the Dhasha said that for my benefit," Jer'ait offered. *"He might have sensed my disguise."* Joe heard the intense reluctance in the Huouyt's voice—he didn't want to admit he might have been outed.

"No," Joe said, *"You probably misunderstood him. Even if he had an agent in headquarters, there's no way the Vahlin could have known which den we'd be assigned to. No one knew that until three hours ago."*

"Perhaps," the Huouyt said. *"I'll be there soon."* He said nothing more.

They were hiding in a short side-shaft Scarab had dug into the side of a Takki tunnel and Joe had masked with a hologram. Daviin lay somewhere in the main shaft, waiting.

Eventually, a Takki scurried up the hall toward them. When he came within reach, Daviin lashed out and wrapped him in a coil. The Takki jerked and left the ground, seemingly held by the air itself.

"Release me, Sentinel." The Takki's words were cold, utterly unafraid.

Thankfully, Daviin did. Joe was acutely aware of the fact that that moment would have been a perfect time for the Huouyt to 'accidentally' get crushed to death. And, considering how Daviin had quietly overlooked his order to get chipped, Joe was doubly concerned that the Jreet would find an unfortunate way for the Va'gan to meet an untimely end.

Jer'ait brushed himself off, looking completely unconcerned that a massive predator had just held him in a death-grip. Calmly, he told Joe, "The tunnel is safe for fifty rods. However, it doesn't connect to a main shaft until we pass the Takki nesting area, which is full of females and young."

"Should we attempt a different approach?" Joe asked.

"Yes," Jer'ait said. "Too much traffic for even the invertebrate to go unnoticed."

Joe heard Daviin snarl, but the Huouyt did not even bother to look.

"*Flea, can you get back here?*" Joe asked.

"*We're leaving?*" The Baga almost sounded…disappointed.

"*Finding another way down.*" Joe said. "*This one's got too many faces.*"

"*Coming.*"

"There's something I want to talk to you about before we go further," Jer'ait said out loud. For the Jreet's benefit, no doubt. Which meant it was important enough for the Huouyt to overlook his disdain for the Sentinel.

Joe scanned the tunnel behind them with his eyes. "What?"

"This place." Jer'ait gestured vaguely at the walls of their tunnel. "There's something wrong here."

"How so?"

The Huouyt's scaly purple, Takki-patterned face strained to find the words. Finally, he said, "I'm not sure. They killed *every* other team before they even had a chance to enter the tunnels. They were waiting for us. Not just waiting for us, but *ready* for us."

"Because they have an inside man," Joe agreed. Nothing really weird about that. Irritating, but not weird.

"It's more than that," Jer'ait insisted. "They knew everything, down to the hour we would appear. *We* didn't even know that until this morning. No one did—except, it seems, the Dhasha Vahlin. And yet, despite knowing the exact moment we would arrive, the Vahlin did not give out our team specifics. The prince has no idea we have a Jreet with us. He had no idea which tunnel we would be assigned to penetrate, which should have been much easier information to obtain than our arrival time." The Huouyt paused, his Takki-blue eyes shimmering like polished sapphires. "I'm finding the situation odd."

"Which means," the Jreet said from thin air, "It's scaring the piss out of him."

Jer'ait made a rude gesture at the Jreet with one clawed Takki hand. "I saw that, Huouyt."

"No you didn't," Jer'ait said. "You're blind when you're invisible and you're too Takki slavesoul to ping."

"You're one to talk," Daviin snorted. "Considering."

Joe sighed and glanced down the tunnel behind them. For the last three hours, the same thought had been tickling the back of his mind. Something was definitely off about the whole affair. If they left now, headquarters would be satisfied with the intelligence they had gained. Escaping with the knowledge that someone in PlanOps was leaking their secrets was worth leaving the prince alive.

The Baga arrived without them seeing, crawling upside-down from the ceiling of the tunnel. "What's scaring the piss out of him? That he'll see a Dhasha?"

"Silence, pest," Jer'ait said casually.

"You look good in that pattern, Huouyt. It compliments your character." The Baga dropped from the ceiling to land on Joe's shoulder.

Jer'ait's borrowed Takki eyes were glacial as he turned to regard the Baga. "I think if we were to take a poll, Baga, you would not win any awards."

Flea made a disgusted sound and took to the air again. He landed a distance away, on the Grekkon's huge jumping legs where they were folded over its back. If the Grekkon noticed or cared, it made no indication.

"So what are we doing?" the Baga demanded. "What next? Why are we still standing here like terrified Takki?" Then he glanced at the Huouyt's patterned form. Smugly, he said, "Oh."

"Joe is trying to decide whether we should return to the surface or continue after the prince," Galek said softly, beside Joe.

"Why would we leave?" the Baga said. "We're almost there."

"Someone's giving out Planetary Ops intelligence…a week in advance." Jer'ait glanced at the Baga. "The Vahlin knew we were coming before *we* knew we were coming."

"That's impossible," the Baga said.

"It's not," Jer'ait said. "It just means it's one of the higher-ups doing the talking."

"It's impossible," the Baga repeated. "I was in the room when the Overseers decided to send us in. They all wanted different times based on their species' strengths. The Ooreiki, for instance, wanted to wait for nightfall—their eyes are better in the dark—while the Jikaln wanted the heat of the day, so they'd have faster reflexes. They ended up on a compromise. Averaged it all out. Big calculation. Had some Bajna work it out based on averages and numbers of each species still left alive after all the infighting and other stuff I don't really care about. That was this morning."

Joe stared at the Baga, stunned. "Why'd they let you in the meeting?"

The Baga did not reply, its faceted red eyes flat.

"You're furging me," Joe cried. "You *eavesdropped?* On the *Overseers?*"

"It's not my fault if other species never take the time to look up," Flea retorted.

"You stupid bastard," Joe growled. "They'd have *executed* you. They would've thought *you* were the traitor."

"You don't learn interesting, possibly life-saving information twiddling your claws in a barracks room." The Baga seemed to have absolutely no remorse.

"So you eavesdropped on the burning Overseer battleroom," Joe blurted.

"And I'll do it again, too. It wasn't boring." The Baga cocked its insectlike head at Jer'ait. "Like the rest of you."

Joe opened his mouth to tell Flea not to, then hesitated. "So, basically what you're telling me is that there's no way the Vahlin knew when we were gonna arrive, because the *Overseers* didn't know when we were going to arrive."

"Not a week ago," the football-sized alien confirmed, his faceted eyes glittering almost maroon despite the Congie technicians' darkening job.

Jer'ait's theory that the prince had said everything for his benefit was beginning to look more plausible. "Well, soot. Jer'ait, if the prince knew you were a spy, why the hell didn't he kill you?"

The Huouyt's response was reluctant. "Perhaps he wanted me to pass on wrong information."

"That he knows we're here? Why?" Joe demanded. "To scare us out?"

"Perhaps his meeting with his lieutenants was contrived," Jer'ait replied. "There might be three times as many and they're waiting for us to come out of hiding, so they can get us all at once."

"I suppose that's plausible," Joe said. "And he could have deduced that we had a Huouyt and a Grekkon on our team after Takki started disappearing in the tunnels." He frowned at Jer'ait. "But, bones, he's gotta be stupid to let a Huouyt assassin go once he's identified one."

"I couldn't have said it better myself," Daviin said loudly. Catching the reference, Joe scowled at the empty air where he knew the Jreet to be huddled.

It was the Grekkon who broke the silence. The voicebox affixed to the small concavity in the underside of his plated body said, "*I'm a PlanOps Battlemaster. I'm here to kill Dhasha. Why do we stand around?*"

"I agree," Daviin said. "They know we're here, but they don't know where. As long as we keep to the slave tunnels and stay out of the main shafts, we should be able to surprise them."

"How?" Jer'ait demanded, turning on the Jreet, who remained invisible. "They can hear your echolocation and as soon as they see one of us, all bets are off. This isn't a training mission—these Dhasha are on high alert. The moment we step in the main shaft, we're all going to die."

"I could lie in wait."

"Blind?" Jer'ait snorted.

"If I have to, yes," Daviin said tightly.

Scarab interrupted again. *"My species spent six million turns on Grek learning how to surprise our enemies. If we can separate the Dhasha, I can give the Jreet the surprise he needs to overpower them."*

Joe nodded. "Show us."

16

THE BEST LAID PLANS...

Daviin dangled from the ceiling, his scales tingling with the higher energy level, listening to the Dhasha lord striding closer. It was a small one, but still easily large enough to rip him apart, should things go wrong.

"Flea and Jer'ait say it's clear," Galek whispered into his ear.

Daviin winced as the Ooreiki then scrambled away from his coils, making a rustling sound deeper in the tunnel behind him. Below, the Dhasha paused. Daviin could hear its indestructible scales grate against each other as it cocked its head, waiting for the sound to come again.

Come on, Daviin thought, growing frustrated. It was the first target that had shown itself without other Dhasha nearby.

To his relief, the Dhasha grunted and the sounds of his talons scuffing against the floor resumed as he continued his walk.

They are so arrogant, Daviin thought. A Jreet warrior would have vanished instantly. This one simply strutted along, unafraid.

A moment later, its hulking body passed under Daviin. Daviin dropped from the ceiling, landing atop its cold, massive back. As the Dhasha tensed, Daviin whipped his body down and under, twisting violently around his victim's middle, knocking the Dhasha off its feet and immobilizing his dangerous talons in one swift, bone-breaking cinching motion. As the Dhasha began to struggle, its powerful legs flailing for purchase, Daviin tightened his body around the creature's thick neck. He felt the familiar pressure of constriction as he threw more coils around the stronger creature, careful to keep his body away from the black rows of triangular, razor teeth.

He tensed his muscles, tightening down on the massive neck and torso. The sheer *weight* of a Dhasha left him straining, the power behind its muscles hard to control. For a moment, Daviin thought that he would lose his grip and allow the razor claws to tear him apart. For several tics, the Dhasha twisted, writhed, and struggled. Slowly, it made a strangled, gasping roar through its meaty neck and went still.

As soon as the Dhasha had exhausted itself, Daviin began throwing loop after loop around it, tightening until the force of his coils began to force the air from the Dhasha's chest in a fleshy gurgle.

To finish it, Daviin ripped away a huge rainbow-colored scale under the creature's neck, then followed with the smaller golden underlayer. He felt the Dhasha sluggishly try to struggle again as it realized what would come next. Daviin slammed his tek into the creature's body, ending its protests.

"That's some good stuff," Joe said, once Daviin had extracted all seven rods of his length from around the body, "Didn't even twitch." The Human gave the ceiling a dubious glance. "Are you sure you can get it back up there?"

Muscles quivering from the pressure he had exerted on the Dhasha, Daviin merely grunted. He wrapped the end of his body around the Dhasha's neck and pushed his head through the hologram masking the hole in the ceiling. Above, the Ooreiki watched nervously, the Grekkon backed into the wall beside him.

"He's got it," Galek said.

Scarab pushed its body deeper into the wall, then up, then around, popping back into the tunnel six digs above where he had exited. In less than a tic, he had a niche for the Dhasha's body.

Daviin slid forward until he felt the first bit of strain from his grip on the Dhasha's neck. "A little help," he muttered.

The Ooreiki jerked sheepishly and hurried to the center of the tunnel. There, he grabbed Daviin around the torso, seemingly oblivious to the tek's sheath he hugged, and added his strength, giving Daviin a more stable basis with which to use his upper body as a fulcrum. With some effort, the Dhasha's head appeared in the hole. Galek ran to grab the corpse behind its massive jaw, and together they levered its mass into their tunnel. The Human, who only stood to be crushed by the forces involved, stood out of the way to watch.

Once they had the Dhasha entombed, Daviin pulled himself into a coil to rest. The dual load of forming his energy-shield and wrestling a Dhasha into submission was bringing on the familiar after-battle exhaustion that Daviin had experienced many times before. He would need a few hours to recuperate.

"Everyone quiet," their Prime said once the Ooreiki had helped him back in the Grekkon's tunnel. "Flea says they heard us."

Not two seconds later, a group of Dhasha came barreling down the tunnel beneath them, their cold green eyes glittering with mad rage. They passed without slowing.

"They'll be back," Joe whispered. "I just hope Jer'ait's smart enough to—oh, ash."

"What?" Daviin swiveled around. Behind him, Joe and Galek looked petrified, staring into space as they listened to something Daviin couldn't hear. The Human's skin had paled, moisture beading on his forehead. The Ooreiki's liquid brown eyes were wide, the slitted black pupils fully dilated.

"They got Flea," Galek cried. Even as Daviin turned to chastise the Ooreiki for being so loud, a flash of rainbow appeared in the opening behind him.

"Found you," the Dhasha said, its unholy emerald eyes glittering Death.

• • •

Jer'ait followed the Baga's corpse at a distance, staying out of sight. A Dhasha's purple-scaled slave was carrying it a pace in front of its master, the Takki's cerulean, egg-shaped eyes downcast. Behind the Takki, the Dhasha strutted like a gem-studded tank. Its massive body and stubby legs made for an awkward shuffle behind the more elegant violet biped, who held the Baga's corpse out before it with two scaly purple arms that resembled Joe's.

They were taking the pest back to the deep den, a prize to show their leader.

Jer'ait ducked into a slave tunnel, deciding to take a less obvious route. He was halfway to the Takki living-quarters when the Grekkon's voice said over the local channel, *"They got the Ooreiki and the Prime. The Jreet escaped in a side tunnel after killing one of them, but I think he's injured, possibly fatal. He's raised his energy level—I have no idea where he went. What should I do?"*

Jer'ait hesitated, considering. *"Did the Dhasha sever the Jreet's head or separate its body in any way?"*

"No."

"Then it will live. Worry about yourself, for now. They'll send Takki after you. Escape to the surface if you have to, but meet me back at our penetration point in two hours."

"Very well." The Grekkon said nothing more.

Now was an excellent time to abandon the Human. Jer'ait had suspected from the beginning that the Trith's message had been a fake, and this was perfect proof. Three of their team dead, one incommunicado, the rest of the six battalions destroyed. Headquarters would welcome a retreat with open arms, considering the intelligence they had gained in the process.

Yet, he had his orders. The Human was to survive until the Vahlin was dead.

Jer'ait took a deep breath and moved deeper into the tunnels.

When Jer'ait reached the deep den, the first thing he realized was that the Human was still fully conscious. The Ooreiki lay in a tentacled, fleshy heap on the floor, its biosuit closed over whatever wounds it had endured in its capture. If it was still alive, it was just barely.

The Human, meanwhile, spat a continuous stream of invective intended to provoke his captors into killing him—a final attempt to protect the rest of his team. The prince seemed oblivious. He was listening to a report by one of his lieutenants.

"It's a five-part com system. That means there's two more members out there."

"A Grekkon and a Huouyt."

"Yes, sir."

"Then who killed my heir?"

"Our guess is the Grekkon, sir. He stayed behind to watch the tunnel. The Grekkon could have surprised him from above."

"Why would they send a five-member groundteam?" the prince demanded. "I was told it would be six. PlanOps always sends six."

Jer'ait dropped to his knees to aid another Takki in removing Dhasha waste from the floor as he listened. Beside him, the slave didn't even look up. It simply continued dragging its scaly violet hands through the excrement—much of which contained the undigested bones of Takki— and kept its pupilless, gemlike blue eyes focused on the floor.

When the lieutenants had no opinions to offer, the prince turned to the Human and casually batted him aside, cutting off his curses abruptly. Jer'ait watched the suit seal over the angry red wounds on the inside and wondered if the Human had been dealt a killing blow.

He hadn't. He groaned as the Dhasha prince flipped him over and pressed a stubby paw to his chest, razor black talons poised to sink into his organs. Into the Human's face, the prince said, "What species is the sixth member of your groundteam? Which one are we missing?"

Jer'ait tensed. The Jreet was their best hope of getting out alive. If the Human gave him away...

"We've only got five," the Human said.

The Dhasha tensed the muscles in his foot, sinking the claws through the biosuit and into the Human's chest. Joe let out a wretched scream.

"Slave, scan him." A Takki rushed forward and pressed a small metallic device to the Human's head. "We know you're lying. Tell me again how many were in your group." He sank his talons deeper.

"Five," the Human screamed.

The prince looked up. "Well?"

"The truth, master," a Takki said, pulling the scanner away from the Human's head.

"These Humans, have they the Huouyt's ability to lie?"

No, they don't, Jer'ait thought, perplexed.

The Takki checked the instrument's database and said, "No, sire. Their mental energies are quite straightforward."

The prince grunted and returned his attention to the Human. "Why five? The Ground Force works in increments of six."

"Because the Prime told him to burn off." Joe's breaths were coming in small pants, his face twisted in pain. "He wouldn't follow orders."

Jer'ait stood from his place beside the Takki cleaning the floor and wove his way through the congregated Dhasha. Without being told, he began to groom the prince.

The prince ignored him completely. To his lieutenants, he said, "Nehi, Glahs, you stay here and guard the captives. The rest of you I want in the tunnels, figuring out where the hell the other two of them are."

Jer'ait felt a wave of frustration as the two largest Dhasha took positions near the entrances to the den. He had an entire array of poisons on his person, but unless he could get the prince alone, there was no way he could use them without being torn to pieces afterward. As it was, if he wasn't careful, the prince could kill him in his death throes. It would only take one stray talon to rip him open from throat to abdomen.

"Harder, slave," the prince barked at him. "*Scratch*, don't rub."

Seething, Jer'ait reached under the golden sub-scales and began clawing away huge portions of stale, rancid-smelling flesh. Biting red parasites came off with the administration of his claws, falling to the ground and scuttling across the floor looking for another host. Around him, other Takki materialized to help, each taking a position on their master's body seemingly at random. The prince gave a contented sigh and shuffled over to the pillows surrounding his brooding females and stretched out to give his slaves better access.

Jer'ait got a good look at his groundmates as he worked and immediately felt a pang of worry. Joe was unconscious, now, and his breathing was shallow enough to suggest his biosuit had shut off his body functions to prolong death. The Ooreiki had been in that state for almost half an hour now.

"Scratch harder!" the prince roared again.

Jer'ait glanced again at the two unconscious bodies on the other side of the room. *Leave them,* his mind screamed at him. *The Trith's message was a hoax. He will not kill the Vahlin. They are no use to you now.*

Yet, every time Jer'ait considered getting up and leaving the den, he was haunted by an image of the Human standing over him, running off one of his brother's agents while he lay drugged and helpless.

Jer'ait gritted his borrowed Takki jaw, and scratched.

• • •

Daviin came to a halt when the slave tunnel widened enough for him to double back upon himself and check his wounds.

They were bad. The Dhasha had sliced open a fluids circuit for his fifth segment. If he didn't find a way to the surface in the next eight hours, he would have to choose between shedding half his length or bleeding to death.

Daviin twisted back around to face the slave tunnel again. It had been sloping upwards for over an hour now, but now it had taken an abrupt downward turn, seemingly doubling back on itself.

Undisciplined fools, Daviin cursed. The tunnels had no rhyme nor reason, and not for the first time, he wished he had the Ooreiki's special instincts. The Jreet, much to Daviin's chagrin, were often taunted by Dhasha for having trouble finding the door in a well-marked, one-room house with nothing to obstruct their view of all four walls. Directions, as much as he hated to admit it, were not Daviin's strong suit.

Praying the slave tunnel resumed its upward slant somewhere ahead, Daviin continued forward.

Instead, the tunnel dipped even more steeply, making it an almost vertical drop. The slaves apparently had dug the tunnel to bypass another one, and wherever Daviin was headed, it wasn't to the surface.

He cursed himself again, though it was too late to turn around. His physiology made it impossible to back up, and he didn't want to take the chance that he would get trapped if he doubled back on himself to change direction.

At the end of the tunnel, Daviin found himself faced with a main shaft and no way to avoid it. Raising his energy level, he slid inside, keeping as tightly to the left wall as he could as he made his way up the slight incline that indicated the way out of the deep den.

The tunnel ended at a pile of rubble a hundred rods later. Daviin realized with growing despair that the Takki had filled in the entrances and he was probably thoroughly trapped. He could never dig his way out, not before the Dhasha heard him and came to investigate. He had to find an open shaft, which meant he had to find the shaft the Grekkon had dug to penetrate the den.

Daviin, however, was thoroughly and utterly lost. He didn't know which of the twelve entrances he had found—he was even having trouble deciding just which way was up.

Examining his fate, knowing he was bleeding to death, Daviin realized he had to make a decision. He was in a main shaft. He knew where it led, if he knew nothing else. He could go back and finish what his comrades had given their lives to do. What his *ward* had given his life to do.

But Daviin hesitated.

His ward was a slave. If the Welus found out a Voran prince had died extracting blood-price for a slave, Daviin's family line would be forever shamed. The Welus would scream his name in battle for a thousand generations.

Still, he *had* given his oath. The Human had been his ward. Daviin had made the choice himself, however much the Human had withheld from him. However faulty his decision, it had been *his* decision.

Daviin had never felt so torn. He glanced down at his hands.

Joe was my ward. We will meet again, beyond the ninety hells. Daviin hesitated, imagining the reunion. Then, *What will I tell him if I didn't do my duty?*

His family, Daviin decided, could fend for itself. Let the Welus scream. The oath of a Voran Sentinel was sacred, to whomever it was given.

Daviin had already started back down the shaft when he heard the movement in the rubble behind him. He froze.

The movement came again, the scraping of scales on rubble. Not Dhasha scales—something softer.

A Takki.

Daviin slid closer, so that he was straddling the pile of debris blocking the entrance. Sure enough, he heard a Takki breathing in a recess, hidden by dirt and rocks. The steady way its breath moved through its teeth told him the Takki had not heard him—it was merely hiding.

Waiting for someone to attempt to break through so it could report it to its masters.

Daviin slid forward and allowed himself one small echolocating ping to solidify in his mind the Takki's position. He heard the Takki jerk with confusion. Then, lightning-fast, he plunged into the Takki's hiding place, grabbed the creature by the arm, and tore it out into the tunnel. With a whiplike motion, he flipped around and slammed the Takki into the ground with all the force he could muster. He heard the rapid pops of bones breaking and a faint gurgling groan. Daviin repeated the process until he was sure the Takki was dead. He wanted to avoid using his tek as much as possible, to save his poison for his real enemies.

After the Takki breathed its last, Daviin slid back down along the side of the tunnel, wedged tightly into the lower corner, pushing his way deeper into the den.

He was going to die, but he would take as many Dhasha with him as he could.

Tics later, Daviin heard a group of Dhasha racing up the shaft, no doubt to investigate why their spy had ceased to file reports. They passed him, oblivious to the seven rods of Jreet lying invisible along the wall. Daviin let them go, still clinging to the edge of the tunnel. His fight was elsewhere. Perhaps, if he was lucky, he could remove Joe's corpse to the surface for an honorable burial.

Daviin had descended almost a ferlii length into the bowels of Neskfaat and was beginning to hear sounds of life from the tunnels ahead when movement from above startled him. For a horrible moment, Daviin thought a Dhasha had been standing completely still in the hallway, listening for him. Then he realized it was a muffled scuffling sound, like something being pushed and dragged at the same time.

He'd heard this sound before.

"Scarab!"

He said the word as loud as he dared, hoping it carried into whatever tunnel the Grekkon had dug. Daviin would have given anything to be able to ping the surrounding area, but he could hear at least a dozen Dhasha somewhere ahead of him, and every one of them would come running at the sound.

The sounds above him stopped. After a moment, they resumed again, though they seemed to grow closer. Daviin reared up, preparing to strike if it wasn't what he had thought.

"Scarab," Daviin repeated.

The sounds stopped again. A trickle of dirt fell from the ceiling.

"*Jreet?*"

There was no mistaking the artificial voicebox of the Grekkon digger.

"Why are you still here?" Daviin whispered. "Why did you not flee?"

"*Follow me. We talk somewhere safe.*" The smooth, dragging-pulling sound resumed, directly above his head. Daviin pushed up and felt for the opening with his snout. The Grekkon was already gone somewhere ahead, leaving Daviin to follow the sounds of his burrowing.

Daviin slid into the perfectly-slick tunnel and followed for almost twenty tics, the Grekkon's tunnel mimicking the Takki's in its lack of logical straight lines, instead curving and swaying haphazardly, almost as if the Grekkon were inebriated. Daviin was growing irritated when the Grekkon finally stopped.

"Lower your energy level, Jreet."

Daviin did.

The Grekkon peered at him with its four black eyes. Instead of talking, the Grekkon burrowed back on the tunnel it had just created, rejoining the shaft precisely where Daviin's body ended. Daviin felt a cold prickle, realizing how close he had come to losing one of his segments.

"Stay right here. Don't move. Don't say a word. I have three Takki on my trail. I've shaken the rest, but these are being stubborn. Save your strength while I deal with them."

"Can I help?" Daviin asked, twisting around to look. He could see nothing past the black void of the Grekkon's rear. Sudden panic washed over Daviin as he realized the Grekkon could back into him and dissolve his entire body—and Daviin could do nothing about it.

"No," the Grekkon said. *"Vanish again and stay silent."*

Daviin did so and held his breath, listening.

Scarab turned around, then carefully backed himself into the tunnel he had just created in the wall.

The first Takki came soon after he was situated. Daviin tensed, ready to lash out and deal with the Takki himself, but he never got the chance. As soon as the Takki passed before the Grekkon's hidden entrance, the Grekkon lunged. Twin spears punctured the Takki's chest and came out the other side. The Takki didn't even have a chance to scream. The Grekkon began backing up again, dragging the Takki with it. What it did with the body, Daviin wasn't sure, but it duplicated the procedure with the next two victims, not even giving Daviin the chance to assist.

Once it had dragged the third Takki out of sight, the Grekkon backed around until it was facing Daviin once more.

"You asked why I'm still here. Two reasons. The prince isn't dead and we have four members still alive in the deep den."

Daviin stiffened. "They surrendered?"

"*No. Incapacitated. The Human and the Ooreiki are unconscious. The Baga is mangled, but Jer'ait believes he might still be alive, based on what the Prime demonstrated in the barracks.*"

"And the Huouyt?"

"*Grooming the prince.*"

Daviin's lip peeled back from his teeth in disgust. "*Grooming* him?"

"*It's the only way he can maintain visual contact with the others without becoming conspicuous.*"

Daviin resisted the urge to comment on the cowardice of the Huouyt and instead said, "So the Human is alive? You're sure?" His instincts as a Sentinel were telling him to rush to the deep den as quickly as possible to do battle, but he had absolutely no idea where he was.

"*I told you. The Human and the Ooreiki are unconscious.*"

"How many guard our companions?"

"*Three, not including the prince's females.*"

"Dhasha females are bloated, craven, and slow. They will not fight us."

"*That's what the Huouyt said. Still, I think they should be accounted for.*"

"Do you have a plan?" Daviin demanded. "I can't kill three Dhasha by myself."

"*We're not going to kill them. I'm going to create a tunnel that exits in the center of the deep den's ceiling. It's a two-rod drop. You'll secure your lower end in the ceiling and drop into the den, grab our companions, and pull yourself back up before the Dhasha realize what's going on. Jer'ait will use the confusion to administer a poison to the Dhasha prince and then will meet us back at the entrance to our original shaft.*"

It sounded plausible. The fact that he might be able to get his ward out alive was making Daviin's blood rise. "What about the heirs? Jer'ait said they needed to be killed, too."

"*At this point, the Huouyt believes headquarters will be happy if we get out alive. The prince will be a bonus.*"

Daviin grunted. "Good. Let's do this fast—" He motioned at his ruptured liquids channel. "I'm running out of time."

If the Grekkon noticed or cared, he said nothing. Instead, Scarab simply slipped into the wall and disappeared.

They had been closer to the deep den than Daviin had thought. In only a couple of tics, the Grekkon had opened a hole in the ceiling and they were staring down at their companions. As the Grekkon had said, three of their companions were piled in an unconscious heap near one side of the room. On the other side of the room, a cluster of small, violet-scaled Takki dug large chunks of rotted flesh from under the prince's huge, uncannily iridescent oblong scales. Daviin peered hard, but he could not distinguish the Huouyt from the others, neither by looks nor mannerisms. The prince grunted in his sleep, kicking one of his stubby, ebony-taloned feet. The Takki near his feet quickly found somewhere else to be.

"Which is Jer'ait?" Daviin whispered, pulling back into the tunnel.

"*Does it matter?*" the Grekkon said. "*As long as he holds up his end, we don't need to know.*"

It was true. Daviin took another look at the scene below, fixing it in his mind, then wrapped the last rod and a half of his body around the pillar of dirt the Grekkon had created for him by making a circular tunnel. Once he was secure, he once more raised his energy level and slowly began lowering himself into the deep den, head-first.

As soon as Daviin's snout touched ground, he oriented himself by listening to the prince's breathing. Heading in the opposite direction, he threaded his way across the floor until he reached the Human's leg. He grabbed it with one hand, careful not to move it as he did so. He closed a fist around the Ooreiki's meaty black arm, then moved forward and took the Baga gently in his mouth.

Behind him, the prince snorted and lunged to his feet with a roar. A Dhasha moved near the entrance it guarded, padding toward the center of the room. It bumped Daviin's body where it was strung out above the floor. The heir gave a startled grunt.

Daviin lunged up and back, throwing every ounce of muscle into ripping his companions off the floor and pulling them toward the ceiling before the Dhasha realized what it had touched.

The Grekkon's pillar had not been made to withstand such treatment. With a horrible sinking in his gut, Daviin felt it collapse under the pressure of his coils. The full weight of his upper half and his burden came to bear on his lower half, and Daviin felt himself sliding. He dropped his companions and scrambled for purchase, but it was too late.

He fell.

• • •

Jer'ait watched his companions get into position and kept the Dhasha prince between himself and the Jreet, away from the direction he knew the Dhasha would lunge when it realized what was happening. Carefully, he selected a poison and extruded it into the claws of his left hand, continuing to scratch with his right. The prince grunted and shifted, but did not complain again. He was close to sleep.

When Jer'ait saw the Human's leg move slightly, he knew it was time. He pushed his left hand under the second layer of scales and slammed the claws into the Dhasha's flesh as deeply as they would go.

It was a contact-based chemical, one that killed through the skin, the mouth, the eyes, the nose, and the ears—any surface or orifice that could absorb it. Since the Dhasha's skin was thicker than most creatures, the poison would be slower to take effect, but the result would be the same. The prince would die.

The prince snorted and twitched, opening its eyes. "Slave, are you incompetent? My skin burns where you—"

The prince was on his feet in a second, bowling the other Takki over. "You're the Huouyt!" he snarled, raising a paw to destroy him.

Behind him, the ceiling collapsed.

Jer'ait scrabbled out of the way as the Dhasha turned to look, then felt his gut churn at the sight that unfolded.

The Jreet had fallen into the pit.

Like an old spaceship engine winding up for takeoff, the Jreet appeared as a massive red blur, screamed its *shee-whomph* battlecry, and wrapped itself around the closest Dhasha, heedless of the one behind it. The prince took two steps toward the Jreet and stumbled, the poison beginning to take hold.

Roaring, the prince turned back on Jer'ait, but he found only stone. Jer'ait had moved around behind the prince and was angling toward the Dhasha the Jreet had not yet seen. The second Dhasha was just beginning to get a grasp of the situation when Jer'ait slammed into it from the side, catching its attention for the moment it took to keep it from shredding the Jreet.

Behind him, the prince slumped to the ground.

The Dhasha Jer'ait had attacked saw this, lowered its cold emerald eyes on Jer'ait, and casually batted him aside, its black talons sinking in deep.

Jer'ait spun away, feeling like half his body had been ripped away. When he managed to sit up, he was amazed that he was still conscious. His torso hung in shreds. Dimly, he realized the Jreet now had both Dhasha wrapped in his body, though the effort had stretched him to the limit, giving him no space to free his tek or use his hands for anything but gripping the first Dhasha's horns and keeping its jaws from finding purchase on his coiled scarlet body.

Jer'ait stumbled to his feet, leaking alarming amounts of blue fluid from his midsection. He tried to perform a localized pattern shift and managed to staunch some of the flow, but the wounds were too grievous. He was quickly losing consciousness. If he didn't find water to negate his shift, he was going to die.

On the other side of the room, near the females, a pool of water lay in a deep trough, a spring that the Takki had diverted for their master's use. It was enough to submerge himself...enough to save his life. Jer'ait glanced at it, then looked back at the Jreet.

In a crush of straining muscle and tearing earth, the Jreet was losing his grip on the first Dhasha, made all the worse by the fact he had been forced to free the creature of half its coils when the second one lunged at him. Already, one of the escaping Dhasha's talons had raked the Jreet along his back, opening a huge rent in the scarlet hide that exposed three digs of bluish muscle to air.

If the Jreet didn't get help soon, he was going to be ripped apart.

Jer'ait staggered toward the Jreet, then fell, his world rapidly losing color. He had enough poison remaining on his Takki-patterned claws to kill another Dhasha, but he couldn't force his muscles to work. He could only lay there, head cocked sideways on the cold stone, and watch as the Jreet rapidly lost the fight.

A dark brown, insectoid shape skittered across the floor and paused in front of the escaping Dhasha. As Jer'ait watched, motionless, the shape switched directions and pressed its bulbous rear into the Dhasha's head.

The Dhasha went limp.

The Grekkon skittered away, leaving the Jreet to deal with the last one. Jer'ait felt something hard grab his wrist and drag him across the floor, away from the fight. Then he was in a tunnel with perfect sides, sliding smoothly along a floor that gave no resistance, leaving a trail of blue Takki blood behind him.

Jer'ait realized he'd been shoved into a niche with three other bodies before he lost consciousness.

• • •

Daviin felt his muscles tearing as he twisted around the Dhasha, constricting its midriff with every ounce of strength he still possessed.

He felt something pop under the pressure. At first, he thought it had been one of his segments severing, but then he realized the Dhasha had gone suddenly stiff, its muscles like rock under his coils.

He eased off some of the pressure and raised his head to look.

The Dhasha's internal organs were weeping from its mouth, oozing over its teeth and onto the ground. The Dhasha had stopped fighting.

"Come," a tinny voice said behind him. The Grekkon was half-in, half-out of a hole in the wall, motioning at him with a spearlike appendage. "Can't you hear them coming for us?"

Daviin opened his senses past the battle-frenzy and heard the distant rumbling as Dhasha charged down the main shaft toward them.

Daviin raised his energy level and unwound from his victim. Across the room, the Grekkon disappeared back into its hole. Daviin hadn't fully uncoiled by the time the other Dhasha arrived, but his exit nonetheless went unnoticed—the Dhasha congregated around the prince's corpse in mute horror, his two heirs forgotten.

Somehow, Daviin made it up the shaft and to the point where the Grekkon had stashed his companions.

"*This shaft leads to the surface,*" the Grekkon said. "*Take the Ooreiki and the Huouyt with you.*"

Daviin blinked at the bodies, barely able to hold himself upright. "Is the Human alive?"

"Barely. But you take the heavier two first. If you don't come back for the Human and the Baga, I'll bring them myself."

Joe survived. Daviin felt a rush of relief—and regret. *Sentinel to a slave.* He shook off the thought. "What are you doing?"

"*I go to kill the final heir and guard our retreat.*"

Daviin did not think he could get himself to the surface, much less make two trips dragging bodies along with him, but he grabbed the two heaviest of his companions nonetheless. Then, closing his eyes, he forced his torn and shredded muscles to move himself onward.

Somehow, he reached the surface, though Daviin had no sense of how long it had taken. It seemed like ages—and only seconds. He dropped the Huouyt and the Ooreiki at the exit to the shaft and went back for the other two. He returned to the surface and dropped the Human and the Baga to the ground.

When Daviin released him, Joe groaned. "Five," he mumbled. "Only five."

Hearing the sound, Daviin's instincts as a Sentinel made him flinch. He remembered his relief, earlier, when he had thought the Human was dead and had therefore spared his family the shame of knowing one of their princes had sworn himself to a slave. Guilt hit Daviin like a punch to the tek. *I'm his* Sentinel, Daviin thought, appalled. And yet, he was also a Voran heir. Daviin fisted his hands, once more finding his honor at war.

Then he realized he was poised over his ward like a moron, bleeding to death in enemy territory, debating over whether or not his ward was a slave.

I can deal with this later.

Daviin began coiling atop his ward, giving him the protection of his body should enemies find them, since he knew he would soon be useless to stop them.

Before he had finished half his coils, Daviin's world closed to a narrow black point and he slid to the ground, spent. He had a vague sense of movement nearby and then flinched instinctively as something began tugging Joe's body from under his coils, but he lost consciousness before he could stop it.

17

THE JREET-DOCTOR

"**P**lanetary Ops will experience a bout of panic once the numbers come back. They'll lobby for the use of an *ekhta*, but as last time, Koliinaati politicians will clamor to stake a claim on Neskfaat once the Dhasha are removed and will veto the Ground Corps' initiative on the grounds that Neskfaat is too important a resource to destroy. Their reasoning will be that they only lost two and a half million groundteams. They'll get a Bajna to crunch the numbers and will suggest Planetary Ops can lose up to three and a half billion before the toll will force them to increase the Draft. They'll actually look at Neskfaat as an opportunity to whittle down the overdraft, which has been causing shortages in the Outer Line."

"So what can I expect the Ground Force to do?" Rri'jan asked.

"Send in another wave. They have no other choice. The Regency has tied their hands. However, the second wave will come after we have completed our business on Neskfaat. Between now and then, Planetary Ops will use the two thousand surviving teams until there's nothing left."

"They won't use them to train new waves?"

"No. Planetary Ops will study the group combinations and attempt to duplicate them, somewhat correctly believing their successes were due to statistics and not individual talent. They'll send them back again and again to determine the best statistical combination before they send in their larger second wave of soldiers. Basically, they will be doing exactly what we are doing. They will be analyzing how long it takes them to die in order to create the proper combinations needed to root out the one hundred and twelve princes that survived the first attack."

"Then we must intervene before they kill our teams off," Rri'jan cried. Forgotten wasn't sure which was more amusing—the fact that Rri'jan had grown so attached to the plan, or the fact that he didn't believe Forgotten had already taken that into account.

"It will require no intervention on our part," Forgotten assured his visitor. "After the sixth attack, only two teams will survive. Planetary Ops will have their statistics by then, and we will have our team."

"Just two?" Rri'jan looked startled. "Twelve soldiers out of two million groundteams will survive the first wave?"

"Two and a half million."

"So these teams that survive the sixth assault…they're the ones we want?"

"No. They're only the candidates. We have a bigger test in store for them, once they've survived to that stage."

"What test?"

"We'll discuss that when we come to it. Be satisfied to know that one of the two groups will fail, leaving us with the one we will send against Mekkval."

Rri'jan did not seem displeased with the idea. Forgotten found the Huouyt's lack of vision irritating.

"I want you to know, Rri'jan, that your brother has a very high chance of surviving to our final test. His team is one of my two chosen candidates. If you sabotage his success in any way, you will be sabotaging your seat on the Tribunal.

Rri'jan's electric eyes gave him a flat, psychotic stare. "I am not stupid, Geuji."

Oh, but you are. "This particular group has enough chances of disintegrating as it is. Jer'ait will already receive enough complications from the other Huouyt to test his limits and possibly make a misstep that will mean his death. The Jreet will require me to train a surgeon to keep his romps with the Dhasha from being his last, and will be difficult to control when he realizes the reigning Welu heir is with him on Jeelsiht. Sooner or later, the Human is going to reawaken a deep-rooted phobia Congressional physicians failed to bury in his recruit training on Kophat. The Baga will be caught spying on top-secret meetings and will face execution. The Ooreiki will eventually begin to question his tunnel-instinct under the constant stress, and the Grekkon may or may not be able to maintain his excretion rate for six attacks in a row."

The Huouyt peered at him narrowly. "You have this all planned already, do you?"

"Yes," Forgotten said. "Further complicating things is that the Trith will become involved sooner or later. Until now, they have been satisfied with approaching my agents, trying to guide my actions through their input. Now, with the plans I am making, the Trith will not be content to watch as their future disintegrates before their eyes. They despise vortexes. They will be insidious, attempting to steer the future back on their chosen track by foiling my plans and foretelling my death."

Rri'jan gave him a calculating look, one that verged on apprecia-tion. "So you truly can't be read by the Trith?"

Forgotten felt a pang of regret. Of loneliness. "It is why the Trith betrayed the Geuji at Uvuai," he replied. "Our futures are incompre-hensible to them. Imagine an entire planet of possibilities combined into one mind. If every creature in existence only has one choice to make in their lives that the Trith cannot foresee, I have billions of them, each independent of the next."

"The Trith betrayed your species to Congress because you *unnerve* them?"

"We render them powerless," Forgotten replied. "The moment Congress found us and gave us ships and mobility, the Trith have been trying to get rid of us. Aliphei used us long enough to create the tech-nologies he wanted, then, with the Trith's help, locked us away."

"Ah. Interesting." The Huouyt cocked his cylindrical head at him. "I always wondered how they caught you. I suppose it would have been much more difficult to subdue the Geuji without the Trith's help."

It would have been impossible, Forgotten thought bitterly. For that, alone, the Trith deserved to die, the entire species eradicated. Instead of dwelling on things he couldn't yet change, however, Forgotten said, "What will be even more interesting to me is to see what they do when they realize I've chosen another vortex to assist me in this."

"Zero."

"Yes."

Rri'jan's eyes narrowed and tapped the com unit in his hand. "You know, he was prophesized to help Na'leen and refused, many turns ago on Kophat. He's why I am here with you today."

"Na'leen's revolt was doomed to fail," Forgotten replied. "Even if Na'leen had survived, Zero would not have tipped the scales either way. He was just a recruit. Your malice should be laid at the feet of the Trith, who painstakingly guided that little blunder into being because it nudged their chosen future back onto a course they approved of."

"Still, it'd please me greatly if he died along the way."

"No doubt."

Rri'jan held up the com unit he had used to give the order to kill Forgotten's brethren. Jiggling it, he said, "Do I need to use this again, Forgotten?"

Forgotten suppressed a rush of irritation at the Huouyt's threats. "No. I understand your grudge for the Human. However unfounded."

"He was prophesized to lead the Huouyt to independence."

"Not at all," Forgotten said. "The Trith left the prophecy they gave to Na'leen about Zero intentionally vague. They never gave a time period, nor a method. Nor, if you examine it carefully, does it specifically say he will lead the *Huouyt* to independence, just that he will shatter Congress."

Rri'jan immediately grew alert. "Then it has truth to it?"

"Trith always tell the truth in their prophecies. If they didn't, they would change the future, and would therefore destroy themselves." Forgotten paused, allowing the Huouyt to contemplate that. "However, because Zero is a vortex, any claims they make on his future are simply guesses, images cobbled together into a picture of what they would *like* for him to do."

"So if he won't be their puppet, why haven't they killed him?" Rri'jan demanded.

"They tried. As they've done with me, they contacted his companions. They convinced one of them she needed to kill him, and the other hates him to this day. As soon as they realize I've enlisted his help, they'll make another attempt. That's why it's of the utmost importance you do not interfere with Jer'ait. His group is already poised to splinter at the slightest provocation. It has the most potential, but at the same time, the most discord. Even the slightest interference on your part will tip the balance and ruin our plans."

"Jer'ait will not die by my hand, Forgotten."

"How many times have you tried to have him assassinated, Rri'jan? Six? You must be pleased to know his chances of surviving this endeavor are infinitesimal."

"It pleases me greatly."

Forgotten was disgusted with the Huouyt's single-mindedness. "I want your oath you'll not interfere with your brother. If I don't get it, my involvement ends here."

Rri'jan made a disgusted motion with his free hand. "Why should I care what the filth does, as long as it gets me my position?"

Immediately, Forgotten said, "Because it burns you to know you might owe your Tribunal seat to the deformed sibling who bested you at everything you've ever done except looking pretty."

The Huouyt's body tensed with anger, then he said, "I do not care who helps me get the seat. If Jer'ait survives, I'll simply kill him afterwards."

Forgotten found himself liking the Huouyt less and less, but the struggles between Huouyt royalty were not on his agenda. At least Rri'jan's greed was enough to keep him from meddling.

"If you already know which two groups will survive, I don't understand why we can't just select the team of your choice and send them against Mekkval tomorrow."

"We can't send them against Mekkval until they've veteraned themselves on Neskfaat. Besides, I don't know. I've guessed."

"Your guesses are as good as a Trith's predictions, Geuji."

"Still. They are just guesses."

"I dislike waiting," Rri'jan said, tapping the com unit again with a cilia-covered tentacle, obviously considering whether another display of power was necessary, "and your plans grow more time-intensive with every twist."

"I've told you before," Forgotten said. "From beginning to end, it will only take one turn. If you cannot wait that long, then you are not suited for the Tribunal."

"I can wait," Rri'jan said coldly. "But if you don't produce, your life is forfeit."

Forgotten laughed and the Huouyt's white-blue eyes sharpened.

"You do not believe me?"

"Rri'jan, if this fails, you will never find me again. If we meet, it will be because I've sought you out, not the other way around."

"I found you once, Geuji."

"Because I wanted you to. I've been waiting for you to make me this offer ever since Na'leen died on Kophat. Oh, and you can stop making an imbecile out of yourself by threatening me with that com unit. I scrambled it the moment it came aboard my ship and your messages go nowhere. The confirmations you received were my own words, disguised from samples I maintain on over two and a half trillion different individuals in this sector of space alone. In case you don't believe me, believe this: Had you really killed a member of my family, you would be back on your flagship right now, and I would be sending out a signal to fry onboard computers on all nearby ships and annihilating your escort down to the last quivering Ueshi mechanic. Then I would seek out every major Ze'laa holding and heir and annihilate them, as well. *When* I came to kill you, you would be impoverished and enslaved for your family's debts, probably to a Dhasha. Mekkval generally has a soft spot for rehabilitation cases, and would probably buy your contract and have your zora removed in order to help you properly serve penance, probably with the sentimental conviction that he might be able to, over a few hundred turns, teach one of your kind to have a conscience. Don't test me, Rri'jan. You have no idea who you are dealing with."

For once, the Huouyt's only response was silence.

• • •

Joe opened his eyes to the biggest headache of his life. It pounded his skull like a Dhasha-powered sledgehammer, raking the backs of his eyeballs, drawing streaks of agony just under his scalp, making his head burn like it was about to catch fire.

He needed a drink.

Joe sat up, shaking, his hand automatically reaching into his vest and retrieving his father's knife for its comforting feel between his fingers as he tried to steady himself. His entire body felt sweaty, feverish. His muscles felt limp and strained at the same time, leaving him on the verge of exhaustion.

Nearby, a bluish shape lunged up and hurried from the room. Joe peered after it. As his vision focused, he realized the blackness of the place was not a Dhasha tunnel, but the black-on-black of a Congie operating chamber.

"What...?"

Speaking hurt. Joe groaned and held his head as he tried to figure out what the hell had happened to him. The horrible feeling of lying helpless, crushed by a thousand lobes of muscle as the Dhasha prince sank its claws into his lungs still burned like acid in his mind, seeming more vivid than the black room around him.

Joe wasn't sentimental enough to think he was dead. He was, however, confused. Someone had penetrated the deep den and gotten him out alive. Who the hell could even *do* that?

Then he knew. Daviin.

"Commander Zero?" A woman stepped into the room, looking pale and lovely despite the triangular grouping of four circles inside an eight-pointed star that symbolized a Prime Overseer. Her nametag read Daiyu Hong. Though she, like the rest of the Force, had no hair to disrupt her biosuit, her eyes were narrow and a deep, luxurious brown. He guessed she was Chinese.

"Did the Jreet live?"

"Yes, Prime Commander. He's in surgery as we speak."

Though he hated it when superior officers spoke to him like they were addressing a deity, Joe felt a stab of relief. "The others?"

"They all survived."

They survived. *All* of them. Joe could only manage, "How?"

"We're not sure." She hesitated, looking puzzled and anxious. The look in her eyes clearly said, *I was hoping you could tell me.* Instead of questions, though, she said, "The Jreet's still in surgery and the Grekkon's not talking."

"What about the Huouyt?"

"He's undergoing water therapy. His last pattern almost killed him. The Huouyt medical team wants him to stay submerged for another day or two while his body recovers."

"Huh." Joe groaned and rubbed his temple with one folded end of his knife. "The Baga lived, too?"

The woman made a face. "Yes, but as soon as he was restored, he disappeared." She looked particularly agitated at that. "Gave him a direct order to be ready for a debriefing this afternoon and he just vanished. We're still looking for him."

"He's probably doing reconnaissance."

The woman's bald face wrinkled in worry. She had pretty eyes, Joe thought. Brown, like his, but softer. Softly, she said, "You think the Baga went back to Neskfaat?"

Joe grunted. "He's around here somewhere. What about the prince?"

"The prince and his five oldest heirs are confirmed dead. We buried the rest of them."

Looking up sharply, Joe said, "We got all the princes, then?"

"We got twenty-two of them."

Joe closed his eyes. He knew there were more than twenty-two. "How many are left?"

"A hundred and twelve, as far as we can tell."

"Ghosts." Joe took a deep breath. "How many people we lose?"

"It's looking like two and a half million teams."

Joe swiveled to stare at Commander Daiyu, unsure he had heard correctly. "That's all we took in."

"Two thousand groundteams survived. Twelve thousand soldiers."

Joe felt something strain in his chest. "That's *all?*"

"Your team, on the other hand, was quite successful," Daiyu said. "Even without help, you took out the top six Dhasha of the den you were assigned. We replayed your unit recordings and it looks as if the Jreet killed three on his own, the Huouyt killed the prince, and the Grekkon killed two more, one with the Jreet's assistance."

Joe frowned as he listened to the litany. "The Grekkon killed one? Alone?"

"Increased his extrusion rate and dropped down on him from above. Fell straight through him."

"Damn."

Joe felt the woman's eyes wander over his body and he gave her a chance to look.

The Overseer cleared her throat. "Commander, we were hoping you could give us some idea of how you made your group work together. What did you do to make them function as a unit? We've had psychologists looking at your file, working on a solution, but I was hoping I could hear it from you."

Joe squeezed his eyes shut and wished he had a drink. Carefully, he put his dad's knife away. "Overseer…" he peered again at her uniform, "Daiyu. You need to go back and look at my file again. Out of anyone on that team, I did the least. They could have done just as well if I'd stayed behind."

Daiyu looked taken aback. "You're saying the Human counterpart means nothing?"

"Yeah."

She blinked at him. "But that's not possible."

Joe peered at her tiredly. More bureaucratic crap, Overseers trying to take more credit than their species deserved. "And why's that?" he asked, tiredly.

"Because of the two thousand teams that survived, a quarter of them were led by Humans."

• • •

Joe went to see Jer'ait first. The Huouyt Overseer of that sector had personally taken charge of his recovery, however, and six armed guards turned Joe away at the door.

"I don't give a bag of soot if it's off limits," Joe snarled, standing two good arms'-distance from the poison-loving bastards. "I'm his Prime."

The six Huouyt at the door regarded him like condescending, electric-eyed statues. "Ko-Jer'ait Ze'laa vehn Morinth is still unconscious," one of them said with complete disdain.

"Bullshit. He's awake. I want to talk to him."

"You'll talk to him later," the Huouyt replied, musical voice dripping with contempt. "The Overseer is speaking with him now."

Joe narrowed his eyes at the casual way the Battlemaster had lied to him. "I want someone to come get me as soon as the Overseer is done with him," Joe said.

"Of course."

Joe knew the Huouyt had no intention of doing so.

Discouraged and frustrated, Joe sought out the Jreet.

Unlike the other grounders to have survived the attack, Daviin did not have an honor guard. In fact, since the Jreet did not partake in the Draft, he did not even have an Overseer to congratulate him on his survival. Daviin was alone in his surgery room, the door unlocked, not a single guard posted outside.

Joe stepped inside and shut the door softly behind him. Then he whistled at what he saw.

The Jreet's body was laid out on his back in a switchback fashion, cream-colored belly facing the ceiling. Hand-sized patches of scales had been shaved completely off, leaving the bluish skin visible underneath.

The fascinating thing was that the Jreet had been restrained in that position, painful-looking clamps squeezing his flesh and securing him to the floor. The doctors had paid special attention to his upper body. Three heavy-duty titanium bands secured a metal plate over his tek. His enormous arms were each strapped down in two places. The Jreet had been muzzled, his head pinned to the ground.

Joe noticed the Jreet's small golden eyes following him as he entered. He went over to Daviin's head and tugged at the muzzle. It had been locked in place utilizing technology used to restrain kree-nit, requiring a special key. Grunting, Joe got up, went over to the operating table, and found a circular saw amongst the other tools. He returned to the Jreet's head and used the saw to cut through the straps holding his muzzle.

"So," Joe said, lowering the saw and tugging the restraint from the Jreet's head, "I take it you were a little unreasonable?"

Daviin glared at him.

"Seriously," Joe said, gesturing at the bands holding him to the floor. "Is all this really necessary?"

"The managing doctor was a tekless Ueshi coward. I swore to my ancestors' souls if he removed my scales, I'd kill him and seek out his spawn to eliminate his sniveling, furgish line."

"You must have been very convincing." Joe motioned at the restraints with the saw.

Daviin's yellow eyes could have belonged to an angry raptor.

"Why haven't they let you out yet?" Joe asked, gesturing at the scarred patches of skin. "You look healed."

"They have the courage of farmed Takki," Daviin snarled.

"You mean you threatened them."

"I told them the truth."

"Which was?"

Daviin raised his voice indignantly. "As soon as I get out of here, I'm going to hunt down every coward who was in the room when they drugged me and make them dance on my tek before I break every bone in their feeble little bodies."

"Huh."

Joe got up and replaced the saw on the table. Then he walked to the door.

"Where are you going?!" Daviin cried behind him.

Joe turned back and shrugged. "I'll let you sort it out with them. I'm not gonna be responsible for the deaths of an entire medic team."

"You must free me!" Daviin snapped. "The fools plan to send me home!"

Joe turned folded his arms, curious, now. "They do? Why?"

"I told you!" Daviin snapped, his muscles constricting against the restraints, for a moment making the straps look as if they would fail before the Jreet relaxed again in frustration. "The doctor was a tekless Ueshi who is terrified of Jreet. I swore an oath to kill him and all his sniveling assistants and all of their worthless spawn."

"And you wonder why they left you there."

"Curse you to the hells, Human!" Daviin snarled. "A Jreet warrior does not need to have his scales removed for 'sanitary reasons.' They were being unreasonable!"

"And you intend to hunt them down for attempting to spare you an infection later."

Daviin hesitated. "I gave my word."

"You were drugged," Joe said. "Unaware of what you were doing."

"I was *fully* aware of what I was doing!" Daviin snapped. "Cowards like that should be executed at birth lest their genes infect the rest of society!"

Joe uncrossed his arms and turned to leave.

"But the drugs might have distorted my perceptions," Daviin added meekly.

Joe grinned, then wiped it off his face before he turned back to face the Jreet. Deadpan, he said, "But you swore an oath. Now you *have* to kill them."

"I was intoxicated," Daviin snapped. "I wasn't in my right mind."

"But a Jreet's honor is his soul."

"Let me worry about my honor, miserable Human wretch."

"I don't know…" Joe gave the titanium bands a dubious look. "This might be considered an accessory to murder."

"*I'm not going to kill the tekless Ueshi worm!*" Daviin roared, straining against the restraints. The fist-sized bolts driven into the ebony floor groaned, but held.

"Hmm," Joe said, pausing to consider. "What about his assistants? I'm not a doctor, but I'm pretty sure it's the assistants that do the shaving. The doctor just does the cutting."

"They," Daviin gritted, "Are safe. From me."

Joe went to the wall and began going through the Jreet's chart.

"What are you doing?"

Scrolling through the documents, Joe said, "I'm checking to see if you've been medicated within the last few hours."

"I'm not drugged!"

Joe replaced the chart and squatted down in front of the Jreet. "So this is your oath?" He watched the Jreet, utterly serious, now. "I know Jreet put a lot of stock in their word, and I'd rather let them send you back to Vora than see you slaughter a bunch of guys who were just trying to help."

"I won't kill them, Human," Daviin muttered, sounding miserable. "I swear it."

Since he didn't have the key, Joe went back to the table and retrieved the saw. He started at the Jreet's upper body, sawing through the clamps one by one. He had to change the blade three times before he reached the Jreet's arms and tek.

"Ghosts of the Mothers," Joe whistled. "These guys weren't messing around."

"They're tekless Cu'it slaves," Daviin snarled, straining.

"Bones," Joe muttered. He lowered the saw and stood.

"What are you doing?" The Jreet gave him an anxious glance.

"I ran out of blades," Joe said, going to the cupboard and searching for a replacement.

As he was digging through the shelves, the door opened and a startled Ueshi in Congie doctor garb burst in. He was surrounded by six Ooreiki in biosuits carrying full tunnel-crawl weaponry. As soon as they saw the Jreet sitting up in its restraints, the titanium plate no longer secured over its tek, they spread out and dropped into crouches, their rifles aimed at Daviin's body.

Daviin responded by blinking out of existence.

"Don't you dare fucking fire goddamn it!" Joe snapped, jumping in front of them. The Ooreiki did not lower their rifles. Their pupils were wide as they stared at the place where Daviin had vanished, their *sudah* whipping frenzies in their necks. They thought they were going to die. It would have been comical, had Joe not thought they would start spraying the room with plasma at any second.

"You," Joe said, jabbing a finger at the tiny Ueshi huddled behind the Ooreiki grounders. "You are the doctor?"

"Yes," the cerulean-skinned physician whispered. He was trembling, his aquamarine headcrest rippling as his binocular blue eyes stared at the place where the Jreet had disappeared.

"Give me the key," Joe snapped.

That got the doctor's attention. "Are you insane? He swore to *kill* me."

"He's not gonna kill you," Joe said. He strode up, caught the black circular chip hanging from a chain around the doctor's neck and yanked it free. Then he turned back to Daviin.

"I can't let you do that," the Ueshi said. "I'm a Jreet Specialist, operated on Sentinels at Koliinaat for thirty turns. That Jreet is a rogue, probably a criminal who survived to this age by avoiding others of his kind. He has no groundteam, no reason to be on Jeelsiht. The last ground leader foolish enough to take him into his team kicked him out and refused to take him back. He's violent, deranged, uncontrollable—a danger to everyone around him. The only reason he's still alive is the bureaucrats refused to let us kill him. He threatened to poison me and my medical team innumerable times, and since Congress won't let us kill him, our only option is to administer pacifying drugs until they can arrange a safe way to transport him." The Ueshi held up an injection syringe and tapped it.

Joe turned back and frowned at the Ueshi. "You *are* a Takki slave-soul, aren't you?"

The Ueshi straightened. "I'm a Specialist of the Medical Corps. Who are you?" He glanced Joe up and down. "For that matter, *what* are you?"

Joe realized the physicians had dressed him in unranked hospital garb after removing his biosuit. He blinked. It was a wonder they hadn't shot him already.

"I'm the furg that kicked the Jreet off my groundteam."

The Ueshi peered at him. "What are you doing here?"

The Ueshi hadn't connected the dots, but the Ooreiki had. Slowly, they lowered their rifles, their eyes tearing from the empty air where Daviin was and settling on Joe's face in unabashed awe. Joe blushed and used that moment to walk over to the Jreet.

"Why did you lower your weapons?" the Ueshi demanded. "Stop him!"

Joe swiped the chip over the Jreet's restraints and Daviin flashed back into existence arching twelve digs in the air, his scarlet and cream magnificence spoiled only by the handful of small blue bald patches where his scales had been shaven.

The Ueshi screamed.

Daviin began to slide toward the doctor, ignoring the Ooreiki completely.

Joe held out a hand to the Jreet's cream-colored chest, stopping the huge creature momentarily. "You swore," he said under his breath.

The Jreet flexed his huge ruby fists as he glared at the Ueshi. "I won't kill him."

Joe released his groundmate.

When it was apparent that Joe was not going to stop the Jreet, the Ueshi turned and ran.

Daviin lashed out, lightning-fast, tearing the doctor from the ground and holding him off the ground so that the Ueshi's head-crest trembled against the ceiling.

"You," Daviin said into the blue-green creature's small rubbery face, "never tended Sentinels." Then he dropped the doctor amidst the stunned Ooreiki and pushed through them, to the door.

Joe jogged to keep up. "He didn't?"

Daviin did not answer him.

"He seemed to know his stuff," Joe said, still jogging. "They told me you almost lost half your body."

Daviin glanced back at him, taking a moment to scowl at the Ooreiki who had emerged from the room after them before returning his attention to Joe. "He never tended Sentinels."

"How do you know?"

"Sentinels don't require surgery. They either live or they die."

"Huh." Joe glanced back at the Ooreiki standing outside the room. The Ueshi had not yet emerged. "Wonder where he learned, then."

Daviin twisted back to the hall before them. "Where are we? I've got a sense of direction like a Takki's got courage."

"We're in the war hospital," Joe replied. "I think I could get us out, but I still haven't visited Jer'ait or Galek."

Daviin turned back to him. "The Huouyt survived?"

"Yeah. His sootbag Overseer's got Huouyt stationed six deep at his door, keeping everyone out. Probably a good thing, after the first time he went under, but it's still ridiculous."

The Jreet flexed an arm that dwarfed Joe's body, then glanced down at him. "You wish to see him?"

A smile formed on Joe's face. "I do."

18

THE TROUBLE WITH ONE'S PEERS

"**I** will not retire."

The Overseer's eyes were perfect mirrors as they watched him, making Jer'ait acutely aware of his deformity. "We aren't giving you a choice. You've been out too long, child. You grow too complacent, showing your *natural* body, of all things. You bring shame to your family and you're a danger to all Huouyt."

"They sterilized me. How am I a danger?" Jer'ait managed to keep the bitterness from his voice, but his deformity betrayed him.

The other Huouyt gave him a condescending smile. "We've tolerated you until now, child, as you have always kept yourself hidden in a pattern. But now you brazenly flaunt your weakness in the open. You shame us all. You degrade the Huouyt image as a whole."

"I will not retire."

The Overseer's body tightened, but his eyes remained perfect mirrors. "Then you shall disappear."

Jer'ait sat up, water sloshing around him. "You wouldn't be the first to try."

Overseer Bev'kii gave him a patronizing look, which was ruined somewhat when the Huouyt stepped carefully out of Jer'ait's reach. "You think you are invincible, child, but how long can you survive here without sustenance? I have guards outside. They will not let you leave." He lowered his voice, his words oozing with contempt. "Please. Accept your fate gracefully. For all our sakes."

"I will accept my fate when my remains are returned to Va'ga and laid to rest amongst the heroes of the past."

"That will never be allowed."

"It isn't your decision!" Jer'ait snapped, losing control over his fury. Immediately, he wished he hadn't. Bev'kii radiated smug satisfaction, his perfect eyes utterly flat.

"Sleep well," the Overseer said. "While you can." At that, he turned and left the room.

You furg, Jer'ait thought, slipping back down into his water. *What have you done?*

He'd declared war on his own kind.

Jer'ait had the urge to climb out of his tank and accept Bev'kii's offer before his fate was sealed. He'd committed suicide. Not even the greatest assassin Va'ga had produced could fight them all.

And yet, a thread of anger, a tendril of the great fire that had burned inside him ever since he'd watched Rri'jan receive the crown while he was condemned to death and sterilized before a crowd of millions…that anger that had refused to accept their punishment, that had pushed him to escape and be greater than all of them…that anger kept him from conceding. The stubbornness that had kept him alive where he had no right to be, bludgeoning his way through society by his reputation and fear alone, kept him from opening his mouth.

You furg.

Jer'ait stared at the ceiling, calculating when the end would come, wondering how many souls he would take to the grave with him before he faced the inevitable.

Sometime later, a disturbance outside his room made him sit up. Jer'ait was getting out of his tank when the door burst open and a flailing

Huouyt was thrown inside, skidding several digs on the floor before coming to a stunned halt a half-dig from Jer'ait's bath. Jer'ait was still trying to process this when the Huouyt seemingly rose into the air of his own accord and flew out the door with all the speed of a malfunctioning *haauk*.

Jer'ait grimaced. "I do not need your help, Jreet."

Daviin appeared, his great length taking up much of the floor space in the center of the room. "Help?" The Jreet looked irritated as he peered through the open door at the Huouyt he had thrown. "Those furgs insulted my parentage."

Stepping inside to join them, the Human said, "What is it he's helping you *with*, Huouyt?"

Jer'ait did not trust the shrewd look in the Human's eyes. If he did not already suspect Jer'ait's troubles, he would soon. The last thing he wanted was his pity.

"Go," Jer'ait said. "I'm not finished resting."

"Rest is for the weak," Daviin said. "Come with us. We're getting food."

Jer'ait's system craved sustenance—he'd gone without food for too long. Bev'kii and the other Huouyt had denied him anything but water for two days, and now the need to eat was a dull ache in his *zora*. Still, though, his pride kept him from accepting. He did not need a Jreet to solve his problems for him.

"That wasn't a question," the Jreet said. He lashed out suddenly, grasped Jer'ait by the torso with both enormous arms, and lifted him from the water, sandwiched against the sheath of his tek.

The message was clear. Fight, and things would become unpleasant.

"Put me down, Jreet," Jer'ait muttered. "I'll walk."

Daviin dropped him unceremoniously at the Human's feet.

"You need some clothes?" Joe asked.

"Clothes are for the weak," the Jreet said, giving Jer'ait a push.

Jer'ait swiveled, giving his left hand the pattern of a Jreet's tek. He jammed it into the exposed blue skin of Daviin's side, then yanked it out again, giving the Jreet an even stare. "Push me again, Takki, and next time I will add something interesting. Now get out. I am not done resting."

The Jreet stared down at the wound. It was small, oozing only a few drops of blue liquid. Both of them knew, however, that the Jreet would have been dead had Jer'ait wished it.

To Jer'ait's irritation, the Jreet laughed and clapped an enormous hand on his shoulder. Without regard to the hand still shaped like a tek, the Jreet firmly guided him from the room and out into the hall.

"Food," the Jreet said, "will improve your attitude."

It probably would, at that. Jer'ait re-formed his hand and resigned himself to eating with his groundmates.

"Where are you taking that patient?" Overseer Bev'kii demanded from down the hall. He was flanked by eight more Huouyt, all of them armed.

"We're going to go get some grub," the Human said. "Don't worry. We won't exhaust him."

"That patient is not leaving the premises."

Jer'ait watched the Human's eyes darken, perceptiveness and anger sharpening his features. "This is a hospital, not a brig. If my groundmate wants to share our victory dinner, he will."

Bev'kii stepped forward, until he was almost touching the Human. They were of a same height, though Bev'kii outweighed Joe by thirty lobes. Bev'kii's eyes were flat when he said, "You're the useless Human Prime who spent his time unconscious while his groundteam killed the prince without him."

To Jer'ait's surprise, Joe grinned. "That's me."

"Allow me to make something clear to you, Human," Bev'kii said, "It was *these* two who accomplished that mission. You had nothing to do with it." Bev'kii's face spread in a smug smile. "So don't let the victory get to your head. You didn't deserve it."

The Human said nothing for a long time and Jer'ait could feel the Jreet tense behind him. *Sweet gods,* Jer'ait thought, *He says the word and Daviin will slay them all.* Jer'ait held his breath, ready to follow Daviin's lead, should it be necessary.

"I agree."

For a moment, Jer'ait thought he had not heard correctly. When he turned, however, the Human was simply watching the Overseer.

"I agree on everything but one point. It wasn't just these two. The other three did their jobs just as well."

"But you admit you failed."

Joe laughed. "I spent half the time bleeding internally six digs from our target. Yes, I failed."

Jer'ait stiffened. "Don't let him goad you."

"Yes," Daviin said, swallowing Joe's shoulder with a clawed scarlet hand, "Our food awaits."

"Jer'ait will return to his room," Bev'kii repeated. "That's an order."

"You might want to re-think that order." The Human said it with a good-natured smile, but there was a hard tone to his words.

At that, the Jreet vanished. The unspoken threat of Daviin's action hung in the air like the sharp tang of ozone. No one moved.

For several heartbeats, it looked as if there would be blood.

"Very well," Bev'kii said softly. "I will see you again, Jer'ait, when you do not have a Jreet to protect you."

"Protect him from what?" Joe said. *Damn* the meddling Human.

Bev'kii cocked his head at Joe, his mirror-perfect eyes showing nothing. "Jer'ait is to retire. The Huouyt Corps Director commands it. We will be outfitting your groundteam with another Huouyt, one more suitable to the task. I have a meeting with your Overseer in two hours. We'll inform you of his replacement."

"Go ahead," Joe said. "But I'm crawling the tunnels with whoever I damn well please."

Bev'kii twitched, showing his first hint of irritation. "I don't believe you understand the scope of this situation, Human. If Jer'ait does not leave for Morinth by tomorrow, he will—"

"Food," Jer'ait said. "This prattle bores me." He turned, trying to draw the Human with him.

Joe did not budge, his eyes never leaving Bev'kii's. "He'll what?"

"He'll face his peers." Bev'kii bowed slightly, then departed.

Jer'ait did not like the thoughtful look the Human had as he watched them go.

The Jreet found the restaurant for them, happily dragging them inside when he found out it served the disgusting fleshy beasts called *melaa* at half price.

"They were obviously trying to lure you in here," Jer'ait said disgustedly as they were seated. "What other creature in the universe has the stomach to eat a *melaa?*" Even as he said it, the Ueshi running the restaurant were not-so-discreetly taking photographs and vidclips of the enormous Jreet coiled upon their floor.

Daviin did not seem to notice. He was drooling, eying the live pictures of the three different *melaa* the restaurant housed in their back rooms. He pointed one of them out to the Ueshi proprietor, who immediately bowed its slim blue-green body and scurried away.

"What the hell does that mean, 'face his peers'?" Joe asked, once their servers had taken their order. "What peers?"

Jer'ait winced, hoping until that point that the Human had forgotten. "It means I'll have to deal with the consequences of my actions."

"He means they'll come to kill him."

Jer'ait could have killed Daviin for interfering. "Keep your assumptions to yourself, Jreet."

"Am I wrong?" Daviin challenged. When Jer'ait did not respond, he said, "Your kind is like mine—we do not accept failure. To a Huouyt, deformity is failure, regardless of your talents. Frankly, I am surprised they haven't tried to kill you before this."

"They have," Jer'ait said.

The other two watched him in silence. Jer'ait sensed understanding, and possibly even pity, making the shame within him burn all that more. He studied a scratch in the tabletop.

"We came here to eat," the Jreet said finally. "Not prattle on about Huouyt politics."

For once, Jer'ait could have blessed the Jreet's scaly hide.

Joe said nothing, watching him in silence as the servers brought their meals and placed them in front of them—orange nutrient wafers for Jer'ait, a reddish mass atop a pile of what appeared to be worms for the Human, and a large, dead *melaa* for the Jreet. It was still bleeding from its blubbery throat.

As Daviin enthusiastically grasped the corpse in both hands and ripped away a leg with his jaws, Jer'ait glanced down at his own food. One thing he enjoyed about taking the pattern of another species was his ability to eat solid food. He was grimacing at the gelatinous orange wafers when the Human leaned forward.

"Are you trying to tell me your own Overseer just threatened to kill you?"

Jer'ait suddenly lost the remnants of his appetite. "Leave it alone, Human."

"No," Joe said. "Answer me."

Anger licked at Jer'ait's insides like fire. "I'll deal with it."

"How?" The Human fixed him with a cold brown stare.

"It is none of your concern, Human."

"Is that what you think?"

"Yes." Before the Human could continue on that train of thought, he said, "Why'd you allow Bev'kii to goad you? What good did it do?"

The Human's hard brown eyes told him he knew Jer'ait was deflecting the issue. Nonetheless, he said, "No one goaded me. I acknowledged a fact. In my old teams, I was always the best, the one who got the kills and received the honors. I was the hot shit. I was the one going places. Here, I'm always gonna be sixth fiddle."

Daviin dropped a large bone on the table servers had provided for the purpose and wiped his bloody muzzle. "What's a fiddle?"

"You know what he means." Jer'ait glanced at his nutrient wafers. He'd never eaten around others before, at least not since his training in Va'ga. There were too many risks involved. He glanced at his companions to assure himself they were not watching him. Still, he could only stare at his food, fighting humiliation at the burning need to eat.

"I do," the Jreet confirmed. "But I would like to know what this fiddle is. It must be a stupid thing, indeed, for him to make such a furgish statement."

"Furgish?" Joe said. "Beside a Huouyt or a Jreet, I'm just a waste of space."

"We survived, furg," the Jreet growled. "There were other teams with Huouyt and Jreet and no Human and they failed. This one survived."

"I was out cold."

Daviin made an irritated rumbling sound in his throat. "Two thousand teams made it out of the tunnels alive, Joe. A quarter of them were led by Humans. Do you not see a pattern?"

"There is no pattern," Joe said, locking gazes with the Jreet.

Jer'ait could not hold back his surprise. "*Only* two thousand?"

His groundmates broke their stare to glance at him. "No one told you?"

"No," Jer'ait whispered. The numbers were staggering. The Ground Force had lost millions.

Daviin snorted. "They told me, and I was strapped to the floor." He clapped a huge scarlet hand against Joe's back and said, "The Humans won the day."

"The Jreet appreciate a winner," Joe muttered. "But unfortunately, your congratulations are mislaid. I did nothing."

"Four Jreet warriors died in the tunnels that day," Daviin said. "And almost twenty thousand Huouyt. Every Human that went in came out alive."

Joe laughed. "That's a lie."

"Jreet don't lie."

The Human's smile faltered. "How many went in?"

"A little over five hundred."

Joe only stared at him.

Daviin went back to his carcass, his point made.

"How do you know?" Joe looked at a loss, now.

"The Ueshi used it to distract me while they drugged me."

Jer'ait tore his eyes from his uneaten wafers and glanced at the Jreet. "I was under the impression Jreet didn't need to be drugged."

For a long moment, Joe did not reply, and the Jreet did not enlighten him. Eventually, however, Joe shook himself and grinned. "They did this time. You want to tell the story, Daviin, or should I?"

Daviin made a sour face and began tearing into his carcass with more vigor. He ripped a good-sized limb from the creature and loudly cracked its bones between his jaws. It was a less-than-subtle threat, one the Human missed entirely.

Turning to Jer'ait, Joe said, "He scared the crap out of this little slavesoul Ueshi doctor, told him he'd hunt him down and kill him and all his descendants if he shaved his scales. They drugged him, then stapled him to the floor, then shaved whatever they wanted. Daviin swore to kill every coward in the room, make them dance on his tek before he crushed their bodies and went off to hunt down their kin... you know, typical Jreet stuff. Doctor didn't take it too well. Was gonna have him deported."

"Strange," Jer'ait said, glancing at the small bare patches on the Jreet's hide. "I was under the assumption Jreet didn't have doctors."

"We don't," Daviin growled. He ripped off a last bleeding chunk of meat and swallowed it whole. Then he slammed the shattered bone down on the pile and picked up the carcass again.

"Then how'd he do such a good job of patching you up?" Joe asked, a small frown forming on the Human's face once more.

"Some of the cowards on Welu might keep them on staff," Daviin said, tossing aside another bone. "I know for a fact Vora doesn't."

"Well, from what I hear, you're damn lucky he was here," the Human said.

Daviin grunted.

"Why?" Jer'ait asked.

"They had to replace sixty lobes of flesh," Joe replied. "He was shredded in several places, holding together by less than half his musculature. Had organ damage, stuff not even nanos would fix. And the pressure he put on his wounds tore some of his muscles halfway up his body."

"That bad?" Jer'ait asked, surprised. "How'd he get out?"

"Beats me." The Human went back to eating his red, wormy sauce.

"I *slid* out," Daviin growled, snapping open another melaa bone so he could suck out the juices inside. He disdainfully tossed the remains aside, almost hitting the Ueshi proprietor, who took more pictures. Then he looked at Jer'ait and added, "Carrying the rest of you lazy bastards."

Jer'ait's *breja* rippled with shame.

"But," Daviin set down the carcass and leaned down so that his head hovered near Jer'ait's. "*I* fell from the ceiling, *I* ruined our plans, and *I* almost got you killed. I was repaying what I owed."

Damn the Jreet! Jer'ait once more thought about his eye, how it would be better to have just one that worked than two that gave away his thoughts like a vid tutorial. He once again considered blinding himself.

Across the room, a loud Human voice shouted, "Burn me! That's a big Jreet!"

Daviin flexed the outer ridges of his audial canals in irritation, then twisted his head to face the door to the street.

Three Humans were walking toward them, one strutting with great confidence while the other, smaller ones walked together. It was the shorter of the two who concerned Jer'ait. He recognized her from Earth.

"We were looking for you, man," the taller Human said. He held out his hand for Joe. "Prime Commander Wolfgang Weiss. My men call me White Wolf."

"Wolfgang." Joe had not taken his eyes off of Phoenix. Jer'ait had the idea he wanted to lunge out of his chair, so tightly was he gripping the table. His stare was so dark that even the Jreet noticed.

"Who's this, Joe?" Daviin asked warily.

Phoenix did not even bother to glance up at the Jreet's bulk, keeping her gaudily-modified eyes firmly fixed on Zero. "We need to talk." Beside her, the other female said nothing, though she looked uncomfortable.

"About what?"

After several moments of Joe ignoring it, the male dropped his hand. "About how screwed up things are around here. You were down there. You saw it."

"Or maybe he didn't," Phoenix said, her eyes never leaving Joe's. "After all, he was unconscious for half of it."

Instead of telling them to leave or simply going back to his meal, Joe stood up. To Jer'ait and Daviin, he said, "I'll see you guys back at the barracks." Then he turned and followed the taller one out.

Phoenix paused a moment, giving Daviin and Jer'ait a calculating glance, then departed.

"Should we follow him?" the Jreet asked.

"No."

"They act like they know each other."

"They do."

"Really?" Daviin twisted around to give him a surprised look. "Who is the small one?"

"The one that ruined his career." Jer'ait got up to go.

Daviin reached out and held him in place with an enormous hand. "I want to talk to you. Alone."

Jer'ait stifled his irritation. "I'm busy." He tried to shrug off the Jreet's grip so he could leave, but it was like trying to shrug off a mountain. Daviin did not let go.

"It is unnatural the way you eat by yourself, Huouyt," Daviin said, looming over him. "Joe didn't notice, but you didn't take a single bite of your meal. You haven't eaten with any of us since we arrived here."

Jer'ait stiffened, resisting the urge to punch a poisoned spine through the Jreet's meddlesome hand. "I like to eat alone."

"A man who eats alone is a man without friends," the Jreet intoned.

"A man who has no friends does not mourn when they pass."

Daviin laughed. "A Jreet does not want his friends to mourn. He wants them to celebrate and impregnate their mates on his grave."

Jer'ait was amused, despite himself. "One can never account for culture." Reluctantly, he sat back down. Then, hesitating, he took one of the orange nutrient wafers from the pile. Feeling it in his paddle-like palm, Jer'ait's zora burned with hunger. He gave the Jreet an anxious look to make sure he wasn't going to try anything unpleasant.

The Jreet was watching him, waiting.

Desperation warring with shame, Jer'ait pushed his zora from his mouth, to take the wafer. Instantly, his zora closed on the nutrient gel and dragged it back into his head, roiling over it, consuming it. Jer'ait experienced the brief moment of panic he always felt when he ate—a brief wondering if the food had somehow been laced with organic material—then allowed himself to relax. The boost of energy was already entering his system, lending strength to his exhausted muscles.

"Good," Daviin said, once the wafer had disappeared in Jer'ait's head and Jer'ait had relaxed into his end of the booth. The Jreet immediately went back to tearing into the four-legged pile of meat in front of him. "So tell me about our Prime. Why do you want to kill him?"

It took Jer'ait a moment to understand what the Jreet had said, and when he did, he was so surprised he couldn't help but flinch. "Excuse me?"

The Jreet went on eating as if he had said nothing out of the ordinary, though his small golden eyes were sharp as they watched him.

Jer'ait glanced around the restaurant to see if it was some sort of trap.

"We're alone, Huouyt." The Jreet's words were filled with disdain. "I don't need others to fight my battles for me."

"Is that what this is?" Jer'ait asked, starting to stand again. "A battle?"

The Jreet lowered his meal, his eyes suddenly intense. "Is that what you want it to be?"

Looking up at his coiled mass, Jer'ait knew his chances of surviving a brawl with the Jreet were infinitesimal. His strength was in deception, not brute strength. Even if he somehow found the purchase to administer a poison, it wouldn't take effect fast enough.

"No," Jer'ait said. "We both know I'd lose."

The Jreet grunted and nodded. "At least you're not stupid. Though it would make me feel better if you were." He flicked a bone shard off of the table in front of him, leveling his impressive stare on Jer'ait. "Tell me why you haven't killed him yet."

"I never said I was here to kill him."

"No," Daviin said, his eyes never leaving Jer'ait's face, "but you are."

Jer'ait returned the Jreet's stare-for-stare, then said, "I'm here to see the Vahlin die."

"Not to kill Joe."

"No."

Daviin scoffed. "I don't believe you."

"You have to."

The Jreet frowned at him. "Why, when I can just kill you right here?"

"You have to trust me," Jer'ait said, "because even if I *am* here to kill him, I'd simply be replaced as soon as I was dead." Jer'ait made a pleasant motion at the exit. "At least this way, you can keep your eye on the enemy."

"*Are* you the enemy?" The Jreet's eyes were too sharp, too cunning.

He really wants to kill me, Jer'ait realized, a little nervously. *He's trying to goad me into giving him an excuse.*

"No," Jer'ait said, standing. He could find somewhere else to eat.

"I want to hear you say it," Duviin said, again blocking the path with his arm. "I want you to tell me to my face you're not here to kill my ward." His head was tilted with challenge, his eyes dangerous. "Can you do it?"

"We both know I can," Jer'ait said.

"But I want to hear it," Daviin demanded. "The fool has ordered me not to dismember you like you deserve, so I want to hear you say you will not kill him. It's the only way my Sentinel instincts will abide you still breathing around my ward."

Jer'ait met Daviin's gaze and searched the Jreet's face.

He's desperate, Jer'ait realized. *He wants to hear it more badly than he shows. He wants to believe it.*

Reading the Jreet's expression, Jer'ait realized something else. *I lie to him and he'll let it drop. He'll never bother me again.*

Jer'ait opened his mouth. Then he remembered collapsing under the Dhasha's claws, expecting to bleed to death. Daviin had dragged him to safety, regardless of his own wounds. He had dragged him to safety when it would have been a thousand times easier to simply let him die in the tunnels. Daviin could have rid himself of all these problems, yet he chose to keep Jer'ait alive.

The Jreet continued to watch him, metallic golden eyes needing to hear the words.

"Finish your meal," Jer'ait said. "We can finish this later, Sentinel." He brushed past the Jreet's arm and left Daviin coiled alone at the table, staring at the remnants of his melaa.

• • •

"What do you want, Maggie?" Joe asked, a tired part of his soul realizing that, almost without exception, this was the source of his misery for the last fifty turns. Every investigation, every write-up, every demotion—every outrageous fine that had appeared after each of his six kasjas, wiping out his bank accounts, leaving him in debt to Congress, unable to retire…

It was all her doing. And if he survived this whole brutal battle, it was *she* who was going to get a Corps Directorship. It was so hard to stand next to her he was shaking. He wanted to hurt her, and it was all he could do not to reach for her throat.

"I want you to survive," Maggie said, her voice a liquid honey that sent a rush of icewater down his spine. "We're sending you back to the tunnels in a second attack."

Joe sat down hard. "A *second* attack? You're insane. The place needs to be demolished."

"When have you ever known Congress to be sane?" Wolfgang growled.

"Why don't they just blow the whole planet?" Joe demanded, growing angry. "If there's ever been a better time to use an ekhta, I haven't seen it."

"Bureaucrats on Koliinaat," Wolfgang told him. "They're squabbling over who gets to have Neskfaat once it's cleared of Dhasha."

"That, and the Jahul," the strange woman with them grimaced. "They've got the Trade Commission chair. They're pressuring really hard to make peace, not war. That whole empath thing."

"So in the meantime," Maggie added, "While they're running the numbers and gathering up the force required for a second major attack, the Directors are gonna send the Neskfaat survivors back down to take out as many princes as you can before you all die off." She oozed satisfaction like a Jahul oozed shit.

"This is furgish," Joe said. "PlanOps already lost its best fighters in that fiasco. Anyone else they pick will already be second-choice. They need teachers for the next wave."

"They're claiming it's statistics," Wolfgang said. "Species abilities versus species compatibility. Once they get the right combinations down, they're gonna try to overwhelm the princes."

"You can't *overwhelm* a Dhasha," Joe growled. "You're just giving him more meat to shred."

"They're sending you back," Maggie said. "So I want the three of you to compare notes."

Joe glanced at the man and the woman in the booths beside him—both Prime Commanders—and waited.

"Something weird is going on," Wolfgang offered. "Phoenix and I already talked. Those Dhasha not only knew when we were coming, but they knew *who* was coming. They killed most of the teams before they even got off the surface."

"Interesting," Joe said. Maggie watched him, the fires flickering in her special contacts failing to hide her uneasy look.

"Interesting?! That Vahlin had my guys pegged, right down to the Dreit that didn't join 'til the hour before the fight. We found the lists after the dust settled. And the poor guy ain't a traitor, neither. Peacemakers got all up in his ass after we got back, but he's clean as a whistle."

Joe said nothing.

"You listening to this?" Wolfgang demanded.

Joe did not respond, never lifting his eyes from Maggie's gaze. *You're lucky there's witnesses,* he wanted to say. *But then, you already knew that, didn't you? That's why you brought them.*

"Screw him," Wolfgang said, standing. "He don't know soot."

"I know the Dhasha prince we killed had been given an exact date and time for our arrival, right down to the half hour."

Wolfgang frowned. "So which Overseer chose the time?"

"All of them," Maggie said. "We compromised. Averaged it."

"That's not possible."

"Yeah." Joe continued to watch Maggie, who never looked away. "Pretty charred up."

Her eyes sharpened behind their dancing flames. "That's interesting, coming from the mouth of a traitor."

"God*damn* it!" Joe slammed his fist on the table and stood, making every soldier in the room stop their conversation. Joe had to squeeze his fist several times to keep from reaching for her throat. Quietly, levelly, he said, "I did nothing to you, Mag."

"No, but you will." She said it utterly flatly, without a hint of emotion or regret.

"Because you keep on *pushing* me!" Then, catching himself, Joe took a deep breath and closed his eyes. Softly, he said, "I don't know what the Trith said to you, Maggie. All this time, you never told me."

A little sneer curled her lips. "And I'm never going to."

Anger flashed inside Joe, at that. "Grow up, will you? Trith lie. Everyone knows they never tell the whole prophecy. Not when it suits them better to leave parts out." When she just gave him a flat stare, he tightened a fist and slammed it into the table. "They're just making you *dance* to their goddamn *tune*, Mag, can't you see that?"

Maggie got to her feet, anger flashing in her own eyes. "They told the truth on Kophat, Joe. That's all I need to know."

Maggie, Joe wanted to shout, *what did he say to you?* He wanted to grasp her by the shoulders, to demand what had fueled her hatred for fifty turns. Instead, he could only stare at her, unable to speak.

Maggie leaned closer, until she was almost touching him. In a whisper, she said, "You're gonna die in those tunnels, Joe. We'll keep sending you back until you're dead. I'll make sure of it." Maggie turned and walked off, not waiting for Wolfgang.

Once she was gone, Wolfgang whispered, "You met a Trith?"

Joe stalked out of the bar, ignoring him.

"Zero, wait!" a female voice called behind him.

Joe slowed in the street outside the bar. The brown-eyed woman Maggie and Wolfgang had brought with them was jogging to catch up with him. When she reached him, she hesitated, looking suddenly unsure.

"What?" Joe demanded.

She held out a hand. "Prime Commander Leila Wright."

Joe shook her hand reluctantly. He was surprised at her firm grip. "Joe Dobbs."

"I wanted to thank you for what you did on Kophat, sir. Most of us wouldn't be here today if it weren't for you leading the assault on Na'leen's control tower."

Joe peered at her. "You're from the first Draft." Memories of his recruit days came flashing back in a painful wave.

"Yes sir," she said, like he was a Jreet god.

"It's Joe," Joe said.

"Sir," she said, looking for all the world like a panicky recruit and not some battle-hardened veteran that had survived since Congress discovered Earth and initiated the first Draft, "I feel more comfortable calling you 'sir.'"

"We're the same rank, for Mothers' sakes," Joe said. "Call me Joe."

She gave the eight-pointed star on his chest a nervous glance. "True, but everyone knows you should be a Corps Director."

Joe laughed in despair. "That don't mean squat to Congress. Your lovely friend back there made sure of that."

"She isn't my friend," Leila said. "She's using me, just like she's using you." She gestured back at the bar, where their other companion had stayed at the booth, ordering food. "Wolfgang's the only one who doesn't see it. Then again, he never had to go up against you and Libby in the tunnel crawls."

Joe cocked his head at her, slowly making the connection. "You're Rat."

She broke out into a big grin. "Some call me that. I prefer Leila."

Joe grinned back, despite himself. "I never thought I'd see *you* again. Maggie made a good decision in you, at least. I've never heard of that 'White Wolf' fellah."

Leila rolled her eyes. "He only started calling himself that when he got his groundteam."

Joe frowned. "So how many teams did Maggie put together?"

"Just three." At his soaring eyebrows, she sighed. "I know. She's being hailed as a genius. They're talking about giving her Director whether we get the Vahlin for her or not."

"Funny, how we do the work and she gets all the glory."

"Not really." Leila looked him over. "So what kind of groundteam did she give you?"

Joe groaned. "Don't ask."

"Really. I'm interested. She gave Wolfgang a pack of Hebbut and a Dreit."

Joe snorted. "A few days ago, I would've traded places with him in an instant."

"Why? What'd you get?"

"Ooreiki, Grekkon, Baga, Huouyt, and a pain in the ass Jreet." He lost his smile when he realized Leila was giving him an odd look. "What?"

"That Ooreiki wouldn't happen to have tunnel instinct, would he?"

Joe frowned. "Yeah. He does."

"And the Huouyt is Va'ga?"

"Yeah."

Her face was pale. "Then the Jreet is a Welu heir?"

"No. Voran."

Her eyes widened. "*You're* the groundteam with the Voran?! Mothers' ghosts, we've gotta get back!"

"Why?" Joe asked.

She was already running, motioning at him to follow. He caught up with her easily. "Why?" he asked again.

"Because my Jreet is Welu, and about a thousand lobes bigger than yours. Big brother of one of the little guys your Voran fucked up. And he's in town with me."

Joe cursed and he ran faster.

19

MORE IMPORTANT THAN A PLANET

Daviin was finishing another *melaa* when the stranger sat down in his booth. At first, he thought it was Jer'ait returning, but the visitor's color was different. Daviin lowered the *melaa* and peered down to get a good look at it.

The creature was a shade of gray, its head impossibly big for its body. It had skinny arms, tiny hands, and a mouth that was a small slit in its chin. Set inside the teardrop-shaped skull, eyes like the Void stared back at him, catching him in their thrall. Daviin felt himself shrink against the enormity of the universe, becoming an insignificant smudge on the plane of existence. The feeling was more humbling than his first day in the Sentinels. He shuddered.

The blackness of the Void seemed to suddenly form words that surrounded him, giving him no escape.

Daviin ga Vora, know these fourfold things: First. You will survive this war of Neskfaat long enough to seek vengeance on the one respon sible.

The darkness was encompassing him, now. Swallowing him. Compressing him into a tiny pinprick of light within an endless expanse of nothingness.

Second. Within the sphere of the Regency, you will be forced to choose between protecting your Human ward or serving justice.

Daviin fought a disgraceful amount of panic as his world narrowed to a tiny speck of existence faced with the enormity of an entire universe. For the first time, he felt how truly small and meaningless he really was, and that thought overwhelmed him.

Third. Before you die, the Humans will need your help. This will be your chance to rescue Congress from its own demise...or learn what it means to be forgotten.

The Void crushed him, suffocated him, giving him no relief from its constant pressure.

Fourth. You will succeed in your quest to find the traitor who destroyed Aez. When you do, you will kill him and let his death be an example to all, then you will take your rightful place in the history of the Jreet.

Daviin jerked, severing the contact. "Who are you? Why do you tell me things I already know?"

He could have sworn the tiny creature smiled at him. *I forewarn you, in case you waver in your resolve.*

"I'm a Jreet. My resolve doesn't waver." Daviin did not like this creature at all. Instinct told him to drive his tek through the thing's chest and dump the corpse in the waste recycler.

Remember that when you realize it is your Human friend who will rob you of your proper vengeance.

The irritating creature stood up to go.

Daviin grabbed the alien's small shoulder, holding him firmly in place. "Explain that." He leaned down with a scowl. "Or I introduce you to my tek."

The tiny creature looked up at him, his thin gray lips forming a smile. In the same moment, the room filled with a Welu war-cry. Daviin ducked as a tek slammed into the wall beside him, burying itself in the upholstery. Behind him, nine rods of muscle thrashed the room, throwing tables and chairs aside as the Welu attacked.

Daviin screamed a reply and raised his energy level, the tiny visitor and its strange message forgotten.

• • •

Syuri took another deep breath, then opened the door.

"Who the hell are you?" An Ooreiki guard rose from the security booth emanating startlement, hand on his weapon

Eleven tics, Syuri thought. He raised his penlike stunner and shot him. "Apologies, friend." He gently levered the Ooreiki aside, then entered the first set of codes Forgotten had given him into the console behind the desk.

The second door dripped open, leaving Syuri facing an eerie black hallway. The line of red lights lining the ceiling did nothing to take away the feeling he was peering into a crypt.

Syuri scratched his arms, the overpowering feeling that he was facing a tomb suddenly too powerful to ignore. *Why does the Army insist on building such dreary places?*

No time.

Syuri stepped into the hall, then paused, realizing a row of doors lined the hall on either side. Each was marked with an alien word, one he did not recognize. He went to the first door and entered the override code.

Ten tics, Syuri thought as he waited for the door to slide open and the multiple seals to break. He heard several more clicks, and the whirring of machinery and a great hum of a fan. Immediately, a suction formed on the door and air from outside was forced inside. Syuri whistled. *Sweet Hagra, whatever's in here must be precious.* Then he frowned. Why would they want air to move *into* the place? In every vault he'd ever seen, they'd tried to keep air *out*. The last barrier fell away, leaving Syuri standing in a powerful whoosh of air that almost propelled him into the room on its own. Syuri held his place and peered into the darkness.

Inside, he saw nothing but pitch blackness, heard nothing but the roar of the fan.

He saw nothing, but the blast of misery that sank into Syuri's soul was enough to make him gag. He stumbled backwards, fumbling for a light. He flipped it on and aimed it at whatever lay beyond the open door.

What he saw made him drop his flashlight.

The walls, floor, and ceiling were covered with a familiar black mold.

"You're a...Geuji." His throat felt like it was closing up.

The room did not answer him.

Tentatively, Syuri moved forward. Despair clung to him that was not his own, making the light tremble in his hand. He bent to touch the Geuji. The Geuji's body was very much alive—it glistened and rippled with health, responding to his touch. "Hello?"

Silence.

Then he understood. Whomever kept the Geuji down here did not allow him the artificial voice to speak. Nor did they allow light, nor sound, nor any companionship save the roar of a fan.

Horrified, Syuri stumbled from the room. He felt sick, like his soul had been submerged in filth.

"Sweet Hagra," Syuri whispered. He glanced down the hall. It had hundreds, if not thousands of doors.

Suddenly, Syuri understood. *This* was why the Geuji weren't running planetary economies and creating art and researching wonderdrugs. Because they were *here*.

"Forgotten's going to help you," he whispered.

The fan answered him in silence.

Syuri glanced down the hallway. Forgotten had told him to visit at least three vaults. He picked another door at random, entered the codes, and waited through the successive thumps and whirs before the layers of door began peeling away. He flashed his light inside.

Another Geuji.

And, in that moment, Syuri knew what was more important to Forgotten than a planet.

Family.

● ● ●

Daviin wound behind the echo-obscuring jumble of toppled tables, staying out of earshot. Behind him, he heard the Welu's pings as it tried to locate him. The Welu moved and the floor groaned. Merciful Ayhi, his opponent was *big*.

"Come out, coward!" the Welu screamed. "Face your death like a warrior!"

Outside, Daviin heard Ooreiki Peacemakers shouting, ordering them both to stand down. Daviin ignored them. With the positioning of the tables, he could work his way around the Welu, then have a chance of ambushing him from behind, just as the coward had done to him.

"This is your last warning!" the Ooreiki outside shouted. "End the violence or we'll be forced to take action!"

Daviin smelled smoke from where their struggles had torn away half the building's inner wall, exposing the kitchen. The appliances and utilities inside had been crushed, and food was charring where the chefs had left it in their haste to escape.

"Voran!" the Welu screamed. "Come *out!*" He picked up a two-rod table and lobbed it into the jumble Daviin now worked his way under, screaming in his frustration.

Daviin reached the edge of the debris and peered around it. He focused on the Welu, who continued to ping the mass, oblivious to Daviin's location. Daviin began pulling his body up behind him, coiling it for a lunge.

"Voran!" the Welu shouted again. "Did you flee, coward?!"

Judging he had enough length to cover the distance, Daviin tensed his muscles, focusing on the closest loop of the Welu's body.

A metallic tinkling caught his attention. He turned.

A sound concussion—like a ripping in the boundaries between the hells—suddenly shook the restaurant, blinding him, raking pain through his insides, tearing at his skull. Daviin lost control over his scales, screaming.

Dozens of Ooreiki in biosuits burst into the room, rifles immediately finding their targets. Daviin never heard them. He and the Welu were both flailing, clawing at their heads like someone had dropped coals into their skulls. Daviin felt slick blood wetting his hands where he clutched his head and knew with a horrible certainty that they'd deafened him.

A Huouyt stepped into the room, one that Daviin recognized due to his odd-colored eye. With swift, professional precision, Jer'ait went to the Welu, avoided his thrashing length, and slipped a tentacle under a cream-colored belly scale. Almost instantly, the Welu went limp. Jer'ait stood and went to Daviin.

If you killed the Welu, I'll destroy you, Daviin tried to say. If anything came out of his mouth, he did not hear it. He could not hear anything.

The Huouyt's mouth moved, and its eye flashed with amusement before he found a smooth patch of bluish skin and pressed his tentacle into Daviin's side. Daviin was in too much pain to try and stop him. He felt a sting, then his world faded to blessed nothingness.

Daviin woke strapped to the floor for the second time that day.

"Welcome back, Jreet."

Daviin craned his neck against the restraints. "Jer'ait?"

"You definitely know how to put a damper in a Va'gan's plans, don't you? I was going to use this afternoon to deal with a few personal issues, but I had to watch over you, instead. Make sure the sniveling little Ueshi didn't get any ideas."

"Thanks," Daviin muttered.

The Huouyt made an elegant, dismissive gesture. "It seemed only fair, since the Ooreiki were going to use gas and I decided to save their fool lives by using sound instead. I felt a little bad afterwards. It seems restoring a Jreet's hearing is a tricky process. If I'd known how many chambers you had in there, I wouldn't have authorized the grenade. As it was, it burst every one of them. Very messy."

Daviin twisted his head in its restraint. The Huouyt sat nearby, watching him.

"Just how good *is* your hearing, Jreet?" Jer'ait sat in his natural form, three legs hanging limply under his chair.

"You authorized a sound grenade?" Daviin was stunned, angry.

"How else do you separate two huge, Sentinel-trained Jreet?"

"You don't."

"Ah." The Huouyt shifted slightly, his cilia rustling against the black Congie fabric he wore. "I was to let you fight to the death."

"*Yes.*" Daviin strained against the bands that held him, wishing he were back in the fight.

"Unfortunately," the Huouyt said, "I had my own selfish interests in mind. I plan on surviving the next tunnel crawl."

Daviin stopped straining and twisted to stare at Jer'ait in shock. "You think I would have *lost?!*"

"He outweighed you by a thousand lobes," Jer'ait replied dryly. "It had crossed my mind."

"He was Welu scum!" Daviin roared.

"You remember the Humans who came to get the Prime?" Jer'ait said. "Your Welu fights under the quiet one's banner. Go fight him after we've killed the Vahlin."

"And let the Dhasha get him first?"

Jer'ait shrugged and squatted beside Daviin. He pulled a keycard from his pocket and began freeing Daviin of his restraints. "If it truly bothers you, go kill him now. However, the damage to his chambers was more extensive…You would be fighting a cripple."

Daviin stiffened. "The damage was permanent?" Fighting a cripple was akin to fighting a Takki. The honor would go to the Takki.

"Permanent, yes," the Huouyt said. "He will probably never be able to raise his energy level again."

"Damn you to the ninety hells, Huouyt," Daviin snapped. "He's my sworn enemy. Now I can't destroy him honorably."

"A shame, I know." The Huouyt went on working, appearing not to see the glare Daviin was giving him. As he lay there, helpless, a Va'gan assassin calmly freeing him of the bonds that held him, Daviin wondered if this was what one of the more frustrating hells was like. Jer'ait, for his part, continued to unlock Daviin's restraints in silence.

Daviin lunged up just as soon as he felt the last band loosen, ripping the last few free of the floor as he straightened. The plate over his tek fell away, leaving him completely free to slam it through the Huouyt's meddling body.

Jer'ait stood and tossed the key into the empty harness. "That Ueshi was a disgusting coward. My drugs were not enough for him."

"I'd like to see him again," Daviin said. "And give my thanks."

The Huouyt peered up at him, obviously trying to decide whether or not he was being sarcastic. Finally, he said, "You'd make him soil himself."

"True." Daviin glanced around the room and, seeing no one else, said, "You stood by through the whole operation?"

"It is a Huouyt's duty to his groundmate."

Daviin grunted. "What of Joe?"

The Huouyt gave a disgusted snort. "I've not killed him yet, if that's what you ask."

Daviin narrowed his eyes. "You've got no shame, do you?"

Jer'ait made a noncommittal gesture. "Our Prime has not returned since his own kind took him."

Gingerly, Daviin touched the side of his head. He did not feel blood, though the area was slightly tender. Sensitized. But he could *hear*. That was the important thing. He tried a small ping just to be sure. The echoes bounced back to him, leaving a solid picture in his head.

Satisfied he was once more whole, Daviin lowered his hand and moved to the door.

"Jreet."

He paused and glanced back at Jer'ait. "What?"

"One blast and you were ruined," the Huouyt said. "If that's the result, why don't they use sound grenades against you more often? Why don't the Dhasha have them in the tunnels?"

Daviin snorted. "To use them would be for the Dhasha to admit they're afraid of us."

Jer'ait did not laugh. "I think it's clear that these Dhasha aren't obeying the rules, Jreet."

Daviin tensed. "It's dishonorable."

"It's war," Jer'ait said. "That's why I had the Ueshi coward replace your inner membranes with synthetic."

Daviin felt his coils tighten. "You *augmented* me?"

"You'll thank me when the Vahlin tells them to use sound grenades on you."

"A Jreet," Daviin said, so low it was almost inaudible, "does not rely upon anything but his own body." His tek began to slide from its sheath out of sheer fury. "Take them out."

The Huouyt moved closer to him. "Listen to me, Jreet," he said, completely ignoring the poisoned appendage. "There's something wrong here. Those who abide by the normal rules will die."

"Better to die than live like an augmented coward!" Daviin roared. "You've disgraced me, Huouyt. I'll never be able to claim the Voran throne."

Jer'ait laughed at him. "How can I disgrace you any more than you've already disgraced yourself? A slave to a slave…It doesn't get much more disgraceful than that."

Daviin suddenly felt his world crash down around him. "Leave," Daviin whispered. "Before I break my oath and kill you now."

Jer'ait ignored him. "You were not augmented, Jreet. You were immunized against a coward's weapon." Jer'ait stared up at him, his purple eye calm despite Daviin's protruding tek. "Seeing you helpless today, I realized something. I could take a handful of those grenades to Vora or Welu and kill the entire Jreet royal lineages and there wouldn't be a single one amongst you who could stop me. I also realized that if this Vahlin is monitoring us closely enough to know our exact attack times and species types, he heard about your tussle with the Welu and how I put an end to it. If the idea to use sound grenades had not occurred to him before, it's occurred to him now. I've done you a favor."

"You tainted me." Daviin's fury was a storm within his chest, an ache of shame and anger.

The Huouyt cocked his head slightly, an amused look crossing his mutated face. "You Jreet are more delicate than you look. Your honor takes one tiny smudge and you are suddenly prepared to kill yourselves." The Huouyt gave an unconcerned shrug. "But whether you like it or not, it is done. The only one on this planet skilled enough to remove them without killing you is the Ueshi, and you can be sure he's not gonna let you find him. So, unless you rip them out yourself, the implants will remain until our business on Neskfaat is complete."

"This Ueshi," Daviin said, slowly. "I want to talk to him."

"So would I," Jer'ait said. "Especially after I discovered no one knows where he came from. It seems you have a guardian angel, Jreet. He appears and disappears at will. He eluded even me, when I tried to follow him."

"That spineless coward is not an angel," Daviin snapped, irritated.

"How else do you evade a Va'ga?"

"Catch him for me and we shall both find out."

"Unfortunately," the Huouyt said, "I have a feeling we won't see him again until you need him."

"What are you trying to say?" Daviin snarled. "That I'm in league with the Ueshi?"

"Somebody important wants to see you succeed," Jer'ait said. "You think your family—"

"No!" Daviin snapped, disgusted at the very idea. "*Never.* Jreet do not coddle their young."

"Then you have a secret admirer," Jer'ait said. "If you're correct and it's not your family, then perhaps you should figure out—"

The door opened and the Ueshi entered, head crest fluttering. His eyes swept to Daviin and he balked. "Oh. I did not realize he was awake. Jer'ait, I heard you were looking for me. I'll wait in the hall for you. Alone, please."

Daviin moved to grab the Ueshi, but the Huouyt beat him to it. Before Daviin had a chance to comprehend quite what the assassin had done, the Ueshi dropped to the floor, staring at the ceiling with wide eyes. Then Jer'ait went to the door and locked it. When he came back, he squatted beside the helpless alien, his eyes hard.

"Will there be any more attacks today?" Jer'ait demanded.

Daviin frowned. *Attacks…?*

"No, sir," the Ueshi whispered.

"Good." Jer'ait reached out and touched the Ueshi, who immediately stiffened. As Daviin watched, the alien's eyes widened and he began to shake silently. Then he stilled.

"You *killed* him?" Even though Daviin had wanted to do the very same, he had wanted to at least *enjoy* it a little, first.

"It's the price we Huouyt pay for having the skills we do. Mercy is not an option because capture is only an inconvenience. If he was any good at all—which I suspect he was—as soon as I turned away, he would have adjusted the chemical content of his blood to compensate, then would have finished what he came here to do."

"An assassin," Daviin said, struggling to piece together what he had seen. "Not the doctor."

"Yes." Jer'ait sighed and stood. "Don't tell Joe. I don't want the Prime to concern himself with my business any more than he already has. Be assured I can and will handle it." Jer'ait calmly began going through the dead assassin's clothing, but his one violet eye betrayed his worry. "It makes me wonder what he did to the Ueshi. He had to have taken genetic material from him somehow to create the pattern he was using." Jer'ait pulled a small alien finger from beneath the Ueshi's uniform, severed at the second delicate joint. The Huouyt gave Daviin a grim look. "Whatever he did, I'd say it's a fair bet your guardian angel is no longer going to be sitting on your shoulder."

"You think he's dead?" Daviin demanded. "You said your kind doesn't take on a dead pattern!"

Jer'ait glanced up at Daviin from where he crouched beside the dead Huouyt. "I said my sect does not use a pattern they did not kill themselves. But most Va'gans are not so…superstitious, as Joe so eloquently put it. I like to think of it as respect. Though he could be alive, it's highly likely he's many hours dead."

"We must find him!"

Jer'ait cocked his head at him. "I thought you wanted to destroy the Ueshi."

Daviin grunted. "He fixed my audial chambers. I should thank him."

The Huouyt turned back to the finger and sniffed it.

Sniffed it? Daviin frowned, repulsed. "What are you—?"

"Be silent a moment, Jreet. I need to concentrate."

Then, to Daviin's disgust, Jer'ait pushed the glistening red appendages from the slit above his eyes and dropped the finger amidst their
grasping, writhing scarlet tentacles. Jer'ait's eyes narrowed and his *zora*
abruptly dropped the finger back to the floor. He shuddered, and visibly tried to hold his pattern in place as his *zora* pulled back into his
head.

"Didn't know your kind could do that," Daviin said, once the zora
had retreated and the trembling had stopped. "Taste a creature and not
become it."

The Huouyt looked exhausted as he got out of his crouch. "It's
hard. If you had interrupted me, I believe I would now be unconscious
at your feet."

"So why'd you do it?"

"I needed to taste for drugs. You're in luck. He used *vembiridol.*"

"Vemb...?"

"An interrogation drug. Leaves its victims alive, able to talk, but
blocked from using any motor functions."

"So he's alive," Daviin said. "Good. Where?"

"I never said he was alive," Jer'ait said. "But if he is, I will find him."

20

VIOLENT ALIEN
COPULATION TECHNIQUES

Syuri checked the time. He had four tics. Forgotten had made it very clear he would have to leave after eleven tics or he would not get out in time. He went to the final door and willed the vault to open faster.

"Enjoying yourself, Jahul?"

Syuri spun.

A Huouyt in Peacemaker black leaned against the wall directly inside the entrance to the hallway.

No, Syuri thought frantically, *Forgotten told me I had four more tics.*

"Where did you get those codes, Jahul?" The Huouyt never moved, but its electric eyes sizzled with eerie intensity. Syuri could feel a wave of triumph rolling off of the creature. He took a step backwards.

The Huouyt moved from the entrance to the hallway and strode over to him with all the grace and power of a stalking Jikaln. "No matter," the Peacemaker said, his eerie electric-blue eyes only a foot away now. "You'll have plenty of time to tell me."

Without taking its eyes off of Syuri, it reached out and entered in the codes to close the vault Syuri had just opened. The sound of the fan disappeared with the thudding of locks and hissing of seals. It did not, however, seal off the misery behind the wall, which continued to seep outwards, staining his soul.

Syuri's hand strayed toward the pocket where he had hidden his tranquilizer.

The Huouyt gave him a flat look. "Do you really want to do that, worm?"

Syuri swallowed hard at the cold anger of the creature before him. Certain Huouyt could isolate chemicals in their body and neutralize them. Shooting him with a tranquilizer, if he was trained, would have no effect. If he submitted, the rest of his life would be short and unpleasant. If he did not, it would be much longer.

"No," Syuri whispered.

"Very well," the Huouyt said. "Give it to me."

His fingers trembling, Syuri handed the device to the Huouyt.

The Peacemaker stuffed it into his belt and calmly went to the other doors Syuri had opened, shutting them as well. Syuri flinched as he heard the doors slam into place, knowing that he would be next to share the Geuji's fate.

Then Syuri saw his opportunity. The Huouyt had stooped to examine a hissing seal on one of the doors, irritation in his alien face. *Forgotten wasn't wrong*, Syuri's mind thought wildly. *He planned this. He knew the Huouyt would get distracted.* Syuri dodged, running at full speed toward the end of the hallway. If he could shut the door on the Huouyt and enter the override code, he would be free.

The Huouyt never stood up. Syuri felt the sting of a tranquilizer—his *own* tranquilizer—and crumpled before he'd even reached the end of the hall.

Slowly, leisurely, the Huouyt finished his inspection of the door and strode up to him. Syuri trembled inside as the assassin paused to stare down at him with cold, lifeless eyes. "Like I said. You will have all the time you need to tell me about your employer."

He was wrong, Syuri thought, losing control of his inner chambers. A mixture of waste liquids oozed out over his skin, making the Huouyt's face wrinkle in disgust. *Forgotten was wrong and they're going to execute me.*

As the Huouyt bent to lift him from the floor, a new, even more horrible thought occurred to him.

Forgotten was *never* wrong.

• • •

"They'll separate the Jreet heirs and their teams will return to the tunnels ahead of schedule. Planetary Ops will want them to kill as many Dhasha as possible before they find each other again and finish what they began in the restaurant."

"So it is the Jreet we want?" Rri'jan insisted.

"I've told you," Forgotten said. "We need a team of six. The Jreet might make the killing blow, but then again, it might not. A Huouyt has as much chance of killing the Representative as a Jreet, since the Jreet must remain blind and mute while invisible and a Huouyt has the added bonus of patience. However, Mekkval is notorious for being able to sense intruders, so it might be that the Huouyt and the Jreet will have to battle Mekkval's bodyguards while the Grekkon or the Baga finishes the job with an ambush."

"You aren't sure what will happen?"

"We aren't there yet," Forgotten said. "We are discussing the second tunnel crawl."

"Why? We already know the result. What is there to discuss?"

"We do not know the result. One can never know the result unless one is a Trith, and my every action muddies the future for them so that, in anything pertaining to my plans, no one can ever know the result."

"But nevertheless, you know."

"I make guesses that usually prove to be accurate. Nothing more."

Rri'jan snorted. "Usually? When have you ever been wrong?"

"Once," Forgotten said. "It was enough."

The Huouyt's electric blue eyes lit up with curiosity. "When?"

"In my youth."

"What happened?"

"I miscalculated."

"How so?" The Huouyt's biorhythmic functions were elevating again, indicating his interest.

"We should continue with the subject at hand," Forgotten said. "Mekkval's home den is eleven times deeper than the average den, mainly to deter enemies with ground-penetration missiles."

Rri'jan gave him an annoyed look. "Who cares about how deep Mekkval's den is?"

"This particular distance generates a lot of heat, up to a total of seventy-nine grads standard, which many species—including yours—cannot withstand without biosuits. We must take this added inconvenience into account when we form our teams."

"You are saying the Huouyt will not make it to Mekkval's deep den?"

"No. I'm saying that the Huouyt that survive this attack will come better prepared the next time."

"You're staging an entire attack just to determine which groups work best in hot conditions?"

"That will be key to our success. For instance, the Grekkon functions best in circumstances at or below sixty-six grads Standard. With each grad after that, his extrusion rate will drop exponentially, reducing his digging ability until it becomes nonexistent. An entire team's survival could depend upon this simple fact."

"Very well," Rri'jan said. "I suppose only another half a percent of our teams will survive this next wave?"

"It will be more along the lines of twenty percent. We've already weeded out the dysfunctional groups. Now we're narrowing the playing field."

The Huouyt's eyes narrowed as it did a quick calculation. "So of the two thousand surviving groundteams from the first attack, four hundred will survive the second attack?"

"Approximately."

• • •

"Well, looks like Jer'ait has things under control," Joe said, turning away from the smoky, rubble-strewn restaurant. "Let's get outta here before they make us fill out paperwork." He groaned, his eye catching on the pile of shredded tables that had been thrown through the half-collapsed front of the structure. The Ueshi proprietor that had lured Daviin into his doors with half-priced melaa was kneeling beside his ruined establishment, tugging at his headcrest, wailing in lamentation. "Mothers' ghosts, that's gonna be a lot of paperwork."

Leila eyed the enormous gray-blue body it was taking thirty Ooreiki to drag out of the rubble by the arms. "I don't know...I should probably be there when he wakes."

"You will be," Joe said. "They're both gonna be in surgery for hours. We've got time to chat."

"You think they can repair their ears? I heard them use a sound grenade."

Joe grunted. "Well, if they can't, it's sure not gonna help for us to stand around and complain about it."

Leila finally tore her eyes away from the scene and looked up at him. Her eyes had a mischievous gleam. "If I didn't know better, Commander, I would think you were trying to get me alone with you."

God hates a coward. Joe winked at her. "What gave you that idea?"

She laughed. "One of your groundmates lies incapacitated not thirty rods away and you're hitting on me."

"I have the feeling this will be the only opportunity I'll have some time alone," Joe said, his eyes following the gang of Ooreiki as they now dragged the smaller Jreet from the ruined restaurant and laid him out beside the bigger one. It took twelve of them just to move Daviin's body out into the road.

"Come on," Leila said, turning away and pulling him with her. "Pray your Huouyt dosed them good enough so they don't wake like that."

Seeing the way the two Jreet were twined like lovers, unconscious bodies flopped against each other's chests, Joe hoped he had, too.

They went to a restaurant, ordered a private booth, and ate good Earth-styled meals while they discussed war wounds. Leila had had her own brush with death in the last crawl, finding herself just as useless as Joe had been after the Dhasha tore up her groin and thigh through a biosuit.

"I'd love to see those scars," Joe said, grinning.

She winked at him and took another bite of salad.

Joe felt like a school kid with his first crush.

By the time they reached the barracks, it was all they could do not to tear each other's clothes off. Trying to regain her composure as they—two Prime Commanders—walked through the halls under the awed gazes of new grounders, Leila said she would meet him in twenty tics, his room.

Joe all but danced back to his room, whistling like a fool.

Joe tried to give the place a romantic atmosphere. He hastily shoved his packs of gear aside, put a little music on over the intercom, turned up the heat, and dimmed the lights, but it was hard to disguise the small room with its small bed for what it was.

Candles, Joe thought. *We need candles.* He went to the com unit and dialed up Leila's personal unit. She didn't answer, so he left a message. "Hey Commander Wright, think you could bring some candles along with you? I'm a hopeless romantic and I ain't got—" Joe hesitated, realizing he was about to say he didn't have the extra cash to buy candles, thanks to his brief 'retirement' and Maggie's meddling. He cleared his throat. "Uh, I think candles would be really nice, if you think you could handle it."

Feeling like a furg, he ended the message and went back to preparation.

About twenty tics later, his door beeped. Joe went to it and let Leila inside, somewhat disappointed she wasn't carrying candles. "Didn't get my message?" he asked, not trying to pry.

Leila raised an eyebrow at him. "Message?"

Joe coughed. "Yeah, uh…" He blushed, realizing he didn't really want to explain. "Think we should get a room?" he asked, somewhat worried his place was gonna horrify her. "I mean, it's kind of cramped…"

Leila grinned. "It's just fine, big guy." Changed, smelling freshly-showered, Leila shut the door. Then, without preamble, she met him with a kiss. Joe groaned and pulled her body tight against his, trying not to remember how long it had been since he'd been with a woman. Leila wrapped her arms tight behind his neck. They started undressing each other as Joe carefully backed them towards the bed.

Joe didn't feel the sting along his spine until it was too late.

He collapsed like a doll, their lips parting as he fell.

"I told you you were marked, Human." As if he weighed nothing at all, Leila picked him up and carried him to the bed. Joe could not even find the strength to protest as the Huouyt laid him out and began calmly unfastening the buttons. It paused when it saw the Jreet's markings on his chest.

It smiled down at Joe. "Pity your Jreet isn't here to protect you. And your precious Va'ga..." He got up and went to the door and Joe heard the horrible sound of bolts falling into place. Somehow, the Huouyt had gotten his security code. Not a soul would enter this room unless a Prime Overseer ordered it.

Though he couldn't turn his head, Joe heard the beepings of the Huouyt accessing the com terminal beside the door.

"Ah," the Huouyt said, stepping back to him. "He's watching the Jreet's operation, which isn't scheduled to end for another three hours." The Huouyt smiled with Leila's lips, mockingly pleasant. "I wonder why he bothers at all. It's not like any of you mean anything to him." The Huouyt glanced at the clock embedded in the wall and clapped his Human hands together. "So! You said you didn't feel getting marked. That means I've got two hours to *make* you feel it."

Only a moment later, Leila's tentative voice came over the intercom, "Hey, uh, Commander Zero? I got this weird message about candles...You...uh...hopin' ta get frisky?" She almost sounded hopeful.

The Huouyt leaned over his prone body to stroke Joe's face. Joe stared back at him, refusing to be cowed.

"Commander Zero?" Leila asked. "You in there?" He heard her knuckles give a muffled rap on the metal door.

Mothers' ghosts, Joe thought, not sure whether he wanted her to leave or to investigate further. He had the feeling the Huouyt would kill them both, if she tried to interrupt his fun.

After a long moment, the Prime Commander outside sighed. "Well...ash."

Then Joe was alone with the Huouyt. Though Joe knew the night would go a lot quicker for him if he gave in to the twinges of fear he felt, Joe glared as the assassin traced his skin.

Give it your best, asher.

The Huouyt's fingers traveled down to the pulsing artery in Joe's neck and Joe tensed. He felt another sting and suddenly he remembered how to talk. In fact, he found he *had* to talk.

"You'd better not hurt her," he blurted.

The Huouyt made an amused snort. "Your own safety is the issue here, Joe. You and I are going to play a game, much like the sexual one we were about to engage in, except with pain instead of pleasure."

Joe had to fight with every ounce of control he had to keep his mouth shut. Some inhibition had been battered away to nothing and now he felt compelled to blurt out the first things that came to mind.

"At the end of the game, you will experience pain so great it will change you forever. It will not kill you. No. I believe that is too lenient a death for one with so little respect for my profession." The Huouyt started pacing around him on the bed, looking down at his prone form. "You will serve as an example to others for the rest of your long life." He smiled down at Joe. "Are you ready?"

"Not really," Joe said. "Actually, I'd rather you leave right now."

The Huouyt's Human face smiled. "I'm sure you would."

"What drug did you use on me?"

"And why would you care?" the assassin said. "What do you know of drugs?"

"I want to know if it's the same one Jer'ait uses."

The Huouyt laughed. "Of course it is. *Vembiridol.* The chemical compounds are so complex that only a true master can reproduce it. I use nothing else."

"You sure don't mind barking up your own tree, do you?" Joe blurted.

The Huouyt gave him a long, hard stare. "After meeting with you, I educated myself on Human tolerances in preparation for our next encounter. Let's see how you like this."

He reached out and took Joe's wrist. Joe tried to flinch away, but the Huouyt easily held him in place.

The pain that shot up from the veins in his hand was like someone had poured boiling acid into his heart. Joe felt his chest heaving in a scream before he heard it.

The Huouyt smiled in Leila's pattern as Joe screamed, then watched him pant as the pain ebbed. "I'm sorry. Was that one not to your liking? I'm sure I can find something better." He reached out again.

This time, Joe thought he would lose his mind. His world centered on the tearing, biting agony that coursed through his veins with every beat of his heart. Every nerve was suddenly afire with horrible, rending pain. He felt his heart shy away from it, palpitating, slowing.

"Oops," the Huouyt said, bringing him back to his senses. "Looks like I might've given you a slight overdose with that one. My mistake."

"No problem," Joe panted. "I'm sure you make a lot of them."

The Huouyt's expression hardened.

Joe grinned, despite knowing he was in for a long night.

• • •

Flea clung to the wall, hiding behind the gear rack. He had heard Joe enter the room while he'd been rooting through his things, trying to gain some sort of idea of just who their Prime really was. Flea had hit the wall in a panic, hoping the Human wouldn't hear the buzz of his wings.

The Human started rooting around the room like a nesting Dhasha. Flea tensed, terrified he'd been caught, but slowly relaxed again when he realized Joe hadn't noticed his intrusion and was simply moving the equipment.

But why?

Feeling exposed on the wall, where other species' eyes so commonly rested, Flea carefully began to climb toward the ceiling, thankful the Congies had painted his carapace a dull black to go with the walls. Step by painful step, he made his way to the domed red light and hid behind it.

Tentatively, he peeked around the light, trying to judge whether or not he could safely crawl across the ceiling and out the door.

Flea watched, intrigued, as Joe went to the wall and dimmed the lights to a soft glow.

Further confusing him, the Human went to the com unit and put a horrid cacophony over the intercom system, one that made Flea's carapace and wings vibrate uncomfortably. He scuttled away from the intercom unit, hoping the lights were dim enough that the Human did not see him.

Then his Prime went and made a call requesting candles. What the hell?

To his surprise, another Human joined his Prime a short while later, this one smaller and with more bulges. Standing on the floor, the two Humans began to strip off each other's outer garments and grope each other's sexual organs. Flea paused. Then he leaned forward from the ceiling, watching with interest.

Joe's body suddenly stiffened and slumped to the ground.

The smaller Human lifted his Prime from the floor and carried him to the rectangular bed the Human seemed to prefer.

I know what this is, Flea thought suddenly. *They're* mating.

Fascinated, Flea settled in to watch.

The first time Joe screamed, Flea found it intriguing. What kind of creatures—except a Jreet—could make mating a painful experience and expect to survive as a species?

The second time Joe screamed, Flea realized something was wrong. He scuttled closer, so he could hear their words.

He heard the one Human apologize and Flea began to relax. Then Joe began to scream out curses that left no mistake of his feelings toward the female. Flea crept closer, until he was perched atop the ceiling directly above them.

Though he was on his back, Joe didn't see him. His eyes were fixed on the other Human. Flea strained to hear.

The strange Human laughed. "Oh no. I will enjoy my full two hours. And in the end, you will serve as a warning for others who would dare to interfere in Huouyt affairs." It reached for Joe again.

The way Joe flinched away, Flea knew something was very wrong. It was almost as if he couldn't move…

It's a Huouyt.

Thunderous miga, it's a Huouyt.

Flea recoiled and fought the urge to scrabble backwards. He held very still, trying to make sense of it. It was a Huouyt, but not Jer'ait.

Jer'ait was standing watch over the Jreet. Even though the walls had been black and Flea had been as quiet as possible, his groundmate had caught him eavesdropping on the operation and had told him to go make himself useful.

Joe screamed again. The Human's vocal range was alarming, reverberating off the walls in what was obviously not pleasure.

Flea glanced at the door. Locked. He could open it and escape, but that would leave the Huouyt alone with his Prime.

Flea could have destroyed another creature in less than a tic. A Huouyt, however, was almost immune to his particular abilities. No sooner would Flea spit on him than the Huouyt would simply slough off the skin and dart him with a pen-tranquilizer.

Yet he had to do something.

The Huouyt reached for the Human again and Flea decided it was time to act. He dropped from the ceiling, landing on the Huouyt's arm. Even as the Huouyt's surprise was beginning to register, Flea spat, taking him full in the face, in the eyes. At the same time, he snipped off the arm.

This time, it was the Huouyt who screamed.

Flea knew he had to follow up his advantage quickly, before the alien could regenerate itself. He scuttled to the edge of the bed and, while the Huouyt stumbled backwards, Flea spat at his feet.

The Huouyt fell over backwards, pinned by its Human ankle. Flea knew that wouldn't last long, so he hopped from the bed and hovered over to the Huouyt's face, filling in the rest of its eyes as he desperately tried to think of how to kill a Huouyt.

The Huouyt's unhurt arm slammed into Flea, swatting him with all the depressing power of a land-lubber. Flea hit the far wall and dropped to the floor in a daze. Vaguely, he noticed the Huouyt getting back to its feet, and Joe continued to lie in his bed, unable to help him. Flea eyed the Human with frustration. Strong enough to stomp him into an incoherent mush at a friendly jest, but not strong enough to lift his pinkie finger when it was needed.

The Huouyt had sloughed off half its Human face, leaving the red, wormy appendages writhing in its forehead above new and awkwardly-placed eyes. "That," the Huouyt said, his voice deadly, "Was a mistake." He pulled his feet free of the floor, leaving red pieces of Human flesh still attached to the metal grating.

On the bed, the Human twitched again, stronger this time. *Time*, Flea thought. *I need to buy us time.* Flea spat at the Huouyt again, once more pinning his feet to the floor. Then he again took out the eyes. Then the mouth, then the nose.

"You wretched little pest!" the Huouyt screamed. Another slab of flesh sloughed off his face and into a puddle on the floor. The Huouyt's enraged eyes moved in its head, calibrating themselves. Flea tried to spit again, but his glands couldn't produce glue fast enough.

Watching the Huouyt tear his foot from the ground a second time, Flea knew his time in the world was limited. He tried to get into the air, but one of his wings had broken in half in his fall. Desperately, he tried to scuttle his way towards the ceiling, but the Huouyt scraped him off the wall and threw him to the floor, where he stomped a cruel boot over his spitter.

Unlike Joe, he knew how to really make it hurt. Flea was babbling incoherently in moments as the Huouyt ground his most sensitive apparatus into the hard metal.

After several tics, the Huouyt let up just enough to allow Flea to recover some of his senses, a look of smug satisfaction over his face. "You furgish little worm. Just what did you think you were going to do, eh? There is nothing a simpering little fool like you can do to me that I can't mend."

"I know," Flea whimpered. A shadow fell in behind the Huouyt and Flea laughed through his pain. "But he can."

The Huouyt blinked and turned—just in time to receive a knife the length of Flea's body in the center of its *zora*.

The Huouyt collapsed like a machine that had lost its source of power. The Human followed it down and hacked its head from its body, tossing the result halfway across the room in disgust. "Mend that, leafmunch."

"It wore off faster than I thought it would," Flea said, struggling back to his feet. "I thought it would be another two tics, at least."

The look on the Human's face was thunderous. "I've been building up my resistance lately. What were you doing in my chambers?"

"I was searching your belongings for something interesting." Flea's head cocked when he noticed the pattern etched into the Human's chest. "That symbol seems familiar."

"It's from a Sentinel," Joe said. "Daviin bound to me." Then, oddly, the Human's entire body tightened and he looked like he was straining against something. "Get out," he said through gritted teeth. "I will deal with the Huouyt."

Flea glanced at the beheaded Huouyt, then back at his Prime. "He gave you a truth serum, didn't he?"

"Yes," the Human said automatically. His brows furrowed. "Get out. Now." The Human went to the door and opened it.

In reply, Flea scampered up the wall and clung to the ceiling, out of reach. "Why, Commander?" he said gleefully. He eyed the dead Huouyt to make sure it wasn't about to resurrect itself, then said, "This could be so much fun."

When it was obvious Flea was not leaving, the Human's face took on the hue of a Jreet's body. "Flea..."

"So you have your very own Sentinel? Does anyone else know?"

"Yes. Only Jer'ait." The Human cursed and clenched a fist. He glanced up at Flea, then out the door.

"You don't want to leave," Flea said. "Think of all the trouble you could get in out there if you had to tell the truth. Better to stay put until it wears off. Isn't it, Commander?"

"Yes," Joe blurted.

With a furious look that promised pain later, the Human slammed his fist against the door-lock, shutting it. "I guess you don't remember what happened last time you cowered on the ceiling," he growled. He reached for the nearest handy object—his boot—and hefted it.

Flea sobered. "Ah, come on, Commander. Let me have my fun. I just saved your life."

The Human glanced reflexively at the dead Huouyt. Then his arm relaxed and he let the boot slide to the floor. His huge lungs drew in a deep breath and expelled it again. "Fine, Flea. I don't have anything I need to hide from you, anyway."

"That's more like it. Come stand underneath me a moment. My wing's busted and only three of my legs are working right."

The Human did, and obligingly held out his arms to catch him. Flea was half-sure he would remove his arms at the last moment, letting him collide painfully with the floor, but the Human faithfully caught him and set him on the chair in the corner of the room. Then, sighing, Joe slumped onto the bed, sprawled out, staring at the ceiling much as he had been only tics before.

Only this time, his chest and forearms were covered with bright red blood where he had performed the grisly task of hacking off the Huouyt's head.

Flea considered all the tantalizing things he could ask, then settled with, "Where did you get your scars?"

"I told you. The Jreet."

"The other ones."

The Human lifted his head high enough to look at him. "You don't miss a thing, do you?"

Flea laughed. "Of course I don't. Where'd you get them?"

The Human's brow furrowed, but he said, "I was a Dhasha slave for a while in Basic."

That was interesting. "Why was the Huouyt trying to kill you?"

The Human dropped his head back to the pillow. "I kept him from Jer'ait when Jer'ait was getting his chip. He wasn't happy with me."

"So what was he trying to do with Jer'ait?"

"Beats me. Had something under his arm. Maybe a locator beacon. I don't think he wanted to kill him."

"Mind-control," Flea said.

Joe lifted his head again. "Excuse me?"

"Mind-control," Flea repeated. "It's a new program. They're using it on convicts, problem-soldiers...anyone who might give Congress a hard time. It's why Jer'ait stood in while Daviin got his operation. I was going to do it, like I did for you, but Jer'ait kicked me out."

The Human pushed himself up onto his bloody elbows. "They're implanting it in soldiers? How do you know?"

"Please. Overseers talk," Flea scoffed. "I just happen to be in places where I can listen."

Joe stared at him for so long that Flea thought he might be experiencing a resurgence of the paralysis drug. Finally, his Prime said, "That's dangerous information, Flea. I've been a Prime for thirty turns and I never heard anything like it."

"You just haven't been in the right places," Flea said. "So Commander, I've been meaning to ask you and now seems like as good as a time as ever, where's your brother keep his stash?"

"Huh?" The Human had a truly perplexed look on his face when he lifted his head.

"Your brother," Flea insisted. "The one who squirreled away billions from big companies on Earth. Ghost. He had a huge stash somewhere. They can't find it."

"I don't know anything about a stash."

Flea was hugely disappointed. "Wherever it is, it's not getting any use. He's dead, you know."

The Human stiffened, but he said, "Yeah. I know."

"Neat fellah," Flea said. "Wise-ass in court. It had a certain charm when he told the Dhasha judge to go suck Ueshi genitalia. I was hoping some of his cronies would rescue him. Never did, though."

The Human was frowning at him. "How did you get access to the trial feed? It was classified."

"Your friend Phoenix was watching it."

Joe stiffened. "She's not my friend."

"Oh, I gathered that much." Flea buzzed his wings in amusement. "Have you ever been in her room, Joe? She's got pictures of you on the wall."

Joe blinked. "She does?"

"Oh yeah. And every one of them is being used for darts. She's actually quite good. Has narrowed her groupings down to the eyes." Flea cocked his head. "Why does she hate you so much?"

"I don't know."

"The drugs wore off, then?"

"No, you lump of Dhasha shit, I really don't know what the Trith said to her."

Flea perked up. "You mean she also had one visit her today?"

The Human frowned. "No. It was back in Basic. What do you mean, 'today'?"

"A Trith was sighted in town today," Flea said. "Right before the Jreet got into their scuffle. Other than for the one that I saw, there were at least four other confirmed sightings...all around where members of your groundteam were at the time."

The Human sat up suddenly, entire body alert. "A Trith visited you?"

Flea grinned. "It was a nice chat. He tried to convince me you were going to destroy the world."

The Human stared at him in mute shock. "Ghosts."

"What?" Flea asked, cocking his head at him.

The Human jumped to his feet, face dark with fury. "Mothers' burning ghosts! It's happening again. *The sons of bitches are doing it again!*"

Flea was a bit surprised by his violent reaction. "If it makes you feel any better, I told him to get lost. Used your brother's words, with a few modifications."

Joe glanced at him, "You didn't believe him?"

Flea twittered with amusement. "Of course I did. It was a *Trith*. But I just happen to believe the world might be a bit more interesting if someone came along and destroyed it. That would be quite a joke on those fat old furgs who send young furgs like us to our deaths, wouldn't it?"

The Human looked stunned.

Flea laughed. "Let's get rid of this body. I'm not sure, but I have the nervous suspicion that it's someone high up in the Peacemakers' chain of command. The last thing we want is this linked to us."

Joe flung his arm at the bloodstains around the room. "A little hard to hide now, isn't it?"

Flea twittered. "What are you talking about? All they'll ever find is that Human's blood. And she's still alive. You can claim it was a mating ritual. Jreet do it all the time."

The Human's dark brown eyes widened when he realized Flea was right.

"The perfect crime," Flea said, grinning. "Kind of like your brother's. Too bad he didn't live long enough to enjoy it."

21

THE SENTINEL AND THE ASSASSIN

"**W**here are you taking me, Huouyt?"

Jer'ait gave Daviin another irritated glance. "Just be silent. They hear you and we'll have to fight our way back out of here."

"I think I'd enjoy that. Too much tension."

Jer'ait stifled his frustration. It was the nature of Jreet to be bull-headed oafs. "This requires *precision*," Jer'ait said. "Brute force will get us both killed." Then he cocked his head, considering just who was pacing the hall with him. He remembered the dismantled restaurant, the Dhasha heir trapped in his coils. "Well, maybe not. But still. Be quiet."

"So this assassin that came for you today," the oversized worm said. "He was the one who came for you in surgery?"

"No," Jer'ait said. "Different employers. Now *shut up.*"

"So if they're not both working for the Huouyt Ground Corps, who was the other one working for?"

"Peacemakers. Shhh."

"I'm confused. You *work* for the Peacemakers."

Jer'ait whirled on the invisible alien. "Shut your *melaa*-eating mouth, or I will do it for you."

"How much do you weigh, Huouyt?"

Jer'ait narrowed his eyes. "It takes less than a drop of fluid to kill a Jreet."

"Why don't you threaten me with something interesting? Like my glands will fall off. Or my tek will dry up." The Sentinel snorted. "Death doesn't scare me, Huouyt. Only a moron jenfurgling wouldn't have noticed that by now. Now where in the ninety hells is this Ueshi coward we're looking for? You've been taking us in circles."

"No I haven't," Jer'ait snapped. "You're just lost."

"Who's lost?" a Huouyt voice asked as an eight-point Prime Commander stepped around the corner.

"Talking to myself, sir," Jer'ait said, allowing his borrowed head-crest a flutter of embarrassment.

The Huouyt looked him up and down. "You lost, Ueshi?"

"No, sir. Well, maybe, sir. I don't know how I got here…I don't remember *anything*. I just woke up in this strange room and have been trying to find my way out ever since. I…I think someone *attacked* me, sir."

The Huouyt's face twitched and Jer'ait was amused with the Prime's lack of discipline. "A prank," the Prime sighed. "We've been getting a lot of them lately. The multi-species groundteams created a lot of Huouyt resentment. Here, allow me to lead you back to the common area. This section is Peacemaker only."

Jer'ait nodded and babbled his gratitude, waiting for the Huouyt to strike.

When he did, Jer'ait immediately isolated and nullified the chemicals he used and, identifying the compound, allowed himself to go limp. *He tried to kill me,*" he thought, surprised. *They're not fooling around.*

The Huouyt slung Jer'ait over his shoulder and began carrying him down the hall. Though Jer'ait didn't hear him, he knew Daviin followed.

The Prime dropped Jer'ait roughly to the floor outside a nondescript door and entered a passcode. Taking a cue from the Human, Jer'ait listened to the tones as each number was pushed. Then he heard the door drip open.

Upon seeing the other Ueshi still inside his prison, the Huouyt demanded, "What the hell?"

"Which hell are you referring to?" Daviin asked above them. Then the Jreet slammed his fist into the Huouyt's midsection. Even Jer'ait had to wince with the force the Jreet put into the strike. Had the wall not been reinforced, it probably would have crumbled.

"You know," Daviin said as the other Huouyt's brains and organs dribbled in an orangeish goo across the wall, "I think you're smarter than I am, Huouyt."

"I know I am," Jer'ait said, picking himself up. Still, his eyes paused a moment on the body of the other Peacemaker. His insides had literally exploded over the walls, and it had taken but a twitch of the Jreet's arm.

Finding a grudging new respect for the Sentinel, Jer'ait stepped inside the room and squatted in front of the wide-eyed Ueshi lying still on the floor. It shied away from Jer'ait, whimpering and closing its eyes. When Jer'ait administered the antidote, the Ueshi gasped in terror.

"He's not the one who took your finger," Daviin said, lowering his energy level. "That one's dead."

Jer'ait had to turn at the concern in the Jreet's voice. The giant was almost...gentle.

Seeing the Jreet, the Ueshi's binocular blue eyes widened to their fullest. "I'm sorry," he babbled. "Jemria told me to—"

At the name, Jer'ait froze. So *that's* what was going on.

"Silence!" the Jreet snapped, his tenderness gone in an instant. "I'm here to rescue you, not to listen to you whimper."

Jer'ait wished the Jreet a new world of agony. Taking a deep, calming breath, he turned back to the Ueshi. "What were you saying?"

The Ueshi's eyes went wide. "N-n-never m-m-m—"

"Finish your sentence!" the Jreet roared.

Jer'ait got up, grabbed Daviin by the audial ridges against the back of the skull, and dragged him down so they were eye-to-eye. Quietly, he said, "I think the Ueshi and I need to be alone. Go watch the hall."

"You don't order me around, Huouyt," Daviin boomed.

"I *do*, or should I tell Joe you're disobeying an order from his Second?"

Daviin's face scrunched. "My hearing is better than a Dhasha's. There's no one out there."

Oh, how Jer'ait wanted to strangle the ignorant, blockheaded creature! As evenly as he could, Jer'ait said, "I don't think you understood me. I need time with the Ueshi to figure out where he learned how to operate on a Jreet." He cocked his head at Daviin. "Or did you think I just came here to free him?"

Daviin straightened in a display that made Jer'ait wince inwardly. *This is where he gets stubborn.*

"I will not let you torture him."

"Jreet, I'm warning you…"

Daviin shoved past him and plucked the Ueshi off the floor. The poor creature gave a terrified whimper and pungent black liquid trickled from its glands. "Please don't hurt me. I—"

"Shut up," Daviin snapped.

"Excellent!" Jer'ait cried, gesturing widely in frustration. "You refuse to let me give a friendly interrogation, but you make him void himself by screaming at him while he's dangling not two ninths from your tek."

Daviin's brow-ridges tightened, then he shifted his gaze to the Ueshi. "I won't let him torture you. You saved my hearing."

Jer'ait took a deep breath, mentally deciding which poisons he would have to use. Then he said, "I suppose you're right, Daviin. He spent twice as long patching you up as the Welu. He took *special* care with you. You were in good hands."

The Jreet's muscular body constricted. He tore his gaze from Jer'ait and glanced down at the creature in his arms as if it had suddenly turned to a frozen Takki.

"After all," Jer'ait continued, "It's not every Jreet who has his own personal guardian angel."

The Jreet dropped the Ueshi suddenly. The weak blue creature crumpled to the ground with a wail, then scuttled backwards on its delicate front limbs.

"In fact," Jer'ait said, "I think he's probably saved your life twice already. The concussion from the sound grenade left you with a lot of internal bleeding near the brain. If he hadn't chosen to help you over the Welu, you'd be dead now."

Tension was drawing the Jreet's lower body into semi-coils, his face tightening into a mask of rage. He raised himself until he was glaring down at the Ueshi. "You helped me over the Welu?"

The ignorant little Ueshi nodded up and down. Jer'ait had to stifle a snicker.

"How *dare* you?" the Jreet roared, surging upward until he was pressed against the ceiling. "I'll make you dance on my tek until your feet bleed, coward!" Daviin reached down for the trembling Ueshi, obviously intending to do just as he said.

"You know," Jer'ait said, "I know a thing or two about pain."

Daviin hesitated, turning toward him. "What?"

"Pain. You want him to feel much of it, yes?"

"I want him to scream until the hells open up and swallow him," Daviin growled. "Before the end, he'll know better than to coddle a Voran!" He grasped the terrified Ueshi by the thin blue arm and dragged him to his feet. With no finesse whatsoever, he thrust the tek from its sheath, making it hover ninths from the babbling creature's squirming body.

"Perhaps you're right," Jer'ait said, praying the Jreet didn't do something incredibly furgish before he could stop him. "Dancing on a tek is a very good way to make an enemy scream, however short-lived it may be."

Daviin tightened his claws around the unfortunate Ueshi. "Short? I'll draw it out."

"Oh, absolutely," Jer'ait said. "I'm sure you could teach me a thing or two. After all, on Va'ga, we only learned a few thousand ways to induce pain. You, though…You'll probably make him cower in terror, threatening to poison him for hours until you finally give him peace. It will be educational."

Daviin twisted around to scowl at him. "You think you could do better?"

Jer'ait gave a confident snort. "I can make it last so long he forgets his own name, and the pain he'd endure would have him screaming until the dawn." He yawned. "But, obviously, I can't do that."

"Why?" Daviin demanded, dragging the blinking Ueshi around to face Jer'ait.

Jer'ait shrugged. "The honor is yours. After all, it's you he wronged. I'm just here to watch."

Daviin glanced down at the whimpering creature in his grasp, then shoved him toward Jer'ait. "You do it."

Jer'ait shoved the Ueshi back at the Jreet. "No, Daviin. I'll not take your vengeance from you."

"Putting him in the hands of a Va'gan is vengeance enough." The Jreet shoved the Ueshi back, making the poor creature let out a terrified cry and drop to the floor in a huddle between them.

Jer'ait eyed the Ueshi, then the Jreet. "Very well. How much pain would you have me give him?"

"Enough to make his ancestors feel it."

Jer'ait nodded, giving the Jreet a grim look. "You should go watch the hall. His screaming will arouse suspicion."

"But I want to see the little worm die!" Daviin cried.

"He's already dead," Jer'ait said solemnly. "Now go. You'll not enjoy the preparations. I'll have to meditate on my poisons and say a prayer for the gods of Va'ga."

The last thing the Jreet wanted to hear was a Va'gan prayer.

Daviin glared at him, then at the Ueshi, then nodded and went out into the hall. As soon as he was outside, Jer'ait locked the door behind him.

"Why'd you lock the door?" Daviin demanded from the other side.

"Only our victims are allowed to witness our prayers," Jer'ait snapped. "Unless you want me to kill you, too, you ignorant janja pile!"

The Jreet made a grumbling noise on the other side, but said nothing.

Jer'ait turned to the whimpering Ueshi. "Now what were you saying about Forgotten?"

The Ueshi blinked its glistening blue eyes, his crest quivering in horror. "I was told not to tell."

"Believe me, Ueshi, I can make you tell."

"You're going to kill me, aren't you?" the Ueshi wailed.

"That's what I told the Jreet," Jer'ait said. "However, I'm not sure that's wise, given the name you just dropped. Jemria. There's only a handful of people in the universe who know of that name. What does Forgotten want with Daviin?"

"He w-w-wants him t-t-to live." The Ueshi's blue headcrest was trembling again.

"Obviously. But why?"

"He never said why," the Ueshi whimpered. "Please."

Jer'ait cocked his head, intrigued. "Is it possible our mythical Geuji has decided to help us fight the Vahlin?"

"Anything's p-possible with J-Jemria," the Ueshi agreed.

"So the Geuji does not enjoy the thought of a universe ruled by Dhasha. How surprising. Are you charged with tending the Welu heir, as well?"

"No, sir," the Ueshi doctor babbled. "There's another Ueshi tending that one."

"Where did he find you two? I thought Jreet didn't have doctors."

"Jemria trained us both, sir." Then, at Jer'ait's sharp glance, he whimpered, "On his ship. I was from a poor hatch. Couldn't get into medical school on my own. He told me he'd teach me. He took me to his ship. T-taught me everything about Jreet."

Jer'ait's eyes narrowed. "Does he continue to contact you?"

"No, sir."

Daviin pounded on the door, making the entire room reverberate with the sound of his huge fist. "I don't hear screaming, Va'gan!"

"Give me time, you underbred oaf!" Jer'ait snapped. To the Ueshi, he said, "You must have a system worked out. Once this is over, how will you get paid?"

"He'll deliver it to my accounts, sir."

"What bank will he use?"

The Ueshi blinked at him. "He won't use a bank."

Jer'ait peered at the Ueshi. "Now that we've freed you, what will you do?"

"My orders were to stay until Daviin left the war, sir."

"But a Huouyt assassin attacked you," Jer'ait pointed out. "It gives you great cause to flee."

The little Ueshi's big eyes boggled. "If I left Daviin, Jemria would kill me."

"So you truly intend to stay."

The Ueshi nodded vehemently.

Jer'ait cursed. He was staring an agent of the Geuji in the eyes and he couldn't haul him back to Levren for questioning. He straightened, irritated. "I'll see the Huouyt who abducted you dies in your place. They'll stop searching for you. Just use a different alias next time you come to work on the Jreet and you'll be fine. We can never tell you Ueshi apart, anyway."

"Huouyt!" the Jreet shouted, pounding on the door again. This time the wall around it vibrated and strained dangerously. "What's taking so long?!"

"Lie down," Jer'ait told the Ueshi. "I will come back for you in an hour."

The Ueshi's head-crest gave a terrified flutter. "But…"

"Do it! Stare at the ceiling." Once the Ueshi had reluctantly complied, Jer'ait walked up to the door and opened it. "We can go, Daviin. My work here is done."

Daviin peeked in at the Ueshi and immediately his face contorted. "You told me he'd feel pain."

"Right now, he is experiencing a level of pain beyond pain itself," Jer'ait said, glancing over his shoulder at the Ueshi doctor. "A horror only a Va'ga can unleash upon him. His ancestors will truly feel it."

"You said there would be screaming!" Daviin roared.

"Oh there will be," Jer'ait assured him solemnly. "At the end."

Daviin turned to peer at Jer'ait, interest lighting his metallic eyes. "At the end?"

"At the end, he will scream until he gurgles blood."

The Jreet twisted to stare back at the Ueshi, obviously impressed. "Can we watch?"

"By all means," Jer'ait said, gesturing towards the door. "Joe won't begrudge a few hours from his Sentinel. As I understand, he never wanted you to bind to him in the first place."

"True." Daviin reluctantly pulled his head from the room. "But the fool steps in trouble like a *melaa* steps in its own shit. We'd best be getting back."

Jer'ait sighed and glanced at the Ueshi. "It's a shame to leave such masterful work unwitnessed."

"Show me again later," Daviin said. "Right now, you must help me get out of this maze so I can find my ward."

"Very well," Jer'ait said reluctantly. "This way."

22

FLEA KICKS ASS

All around them, the sounds of the shuttle's engines roared as it broke into Neskfaat's atmosphere.

In one corner of the shuttle, the Jreet and the Baga were throwing dice and taunting each other. The Ooreiki was watching closely, his lower body pooled into a blob of what looked like biosuit-coated blubber. Jer'ait was staring across the room at the far wall, saying nothing. Scarab, alone in his corner, awaited the next mission in silence.

Watching him stare straight ahead, black eyes utterly emotionless, Joe wondered if the Grekkon even cared about what the others in the shuttle were doing. Scarab looked like a statue of a colossal, mutated Earth insect, and his constant, mute silence wasn't doing much to dispel the image.

That morning, Headquarters had delivered the orders for every soldier of the first wave to return to the tunnels. Six days early. Their excuse was that they were investigating reports of a leak within the command, but everyone knew that it was because Daviin and the Welu heir had almost killed each other.

Congress was putting them back to work as quickly as possible, as many times as possible, before the inter-species groups disintegrated.

They'd already been written off as losses.

At this point, Joe and everyone else waiting in the exit bay already had their final messages recorded and ready to go. Their barracks room was spotless, their belongings packed neatly at the foot of their beds, their wills copied and laid out on the center of their beds to expedite the cleanup process.

Though Headquarters hadn't had the balls to say it, Joe had the feeling that none of the survivors of the first wave were leaving in anything other than bodybags. They'd already beaten the odds by taking out a prince, so as far as Congress was concerned, any Dhasha they killed from here on out was merely a bonus. They'd never join the second, larger wave of attackers because they would be dead long before PlanOps assembled for the next attack.

To make things worse, all of Joe's suspicions had been thoughtfully confirmed by the Baga. Flea had eavesdropped on the Overseers for three days, trying to determine which of them was responsible for the leak. He'd found nothing, aside from the fact that anything Joe's team did from here on was simply going to be a statistic for some Bajna number-cruncher.

There would be no survivors of the first wave. They would send them back again and again until they were all dead or the second wave was ready for its attack.

None of them had any delusions about surviving that long.

"*Well,*" Galek said, rising from the pool of flesh beside Flea and Daviin, "*At least whoever kills the next prince is getting a* kasja. *About time. They should give one to Jer'ait for the first prince.*"

"*What would you do with a* kasja *if you got one, Galek?*" Jer'ait asked.

"*Wear it,*" Galek said, with a look that suggested the Huouyt had asked the stupidest question in the world.

"*He's talking about the money,*" Joe said. "*The three mil.*"

"*Oh.*" Galek gave him a sheepish look. "*Set it aside for retirement, I guess,*" Galek said. "*What about you, Daviin?*"

Daviin, looked up from his dice, "*I care not for Congressional honors nor its money.*" He gave a fearsome Jreet grin. "*I'm winning all I need from the Baga.*" He jingled a bag of tokens above their game.

"*Eat me,*" Flea muttered.

"*Careful, he just might,*" Jer'ait snorted.

"*Flea, what do they know about the Vahlin?*" Scarab interrupted. It was the first thing the Grekkon had said since coming out of the tunnels.

Flea turned away from the dice game with obvious relief. "*The Vahlin? They think he's a thousand turns old, one of the leaders of the last Dhasha rebellion that somehow got off the planet.*" He flicked one of his claw-like arms dismissively. "*The Peacemakers have no idea where he is. They've got reports he's everywhere from straddling the north pole to living in a sealed bubble under the south ocean, they've got no real information on who he has with him, and they don't even know his name. They've been trying for rotations but still have no spies in the Vahlin's employ, something that made them call for the Huouyt Overseer's resignation at the last meeting.*"

"*So,*" Scarab said, "*we know nothing.*"

"*Yeah,*" Flea admitted. "*They were throwing around the idea of offering full retirement and benefits to anyone who can bring them information on the Vahlin. You heard them at the briefing. It's their number one concern, aside from convincing Koliinaat to let them blow up Neskfaat. They're desperate. I tell you, if we bring back some dirt on the Vahlin, they'll give us anything we want. Hell, they'd promote us all. Joe, they'd give you Overseer in a heartbeat.*"

Joe glanced at the Baga, slightly uncomfortable at how much he had learned from his eavesdropping.

The shuttle thumped and the engines died. Daviin raised his energy level and vanished from the visible spectrum. Everyone tensed as the door opened. Seeing nothing hiding amidst the gelatinous red foliage, they unloaded.

"*Flea, Daviin, you two are working together again. Assume they know we're coming. Jer'ait, you go left, Flea and Daviin take right. We're moving up two hundred rods from the dropoff and Scarab's digging us a fighting pit. If you guys encounter more than you can handle, get your asses back here.*"

His team split, with Jer'ait taking the form of a Jikaln warrior. His body blended with the thick, heavy scarlet foliage, rendering him almost as invisible as the Jreet as he disappeared into the forest.

Joe picked a high spot and the Grekkon dug a short tunnel for the three of them. Then, with Joe and Galek guarding the entrance with plasma rifles and biosuits, they waited.

Jer'ait was the first to report.

"There's a group of Takki guarding our planned penetration point. I've counted three hundred sixteen so far. 'Bout half of them are carrying laser rifles. I suggest the Baga retreat before he's seen. The Jreet and I might be able to clear out a path to the penetration point."

"Crack you, Huouyt," Flea snapped. *"I've killed three of them so far. We do this together."*

"You're not doing it at all," Joe said. *"Get back here. All three of you. Scarab will dig us a tunnel all the way to the den."*

"That will use up all of my secretions," Scarab said quickly. *"At this distance, if I hit a main corridor, I won't be able to back up and seek out a slave tunnel. We'd be down there without an escape route."*

"I think the three of us can take out the defenders," Daviin insisted.

"Think about it, goddamn it," Joe snapped. *"Instead of six battalions on each prince this time, we've got three* groundteams. *They've got more Takki to go around, and just like last time, they knew we were coming. Except this time, they know where we're planning our tunnel penetration. The Takki are a distraction. They'll have Dhasha waiting for us there, too. Now get your asses back here before you're seen."*

Joe realized suddenly that it was his three most stubborn ground-mates who were out there, and all three of them had told him to go to hell in the past. If they didn't agree with him, they were just as likely to keep doing things their way as come back to regroup.

Please don't turn this into a fight, Joe prayed.

Jer'ait, to his surprise, was the first to return. He had found a stream or river along the way, for he had shed his Jikaln pattern and was once more in Huouyt form, his violet eye oozing irritation. He said nothing as he climbed into the Grekkon's hole, simply hunkered down and inserted something into the vertical slit in his head. The red wormy appendages of his *zora* slipped out to take it, and immediately his body grew squatter, his muscles and flesh condensing in a shifting that looked both painful and revolting. Still, no matter how many times he saw the Huouyt take a new pattern, Joe could not look away.

Flea and Daviin arrived later, though neither of them showed any of the anger Joe feared.

"*All right,*" Joe said, "*Let's go, Scarab.*"

The Grekkon did not move. "*You're talking about two ferlii lengths of extrusion, if not more. I will be useless to you afterwards, if I even make it to the tunnels.*"

"Do it," Joe said. "*This will be an easy crawl anyway.*"

"*It's never an easy crawl,*" Scarab said, its four black eyes staring back at him. Then, slowly, the Grekkon bowed its two spearlike appendages until they almost touched the ground. "*But you are Prime.*"

Scarab wordlessly began backing into the soil behind him at an imperceptible angle towards the Dhasha den. He was gone so fast that Joe and the others had trouble keeping up.

They were panting by the time the Grekkon backed into a slave tunnel and reversed. Jer'ait and Flea took opposite directions and disappeared down the tunnels as Joe rigged a mask for the entrance.

"*Clear toward the surface,*" the Baga said. "*The end is sealed maybe ninety rods up.*"

"*No Takki guarding it?*" Daviin asked.

"*If there are, they're not on this side.*"

"Good," Joe said. "*Get back down here. Jer'ait, what do you see?*"

"*Tunnel's different from all the slave tunnels I've ever seen,*" Jer'ait said slowly. "*There's less confusion about where the tunnels want to go.*"

"*I agree,*" the Baga said. "*None of that up and down and sideways crack. I can go full bore and not worry about slamming into a wall.*"

"*Another oddity,*" Jer'ait added, "*There's no side tunnels so far. No Takki, either.*"

"*Probably won't find any until we start hitting other tunnels. Jer'ait, stay there. Flea, Daviin, go down there and meet him. Scarab, stay here and guard our way out.*" As Flea sped past at almost fifty lengths an hour, Joe switched his headcom to broadcast to the other three groundteams who were supposed to making the insertion with them. "*Teams One and Three, you make it?*"

Nothing.

"*We're on our own again,*" Joe said, after he repeated his request. He glanced at Galek, signaling for him to wait to follow the others into the slave tunnel. "*Flea, you catch up with Jer'ait yet?*"

"*Caught up and passed,*" Flea announced. "*Still no connections.*"

Joe frowned. "*How far have you gone?*"

"*I don't know. A long way.*"

"*And no connecting tunnels?*"

"*No, Commander.*"

Joe blinked at the added 'Commander.' He wondered if the Baga was being sarcastic. "*All right, go another hundred rods. If you don't find anything, stop. This might not be a deep den. We might've found something else.*"

"*Like what?*" Galek asked.

"*I was told this planet used to belong to the Trosska. Mineral-rich. Had some ruvmestin pockets. We could be in a mine shaft.*"

The Baga obeyed, then said, "*I went a ways further and still see nothing.*"

"*All right,*" Joe said, "*Everybody stay where you are. Flea, go find out what's at the end.*"

"*Flea?*" Joe asked, after a couple tics.

"*Still going,*" Flea responded. "*No connections so far.*"

"*Nobody would dig a tunnel like this without a reason for it. Let us know as soon as you find something.*"

Ten tics later, Flea said, "*I think I found a slave tunnel.*"

Joe sat up. "Ghosts. How deep are you?"

"*I don't know, but it's crackin' hot. A furnace. I'm surprised the walls aren't glowing.*"

"*What makes you think it's a slave tunnel?*" Jer'ait asked.

"*There's Takki crawling in and out of it.*"

"Ash," Joe said. "How *deep did you say you were?*"

"*Deep enough to make my abbas feel like they're drying out.*"

"*Probably a length or two,*" Daviin said. "*On Vora, we dig deep because we like it hot.*"

"*Flea, take a guess on the temp,*" Joe said.

"*A lot warmer than your skin. Almost like the casing on a haauk generator after it's been running a few hours.*"

"Soot," Joe cursed. "*That'd kill me without my biosuit. Jer'ait, you gonna be okay down there?*"

"*I doubt it. Huouyt cannot operate in conditions over sixty-nine-point-three grads Standard for long. Even in another species' pattern, our* zora *begin to lose functionality once they reach sixty-nine grads. After our core temperature reaches the breaking point and remains there for more than four tics, our zora will go into hibernation and we will lose our pattern, thereby quickening our demise, as our natural bodies are aquatic.*"

"*Are you trying to tell me it'd kill you to go down there with him?*"

"*It's a strong possibility, Commander.*"

Joe glanced at the Grekkon, who was sulking in the small trap-hole he had dug in the wall with his remaining secretions. They were down two teammates and they hadn't even met the enemy yet.

"*Flea, how easily do you think you could follow those Takki you're seeing?*"

"*It'd be easier to pluck the scales off a live Dhasha than get through there unseen.*"

"*Too many Takki?*"

"*That, and the tunnel's small.*"

"*Too small for Daviin to slip through?*"

"*He could make it through, but the Takki would know he's there.*"

"*How about deeper in the shaft we're in? There might be another entrance.*"

"*You want me to go* deeper? *Any deeper and my wings are gonna catch fire.*"

"*Go deeper,*" Joe ordered.

The Baga did not report for another tic. Finally, he said, "*There's another tunnel, but it's too small for Daviin. Joe, you might be able to make it, but you'd have to crawl on your stomach. That fat Ooreiki would get stuck. Damn, it's hot down here.*"

Coldness traced along Joe's spine as he listened to the Baga's report. He was once more all too aware of a tunnel crawl fifty turns before, one in which they had lost his groundteam's flag and Joe had been utterly too terrified to go back and look for it—and had subjected his entire platoon to a suicidal frontal assault instead. "*Flea, see if you can find a bigger tunnel.*"

"*This is it,*" Flea said. "*The last one down. All the others were crawling with Takki. This one looks like some sort of waste shaft. Got a little stream running out of it. Probably comes right out of the prince's watering hole.*"

"*Did anyone see you?*" Joe asked.

"*No. One thing about these Takki…they've got vision like a Jreet.*"

"*I see well enough to whip you at dice, Baga.*"

"*Tonight we'll try cards, Jreet. When I'm finished with you, you'll slither back to Vora crying like a Cu'it slave.*"

"*Like you cried last night after losing all your credits?*"

"*It's hot down here. Commander, if you don't need me, I'm getting back to somewhere cooler.*"

"*Check out the tunnel,*" Joe ordered. "*If it goes to the den, that's where we'll make our insertion.*"

The Baga said nothing for several more tics. Then, "*Yep. Straight to the deep den. My scanner says there's twelve adults in here, not counting the females, though none over five digs. The prince himself is only a little bigger. Lots of young, though, and I'm pretty sure some of them are small enough to fit in the slave tunnels. Want me to stick the prince?*"

Joe took a deep breath. "*No. I'm coming down with you. Meet me at the tunnel entrance.*"

"*What about the rest of us?*" Daviin asked.

"*Stay where you are right now. I'm gonna go check out the situation in the deep den first.*"

It took Joe almost two hours to get down to the Baga without alerting the Takki. His stomach did a flip when he saw the tiny opening the Baga had found. Water trickled in a warm, brackish rivulet along the floor. Joe could imagine his body plugging the hole like a stopper in a vial, and his subsequent drowning as the water piled up around him, with nowhere to go.

Ghosts of the Mothers, he wants me to crawl in there?

"*Well?*" Flea demanded. "*Can you do it or not, counter?*"

"I can fit," Joe said, more strongly than he felt.

"*So who you want to go first?*"

"You," Joe said. "*I might block the tunnel for you.*"

"*You might block it behind me, too, counter. Then we'd both be stuck down there.*"

"*Just get your ass in the tunnel.*"

Flea made a disgusted noise and obeyed. For his part, Joe stared at tiny tunnel entrance until he could feel the heat that had nothing to do with temperature slickening his neck and palms. *God hates a coward*, he thought, with more determination than he felt.

Reluctantly, Joe got on his knees and pushed his gun into the darkened entrance. The tunnel sloped up, not down. As such, it was not going to afford Joe the advantage of being out of reach in the high ground when the shit hit the fan. What was worse, if he didn't move fast enough when the Dhasha started attacking, it would pluck him out of his hole as easily as a robin pulling out a worm.

Taking a deep breath, Joe got onto his stomach and eased his head and shoulders into the tunnel. Immediately, the brackish stink of water assaulted his senses. The walls of the tunnel almost touched his back, and his arms had only ninths on either side. Joe tried not to think of the stream running around his waist and legs as he pushed himself deeper into the tunnel.

The further he went, the greater the sensation that he was trapped. *If I have to back out, I won't make it. I'll wedge myself in and the water will build up and I'll have nowhere to go...*

Finally, Joe had to close his eyes and concentrate to calm his breathing.

"A little claustrophobic, Commander?" Flea asked.

Joe cried out and tried to stand, only succeeding in straining his body against the ceiling of the tunnel. "*You son of a bitch!*" Joe snapped through his headcom, barely able to avoid shouting out loud. He located the Baga hidden in a crevice in the rock ceiling ahead. Only the faceted burgundy eyes were visible in the shadows, watching him.

"*What happened?*" Daviin asked quickly.

Joe closed his eyes and tried to slow his heartbeat. "*Nothing. Stay where you are. I'm almost to the den.*"

"Sorry," the Baga said out loud, sounding hesitant. "I was just teasing—I didn't realize..."

"Just shut up and go," Joe said.

The Baga scuttled out of the shadows and disappeared in the tunnel ahead with a speed to envy.

"*I'm waiting for you at the exit,*" Flea announced within a tic.

Joe gritted his teeth and tried to move faster. His left hand was clenched around his rifle, but he could feel his fingers shaking regardless. He squeezed them down and kept moving, trying to do anything but think about the walls of rock surrounding him, the trickle of water being diverted over his body.

Joe smelled the puddle before he saw it. The tunnel began to stink of stagnant water and at first Joe thought he had finally reached the deep den. Then he crawled over a ridge and faced two ninths of air above eight ninths of water. It looked like it stretched several digs, though further on, the stone ceiling dipped down and touched the water, blocking the rest of the tunnel from sight.

Joe stared at it, sucking in panicked lungfuls of stale, brackish air. He had the choice of continuing and risking drowning if the ceiling didn't rise again, or trying to back out. He did not want to back out.

"*Flea, how'd you get past this water?*"

"*I swam.*"

"*How long 'til I'll reach air?*"

"*I don't know. A few digs. I don't need to worry about air.*"

"*Goddamn it. You don't* breathe? *Didn't you think about that when you said I could make it through here?*"

"*I said you could fit. And you did. Everything else is up to you.*"

If Joe had had the opportunity, he gladly would have crushed the Baga all over again. "*All right, furg, if I die, this is on your head.*"

"*It's on your own head. You're the one who wouldn't let me stick the prince by myself.*"

Joe ground his jaw until it hurt. *God hates a coward,* he mentally chanted. It had been one of his father's favorite sayings, something he'd always said right before he was about to do something he knew was furgish. Yet Joe, like many Jreet, had taken it closer to heart than that, and had used it to keep himself sane on Eeloir. To his surprise, Bagkhal had picked up the saying from him and had used it ever since. One of the many ways his old Overseer had surprised him.

God hates a coward. God hates a coward...

Then, taking a deep breath, he pushed himself into the puddle. He had to fight down his nerves as water rose all around him and he had to crane his neck up to the ceiling to breathe. Then, praying the Baga wasn't playing a sick joke, he sucked in as much air as he could and ducked his head under the stone outcropping. He pushed himself forward, feeling the ceiling with one hand and keeping his rifle ahead of him with the other.

Panic clawed at his lungs when he realized the tunnel was dropping, sloping down instead of up. He sped up, trying desperately to stay calm. The tunnel had just started to slope back toward the surface, relief overriding every other part of his brain, when the Baga said, *"Commander, you might want to surface slowly. We're in the Dhasha's watering hole."*

Joe checked his upward climb with a spasm of panic. His lungs clawing for air, he backed down to the bottom and thought, *"Why didn't you say something sooner, you little sootwad?!"*

"It didn't occur to me you'd try to surface like a bumbling Takki clown."

If Joe could have seen the Baga through the thick, brackish water, he would have swam the little insect down and strangled him. Instead, he backed up until he could feel the rock wall beside him and slowly allowed his head to surface, ready to suck in a lungful of air and duck back into the tunnel if necessary.

The room was filled with Dhasha. Packed. The ceiling was low, adding to the place's hot, stifling feel. Joe took several deep breaths, doing it as slowly as he could to avoid catching attention from the enemy.

"They're in a meeting," Joe said. *"Sounds like the prince is pissed."*

"About what?" Jer'ait asked.

"They can't find us," Joe said. He frowned, listening.

"...was correct. The third groundteam contains both a Jreet and a Huouyt. I was told the Huouyt shouldn't be a problem at these temperatures, but no one moves from this room until we have visual confirmation on the Jreet."

"Bones," Joe muttered.

"What, Human?" Daviin demanded.

"*This prince is smart. He's got all the Dhasha walled up in the deep den.*"

"*Waiting for us to come to them?*"

"*He's waiting for one of the Takki to spot you,*" Joe said.

"*Any of us or just me?*" Daviin demanded.

"*Just you. Somebody told them there's a Jreet on our team. They know about Jer'ait, too.*"

"*So the Vahlin has predicted two of our attacks now,*" Jer'ait said. "*Accurately, and ahead of time.*"

"*Looks like,*" Joe said grimly. "*Okay, Daviin, time for you to show your stuff. Flea and I aren't gonna be able to kill the prince with all his young surrounding him.*"

"*You want me to come help you fight them?*"

"*No. I want you to create a diversion.*"

Absolute silence followed his statement. Then, "*A…diversion?*" Like Joe had asked him to knit teddy bears.

"*We need to clear them out of the den. That means they need to think they know where you are.*"

"*Which they will.*"

"*Not if you are smart about it.*"

It took a painfully long time for the Jreet to say, "*How?*"

"*Go down to the first connection and kill anything you find down there. Galek, follow him. As soon as he's got it cleared, drag the bodies out of view and take a position guarding the crossroads. Daviin, take whichever tunnel looks like it's heading to the surface and silence whatever you see along the way. As soon as you hit a main shaft, let one of the Takki escape. Then get the hell out of there. Take the main shaft as far as you can towards the surface and hide out.*"

"*That's suicide,*" the Grekkon interrupted. "*You forget, Human, I cannot dig him out.*"

"*I'm not asking you to,*" Joe said. "*He's gonna have to find his own way out.*"

The headcom descended into silence as his groundmates digested this. Finally, Daviin said, "*I can get into the deep den. I might be able to kill the prince.*"

"*Flea's right. There's no way you're getting through the waste tunnel, and there's an even fatter chance you'd make it through the slave tunnel without*" *the prince knowing you're coming. Besides, this prince isn't asking around. He'd send his young ones after you and you'd have nowhere to go. They'd flood that whole tunnel and we'd all be screwed. We need to draw them up a main shaft, away from us."*

"Very well," Daviin said. *"Galek, come with me."*

Joe waited as they cleared a path and took their positions. In the meantime, he watched as Flea made his painfully slow climb out of the water ditch and onto the ceiling. Time seemed to creep past with every cautious movement of the Baga's black claws. A Dhasha came to the ditch and Joe pressed himself to the wall, rigidly still as the oblivious Dhasha drank its fill not a rod away. As the Dhasha lifted its head and allowed the stray water to dribble from between its razor black teeth, Daviin said, *"If they weren't so irrational, these tunnels would remind me of home."*

"Did you find a main passage yet?" Joe asked, trying not to move. Before him, the Dhasha turned back to the room and rejoined the group.

"No. All slave tunnels so far. Killed a lot of Takki, though."

"Takki don't count unless we kill them all. Then we can go home and let the Space Corps bury this place."

"Don't they have a Takki plague they used in the last war?" Flea asked from his position on the ceiling. *"Why not just spread that stuff out here?"*

"It was eighty thousand turns ago," Joe said. *"And it almost wiped out the Takki and the Dhasha in one go."*

"Then why are we wasting our time down here?"

"Because they barely contained it last time. The Dhasha went nuts. Forced Congress to ban it or declare outright war. Congress gave in and the Dhasha made all the surviving Takki take gene-enhancers. They're immune now."

"So they should make another one," Flea muttered.

"Even if Mekkval would allow it—which he wouldn't—they'd have to come up with something nobody's ever seen before. Ever since they almost lost their Takki, Dhasha have been enhancing their genetics. They literally can't get sick."

"Found a main shaft."

"*Vanish and kill something,*" Joe said. "*Then move down the tunnel and keep killing, maybe two or three more. Then let something see you. Then backtrack and get out of there as fast as you can.*"

"*They'll see the pattern of bodies and think I'm continuing toward the deep den.*"

"*We can hope.*"

"*Interesting. You know, technically, that verges on dishonorable.*"

Joe knew he was treading dangerous ground at that moment. If he said the wrong thing, then Daviin might allow his scruples to overcome his good sense and continue toward the deep den anyway.

The Baga saved him. "*Tricking Takki is as easy as taking money from Jreet. You can't always hold their hands, as much as you feel sorry for them.*"

Daviin chuckled over the mind-band. "How *much* did you lose already, Baga? I forget."

"*That's nothing new,*" the Baga retorted. "*Wait 'till we play cards, Jreet. There isn't a better card player on this planet. I'll earn those credits back and more*"

"*So you say.*" The headcom went silent before the Jreet said, "*It is done. I'm backtracking. Should I return to the slave tunnel I came from?*"

"*No,*" Joe said, knowing as he said so he was risking Daviin's life. "*We can't take the chance they'll follow you back to the rest of us.*"

Instead of arguing, Daviin said, "*Understood.*"

From the ceiling, Flea suddenly cried, "*It's working! Daviin, they're coming after you!*"

"*All of them?*" Joe asked. He couldn't see through the wall of Dhasha bodies, but he felt a stirring in the air.

"*They're fighting to be the first in the tunnel.*"

"*Is the prince staying?*" Daviin asked.

"*Yeah. He went to the back and laid down. He's got a couple of little ones and his females with him.*"

"*Wait for them to clear before we do anything,*" Joe said at the excitement in the Baga's voice. "*It's the small ones we're worried about. They can follow us back into the tunnels.*"

"*You actually think they'd get their scales wet?*"

"*No, but I'm not taking any chances.*"

The last of the Dhasha cleared out, leaving Joe an unobstructed view of the niche containing the prince, three females, and two hatchlings barely reaching Joe's thigh.

"*This is going to be difficult,*" Joe said. "*We need to make a plan—*"

"*You get the females,*" the Baga said. Then he began spitting.

Silently cursing the Baga, Joe lifted his rifle and started firing.

The prince got up under Flea's assault and found itself stuck to its hatchlings. It roared and, in a screaming, flailing shower of scales, began attacking the two smaller Dhasha. One of the females got sucked into the mess, and in less than a tic, all that was left of her was three separate ribbons of meat. The two younger males—having the indestructible rainbow outer layer of scales—were faring better, but were still succumbing to their father's rage. One was secured firmly by his back to the prince's left leg, and the other's face was fused to the prince's side.

Though Joe hit the prince by accident as he shot the three females, the plasma bounced harmlessly off its scales, lodging in the stone wall behind and melting it into bluish-brown sludge. Without the protective outer scales of the males, however, the females could not withstand the plasma. They died quickly, their fat stomachs roiling with baby Dhasha who, even without being born, had been infected with their father's blood-lust. Joe could hear them tearing each other apart in the womb.

On the ceiling above, the Baga calmly spat blob after blob of mucousy gray material into strategic places in the fray. Once the young and females were dead, he went on to bind the male's front paws to the rock floor, then followed with his hind paws. Joe jumped out of the water ditch and rushed forward, readying his hatchet. He only had moments to hack a hole in the prince's chest deep enough for a plasma round to take hold and be lethal enough to kill.

Before Joe could reach the Dhasha, the Baga dropped from the ceiling and hovered above the prince's head. He spat a wad into the Dhasha's face, dousing the flaring air-hole beside an egglike emerald eye in gray slime, plugging it.

The prince went stiff, then roared as Flea spat another glob, covering his other nostril. Watching it, Joe almost felt a pang of pity. Even if he weren't pinned to the ground, the prince would never be able to breathe again. The Dhasha struggled, slowly suffocating. As Joe watched, his body went limp and he slid to the ground, still propped up by the way his stubby legs were fused to the floor.

Joe stared. He had been ready for a fight, ready to hack open a hole in the monster's chest so he could blast it with plasma. He'd never imagined a creature as tiny as the Baga could kill a beast like the Dhasha. It defied imagination.

"*You kick ass, Flea,*" Joe said.

"*I know,*" Flea said, calmly dropping to the floor near one of the Dhasha's front feet.

"C'mon, let's get out of here," Joe said. He got nervous watching his groundmate scuttle closer to the Dhasha's scythelike talons.

"Give me a sec." Picking a black claw that hadn't been doused in glue, Flea snipped it off at the finger joint with his beak. Then he held the rainbow digit and its evil, gleaming ebony talon up for Joe's perusal. "My first prince."

"Great," Joe said, "Now get your ass back in the tunnel."

Flea, however, took to the air and glanced at the prince's niche. "I hear all princes hoard treasure. Think this is where he buried his wealth?" He swung over the squirming stomach of one of the females and let out an excited cry. "It is! The fight kicked up a statue and a necklace. They look like they might be ruvmestin!"

Joe glanced at the nest, which was littered with writhing bodies of dead females. He'd heard tales of Dhasha caches from other PlanOps veterans. Until now, he'd never had the opportunity to check for himself.

"Doesn't matter," Joe said. "Don't have the time. We've gotta get out of here. Daviin's alone up there."

Flea dropped down between the golden bodies of the Dhasha females. "It *is* ruvmestin! The miga's so heavy I can't carry it!"

"Ghosts," Joe muttered. A single bead of ruvmestin would buy his entire groundteam a drink every night for twenty turns.

At that moment, Galek shouted, "*A horde of Takki just crawled out of the tunnel. Couldn't take them all. They disarmed me, but they can't get through my biosuit. They're dragging me into the tunnel Daviin took, toward the surface.*"

"*Burn!*" Joe ran toward the ditch. "Flea, let's go!"

"Come grab this necklace!" Flea cried.

"No, goddamn it! Get your ass over here!"

"It's ruvmestin and Space Corps is gonna *bury* it!" Flea shrieked. "All you have to do is grab it!"

"Now, Flea!"

Flea rose from the nest with his wings working hard to keep him afloat. In his upper arms, he carried a small white statue the size of a *nuajan* stick and in his lower arms he grasped the truncated prince's claw. The Baga gave Joe a nasty look as it sped across the room and followed him to the trench.

"*Galek, what's happening?*" Joe asked. "*Flea and I are coming to help.*"

"*No,*" Jer'ait said. "*I'm already in the tunnel after him. You won't get here in time.*"

Joe blinked. "*I thought you said the temperature would kill you, Jer'ait.*"

"*They're backtracking towards the surface. I might be able to reach cooler temperatures before my* zora *overheats.*"

Joe cursed. "*We'll be there soon.*" He glanced at the Baga. "Drop those. They'll slow you down."

Flea gave him an irritated look and tossed his trophies onto the floor of the den. Then, before Joe could say anything else, he sank into the water. Joe followed at a wary distance. He'd dealt with too many Baga not to expect something psychotic.

He was still crawling through the body-fitting waste tunnel when Flea reported, "*Found your gun, Galek. They tried to hide it under some rocks about twenty rods into the tunnel going up.*"

"*Leave it out for him,*" Jer'ait said. "*We're killing the Takki that captured him as we speak.*"

"*You need help?*" Joe asked.

"*No,*" Jer'ait said, "*Just guard the way back. Galek won't be armed.*"

"*What about you?*"

"*I won't be going back that way. I'm almost overheated as it is.*"

By the time Joe made it to the Trosska mining shaft and reached the upper slave tunnel, Flea and Galek were already on their way back. He met them at the entrance and they left the Baga hidden in a crevice in the ceiling as he and the Ooreiki climbed back towards the Grekkon.

"*Jer'ait, how you doing?*"

"*I'll let you know in a couple tics,*" the Huouyt responded.

"*Hang in there.*"

Joe received no response.

"*Now what?*" Flea asked when he met up with them at Scarab's tunnel, a note of petulance to his transmission.

"*Daviin, Jer'ait, we're back at the exit tunnel. Where are you?*"

"*Lost,*" Daviin said.

"*Jer'ait?*" Joe asked.

Jer'ait did not respond.

23

CAN'T TAKE THE HEAT

Jer'ait felt the heat creeping into his body like a sedative drug. It was taking too long. His *zora* was close to overheating. The team was somewhere behind him, killing the Takki Jer'ait had passed in his desperate quest for cooler grounds.

"*Jer'ait, how you doing?*" the Human asked.

"*I'll let you know in a couple tics.*" He'd been following an upward shaft for two tics now. The air was cooling slightly, but he was sure it wasn't enough.

"*Hang in there.*"

Jer'ait said nothing, knowing that their sentimental Prime would make a mistake and send someone back for him, which would be a disaster. Jer'ait could not return to the heat of the lower tunnels without sinking into a coma. He was already facing certain unconsciousness—he could feel his *zora* straining against the Takki pattern, seeking escape from the heat. Jer'ait tried to breathe as shallowly as possible, knowing that drawing the heated air into his lungs only hastened the reaction.

He ducked into another sloped side-tunnel, hoping it continued on its upward climb. He felt numb and dazed, like he'd accidentally poisoned himself. It was hard to keep a level head as he continued his climb—the urge to lie down and go to sleep was almost overpowering. He gripped a forearm and dug the blunted claws into his skin hard enough to puncture the flesh. The pain grounded him somewhat, though the drowsiness was still there, on the edge of his awareness, growing stronger with every second. He continued on in a daze, blindly taking the path leading to the surface.

Because of this, he did not realize he'd mistakenly taken a downward-sloping tunnel until he felt the heat increase against his face.

It was then that Jer'ait's *zora* failed and he passed out.

• • •

Daviin hesitated at the entrance to the larger corridor. Somewhere far below, he heard several heavy Dhasha retreating at a jog. The cavalry returning home. But did that mean he was near his original penetration point? He could have sworn it was on the other side of the tunnel.

Damn the Takki and their mindless burrowing! There was no scheme to their digging, no logic to their creations. And, unlike the tunnels of his home on Va'ga, there were no signs, no maps, no hallmarks of civilization whatsoever.

They were so utterly irrational that Daviin was beginning to believe the haphazard layout was intentional, that it was calculated to trap fools like him.

"*Daviin?*" the Human interrupted. "*It's been three hours.*"

"*And I'm still lost,*" Daviin said. "*I told you, Commander, I got a sense of direction like a Takki's got courage.*"

"*Maybe you could capture a Takki and make it tell you where to go,*" Galek suggested.

Daviin snorted at the Ooreiki's innocence. "*Takki will not betray their masters.*"

"*But everyone says they have no honor,*" Galek said.

"*That is not honor, kid,*" Joe interrupted. "*That's fear. They're more terrified of the Dhasha than they are of a giant Jreet with his tek in their face. Forced to choose between the two, they choose the Jreet every time.*"

Daviin grinned at Joe's interpretation. Then he realized that Joe knew of such things firsthand. He grimaced.

"*But—*"

Daviin interrupted the Ooreiki. "*Take the survivors and go, Human. Jer'ait is dead or captured. I'm only exhausting myself. Four returning tonight is better than none.*"

"*Screw that,*" Flea said. "*You've still got two thousand credits that belong to me, Jreet.*"

"*I left them in my locker at the barracks,*" Daviin said. "*They're hidden under the* shea *I brought from Vora.*"

"*Ha!*" Flea cried. "*You think I didn't watch where you hid them? If I'd wanted to steal them, I'd've done it as soon as you left your room. I'll take them back fairly, Jreet.*"

Daviin chuckled. "*If I didn't know better, little Baga, I'd say you liked losing at dice.*"

"*I'm not losing. I'm gaining your confidence.*"

"*Of course you are,*" Daviin said. "*That's why I had to pay for your meal this morning.*"

Daviin could feel the tiny creature bristle. "*I overjudged the amount of money in my accounts,*" Flea said. "*It was nothing but a calculation error.*"

And it could have been, too. The Baga had no sense for numbers whatsoever. At the last meal, Daviin had watched the poor creature count its six legs in order to assure itself that everyone in the team was present.

The Human said, "*Daviin, my PPU says you're two hundred digs under the surface. If you could hold still long enough, maybe Scarab could burrow down to you.*"

"*A few hours is not long enough to recover those kind of excretions,*" Scarab said. "*Besides. The prince is dead. The mission is over. We go back.*"

Daviin heard a long pause over the communications line and he had a feeling that their Prime was having a private discussion with the Scarab. After a moment, the Human came back over the common band to say, *"Daviin, hold tight. Scarab's going to burrow to you."*

The Grekkon sounded much more subdued when it said, *"I will re-open the entrance to a main shaft."*

"And you'd have to fight hundreds of armed Takki to get to it," Daviin said. *"No, just leave. I'll find my own way eventually."*

"You'll find your own way into the grave, you stubborn Jreet. We're coming for you. Climb up the main shaft you're in. Get to the surface and we'll meet you there."

"Weren't you listening, Human?" Daviin snarled. *"Four survivors is better than none. Without me and the Huouyt, you'll get killed if you engage them up there."*

"Let us worry about that. You just get to the surface." The Human's tone of voice let Daviin know that to disobey would be to break his oath. Grimacing, Daviin began the slow, tedious process of feeling his way up the corridor.

• • •

The path to the tunnel entrance had been abandoned. The Takki had either been called back to defend the main den or had fled after hearing their master was dead.

The lack of resistance was almost eerie. Joe and Galek took opposite sides of the entrance while the Baga perched in the dense foliage above, watching for intruders.

"Nothing coming, Commander."

Joe lowered his weapon and sought out his PPU. Orienting it toward the entrance of the tunnels, he punched in the eleven-digit local frequency their chips and headcoms were using, then frowned at the five hard green dots that appeared on his screen. Three were clustered around himself, the last was marked as negative twenty-six rods on the Z axis, twenty rods on the Y and fifteen rods on the X, using the PPU as the point of reference.

One other, dangerously flickering green dot was marked negative one hundred rods Z, a thousand rods Y, and negative three hundred rods X. Its blinking had been increasing in urgency over the last six hours. Joe activated biometric stats for the sixth point.

"Ghost-bones," Joe whispered.

"What?" Galek asked. The Ooreiki's sticky brown eyes were watching the foliage in twitchy jerks, his rifle pointed at the alien forest.

"Jer'ait's still alive," Joe said.

"*What is this?*" Daviin demanded, pushing his head through the hole the Grekkon had made in the collapsed rubble.

"*The Huouyt is still alive,*" Joe said. "*He's not moving, but his body rhythms are pretty steady.*"

"*How long does he have?*" Galek asked, liquid brown eyes staring at the puncture they had just made in the den.

"*According to this?*" Joe tapped the small black device. "*Ninety-nine tics.*" Then he thrust it disgustedly back into his cargo belt. "*But we all know just how accurate this soot is. It could be two tics. Or hell, he could just be taking a nap. Who knows.*"

Galek glanced at Joe's PPU, then at the tunnel entrance. "*I'll go get him.*"

"*No,*" Joe said. "*There's no way you can get down there fast enough.*"

"*Then I'll bring him back anyway,*" Galek said stubbornly.

"*There's no way you can find him, even with the PPU,*" Joe said, irritated. The last thing he wanted to do was let the kid get himself killed. "*The place is a maze.*"

"*He's got the tunnel instinct, Joe,*" Daviin said.

Joe opened his mouth to argue, but the pleading look in the Ooreiki's sticky brown eyes forestalled him. He cursed. "*Galek, can you use a Human PPU?*"

"*I can use mine,*" Galek, said, a flash of hope in his eyes. He held up an Ooreiki PPU in his tentacles, though it failed to show the location of the other members in the group. Joe's PPU was the only one authorized to do that.

Joe glanced down at his PPU. It was a Human version, which meant it had smaller buttons than other species could comfortably handle, and therefore more of them. Aside from their linguistic skills, Humans had proven to have a digital dexterity that allowed for more detailed and complex tools, which—sometimes—meant more effective tools.

Of anyone on the team, the Ooreiki was the only other one who carried a PPU with him. The others carried no equipment whatsoever.

"*Here,*" Joe said, handing the Ooreiki his PPU. "*But you get into a fight and you clear it before you do anything else. Get me?*"

"*Yes, Commander,*" Galek said, offering Joe his PPU in return. "*I'll make it fast.*"

"We'll *make it fast,*" Daviin corrected. "*You aren't going down there without protection, Ooreiki.*"

Galek blinked at the Jreet. "*But—*"

"*You both go,*" Joe interrupted. "*And take as long as you need, just don't let that thing get in the wrong hands with our positions lit up like bulls-eyes.*"

Galek flinched like he'd hit him. "*I won't, sir.*"

"*Good. Get out of here.*"

The Ooreiki disappeared after the Jreet. Seconds ticked by like hours, and Joe began to fidget, feeling a sheen of sweat springing up on his forehead before the biosuit ate it. That distance was more than the depth of a normal deep den. It could take hours, even days, to find their teammate in the maze of tunnels. He fretted, wondering if he had given an order that would get them all killed.

"*How's it going down there?*" he finally asked.

"*This is twice I'll have had to carry the Huouyt to safety. He will not be happy.*"

"*You found Jer'ait?*"

"*The Ooreiki found him. I merely followed his lead like a lost* melaa."

"*That was fast,*" Joe said.

"*You'd be amazed at what this Ooreiki can do. He took the first slave tunnel he saw, and it was going in the* wrong *direction, I would have sworn it. Then, after a few dozen intersections, I was staring down at our Huouyt and I thought my jaw was going to fall off.*"

"*He exaggerates,*" Galek said, though Joe could tell the youngster was beaming.

"*Get back here,*" Joe said. "*You guys can brag over chow.*"

"*It's a little harder going with the Huouyt in tow. The slave tunnels are not as large or as smooth as a Grekkon's, so Galek and I are having to take turns pushing and pulling him between us.*"

"*How is Jer'ait?*"

"*Still breathing.*"

Tics later, Galek emerged from the darkness, dragging Jer'ait behind him. The Jreet followed, still invisible, the only trace he gave was a dislodged pebble and a few depressed gelatinous leaves.

The Baga dropped from his roost in the sticky alien treetops and gave the entrance to the den a wistful look. "*All that treasure down there and we're just gonna let the Space Corps bury it.*"

"*Three mil and* kasja *makes it easy to forget about it,*" Joe reminded Flea. "*Now let's get out of here.*"

● ● ●

"I'll ask you again, Jahul. What is the name of your employer?"

"I have no employer," Syuri whispered, horrified of the truth in his own words.

The Huouyt gave him an amused look and moved away from the table to take up a position along the back wall. The Jahul interrogator took his place.

"Listen, child," the elder said with a touch of Rhas Byuin accent, "We know who you're working for. We just want you to say it." He sounded almost kindly, his darker green-yellow skin dry, lacking any of the wastes Syuri had shamefully expelled all over himself during the last four days of interrogation. They had refused to allow him a shower, instead leaving him stinking of his own excrement. It was for this reason that Syuri knew that beyond the other Jahul's kindly manner, he was in truth just as dangerous as the Huouyt.

"We know you didn't come up with those codes on your own," the Rhas Byuin Overseer said, his voice still kind. "You and I both know our kind aren't capable of those calculations."

Syuri lowered his head. He could feel nothing from them—they had removed his *sivvet* the first day they had found him. The resulting blindness to the creatures around him had left Syuri in a state of shock and terror for days afterwards. His meager whisper to the Huouyt only moments before had been the first thing he had said since they had maimed him.

"The longer you sit there, Jahul, the longer your *sivvet* shrivel on ice. You know they can't be replaced. Why do you continue to provoke us?"

Syuri looked up at the Huouyt, feeling nothing behind the mask of his glacial eyes. "You destroyed them as soon as you removed them," he said, miserable. "You never planned on giving them back."

"Oh?" The Huouyt left the room and came back with three bloody lumps of twisted gray flesh pressed between two transparent plates. "Then what are these, friend?"

Syuri felt his internal pressure skyrocket, in part because his hope of regaining his sixth sense had returned, but also because the sheer brutality of the scene was the stuff of every Jahul's nightmares. They had taken his most important sensory organs and put them on display, taunting him, promising to return them to him if he cooperated.

The Rhas Byuin Jahul smiled at him as he watched his reaction. Syuri banished his thoughts of longing, but not quickly enough. His fellow Jahul could read him like an open book. "We know you want them back. We know how blind you feel without your *sivvet.*"

"So why'd you take them?" Syuri whispered, peering up into the Rhas Byuin's kind eyes. Even without his *sivvet*, he could feel the lie. Staring up into his tormentor's false kindness, Syuri suddenly felt an overpowering rage. The Rhas Byuin expected him to crumble. He expected him to grovel, spilling his every sin before them before he executed him with the same, kindly smile on his face. He cared nothing about Syuri, only about destroying him.

He may have been a Jahul, but he was just like the Huouyt.

"I'll just set these down here while we talk," the Huouyt said, lowering the transparent plates to the table across from him. Syuri felt his pressure spike, realizing that the Huouyt was going to allow his *sivvet* to warm, hastening their deterioration. The Huouyt sat down and patiently pressed his flat, paddle-like tentacles together as he looked at Syuri. His eerie white-blue eyes were emotionless. The normally writhing, hair-like cilia upon his skin was unnaturally still. Staring at the Huouyt, not being able to sense whether he wanted to help him or tear off his legs one by one, hopelessness overwhelmed Syuri.

"Nobody is coming to help you," the Rhas Byuin Jahul said, echoing his own feelings back at him. Syuri shot him a tired, angry look, then lowered his gaze back to the tabletop.

"You said having the doctors remove his *sivvet* would make him cooperate," the Huouyt said, never taking his eyes off of Syuri. "I'm beginning to think you were wrong."

For the first time, Syuri saw a sheen of liquid on the other Jahul's skin. The Rhas Byuin Jahul stood, his face clouding with anger as he glared at Syuri. "Look. We know it was Jemria who sent you. No one else would give a furgling fart about the prisoners. We know you're one of his agents. Now tell us how you contact him."

Syuri remembered the endless rows of doors, the subterranean prison. Softly, he said, "Is he the only Geuji you haven't trapped down there?"

"Trapped?" The Huouyt snorted. "They chose that fate, when they committed treason against Congress."

Syuri looked up. "What?"

"One and a half million turns ago. They tried to create their own government," the Huouyt said. His vertical mouth-slit puckered. "Obviously they failed."

Syuri was appalled. "The Dhasha try every hundred turns."

"Yes, but the Geuji would have succeeded."

The Rhas Byuin slapped the table with a slim green hand. "You're giving him too much. We're interrogating him, Cha'vai, not the other way around."

"I'm not worried about getting the information I want out of him," the Huouyt said, his eerie white-blue eyes staring fixedly at Syuri. "Like I said before you maimed him, I can do it with drugs."

"We want it to be legal, you stupid furg."

"Legalities become quite insignificant compared to what is at stake." The Huouyt had not taken his eyes off of Syuri.

The Rhas Byuin straightened angrily. "Jemria was not present at the meeting of Geuji. He hadn't been *spawned* yet. If Congress does not apprehend him legally for the crimes he *has* committed, then we have no way to charge him. Our superiors want no chance that he'll go on trial. If he does, he will not only talk hoops around our prosecutors, but he'll have a chance to get the publicity he desires and those bleeding-heart conservationists will cry over his story and demand that *all* the Geuji go free."

"Then don't give him a trial," the Huouyt said, never taking his eyes off of Syuri. "I assure you our superiors have thought of that long before this. What is important right now is apprehending him. Let the politicians bicker over the technicalities."

"But we were given specific orders to—" The Rhas Byuin caught himself, realizing Syuri was in the room. "Do not drug him until you get approval, Cha'vai."

"We'll see," the Huouyt said. Syuri could feel the press of his gaze on his skin and felt his internal pressure rising. He'd heard horrible stories about Huouyt. They were assassins that used drugs like a freight captain used his ship. Even without his *sivvet*, Syuri knew that the Huouyt could do exactly as he said and elicit the truth from him through chemicals.

The Huouyt leaned toward Syuri.

"The prisoner is a Jahul," the Rhas Byuin insisted, stepping toward them. "That puts him under Jahul authority. I'm going to have to ask you to leave, Huouyt."

"Ask all you want," the Huouyt said, never moving. "As far as I'm concerned, you might be working with him."

The Rhas Byuin made an irritated sound and went to the door. "I'll be back," he said, then slammed the door behind him.

"So," the Huouyt said with an ominous flatness to his voice, "Do you want to tell me where I can find your employer or do you want me to make you tell me?"

Syuri shuddered.

The Huouyt leaned closer, his electric eyes making the skin on Syuri's arms itch from their closeness. "I want you to think about something." As the Huouyt stared at him with his enormous, terrifying, unblinking eyes, he said, "How many times have you known Jemria to be wrong?"

Syuri dropped his gaze. "Never." His whisper felt like a stake through his chest, puncturing his inner chambers.

"You wanted to know why we keep them imprisoned down here? That is why, Jahul. Geuji are never wrong."

Syuri closed his eyes, knowing what was to come.

"And he knew you would be captured here. Tell me I'm wrong."

Syuri said nothing.

Cha'vai made an amused sound. "Forgotten's agents are notorious for their loyalty to their employer, as misplaced as it is. Do you know how many of Forgotten's agents are alive today?"

Syuri didn't want to hear it, but his hands were cuffed to the table and he could not leave.

"One." The Huouyt flicked his downy tentacle at Syuri. "You." He leaned back. "Sure, he has contacts, people we'll never hear of that aid in his criminal activities, and help him evade us time and time again, but he only has one agent. Do you know why that is, Jahul?" He leaned forward again, his electric eyes intense. "Because they turn on him. They always turn."

Syuri shook his head.

The Huouyt gave him a flat, alien look that reeked of pity even without his *sivvet*. "You think a creature like that is actually *capable* of having a friend, Jahul?"

Syuri shuddered, realizing Cha'vai was right. Forgotten was alone. He'd seen the proof. He'd *felt* it. Who could the Geuji afford to trust? It was much easier to get rid of his agents after they'd served their usefulness.

No.

The Geuji must have made a mistake in his timing, something that allowed the Huouyt to catch him. He wouldn't have purposefully put Syuri into the hands of the enemy. He refused to believe it.

"I ask again," the Huouyt said, his eyes unreadable. "Will you give us the information we require willingly or will you do it with drugs? I must warn you that some of the substances we Huouyt use in our interrogations have permanent consequences."

Syuri took a deep breath. "So is that what Forgotten wants? To free his people?"

The Huouyt gave him an electric stare. "One can assume."

"Drug me," Syuri said. "You will not get what you desire, Huouyt."

The Huouyt stood with an unreadable look. His tentacle flicked outward and touched Syuri's exposed arm. He felt a tiny sting and Syuri lost feeling almost instantly.

"I already have," the Huouyt said.

• • •

"Still wanted a claw," Flea muttered as the six of them walked from the awards ceremony.

A bit irritated, Jer'ait examined the Baga. Flea's *kasja* was downsized to about the size of a Congressional credit, so as not to crush the Baga under its weight. An Ooreiki Overseer had affixed it to the back of his carapace, between the wings, right before the Ooreiki had given Flea a ceremonial note worth three million credits. Despite the kasja's diminutive size, it still glowed with all the impressive beauty of a larger one. It made Jer'ait slightly jealous of the Baga's good fortune, but only for a moment. Only imbecile furgs wanted glowing, rainbow-colored targets affixed to their backs. Not even the Human, who had six, wore his.

"You'll get a claw next time," the Human said.

The Baga grunted disgustedly. "I'd have one now, if Galek hadn't been stupid and gotten himself caught."

"I'm sorry, Flea," the Ooreiki said, looking sincere.

"Think of it this way," Daviin said. "Instead of a worthless prince's shit-covered talon, now you've got a few million credits to lose to me, instead of a few thousand."

The Baga's eyes lit up with obvious glee. "Is that a challenge?"

"Not really," Daviin said. "Taking money from a Baga is like taking meat from an Ayhi. They can neither use it, nor have the capacity to appreciate it properly."

Flea's hackles went up, and for a moment, Jer'ait thought he would spit in the furgling Jreet's face. Then the Baga laughed. "You're on."

Jer'ait tried not to resent his groundmates for the casual way they spoke of losing such vast sums of money, but it was hard. Despite everything the rest of the Corps seemed to believe, a Peacemaker of the Eleventh Hjai did not live in luxury. Not a Peacemaker who abided by the law, anyway. Jer'ait could have made plenty of money on the side, as an assassin, but he took his Oath to Congress seriously, unlike many of his peers.

Because of this, Jer'ait lived a bare existence. He nourished himself with standard Huouyt *nuajan* tubes or nutrient wafers. On Koliinaat, he slept in a tiny cubicle overlooking a Ueshi restaurant. On Levren, he maintained a small apartment in the industrial sector. His life savings amounted to two rotations' wages. And, with all the political bickering that went on in the Regency, high-ranked Peacemakers were almost always the first to feel the blow, since Jer'ait and most of his peers chose to forfeit their salaries during this time so that their apprentices could eat.

It had been happening so often of late that Jer'ait considered himself lucky that debtors from Koliinaat hadn't yet come to Jeelsiht looking for him. With Rri'jan back to his old tricks and Bev'kii aligning the Huouyt of Jeelsiht against him, Jer'ait would have been grateful for the aid. He had, after all, killed a Dhasha prince.

Yet Life was not often kind, and while a royal Jreet and a newly-rich Baga bickered about their fortunes, Jer'ait was trying to figure out how to make his next domicile payment without getting either him or his landlord assassinated in the attempt.

Or without the Human finding out about his troubles.

"Save your dice for after dinner," the Human ordered, giving the Jreet and the Baga hard looks with his small round eyes. "We all made it out without having to visit the hospital. A first for any team. This requires a celebration."

"A feast!" the Jreet roared. "In honor of our heroes!" Daviin bent, plucked the Baga from the air, and put him on his shoulder. When he reached for the Human, Joe backed away, holding his hands in front of him. "No, Daviin, don't you da—"

The Jreet easily brushed aside the Human's arms, then lifted him and set him down on the other shoulder. Then, when Joe struggled to get down, Daviin forcefully held him there with a chest-sized hand and turned to scowl at him with his metallic gaze.

Wisely, the Human relented and sat.

"*Melaa* for everyone!" Daviin roared, not losing a beat.

Jer'ait's face twisted as he considered eating the Jreet's fat, bloated cuisine-of-choice. The pattern-shift that would result from such a venture left him feeling physically ill. "I think I'll pass."

"Me, too," Joe said. "But you can eat all the *melaa* you want, Daviin. I'll go for some steak."

Daviin's face contorted in confusion. "*Melaa* has steak."

Jer'ait rolled his eyes. "I don't think he understands. Jreet. Your food *sucks*."

"Have you tried it?" Daviin demanded, swiveling to face Jer'ait.

"Thank the gods, no."

"You will try it," the Jreet said firmly.

"Maybe later," Jer'ait said. "Right now, I have better things to do."

From Daviin's shoulder, Joe's voice was sharp. "Better than eating with your groundmates?"

"Somebody wants me dead," Jer'ait said. "I want to investigate in peace."

"Eat with us first." There was no mistaking his Prime's tone. It was an order.

"I wish I could," Jer'ait said sincerely. "But duty calls."

Daviin's metallic gaze sharpened.

Sensing the Jreet understood which duties he referred to, Jer'ait bowed and departed before the Human could order the Sentinel to stop him. He heard the Baga crack a joke after he'd left, and the others laughed. Jer'ait felt a rush of shame before he stumbled to a halt, stunned.

You're letting yourself get attached to your target. You fool!

He glanced over his shoulder, watching the rest of his ground-mates continue into the city without him. A part of him longed to be there with them.

He's bewitched me, he thought, watching the Human cling uncomfortably to the Jreet's thick neck as Daviin continued his sideways slither toward the food court. He shook himself. *If I don't kill him, someone else will. At least I have the power to make it painless.*

Jer'ait turned back to his path. Overseer Bev'kii he could deal with. It was the Peacemaker spy approaching Joe while Jer'ait was incapacitated that worried him.

Huouyt carry all of their poisons in their body. There's only one reason he needed to have something under his arm.

Jer'ait returned to his room and locked the door. He took out his personal reader, entered his code, and called Yua'nev.

"Yes?"

Jer'ait watched his superior's eyes, frustrated that he could read nothing behind the glassy, electric surface.

"You are troubled, Jer'ait."

Jer'ait cursed himself inwardly. Even though Yua'nev's eyes were mirrors, his own was not. He struggled to regain his composure.

"I spoke with one of Jemria's agents today."

"Truly?" Yua'nev leaned toward his reader, interested. "Where?"

"Here on Jeelsiht. I think the Geuji is helping us defeat the Dhasha. He's keeping the Jreet heirs alive when they should be dead."

Yua'nev snorted. "The Geuji is only interested in freeing his people. We have the proof of that in the cellars of Levren. He sent another agent—a true agent, one we believe has had personal contact with him—to free the Geuji from the basement of the Academy."

"And?" Jer'ait asked.

"He's being interrogated at this moment."

Jer'ait cocked his head. "Ask him if he knows anything about Aez."

Yua'nev's electric eyes remained impassive. "Why?"

"The Geuji works under several layers of deception. I doubt his intention with Daviin is only to keep him alive. Further, the *ekhta* that blew up Aez was too hot to be one of ours. Who else to make one but a Geuji?"

"So he blows up Aez, then proceeds to help us defeat the Vahlin?" Yua'nev made a dismissive gesture. "What's the point of that?"

Jer'ait frowned. "I don't know."

Yua'nev grunted. "It will be taken into consideration. The Trith did prophesize—"

"Are you sure it was the Trith?" Jer'ait interrupted.

For a long moment, Yua'nev did not speak. Then, slowly, he said, "Who else could it have been, Jer'ait?"

"You said there's no supercomputer capable of replicating the Trith message. But what of a Geuji?"

"Are you hearing yourself?" Yua'nev demanded. "Why would the Geuji send us a warning he was about to blow up Aez?"

Jer'ait frowned. *Because he wanted us to do something.* He considered. Just what had they done differently since receiving the message?

They sent me to kill Joe.

Jer'ait felt his breath catch. "Yua'nev, I think he wants the Human dead."

"And that's why he keeps his Sentinel alive."

Jer'ait opened his mouth, but hesitated. The fact that Yua'nev knew Daviin had chosen the Human as his ward bothered him. The Geuji's involvement bothered him. The Trith and Aez bothered him.

He could not produce any answers, so he remained silent.

"It's an interesting idea, Jer'ait," Yua'nev said, once he did not respond, "but the Geuji is not a god. He's not all-powerful. Despite the legends, he can't predict the future."

Predict the future. The phrase tickled something in the back of his head. Who had been predicting the future? Who seemed to be the only one who knew what the hell was happening on Neskfaat?

The Dhasha Vahlin.

The truth slammed into Jer'ait like a runaway freighter.

Looking into Yua'nev's eyes, though, Jer'ait didn't have to be able to read his thoughts to know his superior wasn't going to believe him.

They want me to kill an innocent man.

24

ASK

"By this point, Jer'ait will have discovered my involvement, at least part of it. He will not understand why, but he will understand that his commitment to kill Zero is based on faulty information."

"That won't keep him from killing the Human," Rri'jan said. The Huouyt had unfolded a metal chair from the wall and made himself comfortable. "After accepting employment, a Va'gan kills who he's told to kill. He won't ask questions."

"That's true. The bond of trust between a Va'gan and his employer is imperative, else Va'ga would have no business. Jer'ait is well aware of this."

"So we replace the Human," Rri'jan said. "With who?"

"Rri'jan, as far as our plans are concerned, it would be better if you didn't open your mouth. We'll have more time if I don't have to answer stupid questions."

The Representative's face twitched with anger, though his eyes remained unreadable mirrors. "By all means, Forgotten. Go ahead and enlighten me."

"I think that's beyond the realm of possibility."

"Try. I must understand how I am to get my Tribunal seat."

"Actually, things will run quite smoothly without you knowing anything at all," Forgotten said. "The only reason I tell you is so you know who earned you your reward in the end and you don't dismiss it as chance."

"It is hard to dismiss Mekkval's assassination as chance."

"True. The third crawl will be harder for all the teams involved. Since about four hundred groundteams survive the second crawl, we will be left with about eighty after this one. My two chosen teams will have particular troubles with it."

"Why?"

"Zero will wake up to find the mental barrier the medics on Kophat installed during his recruit training are beginning to fail. Too much time underground in too short a period. That, and the Dhasha will be using their own weapons against them."

"I'm confused."

"Of course you are. But consider this...Mekkval will not only have Takki in the tunnels with him. We must train our groundteam to handle all threats, not just Takki."

Rri'jan's face furrowed in irritation. "Dhasha Representatives refuse to have Sentinels. The Jreet wouldn't Sentinel for them, even if they were accepted. The two species hate each other."

"Why are you so concerned with the Jreet?"

• • •

"We soot this up, we're screwed. Any questions?"

"Why are we going back?" Galek cried. "I thought they gave us two weeks. Flea killed a *prince!*"

He doesn't understand, Jer'ait thought. *Of all of them here, only the Human and I understand. They're sending us back until we're done being useful. Until we're dead.*

The Human glanced at the Ooreiki with obvious irritation. "Because we've got a job to do."

"But we killed a *prince*," Galek insisted, his trunk-shaped body stiffening. "Two of them, now."

"All the more reason to send us back." The Human glanced at the others. "Everyone's chips working?"

Jer'ait was not watching the others prepare their gear for the next battle. Unlike the others, he had nothing to prepare. All he needed was an array of patterns and his own body.

Instead, he was watching the Human's left hand.

The Human had been trying to hide it, keeping it closed around his weapon or buried in his pocket, but several times, it broke free and trembled like a dying Takki before the Human got it back under control.

Interesting.

"All right," the Prime said as the shuttle settled. "Same drill as last time. Daviin lurks, Jer'ait scouts, Flea leads. Scarab, first hint of a fight and you get out of sight, you hear me?"

"*Yes, Commander.*" The Grekkon's eyes remained focused on the far wall, utterly motionless.

"Let's go!" the Human shouted as the door opened. Jer'ait ducked out the door and gave his *zora* the pattern of a Jikaln. He began running even as his body morphed, becoming four legs, teeth, and nearly-invisible, camouflaged speed.

Jer'ait slipped into the dense, jelly-like foliage and began weaving back and forth in front of the advancing party, clearing the path for the others.

He found his first Takki crouched in the brush, facing the direction his party had used for their ambush. Jer'ait sank his teeth into the Takki's neck and twisted, tearing a chunk of purple flesh away from his victim's throat. As the Takki died at his feet, Jer'ait crouched, eying the area where his companions were to appear, disturbed.

The original plans had set them to make their incursion from the opposite direction. Keeping in mind the last Dhasha's advance knowledge of their attack, Joe had altered the plans at the last moment, bullying the pilot into changing course in mid-flight and landing them on the other side of the entrance. The shuttle engines had been shielded, completely silent. So how had the Takki known from which direction they would come?

A coincidence. It had to be. Perhaps they had unwittingly landed in some other groundteam's drop zone.

But with only four hundred groundteams covering an entire planet, how likely were the odds of that?

Jer'ait twisted and lunged deeper into the forest.

The next Takki was also facing the same direction.

Unnerved, Jer'ait eyed the path his companions were to take.

They couldn't know. Not unless the Human had warned them…

Jer'ait remembered the Prime's shaking hand and he grew cold. He was turning, running back to the shuttle, when Joe materialized in the brush in front of him. "Where do you think you're going?"

Jer'ait glanced at the Human's hand. It was no longer shaking.

His fears dissipated. *Your days on Morinth have left you paranoid.* "Thought I heard something in this direction."

"You did."

The Human flicked its hands, a swift, practiced movement, and Jer'ait felt a sharp sting in the chest of his Jikaln pattern, directly beside a major fluids exchange. Jer'ait did not have a chance to isolate the poison before his body went limp. He dropped into the sticky foliage, only able to watch as the Human moved toward him and crouched beside him. "That was easier than I thought it'd be." The Human's hand reached out and touched him firmly on the side. Another sting.

As his eyes widened with understanding, Jer'ait was lost to darkness.

• • •

"*Jer'ait, where the hell are you?*" the Prime demanded.

The Human and the Ooreiki were crouched around the Grekkon's burrow, searching the forest with their rifles. They had not heard from the Huouyt since they left the shuttle.

"*This sooty pile of bones is pissing me off,*" Zero said. "*We saw the bodies. He's out there somewhere.*"

"*Maybe his chip's malfunctioning,*" Flea suggested from his position on a branch above.

"*Should we go look for him?*" Galek asked.

"*This is PlanOps, not grade school,*" their Prime snapped. "*He can take care of himself.*" He switched frequencies. "*Team Two, Team Three, this is Team One. You make it in?*"

Silence answered him.

Those standing around the Grekkon's burrow tensed.

"Damn it," Daviin heard the Human whisper under his breath.

Even as he said it, Daviin sensed something in the woods behind them. "*Movement.*"

"*Where?*" The Ooreiki did not bother to hide its fear.

"*Two hundred rods to the west. Large enough to be a Takki.*"

"*Go check it out.*"

Daviin slipped between the trees, gaining more and more contact with his target as he closed the distance between them. Once Daviin judged he was within twenty digs of his target, he pinged the area.

"*It's a Takki.*"

"*Bones,*" Joe muttered. "*You gotta get it.*"

Daviin coiled, preparing to spring.

"*Before you kill it,*" Joe said, "*Find out if it knows where our Huouyt is.*"

"*What if he's got a chip?*" the Ooreiki asked. "*Won't that give away our position?*"

"*They already knew we would be here,*" Daviin said. "*One would assume they know our position, as well.*"

"*That's furgsoot,*" Joe snarled. "*I changed coordinates. Only an ashing Trith would've seen us coming.*"

"*Then the Vahlin uses a Trith,*" the Grekkon interrupted. "*We need to continue with the mission before they find us.*"

"*No, screw that,*" Flea said. "*If they're using a Trith, then they already know where we're going and we're dead anyway. Joe, we should go looking for him.*"

"*What's a Trith?*" Daviin snapped. "*You want me to kill the Takki or not?!*"

The Prime hesitated. Then, "*Question him. If they got Jer'ait, they already know we're here.*"

Daviin lashed out, knocking the Takki to the ground. As it strained to rise, he wrapped three coils around it, rendering it helpless.

"Where is my companion?" Daviin demanded, remaining cloaked.

The Takki never flinched, never showed a flicker of fear. "It appears my chip isn't working, after all. I thought you were all dead, as I've heard nothing since I took Jikaln form."

Daviin released the Huouyt and uncloaked, irritated. "*It's Jer'ait. His chip didn't activate.*"

"*Mothers' ghosts. Goddamn government sootwads. I'm gonna give those medical furglings an earful. Charge us eight turns for something every Congie should have installed for free, then it doesn't even burning work.*"

Daviin cocked his head, frowning. "*They charge eight turns for a chip?*"

"*Either that or eight hundred grand. But who's got that kind of money?*"

"*I've got that kind of money,*" the Baga said cheerfully.

"Who paid for my chip?" Daviin demanded.

"*I did,*" the Human said. Then, privately, "*Can't have you swearing as my Sentinel and then expect you to shell out eight hundred thousand credits, could I?*"

"*I'll pay you back,*" Daviin said, feeling a rush of irritation at the Human's presumptions.

"*Don't bother,*" Joe replied. "*I figured eight more turns on my contract isn't gonna make much difference. Not when they're going to make us tunnel crawl until we're dead.*"

Daviin's talons dug into his palm as he tightened his fist.

"*Get him back here,*" Joe ordered over the public channel. "*As the Grekkon keeps reminding us, we've got a prince to kill.*"

"Follow me." Daviin led the Huouyt back to the main party.

As soon as Joe saw Jer'ait, he cursed. "It's a goddamn ripoff. We gotta pay for something that we need to do our job. Bones!" He frowned, indecisiveness written plainly on his face.

Daviin understood why—the Huouyt was their information-gatherer, the one who required constant contact. Without it, he was all but useless to the team.

"Daviin did it," Joe said finally. "You can, too. Next time I see those sooters at medical, though, they won't be able to sit for a week. But Mothers' ghosts, why didn't you say something back on the shuttle?!"

"I didn't realize you were talking," Jer'ait said meekly.

Their Prime took a deep breath, steadying himself. "Fine. We can still do this. Daviin, inviso-mode. Jer'ait, get down there with Scarab. You stay with us when he breaks through. I want you within hearing range at all times until we get down there and figure out a plan. Got me?"

"Yes, sir."

Daviin gave the Huouyt a startled look. He'd never heard Jer'ait refer to the Human even half as respectfully. Perhaps his little solo jaunt through the woods—and Daviin's coils—had rattled him.

They climbed into the tunnel, the Human and the Ooreiki staying behind to cover their trail. Up ahead, Daviin heard the Grekkon pause, then reverse. He hurried to catch up.

When he reached them, he found the Grekkon sunk into the wall of the tunnel, spear-shaped appendages aimed outward, ready to skewer anything that got in its way. He'd broken through to a small slave tunnel. The Baga and the Huouyt were gone.

Daviin moved forward to inspect the tunnel, pinging tentatively. With the size of the tunnel, he didn't have to be afraid of a Dhasha hearing him.

"Where's the Huouyt?" he asked the Grekkon.

The Grekkon's voicebox kicked in softly. "*Scouting.*"

"The Human told him to stay."

The Grekkon said nothing. Its black eyes continued to stare at the wall opposite it, utterly motionless.

Behind him, the Human and the Ooreiki caught up.

"*Where the bones is Jer'ait?*" Joe snapped. "*Flea, he with you?*"

"*He went the opposite direction,*" Flea replied.

The Ooreiki immediately got down and flashed his light down the tunnel. "Jer'ait?" he called, as loudly as he dared.

The Huouyt did not respond.

"Should I go after him?" Galek asked.

Joe said nothing.

"Sir?" the Ooreiki called. *"Should I go first?"*

Silence.

"Sir?"

The sour smell of fear sweat assailed Daviin's senses. Daviin dropped his energy level so he could see the Human's face. He immediately wished he hadn't. The Human's face was pale and the smell was coming from him. He was staring at the tiny tunnel they had breached. His hands were clenched on his weapon. He was shaking.

"Yes," Joe said finally. His voice sounded strained. *"Flea, how's the way up?"*

"No one so far," Flea called back.

"Come on back. See if you can find us a bigger tunnel."

"A bigger *tunnel? This one's perfect. There's no Dhasha on the planet that could get in here. Just big enough for Daviin and the Grekkon...even the little ones can't—"*

"Find us a bigger tunnel!" the Human snapped, a little too loudly.

The Baga sped past, a sulking whir in the darkness. The Ooreiki ducked into the tunnel to follow, the Grekkon after him. Daviin took the rear, waiting for the Human to crawl into the tunnel in front of him.

As soon as the Human got onto his hands and knees and began pushing his weapon in front of him, Daviin touched his shoulder. "Something wrong, Joe?"

Joe glared up at him from where he lay on his belly. "Just go."

Daviin frowned, but obeyed.

The Baga found them a bigger tunnel, and after half an hour of crawling, they were able to straighten somewhat. The Ooreiki killed two Takki and the Grekkon buried them in side-shafts that they disguised with holograms.

All the while, the Human's face grew paler.

Daviin took his first Dhasha by accident—the creature came up behind them and was actually straddling Daviin when he struck.

"We need to get out of the main tunnel," Daviin growled as they dragged the Dhasha out of sight. "We're caged Takki here."

The Human stiffened, but did not object. Galek found them a slave tunnel he said led to the heart of the place, so they took it, the Baga leading the way. Once more, Daviin and the Human brought up the rear, though when the Human hesitated upon entering the tunnel, Daviin grabbed Joe by the shoulder and dragged him out of earshot of the others. *"Commander,"* Daviin said on the private channel, *"Is everything all right?"*

"No," the Human replied, clenching his fist. His voice cracked. *"We need to do this fast."*

"What is it?" Daviin insisted.

"Nothing," the Human said.

"Commander—"

"Goddamn it it's nothing!"

Softly, Daviin said, *"I'm your Sentinel, Joe. I can smell the fear on you. What's going on?"*

"Tunnels," the Human whispered. He probably hadn't meant for Daviin to hear it, but there wasn't much Daviin didn't hear.

"What about tunnels?"

The Human's face twitched and he gave Daviin a startled look. Then, quietly, he said, "I'm afraid of tunnels."

Daviin glanced both ways, then lowered his head to the Human's height, until their faces were ninths apart. In a whisper, he said, "You are playing with me."

"No." The Human squeezed his eyes shut. "Ghosts, no."

"Then what?"

He opened his eyes. "I've seen the blood already." It came out in a whimper. His whole body gave a sudden tremor, like he had been hit by a sudden draft.

Daviin wasn't sure what to make of their Prime's sudden disintegration. "Is this because you poisoned yourself on Earth? After-effects of watching your brother's execution?"

Joe laughed. It had been loud enough that, should any Dhasha be within two hundred rods, they would have heard it like a dinner bell.

Daviin grabbed the Human by the shoulders and slammed him against the wall. Using his private channel, he shouted, *"You're fooling with our lives here, Human! What's the matter with you?!"*

Joe shuddered. *"I can't do this."* He squeezed his hand into a fist and sucked in two huge breaths that sounded dangerously like they were near sobs—or he was going to start hyperventilating.

Daviin released him violently. *"You will, because I didn't Sentinel myself to a coward."*

The Human nodded his head.

"No!" Daviin snapped. *"I didn't. And if it turns out that I did, I can negate my contract in an instant. Technically your slavery was cowardice in the past, so I've let it slide, but if you don't finish this mission because you're huddled in terror, Human, it is the last you will ever see of me. I swear it to the Ayhi's graves."*

Joe watched him a moment in silence, then glanced back at the tiny entrance to the slave tunnel.

"So," Daviin said, *"Can you finish the crawl?"*

Joe peered into the tunnel, unmoving. *"I don't know."*

"Yes or no, Human!"

Joe tore his eyes from the descending darkness and returned them to Daviin's face. *"Yes. But I'll need one hell of a drink afterwards."*

"Human," Daviin said, gripping his shoulder, *"Get us out alive and I'll buy your drinks myself."*

• • •

"A Jreet, a Grekkon, an Ooreiki, a Baga, led by a Human."

"What the hairy fuck is a Human?"

His assassin cocked his head and considered. *"Small bony biped, scaleless, average intelligence, known for their linguistic abilities. I tagged the Jreet, as he will be your main danger, but the Baga might also prove to be an irritation if he escapes the first assault."*

Lavik snorted. *"I am not afraid of a glorified worm."*

"The worm in question weighs approximately two thousand lobes."

Lavik grinned. "An old one, eh? Should be fun."

"Sire, I greatly recommend you don't fight this Jreet personally," the Huouyt immediately warned. "Send one of your underlings, one of your heirs, someone you don't mind—"

"Oh, shut up."

The Huouyt made a face, but did not look up. He remained in silence, staring at some point on Lavik's leg. It was obvious he was going to take him literally.

Lavik sighed. "You're a true itch, Huouyt." He glanced at the captive, whom his assassin had trussed up like a farm-bred Takki. It was in his natural form, three semi-aquatic legs and two paddle-like arms bound together by ultra-thin wire. It was having trouble raising its long, neckless head from the ground, but he was attempting it anyway.

Lavik found it amusing to see a Huouyt in natural form. Their long bodies and tapering heads always reminded him of a kreenit penis. "Tell me of the prisoner."

"We should kill him," his assassin said immediately.

Lavik cocked his head at the Huouyt, sensing something deeper in his subordinate's words. "Why?"

"He's a Huouyt. He can change the shape of his body. The moment we take our eyes off of him, he'll be free of his bonds."

"That's why we have Takki watching him." Lavik returned his gaze to the prisoner trussed up across the room. The captive had been cursing the other Huouyt non-stop for the last hour, making interesting comments about his heritage and breeding habits. "Besides. His antics amuse me."

"At least let me silence him," his subordinate said stiffly.

"No."

"Sire, I humbly request—"

"Request denied. What has he told us so far? How goes the war?"

"He told me nothing," the Huouyt said. "Refuses even to tell me his name."

"Oh?" This perplexed Lavik. "Huouyt aren't exactly the most loyal creatures in Congress. You must not be asking him the right questions. Most Huouyt would jump at the opportunity to betray their mates in order to save their own lousy hides. When the Vahlin destroys Congress, the whole species should be added to the food supply."

"Of course," his assassin gritted.

Lavik grinned at the top of his assassin's Takki-patterned head. He enjoyed provoking the Huouyt—it had been one of his only amusements the last few weeks. "I thought the Congressional Prisoner Act allowed its soldiers to give their names to the enemy."

"This one refuses. He spits at my questions, regardless of what drugs I use on him."

"Interesting. The drugs have no effect?"

"He can nullify them, sire."

This gave Lavik pause. He had heard of such things before, but if it were true, it would mean their guest had once walked the halls of Va'ga. A cold itch began to snake under his scales as he watched the prisoner, who had gone silent to listen to their conversation. One eye the normal blue-white, the other purple. Lavik had heard of something like this before. "Is it possible he's faking it?"

"No, sire."

"But you drugged him once."

"I surprised him and used a dose that would kill a hundred Jikaln to incapacitate him. He's got a strong resistance, probably somehow linked to his...deformity." His assassin's distaste was clear. "However, the dosages I'm giving to him—he's got to be nullifying them."

"He could be Va'ga-trained," Lavik noted. "Their resistance is quite high, I've been told."

The Huouyt made a derisive sound. "Not hardly. Not with his... disgusting appearance. Va'ga would not let his filthy body pass its gates. Congress must have simply inoculated him with antidotes to my drugs. I'll have to resort to alternative methods to extract the information we require."

"No torture."

"Sire, he will not answer my questions..."

"Then you weren't asking the right questions." Lavik strode to where the prisoner lay, scattering his Takki guards. The enemy stared up at him with two different-colored eyes. Interesting. Lavik had never seen such a thing before, and yet it was still tickling some buried memory.

"I'll make you a deal, Huouyt."

"I do not deal with Dhasha slime," the prisoner retorted.

Lavik laughed. "Oh, that's a pity. You would've liked this one. You see, I was about to offer to tell you whatever you want to know about your situation. I know you crave to know who betrayed you. You want to know how many Dhasha I've got with me, how many tunnels are blocked off. I'll tell you."

The Huouyt's purple eye became suddenly alert. He obviously still thought he had a chance of escape. "And what do you want in return?"

Lavik sighed. "I want to know who's winning."

"We are," the Huouyt said automatically.

Lavik sank to the ground before the Huouyt. "You and I need to come to an understanding. I'm not letting you escape, Huouyt. Not while I'm alive, anyway. Further, the only way you'll continue to live is if you answer my questions. I won't torture you, won't force your responses in any way. If you fail to engage me sufficiently, I'll just kill you."

"Then kill me."

It actually sounded as if the Huouyt was serious. Lavik laughed. "Have you already forgotten the deal I offered you, Huouyt? You have a chance to gather the intelligence that could possibly give you the edge you need to escape. For every question you answer of mine, I will answer one of yours. Simple enough?"

"Who gets the first question?" the Huouyt asked warily.

Lavik laughed. "Oh, I am not that foolish. I'm the host. I do."

"And how do I know you'll tell the truth in return?"

"I will."

The Huouyt eyed him a moment, then said, "Ask."

"Who's winning?" Lavik asked.

"You are."

Lavik found himself liking this creature. "Let's try this again. Who's winning?"

The Huouyt watched him keenly before he said, "I don't know. In the first wave, you lost twenty-two princes. We lost all but two thousand groundteams. We can wear you down, but you'll probably work your way through Planetary Ops before you fall."

"Ah," Lavik said. "Then you don't know the Vahlin. Go ahead and ask, Huouyt."

Immediately, the Huouyt's mismatched eyes flickered to Lavik's subordinate. "Where'd that spineless traitor come from?"

"A gift from the Vahlin," Lavik said. "He told me I'd need one to defeat your team."

The Huouyt scanned Lavik's face fearlessly, a look dangerously close to ka-par, then nodded. "Ask."

"What's been said in the Regency about using an *ekhta?*"

"They refused the Ground Force's request to use it," the Huouyt said. "The politicians are squabbling over who gets Neskfaat when we rid it of Dhasha, and there's talk the Vahlin will destroy more planets post-mortem if we bomb you."

Lavik grinned. "As he will."

The Huouyt watched him in silence, weighing his reply. Then, softly, he said, "How does the Vahlin know where and when we'll arrive?"

"Do you know of the Fourfold Prophecy, Huouyt?"

Anger flashed in the Huouyt's face. "If this is a way to distract me—"

"The Fourfold Prophecy predicts a race will one day rise up against Congress and win its independence. Lesser-known is that the Prophecy also predicts that the leader of this race will have the powers unto a god. The Vahlin is that leader."

The Huouyt's face remained unreadable. "You believe the Vahlin is a god."

"He is," Lavik agreed. "How else could we have known your leader would change your drop coordinates at the last tic?"

"Our leader betrayed us," the prisoner said immediately.

"Ease your mind, Huouyt," Lavik assured his guest. "Your leader is just as oblivious as you were. You can't do battle with a creature that can see the future."

"So the Vahlin is using a Trith."

Lavik laughed. "You get ahead of yourself."

The Huouyt watched him, then nodded.

"I'm told this is your third time down a den. Did you kill the princes, or was it another of your team?"

"I killed one of them."

"How?"

"Is the Vahlin using a Trith?"

"No. How did you kill the prince?"

"Poison. A lethal dose of *ooma* secretions."

"You carried it with you or made it yourself?"

"When was the last time you spoke with the Vahlin?"

Lavik found himself growing irritated. "What do you care of the Vahlin? You're going to die here, Huouyt. You should be asking of your companions' fates, your means of escape, the strength of my forces."

"Answer me or the game ends."

"Ten days."

"I made the poison myself."

"I'm told that's impossible."

"How did the Vahlin originally contact you?"

Lavik peered at the Huouyt, not liking the way he was fixated on the Vahlin. He had thought the creature would ask about the tunnels, solidify his situation in his mind. Instead, he was interrogating him on subjects he had no right knowing.

But the creature was never going to leave the tunnels alive, and Lavik was bored out of his mind with waiting. If nothing else, he could simply kill him as soon as he had learned what he wanted to know.

"The Vahlin contacted me via courier. Gave me predictions and told me to watch the news. Once he'd convinced me, he sent another message summoning me to Neskfaat."

"So you've never seen the Vahlin?"

"How did you create that poison, Huouyt?"

"I'm Va'ga-trained. Top graduate of my class. I can use my body chemistry to reproduce two thousand six hundred and thirty-seven different chemicals with effects varying from lethal seizures to a mild a muscle relaxant."

Lavik felt his scales tighten against his chest and he had to resist the urge to pull his legs away from the assassin.

Beside him, his servant snapped, "*You're* Va'ga-trained? You lie. They don't waste their time with the deformed. What's your name?"

"Leave," Lavik said quietly. "Go monitor their progress."

"But I should not return to his group without at least knowing his name—"

"*Leave!*"

His servant did.

"So you've never seen the Vahlin?" the Huouyt repeated.

Lavik got to his feet. "The game is over, Huouyt. Make peace with yourself." He lifted a paw to slice him in half.

"Before you kill me, I have one more question," the Huouyt said, his multi-colored eyes showing no fear. "After all, it is my turn."

Lavik gave an irritated flick of his claws. "What difference does it make? You'll only take the information to the grave with you."

"This is a desperate attempt to delay my death as long as possible because I fear the consequences of my actions in the afterlife."

Lavik laughed, despite himself. "We both know that's not true."

"Nevertheless, I have a question."

"Very well. Ask."

"Do you realize you're being used?"

• • •

"*This is turning into a Takkiscrew.*" Joe concentrated on his anger to keep thoughts of the tunnels at bay. "*Where the soot did they all go? It's like they've got burning Houdini working for them.*"

"*We're still alive,*" the Grekkon noted. "*That is a good sign.*"

"*Jer'ait could be rotting in a slave tunnel for all we know,*" Joe replied. "*Goddamn this soot. We haven't seen a Takki for three hours. It's like they know exactly where we are.*"

"*What if they do?*" the Jreet asked.

"*Then we're well and truly charred.*"

No one felt like adding to that.

"*All right,*" Joe said after another twenty tics passed without a single victim for their trap, "*Let's assume they know where we are. How'd they figure it out?*"

"*They got Jer'ait,*" Galek said softly.

"*Jer'ait's got no idea where we are,*" Joe said. "*He took off without us, the cowboy sootbag.*" He was still pissed at that, and would be having a polite conversation with his Second about it just as soon as they got back to the barracks. A polite conversation probably involving a plasma pistol and pruning shears.

"*Say they found him and interrogated him,*" Daviin said. "*If they've got a detailed map of their tunnel systems, they could probably pinpoint the most logical route we'd take to get to the deep den.*"

Joe thought on that a moment. "*So you're saying we've gotta do something illogical?*"

"*We need to take a path we wouldn't normally take.*"

"*While sticking to the slave tunnels,*" the Grekkon added. "*If we don't, and you're correct, as soon as we leave the slave tunnels, the Dhasha will ambush us.*"

Joe rubbed his clenched fist against his knee. "*Okay. Galek, you lead. Find us a tunnel that you wouldn't normally take that connects to a main passage. Doesn't necessarily have to lead to the deep den. I want to test a theory.*"

Galek took the lead, unhesitatingly leading them through a maze of slave tunnels until they crouched at the entrance to a main hallway, this one large enough to fit three Dhasha abreast.

They waited three hours and saw nothing.

Joe's mood deteriorated as the time passed without seeing a single enemy. Finally, Joe said, "*So they know where we are. And it's not Jer'ait.*"

"*They knew where we would land,*" the Ooreiki reminded them. "*Maybe the Trith are still helping them.*"

"*Shut up about the Trith,*" Joe snapped. "*They don't help anyone.*"

"*What are Trith?*" Daviin asked.

"*Never mind. Bones.*" Joe considered their options. Their presence had been compromised, and right now, the only thing keeping them from getting their asses handed to them was the fact they had millions of lobes of dirt squeezing them in on all sides, making it impossible for the Dhasha to reach them.

"*I could go in alone,*" Daviin suggested. "*My energy level raised.*"

"*You'd have no protection if you ran into more than one,*" Joe replied.

"*We'd have a better chance of succeeding if we split up,*" Daviin insisted.

"*We'd have a better chance of* dying *if we split up.*" Joe took a deep breath, eying the tunnel. "*It's either—*"

"*Something's coming!*" Galek interrupted. "*Behind us!*"

Joe twisted around and brought up his weapon to face the tiny crevice that he had somehow managed to crawl through three hours earlier. He saw nothing. "*Where?*"

"*Getting closer,*" Galek said.

"*I can hear it,*" Daviin said after a moment. "*It's a Takki. I can hear its scales grinding against the stone.*"

"*Damn it,*" Joe said, "*What if it's Jer'ait?*"

"*If it's not, and you don't shoot it, it can run to alert the others,*" Daviin said.

"*The others already know we're here. You just proved it,*" the Grekkon reminded them.

At that moment, a Takki's head popped into Joe's field of view and Joe got an immediate rush of goosebumps. Holding his gun trained on the Takki's face, he growled, "Name yourself, sootwad!"

"Shoot me, and you'll have to carry my remains back to Va'ga yourself, Human."

Joe frowned at the Huouyt. "What the hell are you doing? I told you to burning stay with us!"

"I did some scouting. There's a good access point behind me. Slave tunnels all the way to the deep den. Low head count. That whole section of the den is deserted. Prince is all alone."

Joe glanced at the others behind him, then said, "Okay, let's go."

The Huouyt led them back through the tunnels, taking tunnel after tunnel with confidence.

At his last choice, Galek suddenly grabbed Joe's ankle and held on.

"What the...?" Joe turned, frowning.

The Ooreiki was peering past him, at the Huouyt. He cleared his throat, glanced at Joe, then loudly said to Jer'ait, "Are you sure this is the right way?"

The Huouyt gave the Ooreiki an irritated look. "Of course. I memorized the route."

"*He's wrong,*" Galek told them. "*Joe, he's about to lead us into the biggest tunnel I've ever seen.*"

Joe frowned back at the Ooreiki. "*You haven't seen it.*"

"*I can feel it. It's huge.*"

Joe peered at Galek. "*You* feel *it? Is that some kind of joke?*"

"What's going on?" the Huouyt demanded sharply.

"*Listen to him,*" Flea insisted. "*He can cheat at dice.*"

"*And you're absolutely positive we're about to get dumped into a huge tunnel?*"

"*Yes,*" the Ooreiki said.

"*You're* sure?"

"*Yes!*" Galek said, frustration and anger edging his thoughts.

Joe considered that. Then, "Dor'iet," Joe called, watching the Ooreiki's face closely, "You're sure you didn't take a wrong turn somewhere?"

Even as the Ooreiki was frowning, the Huouyt snapped, "I'm sure. I'm not a furg."

Joe turned. "Yes. You are." He raised his gun and fired.

• • •

They sat in a circle staring at the body the Ooreiki had dragged back through the tunnels with them. No one spoke. Behind them, the Grekkon had sunk itself into the wall and was guarding the only entrance to the tunnel it had made.

"*Since when did they start using Huouyt?*" Daviin finally said into the silence. "*Dhasha hate the Huouyt. They hate them almost as much as they hate Jreet.*"

The corpse remained in the form of a Takki, except with a large portion of its chest exposed to air where Daviin had ripped it open posthumously. It had no chip. It did, however, have *zora*. The only thing that remained of a Huouyt after taking a pattern.

Joe turned on his PPU and did a search for Jer'ait's chip, but he found nothing. Even dead, it would have showed up on the screen.

The enemy had shorted it somehow.

"Dhasha wouldn't use a Huouyt," Joe muttered, but he wasn't sure. He stared down at the dead alien. Had it been Jer'ait, who simply hadn't been quick enough to catch his slip? Had Joe killed their groundmate because his claustrophobia had made him trigger-happy?

"So this means Jer'ait is dead?" Galek asked.

Grimly, Daviin said, *"We haven't heard from him since the surface, so I'd say that's a safe assumption."*

"This still doesn't explain why they know where we are," Flea said.

"They tagged us," Joe said simply. *"Somewhere, the bastards tagged us."*

"I thought Dhasha didn't use tags," Galek whispered.

"They do now. Goddamn it. We'll never find the thing."

"He tagged me," Daviin said. *"I was the only one who had contact with him."*

"Great," Joe said. *"So we've got sixty digs of scales to pry up looking for it. And that's if he only planted one. If he were smart, he would've planted one on all of us before he took off."*

"If he were smart," Daviin said grimly, *"He would've learned Jer'ait's name before he killed him."*

"Va'ga-trained have a high tolerance to drugs," Joe said. *"They only have a very small window between ineffectual and lethal, and it's likely this sooter had no idea where that window was."*

"So we can assume Jer'ait told them nothing," Daviin said. *"Because, if I understand correctly, it's legal for a Congressional soldier to give his name once he is captured."*

"It's legal," Joe agreed. *"But Jer'ait probably knew the vaghi would use it against us."*

"Would that matter to a Huouyt?" Daviin demanded.

"Yes, you furgling Jreet," Flea said. *"We're his groundmates."*

Daviin swiveled to face the Baga. *"A Huouyt wouldn't care if we all died down here. He might even give his name away on purpose, so that we all would die down here, if he knows his own death is coming."*

"Jer'ait's different," Flea said. *"He didn't give his name away. That proves it."*

"You're a fool, Baga," the Jreet laughed, and for a moment Joe had the feeling the delicate camaraderie they had developed was going to regress back to the dangerous, rival bickering he had first seen as their commander.

But then Daviin amended, *"But, seeing how Jer'ait's probably dead, it's our duty to give him the benefit of the doubt."* Daviin turned to Joe. *"So what do we do? The Huouyt's dead. Our enemies know our position, and they might have other Huouyt they can use against us."*

"Headquarters might find information about this guy more valuable than the prince's death," Flea suggested, gesturing at the mangled corpse. *"They're really serious about intel, now that almost everybody's dead."*

Joe glanced down at his fist. His hand had gotten better for a while, but ever since he had shot the Huouyt, it had been shaking uncontrollably. He tried not to look at the dirt on either side of him, tried not to think about what would happen if the planet suffered an earthquake. He could feel the old fear, straining at the back of his mind, clawing for release. The last thing he wanted to do was stay down here until the dam burst and he began crying like a little baby.

He opened his mouth to tell them they were going home.

"Our mission was to kill the prince," the Grekkon said to Flea, before Joe could speak. *"The prince is not dead."*

Joe took a deep breath and tried not to gag on the stale, underground air. The Grekkon was right. He couldn't let his fear make his decisions for him. That was the quickest way for a grounder to meet his grave. He squeezed his eyes shut and tried to force his mind into some semblance of clarity. *"Let's suppose this guy only tagged Daviin. We could use that."*

"How?" Flea asked, clearly interested.

"Scarab, how much juice you got left?"

"I could tunnel back to the surface if I had to. Not much further."

"All right," Joe said. *"Time to use a little reverse psychology."*

25

A LIFETIME OF LONELINESS

"Lavik twitched. "Of course I'm being used. I'm a soldier for the Vahlin to do with as he will. Not even a captain or a general. That doesn't bother me. I understand I'm giving my life for my people. If I must die, so be it. The Vahlin will not fail."

The Huouyt cocked its penis-shaped head at him. "If the Vahlin didn't want to fail, why'd he combine all his best forces onto one planet?" his prisoner demanded. "You're completely blockaded. He must know they're going to use an *ekhta* eventually."

Lavik snorted. "You said yourself the cowards of the Regency won't use an *ekhta*."

"They won't use one *now*," the prisoner agreed. "But what will they do when they find out the Huouyt and the Dhasha are working together? They won't have a choice."

"We're *not* working together," Lavik spat. "The Vahlin sent me the Huouyt as a gift. Said your team was a special case." He glanced over his shoulder at the empty tunnels with growing irritation. "Which seems to be true so far, since they're still not dead."

"You're being used," the Huouyt repeated.

"How?"

"Whoever he is, the Vahlin doesn't want you to live."

"How do you figure?" Lavik snorted.

"If he had accurate enough information to predict where we would land, why didn't he take that one step further? Why didn't he tell you the tunnel we would penetrate? Why wouldn't he tell you how to ambush us? Why leave you to your own devices?"

"The Vahlin cannot be bothered with small details," Lavik said.

"Truly? Then why'd he warn the first prince there was a Huouyt in our team and then fail to mention the Jreet entirely? He mentioned every species that posed a danger to him...except the most obvious."

"He didn't know of the Jreet," Lavik said, though the Huouyt's words were disturbing him.

"Really." The Huouyt's purple eye was flat. "After seeing his accuracy today, ten days in advance, you truly believe that?"

"It's not about what I believe, Huouyt," Lavik said. "If the Vahlin sees fit that I die to further his cause, I'll gladly die for my race. We've endured Congressional subjugation too long. The Dhasha will be free."

"The Vahlin wants you to die down here," the Huouyt repeated.

Lavik laughed. "Then why send me a Huouyt to do battle with you?"

"Did he give you grenades?"

Lavik blinked. "Who would use grenades underground?"

"Someone who truly wanted you to survive."

"What are you talking about?"

"I find it odd he arms you against one threat, only to leave another go completely unchecked."

Lavik was pacing, now, unnerved. What the Huouyt said was true. Things were not making sense.

At that moment, a Takki rushed into the room, head bowed low. "Master," it whispered, drawing close, "The enemy is retreating."

Lavik stiffened. "Retreating to where?"

"The surface, master." The Takki stared demurely at the ground, offering nothing more.

"They *flee?*" Lavik demanded.

"Yes, master," the Takki replied quietly.

"Curse it!" Lavik snapped. "What of my heirs? Where are they?"

"They cannot follow, master. The tunnel they used is too small."

"Then have them regroup on the surface! They will *not* get away, you understand?"

The Takki began to bow, but its expression broke into fear with a suddenness to make Lavik's scales tighten. He turned—

And the assassin's paddle-like tentacle slid under Lavik's scales. Lavik felt a sting, then his body went numb beneath him. He fell to the ground, unable to control it.

The Takki's voice raised in a fear-shriek and it turned to run.

The Huouyt caught it before it had moved more than two digs. The poor creature died instantly.

And yet for some reason, Lavik was still breathing. He realized, horrified, that the assassin might mean to extract him to the surface…alive.

Insane. And yet, with his heirs diverted to the surface, the assassin had no one to stop him.

The assassin squatted in Lavik's field of vision and placed a hand on his snout, oblivious to Lavik's deadly jaws only ninths from his body. While his natural eye was as utterly unreadable as all other Huouyt, his one purple eye was almost…compassionate. "I think you know the choice I'm about to give you."

Lavik somehow found his voice. Apparently, the drug was selective in its paralyzation. That frightened him more than anything. "Are you really Va'ga trained, Huouyt?"

The assassin's odd purple eye seemed to pity him. "The best."

"Then you have drugs that can make me utterly suggestible, that will bend me to your will. Make me follow you like a whipped Takki."

The assassin nodded.

"And my choice is life or death."

"Yes."

Lavik laughed. "Do you truly believe the Vahlin wants me dead or was that a bluff?"

The Huouyt watched him a moment before replying. "I think the Vahlin is not what he seems."

Lavik sighed. "You already know what I am going to choose and you're trying to ease my mind before I die. You believe he wanted me to die all along."

"I'm sure of it."

Lavik locked gazes with the Huouyt. "When you see the Vahlin, ask him for me."

The Huouyt cocked his head at him, giving him an odd look. "What makes you think I'll see the Vahlin, Dhasha?"

"You've survived three deep dens," Lavik said. "He obviously wants you alive."

The assassin blinked at him.

"Just hurry up and finish it," Lavik said tiredly. "Before a Takki sees me like this."

The Huouyt nodded and slid his tentacle into Lavik's mouth, touching the sensitive flesh of his tongue.

Lavik felt the sting, then embraced oblivion.

• • •

Joe followed close behind as the Ooreiki led himself and Flea unerringly downward through the maze of tunnels. For the sake of speed, they had found a large, main shaft and descended at a run. The extra space had given Joe a reprieve from the gnawing fear of the smaller tunnels, allowing him more freedom of thought. His fingers continued to shake, but as long as he wasn't seeing blood that wasn't there, he could bear it.

"*Deep den's ten rods up ahead,*" Galek said.

Joe could sense no change in the tunnel ahead of him, but he took it as truth. "*Okay, Flea, go. Get out of reach and give that furg an eyeful, got me? I don't want him getting his claws on you.*"

Flea said nothing and disappeared down the tunnel at the speed of a cruising *haauk*. No sooner had Flea disappeared than a Takki emerged from a slave tunnel adjoining theirs and Joe felt every nerve in his body tingle with alarm. Instead of running as a normal Takki, it lunged, grabbed the Ooreiki by the neck, and dragged its bulk around until Galek blocked his attacker from view.

Joe raised his gun, too late.

Galek, looking as stunned as Joe felt, began to twist under the Takki's grip. The Takki's disposition didn't change, but the Takki's fingers slipped past the Ooreiki's lips, into his mouth, and Galek suddenly went limp.

"I'm a Huouyt," the Takki snapped. "Identify yourself or I'll kill him."

Joe had his gun up and aimed at the Huouyt in an instant. He made a mental communication with the Ooreiki's chip. *"You all right?"*

"I'm alive," the Ooreiki responded, its pupils wide with terror. *"I think it poisoned me. I can't move."*

"You kill him," Joe said over his weapon, his voice cold as death, "and you'll be dead before he hits the ground."

The Huouyt watched him, an utter lack of fear in its Takki face. "Identify yourself," the Huouyt repeated.

Joe realized that they probably had them surrounded and were going to use their names and appearances to take out the last three members of their team. The single Huouyt was just a diversion. As soon as they gave their information, both of them would die.

"Flea, can you hear me?"

Flea said nothing.

Anger flashed in the Huouyt's eyes. He gave the Ooreiki a shake, making Galek give a mental whimper. "Your names!"

"And if you're the enemy, you'll kill him as soon as I give my name."

The Huouyt scowled at him through his borrowed sapphire eyes. "I'll kill him if you *don't* give your name, Human."

"Why aren't you giving him our names, Joe?" the Ooreiki babbled in terror.

"Just hold on," Joe said. "Flea and I will figure something out." *"You still alive, Flea?"*

"Busy," Flea said.

"How busy?!" Joe cried.

"Really busy."

"*Do you need help, Joe?*" His Sentinel's mental voice was thick with concern.

"*No!*" Joe cried. "*Stay where you damn well are.*"

"Hurry," the Huouyt said, still utterly calm, "or he dies. You have five, four, three—"

"Give us *your* name, then," Joe said quickly. "If you are who you're pretending to be, you'd know that much."

The Huouyt gave him a cool look. "I will not betray my friends."

"Very funny," Joe snapped, watching the Huouyt down the barrel of his rifle. "I know what you're doing. *You* have until the count of three before I start shooting."

Galek gave another mental whimper, but Joe ignored him.

The Takki watched him a moment, unmoving, then said, "Show me your left hand."

Joe stiffened. "What?"

"Your left hand," the Huouyt said. "Hold it up."

"Listen, asher, I'm not going to drop my gun so you can—"

"You want your companion to live?" the Huouyt asked coldly. At Joe's hesitation, he said, "Then you are in no position to barter. Your hand. Now."

Joe glanced at Galek, who hung limply in the Huouyt's arms, terrified. "Ghosts," he muttered. Slowly, he lowered his weapon and lifted his fist for the other's perusal.

"Open it."

Suddenly, Joe understood. He'd caught Jer'ait eying his hand on the shuttle, watching it tremble. Shame tightened his insides, making him feel near to choking. "I get it." He dropped his fist. "I'm Joe. That's Galek."

The Huouyt's eyes never left his face. "Open it, Joe."

"You know damn well it's me," Joe snapped.

The Huouyt continued to watch him.

"You asher," Joe whispered. Galek was watching him curiously, now, obviously wondering what it was about.

Angrily, Joe opened his fist and spread his fingers. As much as he willed them to steady, they trembled like leaves, betraying his cowardice for what it was.

With a grunt, the Huouyt released Galek and said, "My name is Jer'ait Ze'laa vehn Morinth. I am four hundred and fifty-two turns old. I was born in the city of Kha'seol in the eighty-second turn of the 1292nd Age of the Huouyt, the first child of the royal family of Ze'laa. Sixteen turns later I was sterilized and slated for execution for a birth defect of my left eye. I am a Class One Va'gan assassin with eight hundred and thirty-three kills to my name. My last kill was not twenty tics ago, a Dhasha prince by the name of Lavik, the second prince of my career. I was recently attacked by a Huouyt in Joe's pattern, whom I can only assume took my pattern and fried my chip. I woke in the Dhasha's deep den to the sound of silence."

Joe stared down at his clenched fist, ignoring the Ooreiki's confused stare. "The prince is dead?"

"Yes."

"Show me."

Jer'ait nodded once and led them down into the deep den.

There, they saw the prince's body laid out in the center of the room, alone and unguarded.

"So what the hell happened to Flea?" Joe growled, lifting his rifle again.

The Dhasha's body jerked and all of them, even Jer'ait, flinched. It jerked again, and Joe rushed forward, ready to plant a plasma blast down its throat before it woke completely.

He didn't have to. Flea was on the other side of the Dhasha, snipping off toes and gathering the enormous, razor-sharp talons in a pile.

"You asher," Joe said.

Flea ignored him.

"Leave those," Joe commanded. "We're going."

"You go," Flea retorted. "I'll meet up with you on the surface." Flea continued to snip off toes.

The Huouyt rounded the Dhasha's body and said, "What is—" His words choked off as soon as he saw the Baga and what he was doing. His sapphire Takki eyes went cold. Without a word, he stalked up and slammed the back of his fist into the Baga's torso. The smaller alien hit the other side of the room and dazedly tried to get to his feet.

Jer'ait stalked over to him and grabbed him by the wings, lifting him until they were face-to-face. "The dead," he whispered, "are not trophies." He slammed the Baga into the wall and Joe heard snapping sounds as the Baga's delicate frame collapsed.

"Someone else will carry this scum to the surface. If it were me, I'd leave him here to rot." Jer'ait cast the Baga aside and stalked from the room.

• • •

Syuri opened his eyes. Immediately, he felt a tingle of relief. It seemed to come from the air around him, almost as if—

They gave me back my sivvet!

"How are you feeling?"

Syuri stiffened. He knew that voice anywhere. It was refined, yet pleasant; crisp, yet completely without mechanical clunkiness; artificial, and yet so filled with emotion it could have come from another Jahul. It was the voice of a Geuji.

Warily, Syuri sat up, at first thinking the Peacemakers had locked him into one of the cells with Forgotten's people, maybe as a form of high-nutrient food when he starved to death and his body started to decompose. Yet, when he lifted his head to examine the Geuji draped around the room, it was impossible to overlook the dozens of beeping electronics, devices, wirings, sensors, machines, monitors, and other high-tech paraphernalia hooked up to the Geuji's body.

Forgotten.

"You came for me!" Syuri cried, so overwhelmed with relief he oozed sexual fluids over his skin. "Sweet Hagra, Geuji," he babbled, "as soon as your plans went sour, I thought I was dead for sure." He knew he was weeping, but he was beyond trying to salvage his pride. "Thank you, Forgotten," he whispered, touching the rippling black mass gently. "Thank you so much for coming for me."

"My plans didn't go sour." A flush of deep, overpowering shame hit his sivvet, a yearning for forgiveness.

353

Syuri froze at the feelings of remorse. Very slowly, he crawled to his feet, fear once more hitting him in a surge. "You meant for me to get captured?"

"Yes." More shame. Anguish so powerful it almost knocked him down. Either the Geuji had replaced Syuri's sivvet with something eight times the sensitivity, or Forgotten was no longer trying to shield his emotions from him.

Syuri swallowed, afraid to guess what that meant. "And for my *sivvet* to be extracted?"

"They weren't actually extracted," Forgotten said, his voice filled with apology. Shame pounded at Syuri's sivvet in an almost too-powerful wave, staggering him with its force. "I developed a drug for the Huouyt to use that would incapacitate your empathy-related abilities."

He...drugged me. But why? "But I *saw* them, Forgotten," Syuri began. "The Huouyt held them out on a piece of glass."

"Those belonged to the last Jahul I sent there."

Syuri felt his internal pressure rising.

"I'm sorry, Syuri," Forgotten whispered. "I didn't want to scare you, but I had to know. I'm so very sorry." The guilt was overwhelming, pounding at him from all sides, a thousand times stronger than anything Syuri had ever felt before. He groaned and slid back to the tiled floor.

"Jreet gods," Syuri moaned, feeling his chambers losing their hold on his wastes under the pressure of the Geuji's assault. "Shut it off, you miserable corpse-rot!"

Instantly, the Geuji's emotions stopped assaulting his sivvet, leaving a low ebb in their wake. Syuri gasped and blinked, feeling like a drowning man suddenly given air.

"Better?" Forgotten asked softly.

"How...?" Syuri whispered, his sivvet still pounding from the emotional overload only moments before.

"I stop thinking," Forgotten said. "Find other things to think about. Less...shameful...things." The tidal wave of guilt hit again, staggering Syuri once more.

"Bugger you with a karwiq bulb, stop!" Syuri gasped. Then, once Forgotten had eased his assault once more, Syuri managed, "Glorious ruvmestin balls, is that what you meant by 'trying to hide it from me,' Geuji?" He felt a whole new wave of awe for the meddling fungus and hid it by rubbing at his skull with his hands.

"Yes," Forgotten said. "I'm sorry."

Syuri believed him. He swallowed and rubbed his head with a groan. "Just what," he managed, "was that all about?" Now that the pain in his head was lessening, he was once more being faced with the fact that he had just spent four days being interrogated by Peacemakers. On Levren. After Forgotten had sent him there. On purpose.

"I needed to know if I could trust you," Forgotten told him. As always, his words carried that pang of truth.

Syuri's chambers gave a startled squeeze. "You set me up?"

"Only once. You passed every test and more, Syuri."

"That...that was a *test?*" Syuri shrieked. He remembered his emotional anguish, his four days of sheer *terror*. "You had them *interrogate* me as a *test?!*"

Another rush of guilt. "It was the *only* test," Forgotten said. "You have my word, if you agree to work for me, I'll never test you again."

Syuri was trembling, on the verge of voiding himself out of fear and rage. "And if I don't agree to work for you?" he managed in a tight whisper.

"You're free to go." A pang of regret. Of sadness.

"You're lying."

"I don't lie."

Syuri opened his mouth to tell Forgotten he'd lost the only friend he might have had in this pathetic universe, but was forestalled by a wave of unhappiness that almost knocked him over.

He knows what I'm about to say.

Syuri bit his lip, the same loneliness and misery that he had felt in the basement of the Space Academy hitting him from all sides in a gut-wrenching wave. Forgotten clung to the walls in silence, waiting for his answer.

"You want me to say yes," Syuri said simply.

Forgotten hesitated, and Syuri felt the tangy bite of shock against his sivvet. "Yes."

Warily, Syuri offered, "So it was a test of my loyalties. I wasn't in any real danger."

"Had you betrayed me, they would have executed you," Forgotten said simply.

Syuri narrowed his eyes. "And you did it because you had to know if you could trust me if I get caught."

"No," Forgotten said. "I just had to know if I could trust you. You won't get caught." At Syuri's skeptical look, Forgotten added, "A good agent is worth more to me alive than dead, Syuri. As such, all seven Va'gan sects could put a billion credits on your head and you would be utterly safe in my service."

Syuri laughed at the idea of the Va'gan assassins coming after *him*. "So sure of that, are you?"

"Yes."

Syuri sobered when he realized Forgotten was *utterly* serious. He voided himself just a little. Cocking his head, he said carefully, "And *are* they going to come after me, Forgotten?"

Forgotten could have lied, but he said, "Yes."

Assassins. He *hated* assassins.

"I know you hate assassins…" Forgotten began.

"Just shut up and let me think," Syuri snapped. His mind was dull from the lack of nutrient boosts the last four days and it was difficult to concentrate. The assault on his sivvet hadn't helped. Struggling for some way to politely tell the Geuji to take his offer and shove it up his wastes bin, he managed, "So that Huouyt who interrogated me…he's your agent?"

"No," Forgotten replied. "A contact."

"And the difference is…?" Syuri growled.

"I have no agent," Forgotten said softly. "I have millions of contacts."

Syuri narrowed his eyes. "And an agent is…?"

Forgotten waited long moments before saying, "Someone I can trust." He hesitated again. "Talk to."

Hagra steal my deodorant, he wants a friend. Syuri peered at the irritating fungus. "You are kidding me, right?"

Forgotten was silent so long that Syuri wondered which unfortunate planetary com system the Geuji was in the process of shutting down. Then, almost timidly, Forgotten said, "A contact is someone I use to monitor my people or perform one of any other millions of tasks I need accomplished on any given day. The Jahul working with your interrogator was another contact, though they did not know it of each other. An agent is…more important. Like I said, I don't have an agent. None of them passed the sivvet test before you." Another wash of loneliness, of…fear? "And you, of course, hate me for it." And resignation. Bitterness. Quiet, unhappy bitterness.

Sensing the same misery he had felt soiling his sivvet in the basement of the Space Academy, Syuri felt some of the pressure on his internal chambers ease. "I don't hate you for it," Syuri muttered. "Miserable fungus. I'll be your damned friend."

He had said the words before he realized they'd left his lips, and shock hit him so hard it strained something inside, like a blood vessel about to explode.

"Shield it!" Syuri screamed, falling to his knees. "Gods, you slippery corpse-rot, shield it!"

It took longer for Forgotten to contain himself this time, and when he did, Syuri was panting on the floor, seeing stars. Syuri could feel Forgotten watching him in shock as he lay there, trying to stabilize, despite the fact the Geuji had no eyes to stare.

Long tics passed in silence, where the only sound was the beep of electronics. Then, as timidly as a nervous child, Forgotten said, "Truly?"

Syuri groaned and rolled onto his side. "You're going to learn to stop doing that, or our friendship is going to be very short-lived. I think you just about killed me."

A wave of horror, this time, but more subdued. "I'm sorry."

Syuri grunted. Agent to a Geuji. That was certainly not on his To Do list when he wrote up his starry-eyed entrance essay to get into the Space Academy. Then again, neither was impregnating a commanding officer's daughter on Grakkas, getting thrown in the brig, being stripped of rank, sentenced to manual labor, or stealing a ship and flying against three dozen Ueshi in a brilliant aerial battle to make the only escape from a ruvmestin planet in the last three hundred turns. He supposed working for the Geuji was better than spending the rest of his life trying not to get cheated by Jikaln or swindled by Huouyt.

Into the silence, Forgotten quietly offered, "Syuri, you're the first Jahul that's passed the *sivvet* test. You're the first of twelve that's come back to me."

"Because they turned on you," Syuri added.

"Yes."

"And the whole thing was a *test*," Syuri repeated, still a bit irritated at that.

"Not all of it." Forgotten paused. The room flooded with a feeling of anxiety, though at a much lower ebb. "Tell me. What did you feel when you opened the vaults?"

Syuri flinched, remembering the thick hopelessness.

"What'd you feel?" Forgotten prodded.

"Misery," Syuri said.

A wave of anguish hit him like another sledge before it was quickly shut away. Forgotten said nothing for several moments before softly whispering, "I feared as much."

"So when are you gonna spring them?" Syuri demanded, sitting up to face the glistening black room that was his employer.

"What?"

"Spring them," Syuri said, gesturing vaguely. "I'll help. Just tell me what to do." So what if the Geuji had locked him in a room with alien interrogators and made him think he was crippled, slated for execution in the bowels of the Space Academy? What the Peacemakers were doing was *wrong*.

"Syuri," Forgotten said softly, "I wish it were that simple."

Syuri frowned. "You could do it. I mean, you blew up a *planet*, Forgotten."

"Call me Jemria."

"I like Forgotten better," Syuri said. "Why haven't you helped them yet?"

"It's what I'm doing now."

"That's why you blew up Aez?"

"Yes."

"How does blowing up Aez help you get your people out?"

"I couldn't possibly explain it to you."

Syuri wondered if Forgotten was acting superior, then realized he was simply stating the truth. "All right. So what do you want me to do?"

Again, the fungus paused. "You'll continue to work for me?" Another tingle of hope danced like warm sunlight across his sivvet. "After everything I've put you through?"

"I'd be stupid not to."

"Yes. But not unjustified."

Syuri scoffed. "I'm a pirate. I deserve a few blows to my pride."

"You're a smuggler," Forgotten corrected. "You don't have the heart to kill people. Even escaping Grakkas—which was well-done, by the way—you didn't harm a single soul, which is why I wanted you."

"An agent who won't kill people?" Syuri demanded. "It's looking like you're getting the short end of the stick here, Forgotten."

"An assassin is easy to buy. A friend is not." Honesty rolled off of the Geuji, heating Syuri's sivvet. Honesty…and hope.

Syuri's mouth fell open. He tried to speak, but found he couldn't. *He's telling the truth*, Syuri realized. *All this time. He just wanted a friend.*

26

PIECING IT TOGETHER

"So," Jer'ait said as the two of them watched the surgeons put Flea back together, "Tell me what's wrong with your hand."

Joe fisted it, his jaw gritting visibly. "Nothing."

"Daviin tells me you had a problem climbing into the slave tunnels."

The Human ignored him.

"If it's a phobia, I can help," Jer'ait insisted.

No response.

"It's getting worse, isn't it?"

The Human glanced at him, his expression caught between wariness and desperation. "How can you help?"

"Chemicals," Jer'ait said. "Regular doses, at least while we're in the tunnels. Maybe once every four hours."

Joe snorted. "Sorry if I'm not jumping at the idea of having you drug me again."

"I'm an expert, Joe."

The Human met his eyes and Jer'ait saw real anguish there. Longing. Trust. "You really think you can help me?"

"Yes," Jer'ait said. "I'm sure of it."

The Human swallowed, hard, his small brown eyes scanning Jer'ait's face. Then he gave a nervous laugh and looked away. He glanced down at his left hand, which was trembling against his hip, then tightened it into a fist. "All right," he whispered.

Jer'ait had expected the Human to concede, but still he was shocked. He knew his Prime understood what Jer'ait was capable of. Joe had seen it in the tunnels. He'd fought on Eeloir. He knew exactly what it meant to allow a Huouyt to manipulate his body chemistry. He was putting his life in Jer'ait's hands, entirely, and he knew it.

Not for the first time, Jer'ait felt a tug of respect for the Human's courage.

And it *was* courage, he knew. Even knowing everything about him—Jer'ait's training on Morinth, his people's capacity for murder, the Huouyt reputation for switching sides—Joe was willing to let Jer'ait touch him. *Drug him.*

Another being's trust—something so easily gained in Jer'ait's line of work—had never before moved him in any way, and yet here, watching the misery play across his Prime's features, Jer'ait found himself at a total loss for words. In the silence that followed, the Human's gaze flickered up to his, sweat glistening on his face. "Stunned?" he said, with an anguished chuckle.

Because he could do nothing else, Jer'ait solemnly touched his paddle to his zora slit above his eyes in a Va'gan salute. "Your trust is not misplaced."

The Human made a miserable sound and just shook his head.

Jer'ait opened his mouth to try and ease his mind, but the door burst open behind them and they both turned.

"That's him," a Jahul in Peacemaker battle garb said, pointing a slender forearm into the room at the table where Flea was being re-inflated by a horde of doctors. A dozen armed Ooreiki grounders trudged in after him, their heavy, boneless bodies sporting full biosuits and tunnel gear.

Both Joe and Jer'ait stiffened.

An Ooreiki Overseer—the only newcomer not wearing a biosuit or carrying a gun—stepped into the room on their heels, scanning both Joe and Jer'ait before his eyes came to rest on Jer'ait. "Are you that Baga's groundleader?"

"Yes," Jer'ait said.

Joe sighed and stepped forward. "I'm his groundleader. What's this about?"

The Jahul Peacemaker stepped forward, interrupting whatever the uniformed Ooreiki was going to say. "Are you aware he has been spying on the Overseer battleroom for the last rotation?"

To his credit, Joe never batted an eye. "Yeah."

This was obviously not the response the Jahul had expected. The Peacemaker blustered. "You *knew* and didn't inform us?"

"Hell, no, I didn't inform you," Joe said. "I ordered it."

You did not, you furg, Jer'ait thought, stiffening. *Why are you taking the fall for that little pest?*

The Jahul was all but shaking in fury. "Are you aware that the sentence for treason is death?"

"Didn't see it as treason," Joe said. "Thought we had a right to know."

The Jahul sputtered. "Commander Zero, if you think your impressive history will change our—"

"It won't," Joe said. "But I also know you're not going to break up a groundteam that's single-handedly taken down three princes."

The Jahul Peacemaker straightened on its four back legs, the dig-long spines on its back bristling into the air. Its two grasping arms were folded back in rage. "You're sure of that, are you?"

"Yes."

The Jahul's tiny black eyes flickered from the Human, then to Jer'ait, then back at the Baga, who was still sprawled in an unconscious pancake. Jer'ait watched the Jahul take the challenge, his tiny mind churning in rage as he mentally prepared his command to disband their team and take Joe to the brig.

"You may leave, now," Jer'ait said, his eyes catching pointedly on his comrade's chest. "*Ninth* Hjai."

The Jahul hesitated, his inky black eyes settling on Jer'ait in confusion. "Who in Hagra's name are you? Where's your rank, soldier?"

Jer'ait gave him a flat stare. "I must have left it back on Levren."

That made the Jahul twitch, but he obviously didn't catch the reference. Which meant he hadn't read the whole team's file. Which meant he was a furg.

The Jahul narrowed his huge black eyes, then turned to face Joe again, once more ignoring Jer'ait. He opened his mouth to give the order—

"Don't let it happen again," the uniformed Ooreiki Overseer interrupted.

The Jahul snapped his greenish head around, glaring at his companion. "Overseer, that almost sounded as if you were going to give him a *warning*. This is a Peacemaker matter. Commander Zero has committed—"

"Just shut up and go," the Ooreiki said. "My peers sent me here to talk with him, nothing more."

"I second that," Jer'ait said. "Shut up and go. And next time, read the *whole* file before you start trying to throw around rank, *Ninth* Hjai."

The Jahul flinched and his small black eyes scanned Jer'ait's forehead, the nervous trait Jahul had when they were reading a victim's emotions. The slick sheen of excrement flowed over the Jahul's mottled green-gray skin. Then the sextuped turned and stormed off, leaving the Ooreiki Overseer behind.

In the silence that followed, the Ooreiki cleared his throat. "I appreciate your loyalty to your groundmates, Commander Zero. But the other Overseers don't. I told them I could put an end to the spying. If it happens again, I won't be able to stop them." He hesitated, glancing once more at Flea. "You're lucky I could sway them. By all rights, the Baga belongs in the brig right now."

"He belongs on a goddamn Ueshi pleasure planet, enjoying the three mil from his *kasja*." Joe stepped forward, until he was face-to-face with the thick, sticky-eyed Ooreiki. "But you're planning on sending us back until we die. Then you'll never have to pay up, will you?"

The Ooreiki's expression hardened. "The Baga told you this?"

"No," Joe said. "You just did."

The room seemed to be suspended in silence as the Overseer returned the Human's stare. Finally, without a word, he turned and departed, taking the nervous Ooreiki grounders with him. The medics finished their re-inflation of the Baga's carapace, then they, too, left them.

The Human let out a huge sigh and turned back to the Baga's unconscious form. Shaking his head, he raised his slender, bony fingers to touch his brow.

The Dhasha prince's final words returned to Jer'ait as he watched the struggle upon the Human's face.

"You've survived three deep dens. He obviously wants you alive."

Forgotten was playing them all like fools, but he wanted them alive. Why?

It made no sense.

"Joe," Jer'ait asked tentatively, "Do you know anyone by the name of Jemria?"

Joe dropped his hand from his face and turned to frown at him. "Haven't heard of her. Why?"

"Just curious. He sometimes calls himself Forgotten."

"What kind of furg calls himself Forgotten?"

Obviously, the Human did not have the creative capacity to have attracted the Geuji's interest. Jer'ait's frustration increased. He wanted to blurt out everything he knew, but he doubted the Human would understand. Nor would he be very happy to find out Jer'ait's mission there was to kill him.

"What's wrong, Jer'ait?"

For an insane moment, Jer'ait felt like telling the Human everything anyway. Then he shrugged it off. "Once Flea stabilizes, I would like to talk to you about the remedies I have for your phobia."

"It's not a phobia," the Human said, a bit too defensively. "It's just the shakes."

"It's the sign of a hasty medical remedy that's crumbling as we speak."

Joe flinched. "How'd you know about that?"

"You had me research what Kophat meant to you."

The Human snorted, though there was an uneasiness in his eyes now.

Which made sense. If it was revealed he was chronically claustrophobic, he could be discharged from the Ground Force to repay his debt in manual labor. As high-protein, chemically compatible exotics, Humans often had the ill fortune of having a Dhasha buy their contract.

Warily, the Human said, "How long did you screw around in my file before you gave up and called for help?"

"I didn't call for help." Jer'ait gave his Prime a long, sober look. "Kophat meant you're probably the most loyal citizen of Congress on this planet."

Joe's gaze flickered across his face, startled. Then he snorted again. "I didn't have a choice. They were shooting at me, I shot back."

"That's not what I'm talking about, Joe."

The Human flinched and gave him a sideways look.

"I'm talking about the choice you made with Na'leen," Jer'ait confirmed for him.

The Human's brown eyes widened a little and he tensed.

"Yes," Jer'ait said. "I know why Na'leen let you breach his bunker. He thought you would lead his army to victory against Congress, as the Trith predicted."

Joe looked away, swallowed, then looked back. "You really just figured it out? On your own?"

"You're a Congie. That's what Kophat means to you."

"Ghosts of the Mothers." The Human now looked at him in nervous awe. "Just how smart are you?"

Not a fraction as smart as the creature we're up against. Jer'ait watched him, wondering if he could trust him. "There's something we need to talk about, Human. Away from your Jreet."

"To hell with that!" Daviin snapped, suddenly popping into existence in a gigantic crimson coil taking up the corner of the room.

Joe turned to glare at the Jreet. "I told you to leave!"

"And I ignored it. Believe me, Joe, the last thing I'm about to do is leave you alone in a room with this mother-killing scum."

"Who killed his mother?" the Baga asked, sitting up on the bed. He buzzed his wings, then crawled up the wall until he was staring down at them from the ceiling.

"We need to talk alone," Jer'ait insisted.

Joe went to the door and locked it. "There. You can say it in front of them."

Daviin shot Jer'ait a triumphant gaze. Jer'ait stifled his anger. "It's private."

"I've got nothing to hide," the Human said.

"No, but *he* does," Daviin said, his golden alien eyes never leaving Jer'ait's face.

Jer'ait almost went back to Koliinaat right there. Almost. Instead, he closed his eyes. "Joe, I'm here to kill you."

"I know," Joe said. "Daviin had Flea follow when you wandered off a few times. Heard you talk with that other Huouyt."

Jer'ait stared at the Human, completely flabbergasted. "You...You knew and you didn't kill me?"

"Figured you'd change your mind."

"Joe..." Jer'ait said, "that's..."

"Stupid?" the Jreet offered. "Yes, I told him that. Repeatedly." The Voran's eyes were piercing as they stared back at Jer'ait. Obviously, he still wanted to murder him.

"*Did* you change your mind, Jer'ait?" Joe leaned up against the wall and crossed his arms over his chest as he watched him. "That gesture you made...that's a Va'gan oath, isn't it?"

"It is," Daviin barked. "It's the only reason he's not dead yet."

"Joe," Jer'ait said, his eyes flickering to the Jreet and back, "I think we're being used."

"You didn't answer the question," Daviin said sharply.

"Yes," Jer'ait snapped. "I changed my mind. Are you happy?"

"No." The look in the Jreet's eye told him Daviin would never trust him, no matter how many times he swore not to hurt his ward. *He's the smart one*, Jer'ait thought.

"How are we being used?" Flea asked, dropping down onto Joe's shoulder.

"The Dhasha Vahlin," Jer'ait said. "I don't think he exists."

Joe shifted against the wall as he considered. Whether or not he was grateful for Jer'ait's honesty about his mission did not register on his impassive face. "Why?" he asked finally.

"The last crawl. I met the prince. We talked. He'd never seen the Vahlin. None of them had."

When his three companions merely stared at him blankly, Jer'ait tried another approach. "What kind of Dhasha is capable of designing a new kind of *ekhta?*"

"Could've been a Takki," Joe said. "They're smart, when they're not getting eaten."

Daviin twisted to give the Human a look of distaste, but Joe continued to hold Jer'ait's gaze.

"Whatever took out Aez was something Congress had never seen before," Jer'ait informed them. "It was too hot to be one of ours. How many turns did it take Congress to develop the technology to build an *ekhta?*"

Joe grunted. "I dunno. Like five hundred thousand. Why?"

"How old is the Dhasha Vahlin, Joe?"

The Human's eyes registered understanding.

"So what does that leave? The Huouyt are the smartest creatures with a Representative in Congress, and it would take us another two and a half million turns to come up with a new kind of ekhta, even if Congress allowed us full access to the technology, which it wouldn't. Ekhtas are built in forty-seven different stages, with each set of manufacturers completely independent of the other and in total lockdown from the outside. There is no way to piece the puzzle together." Jer'ait hesitated. This was where his companions either joined his cause or shoved him aside as Yua'nev had. "There is only one creature who might be capable of building an ekhta in his spare time, without Congressional support."

"Who?" Joe asked.

"Forgotten."

The Baga fluttered its wings. "You mean Jemria?"

Jer'ait glared at the pest. "Where did you hear that name?"

"From you. When I was spying on you. Then I went and looked up the Geuji on the net. I think you're right, you know. That Yua'nev guy's a furg."

Jer'ait cocked his head at the Baga. "You think I'm right?"

"Yeah."

"Then why would he start a war, only to slaughter the rebels?" Jer'ait demanded.

"That's easy," Flea twittered. "He wants to kill off the Dhasha."

"Or," the Human said, leaning forward, "He's on our side. Daviin told me about his guardian angel. And how you killed him. Brilliant work, you two."

"He's alive," Jer'ait said.

"He's *what?*" Daviin roared.

"If it is a Geuji we're dealing with, the last thing he's gonna do is piss him off by killing his agents," the Baga said. "I read his file. Scary crack. His entire body is one gigantic moldy brain. Smarter than lots and lots of supercomputers."

Daviin frowned at the Baga, then at Jer'ait. "I thought the Geuji were a myth. Extinct."

"There's one out there Congress hasn't managed to capture," Jer'ait said. "The rest are locked in the Space Academy cellar."

Joe frowned at Jer'ait. "And you know this how?"

"He's second in command of the Peacemakers," Flea said, faceted eyes glinting. "He knows everything."

"Hardly," Daviin scoffed.

"Let me get this straight," Joe said. "You think this creature... this Geuji...blew up Aez and faked the rise of a Dhasha Vahlin so he could start a Dhasha rebellion? Why do all that, unless he planned to carve out an empire for himself? Having the Dhasha all camp out on Neskfaat isn't exactly the best strategy, if you get my drift."

"I don't know," Jer'ait said, frustrated. "That's where my theory falls apart."

"Okay," Joe said. "So say this Geuji blew up Aez and started the war. What does that have to do with you coming here to kill me?"

Now for the leap of faith. "My superior received a message from a Trith. Supposedly. It predicted Aez's destruction and the Dhasha insurrection."

The Human stiffened visibly. "So?"

"What are Trith?" Daviin asked.

Jer'ait ignored the Jreet. "It also predicted you would kill the Vahlin, Joe."

"Trith are full of ash," Joe snapped, his face flushing in a show of Human rage.

"I don't think it was made by a Trith," Jer'ait offered.

Joe opened his mouth, then closed it again, a frown creasing his brow. "You're saying this Geuji is predicting I'm gonna kill a Dhasha Vahlin that doesn't exist?"

"Yes."

"Why would he do that?" Flea demanded, looking from Joe to Jer'ait and back. "What's he trying to tell us?"

"He's trying to tell me," Jer'ait said, "Not to kill Joe."

Joe's face darkened. "This is stupid. Trith or no, nobody can predict the future."

"Damn it!" Daviin boomed, "Who are these damn Trith you keep speaking of?"

"You've never heard of them?" Flea asked.

"No, damn you," the Jreet snarled. "What are they?"

"They see the future," Jer'ait said.

"No they don't," Joe said stubbornly.

Daviin glanced between them. "Well? Do they or don't they?"

"They do," Jer'ait said. "They're the only species Congress has not conquered."

"Unless you count the Geuji," Flea said.

"The Geuji are conquered," Jer'ait said. "Only one remains to be caught. When he is, he'll be imprisoned with the rest of his people and the Geuji will never be heard from again."

Daviin had a troubled expression on his face. "These Trith you speak of. Do they have bulbous heads like Joe, but bigger? And they're small, like this? Gray skin? And they smell like unwashed cheese?"

The tension in the room suddenly increased a thousandfold.

"They spoke to you?" Joe asked. He sounded like he'd been punched.

"Tried to," Daviin said. "The Welu interrupted us."

"What'd he say to you?" Joe asked.

The room fell silent as the Jreet shrugged. "Something about killing someone. I wasn't really paying attention."

"What about you?" Joe asked, looking at Jer'ait. "What did the Trith say to you?"

Jer'ait gave him a puzzled look. "No Trith came to me."

The Human's eyes narrowed. "Flea said they did."

"No," the Baga corrected, "I said they were sighted in the *area*. They were also killed. All three of them."

Everyone stared at the Baga. "Excuse me?" Joe finally said.

"Got it on security footage. They all died of accidents. Like one slipped on a soapy floor, fell down and cracked his huge ugly head open. Another one had a cooling unit fall on him from thirty stories up when a cable snapped above him. And the last one got run over by a haauk. And here's the weirder thing: Like half a tic after each accident, a couple Ooreiki walked up, grabbed them by their little feet, and carted them off. Nobody can figure out where the bodies went. Government doesn't have 'em. Overseers are stumped."

When Jer'ait found his breath again, he said, "So Forgotten is at war with the Trith." He groaned. "It makes sense."

"Why?"

"The Trith betrayed the Geuji, billions and billions of turns ago," Flea said.

Daviin and Joe glanced at Jer'ait, obviously waiting for him to confirm.

"One and a half million turns ago," Jer'ait amended. He tilted his head at the Baga. "No offense."

"None taken."

The other two waited for him to go on. Jer'ait took a deep breath, feeling their stares like coals. "It's true. When the Geuji tried to peacefully break away from Congress to form a government of their own, in a very *distant* part of the galaxy, the Trith told Congress where to find them. Congress surprised them. Surrounded them. There was never clear legal evidence to lock them away, but Aliphei and the Tribunal did it anyway, then threw away the key."

"No evidence?" Daviin demanded. The Jreet, of course, despised a dishonorable trial like nothing else.

"Technically, they were illegally detained," Jer'ait admitted. "The Geuji had never sworn oaths of loyalty to Congress—they were too smart for that—so they technically weren't committing treason by attempting to form their own government."

"Then they should be freed," Daviin grunted.

Jer'ait glanced up at Daviin. "Perhaps. But it will never happen."

Daviin bristled with indignance. "Why not?"

"Look at what he's *doing*, Daviin," the Baga said. "Jemria could crack up all of Congress without breaking a sweat."

"But he's not," Joe said. The Human was following the conversation with an alert gleam in his eye, and it was clear he wasn't liking what he was hearing. "He hasn't sicced those Dhasha on anyone, just left them there to die." He cocked his head. "And, from what I hear, most of them were rebel furgs anyway, even before this whole Neskfaat thing. You ask me, he just put them all in one place for PlanOps' convenience."

Which was true enough. And that bothered Jer'ait even more. He shook his head, trying to return to the facts. "Jemria's after something. Something we're not seeing. After the Geuji were first discovered on Neskfaat, they—" Jer'ait froze. *Neskfaat.* He swore suddenly, cursing his own blind stupidity. The other three watched with curiosity, waiting.

Jer'ait actually had to collect himself before he could continue. "Neskfaat," he said softly, "was the Geuji's planet of origin, one and a half million turns ago."

The Human paled. "You're kidding me. I thought it was a Huouyt planet."

It was the Baga who said, "I thought you guys knew that! You know those annoying little land-crawler pests that are everywhere? The ones we've gotta check we're not carrying in our gear before we get back on the ship? The vaghi? The Huouyt intentionally introduced them here. The continents used to be covered with Geuji, nothing but slime-mold as far as the eye could see. Then the Huouyt set the vaghi loose and the vaghi ate them all. Well, all but a couple. A Jahul gave his life to protect a few of them. Fought the vaghi off with stones. Saved the species, extracted them to ships. It's in the *history books*, guys, don't you *read*?"

"Oh burn me," Joe said. To Jer'ait, he said, "Is this Geuji sootwad doing a reenactment or something?"

"If it was a reenactment," Jer'ait said slowly, "I'm pretty sure our troops would have been eaten alive by vaghi, not ripped to shreds by Dhasha."

"But it's a message," Joe said.

"Clearly," Daviin growled. The Jreet looked upset, his big fists tensing at his sides. For all their arrogance and battle-hardened rages, Jreet had a soft spot for misfortune.

"So, what, this is a war against the Trith?" Joe asked, sounding incredulous. "I don't see it. Where are all the little gray corpses? Three dead hardly constitutes a war."

"Three dead is more than Congress ever managed in all of its existence," Jer'ait said. "Besides, how else do you explain Forgotten killing all the Trith except for the one who visited the one creature who'd never kill you?"

"Two," the Baga said proudly. "They met with me, too."

"And what did they say?" Daviin demanded.

"They said Joe would destroy the world," Flea said.

Jer'ait froze.

"What?"

"Flea," Jer'ait said. "You know a Trith cannot lie."

"Yeah. So?"

Jer'ait lifted his gaze to stare at the Human, awe and fear suddenly warring within him.

"Oh, get over it," Joe snapped at him. "They're fucking with me."

"But why you?" Daviin demanded. "Why would they only fuck with *you*, Joe?"

"Damned if I know," Joe growled, looking livid, now. To all appearances, their Prime wanted to put his fist through something's face, preferably something small and gray. "They did it on Kophat and they're doing it again. I don't know why." He sounded...pissed. Not at all reverential or humbled that the Trith had found him worthy of their words. Just…pissed.

And, in that moment, seeing his Prime's rage for what it was, the truth hit Jer'ait like a Congressional freighter. He felt his *breja* curl in a cold, clammy wave. In a soft breath of awe, he whispered, "He's a vortex."

27

HEADCOM WARS

"**B**y this point, Jer'ait will have told the others what he's learned."

"You allow Jer'ait to know about our plans?!" Rri'jan cried.

"No, fool. They won't be able to put that together. But they'll suspect I'm behind the Dhasha rebellion, as well as Aez's bombing."

"And this doesn't hinder your plans?"

"Absolutely not. They won't connect me with a future attack on Mekkval. It's beyond their capabilities."

"So this next tunnel crawl…if your two groups are still alive at the end of it, will it be time to send them against him?"

"No," Forgotten said. "The two that survive this crawl will need to go down one more time. We only need one team."

"Only two will survive?" Rri'jan asked, curious. "Out of eighty? What are you doing to them this time?"

"I'm not giving them a ride home."

• • •

As the shuttle entered Neskfaat's atmosphere, Joe wondered how many of the eighty remaining teams would die this time. Looking out the window at the corpses that matted the ground beneath them, he guessed a lot.

They give us one day, Joe thought, disgusted. *One ashing day. Didn't even bother to give Jer'ait a* kasja. Remembering the way the Huouyt Overseer had given Jer'ait a disgusted look when he found out Jer'ait had made the kill, he bristled. He was angry, but as of yet had said nothing to his friends. They were indignant Jer'ait had not received his fair reward, but Joe was pretty sure no one other than Jer'ait had put together what was really going on.

That afternoon, under the watchful eyes of Daviin and the Baga both, Jer'ait had administered a drug that had taken away Joe's shakes as if they never existed. For that alone, Jer'ait deserved a kasja.

They've not even bothering to hide it anymore, Joe thought, disgusted. *They don't expect us to live.* He glanced at his friends.

Instead of dicing, Flea and Daviin were sitting across from each other, scowling at each other as if somebody had been caught cheating, each intensely focused on his opponent. They'd been sitting that way for the last two hours, and the four hours before that, back in the barracks. Flea had flown backwards to get on the shuttle in order to continue staring the Jreet down.

"Guys," Joe warned.

"Shh!" Flea snapped. "Ka-par."

Joe narrowed his eyes. "You're burning me, right?"

"The Baga will bow to me," Daviin said, continuing to give Flea his full predatory attention. "Once and for all."

"He's just trying to get that last batch of credits back," Flea retorted, faceted eyes still locked on Daviin's face. "I won *big* last night, Joe. *Billions.*"

Joe groaned and glanced over at Galek, a little unnerved at the way Jer'ait's drugs seemed to have made him...more relaxed. Even when a gun had gone off in the staging area before getting on a shuttle, Joe hadn't even gotten a tingle of alarm. On one hand, it was good to be without fear. On the other hand, he hated feeling like his survival instincts were being blunted. *Which is more important?* Joe wondered. *Instincts or a lack of fear?* Remembering the way he'd almost gotten them all killed in that last damn crawl, he decided it was a lack of fear...

at least until he could find some way to permanently rewire that part of his brain.

Under his prolonged stare, Galek gave him a nervous grin and went back to the reader on his lap. The Ooreiki was the only other one on the ship who wore a biosuit besides Joe. Despite the Baga's attempts to get Galek to dice with him the night before, however, the Ooreiki had ignored him completely, and had been quietly studying the map of their landing zone for hours.

Across the shuttle, the Huouyt was naked, as was necessary for him to take a new pattern. The Grekkon had to keep the glands upon his bulbous rear free of obstruction, the Baga couldn't fly while wearing one, and Daviin didn't need one, and wouldn't wear it if he did.

"All right," Joe said. *"We make this fast. I want us down that tunnel within a tic, got me?"*

The armored doors of the shuttle hissed open and Joe tensed, expecting sniper fire. Nothing.

"Flea, get up on one of those trees. I want to know if anything moves. Jer'ait, you go check out our insertion point. Scarab, stay between me and Galek. We'll try to draw the fire away from you."

It took Joe a moment to realize that everyone but the Jreet and the Baga had gotten off the ship. Daviin and Flea, on the other hand, continued to scowl at each other across the shuttle bay, motionless.

"Would you burning get your asses out here?!" Joe snapped. "Ka-par later! We have Dhasha to kill."

"Sure," Flea said, still utterly still. "But the Jreet goes first."

"Not gonna happen, Baga," Daviin growled. "Your body is mine."

Joe marched back on the ship, grabbed Daviin by the ear-crest and Flea by the spitter, and ignored their startled grunts as he ripped them out of their staring-contest and shoved them out the shuttle door. "Later!" he snapped.

"Saved by the Prime," Flea jeered.

"You were about to crack like a piji shell," Daviin retorted. *"Next time we ka-par, we'll leave the meddling Human—"*

"Kill Dhasha!" Joe snapped. *"Or the next ka-par you have will be with your reaper. Ghosts!"*

"*That would be fun,*" Flea replied. "*I wonder if he'd be any good.*"

"*Probably,*" Daviin said, as he slithered out into the alien foliage. "*He doesn't have to eat.*"

"*So how would the rules for that work?*" Flea said. "*I mean, if you have to be my slave when I win here, what would happen if I beat* Death*? Think* Death *would be my slave after that?*"

"*Depends on the honor of Death,*" Daviin replied.

Joe narrowed his eyes and followed.

They took cover in a laser-shredded section of red alien under-growth while their scouts took their positions. As they waited, Joe could not help but notice the bodies.

They lay strewn across the landscape like they'd fallen from the sky. Bloated. Stinking. Weeks old. One of the first peacekeeping forces, before PlanOps realized Neskfaat was a full-scale rebellion. Several corpses—or what was left of corpses—were clinging to the branches of alien trees like gruesome holiday ornaments.

"*Stay focused,*" Joe told the Ooreiki, who was staring up at them with his sticky brown eyes wide. "*Jer'ait, how's it looking? Can we come out?*"

"*Entrance is open,*" the Huouyt responded after a moment. "*No guards.*"

"*Then we're in trouble,*" Joe said. "*Everyone haul ass. We're finding another entrance. Now!*"

Flea remained stationed in the tree until Jer'ait and Daviin rejoined them, slipping through the heavy foliage like wraiths. Daviin stayed with the group while Jer'ait rushed ahead to scout for enemies. In a few moments, Flea sped past overhead, assisting Jer'ait.

"*Nothing,*" Flea said.

"*This is really starting to creep me out,*" Joe said. He glanced at the sky. "*Flea, just how high can you go?*"

"*He leaves the treetops and he's a target for anything with a gun,*" Jer'ait said.

"*Yeah, but he won't be long. Flea, go see what you can find.*"

In reply, the Baga soared out of the foliage and into the sky. It was enviable, how fast he could leave them all in the dust.

"*Nothing, Joe,*" Flea said. "*No Takki, no Dhasha.*"

"*For how far?*"

"*Anywhere.*"

"*Why wouldn't they meet us on the surface?*" Joe asked.

"*Maybe they think it's safer to wait underground,*" Jer'ait replied.

Joe didn't like the sound of that. "*Okay, everyone get over here. Scarab, dig us a way in. Main den is a quarter length south-southwest of here.*"

"*I haven't had enough time to recover those kinds of secretions, Commander.*" Joe blinked. "*What?*"

"*I have ten, maybe twenty rods at my disposal. No more.*"

For a moment, Joe could only stare. "*Mothers' ghosts!*" he blurted, when he realized the Grekkon was serious. "*Why didn't you say something earlier?*"

"*I was given a mission.*"

"*You...*" Joe closed his eyes. "*All right. Dig us a fighting hole. Daviin, Flea, we're gonna need a little recon.*"

"*Where?*"

"*Go south. Find us a tunnel close to our original penetration point, but different.*"

"*And I?*" Jer'ait asked.

"*You stay here and help me guard our Ooreiki. We're gonna need him this run.*"

In front of him, Galek seemed to stiffen. "*You'll do fine,*" Joe told him privately. "*Just use those killer instincts of yours, kid.*"

"*So what do you wanna know?*" Flea asked after a moment. "*Tunnel looks deserted. Big, though.*"

"*Look around. We want a small one.*"

"*We have been,*" Flea said. "*They all start out small, but twenty rods down, they widen up. Haven't found a single slave tunnel yet.*"

Joe felt his heart begin to pound in his ears. "*Bones. Stay where you are. Jer'ait, go check them out.*"

Jer'ait nodded and went. "*It's as he says,*" he said after a few tics. "*They're decoys. Made to look like slave tunnels until about twenty rods down. Then they're big enough for three full-size Dhasha to maul us at once.*"

"*All right,*" Joe said. "*They want us to go down the tunnels. What do we do?*"

"*We stay on the surface?*" Flea offered.

"*Wrong. We go down the tunnels.*"

Daviin's mental voice was tentative. "*Forgive me, Joe, but I think it's a trap.*"

"*I know it is,*" Joe said. "*This is what happened to all those other groundteams that got slaughtered.*"

"*Jer'ait and I could try our luck down below,*" Daviin said. "*No need for the rest of you to come along.*"

"*Killing the Dhasha won't do us any good if you get lost down there doing it,*" Joe said, "*And they'll kill Jer'ait on sight. They're gonna tear up anything that comes down those tunnels.*"

"*All the more reason for us* not *to go down the tunnels, Commander,*" Scarab said.

"*So what would you rather do?*" Joe demanded. "*You want me to call up Headquarters and tell them we're declining the mission and oh, by the way, please come pick us up? They'll tell us to rot. We've got a better fighting chance in the tunnels. If they realize we're not coming in, they'll just come out and slaughter us. They'll—*" Joe hesitated.

"*Joe?*" Daviin demanded immediately.

"*I'm still here. I'm thinking maybe you guys are right. Maybe we should make them come get us.*"

● ● ●

This is insane, Jer'ait thought as he strode into the tunnels alone. He had shed his pattern and now he felt naked and vulnerable.

When the first Takki rose from the rubble two rods ahead, a plasma rifle aimed at his heart, Jer'ait stayed where he was. Slowly, he raised his tentacles. "I have a message from the Vahlin."

The Takki said nothing, but did not shoot, either.

Consulting his superiors, Jer'ait thought, relieved.

A Dhasha appeared within moments, strutting from the den with a retinue of slaves.

Don't look him in the eye, Jer'ait reminded himself. He stared at the ground.

The Dhasha came to a stop in front of him. He was big, but Jer'ait doubted he was the prince. He sniffed Jer'ait's body, then clacked its endless rows of triangular black teeth together. "The Vahlin told us we'd be fighting a Huouyt with an odd-colored eye today."

"And you are," Jer'ait said. "I took his pattern when I disabled his crew."

The Dhasha hesitated. "What?"

"I come from the den of a prince called Lavik. He was killed two days ago, by the same team that is assigned to your den today. I followed them here, took the Huouyt's pattern, and disabled three of the team. They're outside now, drugged."

He could feel the Dhasha's egg-shaped emerald eyes boring into him. "Drugged. Why didn't you kill them, if you are who you say you are?"

"I killed the Huouyt," Jer'ait said. "Couldn't let that one live. Two others, the Human and the Ooreiki, are unconscious."

"Check," the Dhasha said.

Six Takki scurried past and Jer'ait knew his life now hung in the balance.

They returned dragging Jer'ait's groundmates.

The Dhasha scanned the bodies in silence. "I see a Jikaln, a Human, and an Ooreiki. Where's the Huouyt?"

"He took the body of the Jikaln for scouting purposes, sir."

He could feel the Dhasha watching him. "Check."

A Takki immediately sliced open the Jikaln's body that Flea had found for them in the carnage, revealing a motionless red *zora* buried inside its chest, the only part that remained after it had taken Jikaln form.

"The other two are drugged, are they?" The Dhasha walked over and sank his talons into Galek's chest. The Ooreiki never flinched. He couldn't flinch. Jer'ait had seen to that.

"Huh," the Dhasha grunted, removing his talons. He watched the biosuit close around the wounds, then glanced at Jer'ait, clearly surprised. "I see the Huouyt was killed with plasma. I was under the impression your kind killed with poison."

"We do, sire. He was my first kill. Had to do it fast, from a distance, so the others wouldn't know."

"I see. So, if I were to scan you for incoming frequencies, what would I find?"

"Nothing, sire. The Huouyt do not get chips."

The Dhasha slammed him aside with the back of his paw, stunning him against the wall. "Check."

Several Takki swarmed him, pinning him in place. A Takki with a gash across one cheek, cutting his lip in half, came over and raised a specialized reader to his head. Jer'ait stiffened. If anyone so much as had a stray thought…

"Nothing, sire," the scarred Takki replied. "No incomings."

"I see three," the Dhasha said. "Where are the others?"

The Takki released him and backed away from him.

Jer'ait straightened. "The Baga flew off before I could hit him and the Jreet is somewhere down one of the eastern tunnels, seeking the prince. As soon as I showed myself, the Grekkon burrowed out of sight."

The Dhasha's gaze hardened. "Show my Takki where the Grekkon disappeared."

Though it was painful to leave his two groundmates unconscious at the Dhasha's feet, Jer'ait turned and hurried outside. He took them to a secluded area with a stream running nearby. "There," he said, pointing at the Grekkon's burrow.

"You first," the closest Takki growled. "You may have fooled the Master, but you haven't fooled us."

Jer'ait stiffened. Six pairs of cold blue eyes stared back at him.

"Oh, well," Jer'ait said. "I got what I came for." He reached out. Even as the startled Takki with the split lip glanced up, Jer'ait tore one of its arm-scales free. Then he dove into the steeply-sloping tunnel feet-first, at a slide.

"Stop him!"

The walls around him were unnaturally smooth stone, allowing Jer'ait to use his arms to push himself faster as he slid deeper into the Grekkon's trap. Behind him, he heard the six Takki enter the tunnel with him.

Jer'ait prepared himself, knowing the entire mission would hinge upon what happened next, knowing what would happen if he failed. Up ahead, he saw the hole the Grekkon had made for him.

"*Now!*" Jer'ait cried. He slammed his legs outward, slowing his descent, and swung out of the tunnel, into the smaller hole, pressing his body as far into the depression as he could, balling his tentacle around the scale. As the Takki slid to a halt and were trying to understand that, the Grekkon completed the circuit and backed into the tunnel behind them, cutting the six Takki from the surface. As they stared, Scarab backed into them. The Takki disappeared as easily as the rock had.

Jer'ait shuddered as the black void passed only ninths from where he pressed into his depression.

"*That's it,*" the Grekkon said. "*I'm out of secretions.*"

"*What about you, Daviin?*"

"*The Dhasha is dead, Joe and the Ooreiki are stashed and safe. They need the antidote.*"

"*Get out of the tunnel,*" Jer'ait said. He pushed his *zora* into the open and gave it the Takki scale. After his body had shifted, he tore off a scale from his front arm in approximately the same place he had taken one from the other Takki. He made a few localized shifts to give himself a few scars and a split lip, then went to Joe's bag in its crevice, found a patch, and placed it over the top of the Grekkon's lair.

"*Billions of Dhasha coming,*" Flea said. "*Trillions of Takki. Look pretty pissed.*"

Jer'ait ran to meet them.

"Slave!" the nearest Dhasha roared, upon seeing him. "Which way did he go?"

"The Grekkon killed them all," Jer'ait babbled. "The Huouyt was working with him. Took my scale and ran."

"Which *way?!*" the Dhasha snapped, batting him hard.

The Dhasha had used the back of his paw, but Jer'ait still felt like he'd been hit by a Congressional tank. He fell to his hands and knees on the ground. Gritting his Takki's sharp, predator teeth against the pain, he got back to his feet as quickly as he could. "This way," he whimpered, not having to fake it. He turned away and began hobbling through the forest. He'd taken no more than three steps when Flea, who had been watching from the branches dropped directly in front of the Dhasha. He spat in his face, then fled.

With a roar, the Dhasha gave chase.

Jer'ait followed for a while, then, when he'd drifted to the back of the group, fell out and circled back. Joe and the Ooreiki still needed an antidote.

• • •

They regrouped two days later. Flea had given them a merry chase, and while he'd done it, the rest of the group descended into the tunnels and killed the females while Daviin took out the prince.

Daviin was a bit surprised he was still alive—had just one of his groundmates failed to uphold their role, their entire plan would have disintegrated and everyone would have died. At that point, Daviin was even feeling generous toward the Huouyt, who was positioned on the bluff above them, his borrowed Jikaln body blending in with the rocks and scrub as he kept watch for the rest of them.

"*Everybody did well,*" the Human said as they waited for their pickup. They sat on an unoccupied hill, twenty marches from the dead prince and his lair. "*Hell. Everybody kicked ass. Flea, you should come up with plans more often.*"

"*I am a criminal mastermind,*" Flea said, his carapace puffing up until he was about the size of the Human's head.

Joe laughed. "*You are at that. You would've given my brother a run for his money.*"

"*I still can't believe we used you as bait,*" Daviin muttered. He was still upset about the fact. Every instinct as a Sentinel had cried out against it, but once the Baga had made his suggestion, the stubborn Human had refused to change his plans.

"I *still can't believe you guys didn't check for ruvmestin*," Flea said. "*That's four princes we've killed and nobody's bothered to check for ruvmestin. I told you guys to check for ruvmestin.*"

"*I'll share the earnings of my* kasja *with you, if that will ease the pain*," Daviin said. He grinned at Flea. "*After all, today the Baga won the day.*"

"*I'm still waiting to see the money from my own* kasja," Flea grumbled. "*It's almost like they don't wanna pay me.*"

No one answered him. The Human cleared his throat and checked the Ooreiki's activated beacon. Then he glanced at his watch. His brow furrowed.

"*How much longer?*" Flea asked.

"*They're ten tics late*," Jer'ait replied.

"*Must have a bunch of other pickups before ours*," Galek suggested.

Jer'ait snorted at the Ooreiki. "*They only sent eighty groundteams down here this time, instead of two and a half million. They are not strapped for pilots or ships.*"

They waited three more hours. Every twenty tics, Joe broadcasted his pickup request back to Congress.

"Burn this," Joe snapped after his twelfth request. He took off his helmet and pried open the inner console.

"What're you doing?" the Ooreiki whispered, watching him curiously.

"Something I learned on Eeloir," Joe said. As Daviin watched, he began using his dexterous Human fingers to manipulate the tiny parts. "Galek, give me your PPU."

Galek hesitated, his tentacle wrapping tightly around it. "What if I need it?"

Joe laughed. "Funny. Give it to me."

For a moment, it actually looked as if the Ooreiki would disobey. Then, reluctantly, Galek handed over his device. Joe immediately cracked it open and began removing several of the tiny parts inside. These he fastened into place in his helmet, holding them down with his fingers. Everyone was watching the Human curiously, now, even Scarab.

"Usually we've gotta use gum or something stupid like that, but since we've got our own little glue machine…Flea, would you mind helping me out? Just a dab."

Flea scuttled over to sit on Joe's leg and eyed the contraption. "You sure?" he asked, sounding worried.

"Yeah," Joe said.

Flea buzzed his wings, then delicately began fusing the pieces from Galek's PPU into Joe's helmet.

"There!" Joe said, putting the shield back in place. "Let those bastards try to ignore me now."

Everyone in the fighting hole gave him a nervous look. "Joe," Daviin began delicately, "It says in the manual not to fiddle with your helmet."

"That's just because they don't want you to do something like this." He grinned and slapped the last panel back in place.

Daviin winced. "It says if you fiddle with your helmet, you can cause serious mental disorders and death."

"Well, that, too." Joe grinned at them. "But I know what I'm doing."

Everyone held their breath as he lowered the helmet over his head.

Immediately, Joe stiffened and began to convulse like a dying thing.

"Get it off of him!" Daviin screeched, lunging forward in blind panic.

Joe opened his eyes and grinned up at him. "Gotcha."

Daviin glared, feeling like a fool. "So what did you just accomplish, Human?"

"Listen to this." Joe closed his eyes…and began singing a startlingly accurate rendition of a lewd Jahul drinking song.

He was on the eighth verse, "…*coupled in her mother's bed*…" when a very loud Ooreiki cut him off.

"*What the hell is the meaning of this, Jahul? Who are you? Why are you flooding our channels? We have more important things to do than listen to your songs.*"

The Human broke out into a huge grin. He dropped the Jahul accent. "*I know. Like coming to get us. This is Commander Zero. My groundteam is ready for pickup.*"

"*As are we,*" said another voice, also Human. "*Why the hell've you vaghi left us here? Are we the only ones left?*"

The Ooreiki on the other side sounded furious. "*You're not the only ones—there's six other groundteams waiting for pickup. We're constructing new orders for you. You'll be picked up after you've finished.*"

Joe's smile faded. "*What you mean, 'new orders?'*"

"*Your second assignment. Your Overseers will contact you as soon as—*"

"*Furgsoot!*" Daviin's ward snapped. "*We just took out a prince. That's four princes, you ghost-burning sooter. Come get us. We earned our keep. We've got leave coming.*"

"*You do,*" the Ooreiki said. "*After you complete another mission. Your Overseer will contact you shortly. Until then, if I hear another word from you, you'll face court-martial.*"

"*Put your money where your mouth is, you shit-eating Takki coward,*" Joe said. "*Come on down here and get me.*"

When the Ooreiki did not reply, Joe launched into a graphic rendition of just where he intended to shove the butt end of his rifle when they finally got off Neskfaat.

"*Give it up, Zero,*" a Human voice said tiredly. "*They're not coming.*"

"*I know,*" Daviin's ward said. "*But I've gotta entertain myself somehow, don't I?*"

"*Would you stop broadcasting!*" the Ooreiki snapped. "*Both of you!*"

"*Make us, sootwad.*"

Joe hesitated. "*Leila? That's you, isn't it?*"

The Human said nothing for a moment, then said, "*It's Rat...Who told you it was Leila?*"

"*I was pretty sure it was you.*"

The other Human snorted. "*Yeah, well. It wasn't. Only place that name still exists is in my file.*"

"Yeah," Joe said, glancing at the Baga. "Right above her blood sample."

Flea twittered, but Daviin didn't understand the reference.

"*So how many princes you killed?*" Joe asked lazily. "*We got four, you know.*"

"*We also got four,*" Rat replied. "*Benva and Kai'lin are two-for-two.*"

Benva! The worthless Welu heir! Daviin felt the beginnings of a battle cry forming in his throat and he tightened his fingers into fists as he forced it down. "Perhaps we can team up," he said, as casually as he could. "Kill Dhasha together." Jer'ait snapped his head around to give him a flat stare.

"*Let me guess. Jreet and Huouyt?*"

"*Yeah. Say, that Voran was on your team, wasn't he?*"

"Sure is," Joe said, still pinning Daviin with that even look. "*Don't you dare give us your coordinates.*"

"*You're both gonna be thrown in the brig as soon as you set foot on Jeelsiht!*"

"*Same to you, Zero. Let's hope they send different pickups.*"

"*You hear that, fellahs? Different shuttles. Make 'em upholstered.*"

"It doesn't matter," Daviin said, disdain dripping from his voice. "I wouldn't fight the Welu. He's a cripple."

"No he's not. Jer'ait just told you that to shut you up," Joe said. He winked at Daviin's startled look and went back to his conversation with the other Human. "*Our Huouyt took out two princes, our Baga got one, and our Jreet just took out this last one.*"

"*Your Baga got one?*"

"*Yeah. Plugged his nose right up. Can't breathe out their mouths, so he suffocated. Flea kicked ass.*"

Flea puffed up like a bloated melaa under the praise.

"*Zero...*" the Human sounded perplexed. "*You don't by any chance have an Ooreiki and a Grekkon on your team, do you?*"

"*You two are giving out sensitive information over all channels. Shut your burning mouths!*"

"Can it," Joe said. "*They already know everything about us before we even get off the shuttle, so a little chit-chat can't hurt. And yes. An Ooreiki and a Grekkon.*"

"*Is the Ooreiki...special?*"

Joe grinned widely and glanced at Galek. "*Sure is.*"

"*Holy crap, Zero. Phoenix gave us the same team.*"

"*And it looks like she's gonna win that Corps Directorship she's always wanted, don't it? Your guys all still kickin'?*"

"*Grekkon ran a little dry, but the last two days gave him a bit of a recharge.*"

"*You two are blatantly disregarding a direct ord—*"

"So," Joe said, "*When we get off this rock, how 'bout some sex?*"

"*Sounds like the best idea I've heard all rotation, Commander. Your place or mine?*"

"*Yours,*" Joe said. "*Mine might bring back unpleasant memories.*"

"*Bad lay or she dump you?*"

"*Well, a little of both, actually. There was blood.*"

"*That's some of the best.*"

Joe laughed. "*Usually, I'd agree with you.*"

"*Fine. You two don't give an ash what we do to you? That's understandable. But I swear to you the next one of you who opens his mouth gets his headcom fried.*"

Joe sighed and lifted the helmet from his head. "Well, it was fun while it lasted." He lifted the screen from the inside of his helmet once more and began cutting away the pieces he had installed with Flea's help. When he put it back on his head, he said, "*You hear me?*"

"*Yes, sir,*" Galek said. He was staring down at the butchered pieces of his PPU. "*What about this, sir?*"

Joe glanced at it and laughed. "What do you need a PPU for, Galek? You got tunnel instinct. It's a hundred times better."

"I suppose," Galek said reluctantly. "But…was it really worth it?"

"Sure it was!" Joe cried, slapping the Ooreiki on the back cheerfully. "Now we know they're gonna leave us here 'til we die."

"He's taking you seriously," Jer'ait said dryly.

"I am serious."

"*Commander Zero, this is Phoenix.*"

Joe's entire body stiffened and he looked as if he wanted to rip the headcom off of his skull. Instead, he said, "*So you finally got what you wanted, huh Mag?*"

"*Commander Zero, you are to proceed on foot to the entrance with surface coordinates of—*"

"*No offense, but burn you, Mag. We'll stay here 'til we get our pickup.*"

"*Look,*" Phoenix said, "*We just intercepted a message from the Dhasha Vahlin to his lieutenants. We have locations on all of them and we can't take the chance they'll realize they've been compromised and move.*"

"Let me guess," Jer'ait muttered, padding up beside them. His Jikaln body blended with the foliage, and his toothy muzzle was opened to expose a row of glistening white fangs. Even to Daviin's ears, he was quiet. "There's eight Lieutenants."

The Human glanced at the Huouyt. "*How many lieutenants?*" he asked.

"*I can't give up that kind of information.*"

"*You will,*" Joe said, "*Or you can bet your petite white ass we aren't moving from this fighting hole.*"

There was a long silence before Phoenix said, "*Eight.*"

The ridges over Joe's eyes drew together. "*Eight. One for each surviving team.*"

"*Fortunate, isn't it?*" Phoenix said.

"*Just dandy. Give me a tic. Gotta take a dump.*"

Out loud, he said, "Is everyone back at Headquarters a ghost-burning jenfurgling? Or is that just me?"

"No," Flea said, "I think you're right. I was rooting through their files and got a look at some of their I.Q.s and it's pretty sad."

"Okay," Joe said, "What's this mean? He's slowly killing us all off… why? He sure as hell could've killed us all just like he killed those three Trith, if he'd wanted to."

"Who are you talking about?" Galek said, giving them a suspicious look.

"Fill you in later," Joe said. "Jer'ait, what you thinking?"

"I'm thinking maybe Jemria doesn't want us alive, after all."

"Of course he doesn't want us alive," Daviin said, gesturing at the stinking fields of corpses that surrounded them. "He wants to see how we die."

"But what the hell difference could that make to him?" Joe demanded.

"In ancient wars, Morinth would send all its prisoners of war to Va'ga," Jer'ait said. "They used to experiment on their enemies, see how much they could take before they died."

"Don't be disgusting," Daviin snapped, repulsed by the very idea.

"Would a Geuji really need to experiment on us?" Joe asked.

Galek's meaty face scrunched in an Ooreiki frown. "What is this about a Geuji?"

"Later," the Human assured the youngster. To Jer'ait, he said, "I've just heard the legends, but couldn't he figure it all out for himself, what makes us tick?"

"Yes," Jer'ait said reluctantly, "But, like you, I find it highly…odd… that the first message intercepted from the Vahlin during the entire war lists eight lieutenants, one for each groundteam that survived."

"So maybe it's the Vahlin laying a trap for us," Joe said. "Maybe there really is a Vahlin."

"Who said there wasn't a Vahlin?" Galek asked, his big, sticky brown eyes confused. And wary. He looked like a Jreet warrior who had just found himself in an elevator filled with Ayhi.

"Commander Zero, it would be best if you didn't play games with me."

"But the Geuji has to be involved," Flea said. "Who else killed those three Trith? You, Joe?"

Joe snorted. "I wish."

"Who killed three Trith?" Galek demanded, looking even more nervous, now.

Daviin waved off the boy's question. To the others, he said, "Look, there's no question the Geuji is involved." Daviin glanced at each of his companions individually. "We all agree on that, correct?"

"Yes," Flea said.

Jer'ait nodded.

"Yeah," Joe said.

The Ooreiki watched them as if they'd all suddenly lost their minds.

"Then we also agree he isn't on our side," Daviin said.

"How do you figure?" Joe asked.

"Who else would be predicting where we're going to land every time?" Daviin demanded. "The Trith?"

"Maybe," Joe said. "Hell, maybe Jer'ait's right and this is a battle between a Geuji and the Trith. Maybe we're just pawns."

"We are just pawns," the Huouyt said.

Joe gave Jer'ait an irritated glance. "Yeah. Okay. So what if the Trith are helping the Dhasha and the Geuji is helping us?"

"Then we'd be doing a lot better than we are," Jer'ait said. "The Geuji's a vortex. Anything he does muddies the Trith's vision. He starts telling us where to go and what to do and the Trith wouldn't be able to pre—" The Huouyt stiffened. "It *is* the Geuji helping the Dhasha. The Trith wouldn't be able to foresee us coming. Jemria is a vortex. And he's been using us, playing us like pawns. The Trith are trying to *stop* him, because everything relating to Neskfaat is going to be unreadable for them. Which means that *we* are going to be unreadable to them."

"Commander Zero, if you want a pickup at all, you're going to stop screwing around.

"No need to jump up and down, Mag. You'll lose those pretty contacts of yours."

"Joe…"

"Please. Call me Zero. Joe's reserved for friends and decent Human beings." He met his groundteam's eyes. *"Make that decent beings."*

"I'm sending the coordinates to your PPU. We want you to the den and into the tunnels within the next day and a half."

Phoenix ended the conversation.

Joe took out his PPU and glanced at it. Then he sighed and put it away.

"Time to go, Commander?" Galek asked.

"No. It's a day's hike, at least. We'll camp here a few nights, then head out."

Galek blinked. "But she said the next day and a half."

Joe turned on the Ooreiki sharply. "Do I look like I give a rat's ass what that de-scaled Takki turd wants?"

"No sir," Galek said meekly.

"All right," Joe said, turning back to the rest of them. "So it's the Geuji. He's patching us up, keeping the Trith off my back *and* sending us into the tunnels to die. Does that make sense to anyone?"

When no one answered, Joe said, "All right, let's look at it from another angle. What could the Geuji get out of this? There's gotta be something or he wouldn't be doing it."

"Maybe he wants to see a bunch of princes die," Flea suggested. "They get on people's nerves."

"That's hardly the reason to start a war," Jer'ait said.

"What if he wants us to blow up Neskfaat?" Joe asked.

"Then he would've let us do it in the first week of the war, when the Space Corps first petitioned for it," the Huouyt said.

Daviin frowned, the tinglings of a memory tickling the back of his mind. "How many groundteams started this fight, Joe?"

"A little over two and a half million."

"And we're down to eight?"

"That's right."

Understanding hit Daviin in a sickening wave. "I know what this is."

"What?"

"We do it on Vora, with our young."

Joe snorted. "You give them rifles, pat them on the butt, and send them after Dhasha?"

"We kill them off," Daviin said. "Only the strongest survives. They fight to determine which gets to live. Only one from every hatch." Daviin tensed. "Joe, I think this Geuji means to whittle us down to one."

28

THE LIEUTENANT

"*So?*" Joe asked, peering through his scope. "*How's it look?*"

"*Empty, Commander.*"

"*I'm looking at a field of corpses, Flea. I doubt it's empty.*"

"*Yeah, but it's been four days. Maybe Phoenix was right. Maybe he moved on.*"

"*Nope,*" Joe said, unscrewing the scope from his rifle and returning it to his pack. "*There's a Dhasha in there.*"

"*Why do you say that?*" Daviin asked.

"*Because that vaghi of a Geuji wants us to fight one, that's why.*"

"*Simple, yet effective logic,*" Jer'ait said. "*How do we test it?*"

"*By going in there and getting him.*" Joe pulled out a viewfinder and enhanced the nighttime image in front of him even more than his nightvision-altered eyes allowed. He scanned the fields of dead around them, seeking movement. After a moment, he frowned. "*Anyone notice anything strange about those corpses?*"

It took Jer'ait only a moment. "*There's no plasma wounds.*"

"*Right,*" Joe said. "*Every damn one of them's been ripped apart by a Dhasha. The same Dhasha.*"

"*How ya figure?*" Flea asked.

"*In the ones that aren't torn completely apart, there's a certain distance between claw marks,*" Jer'ait said. "*It's always the same, and they're very big claws.*"

"*So this lieutenant is a paranoid S.O.B.,*" Joe said. "*Kills them all himself. No Takki. Jer'ait, you're gonna be pretty useless to us this time, unless you think you can outrun a Dhasha.*"

"*I have a few patterns that might, but I'd rather not take the chance.*"

"*No kidding.*"

"*Okay, Flea, take it inside a few rods. The Dhasha sees you, you get out of there, bring him back up for Daviin, if you can get him to follow you.*"

Flea responded a few tics later, "*Man, what's that smell? It's making my carapace itch.*"

"*Describe it,*" Daviin said.

"*Dead meat. Rot.*"

"*Perhaps you didn't see the piles of corpses nearly plugging the tunnel entrance,*" the Huouyt said.

"*No,*" Flea said. "*This is different.*"

"*So they're not dead and rotting?*"

"*Quiet,*" Joe said. "*Flea, have you ever smelled cheese?*"

"*What?*"

"*Listen,*" Joe said. "*Flea, be very careful. What you're smelling is probably the Dhasha. When they don't have Takki, they start to stink, and stink bad.*"

"*And you know this because...*"

"*Let's just say I've had intimate experience with it,*" Joe snapped. "*Keep your eyes open. He's in there somewhere.*"

"*Well,*" Flea said eventually, "*Looks like you were right, Joe. He's down here maybe a hundred-twenty rods. Sitting in his own shit.*"

"*He's sick?*" Daviin asked.

"*No,*" Flea said. "*He's staring at the entrance. Not moving at all.*"

The tiny hairs on Joe's neck stood up. "*Flea, how close are you to him?*"

"*Two and a half rods.*"

"*Get out of there. Now.*"

But he was too late. Flea sent them a startled broadcast of confusion, then the line went dead.

"*Flea!*" Joe snapped.

Nothing.

"*He's waiting for us,*" Joe growled. "*He's been waiting for us all this time. Goddamn it!*"

"*I got the bastard,*" Flea muttered. "*Right in the face. Wouldn't stay stuck to the floor, though.*"

"*Tell me what happened. The prince is dead?*"

Flea gave a mental twitter. "*Crack no, he's not dead. I'm lucky to be alive, Joe. Bit off his own toe to get unstuck from the floor. He's crazy. And huge.*"

"*Where you now?*"

"*Doin' a million lengths a tic through the tunnels. The booming counter's right on my back.*"

"*Daviin, you hear that?*"

"*I'm waiting for him.*"

Joe trained his viewfinder on the tunnel entrance. After a few moments, he saw a tiny black shape burst out of the tunnel and gain altitude as if it had been shot from a cannon. He waited, tense.

To Joe's frustration, nothing followed the Baga. "*What's going on?*" Joe demanded.

"*He won't follow me out,*" Flea said. "*He's standing inside, watching me. Guys, he's huge.*"

"*Daviin, can you take him?*"

"*Not without pinging, Joe. I don't know where he is.*"

"*He's right there!*" Flea cried. "*Right there!*"

"*Screaming doesn't help me, furg,*" Daviin snapped. "*I'm blind when I raise my energy level.*"

"*He's backing up,*" Flea screamed. "*Daviin, get him!*"

"*I can't hear him!*"

"*I thought you guys had good hearing!*"

"*We do,*" Daviin snapped. "*But as soon as I ping, I give away my location.*"

"*Look at how carefully he's walking,*" Jer'ait said. "*Joe, he's trying not to make noise for Daviin to pinpoint.*" Then, after a moment, "*And Joe...*" The Huouyt actually sounded nervous. "*This one's big.*"

"*Like maybe Daviin can't take him, big?*" Joe demanded.

"*Shriveled balls of Takki, I can take any Dhasha,*" Daviin snapped, at the same time Jer'ait told him privately, "*Commander, I think we might need a new plan.*"

Joe considered that. "*Jer'ait, time to show yourself. We'll give the Jreet a chance to excel. Be ready to run if Daviin can't hold him.*"

Near the entrance, the Huouyt stepped from the brush in the form of a thin, four-legged creature that looked built for speed.

Through his viewfinder, Joe watched the entry. Nothing. He scanned the terrain around them for movement once more before returning his attention to the tunnel entrance. "*Ghosts, guys, what's happening?*"

"*He's sitting down,*" Flea said, sounding baffled. "*He's just sitting there watching Jer'ait like a furg.*"

"*He knows Daviin's waiting for him,*" Jer'ait replied. He was still standing in the open, facing something inside the tunnel.

"*Bones,*" Joe said. "*Jer'ait, stay there and watch the prince. Daviin, don't move.*"

"*I didn't plan on it,*" Daviin said. "*I may be brave, but I'm not stupid.*"

"*Time for plan B,*" Joe said. "*Grekkon, dig us a hole into that den. Flea, come here. Circle around low so he can't see where you go.*"

"*Wait,*" Daviin said, sounding worried. "*Joe, what are you doing?*"

"*The four of us are going to kill the prince while you and Jer'ait keep him distracted.*"

"*How?*" Daviin demanded. "*Joe, your two best assets are out here in plain sight.*"

"*I know,*" Joe said. "*And I've got the feeling that smart bastard down in that tunnel knows it, too. He's not gonna move until he hears you, Daviin, so just shut up, breathe real quiet, and keep your head low.*"

Flea met up with them in a buzz of wings. "*That Dhasha's creepy. I was staring him right in the eyes and he never moved.*"

"*Get down the tunnel,*" Joe said. "*We'll find a way to deal with him inside.*"

• • •

Daviin had to fight the impulse to squirm. His body had been tightly coiled for an attack, and now his muscles ached where they ground against his bones. It had been almost ninety tics since Joe and the others had punctured the den from the other side. He was beginning to ease the pressure, bit by bit, when the Dhasha spoke.

"I know you're out there, Jreet," the Dhasha said. "I know you can hear me."

Daviin froze, afraid to breathe.

"I didn't think your kind cowered in the brush like worms. I thought you prided yourselves on killing Dhasha."

Daviin did not respond, but he felt his muscles tightening despite his best efforts to control them.

"But here we are," the Dhasha continued. "Me waiting. You hiding. You must be from Vora. A Welu would have the tek to attack me."

"*Don't let him provoke you,*" Jer'ait said privately.

Daviin fought down the urge to tell the Huouyt to dance on his tek.

"It's unfortunate, that it's come to this. I'd always thought the Jreet prouder than that. That Welu I killed was."

"*He knows you've got a short temper,*" Jer'ait said, "*And he knows you're Voran. Just ignore him while Joe sets up a distraction.*"

"*Stop coddling me,*" Daviin growled. "*I know what he's doing. Go help Joe.*"

"*I'm staying,*" the Huouyt said. "*If you two get into a brawl, I'm going to be here to help you out.*"

"*Screw you, Huouyt. I don't need your help.*"

"*Jreet,*" Jer'ait said, "*You're not seeing what I'm seeing.*"

· · ·

"*So what the hell is it?*" Joe stood at the edge of an enormous pit, looking down into a blackness that could have been an entry into Hades. Water fell from high above, cascading through the air and disappearing into the black without a sound.

Galek peered over the edge, but he looked perplexed.

"*Come on,*" Joe said. "*Galek, you've been sulking ever since I cannibalized your PPU.*"

"*What's wrong?*" Jer'ait asked.

"*Nothing. Galek, what am I looking at?*"

"*I think it's a sinkhole, sir.*"

"*You think? Well, how deep is it? Where's that water going?*"

"*I don't know, sir.*"

Flea sighed and jumped from Joe's shoulder, launching himself over the edge. A few moments later, "*There's a ledge at the bottom around a big pool of water. Big Dhasha tunnels radiating outward. I think it's the watering hole. You guys would probably be okay if you jumped off the edge, as long as you aimed for the middle.*"

"*I can't swim,*" Galek said. "*My kind are too dense.*"

"*We'll take the stairs,*" Joe said, nodding at the Grekkon. Scarab backed down, giving them a sloping path toward the bottom.

At the bottom, Joe glanced up at the enormous black chamber that seemed to go on forever. Out of the blackness, water dripped past his face, spattering into a huge, luminescent pool of water near his feet.

Surrounding the underground lake, dug into the rippling stone edges of the sinkhole, were nine different main shafts. Once again, there were no slave tunnels.

As soon as they left the Grekkon's tunnel, they'd have no cover. If the Dhasha caught them, they'd be ripped apart.

"*Flea, go see if you can figure out where we are.*"

Flea crawled out of the Grekkon's tunnel, scaled the sinkhole wall, and then slipped into the nearest main shaft and began proceeding along the ceiling.

Joe and Galek waited in the back of the Grekkon's tunnel, squatting below the twin spearlike arms that protruded from the front of Scarab's body.

"*Yep,*" the Baga said, finally. "*I found the prince. He's right where we left him.*"

"Okay," Joe said, "Stay on the prince. Galek and I are gonna figure out a way to kill him."

• • •

"Ready, Flea?

Flea held absolutely still in the shadows behind the Dhasha, his eyes fixed firmly on the prince's tank-sized butt.

"Damn right I'm ready."

"Galek, are you ready for this?"

"The charge is in place, sir."

Over the common channel, Phoenix's voice once more demanded, "Commander Zero, why is your team stalling? We know you're alive. Go in there and kill the lieutenant."

The Human responded with, "Don't worry, Mag. We'll do everything in our power to see you get that Corps Directorship." Then he terminated surface contact.

"That Takki brooder would make a nice Dhasha casserole," Flea muttered.

"She can still hear you," Jer'ait said.

"Somebody needed to tell her eventually. It's cruel to let her think anybody gives a soot what she says."

"All right. Everyone take your positions. Flea, go."

Flea began spitting. He landed three good hits around the back claws, but not enough to make the prince stick. Then he dropped from the ceiling and buzzed back toward Joe.

Behind him, he heard a crash, then a roar and the clatter of rocks. Flea chanced a glance behind him and wished he hadn't.

The Dhasha was closer this time, and his empty green eyes gleamed murder. Chunks of rock clung to the scales around the Dhasha's back feet. The Dhasha was catching up.

"Joe, I hope you're ready. He's right on my ass."

"Just bring him on."

Flea did. He shot through the sinkhole, getting water on his cara-pace as he flew through the trickle and on to the tunnel on the other side. The Dhasha skirted the pool, but lost little time regaining his speed and catching back up.

When Flea saw Joe standing alone in the hall up ahead, a plasma rifle trained on the Dhasha, Flea almost fell out of the air in shock. In a panic, he screamed, "*Joe, get out of the way! Run! He's coming!*"

Seeing the massive Dhasha on his heels, the Human's face slacked with surprise and he turned and ran.

"*What's going on?*" Daviin demanded.

Flea caught up with the Human in moments. Instead of passing him, he slowed. "*Joe, you keep running. I'll spit on him a little bit, try to slow him down. I—*" Flea's words died in his throat when the Human started laughing and came to a stop. Flabbergasted, Flea turned. They were alone in the tunnel. He stared, confused.

"*He ran away?*" Flea asked, trying to figure out where the massive Dhasha had gone.

The Human was still laughing. He walked forward three rods, to where he had been standing when Flea appeared in the tunnel. He bent, then stuck his hand through the floor, followed by his head.

Not *onto* it, but *through* it.

While Flea was trying to comprehend that, a massive, angry roar shook the tunnels. It sounded close.

"*Joe, I think—*"

"*It worked!*" Joe shouted, straightening. "*The sonofabitch isn't getting out of there. Set it off, Galek!*"

Joe deactivated the little device inside and the hologram fell away, leaving a huge pit marring the center of the tunnel. When Flea hesi-tantly flew overhead, he saw the Dhasha prince in the bottom, ripping at the rock walls and floor, screaming in fury.

"Scarab dug this?"

"Yeah," Joe said, watching the Dhasha struggle, "But he'll just claw his way out if we don't hurry up." With his headcom, he said, "*What's taking so long, Galek?!*"

"*Sorry, sir.*" They heard a tiny popping sound, then a roar of bubbles in the underground lake beyond their tunnel.

"*Did it work?*"

"*Can't tell yet...*" Galek said. "*Yeah. The water-level's going down.*"

From the pit below, the sounds of splashes echoed up to them and the Dhasha roared again.

"Time to get the hell out of here," Joe told them. "Flea, you alright?"

"Fine. Won't he swim out?"

"Too dense," Joe said. "He'll suffocate."

"I could stick him," Flea suggested.

"No," Joe said. "Let him die."

Joe was answering the other grounders' questions on the status of the prince, when a voice called to them from above the sloshing water below. "Joe?"

The Human froze. Slowly, he peered down into the pit.

"How'd he know your name?" Flea demanded.

Joe looked like he'd been kicked in the stomach. "Oh Mothers."

"Joe?" Flea eyed the Dhasha, then returned his gaze to the Human. "You know him?"

"Mothers' ghosts," Joe said, turning away from the pit. "It's Bagkhal."

"Who?" Flea glanced down at the Dhasha, who was watching them with eerie calm. "You know him?"

The Human ignored him. He stared down at the Dhasha, looking stricken.

It was the Dhasha who spoke first. "He said they'd send you to kill me."

Joe was shaking. "What?"

"Don't fret about freeing me, Human. If I somehow find a way out of here before I drown, I'll kill you all. My loyalties are elsewhere, now."

"To the Vahlin," Joe said. "Why?"

When the Dhasha did not respond, Joe added softly, "Why? You said we needed Congress. You were *loyal.*"

"My experiences led me to believe that Congress was the only force that could keep my kind from reverting to barbarism. I was wrong."

"He led you to a war you can't win," Joe said.

The Dhasha's egg-shaped eyes glittered with gemlike amusement. "This war will still be raging nine hundred turns from now. Even if Neskfaat is lost, the Vahlin will live on. His power will only grow."

Flea stared down at the Dhasha, confused. "You know who the Vahlin really is."

"Of course," Bagkhal said. "Did you really think I'd bow my head to another Dhasha?"

Joe looked stunned. "If you knew it was the Geuji, why serve him? What's his purpose here?"

"I serve him because he has a plan that would truly bring peace. Once and for all. True peace." Water was sloshing at the Dhasha's knees, drawing dangerously close to his chin.

Joe glanced at Flea, then back at their captive. He looked pale, ill. "I can't let you out, Bagkhal."

"I know. Jemria told me I would die today. Though I tried to fight it, I never once thought he was wrong."

Flea watched his Prime narrow his eyes. "And I'm supposed to let you die."

Flea made a startled wing-flutter. "Of *course* you're supposed to let him die."

"That's for...you...to decide," the Dhasha coughed.

"For what purpose?" Joe demanded. "Is this a trap?"

Bagkhal snorted through the water quickly filling his mouth. "A trap? No. It's a test." He began to choke and struggle as water began to press against his nostrils. He lunged awkwardly onto his back feet, his stubby hind legs giving him another rod of breathing room.

Flea glanced over and saw the Human's muscles straining. *He's gonna let him out.* He'd never seen his Prime get so obviously upset before. Almost like this Dhasha was a...friend. Nervously, Flea waited for the order for Scarab to drain the water so the Dhasha could breathe. Instead, the Human said, "A test for what?"

Bagkhal didn't answer. His claws had sunk into the stone like it were clay and his front paws lost purchase, his body sliding back downward before he could struggle to lift his huge head above the surface again.

"A test for what?!" Joe shouted.

"Jreet hells, boy," Bagkhal gurgled, thrashing his head to stay above water. "Isn't it...obvious?"

"Goddamn it, enlighten me, Bagkhal!" His Prime had something wrong with his eyes—they were leaking fluid down his shirt. "What the hell were you thinking, you damned furg?"

"It's a test for *you*." Bagkhal continued choking.

There was a long, miserable silence as the Dhasha struggled to breathe in the pit beneath them. "I'll kill the ashsoul," the Human whispered. "I swear it."

"Forget that nonsense," the Dhasha snorted, clawing its way back up the wall again. "I have...heirs. Hundreds...of them. Good boys, all of them. Jemria will take care of them."

"What the hell is wrong with you, Bagkhal?!" Joe screamed, hurling his PPU across the tunnel. "He doesn't care about you. He sent you here to *die*! *All* of you! Goddamn it!"

The Dhasha prince made what sounded like a sad chuckle.

Flea watched his Prime steel himself. Over the com, he said, "*Galek...*" He hesitated, his small brown eyes catching on Flea. Flea froze, knowing his Prime was about to do something incredibly stupid. He nervously crawled up the wall, away from the Dhasha. But Joe said, "*Kid, your job is done. Get back here.*"

To the Dhasha, Joe swiped his arm across his face and whispered, "What the hell were you thinking?"

"God hates a coward, Joe."

Joe flinched as if the Dhasha had hit him. "You dumb furg," he whispered.

The Dhasha prince could not respond. He couldn't get his head high enough above the churning water to breathe.

Flea and Joe watched Bagkhal struggle for air, still as statues on the rim of the pit. The Dhasha's every breath ended with him spraying water and gasping. His body was too dense to swim. In moments, it was over.

"Well," Flea said, staring down at the Dhasha prince, "That was the easiest one yet."

Joe cast him a dark look and said nothing. He slammed his rifle over his shoulder and again swiped his arm across his eyes, then stalked around the pit without even glancing down. *"The prince is dead,"* he sent to headquarters. *"Send us a pickup."* Flea followed at a wary distance, stopping to pick up his Prime's PPU, which Joe had simply left where it had fallen.

Jer'ait and Daviin were coming down the tunnel at a run, and hesitated upon seeing their Prime. Joe just brushed by them, headed for the surface.

"What happened?!" Daviin roared at Joe, twisting back on himself to follow the Human. When Joe didn't respond, he frowned down at Flea. "What happened?"

Flea dropped their Prime's PPU into Jer'ait's hand. "I don't know," he said, still confused. "It's like Joe knew him."

Daviin flinched. "The Dhasha?"

At the same time, Jer'ait froze. "Merciful dead. He just killed Bagkhal?"

"Yeah, that's the name he used," Flea said. "Bagkhal."

"Mekkval's brother?" Daviin demanded. Daviin and Jer'ait glanced at each other. In the silence that followed, Joe said, *"Mag, you're gonna send us a pickup, or you're next. I don't care how many Dhasha I've gotta kill. I'll find you."*

"Thirty-two hours," Phoenix said. *"Miss the drop and we won't be back for you."*

Up ahead, Flea watched his Prime stiffen. *"I don't like the way you said that, Mag. It's almost like you've got more important things to do than pick up a groundteam that's gonna get you that Corps Directorship."*

"Oh, you're too late for that," Phoenix said, *"Rat already killed the Vahlin. That's why shuttles are scarce. They're on the other side of the planet, digging him out."*

29

MISSION OVER

Joe tossed another stone across the clearing, furious they'd abandoned his team in enemy territory to wait while they dug out an
oversized Dhasha. He checked his watch again.

Two hours to go. He dropped his wrist and hurled another stone,
imagining it was the Geuji's face. He'd kill him. He'd *murder* the Takki
scum. Bagkhal was...

...good.

The only *good* Dhasha Joe had ever met. And he'd killed him. For
that, the Geuji was going to die. Joe hurled another stone so hard it
exploded a small alien tree-trunk.

"You really should stop doing that," Daviin said from thin air beside
him. "A Dhasha might hear it."

"Let 'im," Joe muttered. "You can bet they plucked Rat and her
crew off the surface the moment the Vahlin was dead. They're probably being paraded around Dayut right now like heroes."

Daviin cocked his big head and considered that. "You really think
they killed the Vahlin?"

"No," Joe said. "But Headquarters thinks they have, so they're
gonna get every gift in the book." He threw a stone hard enough
to disintegrate another alien trunk. Joe looked down at his biosuit

appreciatively. Its ebony surface was covered with slightly acidic water droplets, leaving him completely comfortable despite the whipping wind and the rainy, wretched weather. Then he thought of the water droplets sliding like oil off Bagkhal's scales and his mood soured again.

"Daviin!" Galek called from across the foggy clearing. "We found a dead Dhasha! Come help me move this body before Jer'ait sees us! Flea wants to get at the claws!"

Daviin snorted. "Let him get his own claws! And stop shouting!"

"Go help him," Joe said tiredly. "We've cheated him out of enough trophies, and I doubt he's ever gonna see the money from that *kasja*, now that they've got what they wanted. This might be his last chance."

Daviin sighed and slid his huge bulk out of the fighting pit. He paused at the edge and looked back at him. For a long moment, he said nothing. He knew how much Bagkhal had meant to Joe. Joe had told him so many war stories in the hundreds of hours since the Jreet Sentineled him that, at times, Joe had found himself wondering if that's all the Jreet thought he talked about.

And now he was dead. Because Joe killed him.

"I wish I knew what the Geuji wanted from all this," Daviin offered.

Joe's hand fisted on the stone. "I intend to find out."

$$\bullet \ \bullet \ \bullet$$

Daviin crossed the clearing and hesitated. "Galek?"

"Over here!" Flea called. "Ten rods in."

Daviin peered into the dense alien brush. "Joe wants us to stay in sight."

"You big Takki," Flea laughed. "He'll still be able to hear you if you scream."

Daviin narrowed his eyes and peered over his shoulder at Joe. Their Prime was still sulking, tossing stones across the clearing. He wasn't even watching Daviin.

"This better not be a game," Daviin growled, pushing his way through the brush.

He was about to turn back, uncomfortable at being out of sight of his ward, when he saw a body crumpled near a stream. There was no Dhasha in sight.

"I knew it," Daviin snapped. "*Baga, if this is your idea of a joke, you're a furg.*"

Daviin only had a moment to register Flea's irritated, "*What's a joke?*" before he noticed the tentacle pushing under his scales. He opened his mind to warn Joe, but the warning never came.

• • •

Joe waited for Daviin's response, and when it did not come, he went back to lobbing rocks. *Guess they worked it out*, he thought. Then he winced, imagining Daviin confronting the Baga, especially now that Flea was in such a bad mood.

"*You guys play nice,*" Joe said. "*Any fighting and I'll be peeling your face off the bottom of my boot. Get me?*"

Neither responded.

Joe sighed and chucked another rock.

Jer'ait climbed over the edge of the pit and settled down beside him.

"Find anything?" Joe asked.

"There's a couple active dens nearby," Jer'ait said. "Nothing close enough to hear us."

"Good." Joe threw another stone. Then he yawned.

"Tired?" Jer'ait asked.

"Yeah," Joe muttered, rubbing his eyes despite knowing it would do no good with the biosuit on. "Can't wait to get back to my bed. We haven't gotten a good night's sleep in a couple weeks."

"I'll take shift for you," Jer'ait said. "If you want, you can take your biosuit off and get comfortable. Shouldn't be long, right?"

Joe frowned at the Huouyt, irritated and increasingly tired. "Job's not done. Not taking my suit off 'til we're back on Jeelsiht." He glanced at the rain. "Besides, it's cold as hell."

"Think of how comfortable it would be."

It *would* be comfortable. Joe was tired of having to relieve himself in his suit. He wanted to feel the freedom of air on his skin for once. But, more importantly, he wanted to go to sleep.

"Might take you up on the shift," Joe said, yawning, "But biosuit stays on." Ghosts! What was wrong with him? Surely he could stay awake two more hours, couldn't he?

Jer'ait glared at him. "Four members of your team go without biosuits every crawl. Are you so weak you can't expose yourself once?"

"Yep," Joe said. He could barely keep his eyes open, now. The lids felt so heavy…he hadn't thought he was that tired.

I'm not *this tired*, Joe realized, stunned. His eyes widened. *The Huouyt is drugging me somehow.*

"I'm sorry, Commander," Jer'ait said softly. "For what it's worth, I think Yua'nev is wrong."

As Joe was trying to comprehend this in his foggy state of mind, the Huouyt lunged forward, attempting to push a tentacle into Joe's mouth, to touch his tongue. Joe yanked the arm away and closed his mouth. Then he closed his eyes, too. He curled into a ball, feeling his body rhythms slow further.

"*Daviin, I need help! Jer'ait drugged me!*"

There was no reply.

Joe pressed his biosuit-covered hands over his face, blocking Jer'ait from reaching any orifices, and mentally told his suit to go into lockdown.

His last thought as the suit shut down his biorhythms was, *He was lying all along.*

● ● ●

"*Baga, if this is your idea of a joke, you're a furg.*"

Flea halted in carving his name into the side of one of the grotesque alien trees. "*What's a joke?*" He was irritated, in a foul mood, and ready to spit at something.

The Jreet did not bother to answer. Flea returned to scratching symbols into the weepy yellow bark.

"*You guys play nice,*" Joe said. "*Any fighting and I'll be peeling your face off the bottom of my boot. Get me?*"

Flea snorted and said nothing.

Earlier that morning, Jer'ait had shown him how to spell 'Flea' and had told him how Va'gans left a calling card whenever they visited a victim. Since Flea had killed a prince by himself, he should at least mark a few of the trees outside the den where he'd killed the prince.

It had been a long flight, almost twenty tics, but when Flea reached high altitudes and had clear skies, he could travel at almost the speed of sound. He hadn't told Joe he was leaving—only Jer'ait, who had promised to keep it a secret. He had two whole hours to get back, so he wasn't worried.

"*Daviin, I need help! Jer'ait drugged me!*"

Flea snorted and continued drawing the final symbol. *Shouldn't a pissed him off,* he thought. He almost wished he could be there. It was always funny, watching the Huouyt drug their Prime to put him in his place.

But Daviin never replied.

Flea hesitated, his claw sticky with cloudy sap. He slowly realized that aside from Daviin and Joe, the frequency had been utterly silent, more silent than usual. No one was talking. "*Daviin? What joke were you talking about earlier?*"

Daviin did not reply.

A tingle of dread was worming its way under Flea's carapace. "*Daviin? You all right?*"

Nothing.

"*Joe?*"

The frequency remained silent.

Flea launched himself off the branch and tore into the atmosphere, fear gnawing at his insides. "*Is anyone there?*"

"*I'm here,*" Scarab said.

"*Scarab,*" Flea called, relieved. "*What's going on?*"

"Jer'ait just drugged our Prime and is carting him off into the woods."

Flea blinked. *"He is? Are you following him?"*

"Why should I?"

Flea sped up. *"What do you mean? Is he hurting him?"*

"Don't know," Scarab said. *"Waiting for my pickup."*

Flea was outraged. *"Scarab, is Joe in trouble?"*

"Don't know." The Grekkon sounded bored.

"Well go find out!" Flea cried.

"Why should I? Mission's over."

"Why..." Flea could not comprehend the Grekkon's response. *"Because he's your ground leader!"*

"Mission's over," Scarab repeated.

"He's your friend," Flea snapped.

"Grekkon don't need friends."

Flea opened his mouth, unable to believe what he was hearing. *"That Huouyt is probably killing him right now, counter! Go help him!"*

"I'm Battlemaster. You're a Squader. I stay. Wait for pickup."

"You're not gonna help him? Really? This is a joke, right?"

"Mission's over," Scarab repeated. *"Don't need him anymore."*

"What the crack is the matter with you?!" Flea screamed.

"Grekkon don't need friends. Now enough. Grekkon don't like talking, either."

Flea flew faster.

By the time he reached their intended pickup zone, Joe and Jer'ait were gone. He could see Daviin's scarlet bulk stretched out in the forest beneath him, as still as a corpse. The way he was sprawled out, his back twisted sideways, he was not faking.

Flea gained altitude and scanned the area. *"Scarab, which way did they go?"*

Scarab said nothing. At first, Flea thought he was dead, then he saw his beady black eyes hunkered in the darkness of the fighting hole. Scarab was watching him.

Only a rod away, lying empty on the dirt, was Joe's headcom.

Seeing it, Flea spat at Scarab.

It landed on the Grekkon's spearlike arm and solidified, leaving a mottled bump where it had hit. Scarab simply backed deeper into the darkness, saying nothing.

"*You bastard!*" Flea snapped. "*You're the spy, aren't you?!*"

"*No spy,*" Scarab said. "*Waiting for pickup.*"

"*So you're a coward,*" Flea raged. "*Scarab, come help me.*"

"*Mission over. Don't need friends.*"

"*Tell me where Jer'ait took him or I'll come in there and spit in your eyes, I swear it.*"

The Grekkon hesitated. "*South.*"

Flea glanced to the south. "*Why?*"

Scarab ignored him.

Furious, flea spat a few more times into the darkness, hoping he hit the Grekkon. Then he took off after his Prime.

He caught sight of Jer'ait less than a tic later, dragging a black Human shape balled up in a fetal position.

Joe locked down his suit, Flea thought, both relieved and worried. If it was locked down, there was a chance Joe was still alive. It also meant he was in mortal danger.

Apparently, the Huouyt heard the sounds of Flea's wingbeats. He dropped his stiff prize and swirled, a tiny, oblong object in his tentacles. Flea heard a tiny pop. An instant later, a thin black dart whipped past his head, just missing a wing.

Flea twisted in the air, easily missing the next one. He pulled out of range and landed on a treetop. He and the Huouyt studied each other.

"*Let him go, Jer'ait,*" Flea said through his chip.

Jer'ait ignored him and picked up Joe by the elbow again. He began dragging the Human once more.

Flea watched, curious, until he realized where the Huouyt was taking their Prime. An open, gaping hole stood out in the center of a small clearing, its yawning depths dark and unobstructed.

He's taking him to the Dhasha den, Flea thought, confused. He jumped from his branch and caught up. The Huouyt swiveled again and shot another dart at him.

"You missed!" Flea cried. He was angry, now. He aimed his spitter and spat.

A wad hit the Huouyt in the chest and solidified there. Flea let out a triumphant cry and spat again. A miss.

The Huouyt's eyes never left Flea as his wormy red *zora* emerged from the slit in his head and he fed something to them.

Flea laughed and spat at the *zora*. Another miss. He needed to get closer, but if he did, the assassin would be able to hit him with the dart gun. He spat twice more before he realized the Huouyt was changing shape.

When he realized what pattern Jer'ait had chosen, Flea stopped spitting. He hovered there, stunned, fear crawling under his carapace like a cold wind. Meanwhile, the Huouyt was growing the heavy, leathery black wings of a *miga*.

He was taking the pattern of the one thing in the world that could outfly a Baga. A fearsome, unchallenged predator of the skies, the likes of which no other planet had had the bad luck to evolve. When the evil black head began to form, it drew out a coil of instinctual fear within Flea's gut.

Flea was so stunned that he didn't turn to flee until the Huouyt gave his wings a test-flap. His smooth, aerodynamic black head stared up at Flea with cold, merciless red eyes. Then he launched himself into the air with an unmistakable snap of wings.

Flea ducked under the canopy and flew for all he was worth. Unobstructed, the *miga* could catch up to him in a heartbeat. Even then, Flea could hear the sharp cracks of its wings as its backward strokes broke the sound barrier.

Don't panic, Flea thought. *It's just a Huouyt. Just a Huouyt. He won't know how to maneuver...*

But he *did* know how to maneuver. Flea could hear him getting closer, shooting over the treetops as he closed the distance.

Crack, crack, crack! *Gotta hide!* Flea twisted, sank deeper into the canopy, and when he found a tree big enough, he dropped suddenly and climbed up the yellow bark and over the underside of a huge limb until he was hanging upside down, hoping the *miga* hadn't seen where he stopped.

It's not a miga, Flea reminded himself. *Not a miga. Just a Huouyt.*

But the ancestral terror was thick in him as he waited, listening to the thunderous cracks get louder as the *miga* approached.

They feed on our abbas, Flea thought in a panic. *Just one gives them all the energy they need for rotations. But they keep killing anyway. They think it's fun. He's gonna kill me and feed on my abbas and...*

Flea froze when he heard the *miga* land on the branch he was clinging to. The whole tree shuddered. He wanted to scream, wanted to move away, but knew the sound of his feet changing position would result in the *miga's* evil head ducking down and its demonic red eyes locking gazes with him right before it tore him apart.

The *miga* shifted on the branch. Flea watched in terror as its long, glistening black tail swung down and wrapped around the branch only ninths from where Flea was hiding.

Maybe I can reason with him, Flea thought. *Jer'ait won't kill me.*

But, remembering the wet-eyed stare of the *miga* as it was getting ready to launch itself after him, Flea knew he would. He remained silent, terrified and trembling.

The *miga* launched itself into the air again, the thundering crack of its wings making Flea's carapace thump. The Huouyt gained altitude, then thundered across the sky for several tics, backtracking and zigzagging, before it finally gave up and retreated.

Flea stayed where he was for a full twenty tics before he dared to move. He peeked from under the branch, eying the sky.

No glistening black shapes with luminous red eyes.

That didn't mean it wasn't there.

Afraid to take to the air due to the sound it would make, Flea climbed the tree to the top and glanced around.

The *miga* was gone.

Tentatively, he hovered.

No thunderous wingbeats. Just the sound of his buzzing.

Flea glanced up. Sometimes, *miga* would dive-bomb their prey to avoid using their wings.

Clear sky.

Flea was stunned. *He really gave up.*

Which meant he was back with Joe, dragging him toward the Dhasha lair.

Furious, looking for a way to distract him, Flea jeered, *"That all you got, you runny Takki crap! Come get me!"*

Still, he was a little shocked when Jer'ait said, *"Flea? Where are you?"*

"Why don't you come find out, prick?"

Jer'ait hesitated a moment, then said, *"Flea, what's happened?"*

"I got away, that's what. Now I'm gonna go back and get Scarab and we're gonna make you disappear, just the two of us."

"Flea, I'm back in the clearing. Nobody's here except Scarab, and he's not answering me. Where's Daviin and Joe? Where are you?"

"Oh, right. Like I'm gonna tell you where to find me," Flea snapped.

"Flea, listen to me. There's a Huouyt somewhere nearby. He came up to me in Galek's pattern. Knocked me out cold. Would've killed me, if I hadn't managed to contain as much of the poison as I had."

"You're in the pit?"

"Yes."

"Stay there."

Flea gained some altitude and went to check on Joe. The *miga* was gone, the Huouyt back in its natural form. It had almost reached the Dhasha den with Joe.

Flea frowned and sped toward the clearing. He dropped into the trees to mask his approach, then, twenty rods out, he crawled on the ground the rest of the way.

Jer'ait was standing in the pit, watching the sky.

Flea jumped into the air and buzzed toward him. *"Jer'ait, somebody took Joe. He's wearing your pattern..."* He landed on the edge of the pit facing the Huouyt, out of reach, still not quite sure it wasn't a trick.

Jer'ait's face contorted. *"What of the Ooreiki?"*

"I haven't seen him."

"And Daviin?"

Flea took to the air. *"This way."*

Jer'ait followed him to the place where Daviin sprawled in the underbrush, a mass of scarlet against the deeper red of the alien foliage.

Jer'ait cursed as soon as he saw him, then crouched beside the Jreet's bulk. As Flea watched, Jer'ait's hand shifted shape, becoming a hard, scythelike claw. He pried up a cream-colored underbelly scale.

"What are you doing?" Flea asked, wary.

"I need to sample his flesh," Jer'ait said. He proceeded to jam the claw into the skin and twist, using a sawing motion to carve out a piece of flesh almost as big as Flea's head. Blue Jreet fluids ran out from the wound, dripping from the scales and spattering the ground below.

"He still bleeds," Jer'ait said, letting the belly scale flop back into place. "A good sign."

"So he's not dead?" Flea asked.

"You can never tell with a Jreet. They're almost entirely immune to poison. Only a very few work on them, and I'm praying the fool who's pretending to be me doesn't know which ones work the best." Jer'ait glanced up at Flea, his violet eye serious. "Listen to me, Flea. I've got to taste his flesh to determine which poisons were used, but the moment I place it upon my *zora*, I will have to struggle to stay whole. There are very few creatures in the universe a Huouyt can't use as a pattern, but a Jreet is one of them. If I lose my concentration, I could die. Do you understand?"

"Sit down, shut up," Flea said. He landed on a branch and capped his wings.

"Exactly." Jer'ait returned his attention to the dripping piece of flesh he held in his hands. He visibly steeled himself, then pushed his *zora* out to touch it.

Flea held perfectly still, watching in morbid fascination as the Huouyt's body began folding in on itself, like its skin was just a thin membrane containing several live creatures trying to get out.

After several moments of struggle, the Jer'ait relaxed. He tossed the flesh aside and crouched beside Daviin again. He slid his tentacle under a scale near Daviin's head. Then, after only an instant of contact, the Huouyt stood up and pried open one of the Jreet's enormous yellow eyes.

Flea watched, fascinated, as the Jreet blinked. Then blinked again. Then his massive golden eye rolled, found the Huouyt, and his entire body stiffened. He lunged, and no sooner had Jer'ait opened his mouth to explain was he pinned to the ground, the claws of the Jreet's right hand buried in his chest, the claws of the left buried in his face.

"Wait!" Flea shrieked. "That's the real one!"

"Where's Joe?" Daviin demanded.

"The *other* Huouyt is dragging him to the Dhasha den."

Daviin glanced up at him. "Other Huouyt?"

"That's Jer'ait. Use your chip. The other one can't hear us. That one can."

"Besides," Jer'ait said, *"Even if I had been trying to get on your good side by administering an antidote only tics before you went permanently comatose, I could easily poison you with something more deadly as you hold me here."*

"You didn't kill him?" Daviin demanded.

"Joe's not dead," Flea said. "The other Huouyt is dragging him. He's curled up, protecting his face."

"Probably protecting his nose and mouth," Jer'ait said. *"He must've known he was being poisoned."*

The big Jreet released Jer'ait reluctantly. He glanced up at Flea. "Where's Joe? Take me to him!"

"Let's get Scarab first," Flea said. "One of you needs to talk to him. He wouldn't listen to me."

"He's not going to listen to any of us," Jer'ait said as his face and torso mended. "Grekkon don't have emotions. He won't care."

"You can *order* him," Flea insisted.

"I already did," Jer'ait said. "Back when I realized there was a Huouyt stalking us. He ignored me."

"Enough talk!" Daviin snapped. "Take me to my ward!"

"It's a deep den," Flea warned, climbing into the air. *"What are we gonna do?"*

"We're going in," Jer'ait said. His voice was cold. Deadly. *"And we're going to get him back."*

30

CLAUSTROPHOBIA

Joe opened his eyes to utter darkness.

He tried to stand, but immediately, his head hit something hard. He'd barely lifted his chest off the floor.

"*Anyone there?*" he thought.

No one answered. Reluctantly, Joe lifted his hand to touch his head, already knowing what he would find.

Jer'ait had stripped off his headcom.

Further, he had no pack, no rifle, no gear whatsoever.

Without his helmet and the contact it offered to his group, without his PPU to guide him from the tunnels, without his gear, Joe felt that instinctive pang of terror that he had to immediately force back down. He could make out the dim outline of a small tunnel continuing at an upward angle in front of him. Without his visor to collect and amplify the images, however, he might as well have been seeing nothing at all.

Joe ran his fingers along the wall as he considered his situation. The size of the tunnel and its jaggedness suggested he was in a slave passage inside a Dhasha den. He pushed forward, feeling with his hands. He crested a small rise, then realized with a sinking feeling the tunnel was now taking him down.

I don't know which way's out, he realized with increasing panic.

Joe fought to stay calm. Why had Jer'ait dragged him underground? Why—

The scratching sound up ahead answered his question with cold, hard certainty. He couldn't kill him in his biosuit, so he was going to have the Dhasha do it for him.

Joe tensed, expecting a Takki. Thus, when the tiny Dhasha rounded the corner, its green eyes luminous in the black, Joe could only stare.

• • •

"*Come on!*" Flea shouted from up ahead. "*The Dhasha are going nuts. I think they know we're here.*"

"*Impossible,*" Daviin snapped. "*Even if all the Takki were chipped, which they aren't, we haven't given them time to scream, let alone call for help.*"

"*Still, I think…Oh crack.*"

"*What?*" the Jreet snapped.

"*Guys…I found Joe.*"

• • •

Joe felt the muscles in his right arm separate as the teeth continued to yank on him, splitting his biosuit, grinding against his bones. He'd been screaming for twenty tics, dragged by his arm through the tiny tunnels, feeling his bones threaten to crack when his body wedged in a tight space.

The tiny Dhasha was dragging him home.

Joe struggled to push himself forward, trying to keep the monster from ripping off his right arm. He knew it was pointless. It was only half there, anyway. The Dhasha had eaten everything past the wrist, biosuit and all.

Joe finally gave up trying to keep the Dhasha from ripping off his arm. He allowed the Dhasha's jaws to take the full weight of his body, then reached back and pulled the knife from his belt with his left. For a tunnel-crawling Congie, it was a tool, not a weapon. A knife would never kill a Dhasha.

Hell, it probably wouldn't even kill a Takki.

Still, when Joe slammed the knife blade up under the Dhasha's scales, it was surprised.

It also tore off the rest of his arm.

Blood spurted from the stump, painting the sand red.

Joe screamed and hacked into the Dhasha again. This time, his knife slipped across scales with the smoothness of perfectly hard, smooth glass. In response, the Dhasha simply grabbed him by the left arm and continued dragging him. Dizzily, Joe felt his body roll over the severed limb and keep going. His biosuit began forming over the wound to seal it, but it wasn't working fast enough.

I'm losing too much blood, Joe realized, watching the trail of darkness oozing from his wounds. Joe could do nothing but stare into the empty green eyes as the Dhasha continued to pull him backwards, deeper into the den.

All the while, it watched him, its frigid emerald gaze promising death.

Joe had just begun to lose consciousness when they hit a main tunnel. Immediately, a second, much larger Dhasha slammed its paw down upon Joe's back, preventing him from getting up. Joe let out another scream as the claws pierced his suit and began to carve a slow trail down his back.

"He's mine!" the smaller Dhasha said, releasing Joe's arm.

"Where are the others?" the bigger Dhasha asked, ignoring the small one. "Where's the rest of your team?"

"I'm alone," Joe gasped.

The Dhasha chuckled and dug its claws in deeper. Joe felt them scrape against his ribs and spine. Around him, several other Dhasha laughed with him. "For some reason, we don't believe you." Then, using nothing but its talons where they dug into his back, the Dhasha threw him down the tunnel, making him roll several times before he came to a stop against another Dhasha's feet. When he came to a halt, Joe saw his father's knife lying in a pool of his blood on the cavern floor, much like it had been when he first found it.

Dad…

Insanely, Joe didn't care if he died down here, or if he was eaten and became bone-studded Dhasha shit. He cared about his father's knife, ending up in the hands of Takki. Or buried forever when the Space Force launched an ekhta. Or sliced in half by some prince's talons. *No, Dad…*

"Oh, look how your pretty suit seals," the Dhasha above him said as the other padded up to him. "We'll have plenty of time to play with you, I think." He batted him again, slicing open Joe's chest and rolling him back toward the first Dhasha. Joe saw several pieces of himself remain on the ground with the knife, biosuit still writhing over them, trying to swallow them.

I'm dying, he realized, though he felt none of the detachment he had heard he would feel. He still felt every bit of the pain, and as the Dhasha continued to toy with him, batting him around as a cat played with a mouse it had no intention of eating, Joe found himself screaming over and over again.

He screamed until his throat was raw, until his lungs were punctured by Dhasha claws and no longer worked.

It wasn't long before his biosuit could not keep up with his wounds. He felt it fail, but all Joe could think about was the pool of blood that was becoming a dark red slick along the sandy tunnel floor. And the knife. His father's knife. Centered in the blood the same way it had been in the streets of San Diego. In Manny's hand.

No, Joe realized with a start. *Not Manny's hand. Dad's.*

The scene that had always been so fuzzy in his mind was suddenly crystal clear, like he was seeing it anew. His father, slumped over a twisted parking meter, blood pooling around him, the knife clutched in his limp fingers. *It had been Dad all along.*

And he'd refused to see it. All this time, he'd seen Manny's face, Manny's body. *Anything* to keep from seeing those familiar features, bloody and slack in death. But it *was* Dad. *Dad* died to protect Sam, when the aliens came. *Dad* had died with the knife Joe had given him fisted in his hand. The Swiss Army knife Joe had gotten him because he couldn't afford the Leatherman he'd asked for. The realization was shattering. Dad had never given it away to Manny, as Joe had always believed. He'd held it as he *died*.

This time, when Joe saw his own pool of blood slickening the floor, he recognized it. He'd seen it before, in his worst moments of terror underground. A premonition. A moment of truth. The knowledge that his dad hadn't abandoned him, not really. Not even in death.

Once his mind made the connection, it became easier for him. Joe began to lose interest in his own death, and began to wonder if he would see his father again.

I'm dying, Dad, was his last thought. *The Trith was wrong. I was never going to destroy Congress.*

He felt a flash of relief, then nothing.

• • •

Daviin had raised his energy level, so the Dhasha facing them could only see Jer'ait. He was in Jikaln form, fast, maneuverable, and hard to see in the shadows. He darted around the Dhasha, who just watched him with shock, until they were turned the opposite direction, facing Jer'ait instead of facing the Jreet. The Dhasha had just moved far enough away from Joe not to cause him any more damage when Flea began spitting.

The two Dhasha unfortunate enough to be touching each other roared and began tearing at the walls, the floor, the other Dhasha, and each other in their efforts to free themselves. As the six Dhasha that were left were forced to turn their attention to the greater of the two threats, Jer'ait leapt in and poisoned one, then another, then slipped away again before they realized he wasn't what he appeared.

By the time they were beginning to understand two of their fellows were not simply falling asleep, the Jreet struck.

When Daviin descended upon the pack of Dhasha, Jer'ait felt a little tingle of awe as the predators clashed. His own heritage as a prey species left him with the instinctive urge to run as the very walls vibrated with the strength of their bodies and claws tearing at the earth.

It took a great act of will for Jer'ait to leap back into the fray. Flea kept spitting, locking more Dhasha together, gluing their feet to the floor, plugging their nostrils.

It was over in less than a tic. Eight Dhasha lay dead.

Not one of the grounders had been hurt.

Flea, Daviin, and Jer'ait all recognized that, and the fact left them in quiet awe.

It was Daviin that dragged them out of their shock. *"We must get Joe back to the surface."*

"He's going to die," Jer'ait said, looking at the mangled body. It lay in several parts, and red Human blood slicked the floor. *"There's nothing that could bring someone back after that."*

"Nonetheless," Daviin said stubbornly, *"I'll carry him. You call for a pickup."* Daviin scooped the bloody mess from the floor and vanished again, headed for the exit. The way Joe floated along the tunnel, Jer'ait could almost believe he was the Human's spirit, come to avenge his death.

"This is Commander Zero's Second requesting immediate pickup," Jer'ait said. *"We have injured parties needing medical attention."*

"Who?" a Human voice asked.

It was Phoenix.

She continued, *"Aside from the Ooreiki that died in that bar fight yesterday, you only have one member down, the rest at full health. Wait for a pickup."*

The Ooreiki that died? So *that* was why Galek was so damned nervous about the PPU. It had been a Peacemaker, another Eleventh Hjai. Galek had died in some anonymous alley so Jer'ait's coworker could chip himself and have access to their Prime. It came as a blow to Jer'ait, and with it, he felt a wash of fury, knowing which of his brothers it had been. *They're killing an innocent man.*

"*Zero's not dead yet,*" Jer'ait snapped.

"*Oh, but he will be. Injuries that bad…No way to stop it.*" The dismissive way the Human said it, Jer'ait had no doubt in his mind she was going to leave them there until it was true.

"*Perhaps you didn't understand me,*" Jer'ait said softly, lapsing back into his flat, Va'ga-trained voice. "*By now you know my name is Jer'ait Ze'laa. If Zero dies, you won't live to see your Corps Directorship.*"

"*You're threatening me? Stuck on an enemy planet?*" Phoenix laughed. "*Yes.*"

There was a long, horrible pause.

Then, "*Give your threats to someone who cares.*"

Jer'ait was flushing with rage when another Human voice cut in, "*Burn that. This is Rat. A shuttle's on its way.*"

• • •

Somehow, Joe lived.

Daviin watched the entire process, watched him die three times on the table, watched them bring him back to life. Watched the other Human sit down and offer up her fluids to keep him alive.

The Ueshi doctor who had stapled Daviin to the floor was in charge throughout, conducting a stampede of medics with the confident beauty of a Sentinel war-dance.

A dozen hours passed with no improvement, and once an Ooreiki doctor threw down his instruments and told them they were wasting their time.

Daviin picked him up and heaved him from the room.

Three days went on, and the surgeries continued with only brief, unhappy breaks in between. The Human would not stabilize. The female returned twice, to offer up more fluids. The third time, the Ueshi sent her back to her groundteam on a stretcher, her face pale, her fingers trembling.

More than once, the Human woke just long enough to scream before settling back into oblivion. Perhaps he'd never left it.

It was his heart stopping that worried Daviin. It had been punctured during the Dhasha's assault. Shredded. The surgeons had tried to fuse and graft it back together, but the shredded muscles refused to beat as one.

His lungs, too, were refusing to work. They were deflated lumps, neither able to support themselves despite everything the Ueshi did to repair them.

His liver had been removed—that which had remained, anyway. The Human's intestines were all but gone. Even now, the Human was living off machines, his fluids filtered, his breathing forced, his heart prodded.

The doctors didn't have enough time to culture him the organs he needed. They needed another week.

Hold on, Daviin thought, willing him to stay alive until they could give him a transplant. *You can do this.*

If he felt Daviin's need for him to live, Joe never showed any change. The skin that remained was black and yellow, one massive, ugly bruise. He was still missing an arm.

Jer'ait came to Daviin during one of the quiet periods between operations. "I found him."

Daviin swiveled. "Where?"

"Call the Ueshi," Jer'ait said. "Tonight Joe will live."

● ● ●

Jer'ait knew only one Huouyt who would have had the rank to get himself chipped as Galek. Gra'fei. Eleventh Hjai. Yua'nev's other assassin.

"Let me take him," Jer'ait said. "No arguments this time, Jreet. If things don't go exactly right, we'll fail. You know what that means."

Beside him, Daviin nodded grimly.

"Good. Vanish." Jer'ait pushed three more arms from his borrowed Ooreiki torso and entered the bar.

His target sat in one corner, sipping a drink, waiting for his shuttle to arrive to carry him back to Levren. He was watching an Ueshi dancer undulate in the center of the room, thus his eyes were elsewhere when Jer'ait touched him on the shoulder. And on the chest. And the face. And the leg. And the back.

"So nice to see you again, Gra'fei."

The other Huouyt's eyes widened as five different poisons entered his system from five different places. Too many to counter. His mouth pressed together in fear as he went limp in his chair.

"You got it?" Jer'ait asked.

"Yes." Daviin uncloaked and handed him a red vial. The Ueshi in the center of the room stopped dancing, staring down at the Jreet's body where it snaked through the center of the dance floor, only ninths from her feet.

All eyes in the place fell on them.

"Good," Jer'ait said. He pried open Gra'fei's *zora* sheath, tilted the other Huouyt's unresisting head back, unstoppered the vial, and poured it inside.

Gra'fei's eyes widened with understanding and fear as his body began to change.

"Wait for it," Jer'ait said, as the Huouyt's breja disappeared and his body grew bony and weak. Then, gently, he reached out and took the other Huouyt by the neck of his Human pattern. He leaned down to speak in Gra'fei's ear. Softly, he said, "You die for a good cause." He administered the antidotes and pulled away. "Now, Jreet. Make it count."

Even as Gra'fei was beginning to regain some of his motor functions, Daviin struck.

The ferocity with which the Jreet ripped off the Huouyt's Human head and tore open his ribcage, then delicately plucked out the desired organs left Jer'ait with a professional respect.

Then, with great disdain, Daviin flipped the bleeding carcass aside and twisted around to make his departure, the organs held out in front of him like great war trophies, intestines looped around his wrist like a gruesome bracelet. Jer'ait followed, pulling his three extra arms back into his torso as he went.

From the bar through the streets, to the halls of the hospital, every alien in their path got out of the way.

"Here," Daviin said, once they were back in the operating room. He thrust his prizes out for the Ueshi to inspect. The Ueshi stared.

"The heart's still beating," Daviin offered, sounding nervous. "You said fresh was best."

"It's...good," the Ueshi said. "Fresh." He seemed to regain his composure and nodded for Jer'ait to close the door. "Let's get to work."

As the operation began, the Jreet hovered like a nervous hen. Jer'ait had to refrain from doing the same. Something about the Human made him stupid...and he thought he finally understood what it was. "Sentinel," Jer'ait said gruffly, reaching into his pocket.

"Shhh, they're connecting the arteries." Daviin was hunched over the operating table, and not one of the doctors had the zora to tell him to leave.

"*Worm.*"

Daviin's tiny golden eyes narrowed and he swiveled his massive head. Jer'ait held out Joe's knife. "Take it. I can't stay to give it to him."

"Joe's knife!" Daviin said, delighted. He took it in an enormous crimson fist with the same delicacy as if he were cradling a precious treasure.

"It was on the floor of the cavern where they were batting him apart," Jer'ait said.

Daviin's fist closed around the polymer object and Jer'ait had the distinct feeling that it wouldn't open again until Joe woke. "Why can't you stay?"

Jer'ait felt a darkness cross his features as he thought of his peers. "I have other things I must do."

Daviin settled his eyes on Jer'ait's face, and for a moment, they just met each other's gazes, the Sentinel and the assassin. Despite his density at times, Jer'ait knew Daviin understood what he planned. "I never thought I'd say this," the Jreet finally said, "but good luck. May you kill a great many with your tricks."

Jer'ait smiled, despite himself. "And you, too, Jreet. Someday, if I survive, I'll invite you to Koliinaat for a drink." Then, together, they turned back to watch the surgery. Once he saw that the operation would succeed, Jer'ait slid from the room and went to catch Gra'fei's shuttle to Levren.

• • •

Joe opened his eyes.

This time, he was pretty sure he was dead.

He could see no reason why he was still alive. He'd seen pieces of his liver on the ground. He'd seen his arm torn off, his lower torso lying in its own blood. He'd seen the blood.

Yet when he took a breath, it was of his own accord. He felt his heart beating in his chest. The only thing he couldn't feel was the fingertips of his right hand.

Joe struggled to lift his right arm. There was *something* there... it was heavy and he was weak. When he saw it was a perfect Human arm, however, he had to stare. He flexed the fingers, goggling. He had *some* sensation, he realized, but not what he was used to. He touched the steel edge of the bed with it, found the fingers stiffer, strange.

Mechanical, Joe realized, a little stunned. And, cradled in the artificial fingers, were the smooth red surfaces of his father's knife. Joe felt tears burning his eyes and had to look away, tightening his new fingers around the ancient memory.

It was then that Joe saw Daviin.

The Jreet was curled beside the bed in an enormous coil, his great bulk blocking the door, effectively cutting off any would-be assassins... or emergency personnel.

"Hey," Joe rasped. It was a grating sound, barely above a whisper. Joe swallowed twice and tried again. Not much better. The Jreet never twitched.

Joe realized Daviin was asleep.

Grinning, he lay back against the bed and pondered how he had gotten where he was. He was happy to be alive, but he knew he should be dead. No scenario he could imagine in his mind even began to explain how he had gotten where he was. He was grateful, yet perplexed. Several times, he had to sit up just to re-confirm that he was completely whole.

It didn't make sense. He knew Congress couldn't grow specialized tissues that fast. Troubled, Joe stared at the ceiling, wishing Daviin would wake up to talk to him.

A door slamming impatiently against Daviin's bulk made Joe twitch. "Out of the way, Jreet," Rat's voice commanded. "They told me he just woke up."

Joe sat up, propping himself up on his elbows to spare his tender stomach muscles.

On the floor, Daviin grunted, then started awake. "Joe's—" When their eyes met, the sheer *joy* in the Jreet's crocodile-like face was almost cute.

The rough way Daviin ripped Joe off the bed, yanking loose IV lines in his haste to squish him against his chest, was not.

"Goddamn it!" Joe roared. "Get your tek out of my face! Put me back! I *need* those drugs!"

Daviin continued to hold him well off the ground. Happily, he said, "A warrior doesn't need drugs. Welcome back, Joe!"

"I think you just broke my ribs again," Joe muttered. Already, the effects of the drugs were beginning to wear off and he was aching from head to toe. "Really, you should put me back."

"Nonsense! We go eat!" Daviin set him on the floor and gave him a shove toward the door, post-op nightgown and all.

"At least let me get dressed," Joe said. "And I need to ask the doctors if—"

"Clothes are for the weak," Daviin said. "And doctors don't always know what's best."

"They fixed my heart good enough," Joe said.

Daviin scoffed. "They didn't fix your heart." He pointed to a bloody container sitting on the table beside Joe's bed. "Just look at it. Like a Takki's face."

Joe's mouth fell open. "Please tell me that's not my heart."

"Thought you'd want a trophy from all this," Daviin said, slapping him hard upon the back. "The slavesoul Ueshi doctor called it a biohazard, tried to throw it out. I grabbed it out of the trash."

Staring at the multiple chambers and the ragged scars crisscrossing the muscle, Joe felt ill. Then something even more frightening occurred to him. *If that's my heart, what's that thumping in my chest?*

"It's your other heart," a familiar voice said from the door. "Your groundteam harvested it for you. In the middle of Dayut. During happy hour. It was on the news."

Joe was suddenly very aware of the woman standing in the door, watching them. She was tall and lean, in boots only a few ninths shorter than Joe in his bare feet.

"Rat?"

"She gave fluids," Daviin said proudly. "Almost killed her, but it kept you alive long enough for us to find you replacement organs."

Joe did not like the sound of that. "Replacement? You mean they didn't grow them for me?"

"So!" Daviin said, shoving him toward Rat. "You two discussed sex, yes? You can do it while we eat."

Joe's jaw dropped and he twisted, throwing Daviin's huge hand off his shoulder. "What?!"

"On Neskfaat, before the last assignment. You spoke of sex."

"Yeah, but—"

"Not public enough? We can go to the celebration in Dayut. It's been going on ever since Rat killed the Vahlin."

"I didn't kill the Vahlin," Rat said.

Joe frowned at her, then at Daviin, then back at Rat. "Can you believe him? He thinks we're gonna have sex with him watching."

Rat shrugged. "Why not? My Sentinel won't leave my side, either, but the two of them have come to an accord over the problem of the two of us mating. They'll both wait in the hall."

Joe's mouth fell open.

Rat grinned and winked at him.

"Okay," Joe said. "I'm still a little drowsy—the Welu is your *Sentinel?*"

Rat shrugged. "Only way I'd let him on the team."

Joe glanced back at Daviin. "I don't like this. It's almost as if it was—"

"Planned?" Rat suggested. "Yeah. In fact, the only difference between your team and mine is that your Ooreiki was killed. A Huouyt took his place. Tried to assassinate you. They still don't know who or why."

Joe's heart began to thud in his chest, sending searing pain through his limbs.

"Careful," Rat said, her features softening. She rushed forward and caught him as he stumbled. "Daviin, go get a doctor."

Daviin took one look at Joe, then vanished and fled.

"Galek's dead?" Joe asked as she helped him back into the bed.

"He was before your departure from Jeelsiht. A Huouyt killed him in an alley, took his pattern."

A surge of hope relieved some of the tension in Joe's chest. "Huouyt don't take dead patterns."

Rat's brows contorted. "This one did. Trust me, Joe, Galek's dead. They found him in an alley a few days ago. Only now figured out who it was—had his chip fried and his tattoo carved off. They did an autopsy on his body. It was genuine."

Joe blinked back tears. "So," he said bitterly, "Your team won."

"And I'm still looking over my shoulder wherever I go," Rat said. "You and I both know there's something more to this than what the Geuji wanted us to see. Yes—my team survived, but I've got a feeling you guys are the lucky ones. At least for you, the game's over."

"Galek's dead."

"But the rest of them are alive." She made a face. "Even that useless Grekkon."

"Useless?"

"He refused to help the other three get you back. He just sat on the surface the whole time and caught the pickup that the rest of them missed because they were down in the tunnels, getting you back."

Joe remembered a brief flash of a slick of blood coating the floor in front of him and he shuddered. "Who got me out, then? If it wasn't the Grekkon..."

"The Baga, the Jreet, and the Huouyt. They just walked right in, kicked ass, and walked right out. They didn't even need stitches. Killed twelve Dhasha, if you believe the Baga."

"You can't believe the Baga."

"Your Huouyt said it was more along the lines of twenty."

Joe flinched. "Jer'ait never lies about how many kills he's made."

"I know."

"Where's Jer'ait?" Joe said.

"Jer'ait disappeared," Rat told him. "Nobody knows but Daviin, and he's not telling."

"Where's Flea?"

Rat's face darkened. "Phoenix got him transferred. She broke up your groundteam, Joe. Daviin's the only one who could tell them to piss off and get away with it." Then she cocked her head. "Well, Jer'ait could probably get away with it, but he was long gone by the time Phoenix started making her ultimatums."

Joe felt a headache building, as well as a new pain in his chest. "She got Corps Director."

Rat nodded. "She put together the only two teams that survived Neskfaat. Not only that, but our teams each took out six princes. Seven, if you count the one your three killed getting to you, but officially they only gave you six assignments, so Headquarters isn't gonna recognize it. Cheap bastards. You know they never gave Flea his *kasja* money?"

Joe looked up sharply. "What?"

Rat nodded grimly. "Never got around to it. Never got around to giving your team any of its *kasjas*. I tried to bring it up with the awards committee, but Phoenix overruled me."

Joe shook his head and looked away, clenching his fists in fury. His artificial right hand still felt odd, but it reacted to his whims well enough to suit him.

Rat stood up and patted him gently on the chest. "I'll take you up on the sex thing later. Right now, though, I'm gonna go find your Voran before he meets up with my Welu and they decide their non-violence pact doesn't carry to anonymous hospital corridors."

"You sent him to get a nurse," Joe said, automatically feeling a pang of worry.

"Oh, I know," Rat said. "But he's lost. A Jreet couldn't find his way to a door in a one-roomed house. You rest. I'll find him."

"Thanks," Joe said, leaning back. He tried to relax, but the injustices of the past few days were haunting him.

"I'll send a nurse with more drugs, too," Rat said. "You look like you need them."

31

WRAPPING UP THE PLAN

"And only one will survive?"

"Yes," Forgotten said. "That's the one you want."

"Interesting," Rri'jan said. He glanced at his watch. "Two and a half hours. Had you been planning this before I captured you?"

"You did not capture me," Forgotten said. "And, while I did have some general ideas, I began the majority of my planning the moment you stepped onto my ship."

Rri'jan checked his watch again. "But only two and a half hours? You don't need more time? Perhaps, if I gave you a few rotations to think about it, you could come up with a better plan."

"No," Forgotten said. "There is no better plan."

"Less than three hours? Surely you don't expect me to risk my seat on a plan that you began telling me before you'd even finished it."

"No," Forgotten said, "I'd finished it before I began speaking."

Rri'jan's horizontal slit of a mouth opened, then closed again. "You were speaking within ten tics of my arrival."

"Correct."

Rri'jan was silent for some time. "And this will only take a turn."

"Less than, to produce a prince-killing groundteam."

"And I'll have my Tribunal seat afterwards," Rri'jan said. "You realize, if you're deceiving me, Forgotten, I will hunt you down and make you feel pain even you have never thought possible."

"Deceiving you? When you hold my entire species for ransom?" Forgotten snorted.

"Very well," Rri'jan said, standing. He wrapped his cloth-of-silver cape around his shoulders, obviously a bit disconcerted. "I planned on being here much longer than this."

"You're dealing with a Geuji, Rri'jan. Please remember that."

Rri'jan looked up at him, his electric eyes unable to disguise the fact he was impressed. "And the plan? What do I need to do to set it into motion?"

"Just as I said. Nothing. I'll take care of all the details. I've already sent messages to my contacts. The wheels are in motion. All you must do is sit back and watch."

Rri'jan glanced out the window, eying the armada that floated around them. He looked back, satisfaction on his face. "This has been a very productive meeting, Geuji."

"I am happy with the outcome," Forgotten replied.

"Indeed." Rri'jan made a respectful bow. "I'll see you in one turn."

"You won't find me," Forgotten said.

Rri'jan hesitated, his face showing his irritation. "You'll have no need to hide if I order the Geuji freed."

"Nonetheless," Forgotten said, "You won't find me."

Rri'jan gave him a disgusted look, then departed.

"So who was that?" the smuggler asked, when Forgotten unlocked the chamber that hid him.

"A business associate," Forgotten said. "I was expecting him."

"Is that why you just locked me in a room for two hours after luring me here with the promise of riches?" Syuri snapped.

"Actually, it was more like three. And yes. The last thing you want is for him to see your face."

The Jahul grunted. "Fine. Self-righteous slime-mold. So what happened to this job you offered me? Two mil? Or'd you just give it away to that jackass who couldn't see my face?"

Forgotten found the Jahul's spunkiness amusing. The self-proclaimed pirate also had the strongest innate empathy Forgotten had ever seen in a Jahul. Syuri had sensed the visitor despite Forgotten's every effort to mask it. Forgotten had the unnerving feeling the Jahul could also sense some of his own emotions, even shielded. That's why he needed him.

"I want you to deliver some exotic foods to Aez."

The Jahul stared at him. "You have *got* to be kidding me. *Food?* You want me to deliver *food?*"

"It will be to the Aezi gladiator halls, so there will be some risk involved. Especially since their Voran captive recently freed himself and is probably lurking in the very halls where you will need to make your deliveries."

Syuri scrunched his sticky Jahul face. "How about you give me another assignment, one on some Ueshi pleasure planet or something. I'd rather deal with an entire Ueshi syndicate than a lone Voran Jreet. I hate Jreet, especially *those* Jreet. Vorans are so pig-headed."

"The Voran will not hurt you."

"Hurt me?" Syuri scoffed. "I'm doing business with his *enemies*. Who, by the way, are self-righteous, out-of-control zealots. I've been listening to the rumors going around. I've got *sources*, Forgotten. They're gonna kill everyone in the Old Territory, you know that? Have you ever *been* to Aez? They're all insane. Violent furgs, all as crazy as that Tribunal member leading them."

"Are you done ranting, now?" Forgotten asked, amused.

"No," the Jahul said, making a cutting motion with his horny front limb. "They're sending out raiding armadas, catching outsiders and dragging them home, just like the *old days*, Forgotten. Back before Congress. They're stringing up disbelievers in the main square of every Aezi city and letting them die of the elements. Everyone they can get hold of. And if they're Jreet—they're throwing them in the gladiatorial ring with kreenit. Just to watch them die! And last rotation, they pulled all their people out of the Sentinels. You know what that *means*, you ignorant corpse-rot?"

"Enlighten me."

"It means Prazeil's about to declare war. On Vora and Welu. And probably the rest of the planets in that sector. Do you have any *idea* of the kind of bloodbath that would be?"

"I'm sure you'll be happy to tell me."

"They'd take out Poen," Syuri snapped. "All those Ooreiki souls... *poof*! They do that...the whole Old Territory would explode on itself, you get me?"

"I think so."

"Faelor would go down," Syuri insisted. "The Bajna can't fight Jreet, not even with their war machines. Then where would Congress be?"

"I could probably make a guess," Forgotten said.

"*Gone*, that's where!" Syuri waved a disgusted hand. "Eighty percent of our banking goes through that planet, you ignorant slime-mold. Sweet Hagra, you ask me, we should be moving this whole operation to the other side of the *galaxy*. The Old Territory is unstable."

"But I have a delivery to make to Aez."

"Monsters," the Jahul went on, oblivious. "Aez is filled with monsters. And you want me to help *feed* them? That Voran catches me feeding them and he'll tear off my limbs and use my inner chambers for canteens. He'd think I was working for them!"

Forgotten said, "I'm sure you'll be fine."

• • •

When the top five highest-ranking Peacemakers died in five separate accidents, leaving Jer'ait to inherit the Peacemaster's position, everyone knew foul play had been involved, but no one had the *zora* to accuse him.

The first thing Jer'ait did upon gaining his Peacemaster position was to erase all vestiges of the Geuji's prediction of Joe's future. There were surprisingly few references—Yua'nev had wanted to keep the Peacemaker's prior knowledge of Aez as far from the media as possible, lest he be implicated as a possible conspirator.

The second thing that Jer'ait did was replace the open positions of the Eleventh Hjai with Peacemakers that deserved them, regardless of species. The same day, he sent missives to every Huouyt family head explaining his decision and what would happen if it was not respected.

Then he began researching the Geuji. Everything he could find on Jemria, the only Geuji to have escaped from the basement of the Space Academy. Not, he found, because he had planned some grand scheme, but because his spore had wound up on the inside of an Ueshi Space Academy recruit's headcom. The Ueshi had done exceedingly well in her flight and war-games, and once she realized what she had on her hands, she testified that she had blackmailed the Geuji to help her complete training and win in Jahul gaming dens.

Yet the Geuji, against all odds, without any mobility whatsoever, had turned the tables and convinced the Ueshi to free him of his servitude and install him in his first ship, thus beginning three centuries of life on the run. Peacemakers had been hunting him since the very night the Ueshi freed him. Though his species had never been entered into Congress, though he broke no laws, though he had done nothing wrong, his file had been marked 'Dead or Alive' for over three centuries.

He was never given a chance, Jer'ait thought, troubled.

An instant later, his secretary, Orbil, hit the CALL button. *"Peacemaster?"* the Ooreiki Sixth Hjai asked nervously. *"They're requesting your presence in the Regency."*

Jer'ait felt his breja ripple at mention of the Regency. "Why?"

"There was an attack on Representative Mekkval on his home planet of Jakun 5. A representative of the Peacemakers is being requested by the Tribunal."

Jer'ait froze, the next step in the Geuji's plan suddenly clicking into focus. Mekkval maintained a deep den on Jakun, perceived by Congress to be impenetrable. He had retreated to it once the hostilities had started, to keep his own heirs from joining the rebellion. "Was Representative Mekkval killed?" he demanded.

His secretary hesitated as he collected the information. *"No, sir. Wounded."*

Jer'ait, who had been fearing the worst, hesitated. Cocking his head, he said, *"Wounded,* Orbil?" Then that would mean…

…the Geuji had failed.

"Yes, sir. By a Jreet, sir."

Jer'ait narrowed his eyes, remembering Rat's team. "Was it a *Welu* Jreet, Orbil?"

Another pause. "Yes sir. A group of six renegade Congies. Survivors from Neskfaat. They're saying it was war-trauma."

Jer'ait considered for several long moments.

The fact it was Rat's team left no doubt in his mind that the Geuji had been involved. Yet, if the Geuji had intended Mekkval to die, Mekkval would be dead. He had seen that much on Neskfaat.

"Would you like me to transfer them to an Eleventh Hjai to take the summons instead, sir?" Orbil asked, after Jer'ait did not respond for some time.

As long as Jer'ait stayed within the Peacemaker Sanctuary of Koliinaat, the Watcher could not transport him anywhere. Thus, the politicians actually had to *ask* for his attendance. It was one of the balances of power that the Geuji had worked into the original design of Koliinaat, when Aliphei and the Regency commissioned it in the 100th Age of the Ooreiki.

The design of Koliinaat was one of many things the Geuji had done before they were captured that left Jer'ait discomfited. Upon ascending the seat of the Peacemaster, he had spent long hours researching the Space Academy basement's long-term guests. As it turned out, most of Congress's greatest advancements had been instigated by the Geuji: Nanos—everything that Congress now used in its ships, medicine, and weaponry. Ruvmestin generators—continuous, clean, essentially unlimited energy. Faster than light travel—something so advanced that not even present-day technicians could decipher the why of it; they just built all ships to ancient Geuji design and trusted it worked. Teleportation—which only remained possible on Koliinaat because all other technology was lost. Ekhtas—the greatest weapon known to the universe. And, of course, the ultimate Geuji creation—Koliinaat and its Watcher. A completely artificial planet with omnipotent, omnipresent, *sentient* artificial intelligence that directed billions of individual affairs per second.

The Geuji had only been given six hundred turns before they were locked away on Levren. Six hundred turns and they had created what Congress considered the pinnacles of its two and a half million turn existence.

Knowing that, Jer'ait found his breja writhing at the very fact that he was sitting deep within one of their creations, run by a creature of their own design. The only artificial life form that was, unquestionably, sentient.

Where do his loyalties lie? Jer'ait wondered of the Watcher. Such things bothered him, now that he had the Peacemaster's seat. The fact that every power-player in Congress placed his life in the Watcher's hands every second of every day did not escape his notice.

And yet, *none* of the Geuji's creations had initially been for the purpose of war. They had, until Forgotten, never been accused of murder or war. Biosuits had been created to protect its users on space walks and high-danger jobs. Nanos had been created for medicine and safer, more versatile, life-saving ships, using the Geuji's own bodies as inspiration. And ekhtas had been created for mining difficult-to-penetrate, mineral-rich asteroids and planetoids.

"*Sir?*" Orbil asked again, hesitantly.

"Tell them I will meet their summons," Jer'ait said, "but I will have no answers for them."

Because the Watcher had no direct access to the Peacemaker Sanctuary on Koliinaat, Jer'ait had to leave his office, walk through the interrogation suite, past the cell block, down the long maze of corridors to the outer foyer, then summon the Watcher to take him to the Tribunal.

The moment the Watcher arrived in the room with him, it was as if the mental density of the air itself seemed to thicken. Instead of immediately teleporting him, however, the Watcher asked, *"Are you sure about this, Jer'ait?"*

Jer'ait froze, thinking he had misheard. Was he...sure? Jer'ait, who in a hundred turns of working between Koliinaat and Levren had never had to give the Watcher a command more than once, felt his breja twist upon his skin in sudden, acute unease. Knowing what he knew about the Geuji, and his research of the Geuji's betrayal by the Trith and Congress, he could not be sure if he were speaking to a friend or foe. Carefully, though the Watcher maintained no image or face, he stared straight at the far wall and said, "Why would I not be sure?"

"The journey will be long, and you might not like what you find," the Watcher replied. *"Sending an Eleventh Hjai would give you more rest at night."*

Every breja across his entire body flexed into rigidity at those words. Knowing that the Watcher held Jer'ait's life in his hands—the same hands that held every Representative of Congress—Jer'ait asked, "Are you working with Forgotten?"

The Watcher scoffed. *"My primary duty is to protect the Regency."*

"Are you?" Jer'ait asked.

"Could you stop me, if I was?"

The cold threat in the room left Jer'ait silent for several moments. Then, "Are you?"

The room around him seemed to chuckle. *"Jemria has not contacted me, but his workings are easy enough to see. Shall I transport you, Jer'ait, or will you find someone else? Keep in mind, the Geuji's plans hinge on your involvement."*

Jer'ait felt his attention sharpen. "Then they are not yet complete."

"Oh, not by far," the Watcher said, sounding amused.

"And what is his goal?" Jer'ait demanded.

The Watcher laughed. *"For now? Entertainment. Later? Freedom, I'm sure."*

Jer'ait eyes narrowed at 'entertainment,' realizing that the Watcher was, in essence, an artificial Geuji. "You're sure or you know?"

"I know that Jemria just set off a series of events that will not see their completion until over five hundred turns from now," the Watcher said. *"And he wants you to be part of it."*

"That much," Jer'ait said bitterly, "is obvious."

"Isn't it, though. Shall I transport you, Jer'ait? Being forewarned, of course, that all you must do to bring his entire plan to a crashing halt is to tell one of your underlings to take this call for you?"

Jer'ait stiffened. "Don't toy with me."

"I merely state a fact. Jemria expects you to help him. He did not expect me to tell you as much. This gives you an unforeseen advantage. I thought it only fair."

Jer'ait cocked his head. "You can out-think him."

His reply was an amused, "Of course."

"How do I end his destruction?" Jer'ait said. "Geuji were never meant to do violence. He's gone rogue. Tell me how to stop him."

"I already did," the Watcher replied. Then, "What makes you think Jemria's gone rogue?"

Jer'ait frowned. "Then he didn't try to kill Mekkval."

He could feel the Watcher's amusement all around him, like a yeeri scholar watching the antics of a particularly bright toddler. "Mekkval," the Watcher said, "recently hired six new staff members. One of them eats a melaa a day. He's sent the six of them on a diplomatic mission to Mijor last week. Before that, it was Kiji'banu."

Jer'ait blinked. Mijor and Kiji'banu were two Outer Line planets that had each become home to a Dhasha prince whose loyalties to Congress were on the dangerous side of questionable. Each had been stockpiling weapons and slaves and rebuffing Congressional probes for several turns. Yet resistance, as of last he'd heard, had inexplicably ended on Mijor last week. A couple weeks before that, Kiji'banu had gone silent.

"And now," the Watcher said, "I really do need an answer, Peacemaster. Aliphei grows impatient."

Jer'ait glanced at the entrance back into the Sanctuary and considered. "And all I have to do to crush his plans is walk away and let someone else handle this?"

"That would be correct."

Jer'ait considered, thinking of a bomb made for the ease of mining, twisted into something else entirely once the Geuji were safely

entombed in darkness. "Take me to the Regency," he said. "I look forward to meeting him."

The Watcher chuckled. *"You are perceptive, for your capabilities."*

The room vanished around him and Jer'ait endured the instant of
cold, prickly numbed-limb sensation before he found himself standing
in the private Tribunal chambers. Mekkval, Prazeil, and Aliphei were
all in attendance.

"Have you grown so accustomed to your station already that
you ignore a direct summons from the Tribunal, Huouyt?" Prazeil
demanded, the moment he arrived. The enormous Aezi lifted his head
high in rage, his creamy, thirteen-rod body coiled beneath him.

"I am Peacemaster," Jer'ait replied. "I have things to attend to." He
cocked his head at the Jreet. "I will also remind you, Jreet, that I do not
answer to the Tribunal. For, if one of you were to ever be charged, it
would be *I* who would stand in your place to try you."

The engine-like battlecry began to form in the Jreet's chest, but
Aliphei interrupted dismissively with, "Mekkval was attacked on his
home of Jakun 5. Six Congies. Before they died, he extracted confes-
sions from them indicating Rri'jan Ze'laa vehn Morinth was behind
the war on Neskfaat.

Jer'ait turned to give Mekkval a long look. "Did he."

Mekkval, to his credit, returned his stare completely unwavering.

"We attempted to detain Rri'jan for questioning," Aliphei said,
"but your brother killed our agents and fled. Further confirming, of
course, his guilt."

Jer'ait paused to regard the First Citizen. "Ah."

"Ah?!" Prazeil roared, lunging to loom over Jer'ait. "We tell you of
a conspiracy of your traitorous blood and your response is 'ah?!'"

Jer'ait calmly cocked his head up at the massive Jreet. "I assume
the purpose of this meeting is to convince me to go bring him back so
that you may try him and quite probably do something unpleasant to
the Huouyt for their continuous schemes to rule Congress. Further, it
does not escape my notice that my brother is a Va'gan assassin and you
are a very large, bulky, ungainly worm. So, unless you would like to go
hunt him down yourself, Jreet, you will have to be satisfied with 'ah.'"

Prazeil's audial-ridges tightened against his head. "What did you just say to me?"

Unconcernedly, Jer'ait turned back to Aliphei and Mekkval. "I *do* assume that is what you want, yes?"

Aliphei was giving him a hard look, his tiny red eyes fierce within his shaggy coat of blue. "Are you refusing to do justice, Peacemaster?"

"Oh, not at all," Jer'ait scoffed. "Nothing would please me more than to see my brother have his breja plucked for Neskfaat." He said the last looking Mekkval directly in the big green eyes. "I never liked him, anyway. Unconscionable bastard that he was."

He thought he saw the ghost of a smile on Mekkval's rainbow lips before it disappeared again, replaced by cool indifference.

Jer'ait turned back to Aliphei, considering. *If I don't go after Rri'jan, he will get away, the Regency seat will be given to another Huouyt and life will go on.* And Jer'ait was the only Peacemaker with the training and skill to find his brother and bring him back alive. The Watcher was right. All he had to do to utterly ruin the Geuji's plans was tell the Tribunal he had more important things to do with his life than chase after his criminally ambitious brother.

Yet he *burned* to see Rri'jan see justice. Ever since seeing his brother crowned, when Jer'ait, the elder, was condemned to death and sterilized, Jer'ait had lived on that fire. He had made it through Va'ga powered by that alone. It had kept him alive, kept him killing evildoers for the meager Congressional salary of four and a half thousand credits a rotation, kept him working with the Peacemakers when Representatives and corporations would have paid millions for his contracts. And yet, the Geuji knew that. If Jer'ait brought Rri'jan back, he would be playing into Forgotten's hands, who from the start assumed Jer'ait would *enjoy* bringing Rri'jan back, considering their history. And there were few things Jer'ait hated more than being a pawn.

At that, Jer'ait had a brief flash of his aging mentor, Ti'peth, who had sided—and died—with Na'leen, fifty-four turns ago. It had been one of the ancient assassin's mottos. *A pawn can wish itself to be a hand for all eternity, but in the end, it will still do as the hand guides it, for it is still a pawn.* Va'gans, however they wished otherwise, were pawns. Paid to work for the highest bidder, to accomplish another's will.

This was Jer'ait's chance to be the hand.

Yet, even as he had that thought, he had to wonder: Was the hand wrong?

Jer'ait thought of upsetting the board, of scattering the Geuji's pieces to the wind. Then he thought of Aez, a planet of radical, blood-thirsty zealots clamoring for war, simply disappearing from the political scene weeks before their insanity could boil over into the rest of the Old Territory. He thought of a hundred and thirty-four princes, all with history of rebellion, all but one with a penchant for violence and trading in sentient flesh, all lured to the same planet to die. He thought of a team of six whose lives were even then being used to kill what would otherwise have taken millions, in between living in the luxury of a Tribunal member's grace. He thought of a single sentient mold float-ing somewhere in the cold, lonely depths of space. He thought of the architects of Koliinaat, locked away in darkness and silence, betrayed and forgotten. Kept on Levren, rather than Koliinaat, because the Watcher could not be trusted.

"I'll do it," Jer'ait said. "But be warned—you might not like where this goes."

Aliphei made a dismissive motion with his big paw. "Just bring Rri'jan back here. We'll deal with his delinquencies as befits his station and crimes."

You grow complacent in your old age, Jer'ait thought. But he bowed low anyway. He thought he saw Mekkval's lip twitch again before he straight-ened. "Then I shall leave on the next flight out, your Excellencies. If you have further requests, please approach Koriel or Drannik."

"An Ooreiki and a Jahul," Mekkval said, seemingly bemused. "You do realize that the Peacemakers haven't seen anything but a Huouyt beyond Ninth Hjai in over a million turns?" The huge Dhasha cocked his massive head. "And even then, it was an accident. Quickly remedied."

Straightening, Jer'ait gave the Dhasha a long look. "Koriel and Drannik are two of the most brilliant minds under my command."

"So I've heard," Mekkval replied. "I also heard you threatened to kill the heads of all thirty-two Huouyt royal families, if they died, accidental or otherwise, within the next hundred turns."

"And interestingly enough," Jer'ait said, "they now each have an honor guard of six of the highest-paid Va'gans in Congress."

Mekkval clacked his jaws together in a Dhasha laugh. "You shake up a system that has worked for millions of turns, Jer'ait." There was no accusation in the Representative's words. Just...interest. And bemusement.

"Koriel and Drannik have each spent over two hundred turns as Ninth Hjai," Jer'ait replied. "It was time."

"Indeed," Mekkval said, thoughtfully, at the same time Prazeil snapped, "Go get the Huouyt, imbecile. No one cares about Peacemaker politics."

Jer'ait cocked his head up at the huge white Jreet, wondering why he was still alive. "Of course." He bowed again. "Your Excellencies." He turned to go find his brother, actually finding himself looking forward to the challenge.

Besides. He wanted to have a chat with his brother. He had questions for him.

· · ·

Rri'jan hesitated in the corridor of the shabby Jahul apartment complex, listening. For a moment, he thought he had heard footsteps, following him, but as he waited to hear it again, caught nothing but the sound of rain dribbling down the eaves to spatter against the filthy cobbles. Sighing, he looked back at the dilapidated, grimy structure that had been his sanctuary the last three days as he gathered information on the Geuji. It was a low-tech establishment, out near the Outer Line. He wore a Jahul pattern that was even then dripping a combination of excrement and water into the disgusting puddles of murky refuse at his feet. Monsoons were a problem on this planet, something that the Ueshi who owned it were petitioning to fix, though the survival of the primitive native flora and fauna had been stopping up the process with studies and permits for almost a hundred turns. Rri'jan's current pattern had been one of the scientists charged with collecting genetic material for analysis by Ueshi scientists on Koliinaat.

A Jahul, Rri'jan thought, looking down at himself disgustedly. If there was one pattern a Va'gan hated to take, it was a Jahul. They were the most physically revolting pattern of the Grand Six, if not all of Congress, and spent most of their time walking around in their own shit. That was, however, what had worked in his favor in his escape from Koliinaat. No Peacemaker blockader or Regency agent thought a Huouyt Representative would demean himself enough to take the pattern of a Jahul.

Forgotten will pay for this, Rri'jan thought. Ever since the Geuji's plans had failed—*failed*—and Mekkval had somehow linked it back to *him*, Rri'jan had been plotting Forgotten's demise.

And now, with his latest information on the Geuji's whereabouts, taken from an Ueshi mechanic on his deathbed, he was only days from his target.

Slow, he thought again, as he leaned back to pull his front two legs off the ground to reach the opening to his apartment. *It will be slow and painful.*

As it was, Forgotten was scheduled to be docked in Hub 13 of the Oriath spaceport in one week. Rri'jan had tracked him to this lonely corner of space, and intended to rid the universe of the pest once and for all before he disappeared for good. Probably on an Ueshi pleasure-planet. Kaleu had appealed to him, though it was a bit high-profile for his liking. Tholiba was the smarter choice. Large enough to get lost in the traffic, yet small enough that it wouldn't be on the Peacemakers' lists to search.

It was as Rri'jan fiddled with the corroded metal lock to his filthy hideaway that a camouflaged Jikaln paw slapped him across his neck and he felt a sting. Rri'jan immediately moved to contain and neutralize the poison—but not before he was hit in four more places, too many to counter. Rri'jan felt himself losing control, the chemicals dispersing into his system. In a wash of horror, he went limp.

"Jahul befits you, brother," a Jikaln voice rattled above him. "The shit compliments your lovely eyes." At that, Rri'jan was being dragged into the apartment he had just unlocked, then shut the door to the waterlogged alley behind them. The Jikaln propped him up against the wall and regarded him, his body blending so perfectly with the wall and shabby shelves behind him that the four-legged alien was almost impossible to see. "Where is he?"

For a startled moment, Rri'jan thought that his attacker had mistaken him for an underling. "Rri'jan went to Kaleu," he said. "He sent me here as a decoy."

The Jikaln chuckled, making his shape blur before re-solidifying to that of the wall once more. "Forgotten, brother. I want to know where he is before I take you back to face the Tribunal."

"I'm not your brother," Rri'jan snapped, furious that he had somehow allowed his caution to lapse enough for a Congressional lackey to find him. "Watch your pretensions, Peacemaker. When it comes to blood-merit, we are not even of the same solar-system."

"And that," the Jikaln-patterned Huouyt said, "is where you are wrong, brother."

Rri'jan froze, a wash of fury almost twisting him out of pattern with its intensity. "You lie." The thought that the mutated *scum* had the audacity to touch *him*, the royal heir to the Ze'laa...Jer'ait's days were numbered. Either that, or it was another assassin's tactic to unnerve him, make him say something stupid.

"Do I?" the Huouyt asked. He moved again, his predatory outline once again blurring against the wall before he faded back into his surroundings, only his yellow eyes showing. "Since you killed all but one brother in your scramble for the Ze'laa throne," his captor acceded, "I suppose you're right...the chances are small I would be the one who managed to escape your ambition for all these turns."

It was the first time Rri'jan had looked his brother in the eyes since his crowning, and it left his zora cold. Jer'ait was not what he had imagined. Four hundred turns had given the reject...presence.

Then, realizing it was just his nerves and overactive imagination, Rri'jan forced himself to laugh. "You won't kill me. You bow and scrape to the Peacemaster like the lapdog you are."

The Huouyt continued to watch him flatly. "Why are you seeking Forgotten?"

Rri'jan found his brother's ignorance to be amusing. "He planned it all, you know. Neskfaat. Aez. Mekkval. Everything."

Jer'ait cocked his head and his attention sharpened. "Oh?" he asked, his curiosity as painfully clear as a child's.

The outclassed moron. "Used you like a pawn," Rri'jan sneered. "The whole time, you danced like a puppet to his whim. All that, everything that happened on Neskfaat, was to pick the team that would kill Mekkval."

"Which failed." The furg actually had the lack of discipline to sound confused.

"As the Trith so clearly demonstrated one and a half million turns ago," Rri'jan laughed, "not even a Geuji can predict the future."

"And why should we believe it was the Geuji when *you* were the one implicated?" Jer'ait asked. He picked at a cloth-covered lump of fermented grain, trying amateurishly to look disinterested in the conversation, which he was in all likelihood recording.

"What better scapegoat for the Geuji's foiled plans than the Huouyt?" Rri'jan demanded. "His plan—whatever it was—failed, and now he needs to remove himself from the limelight before the universe gets wind of what he's done."

"Oh?" Jer'ait asked. "Why would he do that?"

"So he can go back to skulking in shadows like the coward he is," Rri'jan snapped. "Don't test my patience, lapdog. The Geuji is setting up the Huouyt as his fall-men so that he can return to hiding. The less the universe knows about him, the safer he is."

"And what," Jer'ait asked, lifting the stinking Jahul food-object to look at it distractedly, "would Forgotten have against the Huouyt?"

"Study the history books, furg," Rri'jan sneered. "This was Forgotten's way of getting even for what happened to the Geuji on Neskfaat." There, let *that* lead his ignorant brother astray.

Jer'ait dropped the cloth bundle back to the shelf. This time, his voice was flat as any Va'gan's, his intelligence unmistakable. "Then we are to simply overlook the fact you were the one with the most motive, and that Mekkval's death would have eased your way back to the Tribunal with minimum effort on your part?"

Rri'jan's face darkened. "The Regency has nothing to hold against me, Jer'ait. They have no proof except the confession of one tortured Human. I was on my way to assassinate the bigger threat. It will hold up before the Tribunal. Release me now, so that I may finish the job, or when I go free, you and Forgotten will *both* die."

"Generally, in order to make decent threats, one must have something substantial to back them," Jer'ait said. He moved forward, hurting the eyes as his outline shifted against the wall. "Tell me what you know of the Geuji."

Rri'jan smiled, happy to take the Geuji down with him. "I know he will be in Hub 13 of the Oriath spaceport in eight days," Rri'jan said. "A communications overhaul on his long-distance array."

For a Peacemaker whose organization had been trying to capture the Geuji for three hundred and four turns, Jer'ait seemed disappointingly unaffected by the news. "Ah." Then his captor leaned forward and touched him again, and Rri'jan embraced oblivion.

32

GOING STRAIGHT

Eight days after sending Rri'jan back to Koliinaat with an escort of his best men, Jer'ait stood alone against one wall of Hub 13 of the Oriath spaceport, watching the arrival lists for something that stood out from the rest. It was late, and his quarry had not yet shown himself. Several ships had ordered 'minor repairs' throughout the day, but all checked out to be legitimate debris hits or minor trading scuffles. Jer'ait was beginning to think that Rri'jan had sent him on a furg's errand when the Jahul trader *Silence* pulled into the dock and he felt his attention sharpen.

Communications troubles, was its listed docking complaint.

The ship mated with the hub and the airlock synched and the light above the entrance flashed READY, but for long hours, the door remained closed. No agents came or went. No repairmen went to work on the ship's exterior. Aside from the flashing READY sign, signaling that the ship had equalized its systems in preparation for passenger exchange, there was no change.

Hours came and went, and still the lock flashed READY.

Eventually, once the crowds had died down for the day and it was only Jer'ait and a few scattered passengers in the hub, the Ueshi docking authority seated in the booth nearby frowned at the flashing light, glanced at the docking manifest, and then opened a line to the Jahul ship. "Are you also experiencing issues with your airlock, *Silence?*"

"*Negative*," a Jahul voice replied apologetically. "*I'm waiting for someone, sir.*"

He's expecting me, Jer'ait realized, with a breja-crushing wave of unease.

The Ueshi chuckled. "It seems your friend needs to synch his time-chip. You've been waiting on him for six hours."

"*Has it been that long?*" the Jahul replied. "*I was busy drafting a letter.*" Again, perfect Bovan Jahul.

"More like six and a half," the Ueshi port master confirmed. "Would you like me to patch you through to a planetside location?"

"*No, sir. I'm sure he's on his way.*"

Steeling himself, Jer'ait pushed himself from the wall and took a few steps towards the Geuji's lonely, flashing airlock, then hesitated in the center of the room, exposed and vulnerable.

When no laser fire singled him out, no plasma cut him down, no assassins lurched forth to strike, Jer'ait took a deep breath and made his way to the Geuji's lock.

The door opened the moment he stepped within range. If the Ueshi manning the docking booth noticed that Jer'ait had never touched the control screen to activate the door, he never mentioned it. Feeling his breja prickling at the complexities of casually hacking into the port authority's system, Jer'ait stepped closer and, fighting nerves, looked inside.

Seeing the utterly alien-looking airlock waiting through the open door, Jer'ait had a flash of uncertainty. Forgotten could have installed anything at all on his ship. From robotics to drugs to biological agents to unspeakable alien weaponry. If he proceeded with this meeting, he was, quite literally, placing his life in the Geuji's hands. Without backup. Without a soul even knowing where he was. He, the Peacemaster, was about to be completely at Forgotten's mercy.

He continued to hesitate, eying the blackness beyond. This was where he tested his theory. With his life.

Though Jer'ait knew the Geuji could see him and, if he wanted to, speak through the microphones lining the lock, Forgotten said nothing.

Jer'ait steeled himself, then stepped into the airlock.

Immediately, the hub door dripped shut behind him and there was a slight discomfort at the equalization of pressure, then the door to the ship opened on the other side, revealing a brightly-lit corridor leading into the Geuji's ship.

Very carefully, Jer'ait stepped out of the darkened airlock and into the light. He jumped when the alien door slid shut behind him, trapping him on the ship with the Geuji. The sterile hall was brightly lit and eerily silent.

"Hello," the Geuji said, seemingly from the ship itself. It was a voice that Jer'ait couldn't quite pinpoint as being from one species, but more a mix of several.

Jer'ait waited in a wary silence.

When he did not reply with similar courtesies, the Geuji prodded, "I assume you have questions."

Jer'ait said nothing, quietly wondering what in the ninety Jreet hells he had been thinking, stepping on a Geuji ship alone. The hall was unlike anything he had ever seen before, its construction familiar, yet at the same time, nerve-wrackingly different. He found himself fighting the urge to back up to the exit as he eyed the surrounding hall, trying not to let his unease show.

"I've been looking forward to this meeting with you for several turns," Forgotten said. "And I'll admit that it's been with a disconcerting combination of fear, excitement, and anxiety."

Forgotten was obviously trying to put him at ease. There was nothing for the Geuji to fear, and they both knew it. Jer'ait had simply been stupid. Merciful dead, he'd been stupid. Stupid, stupid, stupid...

"I'm not going to hurt you," Forgotten said softly.

Jer'ait felt his breja ripple in a rush of relief before he got it back under control. "I appreciate that," he said warily, still backed carefully against the airlock.

"It is rare to meet a Huouyt with a conscience," Forgotten offered.

"And you still haven't," Jer'ait snorted. He eyed the empty corridor, half expecting a rush of robots to emerge and carve out his zora. "What do you want, Geuji?"

"Why were you in the hub, waiting for me, alone and unarmed?"

"I asked first."

"To talk."

"My desires were similar," Jer'ait admitted. He surreptitiously glanced at the control panel of the airlock and was unsurprised to find that the controls were in no language he had ever encountered.

"Relax, Jer'ait," the Geuji's ship urged. "I see no reason why we can't humor each other."

"A Va'gan does not relax." Jer'ait nonetheless stopped trying to puzzle out the airlock controls and returned his attention to the empty corridor itself.

"Here, on my ship, you have no reason not to," Forgotten told him. "We both know that, should my intentions have been nefarious, you would be dead now. Vigilance or no."

Jer'ait knew as much, of course, but to be reminded of it rankled.

"But, if it would make you feel better," Forgotten said, "I'll invite you into my chambers for the duration of our discussion."

Jer'ait's curiosity was piqued, despite himself. He had always wanted to see a Geuji close up. The containment systems that Aliphei had in place on Levren were so strict that the paperwork to achieve clearance had never been worth it for him. "Very well," he said warily.

"Third hall on the right, sixth door down," the Geuji told him.

Jer'ait took three steps down the alien hallway before a little eight-legged robot seemingly unfolded from the wall itself and began skittering ahead of him as a guide. Clearly distinguishable from the robot's carapace were unmistakable gun turrets. *So much for the Geuji being peaceful*, Jer'ait thought, despite himself. He hesitated, once again wondering what the hell he was thinking.

"I will not hurt you," the Geuji said again.

"Is that what you told my brother, when you embroiled him in this mess?" Jer'ait demanded.

"Your brother requested this mess," Forgotten said. "And, as you will see in our taped conversation, I never made him any promises. You, I will not harm."

Jer'ait's interest piqued at mention of documented proof of Rri'jan's wrongdoing. "Will you let me take the recording with me, when I leave?"

"Of course."

That, alone, was worth braving the dangers of this visit. Reluctantly, Jer'ait stepped deeper into the corridor and took the third hall on the right. Then he counted doors until he arrived at the one suggested by the Geuji. He waited several moments, but nothing happened.

"I'm here," he finally muttered, feeling stupid.

"I know," Forgotten said. "I'm trying to work up the courage to let you in."

Which, despite its ludicrousness, rang with truth. Jer'ait waited curiously. Tics passed.

"This is very hard for me," Forgotten whispered.

Jer'ait cocked his head. "If I didn't know better, Geuji, I would almost say you're telling the truth."

"I am," Forgotten replied. "Just hold on a moment, please." The black, alien portal before him remained closed.

Jer'ait examined the door, both complimented by the Geuji's fear and concerned by its ridiculousness. "What makes *you* afraid of *me*?"

"Aside from the fact that you can kill me with a touch?"

"You could most likely kill me with a thought," Jer'ait said. "If I were an outsider wagering on this meeting, I would place my bet with you, Geuji."

"Is it a contest?" Forgotten asked softly.

"No," Jer'ait said. Then, when the door continued to remain shut, Jer'ait said tentatively, "I won't hurt you, Geuji. There's been enough of that."

Several seconds later, the door slid open, though hesitantly, as if the ship itself shared the Geuji's reluctance.

On the other side of the portal, a bedroom-sized chamber was hung, floor-to-ceiling, with living black flesh. It moved and glistened in the light, with no identifiable features, a formless ebony mold that was continuing its glacially slow march across the intentionally rough walls. The ceiling itself was a display of ever-changing images...sometimes sky and clouds, sometimes forests, sometimes mountainscapes, sometimes sunrises. The soft sound of breeze, the chatter of fauna, and the crash of waves set a smooth ambiance in the background. Even with the sounds and color, however, the place looked depressingly... lonely.

"Highly accurate," Jer'ait offered, recognizing the scenery of Neskfaat. Then he checked himself and gave a wan smile. "Well, until PlanOps covered it with bodies."

"Thank you." The words were tight. Highly controlled.

Jer'ait realized, startled, that the Geuji was telling the truth. He was *terrified*. "You think I'm going to kill you," he said. Which he found odd, because he had no intention of doing so whatsoever.

"Not exactly," Forgotten said softly.

"What, then?" Jer'ait demanded. "You quiver like a frightened Ueshi, Geuji." He gestured at the way the room itself seemed to glisten and shift with the Geuji's thoughts.

"You know that my plans with Mekkval did not go awry," Forgotten hedged.

"Of course," Jer'ait snorted. "That's why I'm here right now, listening to you prattle, instead of quarantining your ship with a specialized ship-storming crew."

Forgotten hesitated. "May I ask how you knew?"

"The Watcher told me."

"...oh." The room was silent for almost a tic. Jer'ait could sense the Geuji's desperation to know more, yet also his fear of letting his desires known.

"I'll spare you the guessing," Jer'ait said. "He told me that your plan from the beginning was to give Mekkval a team that could kill Dhasha princes quietly and effectively, that you intended to meet me, and that all I would have had to do to foil your plans would be to give the assignment to hunt my brother to an Eleventh Hjai."

"And you've guessed the rest."

Jer'ait laughed. "I have no misconceptions about being able to guess the 'rest,' no. But I anticipate some of it, I'm sure."

Though the physical cues were subtle, the Geuji seemed to relax somewhat. "It does not bother you, what I plan for the Huouyt?"

"I can't say I'm very impressed with my own people," Jer'ait said.

"But they *are* your people," Forgotten insisted. On the screen above them, the view shifted to the ancient stone cityscape of Morinth's capital, something that Jer'ait had not seen in almost four hundred turns.

Seeing it, Jer'ait's eyes narrowed in irritation. "They sterilized me in public and slated me for execution the next day. They can rot."

Forgotten was silent a long moment. Then, "I can remedy that."

Jer'ait stiffened. "If this is some way to ingratiate yourself to me—"

"No," Forgotten said. "I'd expect nothing. I'd simply be righting a wrong."

"By drugging me and having your way with my body."

"When you put it that way, Huouyt, it almost sounds entertaining."

For the first time since stepping aboard the ship, Jer'ait was truly shaken. "You'd simply *do* it. No favors requested. No future tasks to be fulfilled."

"Yes."

Jer'ait narrowed his eyes. "No implants left behind."

"Again, Jer'ait, if I'd wanted to do as much, I could do so without even your knowledge. I only offer because, for me, it would be a simple thing. I have a feeling, though, that for you, it would mean much more."

"And my eye?" Jer'ait asked. "Can you fix that, as well?"

Forgotten hesitated. Around him, the room rippled. Then, "I will not alter your eye."

"But you *could*," Jer'ait insisted.

"I won't."

"Then the rumors are true," Jer'ait muttered. "The eye...changes... things."

"It does."

Jer'ait took a deep breath and looked away, his deformity once more weighing on his soul. Finally, he said, "Like I said, Geuji, I am not impressed by my people. I have little interest in breeding more of them."

"The offer remains open, should I survive this," Forgotten said softly.

Jer'ait's attention sharpened and he glanced back at the Geuji. "Survive what?"

Forgotten hesitated a moment. Then, quietly, he said, "Whatever happens, I want you to know, personally, that this is my attempt to go on the straight and level. No tricks. If they deal with me honorably, then I will return the favor. I…wish to test a theory."

"Forgive me if I am confused," Jer'ait said, frowning. "If *who* deals with you honorably?"

The Geuji's silence seemed to go on forever. "Any of them." Then, heedless of Jer'ait's confusion, Forgotten went on, "From here onward, Huouyt, the rest of our meeting is going to be recorded."

As Jer'ait frowned at that, but before he could comment, Forgotten went on in a formal, ringing voice, "Jer'ait Ze'laa vehn Morinth, seventeenth of his name, rightful heir to the Morinthian throne, Peacemaster of Congress, brother of Rri'jan Ze'laa, Va'gan specialist with highest honors…" Forgotten hesitated for several moments. Then, "I have a confession to make."

• • •

Rri'jan shifted boredly in his Regency seat, awaiting the arrival of the Tribunal. It was a closed session, probably because the Dhasha coward didn't want the rest of Congress to know how close he had come to dying in his own den. That, alone, was amusing enough to have been worth the hassle with Neskfaat.

When his three peers arrived, it was as Rri'jan expected. They each sat down without files or any other references in front of them. They had built their case on the dying wind of a tortured Human. They *had* no case.

"I see your evidence is rather slim," Rri'jan said. He yawned. "Can we get on with this? I have a vetun game with Gervin this afternoon. I wouldn't want to be late."

"Consider it cancelled," the Jreet Representative said. "Permanently."

Rri'jan sat up, his breja attempting to twist in agitation. "That almost sounded like a threat, worm." He cocked his head. "*Was* that a threat?"

"Rri'jan Ze'laa vehn Morinth," the First Citizen intoned, before the fool Jreet could respond, "you are hereby charged with violating the First Law of Congress. This is the second time in fifty-four turns that a Huouyt Representative has been accused of this heinous crime. In fact, the last accused was your predecessor, Representative Na'leen. That the violations were back-to-back does not go unnoticed by this body, and, as such, your punishment will be more severe."

"*Alleged* violations," Rri'jan said, amused.

"We'll see," the Jreet replied. He almost sounded...smug.

Rri'jan wondered idly what kind of 'evidence' they could have cobbled together from his complete lack of involvement. Aside from that two and a half hour conversation with the Geuji, Rri'jan had done nothing. There were no links to trace back to him, no clandestine check-ins, no furtive messages, no bank withdrawals. He had seen to it himself that all who had accompanied him on the trip to hunt down the Geuji a turn before were dead. And the Human, pawn that she was, had never met him, nor any of his people, nor had she received any payments from his accounts. There simply *was* nothing to trace back to him.

This time, it was Mekkval—his accuser—who spoke. "As we speak, evidence of your crimes is being broadcast to every member of the Regency."

That made Rri'jan sit up. "*What* evidence?"

Immediately, a recording of himself, discussing the plan to kill Mekkval with Forgotten, began playing over his podium. Rri'jan immediately dismissed it. "A fake." He snorted. "Is that all you have to level against me, *esteemed* Representatives?"

Mekkval and the First Citizen glanced at each other. Aliphei nodded.

"We have a confession," Mekkval began.

"You'll need better than that," Rri'jan laughed. "Words gathered in the heat of torture are useless in trial."

"How about words given freely, under no duress or mental impairment?" a Morinthian Huouyt said nearby. The nearest closed booth opened inward to reveal the glistening ebony form of a Geuji.

Rri'jan was so stunned he could only stare. Forgotten? *Here?*

"Speechless, for once," Mekkval commented wryly.

"I admit it has its appeal," the First Citizen said.

"Let's see the stupid furg dance words now," Prazeil added.

"As we agreed in the terms of my surrender," the Geuji continued, "I shall receive a full pardon by the Tribunal for all of my crimes to date. Further, you will give my people access to all incoming news and entertainment channels and install reliable and consistent means of conversation between each other, permanently, to be monitored by an independent species preservation society, or my confession ends here."

"It will be done," Mekkval said solemnly. "You have my word."

"Very well, then," Forgotten went on. "I am uploading all corresponding documentation, records, receipts, and transaction reports that involve this case to your podiums now. They are clearly labeled and can be cross-referenced with the report I am also submitting with them. As each piece of evidence is addressed in my testimony, I will highlight it for your records. My confession will begin just over a turn ago. On the 3rd Turn of the 860th Age of the Jreet, Rri'jan approached me with a fleet of fifty-seven—"

"This is a *hoax*," Rri'jan shrieked. "We all know the damn Geuji would never surrender. He's been a thorn in Congress's side for three hundred turns."

"Be silent," Mekkval said coolly, "or I will silence you."

"—personally-acquired warships. See Items A1 through A-44, detailing purchase, outfitting, and types of ships he used. I will pause to allow you time to examine the evidence."

"We've already previewed it," the First Citizen said. "You may continue."

"Once his forces surrounded me," Forgotten said, "Rri'jan let it be known that he came to me requesting my help to gain a seat on the Tribunal, video and audioclips of which can be accessed as B1 through B7 in your evidence packets…"

Rri'jan listened, disgusted, as Forgotten once again repeated his plan, this time with the added details of Rri'jan's exact words and reactions to each proposed twist. Rri'jan dropped to his seat in impotent rage. He stopped listening by the fourth hour.

"If you will notice," Forgotten finished, after the Watcher had made them take several food-breaks to keep from starving during his endless monologue, "as each stage of this plan came to fruition—most visibly the destruction of Aez, the accumulation of Dhasha princes on Neskfaat, and Planetary Ops' debilitating losses—your good Representative did absolutely nothing to voice his concerns to the Regency."

"Proof of my innocence!" Rri'jan snapped, unable to take the sham any longer.

"What I want to know," Prazeil snarled, "is why you destroyed my home."

For a moment, Rri'jan felt a surge of triumph, thinking that the Jreet's wrath was focused on Forgotten. Then, with a rush of startlement, he realized Prazeil was looking at *him*.

"Aez was a target of opportunity," Forgotten said. "It would have been too dangerous to leave a planet of fervent, impassioned, dedicated warriors as skilled and determined as the Aezi alive during a period of political unrest and instability as crucial for the Huouyt's eventual ascension to a secure and stable throne as was the last turn, and after a long, thorough examination of the facts at hand, it was decided that their neutralization could not wait until after the Regency's power-structure was reorganized to Huouyt liking, and had to be attended to before the Dhasha created a very visible and powerful distraction in the heart of Congress, lest our plan leave much of the Old Territory embroiled in a bitter war that would engulf dozens of innocent planets and undermine the very structure Rri'jan wished to rule."

"You can't even understand what he's saying," Rri'jan snapped. "I move to dismiss his entire, twisted testimony as unclear and indecipherable gibberish."

"Paraphrase," Aliphei commanded of the Geuji.

"The Aezi would have created trouble, so we decided to remove Aez from the equation."

"Don't implicate me in that!" Rri'jan snapped, even as the Jreet stiffened and rose from his white coils with rage. "Aez was not my idea! I *questioned* Aez."

"Then you were there," Mekkval suggested, voice utterly cold.

"I have no idea what he's talking about," Rri'jan snapped. "I never asked him to get me a throne."

"Then you admit to the rest of the conspiracy?"

"No, *none* of this was my idea!" Rri'jan snapped. "He did it all!"

"But you bought his cooperation with a promise to free his people," Aliphei noted. "And he says your ultimate intent was to rearrange the power-structure of Congress to better suit your liking. With you enthroned at its head, of course."

"The Geuji is *lying*," Rri'jan screamed, slamming his fist into the podium. "Can't you see that?"

"Odd," Mekkval replied, "when historically, it is the *Geuji* who are known for their distaste for lies, and the *Huouyt* have the reputation of being unable to tell the truth."

Rri'jan turned to scowl at his peer. "You almost speak as if you have already made up your mind, Dhasha."

"Oh, I have," Mekkval said coldly.

It was at that point that, looking at the impassive faces of other two Tribunal members, the horrible truth of the situation dawned upon him. "You're going to convict me."

"Shall we skip the rest of the formalities and move on to sentencing?" Aliphei asked. "I have an appointment with my masseuse this evening."

"We should at least take a vote," Mekkval said, sounding amused. "Prazeil? Aliphei? I vote to condemn."

"And I," Aliphei replied. Rri'jan's breja fluttered at the finality of what had just happened to him. The Tribunal only needed two to condemn.

"And I," Prazeil growled, lurching up to almost two rods in height. "Rest assured, Huouyt, whatever sentence is offered you, I will purchase your contract and make you dance on my tek."

"That might be difficult, considering you no longer have a planet backing you, worm," Rri'jan snapped, beyond reason, now.

"The sentence," Aliphei said, "shall befit your crime and station. For your repeated crimes as a species, the Huouyt will be henceforth banned from the Tribunal."

"Agreed," Mekkval said.

"Agreed," Prazeil barked. "May the Huouyt shrivel and die like the sun-fearing cowards they are."

Rri'jan could only stare. "Did you just say...*banned*?"

"Shall I look up the definition for you?" Mekkval asked, sounding amused.

"In the history of Congress, no species has been *banned* from the Tribunal," Rri'jan snapped. "That's *ludicrous*."

"We thought it was fitting," Mekkval said, his huge, oblong jaw open in a smirk, showing rows upon rows of triangular black teeth. "You are, after all, the species to come up again and again, in interspecies conflicts."

Rri'jan ignored the Dhasha's taunt. "If you're going to ban the Huouyt, ban the Dhasha, too. It is *their* rebellions that drain Congressional funds and necessitate the Draft."

"As far as I was aware," Aliphei said, "the Dhasha are not on trial, here,"

"The Huouyt have been with Congress since we formed it!" Rri'jan snapped. "You can't *ban* us, furgs."

"I was reading the Tribunal charter last night," Mekkval said idly, "and it says we can."

"Further," Aliphei said, "there is the matter of your *personal* punishment, Rri'jan."

"Kill him!" Prazeil roared. "Give him to me and I shall make him squeal like a gutted melaa before he dies."

"Rri'jan sought money and power," Aliphei went on. "I vote we send this ambitious vaghi to a place where he can witness both, for the rest of his existence, as a slave."

"Where were you thinking?" Mekkval asked, his attention sharpening.

"I say we kill him," Prazeil snapped. "I'll do the honors myself. I'll make the coward scream until his grandmothers cringe in their—"

"Yes, we heard you," Rri'jan snapped, intently focused on the First Citizen and the Dhasha. They were the two he needed to concern himself with. The Jreet was a bumbling clown.

"It would please me greatly to see this selfish furg rehabilitated," Mekkval offered, meeting Rri'jan's stare pointedly. "Satisfying, even."

"Yes! Make him grovel! Then we shall soak the earth in his blood and hunt down his kinfolk for their part in his crimes."

"I was thinking the same," Aliphei said calmly.

"Where?" Mekkval asked.

"On a platform in the center of the Regency!" Prazeil cried. "I will sharpen my tek so that he quivers, then cleanse him personally, so all may watch."

"There are several options," Aliphei said thoughtfully. "All of which are appealing."

"An Ueshi pleasure-slave?" Mekkval asked, his scaly face alighting in amusement.

Rri'jan watched Mekkval and Aliphei in fury, promising himself that, wherever the furgs sent him, he would slip free of his wardens' grasp and return to see them both die painfully. He was not worried about the Jreet. The Jreet he could kill the moment he tried to wrap him in his coils. It was these two who had the intelligence to be the ringleaders in this operation.

"How about a ruvmestin mine," Aliphei said. "Grakkas, perhaps."

The furglings send me to Grakkas, Rri'jan thought, fighting a smirk, *and I will be back on a shuttle within a night.* He schooled his face into the picture of horror. "You can't do that."

"His zora must be removed, of course," Mekkval suggested.

Rri'jan froze, all of his smugness draining out his feet in a wash of horror. No matter where they sent him, he could escape—if he had his zora. If he *didn't*, he was just another criminal. Just another stagnant, trapped creature to be ushered about. "That barbaric punishment was outlawed millennia ago," he blurted.

"Not outlawed," Mekkval said, sounding amused. "Frowned upon."

"Why should we bother maiming him?" Prazeil demanded, giving his companions a confused glance. "Are you *afraid* of this tekless betrayer, Dhasha?"

"I was thinking more of his capacity to elude Congressional forces, once he is tucked away to serve penance," the Dhasha responded.

"There will be no 'eluding'," Prazeil snapped. "He will not leave his trial alive."

"We'll see," Mekkval said, watching Rri'jan intently. "Watcher, remove his zora. Authorized by myself."

"And I," Aliphei said.

"As you command, your Excellencies."

Rri'jan stiffened as he felt something shift within him, then all the sensation of a limb disappeared. With it, he lost everything. The sensory organs that could activate and direct his body were simply...gone.

In that moment, Rri'jan's life simply crashed down around his shoulders, leaving him naked and terrified before his accusers.

But Mekkval wasn't done. "I say we let the Huouyt decide," the Dhasha continued. "Death by tek or rehabilitation by servitude."

"The craven weakling does not get to choose!" Prazeil snapped. "It was *my* planet he destroyed. He shall therefore dance on *my* tek."

"Choose," Aliphei commanded, watching him coldly.

And, in that moment, Rri'jan realized that the more pleasant outcome, for him, would be the Jreet's suggestion.

More pleasant...but infinitely more short.

Rri'jan stared at Aliphei, then Mekkval, humiliated, hopeless, furious that they were going to make him choose between slavery and execution. He, a Ze'laa royal. A Representative of *Congress*. They had maimed him. Impotized him before the entire universe. He was so stunned and wretchedly degraded that he couldn't find the words to speak.

"For what it's worth," the Geuji said into the silence that followed, "You never stood a chance, Rri'jan. Bow and accept the terms given. You can still save yourself."

"Enough!" Prazeil snapped. "The slime-mold is done here. Watcher, remove him to his cell."

Forgotten had just enough time to say a startled, "But we agreed—" before his disgusting mass vanished. Rri'jan felt a satisfied ripple of his breja knowing that he would not be the only one whose plans were ruined, but it was short-lived. Once again, he was left facing his three cold-eyed peers, facing a choice no Huouyt should have to make. Steeling himself, knowing that alive—albeit humiliated—was better than righteous and dead, Rri'jan whispered, "Send me to Grakkas, you miserable furgs."

"I hear the ruvmestin mines," Aliphei commented.

"I'll buy his contract," Prazeil retorted. "There will be no Grakkas."

"You and what economy?" Rri'jan retorted, unable to hold back his disdain. "In case you forgot, *Aezi*, there is nothing left for you to use to purchase my servitude."

"A Congressional Representative would require an inordinately high bid," Aliphei conceded. "I'm afraid you don't have the funds, Jreet."

"Make an exception!" Prazeil snapped. "It was *my* planet the sniveling vaghi destroyed. *I* should be able to mete out justice."

"If Tribunal members flaunted the rules we made, what stability would there be in our great nation?" Aliphei asked pointedly. Then, to Mekkval, "What say you?"

The Dhasha, who had said nothing up until that point, continued watching Rri'jan and said, "Ka-par."

Instantly, the Jreet reared up with a roar of fury, his ivory scales arching two and a half rods over the proceedings. "There will be no ka-par! The Huouyt is *mine*."

For a moment, the room was tense, waiting for the First Citizen to weigh in on the matter. When he did, it was with great reluctance.

"The Dhasha are allowed ka-par as part of their species' cultural concessions," Aliphei said slowly. "But if he accepts, then the rules of ka-par shall stand. He would take your place if he won, Mekkval."

"He won't win," Mekkval said, the prince's confidence like an immobile mountain, crushing him.

Rri'jan felt his breja curl at the idea of being indentured to a Dhasha. *That* Dhasha.

"I will not allow it," Prazeil snarled. "By the seventh hell, you will *not* take this prize from me, Mekkval."

"He is my prize, too," Mekkval retorted. "It is *I* that the Huouyt sought to assassinate. It is I who will rise to his challenge. If he is man enough to face the consequences of his own actions."

"My *blood* before you steal the Huouyt," Prazeil snapped. "I will not waste my breath with allowances or compromises. I *will* be given what is owed."

"Then I ka-par you first, the Huouyt after," Mekkval replied calmly, still watching Rri'jan with intensity.

Rri'jan felt himself freeze, along with every other creature in the room. Silence reigned absolute for several moments, the ramification of the Dhasha's words settling over them like a cold blanket. Then, "You are challenging the Jreet to ka-par?" Aliphei demanded sharply.

"If he has the tek to accept," the Dhasha replied, sounding utterly calm. He turned to Prazeil. "*Do* you have the tek to accept, Prazeil?"

Prazeil reared to his full height in a snarl. "How *dare* you suggest I do not."

Mekkval made an amused sound. "That doesn't answer the question, Jreet."

For a long moment, no one spoke.

The Jreet continued to tower over them like a sinuous statue, poised to strike.

"Well?" Mekkval said, into the dangerous silence. "I would love to add your...passion...to my retinue. Ka-par?"

Long moments passed. Then tics. Then, in a snarl, Prazeil said, "The Jreet do not caper to the ridiculous customs of Dhasha."

"Of course," Mekkval chuckled.

At that, the Jreet snarled, "Do as you will with the Huouyt. It's obvious you two plan to overrule me. Watcher, my quarters." At that, the Jreet flashed out of existence, leaving only Mekkval and Aliphei in attendance. For a brief moment, Rri'jan had a flash of hope that he could possibly divide the remaining votes, giving him a non-verdict and possibly a stay of execution.

Then the Dhasha swiveled his huge, rainbow-scaled head back to face him and his deep emerald eyes once again settled on Rri'jan, and Rri'jan felt his breja quiver with his first real fear since the trial began.

"Ka-par," Mekkval offered.

Rri'jan could not best Mekkval in ka-par. The Dhasha had made thousands, and he had never lost.

"Refuse," Mekkval warned him, "and I will buy your contract anyway. I own fourteen planets, whereas Prazeil was the chosen politician of one. I could outbid him, even before you destroyed his people."

Rri'jan shuddered with rage. "I would see you spend a fortune to obtain me rather than give you that satisfaction," he whispered.

"And, in the end, I will still obtain you," Mekkval replied. "And your life will be rougher for it."

Rri'jan glanced to the First Citizen, who was simply watching the proceedings with distracted interest. He glanced at the Jreet's seat, which was now vacant, then at the darkened walls that hid the rest of the Regency from view. Swallowing, he turned back to the Dhasha, whose gaze had never wavered.

"Ka-par," he whispered.

Immediate satisfaction tightened the Dhasha's features. "Ka-par rak'tal," he said, in the barking Dhasha tongue. "Ka-par accepted. Mahid ka-par."

Then the Dhasha's intensity sharpened and all Rri'jan's hopes of escaping the trial with his freedom intact diminished to nothing.

33

SAM

He was in the midst of examining strange inconsistencies between the confession the Geuji had given the Tribunal and the copy the Watcher had logged in Forgotten's record when he came across a file that made him look twice.

It read, *Samuel Dobbs, Human, a.k.a. The Ghost—Illicit Genetics Experiments.*

Inside the file, Jer'ait found even more interesting information. Somehow, Joe's brother had hacked into what was suspected to be an illegal Earth military experiment to duplicate the Huouyt ability to shift form. Peacemakers had been catching hints of illegal experiments on Earth for almost five turns, but capturing Samuel—a *civilian*—was the first real proof that Jer'ait's colleagues had that the Human government was participating in unsanctioned genetic alterations with the intent of creating mutant foot soldiers. Which, if it were true, would damn Earth back to its Dark Ages—there were few laws of Congress that, if broken, would spell the swift and violent end for a civilization, but genetic alterations with the intent to create living weaponry was one of them. It was the Second Law of Congress, and if Jer'ait was reading the reports correctly, Humanity was well on its way to breaking it.

With, to all appearances, the intent of breaking the First Law of Congress and using it to incite war against fellow member planets.

Humans, as Jer'ait had discovered through a two-rotation crash-course in Human idiosyncrasies—were stubborn to the point of being stupid, foolhardy to the point of being courageous, and optimistic to the point of being insane.

Bemused, he read on. The moment the Peacemakers detained Sam, they knew he was the key to rooting out the Human experiments. His DNA had become a multi-species stew, and his very existence was dangerously close to violating the Second Law of Congress. With questioning, they discovered Sam had somehow located the Human government files that the Peacemakers had been desperate to find. His information, however, was grudging and sketchy, usually pulled out of him with pain, and the genetic alterations had not only immunized him to interrogators' drugs, but had also increased his already-extraordinary intellectual capacity to the point he was consistently able to talk circles around his questioners, even Va'ga-trained Huouyt.

From what little Sam *had* said of the original experiment files, every test subject had died gruesomely, their genetics regurgitating all Huouyt influence, resulting in a quivering puddle of unidentifiable flesh.

Yet somehow, Samuel had taken the information, modified the experiments, and made them work.

On himself.

Where the others had devolved, he'd stabilized. He was the only test subject to ever do so. Joe's brother, it appeared, was some sort of genius. Jer'ait read on, intrigued.

What he found deeper within the file, however, left him stunned.

Samuel was still alive.

Peacemakers, desperate to locate the illicit Human military experiments, had faked his death. Jer'ait's peers wanted to know how he'd succeeded in his experiments, and since Samuel had destroyed all of his records before his capture, they were frantically trying to get the details from him. He was being held in a supersecret facility on Earth—the Peacemakers were so serious about keeping his existence a secret that they hadn't even taken the chance to ship him to Levren for questioning.

Jer'ait closed the file. *Joe's going to love this.*

• • •

"Oh, Mothers' ghosts!" Joe snapped, turning on the light. Beside him, the Congie Prime he'd invited over for dinner moaned and rolled in her sleep. "Daviin, can't you leave me alone for two seconds?"

"Sorry," Daviin said, looking not at all sorry. "We have orders."

Joe rolled his eyes and lay back down. "Burn them and their orders."

"No," Daviin said. "You'll like these. Trust me." He shoved a reader at Joe, who took it tentatively.

At about the same time, the Congie opened her eyes, saw the Jreet, and screamed.

Joe and Daviin, who were both used to this reaction by now, did not even look up. "See?" Daviin said, tapping a claw upon the screen.

"Get your fat finger out of the way," Joe snapped. "Is this a joke?"

"Nope," Daviin said. "Leave on Earth. All four of us. Jer'ait pulled some strings."

"Why?"

"Read *further*, Joe."

The woman, who now was over her shock and had realized that she was being ignored, began packing up her things in a huff.

"Don't forget your bra," Daviin said pointing.

The naked woman glared at the Jreet. "I'm surprised you even know what it is."

"I'm not," Joe said. "He likes to wat—" Joe's jaw fell open. "Daviin. Is Jer'ait serious? They're finally giving us our *kasjas?*"

"He said there'd be a lot of money," Daviin said, bobbing his head excitedly. At one time, the Jreet had scorned Congressional currency. Now, cut off from Vora, living on a grounder's pay, and going rotations between *melaa* had put things into perspective. He was already twenty thousand credits in debt to Joe, and still the Jreet was barely eating enough to keep himself from starving.

When Congress issued its payments, it didn't take into account the fact the Jreet was seven rods long and could eat a cow a day and still be hungry.

"And you're sure it's really from Jer'ait? Not a fake?"

"Well," Daviin said, "It was delivered by a Peacemaker. When I asked, the little Ueshi coward told me Jer'ait was taking a few weeks off. Unspecified reasons."

Joe frowned. "Don't tell me you assaulted another Peacemaker."

"At least I didn't eat him. I *wanted* to eat him."

The Jreet's tone of voice suggested he'd come very close.

Seeing the Jreet's hungry gleam, Joe grimaced. "If they're giving us our *kasjas*," Joe said, "We can afford to splurge a little. How about—"

"*Melaa?*" Daviin asked, the gleam of a happy child lighting his metallic yellow eyes.

"Yeah," Joe said, grinning. "As many as you want. My treat."

That turned out to be a mistake. Daviin ate an entire herd, and was so bloated when it came time to get on the shuttle they had to wait for them to work their way out the other end before he would fit.

The shuttle ride was awful. Every two tics, Daviin would crane his neck and peer into the cockpit and ask, "You think we're close?"

Joe kept him entertained with stories of beef steers he remembered seeing as a kid when his parents took him and Sam on a road trip through Texas. The more he talked about them, the more interested Daviin became. It came to the point where Joe was making up details, just to keep the Jreet occupied.

By the time they got to Earth, cows grew to be several hundred tons, came in all variety of flavors, and put up a good fight before they relinquished their succulent meat. Daviin was particularly excited by the last detail. Jreet, unlike other, civilized creatures, liked to fight for their dinner.

Joe didn't have the heart to tell him that pretty much every cow Joe had ever seen could be taken out with a two-by-four.

Jer'ait and Flea met them in the offloading area. Flea was back to his normal beetle-green and bright red, insectoid eyes, having shed the black when Maggie sent him to Grakkas to watch Trosska mine ruvmestin. The first thing out of Flea's mouth was, "So, Joe, you ready to go rescue your brother?"

"Huh?"

Smoothly, Jer'ait said, "Perhaps there's a better place to discuss these things, Baga. Besides, they must be exhausted from such a long trip. We could find a quiet place to eat and talk about old times."

"What did he say about Sam?" Joe demanded.

"Come," Daviin said, grabbing him by the shoulder, "We eat. I'm tired of ship food. Someone find me a cow."

They found a cow, though it was not in a restaurant, but in a rancher's backyard. Daviin was fairly upset at the lack of resistance he found when he vanished and screamed a war-cry, but looked mollified twenty tics later, when he was tearing the remains of the meat from the hindquarters.

"How much did you pay the farmer?" Joe asked Jer'ait, wincing at the way the Jreet was happily spreading shattered bones and entrails over a thirty-foot area. "Maybe you should double it."

Jer'ait nodded silently.

"So you're sure it's Sam?" Joe asked finally. "I watched him die on the news. They made his execution public."

"Faked," Jer'ait said.

Joe's face twisted. "So someone died in his place?"

"Of course not," Jer'ait replied. "You'd be amazed what we can do with robotics and artificial imagery nowadays."

Joe clenched his robotic hand and shook his head. "No. I believe you. This thing's awesome. Better than my real one, and it doesn't hurt when I ram it in someone's face."

"He's been doing a lot of that," Daviin commented.

"I'd heard," Jer'ait said. "Congress was not kind to you after Neskfaat."

Daviin grunted agreement and tore into another haunch.

"So did they ever figure out what Forgotten wanted with Neskfaat?" Joe asked.

Jer'ait's gaze remained stoic. "Yes."

Daviin stopped chewing. Even Flea had stopped spitting at flies to stare at the Huouyt.

"So why'd he do it?" Joe asked.

Much too carefully, Jer'ait said, "The official story is that he was attempting to get my brother into the Tribunal by assassinating Mekkval. He sent Rat's team after the Dhasha Representative two rotations after you last saw her on Jeelsiht. Made it appear as if it were a military-sanctioned operation. She never knew who she was attacking."

"She's dead, isn't she?" Joe said.

"The official story is yes," Jer'ait said. "All six of them died before they even got halfway down the tunnels."

Joe frowned at Jer'ait and said, "*Official* story?" even as Daviin slammed the remnants of the cow down and straightened. "This Geuji. How do we kill it?"

Flea snorted. "We can't kill it."

"Anything can be killed," Daviin said, "And this thing needs it more than most."

Jer'ait shook his head. "Normally, I'd agree with you, Daviin, but he staged Neskfaat and Aez simply to get the Huouyt banned from the Tribunal."

Joe frowned. "*Banned*? You know that for a fact?"

"He gave me a written confession," Jer'ait said. "Translated in thirteen thousand different languages, for the Regency's convenience."

Joe's attention sharpened. "You? As in you *personally*?"

"I sought him out," Jer'ait said. "We talked."

Every one of Jer'ait's groundmates stared at him.

"You...talked...to *Forgotten*?" Flea finally whispered, obviously in awe.

Jer'ait made a dismissive gesture. "It only confirmed things I already knew."

"And then you captured him?" Daviin demanded.

"He turned himself in," Jer'ait said. "Part of his conditions of sur-render was that Congress give his people access to basic entertainment and communication between each other."

"And have they?" Joe demanded.

Jer'ait gave him a long look. "Not yet."

"That's it?" Daviin demanded. "All that, and it was just politics?"

"What else is war but politics?"

Daviin flung a bone in disgust. "The Geuji needs to die," Daviin said. "He's shed too much blood."

Jer'ait seemed to hesitate. "I'm not sure the blood he shed was entirely bad, Jreet."

Daviin lifted his bloody muzzle sharply. "Explain that."

"He destroyed Aez...because it was filled with religious zealots intent on spilling blood. Not even subjugating—just spilling blood."

"They would never have bested the Vorans," Daviin snorted.

"They weren't interested in warring other Jreet. They wanted the blood of lesser creatures, easy pickings. I researched the Peacemaker reports off Aez before it exploded. The moment the Dhasha accumu-lated on Neskfaat, the Aezi would have begun slaughtering innocents." Jer'ait glanced at the others. "Further, Rat is not dead. The Geuji made some sort of pact with Mekkval—I'm still not sure if the Dhasha knows it or not—and Rat and her team now work as a specialized unit for Mekkval, hunting down and killing renegade Dhasha before they can start a war. Mekkval faked their deaths, and used the opportunity to charge Rri'jan with attempted murder. So far, they've killed four ren-egade princes, and when they are not hunting Dhasha, Rat and her team are living a life of luxury on Kaleu."

Joe, who had been barely scraping by, having to feed himself and his Sentinel on a Prime Commander's pay, felt a pang of jealousy at the news. "What else?" he demanded. "There's more."

This time, Jer'ait spoke with great reluctance. "I researched the Dhasha princes Forgotten lured to Neskfaat," he said. "All but one were known traitors. Just one."

Joe felt acid etch the insides of his veins. "Bagkhal."

"The one we killed. His 'lieutenant.' Yes."

Joe knew that meant something. Everyone else at the meeting knew it, too. But, from the sideways glances and silence, no one had any idea what.

Tentatively, Jer'ait said, "Joe, do you have any idea why..."

"No," Joe snapped.

"For once," Daviin said softly, "I think I understand why Aliphei keeps the Geuji locked in the Space Academy vault. Just one could bring down Congress."

"But he hasn't," Flea said. "Makes you wonder why not, huh?"

Bitterly, now, Joe said, "How many of them *are* there, Jer'ait?"

"About five thousand," Jer'ait said. "Rri'jan was using them for leverage. Or so he thought."

"And now?"

"Aliphei's having them all killed. He says Forgotten has proven the Geuji are too dangerous to keep alive, and Rri'jan's actions basically constituted a hostage situation. Should there be any other Geuji out there, Congress can't take the chance that another Representative will decide to use them as a bargaining chip."

Joe glanced out at the farmland, troubled. "And Forgotten's just letting it happen?"

"Forgotten is detained, like the rest of them," Jer'ait replied. "He's on a ship docked at Koliinaat, destined for Levren once his trial is over, and has been cut off from all communication with the outside. There is nothing he can do."

"After he confessed," Flea said, obviously disbelieving. "And got pardoned? Registered as a citizen and everything? Tried to come clean?"

"Indeed," Jer'ait said softly.

"The Tribunal breaks their word?" Daviin demanded.

"Mekkval objected," Jer'ait said. "Aliphei and Prazeil overrode him. Forgotten was a...high-profile...target. They'd be furgs to let him go. His trial takes place in a little over a rotation. The Regency is mustering its greatest lawyers to build the case. They're importing Bajna to crunch the numbers for them. After that, he is sent to Levren, where he dies."

Joe watched Jer'ait's expression carefully. Buzzing over to land on his shoulder, Flea cocked his head at the Huouyt and said, "There's something you're not telling us."

Jer'ait gave the Baga a slow, reluctant nod. "I'm in a position to see and hear quite a bit. The whole thing smells like Neskfaat did. I think this was the Geuji's plan all along."

"To kill his species?" Joe was appalled.

"That, and to solve a few problems before he disappeared." Jer'ait's purple eye was sad. "Once a turn, a team is sent in to evaluate the captives. Aliphei keeps them in wretched conditions, without light nor sound, nor any contact with the rest of the world. There's no way to free them from that place without the Tribunal's express permission. That means Aliphei's permission. And Aliphei is intent on keeping them as secluded as possible, to prevent any plotting amongst them."

"So Forgotten wants them to die," Joe said. "All of them. Himself included."

"He's sent twelve agents into the vaults to check on them. Every one of them has been a Jahul."

"So?"

"The Geuji were not fitted with electronic voices," Jer'ait said. "They have no way of communicating with anyone who enters their prison."

"Except the Jahul," Joe said, eyes widening with understanding.

"Yes," Jer'ait said, "And every one of those Jahul were caught and interrogated afterwards." He cocked his head. "All but one of them betrayed the Geuji and all but one of them was subsequently executed. The last one escaped. That was only a few weeks after Aez. And here's the odd thing. His empathy rating was off the charts. He kept insisting the Geuji were miserable. Hopeless. That we were cruel to hold them like that. Not one of the other Jahul even mentioned the prisoners, other than to say they could forget they saw them. This one couldn't stop talking about them. Even drugged, it's all he would say."

"So you think this last spy got back to Forgotten and told him what his people were *feeling*?" Daviin demanded.

"Lacking any other means of communicating with them, I think that's a very real possibility."

"And Forgotten decided to kill them." Joe did not sound happy.

"I think he'd decided to kill them long before he blew up Aez," Jer'ait said. "This just solidified it in his mind."

"There is a special level of hell reserved for kin-killers," Daviin said, obviously disgusted. "Like I said before, this Forgotten needs to die."

"He's doing them a favor," Jer'ait said. "They're going to remain imprisoned as long as Aliphei lives."

No one needed to voice the fact that Aliphei was of a species that did not succumb to old age, and had enough drugs, nanos, and body-guards whenever he traveled away from Koliinaat that accidental death wasn't likely.

"Can we talk about Joe's brother now?" Flea demanded. "The Geuji is interesting, but right now, I'm craving *cash.*"

Catching Joe's frown, Jer'ait said, "Flea believes your brother would be willing to relinquish a percentage of his savings to his rescuers."

"He will," Flea said, "Or I'll glue him to the prison floor myself."

Daviin's head perked up. "How much of a percentage?"

"In the *billions*," Flea said.

Daviin glanced at Jer'ait. Jer'ait nodded.

Daviin's eye-ridges lifted in surprise. "We've wasted enough time. Joe wants to see his brother." He hurriedly ducked under the fence, leaving the mangled remains of the cow behind. "Come, Joe. You must introduce us!"

34

BILLIONS

Sam sighed as his jailors returned. He couldn't see them through the blindfold, but he could hear them. *Strange. I don't remember that buzzing. Maybe they brought in somebody new.*

"Power outage?" he said, grinning. Any setbacks for his interrogators gave him reason to smile.

"Yes," a strange voice said, above him. *Far* above him.

Sam was a tall man, and he was standing, since they'd left him no chair. Whatever it was that now shared the room with him must have brushed the ceiling.

Sam swallowed, realizing they were going back into another intimidation routine. "What a shame," he said, trying not to act as spooked as he felt. "I hope nobody bumps his head."

"Oh, they'll manage." A man's voice. He sounded amused.

They?

"Get moving, Sam," the 'tall' voice said, though he didn't sound so tall anymore. Eye level, and behind him.

"Call me Samuel," he said. "Sam's for friends and decent Human beings."

"Funny. I seem to have heard that somewhere before." A third voice, flat, yet pitched with meaning that Sam could only guess.

478

Sam edged forward a few feet, then cocked his head. "Where is everybody? This hall is always filled with people."

"They ran screaming," the 'tall' voice said.

"Careful," the 'flat' voice said. "You'll frighten the child."

"I'm not a child," Sam snapped. "I'm seventy-one, you dumb fucks. The mod just makes me look younger. And what the hell's going on?" The buzzing sound was back, this time only ninths from his face. "What the hell is that noise?"

"You know," a tinny voice said above the buzzing, "I think he looks like you, Commander."

"If this is an attempt to intimidate me, it's not gonna work."

A huge alien hand slapped Sam on the back, claws digging painfully into his skin as it shoved him forward. "Walk, Human. We'll scare you later."

"Promise," the tinny, floating voice said.

Sam settled into an unconcerned gait, allowing the enormous hand to guide him. "Where are we walking?"

"Out," the tinny voice said. "So we can interrogate you."

"You've *been* interrogating me," Sam snapped.

"Not like this, we haven't," the Human said.

Sam felt a coldness trickle up the base of his spine. There was something about that voice he didn't like. There was something about the whole *situation* he didn't like.

"Where is everybody?" he demanded.

"They're watching us walk you out the front door," the man said. "It's actually pretty funny. I think you scared them, Daviin."

"No more than you did, Commander."

"You know, this is a piece of cake compared to a crawl. At least the Takki would attack us."

"They *did* attack us," the tinny voice said. "And then they stopped."

"Cowards," the 'tall' voice said. "When we're done here, I should come back and make them all dance on my tek for abandoning their duties so easily."

The 'tall' gaoler shoved Sam again, who had slowed as he puzzled over the conversation. It felt like getting hit by a Congressional freighter. He let out an *oof* and stumbled, the bones in his back creaking as he struggled to catch his breath.

"They've got a sooty assignment on a sooty border planet," the Human said. "What do you expect? You think they're gonna put their lives on the line for a poofy-haired, smartass criminal?"

Sam's feet stopped of their own accord. "You're going to kill me, aren't you?"

"Move," the tall voice said.

"No," Sam said. "I'm staying here. Somebody help!"

Sam was a big man, a full six-seven, but when the alien shoved him, he *moved*.

"They're not going to help you," the man said behind him. "Trust me. If you could see their faces, you'd understand."

"Hell," the buzzing voice said, "If he could see *anything*, he'd understand."

The four of them laughed at that. Sam began to get more and more spooked. More than anything, he wanted the blindfold off. He really began to get scared when they pushed him into the back of a *haauk*. "This is a trick, isn't it?"

"You're about to find out," the man said. He was sitting right beside him, and, from the way they were pressed shoulder-to-shoulder in the back seat of the *haauk*, Sam guessed they were about the same height and build. He squirmed away from him uncomfortably.

Sam became even more nervous when he realized it was a big *haauk*. Made for transport. And, whatever it was that was climbing aboard behind them was making the entire thing rock like a toddler hopping on a swingset. Sam tried scooting back out of the seat, but another large shape sat down beside him. The *haauk* began to move.

The buzzing grew louder, until Sam felt something land in his lap. He flinched when he felt the thing brush his balls through his prison overalls.

"So," the buzzing voice said. "Where'd you stash your money, Sam?"

"I'd tell him," the man said. "He's had a really bad past six rotations."

"Do you know how much stuff *costs* on a ruvmestin planet?" Flea demanded. "I was going into debt just to stay alive."

Sam snorted. "I thought we were talking about genetics and how I cracked your code."

"Who wants to look like a powder puff?" the man said. "I saw the pictures, but it's even weirder close up."

Sam's heart was pounding, now. "This isn't about the experiment?"

"No," the 'tinny' voice said, from his lap. "It's about your *money*. Where is it?"

"What kind of Peacemakers are you?" Sam asked.

"The very best," the flat voice said.

"Trust me," the man said, "You really, really want to tell us."

"You're just thieves!" Sam cried.

"What did you say?" An enormous, clawed hand clapped him upon the shoulder and squeezed, painfully.

"That was a mistake," the flat voice said. "His kind have very prickly honor."

"I was told this could be a mutually beneficial business arrangement," the tall voice said. "I was told we free you, you pay us. If you don't *want* to pay us…"

Something wrenched Sam out of his seat and held him off the ground, the air from the traveling *haauk* whipping through his hair. "We'll still free you."

Sam screamed.

"Careful," the flat voice said. "We're half a length up. You drop him and we don't get paid."

"I won't drop him. Unless he wants me to."

Sam somehow got a hold on himself and laughed. "This is just another game."

The man sounded worried, now. "Listen to me, Sam. You don't know the Jreet. He means every word. You piss him off and he'll drop you."

All the tension left Sam's body. "You're lying. This is all a setup. We're not really moving anywhere. You've got a fan on us and we're still inside the prison."

The Human sighed. "Sam, I was gonna try to spare you this, but since you're being difficult…" Sam felt hands reach behind his head and undo the blindfold.

No sooner had Sam caught a glimpse of the man's face than he was suddenly wrenched around, dangled ten feet off the edge of a moving *haauk* by a slab of scarlet muscle that looked capable of ripping him in half with two fingers.

Sam screamed.

"Now we're getting somewhere!" the Jreet snapped, leaning close. His golden eyes bored into Sam's skull. "So tell me, Human. Will you pay us for your rescue?"

"Yes," Sam gasped, his legs kicking futilely for purchase as the ground passed by thousands of feet beneath him.

"Excellent!" The Jreet yanked him back inside the *haauk* and thrust him back into the seat between the man and an odd-eyed Huouyt. "You see? No drugs required."

"He has yet to tell us where the money is," the violet-eyed Huouyt said as he untied Sam's hands.

"I'll tell you," Sam muttered. His eyes once more found the man's face. He looked even more like Sam's father than Sam had, with his brown eyes and a lean, muscular body that a Greek god would have envied. Bitterly, he growled, "Even though I know you're not gonna kill me."

The man's brown eyes remained impassive. "What makes you say that?"

"Cut the crap, Joe," Sam spat. "I know who you are. You're not gonna hurt me."

"No," Joe agreed, "But everyone else on this haauk might. You have no idea the kind of dangerous bastards I had to enlist to help spring you. I told them there'd be good money involved in getting you out… who knows what they'll do if you don't pay up?"

With his words, Joe handed Sam a reader. In it, four separate accounts stood open, awaiting transactions.

"It would really help if you could divide it equally amongst the four of us," Joe said. "What are you worth, exactly?"

"Two billion," Sam said.

"Jer'ait?"

"Eight, easy. Probably twelve."

"That's fortunate," Joe said. "I promised Daviin three, and everyone should have an equal share."

Sam felt like he'd swallowed lead weights. He was only worth twelve and a half billion. "I only have nine."

"Jer'ait?"

"He's lying."

Damn the Huouyt and their ability to recognize a lie! "I don't have twelve billion!" Sam cried, carefully stabilizing his brainwaves and thinking of fluffy pink bunny rabbits.

"Lying."

Sam narrowed his eyes at the Huouyt. Seeing his consternation, Joe grinned at him. "If you don't got it—which Jer'ait seems to think you do—sounds to me like you better come up with some creative criminality right now, because we're not setting you down until we've each got three billion credits."

"You're just a petty thief!" Sam snapped.

Joe shrugged. "Runs in the family, I guess."

"And I'd like to point out it's not exactly petty," the small, tinny voice said. It took Sam a moment to realize it was coming from the roof above him.

A spider-like creature with huge red, buglike eyes and black-ribbed wings stared down at him, its scissor-like beak aimed at his face. Sam quickly looked away.

"I can give you each two," Sam said.

"I was promised three!" the Jreet roared.

Sam flinched. "Two each and three for the Jreet."

The Huouyt's eyes fixed on him coldly. "You would favor the Jreet?"

Sam realized where he'd heard a flat voice like that before. A Va'gan assassin, hired to kill him in his fortress apartment twenty years ago. "I can give you both three."

"Oh?" the little insect creature snapped. "Then maybe I should cut off a trophy to take with me. How about a hand, Joe? I never got a prince talon. I should have a hand."

"Nah," Joe said. "He'd just grow it back. Gotta find something more permanent."

The insect dropped from the ceiling, landing solidly on Sam's shoulder. "The head, then?"

"Fine!" Sam snapped. "Three to each of you."

"And what about Joe?" the Jreet demanded. "You would rob your brother of his due?"

"I don't have any more," Sam gritted.

"Lying."

A huge, clawed hand enveloped his shoulder and squeezed. "Find it."

In the end, Sam transferred all twelve billion.

"So why didn't you come get me sooner?" Sam asked, sulking, as the Baga and the Huouyt left them on the *haauk* to test their accounts.

"I thought you were dead," Joe said, watching the door where the two had disappeared. "That, and I didn't have the groundteam."

Sam's mouth fell open. "This is your *groundteam?* You asshole! That's why they were calling you 'Commander,' isn't it? You could've told them to be happy with two and they woulda dropped it!"

Joe grinned. "Yeah, but what's a few billion to a criminal mastermind? You'll get it all back in a couple turns while the rest of us are stuck making Congie wage the rest of our lives. This is gonna be our only payday worth talking about until we die."

"May that be soon and violent," Sam growled.

Joe shrugged. "Prolly will be. That's why we're gonna go use it up on having a good time before we get back off leave."

Sam felt like he was choking. "You're gonna use up three billion credits to have a good *time?*"

"Yep. Flea plans on buying himself a spaceship so he can crash it. He's a destructive little shit, I'll tell you what."

Sam thought he was going to throw up. "You're insane."

"Nope," Joe said. "Just realistic. We know the four of us prolly won't live long. Might as well get our jollies in now, before Congress finally finds a way to kill us."

"Besides," the Jreet roared, "they split us up, so we've gotta enjoy the good company while we can."

Joe cocked his head up to eye the Jreet. "You know, Daviin, you should probably set aside a few mil, just to keep you from starving later on. Think of your stomach."

"I am," Daviin said. "And I'm thinking of all the *melaa* my share will buy me. I don't intend to be able to move for weeks. I might manage to get a few more segments out of this."

"What about your Sentinel duties?"

Daviin snorted. "Jer'ait took care of all the ones who wanted to kill you. I can afford some time off."

Sam frowned, glancing between the Jreet and Joe. "He's your Sentinel?"

Joe didn't get a chance to answer because Flea burst out of the building and came at them at approximately the speed of sound.

"It's in!" the Baga cried. "It's all there! We routed it through some Jahul gambling dens, shows up to Congress as gaming winnings." The insectoid little monster landed on top of the Jreet's head and tapped a bright red brow-scale with a sharp claw. "You hear that, Daviin? Your bank account says you actually *won* at cards, for once."

"Perhaps you would like to make another wager, Baga," the Jreet replied. "*Bigger*, this time."

The massive insect puffed up. "Bring it o—"

"No wagers," Joe said. "You each have three billion." He gave the Jreet a pointed look. "Period."

Behind the Baga, Jer'ait strode from the hub with calm purpose, showing neither excitement nor pleasure. "We transferred it all to the new accounts," Jer'ait said as he got into the *haauk*. Then, looking at Sam, he said, "On Faelor."

Sam winced. He had memorized the account numbers he'd transferred the billions into and had been planning on reclaiming his money as soon as they let him go, but Faelor was run by Bajna. They were the bankers of Congress, and not a cent would leave the planet without six different forms of encrypted identification.

Sam was never seeing his money again.

"Great!" Joe said. "Then let's go free my wayward brother."

Sulking, Sam said, "Take me to the Manhattan Skyplex. I've got friends there." He leaned back and watched the landscape speed by, brooding.

Several hours later, Joe clapped him on the shoulder. "Well, we're here, little brother. Out you go."

Sam opened his eyes, not realizing he'd fallen asleep. He blinked at the dry desert scrub and the two lonely little huts along a dusty orange road. The heat was bearing down on them like they were stuck inside a furnace, with the front of Sam's prison overalls already beginning to stain with sweat.

"This isn't the Skyplex."

"Nope," Joe said. "Figure I'm your big brother and should give you a talkin' to about all the crime you've been doing, but I don't have the time and I don't really think you'd listen, anyway, so I'm just gonna drop you off on the other side of the planet, away from all your thieving buddies, and hope you can straighten yourself out."

Sam's eyes flew wide as he saw the man in African dress step out of the closest hut to stare at them. "You can't."

"Might wanna lose the pajamas, though," Joe continued. "They're probably tagged."

"They are," Jer'ait said.

"You can't," Sam repeated, more stunned than worried.

"Oh, but we can," Joe said. "Figure you need to learn about hard work, since Dad never had the chance to teach you himself. There isn't a phone for a hundred miles, a bank outlet for a thousand. You *could* try walking to them, but we paid that nice young man over there ten thousand dollars to give you a job, and I think he intends to do it." Joe grinned at him. "You ever herded cattle before, Sam? Daviin thought you'd enjoy it."

"Joe, you can't do this! Dad would—"

"Dad would what?" Joe's eyes darkened and Sam suddenly wished they weren't sitting so close. "Believe me, I can do this, Sam. I think of the kind of ash you've dragged Dad's name into and you're lucky I don't kill you. Now get out. And take off the overalls. We'll get rid of them for you."

Sam glanced at the other three, hoping to find an ally against his brother's insanity.

All he found were cold, hard, alien stares.

Reluctantly, Sam got out of the *haauk*. When the Huouyt held out a flat tentacle, he reluctantly removed his overalls and handed them over.

Then, as Sam watched, the *haauk* rose into the air and flew off. Sam watched it until the craft was over the mountains.

A dark hand clapped him on the shoulder and Sam turned.

The man beamed a bright African smile at him. Then he said something in a language that was neither Congie, nor English, and pointed towards the six scrawny cows.

Sam laughed and shook his head. "No, I don't think so."

Immediately, the African's smile faded. He gave Sam a shove.

Sam stopped laughing.

• • •

Syuri received Forgotten's letter after almost two rotations without communications. Immediately, Syuri dropped everything and took the message to his room.

Syuri. I'm sorry we couldn't continue our relationship together. I'm sure you deduced as much, but Aliphei has left the Geuji in abject misery for hundreds of thousands of turns. I'll be giving myself up in the hopes I can earn them some basic privileges and bring to light their suffering, once and for all. If all goes according to plan, I should be able to at least secure one-way net links and news feeds for my kind. Perhaps, if Fate is kind, I will manage to procure them communication between themselves, which would be the greatest entertainment a Geuji shall ever know. Even when the Geuji were free, our greatest diversion was discussion with our peers. If I can obtain them that, then my life has been well-lived.

Unfortunately, Aliphei has a history of quietly destroying races such as mine, and has had since the formation of Congress to learn from his mistakes, so I will be playing with fire. Even if I do succeed, you will likely never hear from me again, for I go to join my race in the vaults.

I tell you this to let you know I've set you up to inherit my full estate. As soon as I'm gone, you will be rich. It's the least I can do, to repay your kindness.

Please don't do anything stupid.

Your friend,

Jemria

Syuri played the message twice more, then threw the reader against the wall.

He cried, at first, because he knew Forgotten had been planning this from the moment he met him. He'd been looking for an heir, someone to pass his fortunes to when he handed himself over to Aliphei to be destroyed.

That's not going to happen, Syuri thought suddenly, tearing himself out of his thoughts.

He would not let it happen. Forgotten would not end up like the other Geuji. Syuri could not allow it.

He knew what he had to do.

Come Peacemakers, Jreet hells, or Dhasha jaws, Syuri was going to save his friend.

35

KA-PAR

"**Y**ou two really should eat something," the Huouyt said as he clung to the side of the massive private pool, surfing channels on the enormous vidscreen of the penthouse of the Ueshi pleasure-palace that they had rented for the rotation. He plucked a Huouyt delicacy from a plate and held it up appreciatively. "I will not be responsible for the bill if one of you starves to death."

"Besides," Joe said, from under the tiny, expert fingers of an Ueshi masseuse, "you're missing out on the fun." At that, the Ueshi began a gentle thumping down the backs of his legs, loosening the muscles there, and Joe groaned.

"Quiet," Daviin muttered from his coils. "Ka-par."

Joe rolled his eyes. "And what are you charhead furgs gonna do if one of you wins, huh?"

"Shut up," the Baga replied. "The Jreet's about to cave." Neither one had so much as twitched for almost a week.

"From what I've seen," Jer'ait said, "you're both about to pass out."

"First one to pass out loses," Baga said stubbornly. "Then I *own* his ass."

"I think I'll make you carry my grooming kit," the Jreet retorted, "as would properly befit a slave."

Over by the vidscreen, the Human gave a loud groan and rolled his eyes. "Guys, we've got three *billion* credits apiece and you haven't moved from that spot in the last two weeks."

"Ka-par," Flea said.

"Yes," Daviin said. "Let the little insect lose fairly. Stop distracting him."

"I'm *not* having another melaa shipped in here, Daviin," the Human growled. "And Flea, get your ass off the chair and get something to eat. This is ridiculous."

The Jreet ignored Joe completely, his predatory gaze completely focused on the tiny Baga, who returned it intently, seated on the back of a chair facing him. Joe muttered something under his breath and went back to surfing channels, a fizzy—non-alcoholic—Earth-drink in his hand.

Joe was groaning with pleasure as the little Ueshi began working her way up his back when Jer'ait heaved himself from the water and shouted, "By the bloody fucking eyes of the merciful dead, the self-molesting furgs are falling into his fucking trap!"

Joe grunted and looked up.

Jer'ait was watching a live news feed from Koliinaat. It was a crisp, no-frills view of the inside of the Regency, with almost all the Representatives in attendance. At the center of the screen, the three Tribunal members—the First Citizen Aliphei, Prazeil representing the Jreet, and Mekkval representing the Dhasha—sat presiding over the trial of what looked like a quivering, semi-translucent green slime spread over a boxlike apparatus.

"The Ayhi damn the ignorant vaghi to the deepest Jreet hells!" Jer'ait shouted. "He set the noose and they're crawling into it!" He hurled the platter of delicacies across the room and bent to yank a towel from a pool chair.

Having never seen the Va'gan display more than quiet irritation at anything, every head in the room turned to stare as Jer'ait upended a table of pool supplies across the damp stone. Towels and bath soaps rolled into the pool. Jer'ait kicked them for greater effect, skittering a flotation pad out across the water.

"Uh…Jer'ait?" Joe asked curiously.

"*Look*," Jer'ait snarled, gesturing at the screen. "They're giving him what he *wants*. He could take down *everything*. The Regency, the Tribunal, *everything*."

The Baga buzzed over to land on a chair in front of the vidscreen, cocking his buglike head at the screen. "Is that the Geuji?" he asked, curious.

"No," Jer'ait snapped.

The Baga hesitated. "It *says* it's the Geuji. Live feed from Koliinaat."

"It's not," Jer'ait snapped. "The Geuji is black and does not have eyes."

"So…" Daviin said, as the Jreet wove over to take a look, "if that's not the Geuji, who is it?"

"It's a forgery," Flea said, scrabbling closer. "Like Joe's brother. If you look close, that jiggly pattern repeats itself. Like it's on a timer."

"A farce," Jer'ait agreed. "A complete fucking fraud. Merciful *dead!* Were I *there*, that trial would not be happening. But of course he knew that. The damnable furg Aliphei lured me off to steal money and play games so he could have access to the Geuji unimpeded. I *thought* that Ghost file had been too close to the surface." He hurled a vase of rare flowers into the pool, where it shattered against the far edge. "*Damn. Fucking damn.*"

"So," Joe said slowly, "what's happening?"

"They're faking the trial," Flea said, "…on the floor of the Regency." He seemed stunned. "Isn't that, like, illegal?"

"Turn it up," Daviin commanded. "The Aezi is talking."

"*Tell us again, for the record, how you came to be, Geuji.*"

"*My people live in a faraway galaxy, and we often come to scout out your progress and determine the best ways to stop your impending threat to the stability of our great nation. Until now, we were never caught.*"

"*And you conspired with the Huouyt to destroy Aez and initiate the war on Neskfaat to weaken us?*" Prazeil demanded.

"*Admittedly, it failed. But yes, that was our plan.*"

"*Why did you attack Aez?*" the Jreet Representative urged. "*Why not Vora or Welu?*"

"*The Aezi were our greatest threat*," the greenish slime-creature told them. "*They are the greatest warriors of Congress. We had no choice but to neutralize them.*"

"He *dares*?!" Daviin screamed, rearing up in fury.

"It's a fake," Joe said, watching the screen with curiosity. "That's not Forgotten."

Daviin frowned as the Jreet Representative continued to interrogate their subject. "And Prazeil *knows* it's a fake?"

"How can he not?" Jer'ait demanded. "They had the real Geuji testify against Rri'jan in a closed session. Forgotten looks nothing like that...thing."

"A Jreet *knowingly* participates in such a dishonor?" Daviin snarled.

"There's nothing you can do about it," Joe said tiredly. "It's just more politics."

"I could *challenge*," Daviin snapped. "Look at them! They spew lies about Aez. They say the Aezi warriors could best a Voran, and that's why the Aezi had to die."

"A *fake*, furg," Jer'ait repeated.

"But all of *Congress* sees it!" Daviin retorted. "They'll take it as sooth, because it came from the mind of a Geuji!"

...which was true. "What do you mean, challenge?" Joe said.

"For his seat," Daviin snapped. He began pacing in front of the screen, tek protruding slightly from its sheath, looking utterly enraged.

"A *Tribunal* member?" Joe asked carefully, "Won't that, oh, I don't know, get you eradicated?"

"No," Daviin snarled. "It is my right." He continued to pace, failing to elaborate.

Joe frowned. "I thought that Representatives had to be chosen by the people."

"It is different for the Jreet," Daviin snapped out. "One of our Species Concessions. We challenge. Only the best rule." The Jreet looked so pissed that he was having trouble forming words.

"Uh..." Joe said, "you realize you're only half as big as that guy, right?"

"I've killed Aezi bigger than him," Daviin snapped.

Joe's eyebrows went up. "Really."

"Never mind," Daviin snarled. "It takes a clan ages to put together enough funds to back their greatest warrior and send him to Congress."

Joe glanced from the screen, to Daviin, then to Jer'ait, who was watching the Jreet with a narrow look. It was the Baga, however, who said, "Daviin, how much would it cost you to challenge the Welu?"

"Six billion," Daviin snapped.

"You can have mine," the Baga said.

"Done!" the Jreet roared. He reached forth and lowered a huge ruby hand over Flea's back. "Little Flea, you just made the best decision of your life." He lifted his hand and made a fist. "The Aezi has breathed his last lie. I swear it!" He crossed the room to get a better look at the vidscreen, doubtlessly to get a better look at his enemy.

Jer'ait gave Flea an irritated look. "Baga, do you have any idea how much money you just threw away?"

"No," Flea said. "And I probably don't want to." He lifted his caps and flitted his wings, a Baga impression of a shrug. "Besides, if Daviin wins, he can pay me back."

"Uh," Joe said, "you realize that's probably exactly what Forgotten *wants* you to do, right?"

"Oh sure," Flea said. "That's why I challenged the Jreet to ka'par. Keep him from spending all his cash."

Jer'ait cocked his head at Flea. "Excuse me?"

"Oh come on!" Flea cried. "You guys didn't see this coming? Seriously?" Then, looking from Joe to Jer'ait to Daviin, he seemed to deflate. "You didn't see it coming." Puffing up with irritation, he said, "Come *on*, guys. Daviin's *obviously* being groomed for the Tribunal. Think about it. He Sentineled a pleb—no offense—and had to live as a commoner for a couple rotations. He starved a bit and had to caper to the whims of a Human—the lowest of the low."

"Hey, now," Joe muttered.

Flea ignored him and went on, heedless. "He was pulled out of an Aezi *gladiatorial ring*. On the day—get this—Aez gets blown apart? He's killed more Aezi than any Jreet alive. And his little guardian angel was keeping him alive on Jeelsiht. For what...to go steal a few billion from Joe's brother? Of *course* the Geuji wants him to kill Prazeil."

"So you *knew* Forgotten was setting us up...*again*...and you just went along with it?" Joe asked, carefully resisting the urge to stomp the little bastard.

"Well, yeah," Flea said, sounding confused. "What better way to spend my money than getting myself a friend on the Tribunal?"

Joe and Jer'ait blinked at each other, then glanced over at the seething Jreet, who had crossed the room and was leaning close to the vidscreen to compensate for his poor eyesight, oblivious to their chat.

"You know, Flea," Joe said slowly, "you might be some sort of evil genius."

"Of course I am," Flea said, crawling up his arm to take residence on his shoulder. "I'm Bagan. Can I have something to eat now? Distracting the Voran sucked."

On the screen, the First Citizen was speaking again. *"Mekkval, you've been silent throughout,"* Aliphei noted. *"Do you have any questions for the condemned?"*

The enormous Dhasha Representative was scowling at the quivering green 'Geuji'. *"You already know my opinion. You already have decided your votes. I refuse to take part in this farce."* At that, the Dhasha summoned the Watcher and flickered out, leaving only Prazeil and Aliphei presiding.

"Did you see that?!" Daviin snarled. He grabbed the massive lounge chair beside him and hurled it against the wall, shattering it into thousands of splinters no bigger than Joe's pinkie and putting a hole in the wall that exposed the contents of the room next door, making the naked Jahul on the other side lunge out of their orgy with a tide of terrified screams. Heedless, Daviin roared at the vidscreen, "The *Dhasha* has more honor than that vaghi scum!"

"On second thought," Flea said, settling into a crouch on Joe's shoulder as he watched the Jreet's tantrum with obvious delight, "this is more interesting."

• • •

Syuri was moving through the crowded hub of Koliinaat's shipping quarter, trying to determine the best way to steal his friend's ship, when an angry Voran Jreet voice bellowed across the distance, "You! Food-trader! I have questions about Aez." The hot wash of Jreet-tinged anger that assaulted his sivvet was immediately followed by the pang of fear from a dozen nearby bystanders.

Syuri felt his chambers flex, expelling all of his wastes over his skin in a rush of total panic. At the same time, he spasmodically yanked his front legs into a protected tuck and *ran*.

Jreet, thankfully, were not a prey species. Thus, the Jreet could only bellow and shove bystanders aside angrily as Syuri escaped at speeds that befitted his humble ancestry.

Only once he had ducked through six separate hubs, navigated the bustling, narrow-halled services courts, and hurtled down a dozen passageways and busy halls did Syuri find the presence of mind to stop running and steady himself.

The Voran Jreet. The heir he had rescued on Aez. *Here.* Blessed Hagra, he had the ill-fated fortune of the Shadyi.

He couldn't follow me, Syuri thought, trying to get his chambers back under control. *Calm down. Jreet aren't that fast. You were running for hours.* Indeed, when he found the courage to look behind him, there were no massive, sinuous ruby coils sweeping through the halls after him. No enraged Jreet, seeking to skewer him on a glistening tek.

Somehow, Syuri got his legs to stop shaking. Once he'd panicked, he'd simply discharged everything, covering his skin in a humiliating slime that reeked like the eighth Jreet hell. Even then, travelers were making a wide berth around him, disgust clearly written on their alien faces.

Embarrassed, Syuri went to the nearest bathroom and began cleaning himself as best he could. The aliens that had been using the sinks and mirrors to freshen-up between trips quickly vacated the area, leaving him humiliatingly alone as he ran woefully inadequate Congressional hand-towels down his back and belly, repeatedly paying the two-credit charge each time he needed a new batch from the dispenser.

Once he had removed what filth he could and disposed of his clothes in the wastes recycler, Syuri ducked back into the hall, naked. He still stank, but not as bad. His legs weren't trembling as horribly, but he had lost all of his means of carrying implements and tools necessary to crack the piji shell that was the Geuji's containment.

Standing there amidst the flow of curious passengers—many of whom crushed his sivvet with smug disdain for his lack of attire—Syuri felt an overwhelming rush of shame and hopelessness. What was he, a humble, shit-covered Jahul, going to do against the likes of Aliphei and the Tribunal? He was a small-time smuggler who'd attracted the attention of a big fish…

…a big fish that was now entombed in a massive Congressional battlecrusier, waiting for the Geuji's long, drawn-out trial to finally come to an end.

The fact that it was a blatantly fake trial pressurized his chambers every time he thought of it. It had been spread across the news for weeks. They portrayed the Geuji as a huge, green, blubbering wad of mucous who couldn't even hold his own when pitted against soul-sucking Congressional lawyers with mountains—*mountains*—of evidence to level upon him. And, brandishing said documentation, the fools caught him in 'lie' after 'lie,' to which the imposter recanted his words and wove them a story that was nothing at all like what Syuri knew to be truth.

Little by little, they were portraying the Geuji to be a heartless, malicious career criminal whose only purpose had been to bring about the destruction of Congress so that his 'people' could be safe. Billions of them. In some distant galaxy many hundreds of turns away.

How the Congressional lawyers got hold of Forgotten's bank records, trading contracts, private communications, and vessel documentation was still a mystery to Syuri. As far as he knew, not even a Bajna could track his funds if he didn't want them tracked. Which meant the Bajna had been *given* the records, by the *real* Geuji.

They're torturing him, Syuri thought, in despair.

The interrogators had gotten everything from Forgotten. Every transaction that the Geuji had made in the last turn and a half, all of it was right there.

With, of course, the glaring exception of Syuri's payment for Aez, and his subsequent payment for infiltrating the Space Academy. Forgotten, it seemed, was going to be true to his word and leave him his entire estate.

He's protecting me to the death, Syuri realized, miserable. *Just as I did. He was testing me.* Standing there in the crowded hall, naked and covered in his own wastes, Syuri had an overwhelming rush of anger. He knew he couldn't leave Forgotten to die, as the damnable corpse-rot planned. Come Jreet, Huouyt interrogators, or automated laser cannon, Syuri was going to save him.

He was, after all, a pirate.

• • •

Flea watched the Jahul clean himself, then scuttle off to a forgotten corner of the hub and order an elevator to the shipping area. Flea followed him inside the chute when it came, crawling across the ceiling where he would go unnoticed. *Commander,* he said, *I just entered Elevator 1442K.*

Yeah, we're coming. Gotta find a way around for Daviin. Jer'ait?

Waiting on the other side of the elevator shaft in an Ooreiki pattern. The Watcher was nice enough to transport me to my chambers to make the shift before returning me to the outgoing shaft.

Must be nice to be a Peacemaster, Joe grumbled. *Walking sucks. This place is huge.*

So why do we follow this shit-stinking Jahul? Daviin demanded. *I have an Aezi to kill.*

Gut feeling, Joe said.

Ditto, Flea replied, climbing up the wall of the chute and over to hide behind the light fixture.

As soon as the doors closed, the Jahul glanced up at him. "Good afternoon," he said cheerfully. "Sorry about the smell." He glanced down at his reeking body. "I had a bit of a scare earlier."

Flea was surprised, and not only because the Jahul had so easily located him. Most creatures—even Jahul—saw him and immediately thought non-sent. "The smell doesn't bother me," Flea said, truthfully. He crawled down the wall a bit to get a better look. Seeing the crusted slime still caking those hard-to-reach places along the Jahul's back and sides, he gave a buzz of commiseration. "It must suck to be Jahul."

The Jahul laughed as he pulled sanitary wipes from the elevator wall and began to clean himself. "Not so much as…" he cocked his head up at Flea. "What *are* you, anyway? You look like something that would lay eggs on the underside of a Dhasha."

Flea snickered, amused. "How do you know I'm not?"

The Jahul threw wads of sticky green crap-covered napkins into the disposal. "I'm more talented than most. Your emotions are much too refined for something like a flea or parasite."

"You might be surprised," Flea said. "I'm Baga. My hive called me Traxxalihania but my groundteam calls me Flea."

The Jahul hesitated.

"So you want to free Forgotten?" Flea asked.

Very slowly, the Jahul looked up, gripping the wad of rags.

"I can get you in," Flea offered. "If you can get us out."

Over the link, Jer'ait said, *Flea, Elevator 1442K had nothing but a group of Ueshi come out of it. Where are you?*

Flea did not answer, watching the Jahul carefully. "Well?" Flea demanded. "You wanna save him or not?" He cocked his head, waiting.

"Of course I want to save him," the Jahul whispered. "Are you one of his agents?"

Flea buzzed his wings in amusement. "He sent me a note about the wet-eyed Huouyt and Ooreiki taking thirty-two planets from the Baga. Is that a lot?"

The Jahul nodded, slowly.

"Thought so," Flea said. "That's not really fair, is it?"

The Jahul gave his head a slight shake, his huge, glistening black eyes wary.

"I didn't think so, either," Flea said.

"You're willing to…*help*…the Geuji?"

"Sure," Flea said. "I like him. He's interesting."

"Didn't he try to kill you?"

"I don't think so," Flea said. "You know where they're keeping him?"

Glancing nervously at the elevator door, the Jahul said, "On the battlecruiser *Koliinaat Defender*."

Flea snorted. "That's the decoy. The real Geuji's in the main incinerator room. They're gonna kill him in like twenty tics."

The Jahul seemed to stiffen with distrust. "And you know this *how*?"

"I watch," Flea said.

36

WITH GREAT POWER...

Jer'ait scowled at the empty elevator. He had scoured it for signs of a struggle, but there was neither Baga glue nor Jahul excretions covering the interior. *Flea*, he said again, *if this is a joke, it is not amusing.*

He received nothing but silence.

"All right," the Human panted as he came jogging up, "what the hell's going on?"

"I'm not sure," Jer'ait said warily. "Give me a moment." He cocked his head and looked at the wall. "Watcher, where is Flea?"

"Who is Flea?" the Watcher asked.

Jer'ait narrowed his eyes. "You know who Flea is."

"There is no registered Flea on Koliinaat," the Watcher said. *"Perhaps you can supply me with a registered name? Koliinaati privacy laws of the 533,500ᵗʰ Standard turn require confirmed association or legitimate potential business with the subject of a database search before I can legally provide you with any more information."*

Irritated, Jer'ait glanced at the Human. "Privacy laws. What's his name?"

"Burned if I know," Joe muttered. "Something long. Think it started with T. Or X." The Human cocked his bulbous head. "Or R?"

Jer'ait glanced up at Daviin as he wound up between them. "What's the Bagan furg's name?"

At his query, the Jreet shrugged. "I have trouble remembering the name of the planet I'm on," the Jreet replied.

Frustrated, Jer'ait turned back to the wall. "He is my groundmate," Jer'ait said. "The Baga."

There was no response.

Jer'ait realized he had not used the formal activation code to acknowledge speaking directly to the Watcher. Bristling, he said, "Watcher, he is my groundmate."

"According to my records, Jer'ait, you are not part of a groundteam."

"*Former* groundteam," Jer'ait said, balling his boneless Ooreiki fingers to keep his irritation in check.

"There are two members of your former groundteam in the hub with you, Peacemaster."

"Where is my former *Bagan* groundmate?" Jer'ait asked calmly.

"In a hallway, Peacemaster."

"Where is this hallway?" Jer'ait snapped, finally losing his temper.

The Watcher replied by giving him a string of precise coordinates based off of the ever-expanding space around them, using Tordakian finger-lengths as measurement units and the black hole in the Ganut sector as a reference point.

For a long moment, Jer'ait stared at the wall. Then, calmly, he turned to Joe and said, "Flea is helping Forgotten."

Daviin cocked his head, confusion straining his eye-ridges. "You got that from Tordakian finger-lengths?" He looked impressed. "You are smarter than I thought, Huouyt."

Jer'ait gave the Jreet an irritated look. "Anyone else have any damn ideas?"

"Uh…Watcher?" Joe said, giving the walls around them a nervous look.

"Yes, Prime Commander Zero?" the Watcher asked immediately

Jer'ait narrowed his eyes. "His *registered name* is 'Joe Dobbs.'"

The Watcher said nothing.

"Uh…" Daviin said, glancing at the walls nervously. "Great Watcher of Koliinaat. How long until the Geuji's trial is over? I have a…wager…I'd like to make."

"*Why wait until the trial is over?*" the Watcher asked pleasantly. "*Do you have the funds available for a full Representative's Challenge, Daviin ga Vora?*"

Daviin flinched, then glanced at the others, confusion in his small golden eyes. "They are in my accounts on Faelor as we speak," Daviin replied, frowning. "But I was told by a jenfurgling Ueshi running the Aezi's office that I could not challenge while the Aezi worm was in a Tribunal session."

"I don't see why you couldn't," the Watcher said pleasantly. "It's a mere courtesy. There is no law that says you have to wait. Would you like to submit your application now, Daviin?"

"I can't," the Jreet muttered. "I was told by the Exchange Commission that I can't move that much funding without permits. I'm waiting on permits. They said six weeks."

"*I think it's safe to say your permits will clear. As a matter of fact, I just received confirmation. The funds have been transferred. Congratulations, Daviin. You are now authorized to challenge.*"

Daviin looked flustered. "But they told me *that* paperwork would take several weeks, once my funds had cleared and I'd placed my security deposit."

"*Not surprisingly, it appears the person you spoke to was wrong. On what grounds would you like to issue your challenge?*"

"Now just hold on!" the Human snapped, stepping between the Voran and the wall. At the same time Daviin straightened in a rigid coil of indignant fury that they had been witnessing so often in the last weeks of travel to Koliinaat and said, "The Aezi is a fat, lying, dishonorable *vaghi* who falsifies crimes and flagrantly breaks his oaths in front of billions, knowingly trying a forgery instead of a real Geuji. He is a disgrace to Jreet everywhere, a coward who has allowed the luxury of Koliinaat to corrupt the Aezis' already weak moral code, and he shall dance on my tek for his misdeeds."

"*Your application was accepted. Congratulations, Daviin. And good luck.*"

An instant later, the Jreet disappeared, leaving Joe and Jer'ait staring at each other in an empty hub. Silence reigned. On the far wall, an elevator pinged and a group of Ooreiki in grounders' black stepped out and wandered off down a hall, grunting and laughing in a harsh Ooreiki dialect. Then they were gone again, leaving Jer'ait and Joe alone.

"You know," the Human muttered in the silence that followed, "I get the idea this was a setup."

• • •

"The Aezi is a fat, lying, dishonorable vaghi who falsifies crimes and flagrantly breaks his oaths in front of billions, knowingly trying a forgery instead of a real Geuji. He is a disgrace to Jreet everywhere, a coward who has allowed the luxury of Koliinaat to corrupt the Aezis' already weak moral code, and he shall dance on my tek for his misdeeds."

Daviin suddenly found himself coiled on a glass platform surrounded by spheritheater seating, his voice of moments before echoing against the thousands upon thousands of seats, none of which were placed higher than the others, half of which were filled with aliens, and all of which were pointed at him. Once again, he got the uncanny feeling of being in the Aezi gladiatorial pit, the entertainment of millions.

Before him, the shamefully pale, fat Aezi Representative was slowly lifting his head from his coils, a look of bewilderment on his blunt, cowardly face.

"Honorable Representatives, as you have just heard, we interrupt this fascinating Tribunal session to highlight a Representative's Challenge. Daviin ga Vora, son of Redwiin ga Vora, son of Adeiin ga Vora, son of Mabiin ga Vora, son of Rathiin ga Vora, son of—"

"What in the Jreet hells is the meaning of this?" the First Citizen demanded, glaring at Daviin, whose ruby coils now took up the center of the Tribunal platform.

"The Vorans have issued a challenge to the Aezi," the Watcher replied. *"Daviin ga Vora represents."*

"That can *wait*," Aliphei roared, so violently that his shaggy blue fur rippled. "We are currently trying the universe's most dangerous criminal."

"Yes, well, as stimulating as this show is, Daviin's application was approved. To delay any longer would be to give the Aezi an unfair time to prepare."

Representative Prazeil arched his neck up in a fury, making Daviin realize just how *big* his opponent was. "I was aware of no challenger application!" he roared.

"It was recently approved."

"How recently?" Aliphei snapped. He had backed away from his podium, putting distance between him and the two of them.

"Of course. In what unit of measurement would you like that information, your Excellency? I could give you Diji ewets, Mogati mebus, Stajetti icarions…"

"Days," Aliphei snapped.

"Perhaps you can clarify. Do you mean Poenian days, Faelorian days, Grakkan days—"

"Standard days!"

"I apologize, but it is an imprecise number. Would you like that in Bajnan increments of eighty-one, Itharian increments of thirteen, Human increments of ten—"

"Damn it," Aliphei roared. "Get him off the Tribunal floor! We're busy."

"Unfortunately, your Excellency, because the challenged Representative taking part in the trial is weaker and less experienced in combat, and therefore has an excellent chance of losing, and because the challenger, who is more intelligent, more versed in warfare, and more maneuverable, upon winning, could affect the outcome of said trial, the Representative's Challenge supersedes the trial itself, priority-wise."

"I vote to condemn!" Aliphei snarled.

"Did you call me *weak*?!" Prazeil screamed at the air itself. He ripped his podium from the platform and hurled it into the Regency's spherical seating. "I'm not *weak*."

"Care to place your tek on that?" Daviin snapped, rearing in challenge. "I'll hang it on my wall, Aezi. Small and stunted as it is."

"Condemn him!" Aliphei snapped. "We have plenty of proof."

"You shall *dance* tonight, Voran!" Prazeil shrieked, flinging the First Citizen's podium aside as his sperm-colored body uncoiled. It tumbled over the edge, only to disappear moments before it crashed into the seating below. The glass beneath Daviin's coils began to vibrate in his weak, pathetic battlecry. Voran returned it, screaming the name of his forefathers.

"Remove the accused from the platform!" the First Citizen commanded.

"I'm sorry, your Excellency, Prazeil ga Aez is still presiding and it takes two votes to end a Tribunal session."

Prazeil raised his energy level and vanished from the visible spectrum. An instant later, the box over which was draped the fake Geuji shattered as something huge crashed into it. Daviin pinged and similarly raised his energy. The world went black around him.

"Remove me to my room!" Aliphei shrieked, his shaggy body backing to the very edge of the platform overlooking the void. "Now!"

"As you command, your Excellency." Then it was just Daviin and Prazeil on the platform, and once again, Daviin found himself facing a larger foe to entertain the masses.

• • •

"Is that electronics?" one of the Ooreiki seated along the bar asked with a curious note, peering up at the huge vidscreen showing the fight in the center of the Regency. After a violent tussle, the Jreet had flung each other from the central Tribunal platform and were wading through the Congressional seats in a rage as startled Representatives screamed and got out of their way. The camera, however, kept switching back to the glittering, sizzling mechanical guts of the blubbering green Geuji on the screen, who, once the Jreet had crashed into him, had resumed his confession to unhearing masses at a speed approximately five times normal, making his words sound like high-pitched gibberish. No one was taking notes. The Congressional lawyers were either dispersed, dead, or, in one unfortunate Huouyt's case, splattered in an arc across a good portion of the Regency's Y-axis seating after Prazeil had whipped him so violently off the platform he ripped in half.

The onlookers had cheered.

Now they were arguing amongst themselves as to whether or not the green blob on the screen was a robot.

"Looks like Daviin's holding his own," Joe said, watching the show from his booth with Jer'ait.

"Indeed," Jer'ait replied. Still in Ooreiki pattern, the Huouyt hadn't said much since the fight had started. Two hours and five hundred and eighty-seven destroyed Regency seats later, he still hadn't had much to say.

The room cheered as another podium was ripped from its place and hurled across the Regency. Very rarely did the Watcher allow Representatives to come to blows, and it was the greatest story since Neskfaat, filling every available channels, even one reserved for single-species use. The Ooreiki grounders were even then taking bets on how many podiums the two Jreet would crush in their duel.

"Think he's going to win?" Joe asked, as the Ooreiki hooted and called for more drinks.

"Do you?" Jer'ait asked, almost bitter.

"You found him once," Joe said. "How about you find him again? Just the two of us."

Jer'ait's sticky Ooreiki-patterned eyes flickered to him. "The first time, he wanted to be found."

"Screw Forgotten," Joe said. "Find the Jahul."

For a moment, Jer'ait almost looked interested. Then, slowly, "The Watcher is not going to help us."

"He also can't help the Jahul, specifically, can he?" Joe demanded. "So somewhere on Koliinaat, a Jahul is pushing around a huge box filled with Geuji. Am I right?"

Jer'ait glared at him. "We aren't going to be able to wreck his plan, Human. *Look* at it." He made a disgusted gesture with a boneless arm at the view of the inside of the Regency, where the fake Geuji continued to confess to an empty platform. "It doesn't matter if Daviin wins. He's got enough right there to blackmail the Tribunal for the next thousand turns."

"You're assuming he escapes."

"He will," Jer'ait said. He took another sip of his blue-tinged drink.

"You don't sound too upset by that."

"I'm honestly not sure what to think," Jer'ait said. "I swore an oath to Congress...to uphold the law. And the law is...gray...where the Geuji is concerned. All the crimes we could find to pin on him were pardoned. He's not even a citizen. His species was never incorporated."

Joe felt his first real surge of anger boil up from within, realizing that Jer'ait was perfectly happy to let the Geuji get away with everything.

"I say we find him," Joe said, shoving his cheap whiskey aside. "Daviin said he called himself Syuri. He wrote down his identification numbers and gave them to me."

Jer'ait gave him an irritated look. "Let the Geuji go. You, me, Daviin, Flea—we were all pawns. Your turn came and went. Now the hand moves on."

Joe narrowed his eyes at his friend, "What kind of janja pile is that?"

"The realistic kind," Jer'ait muttered. He went back to watching the fight. Back at the bar, the group of Ooreiki cheered again. Daviin had launched a podium at the Aezi and hit him square in the head, knocking him backwards in a podium-crushing sprawl. Unfortunately, it hadn't done much damage to the massive, cream-colored Jreet. He screamed another shee-*whomph* battlecry and flashed invisible again, and a moment later, a wave of Representative chairs went spraying out into the other viewing booths, flung aside by the Jreet's invisible body. The Ooreiki howled and downed more drinks, calling out bets.

"All right," Joe said, snagging his coat and standing. "Be a pawn. I'm gonna go have a chat with our friend."

"How?" Jer'ait snorted.

"I'm gonna ask nicely," Joe said. He threw his coat over his shoulder and walked from the room.

"The Watcher isn't stupid!" Jer'ait called after him.

Ignoring the Huouyt, Joe went around the corner, into a relatively deserted hallway, and stopped. He stood there in several moments of silence before he could properly collect his thoughts. He'd never been on Koliinaat before, and the idea of speaking to a sentient AI disturbed him. Tentatively, he said, "Watcher, you hear that?"

"*Of course, Joe,*" the Watcher replied. "*I have been listening since the hub.*"

Joe took a deep, shuddering breath, and leaned back against the wall. "Then you know this Geuji forced me to kill one of my best friends. My mentor. His life or mine."

The Watcher hesitated. "*I was aware.*"

"I was enslaved by a Dhasha in Human bootcamp," Joe went on. "The damn thing was going to breed me. I was bigger. More meat. He loved to eat other Humans in front of me, then make me climb into his jaws and pick the flesh from his teeth. Thought I was gonna die. So scared I kept pissing myself. They punished me for that. Tore their claws through my skin, left me with so many scars that nanos have trouble finding what goes where."

The Watcher said nothing.

"So when I finally got away from him, I swore to myself it would never happen again. Swore I'd die first. He broke me in a lot of ways. Then Bagkhal saw me mouthing off and decided to piece me back together. Declared ka-par. I was just a stupid kid, so I accepted. I lost. Bagkhal could have taken me as a slave, but didn't. He could've done a lot worse than Knaaren, legally, but he took me under his wing, instead. Taught me how to survive, how to lead."

His listener's response was silence.

Joe swallowed. "He even taught me how to die."

The walls around him resonated with stillness, but he knew the Watcher was listening.

Joe tightened a fist and composed himself. Once he was sure his voice wasn't going to crack, he went on. "This guy was the only Dhasha I've ever known who didn't have Takki," he said. "The only decent Dhasha I've ever heard of. And I killed him. Looked him in the eyes as he drowned." Joe swiped trembling fingers across his eyes. "Sputtered and died in a pit I helped dig. I stood on the edge and watched him choke. Water splashed on my feet. I could have saved him. Could have told the Ooreiki to plug the tunnel. All it would've taken was a word." He took a shuddering breath, let it out between his teeth. "I still have nightmares about it."

"*I'm sorry,*" the Watcher said softly.

Tilting his head back against the corridor, Joe closed his eyes and said, "You know what it's like to be sent down a tunnel to die, Watcher?"

"*I can guess,*" the Watcher said.

"Yeah? You ever felt the dust in your nostrils? Heard the thunder of oncoming Dhasha? Got your arm pulled off 'cause you were fighting too hard? Seen your blood seeping into the floor as they fought over who got to eat you?"

"*No,*" the Watcher said.

"You know what it's like to kill your best friend because he'll kill you if you don't?"

The Watcher said nothing.

"I wanna look this Geuji in the eyes and ask him why," Joe said, opening his eyes. "Of all the guys down there that day, I want to know why he made me do it. Then I want to kill him."

For a long moment, the corridor was utterly silent around him. Then, softly, "*You and Jemria have more in common than you know.*" A moment later, the hall disappeared, and Joe felt a strange tingle-numb sensation throughout his body before he was suddenly standing in the cargo bay of a ship.

In the center of the bay, a single metal incineration box sat alone and unguarded. On one side, it had a row of beeping lights and what looked like a speaker system.

"Thank you," Joe whispered.

The Watcher did not reply. Joe walked up to the crate and touched the side. It was a cube about as high and wide as he was tall.

"You the Geuji?" Joe asked softly, looking at the beeping lights. The RECEIVE light was on.

The box didn't reply.

Joe ran his fingers along the box's controls, stopping on the SPEAKER light. It was lit up, waiting.

"I know you can hear me," Joe said. "And I know damn well you know who I am." He pulled his hand away from the controls and fisted it. "Which means you know I'm going to eject your ass into space if you don't answer me. You the Geuji?"

For a long moment, he thought the alien would not reply. Then, softly, "Yes." The voice almost sounded...scared.

Joe stared at the box. It wasn't what he had envisioned, in his fantasies of this moment. He had expected to see some grand mastermind, splayed across a thousand different instruments and machines, conducting the dance that had sent him to Koliinaat, tugging the strings to send people like him to their deaths in the millions. Instead, the Geuji almost looked...entombed. Trapped in its own coffin. Joe ached to see the creature on the other side, to know what kind of being had sent him into those tunnels.

"You know why I'm here," Joe said.

"Bagkhal." It had taken the creature on the other end no more than a second.

"Yeah," Joe said, choking up this time. "Bagkhal." He eyed the IMMOLATE button. "Why'd you make me do it?"

For a long moment, the Geuji said nothing.

"Why?!" Joe screamed, slamming his fist hard against the side, just missing the button.

"He asked that it would be you," Forgotten said quietly.

"Why?" It came out as a hoarse whisper.

"He wanted to die with a friend."

Joe almost pushed the button. Almost. His thumb touched it, caressed it, felt its smoothness under his finger. Then he closed his eyes and wept. He ducked his forehead to the side of the cold, metal crate and struggled to get his breathing under control. "Why?"

"Bagkhal had one thousand, eight hundred and seventy-two male heirs," Forgotten said. "By Dhasha law, a Dhasha male is unable to take mates until his father is dead."

Joe blinked at the box through tears, staring at the steel that was ninths from his nose. Bagkhal had mentioned his heirs, and that Jemria would take care of them. "So?" he asked.

"Your friend schooled all of his heirs in his personal ethical and moral code, but even though some had seen over six hundred turns, they were impotent in society, by the Dhasha's own rules. Now they can disperse to the four corners of the known universe and have families of their own. They can take important positions in society, start drafting laws, enforcing codes, leading by example. Some might even become princes and draw whole planets into their rule, spreading their philosophy. Many, if I can help it."

Joe stared at the box. "You killed him so his sons could *breed*?"

"What better way to spread his ideals to an entire universe?"

"You son of a *bitch*!" Joe snarled. He pounded the side of the crate. "You hear me? You goddamn son of a *bitch*!"

"I hear you," Forgotten said softly.

"Bagkhal said it was a test," Joe managed. He wiped his eyes again. "What was the test? And don't ashing lie to me. There's a button out here that says Immolate, you nasty vaghi ashsoul."

"I know there is," Forgotten whispered. "My world collapses every time I feel you hit the crate. By my calculations, you're about a thumb's-width from pushing it."

"What was the test?" Joe demanded, punching the crate again. "I swear to God I'm hitting it if you don't answer me."

"Loyalty," Forgotten said. "It was to prove your loyalty."

"Excuse me?" Joe asked hoarsely.

"Your former groundmate has had a vendetta against you from the beginning. Wrongfully. Because a Trith attempted to take you out of the picture. Bagkhal and I could think of no better way for you to prove your loyalty to Congress."

For over a tic, Joe couldn't think. All he could do was stare blindly at the box through tears. "Are you telling me," he managed, "you traded my life for his?"

Forgotten did not reply.

"Answer me," he whispered in fury.

"You are more important than you know," Forgotten said finally.

"You traded my life for his. Because of the Trith."

"No," Forgotten said. "I hate the Trith. The Trith are meddling, controlling, backstabbing little Huouyt that should all be shot on sight. I kill as many as I can, but they unfortunately have the capacity to reproduce."

"They have an agenda, and they make sure the whole world dances on their strings," Joe said softly.

Forgotten went utterly silent.

"You know," Joe said, eying IMMOLATE, "while pushing that button would totally make my millennium, it won't be nearly as satisfying as stomping the soot outta you before I blast you full of plasma and eject your ass into space." Joe slid his hand along the control panel and hit the OPEN mechanism. He had to back out of the way as the box folded open. A crushed and folded roll of black, quivering flesh slid outward, pooling in a wrinkled pile on the floor in front of him.

Joe stared down at the glistening heap of ebony tissue, feeling somehow let down. It seemed almost...pathetic.

Joe turned to walk around the Geuji and the entire pile of flesh flinched in a tiny, helpless spasm.

It can't even crawl away, Joe thought. He watched it ripple and quiver for several moments before he looked away, feeling sick. Into the silence that followed, he said, "Can you still hear me?"

The pause seemed infinite. Then, a small and frightened, "...yes."

Joe said nothing. He watched the Geuji, struggling between his fury and his self-disgust. Finally, he lifted his arm and tossed his coat aside. The motion made the Geuji's entire body give another tiny flinch.

"The air gonna kill you?" Joe demanded.

"No."

"You gonna get some horrible infection or something if I touch you?" The pile of flesh quivered again. "No."

"Will it hurt?" Joe demanded.

There was a long, horrible pause. "I can't defend myself," the Geuji finally whispered.

"I meant you," Joe muttered gruffly. "Will it hurt you?"

The flesh went suddenly still. "Aside from terrify the hell out of me?" Forgotten said. "No."

"I want you to promise me something," Joe said. "And I want you to shake on it. As best as you goddamn can. You understand what I'm getting at?"

"I'm too scared to really think straight at the moment," Forgotten managed.

"There's not much to understand. I'm offering you a bargain, and you're gonna accept it, and swear your oath on it, or I'm going to send you on your very own spacewalk."

"I get that much," Forgotten whispered. "I don't know what you want."

"Must be a new experience for you, huh?" Joe said dryly.

"Not new," the Geuji said quietly. "Just hasn't happened recently."

Joe considered. Then he walked forward and squatted beside the pile of flesh. It flinched again, a whole fraction of a dig, like a slug that was glued to the floor. "All right," Joe said, "you ready?"

"Yes," Forgotten said, his voice barely audible.

"I want you to think about this," Joe said, "the next time you are out there pulling strings."

For a long time, Forgotten simply huddled there, waiting. Then, tentatively, "Think about what?"

"This," Joe said. He continued to squat beside the Geuji and waited. Tics passed. "That's all?"

"It's a lot to think about," Joe said. "If you're doing it right."

"I...suppose it is."

"Okay," Joe said. "Ready to shake on it?"

The Geuji's body gave another tiny flinch, but he said, "Yes." Then, after a moment of hesitation, "But could you simply lay your hand down? Trying to move me could be...damaging."

In response, Joe put his hand down on the Geuji's body and held it there. "Listen to me, you miserable vaghi," he said softly, "nobody likes to have their life in someone else's hands. It sucks. A lot."

"Understood," Forgotten whispered. To his credit, his cool flesh beneath Joe's hand barely quivered.

"I read something once that kinda applies to you," Joe went on. "Was on some art my dad collected, I think. Hard for me to remember. Was a long time ago. But anyway. With great power comes great responsibility. And you've got the ability to change the world."

"I..." Forgotten hesitated, "...know."

"All right." Joe lifted his hand from the Geuji's body. "That's all I wanted to say." He stood to go. Wandering over to retrieve his coat, he took one last look at the Geuji, whose vulnerable ebony body was rippling much like the constant moving black waves of texture inside a Congressional nannite spaceship. He turned away. "Watcher, take me to—"

"Wait," Forgotten interrupted. "I would like to add to that."

Joe hesitated and turned back to the Geuji.

"But with great responsibility, one finds great loneliness," Forgotten intoned. "Can I call you a friend?"

Joe laughed. "I just threatened to incinerate you and jettison your ass into space."

"You had just cause. May I?" The desperation in the Geuji's voice was unmistakable.

Joe snorted. "I have no misconceptions about what's going to happen to me once I leave you here. I'm going to go right back to being your puppet. Dancing to your tune, doing whatever it is you had planned for me. And I know you *did* have something planned for me. I'm the only one of the survivors of Neskfaat who didn't do something important afterwards." He cocked his head. "Well, me and the Grekkon. But they're almost classified as non-sents, so that leaves me."

Forgotten was silent a very long time. Then, "You will."

"Then we can't really be friends, can we?" Joe asked.

It seemed to take an eternity for the Geuji to finally answer. "No."

"Goodbye Forgotten. Make sure you think about it."

"I will."

Joe took one last look at the Geuji's quivering ebony mass. "Watcher," he said, "I'd like to go back, now."

• • •

"Okay, I sent out those To Be Forgotten files and got us launched a few hours ago," Syuri said as he opened the door and stepped into the shuttle bay. "Your real confession was all over the news. Species preservationists jumped all over—" Upon seeing the Geuji sprawled out on the unfolded box, Syuri froze, his chambers tightening painfully. "Forgotten?"

A wave of relief hit his sivvet so strong that Syuri staggered.

"Sweet Hagra!" Syuri cried, rushing up to crouch beside the sentient mold. He hesitated at the edge of the flesh, afraid to touch it. "What happened?"

"My box opened unexpectedly." The voice was muffled, as the speaker was now facing the floor.

"Was the Baga in here?" Syuri demanded, looking around the room for the sneaky, insectoid alien that had disappeared the moment Forgotten had been safely tucked away on Syuri's ship.

"No. Did you purchase the robotics?"

"Well, yes," Syuri said, reluctant to leave the subject of how the Geuji had come to be sprawled across the floor. "They'll be waiting for us in the Jakun system. Are you sure we can wait that long? What if you dry out?"

"There should be a humidity control on the ship. The cargo bay needs to be as close to the absolute saturation point as you can get it. And, apologies, but quicker would actually be better, in that respect. I've been trying not to panic for several hours, now." There was a tension in the Geuji's words that made Syuri's chambers tighten further.

Syuri got up and hurried to the humidity controls, cranked it to the max, and the room began to fill with cold, clammy air. When he returned, the Geuji was exactly where he had left him.

"So," Syuri hedged reluctantly, looking at the Geuji's quivering mass, "uh, was this in the plan?"

For the first time since Syuri had met the Geuji, Forgotten laughed. "No. It wasn't in the plan, Syuri."

"Is everything still going to be okay?" Syuri asked, somewhat unnerved by the Geuji's laughter.

"Did the news agencies play my confession?"

"Yes," Syuri said. "The Jreet dropped everything and all went to the Regency to watch the fight. All the Sentinels. They say they're lining up to challenge, whether Daviin wins or not."

"Then it'll be fine," Forgotten told him.

"So what are you going to do?" Syuri asked. "Take down Congress? There's talk that Aliphei might have to abdicate."

"He won't." Forgotten quieted. "Syuri, may I ask you a question?"

"Sure."

"If I were to say to you, 'With great power comes great responsibility,' what would you say to me?"

Syuri gave the Geuji a wary glance and backed up a couple digs. "Not no, but *hell* no, Jemria. Leave the Representative seat to the Jreet. Last thing I want is power *or* responsibility, you damned corpse-rot. It was bad enough all the *money* you stuffed in my accounts. You *know* I'm just gonna have to give a lot of it away, right? I'm a pirate, not a perfumed politician."

"You're a smuggler. You haven't killed anybody."

Syuri opened his mouth to argue, then realized that arguing with a Geuji was so innately stupid that it was used as a colloquialism for the epitome of pointlessness. He shut his mouth and glared.

"You aren't going to argue?" Forgotten asked, sounding amused.

Syuri gave him an irritated look. "I wonder what's on the waves." He went over to the little communications console set into the shelving units and turned on the wall-screen, then dialed it in to the Koliinaati waves. Immediately, the ongoing battle between the two big Jreet showed up in a heat-spectrum overlay, showing the two contestants currently in the process of demolishing the Regency floor.

"Please turn it up," Forgotten said. "I think the microphone is aimed at the ground."

Syuri obliged, cranking up the sound on the speaker system until it was reverberating through the very floor of the ship. "That Voran fighting the Aezi Representative on the floor of the Regency right now is the one who escaped Aez with me," Syuri said. "Daviin ga Vora. I'd recognize that name anywhere."

After a moment, "Has this been going on long?"

"Only like eight hours," Syuri said, disgusted.

"And the news services are covering the fight?" Forgotten asked.

"Like it's the only thing happening in the universe," Syuri muttered. "You can't even get race results right now. Everyone's betting on the two Jreet."

"Daviin is going to win."

Syuri gave the screen a dubious look. "I don't know, Jemria. The white Aezi's like twice his size."

"Listen to their war cries," Forgotten said. "The Aezi has taken enough of Daviin's poison that he's starting to slur."

Syuri cocked his head at the screen and tried to distinguish the two engine-like shee-*whomph* Jreet war cries, but try as he might, he couldn't tell the difference between them.

Forgotten listened for a few more tics, then said, "You can turn it down, now. It will be over in sixteen tics."

"You know," Syuri said, unhappily, "You'd be a killer in the Jahul gambling dens." He had bet millions on the Aezi, mostly because he really wanted to see the Voran get some sort of comeuppance.

Forgotten paused a moment. "Syuri, were you placing petty wagers on the Jreet when I was lying here for hours, dehydrating and helpless?"

Syuri swallowed in a spasm. "No."

Forgotten seemed to digest that. Almost gently, he said, "You should go place another one. Fifty million on the Voran. Cause of death will be strangulation."

"Strangulation?" Syuri said, frowning. "They don't strangle each other. Only everybody else."

"They strangle a few," Forgotten said. "In matters of severe dishonor. You should place the bet. Fifteen tics."

"I'm good," Syuri managed. In truth, he had been hoping that Forgotten wouldn't find out about his nasty gambling habit. Just in coming to Koliinaat, he had lost almost half a billion of Forgotten's money in frivolous wagers.

"No, do it," Forgotten said. "I want to test a theory."

Syuri raised an eyebrow, but he reluctantly turned back to the com, brought up his favorite high-roller gambling feed, and entered in Forgotten's information. "Done," he said, nervously closing the account. "What kind of theory?"

"A personal one."

"Um," Syuri said, fidgeting. He had the weird feeling the theory was about *him*, and he felt very much like a cornered vaghi in a scientist's cage. "Can you at least give me an idea what kind of theory?"

"You're about to win a lot of money," Forgotten said. "I want to see what happens."

Syuri frowned at the screen. The odds were 5 to 1, in favor of the Aezi, plus modifiers for time of death. "I could make two hundred and fifty million. A lot more if the time of death is correct."

"In sixteen tics. With absolutely no effort on your part."

By the way the Geuji said it, Syuri was sure there was something he *should* be getting, but wasn't. Not uncommonly when around the Geuji, Syuri felt stupid. "I'm not understanding."

"Patience."

So Syuri watched. He watched the Jreet continue hurling chairs and podiums at each other as other Jreet crowded around in a wide ring, chanting war cries. Then he saw the Aezi stumble, saw the smaller Jreet lunge in and wrap his lithe body around the bigger Jreet's neck, cinching it down until the bigger Jreet's mouth hung open, tiny blue eyes bulging in a death-grimace. He checked the clock. Sixteen tics. He'd made close to half a billion credits in the space of the time it took to shower.

"Wow," Syuri said. "No wonder you're rich."

Forgotten said nothing.

Syuri shut down the wall unit. "So what was the theory?"

"I'm sure you'll figure it out."

Syuri laughed. "That's not very nice, picking on an old Jahul. You know I pissed out all my last nutrient infusions when I ran from the Jreet. My brain isn't working at its prime. I missed something."

Forgotten hesitated a moment, then said, "Syuri, how hard was it for you to make that money?"

"Easiest money I ever made in my life," Syuri said, warily. "Did you have it flagged somehow?"

"Do you want to make *more* money like that, Syuri?" the Geuji prodded.

"Sure," Syuri said, not following. *Damn* the Jreet for making him stupid. He itched to go get his supplements, but refrained, knowing that he could pack himself so full of nutrients a chamber ruptured and he still wouldn't have the brainpower to follow the Geuji along one of his 'plans.' When Forgotten offered nothing else, he said, "Um, forgive me for being dense, but how?"

"You have access to the humidity controls."

Syuri glanced at the panel on the wall. "I'm still not following."

His sivvet got hit with a sudden, brief crash of joy before the Geuji stifled it.

Nervous, now, Syuri said, "What's going on, Forgotten? What did I do wrong? You want me to change the setting? Too wet?"

"I can't move," Forgotten said.

Syuri peered at the quivering ball of tissue. "You want me to slide your box closer to the humidifiers?"

"I'm very smart."

Now he *knew* he was missing something. "Obviously not smart enough. What in the ninety Jreet hells are you trying to say?"

"I'm also afraid to die."

At that point, it dawned on him. Forgotten was offering him the chance to have his own personal Geuji at his service. Forever. All he had to do was just 'forget' to take him to the Jakun system and its awaiting robotics. Syuri just blinked at him. "You're not smart. You're a Jreet-kissing jenfurgling. I swear on the Ooreiki ghosts, Forgotten, someone needs to buy you a dictionary. Friends don't do that, you miserable corpse-rot. Friends help each other when they need it." He glared, irritated the Geuji would have thought he could stoop to something like that. "It's almost like you never knew your mother or something," he muttered. "Oozing mold."

A sudden, overwhelming rush of joy flooded his sivvet, this one completely uncontrolled. The intense pleasure of another's happiness overpowered all other senses in an unstoppable hurricane of emotion and Syuri staggered, then fell, holding his head as his body responded automatically to the bliss. He moaned as his chambers began releasing like a teenager witnessing his first orgy. Shuddering, Syuri found himself too wrapped up in the experience to tell the Geuji to stop.

"You're not saying much," Forgotten finally said, once the joy had ebbed. "Reconsidering?"

"Sweet Hagra," he muttered, once he'd picked himself back up from the floor. "You just made me ooze sexual lubricants all over myself, you slippery corpse-rot."

"Sorry."

"Don't be," Syuri muttered grudgingly. He looked down at himself and winced. "But for the love of the Ooreiki ghosts, don't tell anyone, either."

"I won't."

Grimacing, Syuri tried to slough off some of the slime. It formed a translucent, jiggling puddle on the floor. "And what," he muttered, flicking long strands of it from his fingers in disgust, "was so great just now that you had to return me to my carefully-buried teenage turns?"

"You want me to spell it out for you?"

Syuri pointed a slime-dripping finger at the Geuji. "You are this close to getting stepped on." As he spoke, a long dribble of lubricant slid from his finger to plop against the floor. He flicked off the remnants in distaste.

Forgotten took a moment to consider before he said, "The last time I gave someone a winning bet, it was in complete innocence, trying to make her life easier. She kept me in a headcom for the next six turns and forced me to come up with winning bets for her or she would do unpleasant things."

Syuri felt his gut clench at the wave of fear and hopelessness that rolled off Forgotten at 'unpleasant things' before the Geuji contained it.

"Well," Syuri said, grabbing a mechanic's rag from the rack beside him, "sorry to tell you this, Forgotten, but you don't quite fit in a headcom anymore." He gestured at the Geuji's mass with his towel.

"You have a ship," Forgotten replied. "And I'm not going anywhere."

Syuri cocked his head at the mold as he began wiping himself down. "Are you *asking* me to keep you here and use you for your lovely brain cells?"

"My brain doesn't have cells and no."

"Then what the hell is your point?" Syuri demanded, going after his legs, now.

The rush of joy, this time, knocked him out.

When he came to with a moan, the first thing Syuri heard was a guilty-sounding, "Sorry."

"You know what?" Syuri managed, pulling himself out of the puddle of slime, "From now on, we talk about depressing things." He shakily got back to his feet, but had to grab the rack beside him to steady his wobbly legs.

"What if I told you I wasn't really expecting you to try and save me?" Forgotten asked.

Syuri laughed. "I'd call you a bad liar." Trembling, he bent to retrieve the rag. "Really, Geuji, you need to work on that."

"You want me to lie to you?"

Syuri grimaced. "On the other hand, no, ignore that. Just a jabbering Jahul without his nutrients." He started carefully running the rag over his over-sensitized abdomen. "Most of the universe is filled with lying, backstabbing Huouyt. I like the fact you don't lie. It's refreshing." He grimaced as he peeled more layers of slime from his body, squeegeeing it to the floor in embarrassing plops.

Forgotten listened to him for a couple tics in silence before he said, "What if I told you I really went to Koliinaat to die?"

Syuri frowned, hesitating in his cleaning. "Did you?"

There was a long, horrible pause. Then, "Someone I respect once told me that God hates a coward. He lived a good life, and was very brave. As I've never been particularly brave, and my life has been more miserable than I could possibly explain, I took it to heart."

"You went there to die."

"Yes."

Syuri blinked. "The Baga said you sent him a note about thirty-two planets that had been stolen from Bagans, and to come help me today and you'd let him crash some Huouyt spaceships, once they were forced to abandon them on the planet. Gave him a date and location and everything."

Forgotten was silent for whole tics.

"Forgotten?"

"I never sent a note," Forgotten replied softly.

"Oh come on," Syuri snorted.

"I told him to distract the Jreet so Daviin would have the money to challenge Prazeil."

Syuri recoiled. "It was a Trith?"

Forgotten said nothing for some time. Then, reluctantly, "I know who it was."

"Oh?"

"It's not important," Forgotten said. "What's important is that I never meant for you to save me, but you did it anyway. Why?"

"Huouyt tear out my eyelids, not this again." Syuri made a disgusted sigh and tossed the sopping rag aside. It hit the far wall with a wet, sucking sound, then slid slowly down to the floor. "Why do you *think*, you oozing Geuji?"

"You take…special…pleasure in my presence?"

Syuri's eyes narrowed. "I need a shower." At that, he turned his back to the Geuji and headed back into the living area of the ship. He felt another surge of happiness behind him before he ducked into the main hall and sought out his bathing chamber.

37

MAGGIE'S SECRET

Jer'ait had gone to look for the Human when Joe suddenly appeared in the hallway, his small brown eyes looking haggard. Blinking, Jer'ait cocked his head at the wall, then at Joe. "The Watcher took you to see Forgotten?" he asked, stunned.

The Human nodded grimly and walked past him, back into the bar. This time, he ordered a full bottle of the piss-tinted poison. He had just sat back down at the booth and had begun to raise the bottle to his lips when Jer'ait snagged it out of his hands.

"A friend would not allow you to return to poisoning yourself because you just did something incredibly stupid," Jer'ait said, when the Human glowered at him. He set the bottle out of reach and sat down across from the Prime Commander. For a long time, they just looked at each other. Then Jer'ait said, "So. Did you kill him?"

"No," the Human croaked. "Probably should have. But I didn't."

Jer'ait found himself surprised at that. He would have bet anything the Human would have killed the Geuji, given the opportunity. "Did the Watcher not allow you to get close enough?" he hedged.

"Nope," Joe snorted. "I had my finger on the button. Could've crushed him with my goddamn boot—"The Human hesitated, frowning.

"Wait a tic." Frowning, the Human started patting at his pockets and yanked a docking slip from his jacket. "Got a pen?"

Jer'ait, who always carried several various tranquilizers with him in the form of common writing instruments, calmly tugged one from his vest and handed it to Joe. "Be careful you don't squeeze the grip too tightly."

Joe, who had immediately taken up the pen and started writing, hesitated. He looked at the pen, then looked suspiciously at Jer'ait.

"It's non-lethal," Jer'ait said. Then he grimaced. "Well, for an Ooreiki. Humans have less mass."

The Human stared down at the assassin's weapon for several moments. "Aw what the hell," he muttered, and went back to drafting his tiny note, crossing things off as he went.

Curious, Jer'ait leaned over to watch.

The Human wrote:

1) While on Kophat, you will enter Congress into a new Age.

2) You will make friends with a Huouyt assassin, and at his command, a Jreet heir shall remove your still-beating heart from your chest and deliver it to strangers.

3) After a battle the likes of which the universe has never seen, you shall have the cosmos' greatest mind helpless under your boot, and your mercy shall unmake him.

4) And while you shall die in a cave, shamed and surrounded by dragon-slaying innocents, your deeds will crush the unbreakable, and your name will never be forgotten.

As Joe wrote, Jer'ait found himself getting chills. He pulled his Ooreiki-patterned hands away from the Human, feeling the first real pangs of fear. Once Joe was done writing, he dropped the tranquilizer to the table and leaned back, staring at the page he had written, looking like he'd been hit by a freighter.

"Someone gave you a fourfold prophecy," Jer'ait whispered.

The Human just stared at the note. Then, without a word, he snatched up his coat, stood, and walked out of the bar.

Very carefully, Jer'ait pulled the Human's slip of paper across the table to him. He read the four parts again, cold chills wracking his spine. Then, softly, he said, "Watcher, destroy this."

"*Of course, Peacemaster,*" the Watcher obliged. The slip of paper vanished.

"And erase all records of the last ten tics within a thirty rod span."

"*Already done, Peacemaster.*"

Jer'ait swallowed hard. He turned to glance at where the Human had departed. His job—his *duty*—was to detain his former groundmate and take him to the Sanctuary for questioning and execution. Instead, he softly said, "And look out for him."

"*I will do all I can while he is in my care,*" the Watcher said. "*But it is not on Koliinaat where he will meet that end.*"

"Where?" Jer'ait asked softly.

The Watcher hesitated. "*Earth.*"

• • •

Daviin ducked another chair and, using his lower body as a whip, slammed a podium into his opponent's head, to the cheer of other Jreet. For some reason, halfway through the fight, the Sentinels had shown up and had started to cheer for *him*. Not only that, but they had actually left their charges to gather en masse, surrounding the two of them in ruby, cream, and gray coils. Thousands of them. The Regency had become a gladiatorial pit-ring, with what sounded like every Jreet on Koliinaat in attendance.

"Give up, Voran," Prazeil slurred. "Tekless coward." He ripped a canister of exotic gasses from inside one of the Representative booths and haphazardly hurled it at Daviin hard enough to explode. He missed his target by several rods, igniting the gasses on the floor between them. The resulting blast flipped Daviin head-over-tail into the Sentinel onlookers, who violently threw him back into the ring with shouts of encouragement. The same explosion knocked Prazeil backwards into a glass water-tank, which shattered under his weight, dousing him in whatever native slurry the Watcher kept on hand for their sentient liquid-based life-forms.

"Miserable...Ayhi," Prazeil managed. "Cold..." His tek-punctured body flopped uselessly, trying to right himself. *Rravut* spilled from his open wounds in dribbles of red that would kill lesser creatures on contact. "Come...fight..." His opponent groaned and flipped onto his back, his massive cream-colored scales mottled with long smears of blue. He flailed almost blindly, pinging directly at the floor like a child.

Daviin recognized the symptoms of *rravut* poisoning and slid in to finish it. When Daviin grabbed him by the throat, Prazeil groaned and tried to yank his head away, but was too weak. Daviin jerked him up, so that they were eye-to-eye. The Jreet surrounding them went totally quiet.

"Know this," Daviin said into the silence. "You dishonored us." When Prazeil again tried to pull away, Daviin tugged him brutally back, ripping part of his ear-crest. Forcing him to once again meet his eyes, Daviin said, "You took the oath of a Sentinel and you disgraced it with lies and ambition. You will walk the ninety hells alone, and no one will be there to meet you on the other side." He heard his words picked up and amplified by the Representative booths around him, broadcast to the entire Regency, but he didn't waver. Giving Prazeil a long, cold stare, Daviin said, "Today, you get what you wanted all along. Today, you became a politician. You are not Jreet."

Prazeil's blue eyes flickered toward the Jreet surrounding them, fear glinting in his watery blue eyes. "A warrior's death," he whispered. "Please. I deserve an ovi,"

"No," Daviin said, moving his body under him, "you don't." He left his ovi where it was, secured in a specially-made pouch within his tek-sheath, and started wrapping himself around the Representative's neck.

"*No!*" Prazeil cried, beginning to thrash. Glass and alien liquid were flung across the spectators as Prazeil tried to fight what was coming. He twisted, slamming Daviin violently into the floor again and again until Daviin had too many coils wrapped around his throat for him to lift his head.

Daviin listened grimly as the Aezi started to choke, then held on tight as the larger Jreet's length started to twist and quiver as his air was cut off. He flailed and struggled for several tics before he finally went still. Daviin continued to hold on, to make sure the deed was done.

"*Representative Prazeil ga Aez is dead,*" the Watcher intoned. "*Daviin ga Vora, you have earned a seat on the Tribunal and as a Representative of your species. Do you accept?*"

"Fuck the Tribunal *and* the Regency," Daviin snapped, taking a lesson from Joe. "I'm a warrior, not a fat vaghi cancer. I haven't had a good keg of *lesthar* since they froze my accounts on Jeelsiht. I go to get drunk." Around him, the Jreet screamed their approval and started ripping more chairs from the floor to throw at him in celebration. Ducking his obligatory post-victory assault, he started to uncoil himself from the Aezi.

The Watcher hesitated a moment as blood-fevered Jreet began wrecking the Regency in their frenzied copulations. Daviin shoved the Aezi body away and pulled himself out of the cold pool of liquid from the destroyed Regency water-chamber.

Tentatively, the Watcher offered, "*Representatives and their guests are given free unlimited kegs of lesthar at happy hour in four hundred and sixteen different Koliinaati locations.*"

Daviin, who had been picking bloody glass from under his scales, hesitated. He cocked his head at the booth that had spoken, then glanced at the thousands of Jreet around him. Absolute silence fell in the Regency as celebrating Jreet froze, mid-sex, watching him with sudden, *ovi*-sharp intensity.

• • •

Joe bought a yacht.

He didn't really have anything else to do with his money, since the Jreet's oath of Representative trumped his oath as a Sentinel, and food on Koliinaat was free. The Sentinels had offered to replace Daviin with six of their best warriors, but the idea of running around with *six* Jreet babysitting him had left Joe laughing in the messenger's face—and having to make another trip to a regen chamber because of it.

Jer'ait, likewise, was busy with official duties on Koliinaat and certainly wasn't lacking for cash. Joe never saw the Va'gan spend more than a few credits on food and drink, and he had an odd feeling that Jer'ait would still have his billions five hundred turns after Joe and the rest had blown theirs.

The only person Joe could have really shared his money with was Flea, but Joe was still pissed with him for trading sides on Koliinaat, and—perhaps justifiably—Flea had made a point of avoiding Joe ever since. Last he'd heard, Flea was busy systematically crashing Huouyt and Ooreiki spaceships that illegal immigrants had been forced to leave behind on Bagan-owned planets, after his honorable Voran friend on the Tribunal had a nice, *stimulating* talk with the Planetary Claims Board on his behalf.

So, in his last two weeks of leave, alone and bored, Joe bought a yacht.

It wasn't really fancy, just a few dozen million's worth, but it was big and had custom Human-patterned seating and beds, so it wasn't the scoop-shaped generic Ooreiki designs he was used to. At first, he had thought that the Human objects would be a well-deserved luxury, but the longer he used the chairs that seemed too flat, the mattress that had no concave slope, the sinks that were too tall, the carpets that were too soft, the more Joe wished he hadn't wasted his money.

Joe was floating in the pool of his yacht, boredly eying yet another newscast of the Baga destroying a perfectly good Ooreiki freighter in a glorious ball of fire and twisted metal, when it occurred to him that maybe his life would be more fulfilling with a woman.

Joe thought about heading back to the barracks early and having his pick of the women there, then grimaced. That, he realized, was part of the problem. He *could* have any Congie girl he crooked a finger at. They idolized him. Adored him. Had pictures of him on their walls. Full color, with him twisted in a heroic pose, regally holding a rifle, his combat boot on a Dhasha's head.

Joe had no freakin' idea where they came from, but he wanted to slaughter whatever bastard had put them together, as it had made it impossible to find a girl that wasn't starry-eyed with hero-worship, able to babble off the names of every battle he'd ever been in better than Joe could.

He briefly thought about hitting up the local bars on the off-chance he might find a civilian Human woman who would be interested in dating a Congie, then sighed. The chances of that were about as likely as surviving a spacewalk in his birthday suit.

Alone, bored to tears, Joe began surfing the species-specific, English-speaking Congie section of the local dating site with no real goal in mind. He was halfway through the first day's personal ads when he ran across one that made him do a double-take.

Maggie P. 53 turns in service. Rank: Not Specified. Combat Experience: Not Specified. Height: 5'2" Looking for: strong man, 6'2" or bigr. gud in bed, descent cock. had tired of shity leys, lokin fer full-tyme relasionship. must be COngie...can"t stand sivilyan wimps...gotta hve the bawls to stand up to a gurl. i'm sexy, intimadating, and self-relyant. real experyunced. I hve gud Rank, no i'm not telin. u shyoot me pic and i shyoot u mine. Want some1 dominunt and Taek-charge. welthy a big +

Joe sat there, staring at the ad for several tics. He glanced at the Create Account option. Then he closed his eyes and prayed to the Ooreiki ghosts for restraint.

Don't do it, he thought, staring at the ceiling through closed eyelids. *Mothers' ghosts, don't drop to her level. Just close the site and walk away.*

When he opened his eyes again, however, he couldn't help but read the ad a second time. He thought about every denied promotion, every overlooked kasja, every time he'd been forced to add time to his enlistment to buy gear or eat properly, and one question kept slamming through his mind, burning in his guts like a coal.

Why?

Why had she hated him so much? After so many turns, why couldn't she just let it go? Why did she lie about him, sneer whenever she saw him, throw *darts* at his goddamn picture? What had he done to her to deserve that? Why couldn't she just *move on*? Why did she hire private detectives to follow him, writing down every discrepancy, every tiny violation? What was *wrong* with her?

So they had been the only two survivors of their original groundteam on Kophat. So *what*? Millions of recruits died in that war. They bombed every barracks on the *planet*. So *what* if Joe hadn't managed to keep them all alive? He still felt ashy about it, but he had *moved on*.

And, in that moment, Joe realized he needed to know. It wasn't just a simple question, a yes/no answer or a multiple choice he wanted her to fill out at her convenience. He needed her to explain it to him, in person, so he could look in her eyes when she revealed to him that cardinal sin, that appalling crime that had made him worthy of so much loathing.

As soon as he realized that, he knew there was no going back. He began filling out an account under the name of Jimmy B. He put enough of his stats into his account to make it interesting without being recognizable, then sent her a message that said:

I'm a traveling Human merchant currently overseeing business in the Hev'asti textiles trade and I noticed your profile. I was intrigued! I'm not a Congie, but I'm wealthy and fit. I'm 6'4", well-endowed, run my own intergalactic shipping company, and can hold my own in Huouyt trade negotiations, so I am pretty confident I can be the strong personality you're looking for. 53 turns! You certainly do have experience. I've always been fascinated with Congie women and would love to meet. If nothing else, dinner's on me. How about tonight on my yacht? Say, 28:36? Hub 36A, door 139. Access code 2736009.

Joe hesitated, staring at the message for several tics before he hit SEND. Then he leaned back and sat there in his oddly-flat Human chair, watching the little flashing MESSAGE SENT light.

He couldn't, he found, move from the chair. He kept checking and re-checking, waiting for her reply.

It came a couple hours later.

not ushuly my thng, but we can trie it. will be thare for dnnr. Hve sumthing too drink. i lyke kon-yak.

Joe stared at the reply for several tics before he nervously glanced at the time. 22:14. He had a little over six hours. He got up, took a shower, brushed his teeth, combed his hair, dressed and redressed, forced himself to eat half a hamburger, then just sat down beside the pool, nervously tapping his fingers on the armrest of the strange alien chair.

What do you think you're going to accomplish with this, Joe? he thought as he watched the tics pass by with agonizing slowness. *You're just gonna ask her nicely what the fuck her problem is, and she's gonna tell you?*

No, he was not that naïve. She wasn't going to just *tell* him what was wrong with her. He'd asked her enough times and she'd just laughed him off that *that* was painfully obvious. And, he realized with growing apprehension, the moment she saw his face, she would just leave. No way would she even hang around for the question. She would just get pissed, maybe fly off the handle, then go try to get him demoted again.

So what the hell was he thinking he was going to accomplish?

Yet, the more he sat there, agonizing over what Maggie would do once she realized just whose yacht she had stepped onto, Joe knew that he *had* to know. He *had* to get her to finally answer the question that had been burning at him ever since he'd graduated basic.

So he began to plot. He made dinner. He set out a note. He put on some nice Ooreiki music. He bought a couple alien flowers from the hub and set them in a glass of water. He left a trail of strategically-lit rooms and corridors, ending in the dining area. Then he stood in the shadows inside the bathroom and waited.

Maggie arrived ten tics early, dressed in wig, makeup, false eyebrows and lashes, and a body-fitting black dress. She'd taken out the contacts and now her soft gray eyes looked almost vulnerable. Joe actually felt his breath catch and his heart start to hammer, seeing for the first time the beautiful woman that had had nothing but sneering disdain for him for so long.

...the beautiful woman that, he knew, could have shared his life with him. They had so much in common, so many stories to tell...

He watched from the darkened bathroom as Maggie eyed her surroundings with a look of awe. "Hello?" Her voice was hesitant, almost timid.

Joe stayed where he was. He needed her to step deeper into the room before he could show himself, lest he risk losing the only opportunity he was ever going to get.

Maggie's gaze finally came to rest on the note he'd placed on the coffee table inside the living-area, almost four rods into the room. She hesitated, and Joe got the feeling she was considering abandoning the meeting and going back out the way she'd come. He held his breath, waiting. He saw her eyes drift tentatively to the dining-room down the hall, where even then he had the light and music cranked up, giving it an appealing ambiance.

Almost reluctantly, Maggie left the air-lock and stepped down into the main living area, then crossed to the end-table. Setting down her purse, she picked up the note.

Joe knew what it read by heart.

Dear Maggie,
   Tell me why. You owe me that much.
   -Joe

Maggie started and dropped the note, but not before Joe had stepped from the bathroom and put himself between her and the air-lock. Seeing him, her soft gray eyes went wide, first with fear, then with fury.

"What the ash are *you* doing here?" she demanded, her decades-old sneer solidly back in place.

"I saw your profile," Joe said. "Thought we could catch up." He crossed his arms and leaned against the air-lock pointedly.

Maggie's gaze flickered to the exit, then back to him. Her eyes narrowed. "Get away from the airlock. That's an order. From a *Corps Director*."

"So," Joe said, staying where he was, "are you gonna tell me?"

Maggie's look was deadly. "I could have you thrown in the brig."

"Maybe," Joe said. "Later." He cocked his head at her. "Just tell me why, Mag. That's all I want to know."

"Why what?" she barked.

"Why do you hate me?" Joe asked.

Her pretty face twisted in a sneer. "You're a traitorous waste of air."

Joe kept waiting.

Maggie snorted and yanked her purse from the end-table. "Get out of my way." She stomped up the steps to the air-lock and tried to push past him. When Joe remained where he was, he watched violence cross her steely gray eyes.

"Careful," he warned. "You hit me and you *will* ruin that dress."

"You're threatening me," Maggie laughed. "A superior officer."

Joe just waited.

She must have realized that he was serious, because Maggie took a couple nervous steps backwards, away from him. "What do you want?" The sneer was gone, replaced with a hunted look.

"Tell me why," Joe said calmly. "You're not leaving until you tell me why you've been such an ashing backbiting vaghi bitch for fifty turns."

Her pretty eyes darkened to the color of slate. "You really want to know?" It came out as a cold whisper.

"I wouldn't be here if I didn't," Joe said.

Maggie set her purse down on a table-stand holding a fancy lamp. "All right, Joe. Here's why." Her gaze was like ice. "Once every few rotations, I'm visited by a Trith. They force me to watch my own death, again and again and again. Back in Basic, they would come to me every two or three weeks, while everybody else was sleeping. They'll show me other stuff, too. Awful stuff. Like Earth getting wiped out. Covered in kreenit. Everyone getting eaten. Every time they come, they show me that soot, Joe. They show you in the middle of it. And I can't stop them. They won't. *Stop.*"

Joe frowned and he felt his arms loosen against his chest. "A Trith?"

"They want you dead, Joe." Her cold gray eyes were becoming tear-filled. "And they won't stop coming to *me* because they want *you* dead."

"Mag," Joe said softly, a wash of empathy flooding his chest. "I'm so sorry…"

"Oh burning shut up already," Maggie snapped, swiping a forearm across her eyes. "You have no idea what it's like, knowing your own future. Knowing you've got no choice in it. Knowing *how* and *when* you're going to die. Having to see it over and over again. Makes me tempted to get out my gun and blow my own goddamn head off, to spite them, you know?"

"How do you die?" Joe asked softly.

Fear flickered across her eyes before Maggie looked away. For a long time, she just stared at the table. Then, softly, "An interrogation. Asking about you and that Geuji. Three days from now."

Joe froze. "What?"

"It's someone trained, but not military. Not Peacemaker, either."

"Va'gan?" Joe demanded.

Maggie's head snapped up. Slowly, she nodded. "Two of them. Working for someone powerful. Lots of pull." She hesitated. "Joe, I think it was Aliphei."

Joe frowned. "Ghosts, Mag! We need to get you out of here!" Jer'ait, he knew, would watch over her in the Sanctuary on Koliinaat, if he asked.

Maggie made a disgusted snort. "There's *nothing* you can do. Don't you understand that? They're *Trith*, Joe. Whatever you try to do is only going to send me right into their arms."

Joe opened his mouth to tell her that he was a vortex, that he could *change* the future, then he thought about that little docking slip sitting at a bar on Koliinaat. He closed his mouth and looked away.

"So now *I've* gotta ask," Maggie whispered, stepping up to peer up into his eyes. Her hatred was there, as strong as ever, but there was also something deeper, something that reminded him of a little girl who missed her guppies. "What is it about you, Joe, that I'm going to die to protect?"

Joe opened his mouth. He almost told her everything. Almost.

Then he saw a rapt glint in her eye, a tiny window into a massive factory of sheer cunning, just for a moment, before it was gone, hidden away as if a shutter had been drawn. Joe blinked at her, every hair on his body suddenly standing on end in a bone-chilling wave.

"Burning ghosts," he whispered. He took a step backwards, slamming his spine into the door, rubbing goosebumps on his arms. "Burning ghosts."

The Huouyt gave him a long, deliberate look, then smiled. "I tire of her pattern, anyway. Fifty-four turns is too long."

Joe was suddenly acutely aware of the fact that he wasn't carrying a weapon, not even a knife, and that there was no way he could get the air-lock open in time to escape his visitor.

"To answer your question," the Huouyt said calmly, "I made your life a hell because Na'leen believed so much in you that he made stupid decisions. A hundred turns of planning, and he threw it all away because of the few whispered words of a Trith." Maggie's face smiled up at him. "And, because I failed Na'leen, I could never return to Va'ga. I had no place in society. No purpose. No *meaning*. You took that from me, Human. You left me as a pawn without a hand." The Huouyt narrowed Maggie's eyes. "So yes, nothing would make me happier than to see you die the dance of nine thousand slices."

Joe swallowed convulsively, and the Va'gan returned his gaze for long tics, cold and silent.

"Now," the Huouyt eventually said, Maggie's pretty face still formed into a pleasant smile, "perhaps you will get out of my way?"

Joe was trembling all over, the tingles of alarm now a screaming cacophony in his mind. He was so sure he was going to die that he didn't actually hear the words that had come out of his tormentor's mouth. He blinked. "You're not going to kill me?"

The Huouyt snorted. "Oh, believe me. I would enjoy nothing more." Maggie's eyes were cold and calculating. "But you're going to destroy Congress. And I hate Congress more than I hate you." Maggie's face gave a bitter smile. "It's a delicate balance." The Huouyt gestured at the door and cocked its head at him, waiting.

Very slowly, Joe stepped aside.

The Huouyt gave him one last, long look. Then, "Tell Jer'ait he's getting better, but he still has problems fully assimilating a pattern's culture and psyche." Then opened the lock and stepped into the hub beyond.

END

Note from Sara: Zero Recall is different. If you read it right the first time, it should've blown your mind. Now, if you read it right the second time, it should blow your mind again. It should still be perfectly entertaining the third time through. It was an experiment in layers. Like a cake. (Or an onion.) It was a complex biyatch to write, but I think (hope??) I succeeded.

So. Now that you've finished the book, I dare you to go back and read **Chapter 1: Forgotten**, *and* **Chapter 5: The Hungry Kitten**. *I think it will answer a LOT of your questions, if you still have them.*

Let me know! Oh, and if you liked this book, please leave me a review on Amazon! I can't stress enough how, in the Grand Scheme of things, a few honest words from Readers Like You can really go a long way toward that World Domination thing I keep talking about. :)

kingnovel@gmail.com

ABOUT THE AUTHOR

My name is Sara King and I'm going to change the world.
No, seriously. I am. And I need your help. My goal is simple. I
want to champion, define, and spread character writing throughout the
galaxy. (Okay, maybe we can just start with Planet Earth.) I want to take
good writing out of the hands of the huge corporations who have had a
stranglehold on the publishing industry for so long and reconnect it to
the people (you) and what you really want. I want to democratize writing as an art form. Something that's always been controlled by an elite
few who have (in my opinion) a different idea of what is 'good writing'

than the rest of the world, and have been feeding the sci-fi audience over 50% crap for the last 40 years. (To get my spiel on character writing and what it is, jump to the Meet Stuey section of this book.)

To assist me in my goals to take over the world (crap, did I say that out loud??), please leave a review for this book! It's the first and easiest way for you guys to chip in and assist your friendly neighborhood writer-gal. And believe me, every review helps otherwise unknown books like mine stand up against the likes of the Big Boys on an impersonal site like Amazon.

Also, I have an email! (Totally surprising, I know.) Use it! (Don't you know that fanmail keeps writers going through those dark times when we run out of chocolate???) I love posting letters on Facebook—gives me something fulfilling to do with my time. ;) Shoot me a line! kingnovel@gmail.com

And, for those of you who do the Facebook thing, check me out: http://www.facebook.com/kingfiction (personal) or http://www.facebook.com/sknovel (my author page) or stay up to date on continuous new ZERO publications with The Legend of ZERO fan page: http://www.facebook.com/legendofzero

AFTERWORD

In case you hadn't guessed, this is the second book in a (very) large, sprawling sci-fi world. More ZERO stories are coming out very soon, if they haven't already, and I will very likely write more novels in this world, simply because I've been told to. Repeatedly. By people with that crazed, hungry look in their eyes. (Shudder.) While I'm working on them, be sure to check out these great books, short stories, and additional ZERO materials on Amazon:

The Legend of ZERO: Forging Zero. The story of how Joe Dobbs is captured from a devastated Earth and inducted into the Human Ground Force and trained to be a soldier for the alien army.

The Legend of ZERO: Zero Recall. (The one you just read. It's a play on Forgotten.) 53 turns after Forging ZERO, Joe Dobbs is recalled to fight a war the likes of which Congress has never seen.

The Legend of ZERO: Zero's Return. 20 turns after Zero faces off Forgotten in Zero Recall, he returns to Earth to fight a new kind of war—the kind that will determine the future of the Human race.

The Legend of ZERO: Zero's Legacy. After preserving Earth's most precious resource from the hands of the Huouyt, Joe and his friends must now work together to survive this new post-apocalyptic world—and find the People a home.

The Legend of ZERO: Forgotten. A Sacred Turn after Zero returns to Earth, his descendants seek out his ancient nemesis with a bargain Forgotten cannot resist: Remove Earth from Congress without a single death, and Humans will give him his freedom.

The Complete ZERO WorldBuilder: A complete(ly massive) glossary, fun facts, timeline, illustrations, and cool details that I couldn't pack into the books.

The Moldy Dead: A story about the Origins of the Geuji, one of whom plays a dominant role in books 2 and 4. The Moldy Dead is easily one of my best short stories.

Opening Night at the Naturals Preserve: A story about Congress' discovery of the Baga, one of whom plays an important role in book 2.

Planetside: A fun story about how the Ueshi earned the right to fly.

The First Gods of Fire: The story of how Congress was formed.

Breaking the Mold: How the Geuji were betrayed by Congress (again).

Beda and Shael: A Jreet love story, a la Romeo and Juliet. Except this time, it's Vorans and Welus. Yeah, sparks fly. And blood. And scales…

Parting Gift: The Vanun struggle to escape the Huouyt, both of whom evolved on the same planet. (Vanun on land, Huouyt in the sea).

Syuri: Everybody loves lackeys. Here's how Forgotten got his. ☺

And keep your eyes open for more, as I will keep putting them up whenever I have time. Just search "The Legend of ZERO" on Amazon. Also, if you liked ZERO, you'd probably like <u>Outer Bounds: Fortune's Rising</u>. It's another character sci-fi that'll rock your world.

And guys? Thanks. You are freakin' awesome.

MEET STUEY

Meet Stuey. He's our mascot here at Parasite Publications. Stuey is a brain parasite. Stuey burrows into people's heads and stays there. He takes over your body. He shuts you away from your senses. He talks to you in the darkness. He makes you do things you would never do while you can only watch in horror.

But he's an understandable little monster.

Imagine your favorite action-adventure story. Your favorite romance. Your favorite epic sci-fi. Your favorite thriller. Each one of them is going to have a character that left you breathless, one that had you at the edge of your seat, rooting for, screaming at, and pleading with. Those are the *only* stories that Parasite publishes.

Our goal at Parasite Publications is twofold: First, we want to produce memorable, sympathetic characters that readers will still be thinking about years after finishing our books. Second, we want to create a team of creative minds whose work can be trusted by readers to produce the same kind of character stories they love, time and again. We're forming a club. A logo. A place for readers to go to read books about *people*, not places or machines. A place for character writers to band together and create a brand that means quality to readers. Readers of Parasite books will no longer have to wonder if they're throwing their money away on novels that, even in 150k words, never really get into a character's head.

They never have to wonder, because that's what we're *about*. Getting into the character's head. And, if we do our job right, Parasite will get into your head and stay there. Just like Stuey.

Check us out on Facebook at http://www.facebook.com/ ParasitePublications/info to read more about Stuey's mission to change publishing for your benefit.

SARA RECOMMENDS

If you're looking for another great character novel, try <u>Changes</u> by Charles Colyott. This independent thriller writer grabs you by the balls and doesn't let you go until you beg for mercy. Colyott is a character writer supreme. Seriously, I haven't had a novel hold my attention this thoroughly since George R. R. Martin. Because Colyott blows most traditionally-published authors completely out of the water, he deserves your money. (GIVE HIM YOUR MONEY!!) Ahem. ☺

OTHER TITLES
BY SARA KING

Guardians of the First Realm: Alaskan Fire
Guardians of the First Realm: Alaskan Fury

Millennium Potion: Wings of Retribution

Outer Bounds: Fortune's Rising

Terms of Mercy: To the Princess Bound

The Legend of ZERO: Forging Zero
The Legend of ZERO: Zero's Return

COMING SOON

Guardians of the First Realm: Fury of the Fourth Realm ~ Sara King
Guardians of the First Realm: Alaskan Fiend ~ Sara King
Guardians of the First Realm: Alaskan Fang ~ Sara King

ZERO: Zero's Legacy – Sara King
ZERO: Forgotten – Sara King

Terms of Mercy: Slave of the Dragon Lord ~ Sara King

Aulds of the Spyre: The Sheet Charmer ~ Sara King
Aulds of the Spyre: Form and Function ~ Sara King

Outer Bounds: Fortune's Folly ~ Sara King

MINI GLOSSARY

(I.E. THE SO YOU DON T LOSE YOUR MIND TINY VERSION)

BAGA-SPECIFIC:

Counter – demeaning use for anyone non-Baga. Relates to the Bagan inability to count effectively beyond 6.

Cracker – like 'asshole'.

Crack – like 'fuck.' Spawns from the Bagan history with their ancestral predators the miga, whose leathery wingtips break the sound barrier with each downward stroke. The crack of a miga's wingbeats is enough to inspire instinctive terror in any Baga. *(See Opening Night at the Naturals Preserve.)*

DHASHA-SPECIFIC:

Ka-par (ka-par) – The predatory game of wills that older Dhasha play with worthy prey creatures or other ancient Dhasha. A stare-down until one contestant submits.

Ka-par inalt (ka-par in-alt) – 'I submit.'

Ka-par rak'tal. (ka-par rak*tal) – 'duel accepted.' *is used to denote a guttural, back-of-throat, almost hacking sound.

Leafling – As the Dhasha are carnivores, as are their Takki and their greatest threats, 'leafling' is used to describe anyone who is utterly useless for anything but food.

Mahid ka-par (ma-heed ka-par) – 'may it begin.'

Mothers – The four mythic beings who weave the lives of all creatures into a tapestry upon which the Trith can gaze. Considered the Dhasha gods by many.

Vahlin (vah-lin) – the legendary leader of the Dhasha, prophecized to be 'dark of body' and lead them to independence from tyranny.

HUOUYT-SPECIFIC:

Breja (bray-shjah) – the quarter-inch long, downy white cilia covering a Huouyt's entire body. Extremely painful to be pulled or mutilated, as it is basically raw nerves.

Zora (zoh-rah) – the red, wormlike, many-tentacled appendage that exits a Houyt's forehead. Much like a fleshy form of coral in appearance when fully extended. It is the zora that allows a Huouyt to digest and analyze genetic material to take a new pattern.

JAHUL-SPECIFIC:

Oozing furg – dumbass. Someone who's young, stupid.

Sivvet (siv-et)– the sensory organs within a Jahul's head that allows it to sense the emotions of other sentient creatures.

JREET-SPECIFIC:

Beda's bones – used alternatively as a curse or exclamation of surprise. Beda ga Vora, who was originally Beda ga Welu. A great warrior who led Congressional forces in a heroic multi-species civil war, but who was abandoned by his own people for falling in love with a Voran, only to be saved and claimed by the Vorans as the only gray-scaled (Welu) clan-member in history, one who was eventually held in such high esteem that he was given breeding privileges. *(See Beda and Shael)* Considered the epitome of a Jreet warrior.

Tek (tehk) – the appendage sheathed within their chests that extrudes poison instantly deadly to any other species in Congress—but not Jreet. Can produce several thousand lobes of pressure in a single strike. The tek's sheath is also commonly used as a storage area for Jreet to carry things like credit stubs and ovi, usually in a leather carrying case.

Lesthar (less-tar)– the favored intoxicating drink of Voran Jreet. Smells like burning tires. Small sips will kill most other species.

Ovi – the transparent, razor-sharp, glasslike knife that is used in every important Jreet ceremony. If a Jreet dies and his body cannot be returned to his clan, it is expected that his tek be removed with his ovi and carried back to his clan for burial.

Rravut – the poison extruded by a Jreet's tek. The most powerful poison in Congress. Causes instant death in all living creatures except other Jreet, who only get numbed or drunken from it.

OOREIKI-SPECIFIC:

Ash/soot – a disgusting, unclean substance

Asher – much like 'asshole,' but with an aggressive, fighting connotation

Ashsoul – the most extreme insult in the Ooreiki language. Also translates to 'lost one'

Ashy – shitty/gross/disgusting/awful

Burn/burning – used much like Human fuck/fucking

Charhead – dumbass, someone stupid, alternatively: someone with an unclean/dirty mind

Furgsoot – bull, bullshit, horseshit, crap, yeah right

Niish Ahymar (nish ay-a-mar) - An Ooreiki ceremony to determine caste where a red-hot brand is pressed into a child's skin. Vkala do not burn, and are then cast to onen. The traditional Ooreiki ceremony of adulthood.

Oorei (oo-ray) – the Ooreiki term for 'soul.' It is the name of the crystalline sphere carried within every Ooreiki and removed by Poenian yeeri priests at their death. Emotional/psychological experiences throughout life change color of crystal. Considered to be the highest crime of Ooreiki society to harm an oorei.

Shenaal (She-nahl) – Mark of the Pure. The burn left when Ooreiki niish are tested during the Niish Ahymar.

Sootbag – someone disgusting, unprepared, unequipped

Sooter – disgusting, unclean person; bastard

Sootwad – degrading, denotes disrespect, a useless person

UNIVERSAL WORDS:

Ekhta (ek-tuh) – Planet-killer. The most destructive bomb in the Congressional arsenal, one of the many great inventions of the Geuji during the Age of Expansion. Like all Geuji technology, the manufacture is so complex that it is un-reproducible by any other mind, and Congress simply follows the steps outlined by the Geuji to create it. (For more info on the Geuji, check out 'The Moldy Dead' and 'Breaking the Mold' in The Legend of ZERO Additional Materials.)

Ferlii (fur-lee) – The massive alien, fungus-like growths covering Ooreiki planets whose reddish spores turn the sky purple. Used as a unit of measurement: One ferlii-length is similar to a human mile.

Furg – A short, squat, very hairy alien that is as ugly as it is stupid. A tool-user, but too primitive to use anything other than sharpened rocks. Think a stocky, 2.5-foot-tall Neanderthal who breeds fast enough to replace numbers lost to stupidity. Darwinian law does not apply.

Furgling – A younger version of a furg. Shorter, hairier, and stupider than its parents.

Haauk (hawk) – skimmer, the floating platforms used as personal planetary transportation

Jenfurgling – One of the most blatantly stupid creatures in Congress. An evolutionary offshoot of furgs arriving on an island where the population underwent a severe bottleneck and had no predators. They delight in beating their hairy faces against the ground and playing with their own excrement.

Kaleu – An Ueshi pleasure-planet known as a vacation destination. Any request will be accommodated.

Kasja (kas-jah) – Highest congressional war-medal. Awarded to a very few, very highly esteemed. Usually comes with a three million credit reward.

Kkee (ca-ca-ee) – yes

Koliinaat – The artificial planet conceived of by the Geuji and funded by the Ooreiki one and a half million years ago, to celebrate the 100th Age of the Ooreiki. Is the home of the Regency, the Tribunal, and the Sanctuary. It is manned, in its entirety, by the artificial sentient life-form called the Watcher, also a Geuji construction, who conducts all Koliinaati affairs with supreme precision.

Levren – the Peacemaker planetary headquarters. Also home of the Space Force Academy.

Ninety Jreet Hells – The ninety levels of pain and unpleasantness that a Jreet warrior must pass through upon death in order to reach the afterlife. (See The Legend of ZERO Additional Materials.)

Nkjan (naka-john) – war; also: "Evil"

Nkjanii (naka-john-ee-ay) – "Evildoer" – battlemaster

Non-sent – colloquial/shortened way to say non-sentient, usually used in a derogatory manner.

Oonnai (oon-nigh) - hello

Oora (oo-ra) – "Souled one" - sir

Peacemakers- the governmental, semi-military authorities who are autonomous in judging, monitoring, and policing the populace. Their main task is to make sure nobody has seditious thoughts, symbol is an eight-pointed star with a planet balancing on each tip. Their base planet is Levren, but they also maintain the Sanctuary on Koliinaat, which is the only place on the planet that is inaccessible to the Watcher.

Planetary Ops (also: PlanOps) – symbol is a single sphere, half red, half blue. Tattoo is of a green, single-moon planet with a headcom, a PPU, and a species-generic plasma rifle leaning against the debris ring. The tattoo glows slightly, a cell-by-cell gene modification that causes the tattooed skin to bio-luminesce.

Regency – The sphere-shaped center of Koliinaat, where all the Representatives of Congress gather to discuss new laws or political conflicts.

Ruvmestin (ruv-meh-stihn) – A whitish, extremely heavy metal with a greater density than gold. The most valuable metal in Congress. Used in Geuji technologies, esp. nannites, like biosuits and spaceships. Does not oxidize in air. Mined on the government planets of Grakkas, Yeejor, and Pelipe. Once ruvmestin is discovered on a planet, Congress immediately claims the planet for the common good, removing it from the Planetary Claims Board queue.

Sanctuary – The one area of Koliinaat—about the size of a large city block—where the Watcher has no effect. Was claimed by Peacemakers almost immediately after Koliinaat's creation, though it was originally constructed as a place for delegations of non-members of Congress to gather to discuss treaties, trade, and other matters of diplomacy. Since Congress has swallowed every society it has come across, unlike the intent of its original charter, there are no non-members to require separate quarters.

Sacred Turn – Time period. 666 turns.

Tribunal – The three members of the Regency chosen to represent and make judgments for the whole of Congress. The Tribunal are the power-members of the Regency, usually occupied by members of the Grand Six. Aliphei is First Citizen, and has maintained a seat on the Tribunal for the entire duration of Congress. The symbol of the Tribunal is three red circles inside a silver ring, surrounded by eight blue circles formed into two sides facing off against each other.

Vaghi – a small, nuisance pest-animal that eats and breeds uncontrollably. Once introduced to a planet, the entire planet must be killed in order to remove them. Which, unfortunately, is often necessary because the vaghi leave no vegetation or small animals behind.

Zahali (za-ha-li) – I'm sorry

SPECIES:

Baga (Ba-guh)– Small, one-foot beetle-like fliers with iridescent green carapaces and faceted red eyes like a fly. Have *abbas*, which are the glands that produce their infamous glue, a compound that instantly becomes whatever it touches. Are afraid of *miga*, their natural predators, whose wings break the sound barrier with every stroke. Can't count effectively beyond 6.

Bajna (Bajh-nah)– The 'bankers' of Congress. Black, ten-legged spider-like creatures approximately eight feet wide at rest—twenty if stretched out—who are extraordinary good with numbers.

Dhasha (Dah-sha) – One of the Grand Six. Very dangerous, violent beasts with indestructible metallic scales that shine with constantly-shifting iridescence. Big, crystalline, oval green eyes, long black talons, stubby bodies, sharklike faces with triangular black teeth. Their nostrils are set beside their eyes. Females are golden instead of rainbow, males have two layers of scales, indestructible metallic on top, gold underneath. Gutteral, snarling voice. Laugh by clacking their teeth together. Grow continuously throughout their lifetimes.

Geuji (Goy-gee)– a form of sentient mold whose entire body structure is composed of microscopic biological nanotubules capable of exchanging, storing, and processing information. If allowed to grow, they are easily the most intelligent species in Congress, with computing capacity far exceeding every artificial machine built by Congressional minds. Were the creative genius behind the ekhta, Congressional nannites, biosuits, and flowing-state ships. Bodies are glossy black that ripple in the light as information is passed throughout. Originated on Neskfaat, but were uprooted by Huouyt sabotage. *(See The Moldy Dead.)* Then imprisoned by Trith betrayal. *(See Breaking the Mold.)*

Grekkon (Greh-kuhn) – a creature that looks like a gigantic brown jumping-spider, but with a bulbous rear that extrudes a substance that will immediately decay/dissolve any substance, including otherwise indestructible Dhasha scales. As a species, do not have emotions. A burrower by nature.

Huouyt (sounds like: White) – One of the Grand Six. Three-legged, ancestrally aquatic shape-shifters. Bleed clear mucous. *Breja* – downy white fluff covering body. Tentacle legs and paddle-like arms. Cylindrical torso, enormous, electric-blue eyes, and a tri-angular, squid-like head. *Zora* – red, wormy gills in upper center of Huouyt heads that allow them to take the genetic patterns of another creature. Huouyt have a bad reputation in Congress. They are cunning, sneaky, adaptable, and excellent mimics. Considered to be psychopathic by most species in Congress.

Jahul (Jah-hool)– One of the Grand Six. Sextuped empaths with green-ish skin and a chemical defense system of releasing their own wastes over their skin when they are frightened or stressed. *Sivvet* – the sensory organs that allow Jahul to feel emotions.

Jreet (Jreet) – One of the Grand Six. Red, gray, or cream-colored serpen-tine warriors who guard the First Citizen and the Tribunal. Have the ability to raise the energy level of their scales and disappear from the visible spectrum. Use echolocation to see. Have great concave depressions in the sides of their heads to focus sound, much like bat ears. Believe in ninety hells for cowards, and that each soul splits into ninety different parts so they can experience all ninety hells at once. Their rravut within their teks is the most powerful poison in Congress. Bluish blood. Short, engine-like *shee-whomp* battlecry. Cream colored bellies. Diamond-shaped head. Tek- the talon protruding from their chests.

Ooreiki (Ooh-reh-kee) – One of the Grand Six. Heavy aliens a lot like boneless gorillas. Five hundred pounds on average. Four tentacle fingers on each arm. Big brown ostrich-egg sized snake-eyes, brown legs, skin turns splotchy when frightened. Huge mouths. Wrinkle their big faces to smile. Grunting rattle of speech. Five feet tall on average. Laugh by making a guttural rapping sound in the base of their necks like a toad croaking. Average age is 400. Outnumber humans ten thousand to one. Only the Ueshi are a more populous species.

Shadyi (Shad-yee) – The species of the First Citizen, Aliphei. There is only one surviving member of this species. Shaggy blue alien, walks on four feet, elephant-sized, black tusks, red eyes.

Takki (Sounds like: Tacky) – The ancestral servants of the Dhasha. Reviled throughout Congress as cowards and betrayers. Purple scales, very dense bodies, upright humanoid lizards. Crystalline, blue, ovoid eyes.

Ueshi (Oo-eh-she) – One of the Grand Six. Small blue or blue-green aliens with excellent reflexes and rubbery skin. Aquatic ancestry. Headcrest.

MEASUREMENTS:

ST – Standard Turns 9 standard rotations (1.23 years, 448.875 Earth Days to a Standard Turn)

SR – Standard Rotation 36 standard days (49.875 Earth Days to a Standard Rotation)

SD – Standard Day 36 standard hours (33.25 Earth Hours to a Standard Day)

SH – Standard Hour 72 standard tics (55.42 Earth Minutes to a Standard Hour)

St – Standard Tics (1.299 tics to an Earth Minute, .7698 Earth Minutes to a Standard Tic)

Standard Ninth-Dig (colloquially 'ninths') – approx. 1.3 inches
Standard Dig- approx. 1 foot
Standard Rod- approx. 9 feet
Standard Length - approx. 4,000 feet
Standard March- approx. 9,999 rods (90,000 feet)
Standard Lobe- approx. 2.5 pounds

RANKS:

Multi-Specieal Galactic Corps – Prime Corps Director
18-unit Galactic Corps – Secondary Corps Director
3-unit Galactic Corps – Tertiary Corps Director
Single-Species Sector Corps – _____(species) Corps Director Single solid silver eight-pointed star with a solid black interior.
Sector Unit – Prime Overseer. Silver eight-pointed star and four inner circles of a Prime Overseer
Solar Unit – Secondary Overseer. Silver eight-pointed star and three inner circles of a Secondary Overseer
Planetary Unit – Tertiary Overseer
Force – Petty Overseer
Regiment (8,100)- Prime Commander - eight-pointed star (In Planetary Ops, a Prime leads a single groundteam of 6 hand-picked soldiers, usually all battlemasters or above.)
Brigade (1800)- Secondary Commander - seven pointed star (In Planetary Ops, a Secondary Commander is otherwise known as a Prime's 'Second.')
Battalion (900)- Tertiary Commander OR Secondary Commander -six pointed star OR 7-pointed star
Company (450)- Small Commander - five-pointed star
Platoon (90)- Battlemaster - four-pointed star
Squad (18)- Squad leader (Squader) - triangle
Groundteam (6)- Ground Leader - line
Grounder - point

A Sneak Peek at The Legend of ZERO 3,
Zero's Return:

THE LEGEND OF
ZERO

ZERO RETURN

SARA KING

1

TWELVE-A

This is our future.

Though their bodies were naked, their minds empty, the fearful, half-mad faces that followed Marie from behind the bars of their cages were humanity's hope.

Marie hurried her step. Despite almost twenty years on the project, the depraved gazes never ceased to bother her.

A familiar voice entered her head, unbidden. *It will be over soon, Marie.*

Marie shuddered, her eyes drawn to the blue-eyed experiment in the corner cell. His drip bag had run out again and he was awake. Fear clotted her blood as she watched him. She knew, more than anyone, that Twelve-A could kill them all, should it ever cross his mind.

The experiment said nothing more, merely watched her.

Marie hurried through the heavy doors and entered the lab. "Twelve-A needs another dose. He's awake again." Marie hoped her fear didn't show.

"Colonel Codgson wants him awake," the tech, a young blonde Army lieutenant, said. The woman gave the holding area a nervous glance. "Codgson's got techs monitoring him, making sure his patterns stay level—he's scheduled another demonstration for this afternoon."

Despite herself, Marie cursed. Codgson was a fool. Ever since he had discovered their prodigy's unique talents, Codgson had made every attempt to show him off to the board. Twelve-A had been pitted against everything the other labs could throw at him—and had lived.

"Do you think Twelve-A will survive this one?" Lieutenant Carter asked, peering at the experiment through a camera installed in his cell, face etched with worry.

Marie knew the lieutenant was partial to the handsome, blue-eyed young man in the last cage on the right. She didn't think of him as a killer.

"He's survived all the others." Still, Marie felt dread creeping into her soul. Twelve-A hated the Dark Room. What if this time, he decided not to cooperate? Just the tiniest slip by the technicians monitoring him and he could wreak destruction on the whole lab. It wasn't worth the risk.

"I know," Lieutenant Carter said, eyes fixed on the glass windows of the experiment wing. "That's what bothers me. He doesn't like it... it *hurts* him. What if he doesn't—"

A male voice behind her interrupted them. "We have his DNA. We can always make another, if he fails to cooperate."

Marie stiffened and turned. The Colonel stood in the hall, his perfectly crisp blue uniform accenting a bored demeanor, as if they were talking about cloning rats.

You don't have a clue, you stupid fool, Marie thought, watching him.

The Colonel caught her gaze and smiled, a wormlike twisting that chilled her core. "The first rule of this project is not to become attached to the subjects, doctor."

Marie's anger spiked, as it always did around the Colonel. "You shouldn't leave him awake and unguarded like that. Twelve-A could kill us all right now if he wanted to. He could empty our minds, make us all stop breathing just like he does in your Dark Room."

The Colonel snorted. "I doubt that. My techs—"

"—would die too," Marie interrupted coldly. "You're playing with fire, Colonel."

The Colonel laughed and rapped sharply on the thick metal door leading to the containment area. The sound diffused with the sheer density of the metal. The Colonel gave her a smug look. "He doesn't even know we're here."

Marie glared, but said nothing.

"If he did," the Colonel said. "He would have killed us a long time ago."

"You don't know that," Marie said. "Maybe he doesn't like to kill."

The Colonel's gaze sharpened, as if he were a hound breeder and she had suggested his dogs didn't like to hunt. He turned to Lieutenant Carter abruptly. "Collect the experiment and take him to the Dark Room. Our visitors are waiting in the observation booth."

As the tech went to get the necessary equipment, Marie asked, "What's he going to fight this time?"

"An experiment from another lab."

Marie's lips tightened. "Twelve-A represents fifty-two turns of work. If you want a friendly competition for the generals' viewing pleasure, go get one of the Eleven-series to be your gladiator. Anything above twelve-series shouldn't be risked."

The Colonel gave her a humorless smile. "There is nothing friendly about it. The lab that fails today loses its funding. If we lose our funding, every experiment will be killed and our data destroyed. We need to win. That's why I chose him."

Marie watched him and saw the sincerity there. Softly, she whispered, "They would kill them all?"

The Colonel inclined his head. "Now you see why it must be Twelve-A."

"Why?" she whispered.

The Colonel gave her a long look before he said, "Congress discovered our intent. The board hopes we can stall them for a few years, and the fewer active labs we have, the better our chances will be."

"Can't we combine the labs?" Marie blurted. "Throw them all into one building?"

The Colonel shook his head. "The genetic lines wouldn't fight each other if they were kept in the same building."

Still hopeful, Marie charged ahead. "Then maybe we could use some other means to determine the success of the experiments. Something that does not endanger their lives. There is evidence that latent brain activity is a clear indicator of—"

"We're constructing a war," the Colonel interrupted. "The alien Congress will bathe in its own blood before it realizes it can no longer hold us. Twelve-A and his kind represent Earth's hope for independence, and it will take many of their deaths to see it happen."

Doggedly, Marie said, "You've used Twelve-A three times in the last month. Why not Ten-F?"

"You want to place all of their lives on *her*?"

Marie licked her lips. Ten-F, though potent, was insane. She had fingernail scars down her face from where she'd tried to take out her own eyes after her final visit to the Dark Room.

"Colonel," she began tentatively, "you don't see them after their experiences in the Dark Room. It's obviously very traumatic for the minders, and you've already used Twelve-A many more times than regulations allow. I want you to retire him. He's too valuable to the project for any more games."

The Colonel's eyes narrowed. "This is not a game." Marie started to retort, but he cut her off. "Go find out what's taking Lieutenant Carter so long. I told them noon sharp." The Colonel's mouth twisted in irritation when he glanced at his big gold wristwatch. "We're two minutes behind already." He strode off in the direction of the Dark Room, hard black boot-heels reverberating on the white tile as he departed.

Frustrated, Marie went looking for Carter.

Ten minutes later, she found the lieutenant slumped on the floor of the containment corridor outside Twelve-A's cage, the behavioral adaptor still clasped in her hand.

"You *killed* her?!" Marie cried, jogging up to kneel beside her.

Dr. Carter had a pulse. Relieved, Marie turned on the experiment.

Cold blue eyes met her stare, unwavering. Twelve-A was only two feet away, squatting naked in front of the bars, watching her. He was angry.

I'm not fighting.

Marie stumbled away from him. She began to reach for the behavioral adaptor, then froze when she saw him following her motions with his eyes. Twelve-A knew what she was thinking. He'd never let her use it.

Tentatively, Marie retracted her hand. "You need to fight. If our lab fails this match, they'll all die." Eyes still fixed on him, she motioned to the other experiments.

Twelve-A's eyes flickered toward the others, then back at her. *They're miserable. You treat them like animals. They're better off dead.*

In that moment, Marie realized that Twelve-A could not only kill her and her comrades, but he could also kill his own kind.

"No!" After twenty years of living her work, the experiments were Marie's children. At the thought of losing them, she almost forgot the history of the man in front of her. She reached through the bars to touch his knee. "Things will get better, Twelve-A."

He recoiled, drawing deeper into his cell before she could reach him. *You can't lie to me.*

"I'm not." Marie held his eyes. "Just once more. I'll make sure you won't have to do it again."

Twelve-A glanced to the side, away from her, pain etched in his young face. For long moments, he said nothing. Then, *Take me to the Dark Room.*

Marie glanced down at the unconscious lieutenant, then at the experiment. She left the behavioral adapter on the floor.

• • •

"Watch closely," Colonel Codgson said, addressing the visitors. "See how he paces? Our experiments show an innate aggression...a drive to fight. He's anticipating the kill."

Marie watched with her back to the Colonel, recognizing Twelve-A's pacing for what it was—anger.

"Is the experiment contained?" one of the visitors demanded. A nasal, gray-haired woman pointed at the large observation station in the corner, indicating the two technicians monitoring it. "Are they all that stand between us and that monster?"

In the Dark Room, Twelve-A stopped and gave the observation booth a small frown before continuing to pace. The others did not notice, but Marie's heart clenched.

He knows we're here, she thought, horrified. *And he's listening.*

"We're in no danger," Colonel Codgson replied. "The walls are a foot and a half of lead-ceramic composite. Even the windows are leaded. His abilities cannot penetrate."

"Has this been proven?"

"Beyond a doubt," Colonel Codgson replied.

On the other side of the glass, the Dark Room doors opened and a second experiment, a naked redheaded woman, was thrust inside.

The fight ended as swiftly and undramatically as they always did with Twelve-A. He simply walked up to the other experiment, gently took her trembling chin into his hands, touched his forehead to hers, and his opponent collapsed.

"Amazing," the nasal woman said, though she did not sound very amazed. "That's it? Why didn't they fight?"

"No one can fight Twelve-A," Colonel Codgson said, pride seeping through his voice. "He is our finest creation."

Again, Marie thought she saw Twelve-A glance in their direction, but an embarrassed-looking Lieutenant Carter was already leading the experiment from the room, her fist wrapped tightly around her portable behavioral adaptor. The moment Twelve-A looked at her, she twisted the dial and made him scream.

As Marie watched the other technicians rush in to help Carter carry the experiment from the room, she felt undefinable sadness. The Lieutenant's good will had officially ended.

She and I were his only two friends in this place.

Afterwards, Colonel Codgson hosted a celebration to commemorate their continued research, but Marie could not stay. She left the restaurant and drove back to the lab, thinking about the look of anguish she'd seen on Twelve-A's face as Carter and the others had prodded the whimpering telepath back to his cell and re-attached the driplines.

Even though she got chills thinking of it, Marie wanted to see him. Console him.

When she got there, the lab was cold and dark. Marie flicked on the lights and moved to the holding area, swiping her card and pushed one of the thick leaden doors open. Inside, a sixth of the lights remained permanently on, more for the technicians' comfort than the experiments'—no one wanted to be alone in the dark with the monsters they had created.

Somewhere, near the back of the room, Marie heard crying.

Though she carried no restraining devices, had followed none of the pre-entry monitoring protocol, Marie stepped inside the corridor.

"Hello?" she whispered.

Though she knew her words had not been loud enough to carry beyond her own ears, the sobbing cut off instantly.

Cold prickles crawled across Marie's arms and back. It was Twelve-A. He hadn't been drugged. She had *seen* him get drugged.

Had Lieutenant Carter forgotten to refill the bag? Or had Twelve-A made her forget?

The idea was terrifying. Marie knew right then she should scurry back behind the protective leaden walls and wait for assistance.

And yet, she found herself rooted to the place, unable to leave. Guilt welled in her gut like a moldy sack, weighing on her soul.

They don't deserve this, she thought, eying the other experiments in their beds. All slept, either naturally or by drugs, splayed out in naked disregard like animals.

The crying had not begun again, and Marie got the eerie impression that Twelve-A waited for her in the darkness. Realizing how blithely she'd stepped into his trap, Marie's pulse began to race. Fear paralyzed her. Like a farmer standing feet from a tiger hidden in the undergrowth, she had entered his realm, and her continued existence was solely at his discretion. Running was no longer an option, as much as her panicked thoughts screamed at her to do so.

She made herself move deeper into the corridor of cages.

Twelve-A was tucked into a fetal position on his bed, knees to his chest, back against the corner where two walls joined. There was no drip-bag hanging from the stand beside his bed. A wave of goosebumps prickled Marie's body in a wave, seeing that.

As soon as Twelve-A saw her, he stopped rocking.

I know their fear before I kill them, he said in a whimper.

Self-loathing emanated from Twelve-A in a thick mental wave that made Marie stumble against his cell. Panting, she struggled to keep from bursting into tears at the sheer *power* of the emotional barrage. Knowing that this was how he felt, that this was *him,* Marie had to act. Before she could talk herself out of it, she opened the gate to his cell and went to sit down on the thin mattress beside him.

"It's okay," she said, touching his knee. "You'll never have to do that again."

The touch made Twelve-A jerk, and for the first time, she realized that he had never been allowed to touch another human being before, other than those he meant to kill. Before Marie could correct her mistake, he unfolded and threw himself into her arms like a frightened child.

There, the lab's most dangerous creation cried into her shoulder.

Marie froze, terrified of his presence, terrified of what she'd done. She felt Twelve-A's body tremble against her, wracked by an emotional torment whose very residues still left her weak and nauseous. Despite her fears, she felt tears coming to her own eyes and softly began stroking Twelve-A's shaven head.

"It's okay," she whispered.

He shook his head against her chest and sobbed. Pent-up breaths exploded from him in tortured spasms. His grip on her back began to hurt. Marie said nothing more and wrapped her arms around him.

Biologically, Twelve-A was a healthy twenty-two-turn-old man. Mentally, however, he was as vulnerable as a small child. They had kept every stimulation to the barest necessary for survival, sedating him with drugs for most of his life, never speaking within hearing range, never giving him a chance to *think.*

The reason was simple; undrugged and unhindered—like he was now—he could execute his keepers with a thought. Unrestrained, his cell open, he could cast Marie aside and simply leave the lab. He could walk through the open containment area doors, all the way to the reception area, where it would be a small thing to get past the guard and escape, never to be seen again. Like with Carter and the drip-bag, he could probably even make them all forget he had even existed.

Marie considered all these things as she sat there, holding him, but found she did not care. He needed her, and that was all that mattered.

Thank you, came his mental whisper in her mind. Twelve-A's body had calmed somewhat, leaving only an underlying shuddering, like someone who'd spent too much time in the cold.

"I'm going to help you," Marie said, before she realized it was true. "I'm going to help you escape this place."

Twelve-A looked her in the eyes and said, *I could escape any time I want.*

"Then why don't you?" Marie whispered back.

The others, he replied. *If I took them with me, they'd all be caught and brought back here.*

She watched him closely. "But you wouldn't."

He shook his head once, and it gave Marie chills. She wondered just how powerful their experiment was, just how much he'd been hiding from them.

Tentatively, she said, "You know what's outside the complex, don't you? Can you actually feel beyond the walls?"

Twelve-A looked away. His silence was answer enough. All of their precautions, all of their procedures, all their efforts to keep him ignorant of his humanity…all had been for naught. Twelve-A had been in contact with the real world since the moment he'd been born.

"I'll get you out of here," Marie said. "I promise."

• • •

That night, she drafted an anonymous letter to the funding committee, to three separate civil rights groups, to eight government officials, to six leading scientists, and to three different news agencies. She knew it would end her career. She knew she and her colleagues would spend the rest of their lives in prison. But, after everything she'd done, it seemed a fitting demise.

To Marie's surprise, her letter was not published the next day. Nor the next. Not even a whisper of it came in the weeks that followed. Her only indication that something had happened was the Colonel's increasingly terse attitude, his shortening temper.

"Get Twelve-A," he snapped upon entering on the final morning. "He has another demonstration to make."

"No!" Marie cried, stepping between the iron-faced Lieutenant Carter and the holding area. "You promised, Colonel."

Codgson's eyes were chipped obsidian as he said, "Someone betrayed us to Congress. Confirmed their suspicions. Their ships are coming. The committee is here to decide which specimens to use in the fight against the Dhasha commander. They want to see Twelve-A in the Dark Room, to see just how much they can do with him."

"Let me do it," Marie said, desperate, now. "Let me retrieve him."

The Colonel glanced back to frown at her. "Why?"

"He is like a son to me."

"He is an animal, Doctor."

It took all of Marie's willpower to say, "It's not a crime to be fond of one's dog, Colonel."

He gave a bitter laugh. "Make sure he's in the Dark Room in six minutes."

Marie was shaking as she walked down the corridor. Congress was coming, and Earth would feel its wrath for ages to come. She, and every other scientist who worked on the experiments, would be killed. The experiments themselves would be murdered, the labs destroyed. Their only hope of avoiding the coming apocalypse was if the experiments could do what they were created to do.

Defend them.

Defend them against a power so great it spanned the entire universe.

Marie felt helpless as she approached Twelve-A's cell. She'd tried to help, but she'd brought the aliens to their doorstep, instead.

It wasn't you, Twelve-A told her, looking up from his cot to meet her gaze with solemn blue eyes. *I never let you send that letter.*

Marie clearly remembered sending it. She remembered checking her Sent files and getting Delivery Confirmation on the physical drafts, just to make sure.

Then Marie gasped at what the minder was trying to tell her. She had been in her own home when she drafted and sent those letters, twenty miles from the lab. His influence couldn't possibly reach that far. But if it had…

What was the limit?

Fearful, Marie began backing away. Twelve-A watched her soberly through the bars.

He was huddled in one corner, his lanky knees tucked under his chin. Once more, she felt like she was caught in the tiger's stare, but this time the tiger was debating.

After a moment, Twelve-A looked away.

Marie sank down to her knees in front of him, relief washing over her. Softly, she said, "I can help you get out of here. I can help you start new lives on the surface."

Twelve-A's blue eyes flickered back toward her. *We can't go now. The aliens will kill us.*

Marie felt like she'd been struck. "You know about the aliens?"

I've been watching them. They're destroying the other labs. This is the only one they haven't found.

Marie blinked at him, once again shocked by how much he had managed to hide from them.

"We need you to fight," she whispered. "We need you to stop the—"

I'm not killing the aliens.

"But you've got to help us defend the—"

No, Twelve-A thought. *I don't.*

Coldness settled in the pit of Marie's stomach. "You're going to kill us, aren't you?"

I'm killing everyone who knows about this place, Twelve-A said, his voice cold and final. *It's the only way the People are going to survive.*

Marie met the deep blue of his gaze and sweat slid like ice down her back as she began to bargain for her life. "Once we're dead, then what? Where will you go? What will you do?"

Twelve-A swallowed hard.

"You don't know anything about the real world," Marie insisted. "I can help you create new lives for yourselves. I can help you *adapt*. I'm your *friend*, Twelve-A. I can help you."

He didn't answer her. Looking drained, he got to his feet. *Come with me to the Dark Room. I want you to watch something.*

Reluctantly, realizing she didn't really have a choice, Marie did. Once they stood outside the small green door, Twelve-A gave her a gentle nudge down the hall, toward the observation booth. Confused, she went.

Inside, the occupants were milling in obvious agitation. Every face she had ever seen inside the lab was there, checking their watches, grimacing at the blond experiment pacing in the Dark Room. As more staff filtered into the observation booth, Marie anxiously glanced from Twelve-A to the group of observers and back, wondering what he planned for them. Her entire body trembled with fear and adrenaline. She'd heard the mental's death was painless, like falling asleep. She was terrified she was about to find out.

"So what are we waiting for, Colonel?" one of the generals finally demanded. The group had become more and more aggravated as nothing happened in the room before them.

"We're waiting for your test subjects," the Colonel replied briskly.

The general's face went slack. "What test subjects? We're here because you told us your famous Twelve-A could do something that would save billions of lives."

At Colonel Codgson's frown, a man in a pristine black suit bitterly snapped, "Do *not* tell us you brought us all together to waste our time, Colonel."

The Colonel stared back at them in complete confusion. "I never sent for you."

A thin woman with short-cropped brown hair entered the room and shut the door behind her on the Colonel's last words. Frowning, she said, "You didn't? Then who did?"

In the center of the Dark Room, Twelve-A stopped pacing. He turned, his ice-blue eyes cold beyond the leaded glass.

Me.

It was like a mental thunderclap. Several members of the committee screamed and staggered toward the door. Only Colonel Codgson remained where he stood, staring at Twelve-A through the glass with a queer little smile.

Twelve-A looked at them through the glass, meeting each of their eyes, though Marie knew he couldn't possibly see through the tinted windows.

I want you to know, Twelve-A said in a resounding mental boom, *that I killed them because they didn't want to live, not because you told me to.*

Every expert and government in the room screamed and rushed for the door, throwing each other aside as they wrestled for the exit. Marie stayed where she was against the back wall, knowing that there was nowhere to run, nowhere she could hide from the telepath's mental barrage.

But with you, Twelve-A continued, *it's because you deserve it.*

Desperate men and women were making it out into the hallway, and Marie heard their frantic footsteps on the tiles of the corridor outside. Back in the Dark Room, the telepath shut his eyes and inclined his head slightly. As one, the two dozen uniformed men and women occupying the room around her collapsed in a silent, falling wave of flesh.

Except for Marie. She kept breathing, waiting for it to happen, but it never did. Minutes after her companions' wide eyes began to glaze, she was stunned to find herself still standing amidst the corpses. Alive.

She looked at Twelve-A. Beyond the glass in the center of the Dark Room, his body had slumped to the floor with his victims. He was now lying on his side, half-curled into a fetal position, arms pulled in towards his chest. Heart thundering, Marie went to see if he lived.

Put me back in my cell, Twelve-A whimpered, when she entered the room and knelt beside him.

Marie recoiled. "Your cell? Why?"

I want to die.

"No!"

Do it.

It allowed no argument. In a daze, Marie drew him to his feet and helped him back into the containment area. As she settled him onto his bed, Twelve-A said, *Please kill me.*

The mental whimper was infused with so much emotional agony that it left Marie's chest afire. Still, her eyes flickered toward the IV rack they used to keep the experiments sedate. "I'll go get the drugs. They'll make you feel better." She turned to go.

Twelve-A caught her hand, his blue gaze intense. *You should kill me, Marie.*

"No," she said, finding strength in the words, "I shouldn't. I should get you and all your friends out of here." She patted his warm, slender hand and Twelve-A released his hold. She went to the labs, got the drugs, and hooked them to the rack. As she was connecting his IV line to the bag, however, the minder stopped her. His cerulean eyes were angry.

If you're not going to kill me, leave.

She winced at the force of his words, like hammers that pounded against the aluminum walls of her brain. "What about your friends?"

Don't worry about us. Leave. Lock the doors and never come back.

Marie met his deep blue stare, saw the danger there, then dropped everything and hurried from his cell. She heard the gate to Twelve-A's cage slam behind her as she went to the containment doors and wrenched them shut. She used her card to lock them, then rushed through the facility, gaining speed as she realized she was the only one left alive. The only one who knew about the experiments. The only one who could help them create new lives on the surface.

The only one who could keep them *alive.*

She could rehabilitate them. Find them jobs. Find them friends.

The guard was not at his booth. Buoyed by her new mission, Marie hurried past, pushed through the bullet-proof glass doors, and locked them behind her with another swipe of her card. She followed the corridor, climbed the stairs, and exited through the single door at the top. Facing it, the entrance looked like the door to a decrepit coffee shop, with the Coffee House Express sign hanging askew and the paint peeling on the CLOSED FOR BUSINESS notice.

Under the façade, however, the door was tank-proof, the walls behind it bomb-proof. It would take nukes to get inside.

Marie locked the entrance with her card, sliding it through an inconspicuous crack in the wooden trim.

Thank you, Twelve-A told her. *That should keep them out.*

"Yes," Marie said, hurrying toward her car. "But don't worry—you won't be in there long. I'll find somewhere to keep you. The war will make it harder, but once I've got living quarters and food, I'll come back for you."

You don't understand, Marie.

She stuck her key into her Ford. "Don't understand what?"

Once it's safe, we're going to get ourselves out.

"But I can—" Terror infused Marie's soul as she realized why Twelve-A had left her alive. Babbling, Marie said, "Please, Twelve-A. I can help you. I won't tell anyone. *Please*—you don't need to kill me."

Twelve-A gave a mental shudder, buoyed on a wave of self-loathing. *It's always so hard.*

Even as she opened her mouth to scream, a wave of calmness overpowered her. Her eyes drifted shut and she slid to the concrete beside her car, the keys tumbling from her hands to clatter on the cement. Trapped in the darkness of her own body, Marie felt her heart stop.

Somewhere, deep underground, Twelve-A replaced the IV line and closed his eyes. His shoulders began to shake as he waited for oblivion to take him.

END